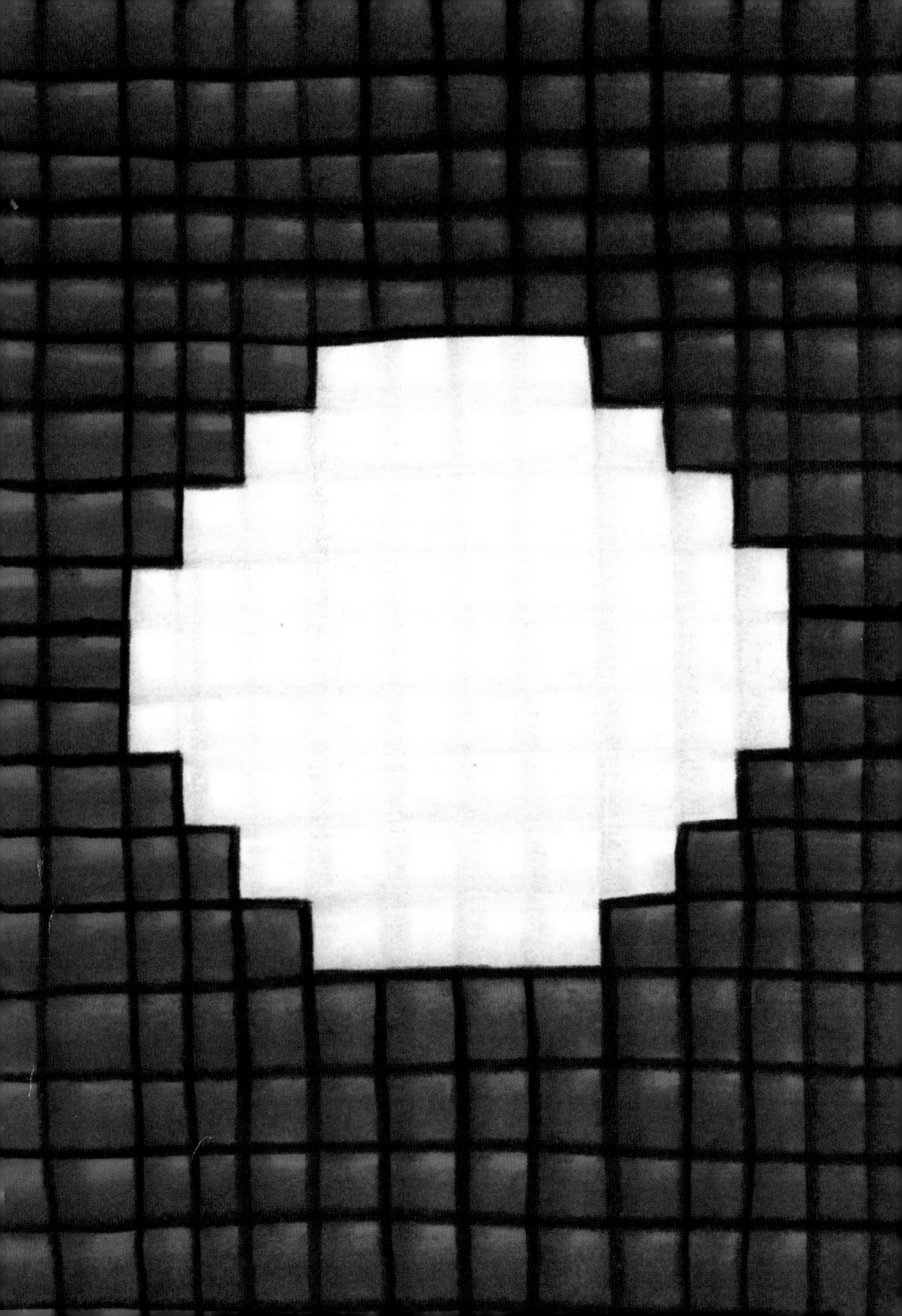

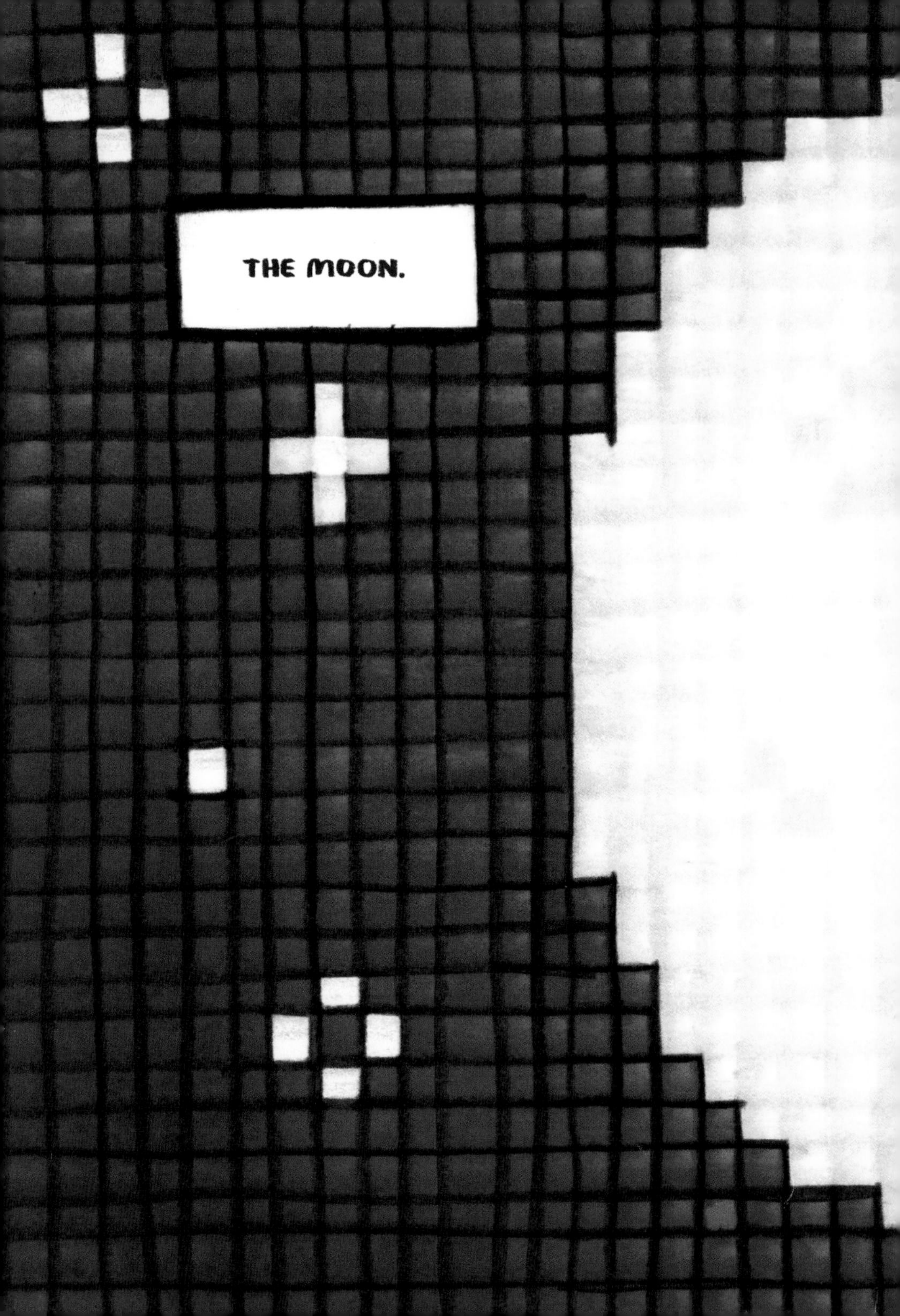
THE MOON.

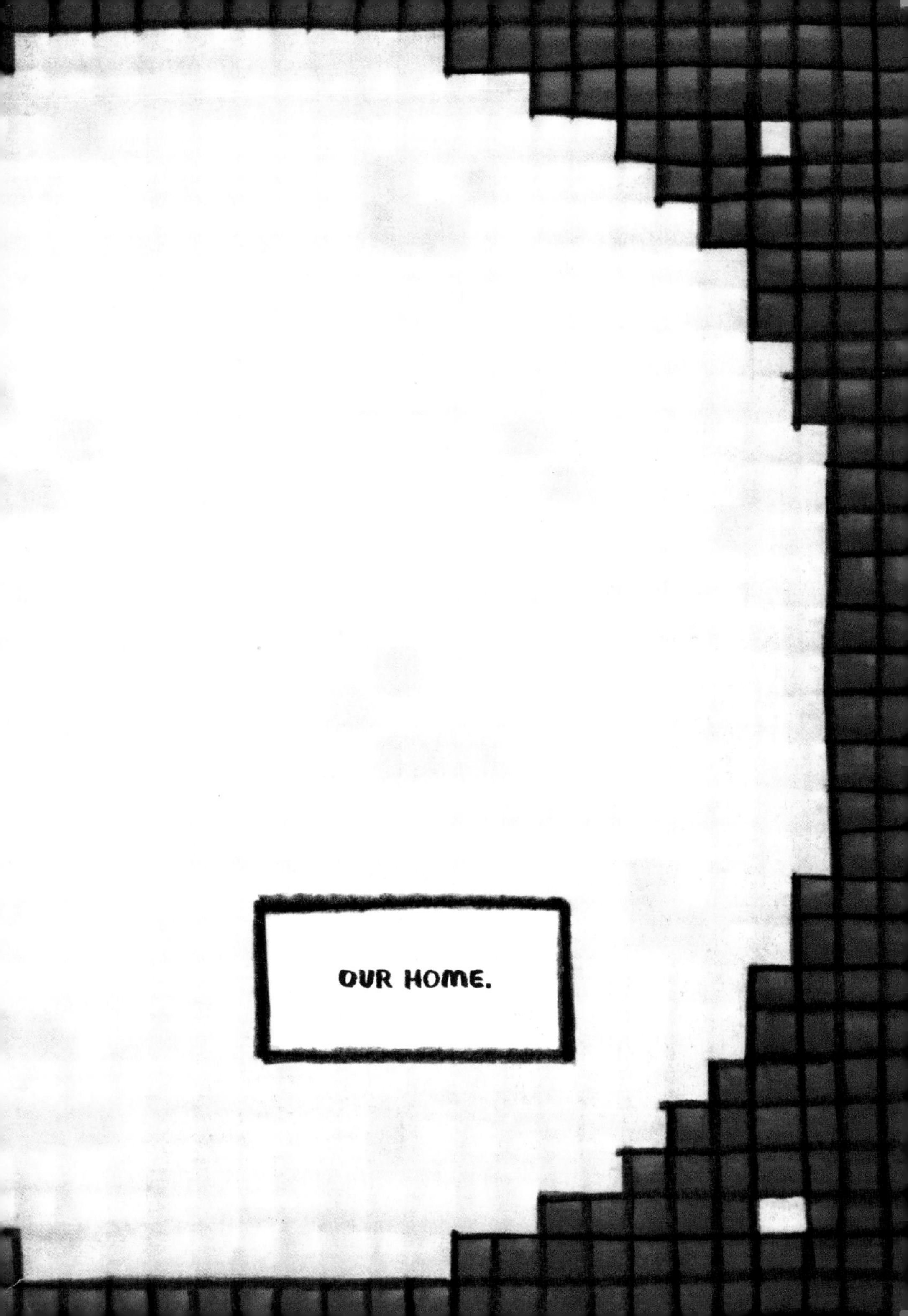
OUR HOME.

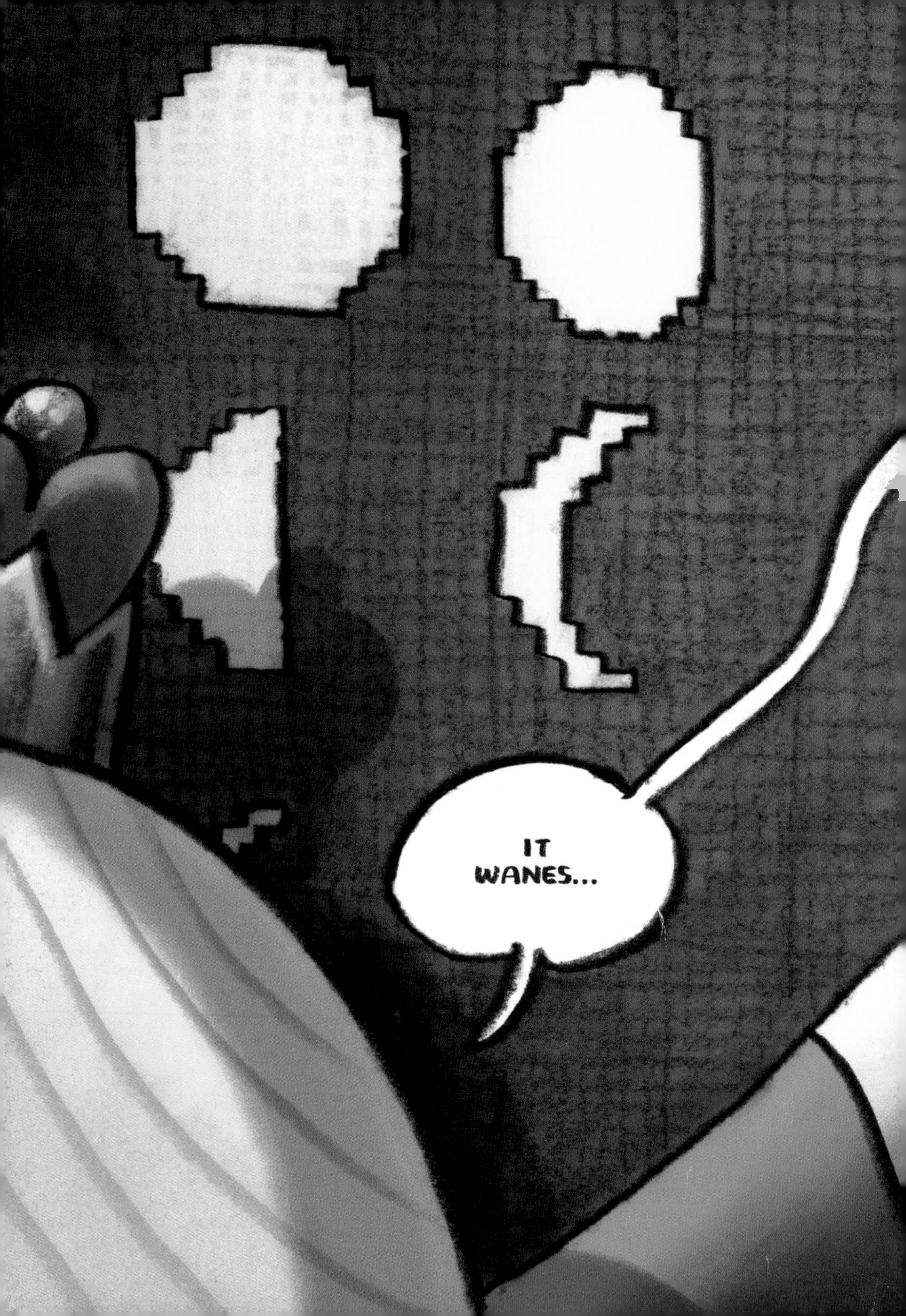
IT WANES...

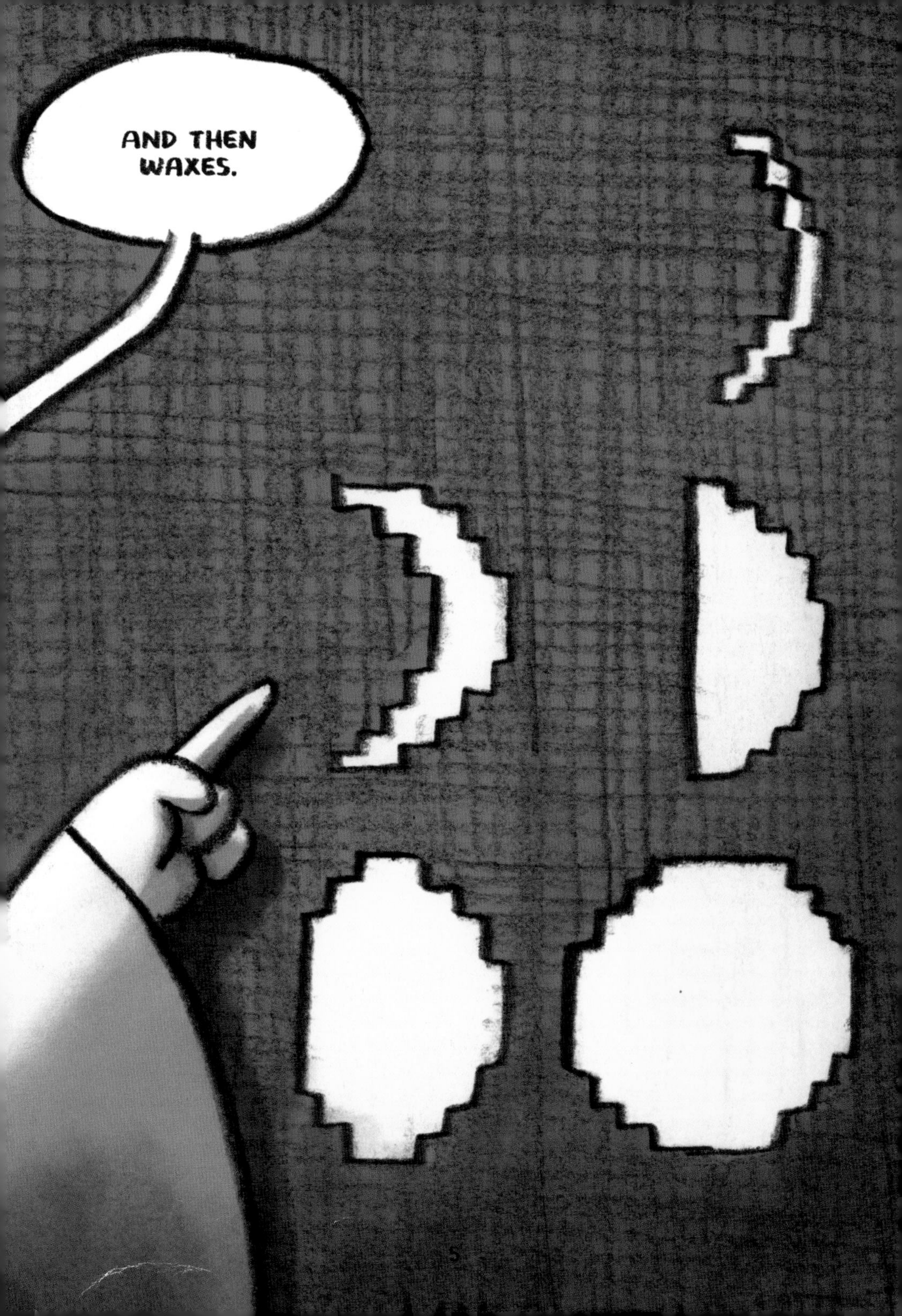
AND THEN WAXES.

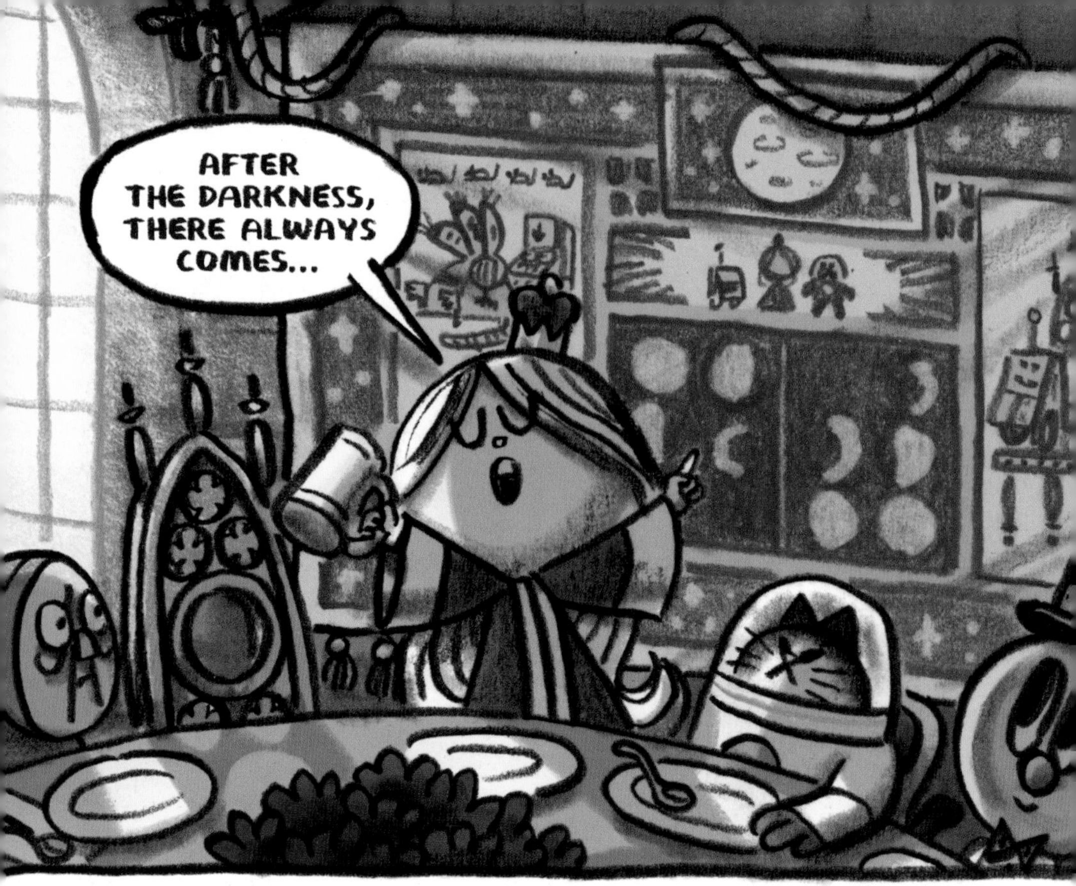
AFTER THE DARKNESS, THERE ALWAYS COMES...

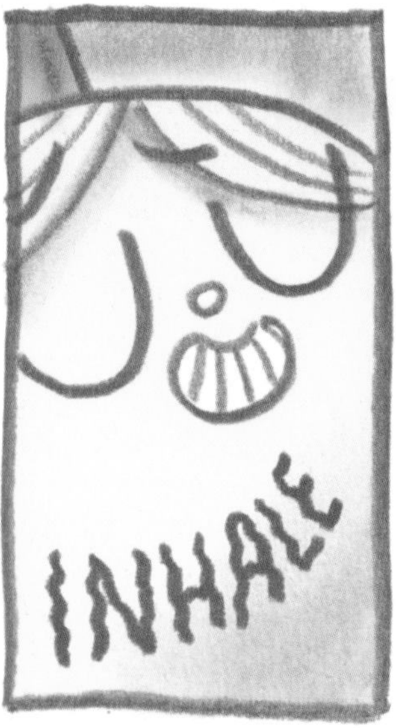
INHALE

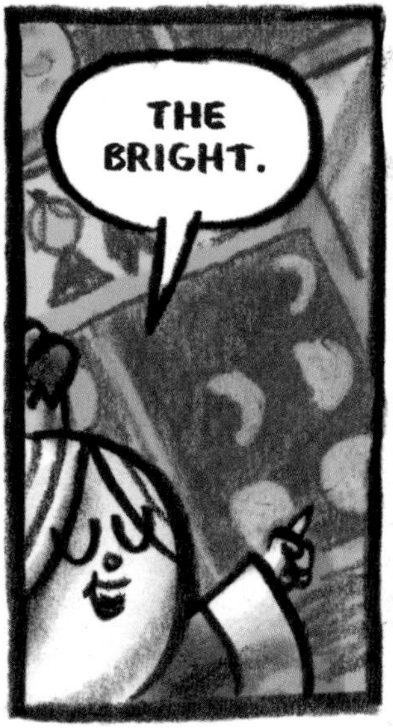
THE BRIGHT.

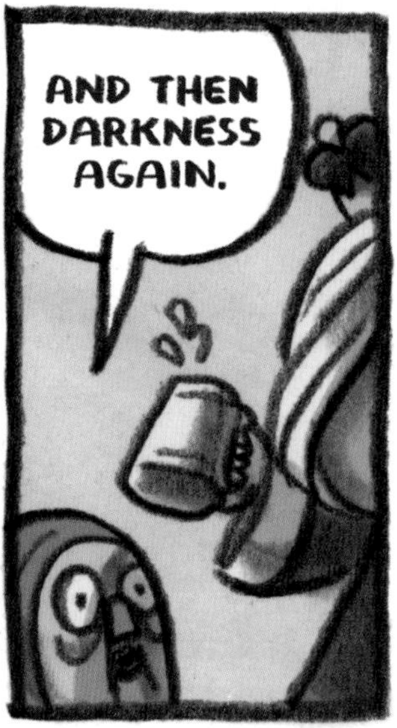
AND THEN DARKNESS AGAIN.

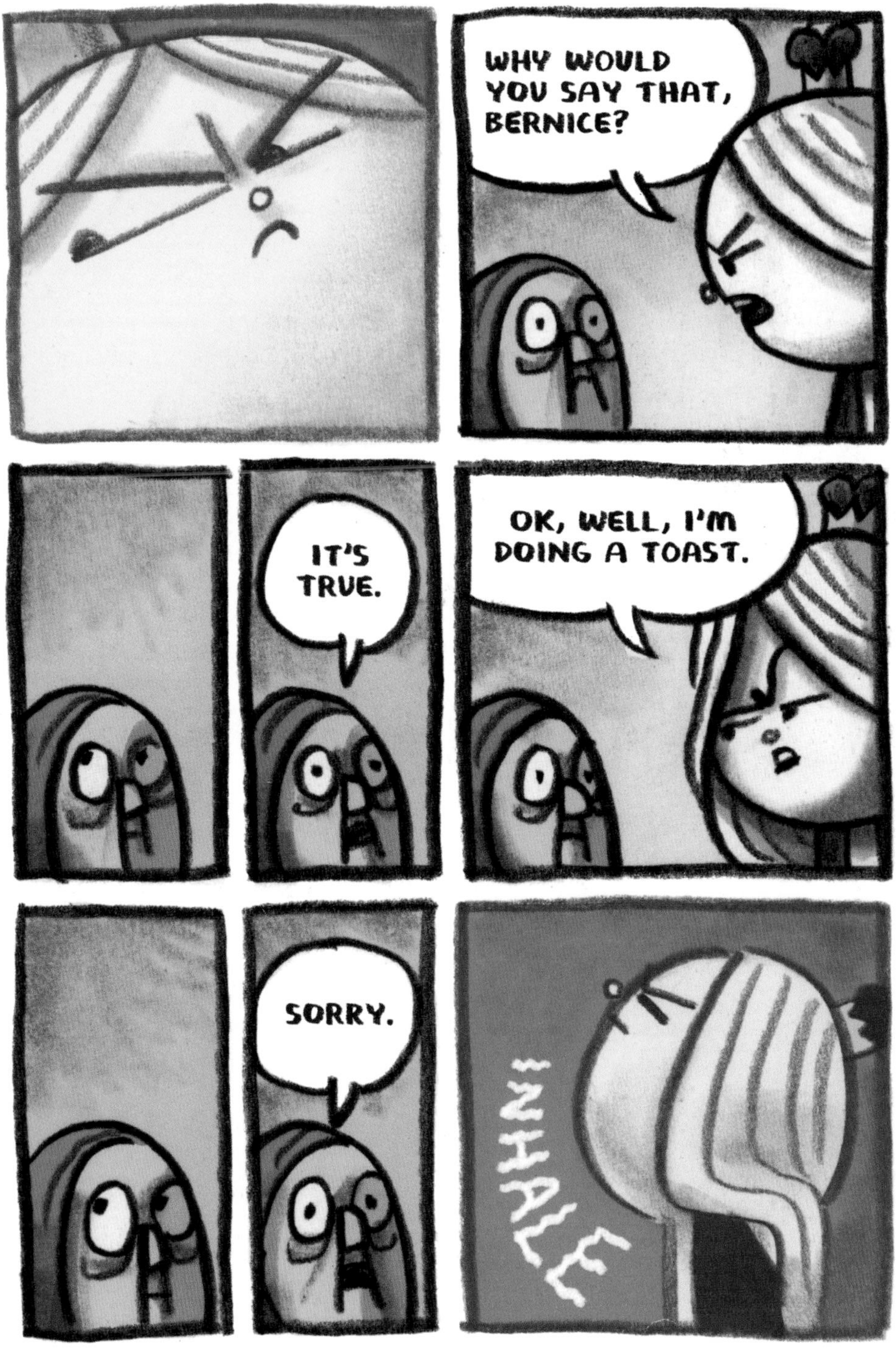
WHY WOULD YOU SAY THAT, BERNICE?
IT'S TRUE.
OK, WELL, I'M DOING A TOAST.
SORRY.
INHALE

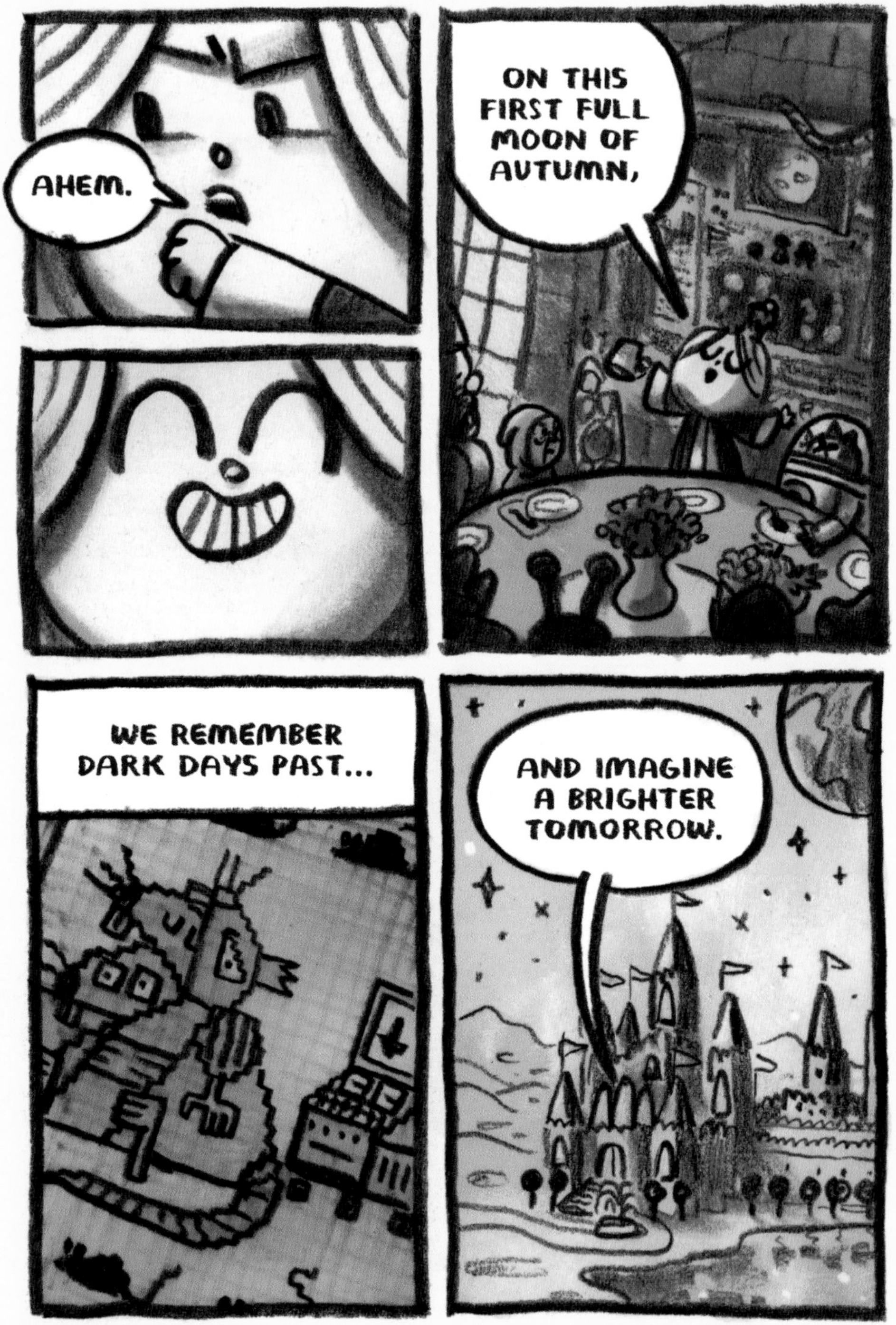
AHEM.
ON THIS FIRST FULL MOON OF AUTUMN,
WE REMEMBER DARK DAYS PAST...
AND IMAGINE A BRIGHTER TOMORROW.

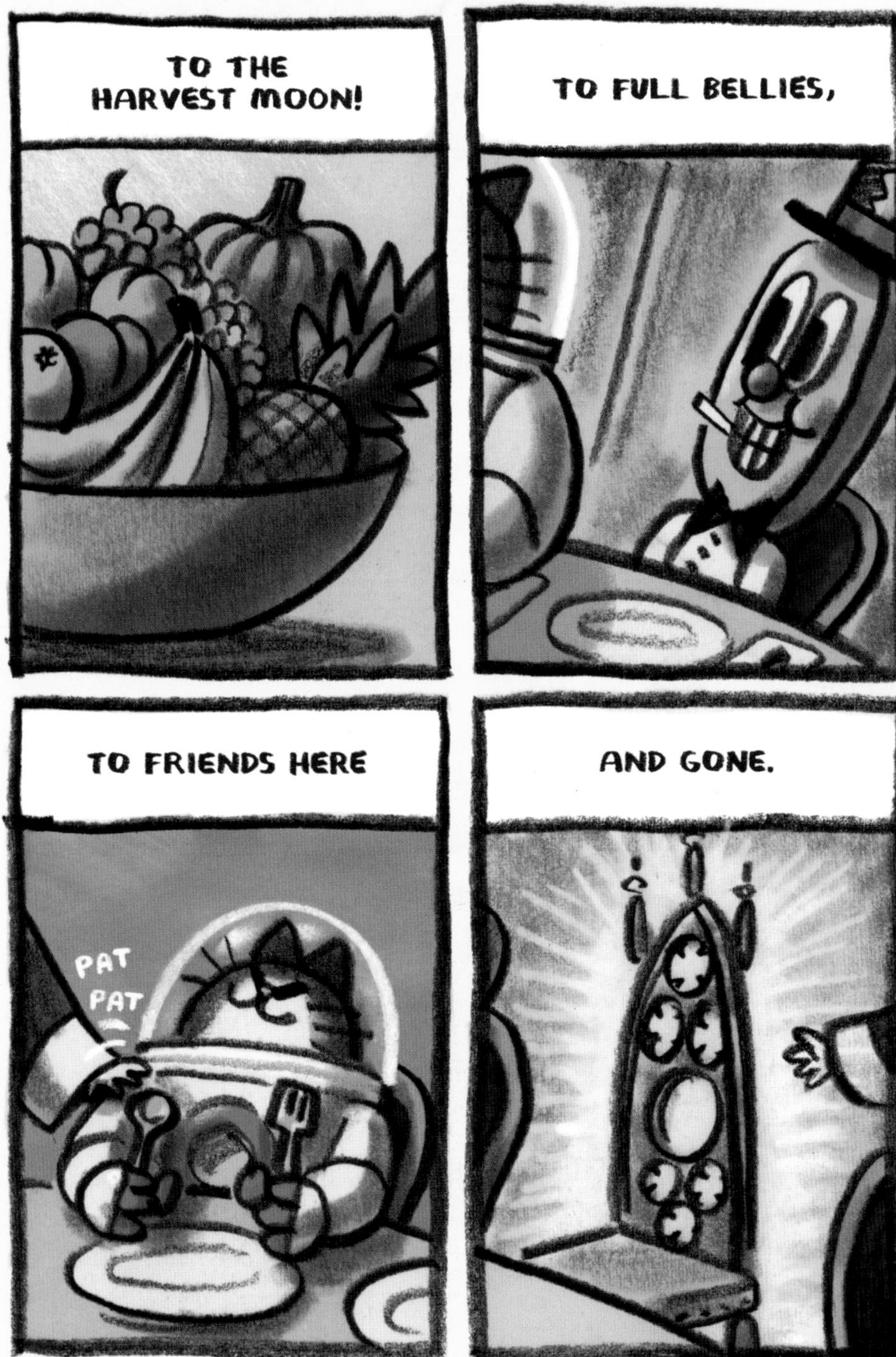
TO THE HARVEST MOON!
TO FULL BELLIES,
TO FRIENDS HERE
PAT PAT
AND GONE.

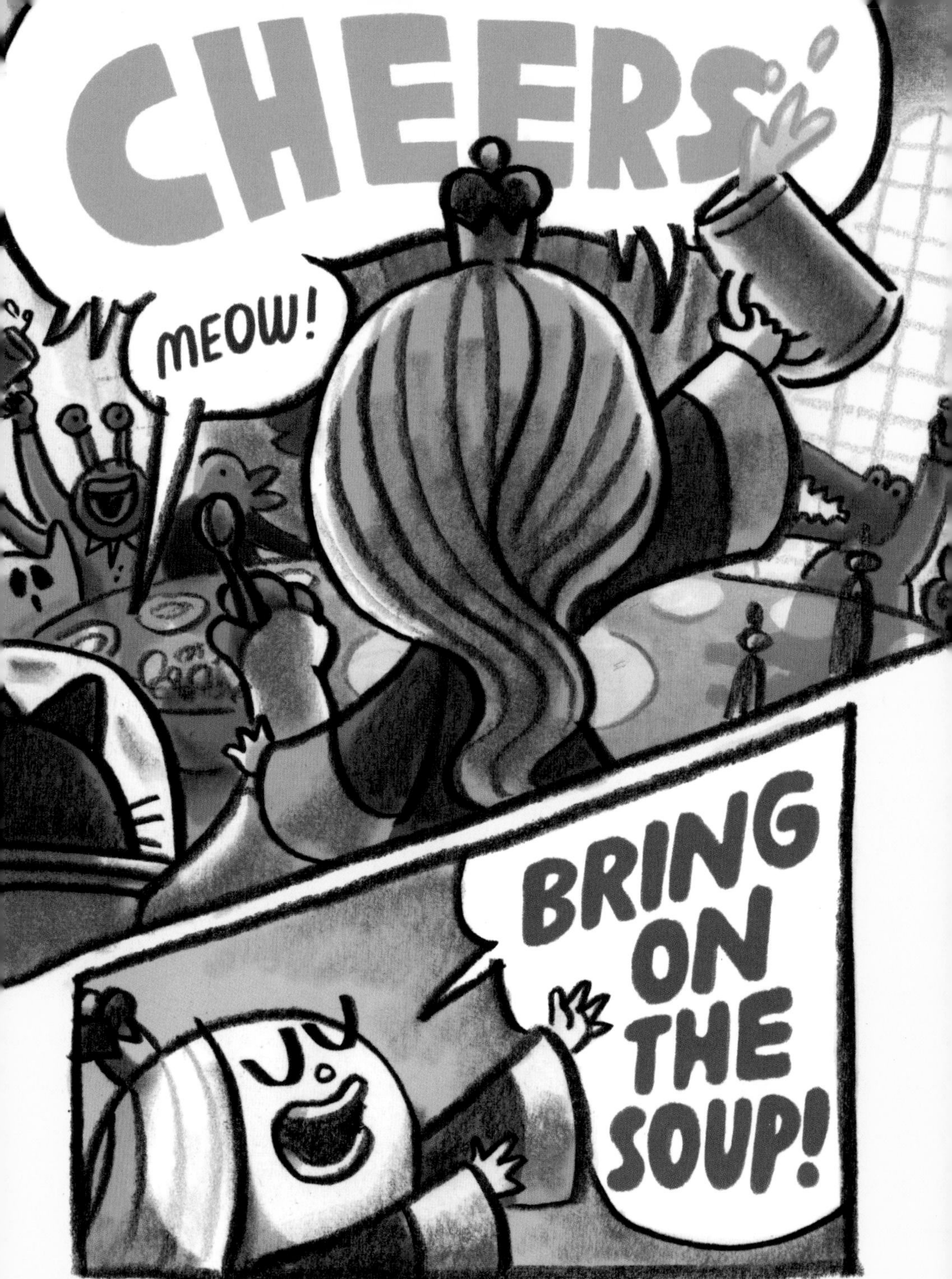
CHEERS!
MEOW!
BRING ON THE SOUP!

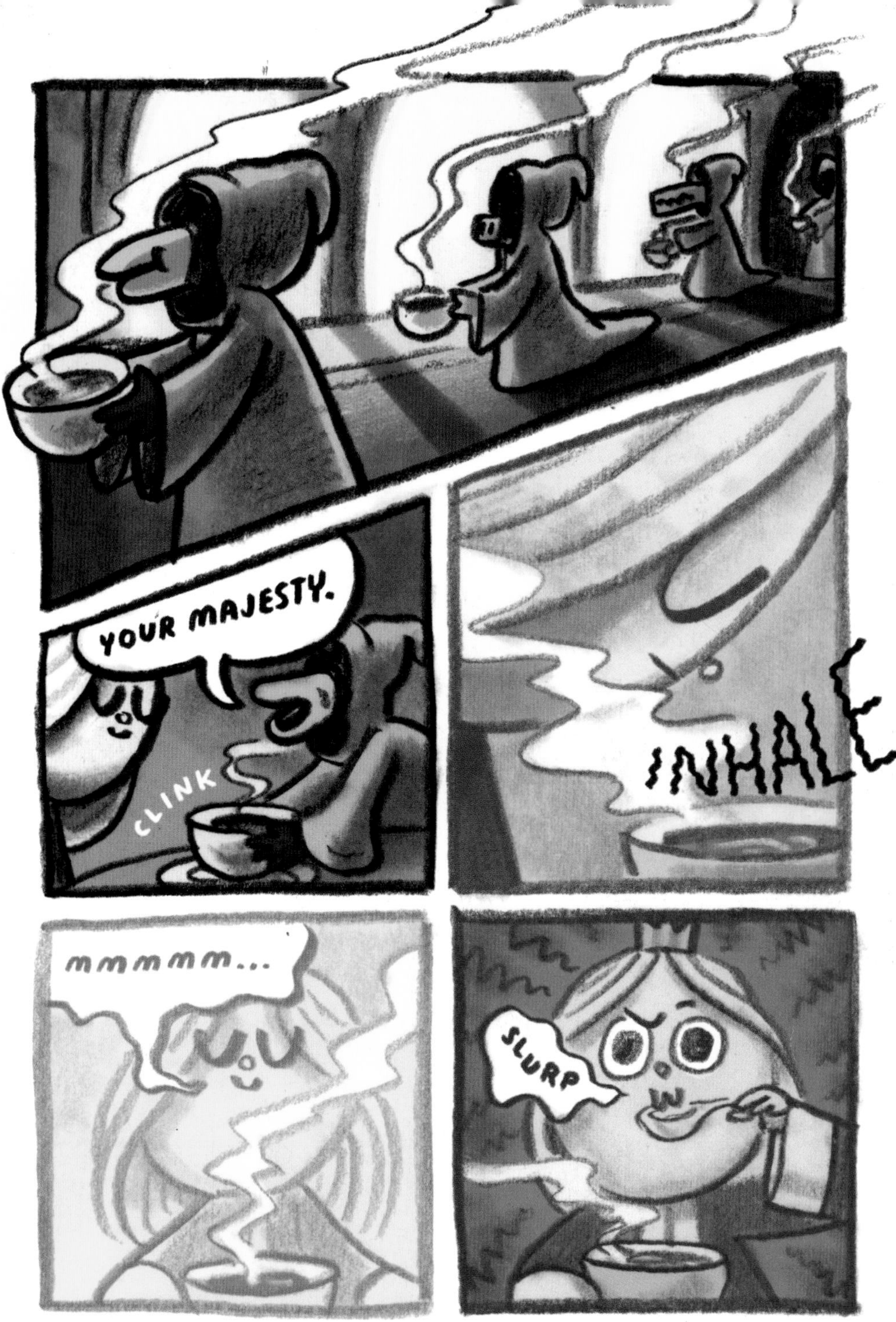
YOUR MAJESTY.
CLINK
INHALE
mmmmm...
SLURP

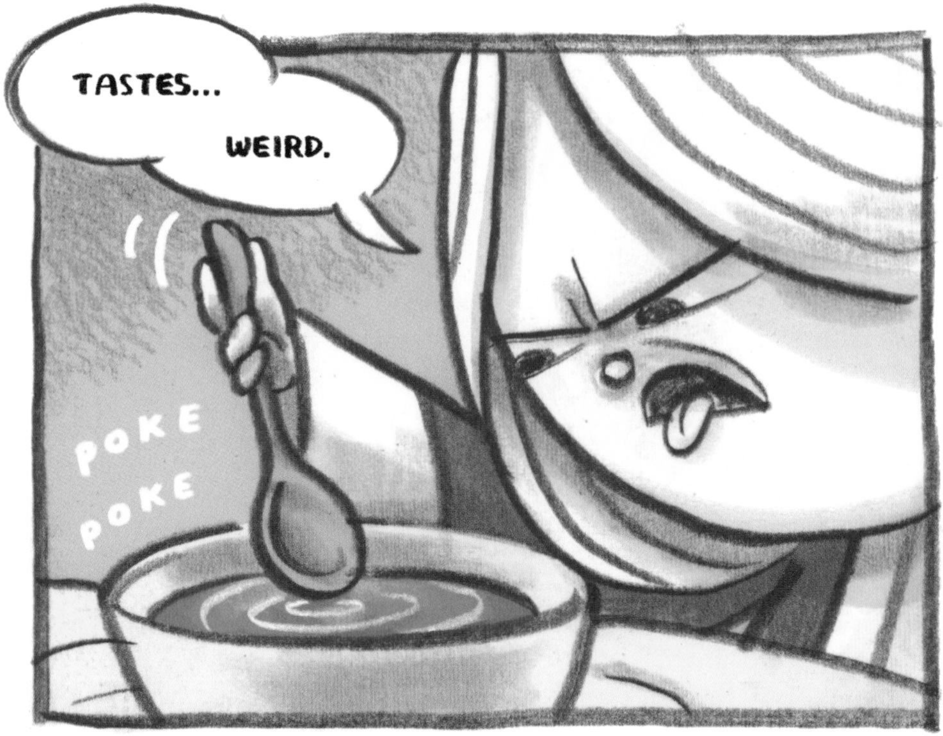
TASTES...
WEIRD.
POKE
POKE

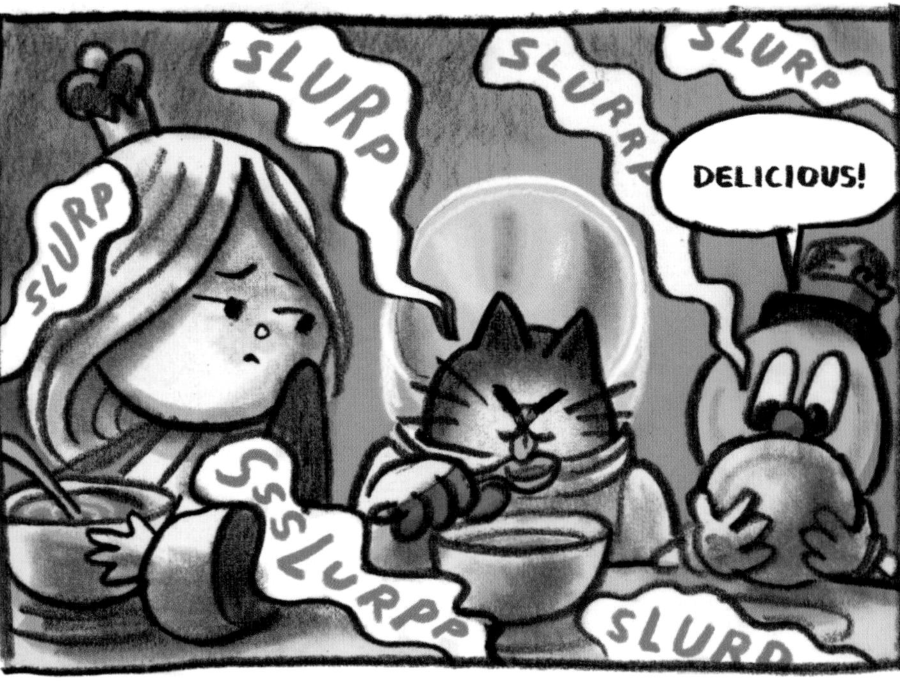
SLURP
SLURP
SLURRR
SLURP
DELICIOUS!
SSSLURPP
SLURP

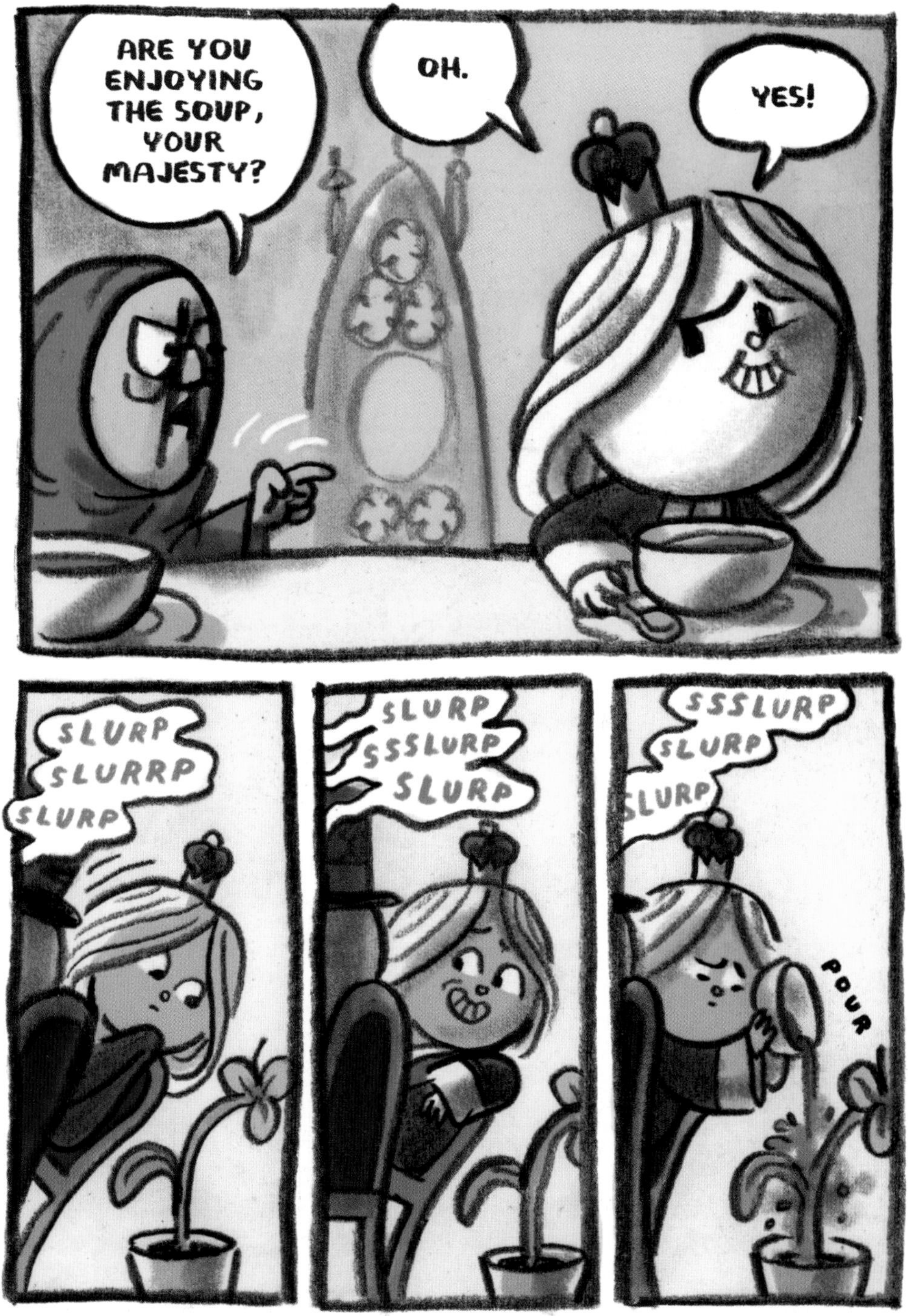
ARE YOU ENJOYING THE SOUP, YOUR MAJESTY?
OH.
YES!
SLURP
SLURRP
SLURP
SLURP
SSSLURP
SLURP
SSSLURP
SLURP
SLURP
POUR

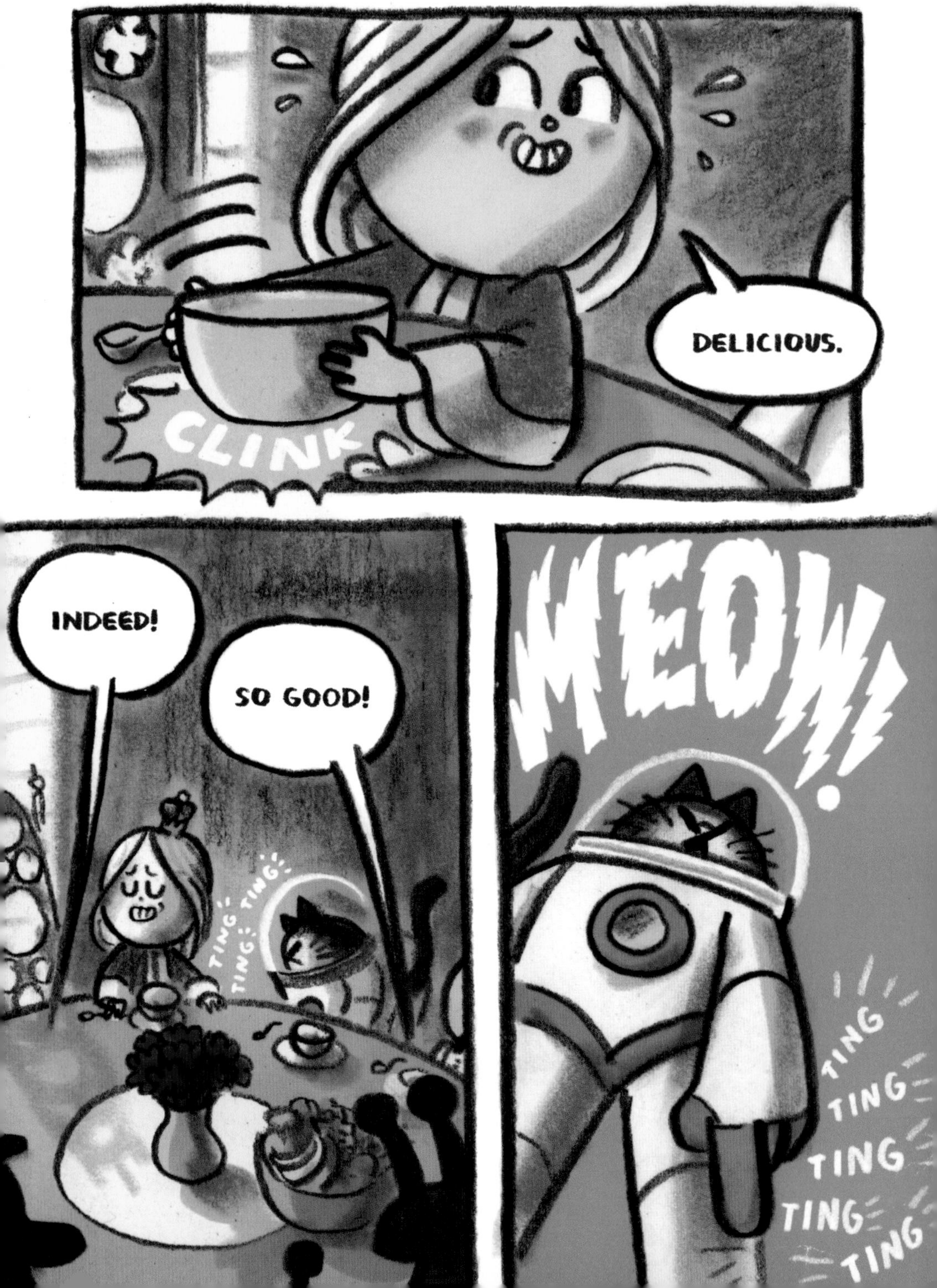

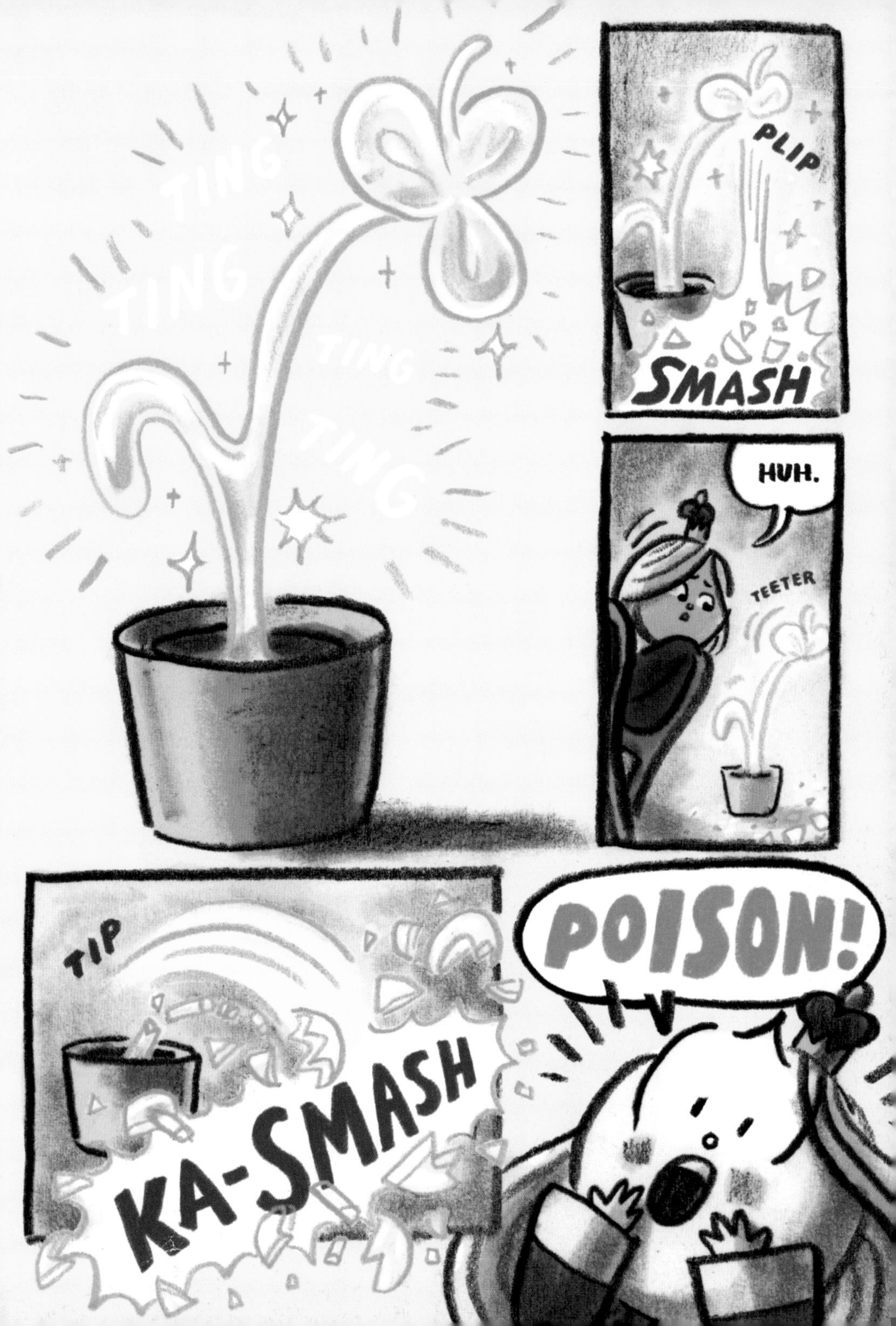
TING
TING
TING
TING
PLIP
SMASH
HUH.
TEETER
TIP
KA-SMASH
POISON!

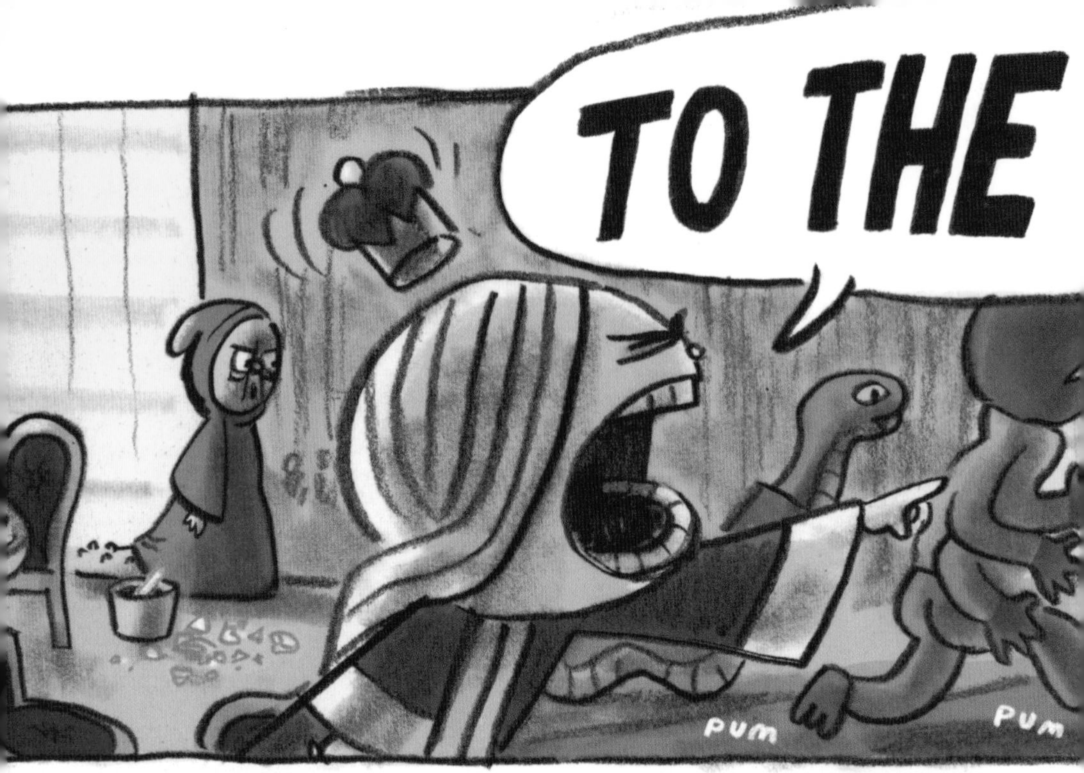
TO THE
PUM
PUM

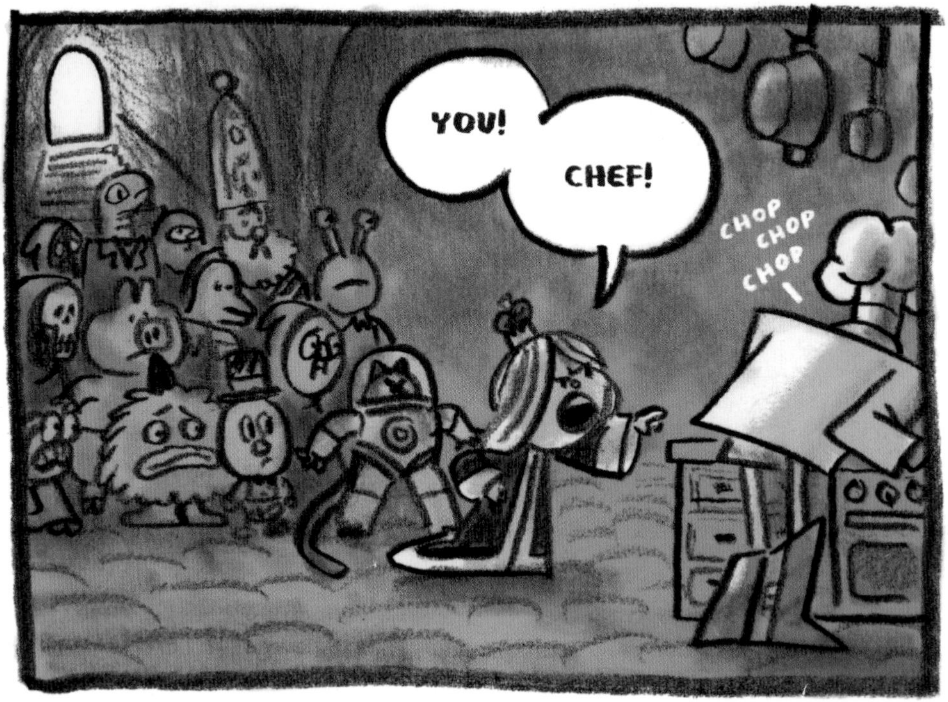
YOU!
CHEF!
CHOP
CHOP
CHOP

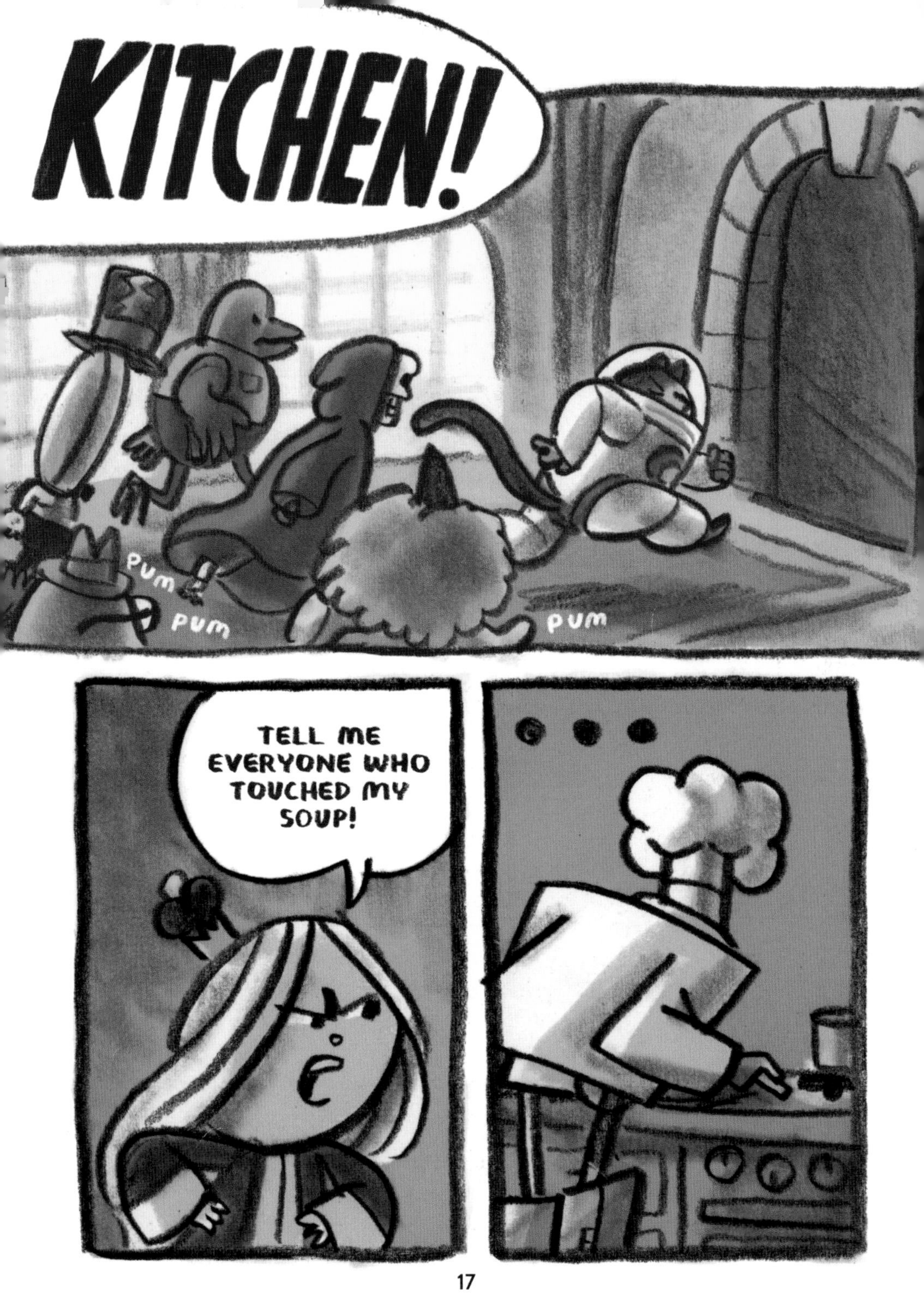
KITCHEN!
PUM
PUM
PUM
TELL ME EVERYONE WHO TOUCHED MY SOUP!

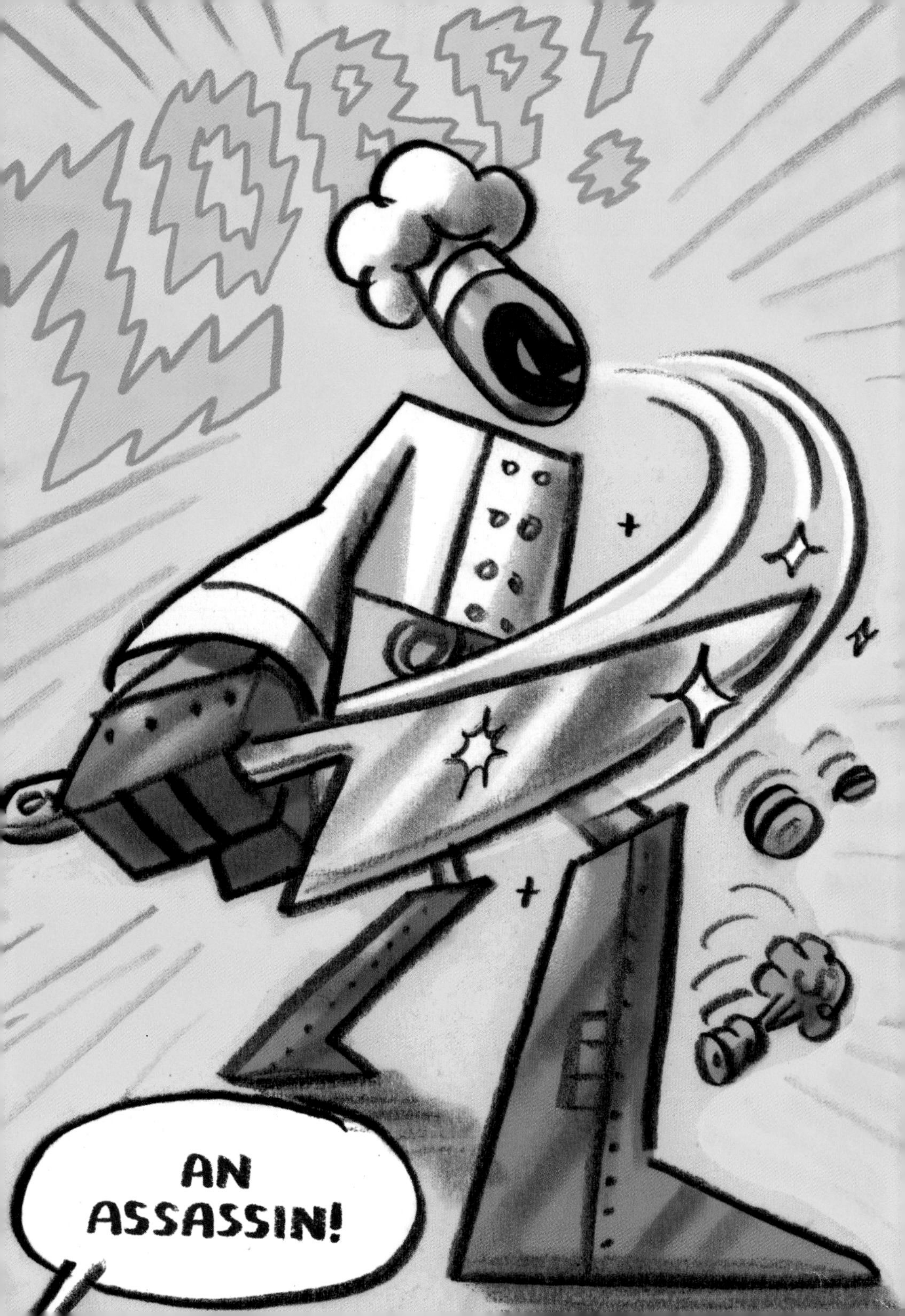
AN ASSASSIN!

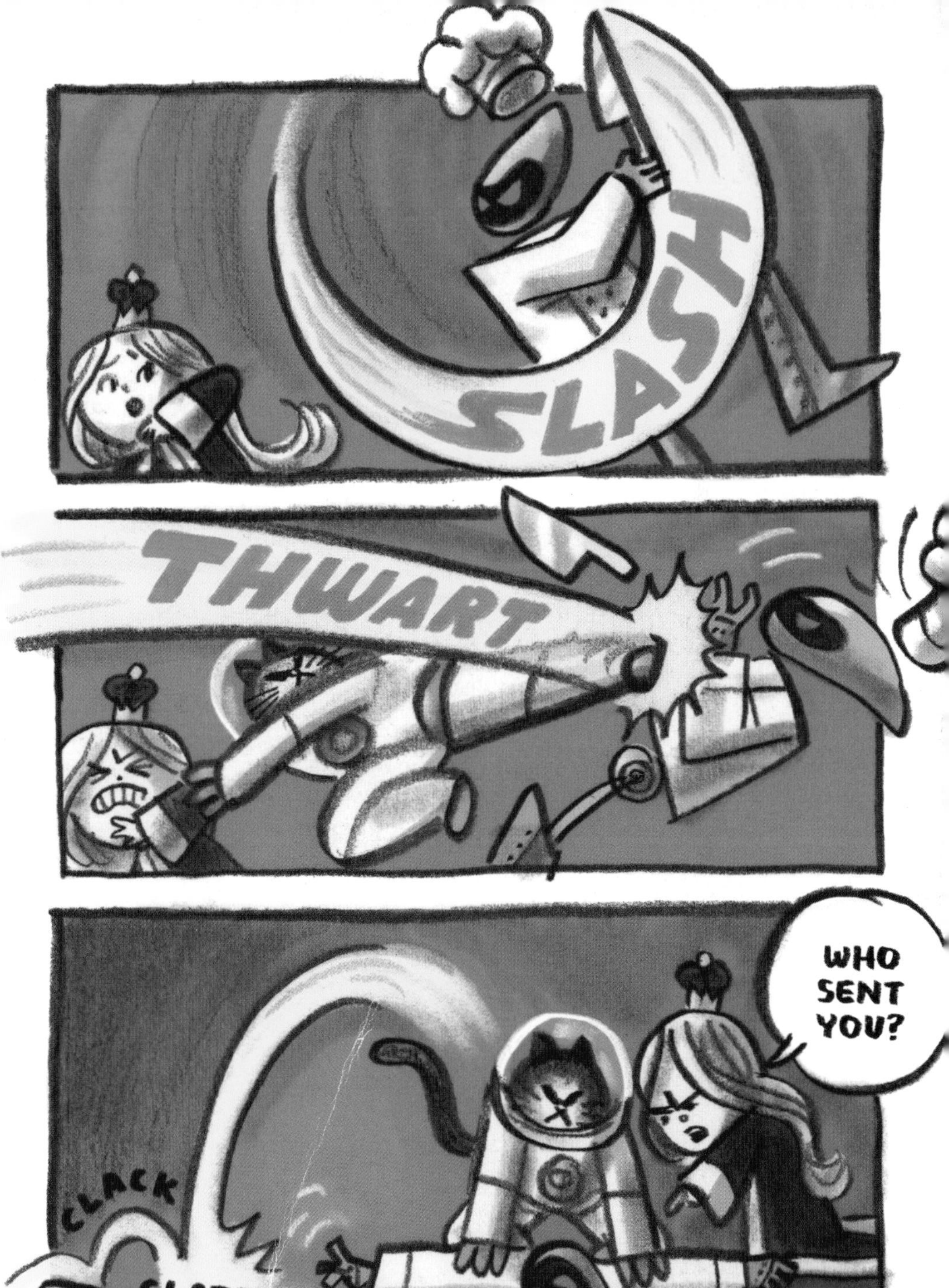
SLASH
THWART
WHO SENT YOU?
CLACK
CLATTER

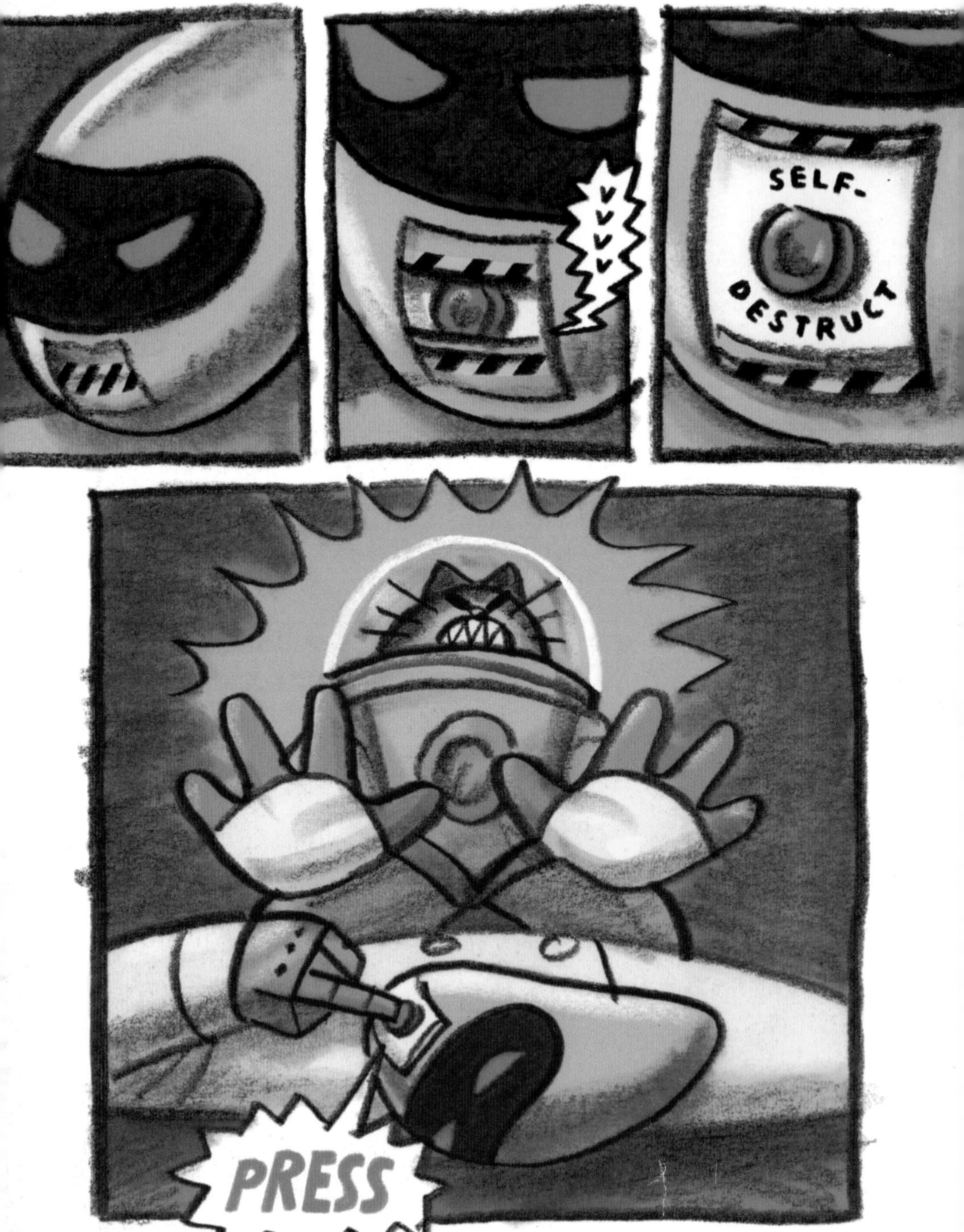
VVVVV
SELF-DESTRUCT
PRESS

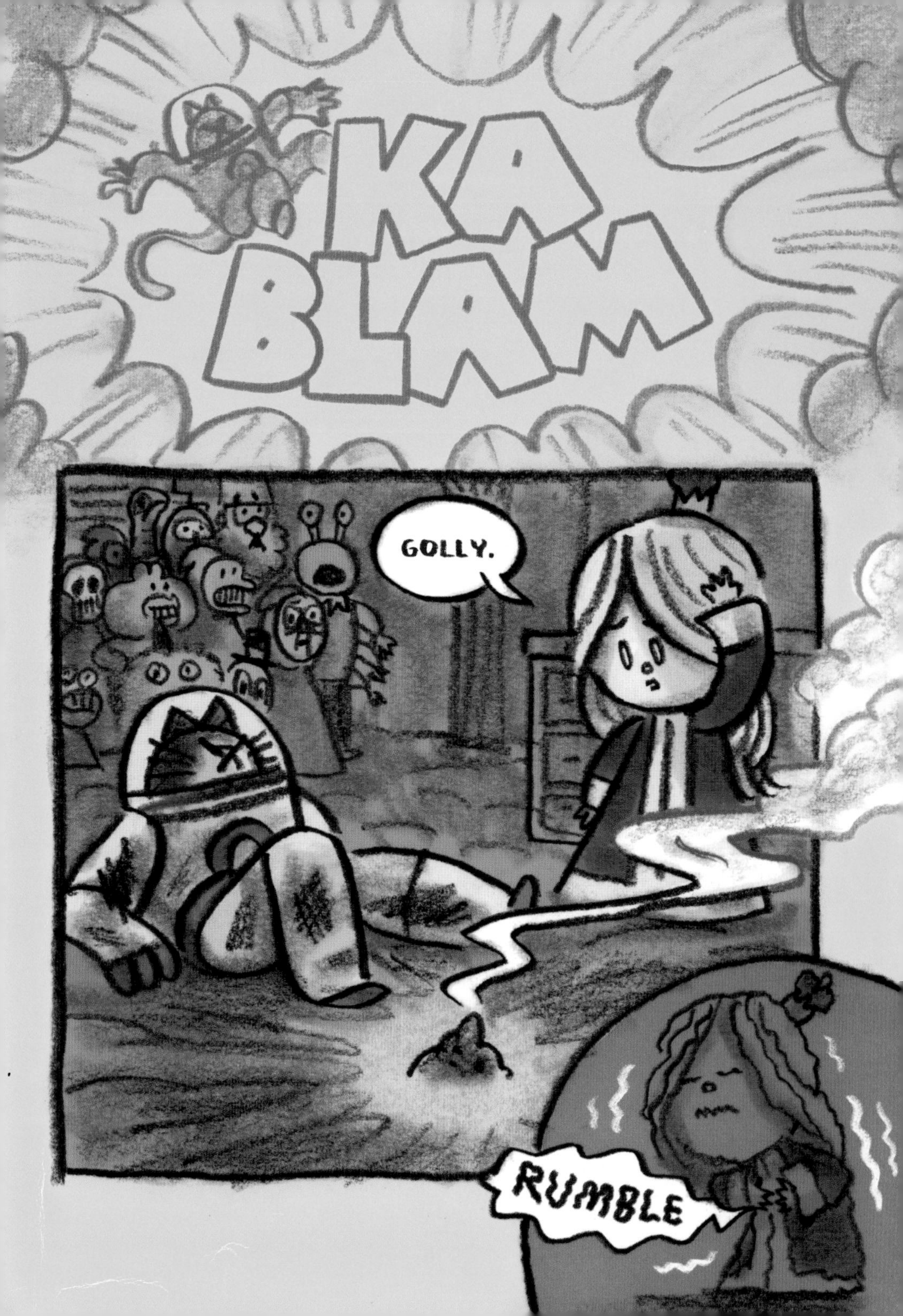
KA BLAM
GOLLY.
RUMBLE

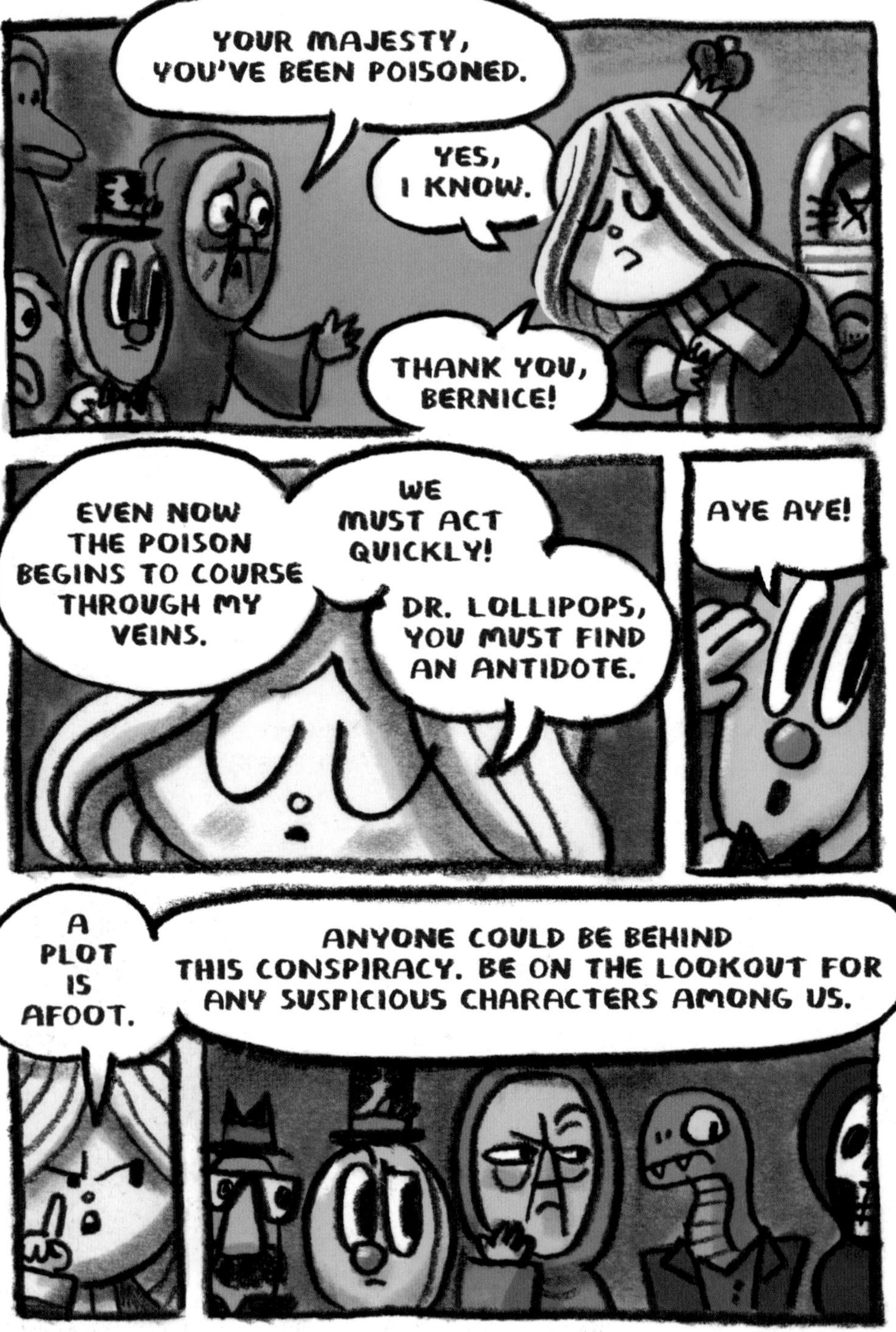
YOUR MAJESTY, YOU'VE BEEN POISONED.
YES, I KNOW.
THANK YOU, BERNICE!
EVEN NOW THE POISON BEGINS TO COURSE THROUGH MY VEINS.
WE MUST ACT QUICKLY!
DR. LOLLIPOPS, YOU MUST FIND AN ANTIDOTE.
AYE AYE!
A PLOT IS AFOOT.
ANYONE COULD BE BEHIND THIS CONSPIRACY. BE ON THE LOOKOUT FOR ANY SUSPICIOUS CHARACTERS AMONG US.

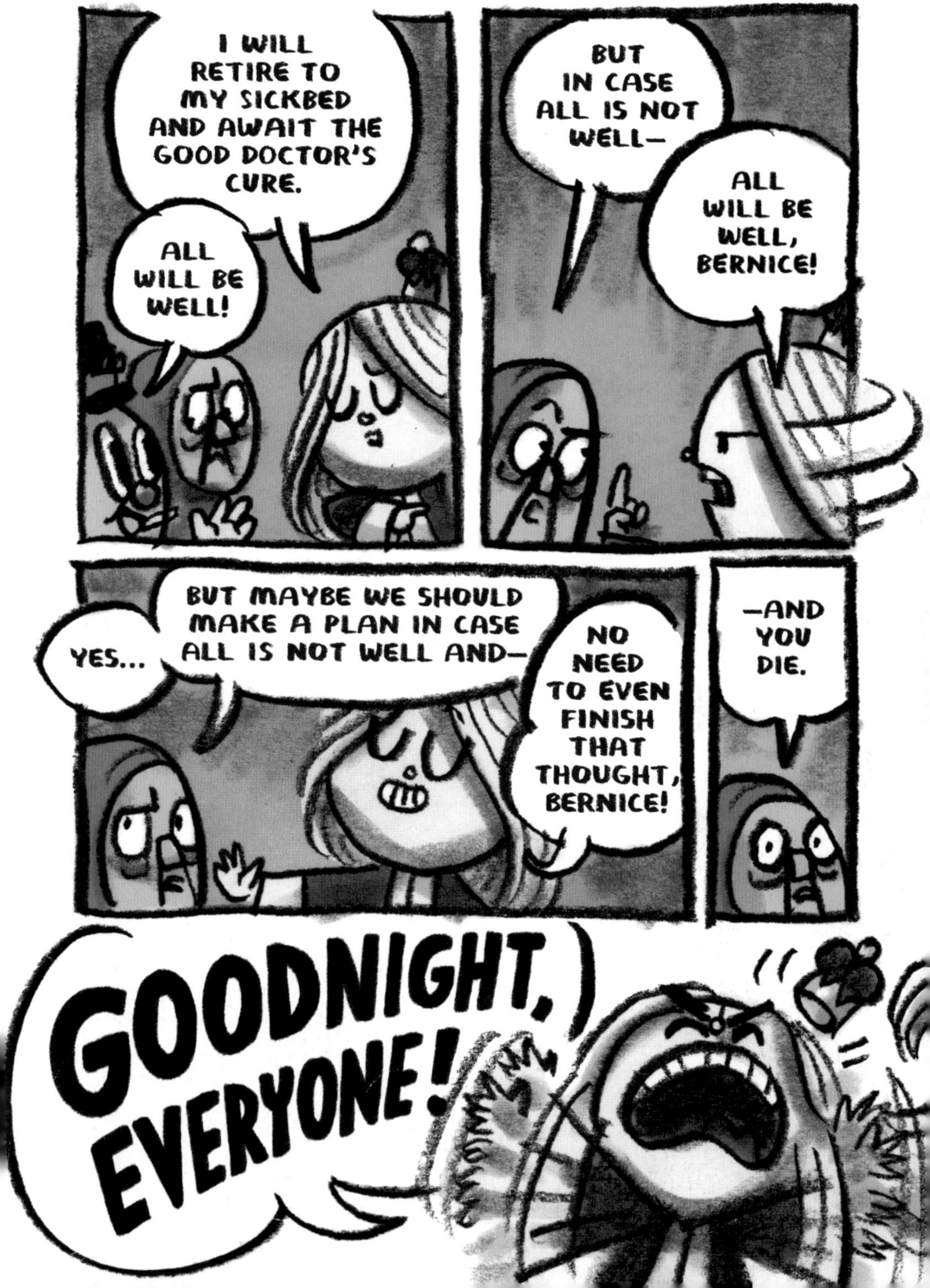
I WILL RETIRE TO MY SICKBED AND AWAIT THE GOOD DOCTOR'S CURE.
ALL WILL BE WELL!
BUT IN CASE ALL IS NOT WELL—
ALL WILL BE WELL, BERNICE!
YES...
BUT MAYBE WE SHOULD MAKE A PLAN IN CASE ALL IS NOT WELL AND—
NO NEED TO EVEN FINISH THAT THOUGHT, BERNICE!
—AND YOU DIE.
GOODNIGHT, EVERYONE!

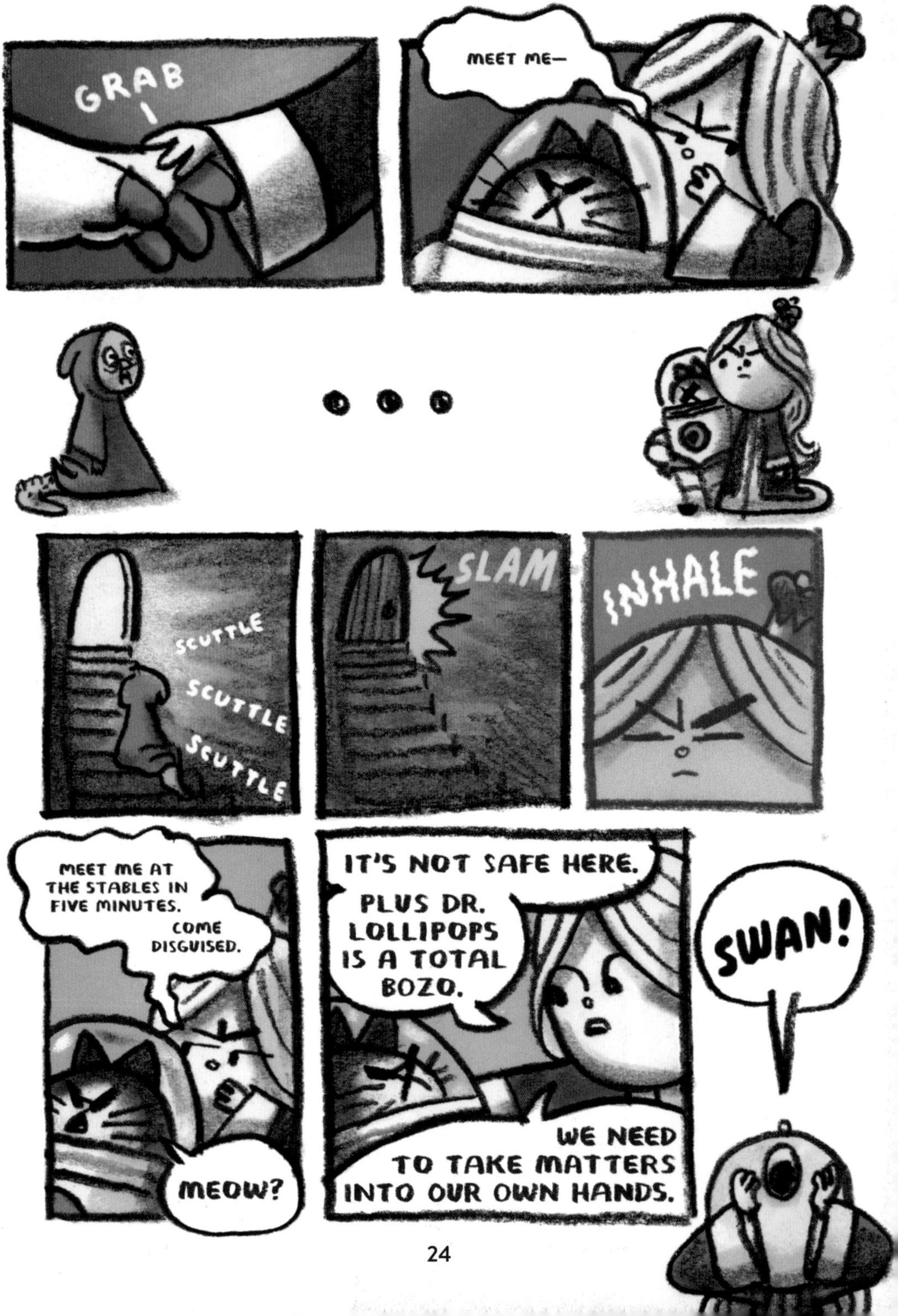
GRAB
MEET ME—
SCUTTLE
SCUTTLE
SCUTTLE
SLAM
INHALE
MEET ME AT THE STABLES IN FIVE MINUTES.
COME DISGUISED.
MEOW?
IT'S NOT SAFE HERE.
PLUS DR. LOLLIPOPS IS A TOTAL BOZO.
WE NEED TO TAKE MATTERS INTO OUR OWN HANDS.
SWAN!

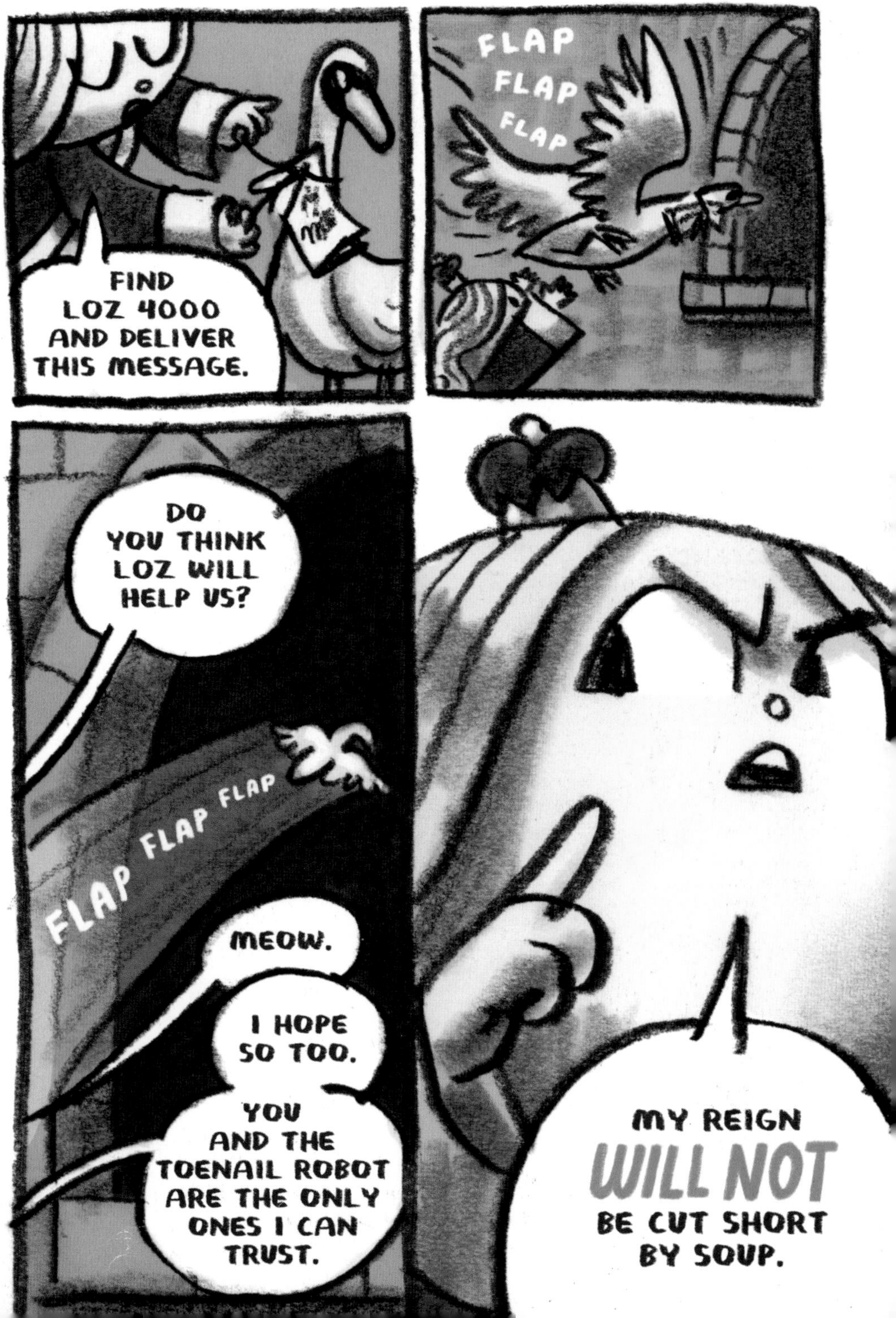
FIND LOZ 4000 AND DELIVER THIS MESSAGE.
FLAP FLAP FLAP
DO YOU THINK LOZ WILL HELP US?
FLAP FLAP FLAP
MEOW.
I HOPE SO TOO.
YOU AND THE TOENAIL ROBOT ARE THE ONLY ONES I CAN TRUST.
MY REIGN WILL NOT BE CUT SHORT BY SOUP.

SHAWN & MAC

PRESENT...

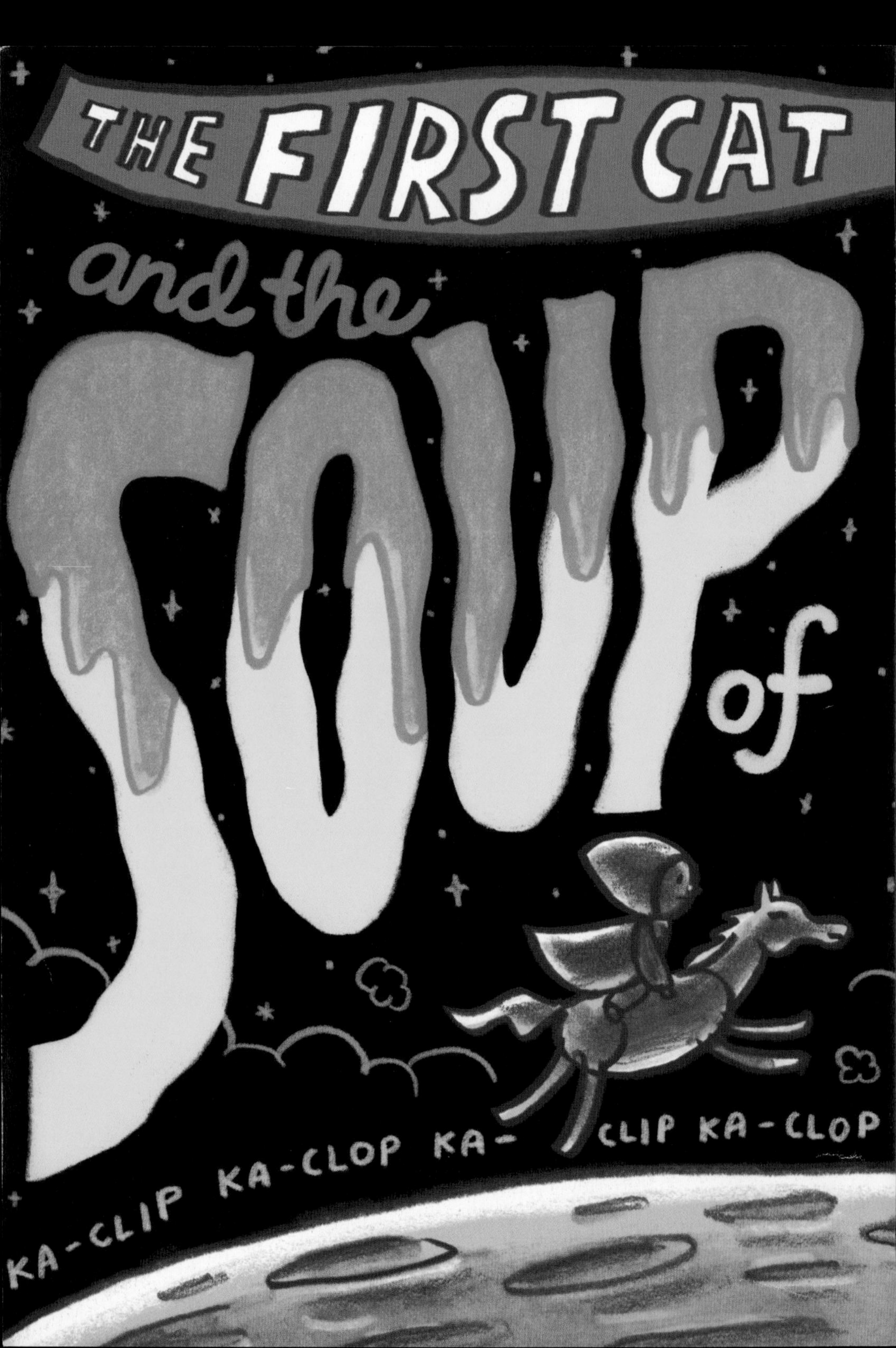
THE FIRST CAT
and the
SOUP
of
KA-CLIP KA-CLOP KA-CLIP KA-CLOP

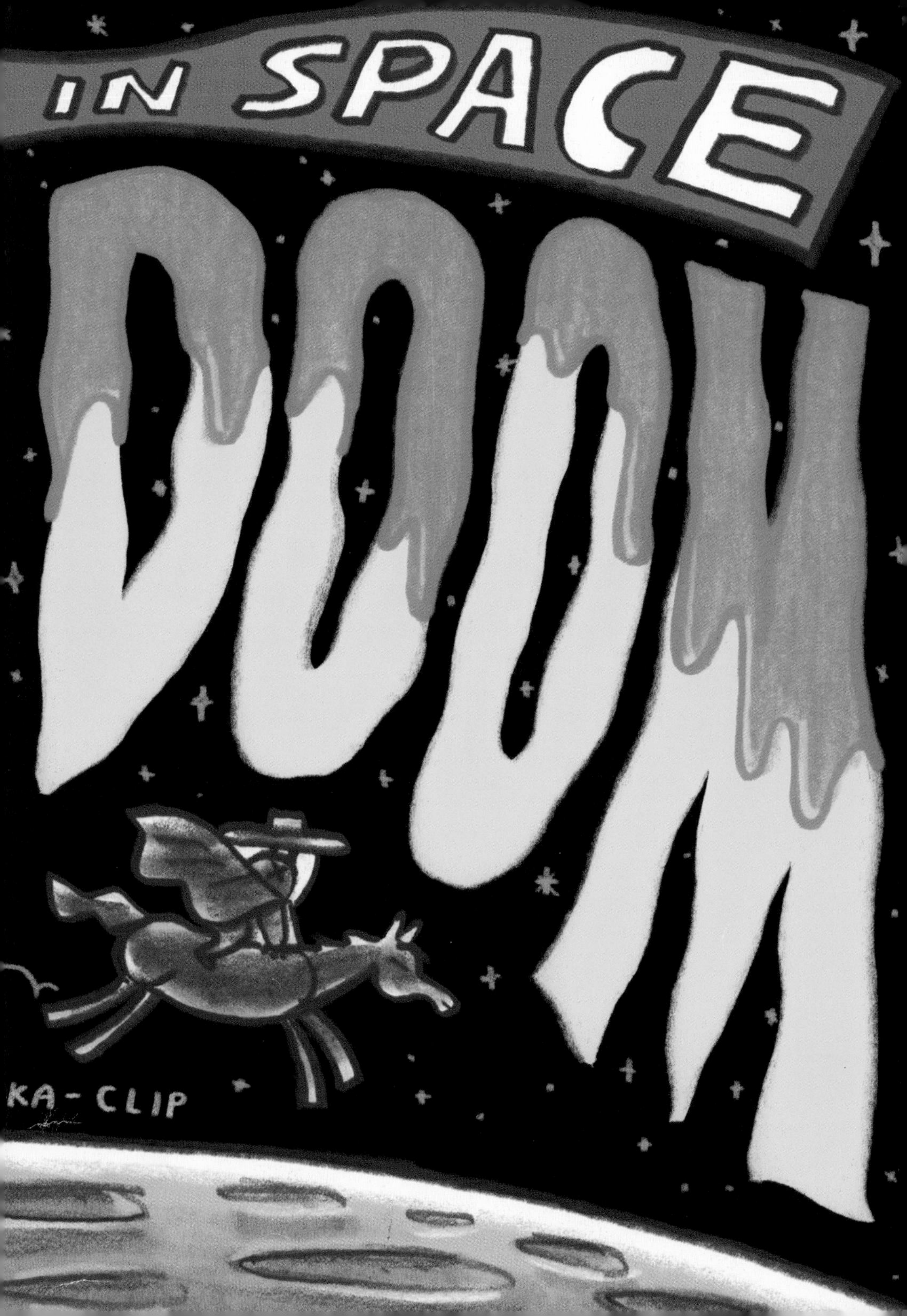
IN SPACE
DOOM
KA-CLIP

# CHAPTER 1

# HARVEST MOON

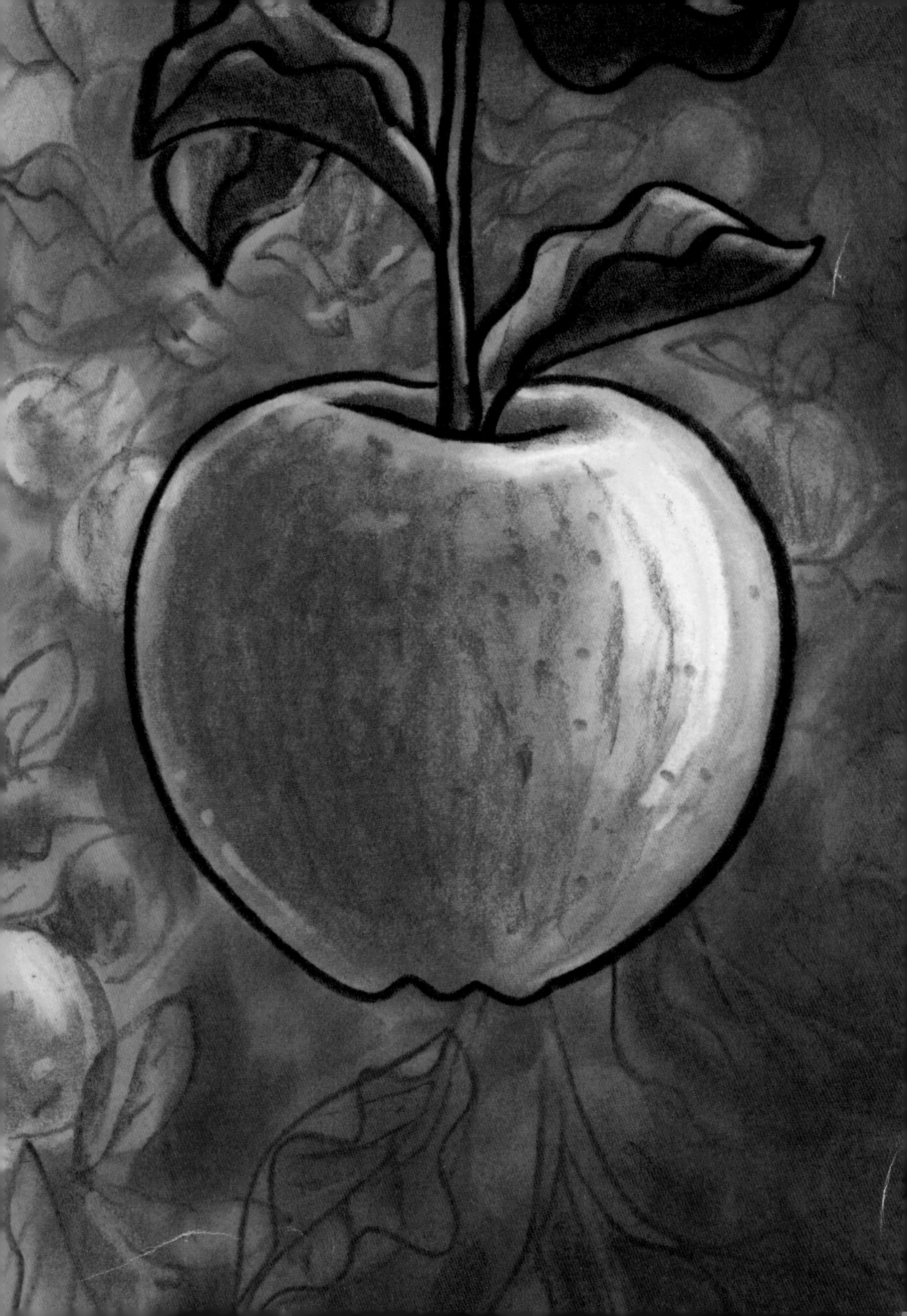

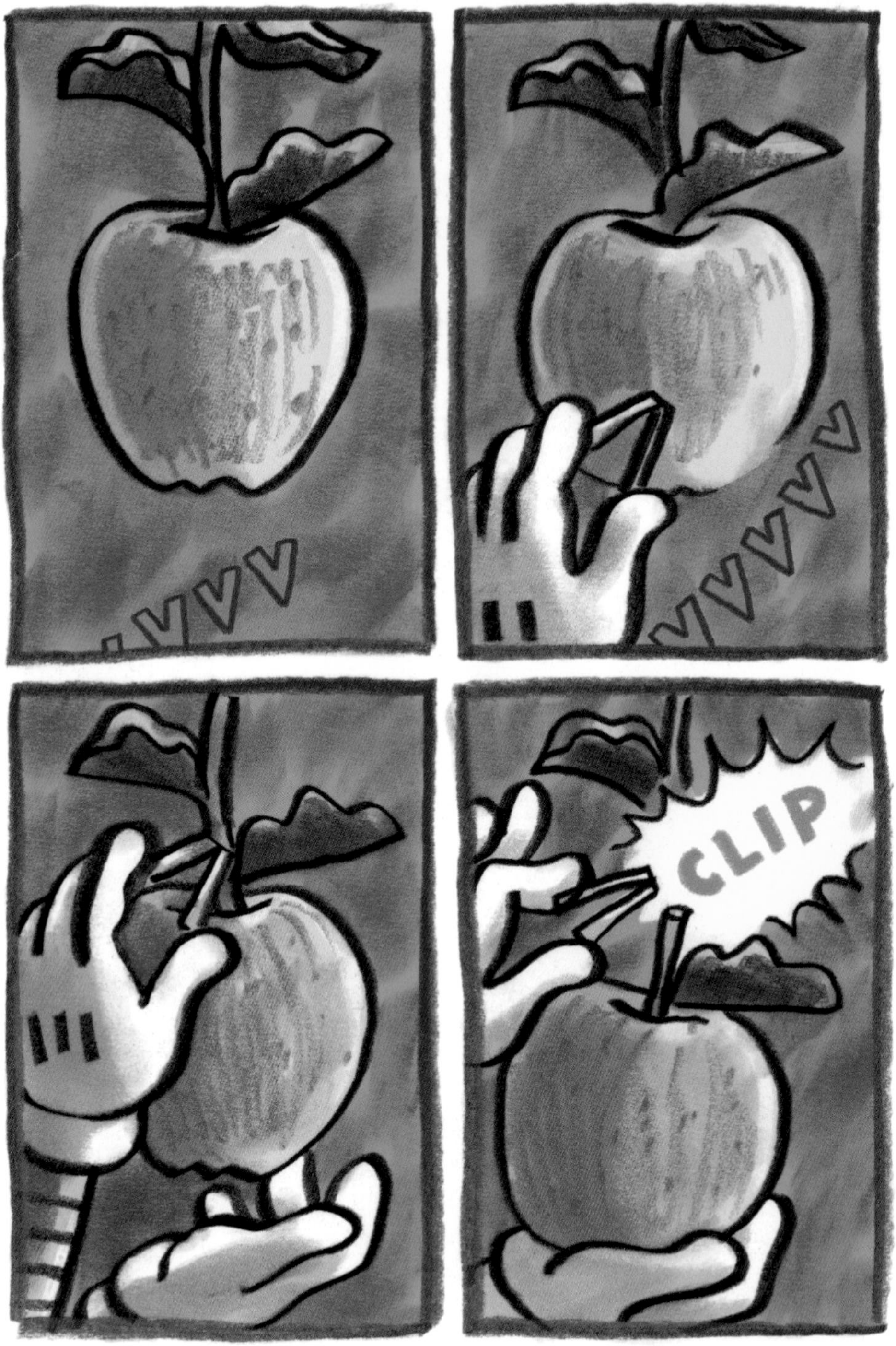
CLIP

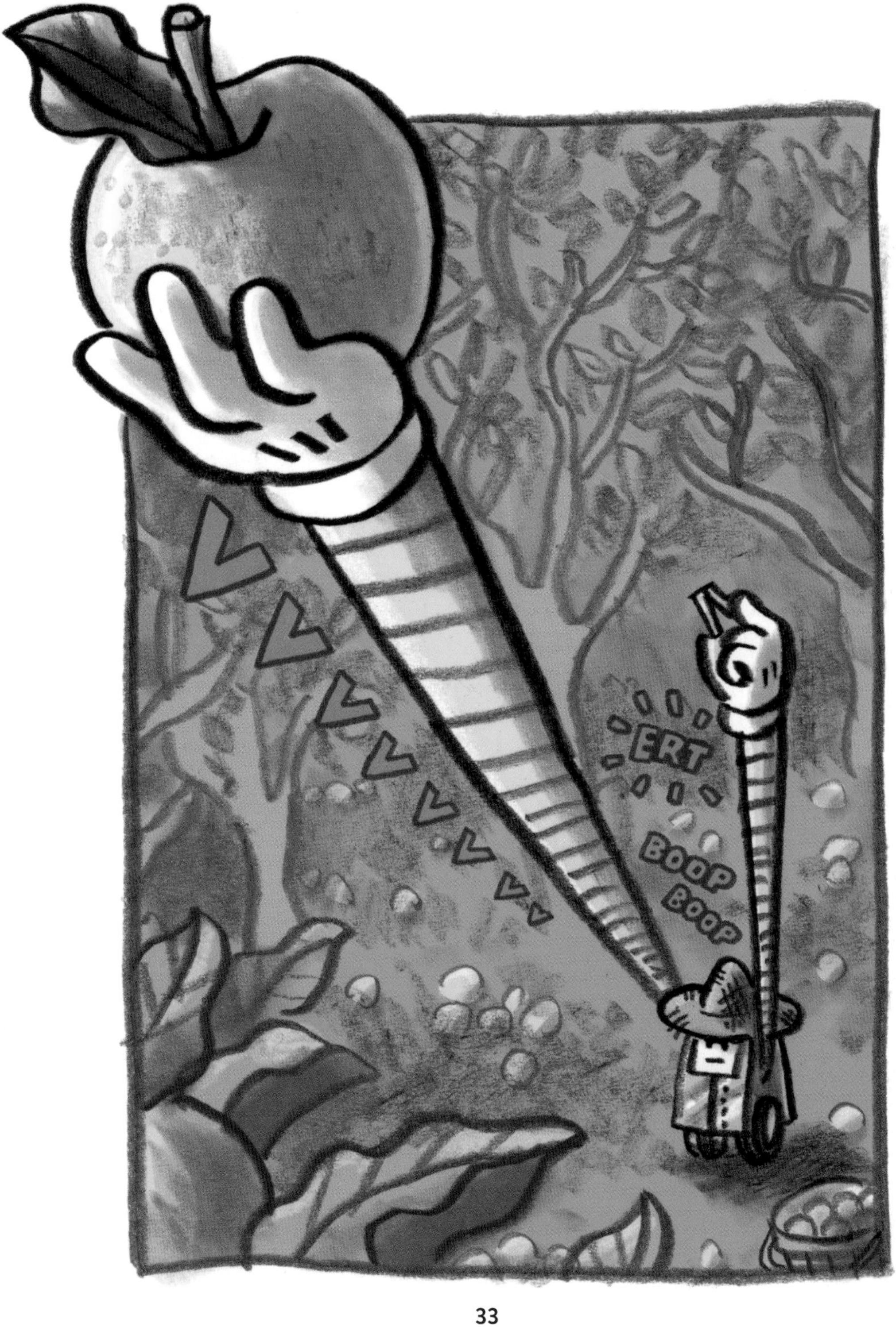
ERT
BOOP
BOOP

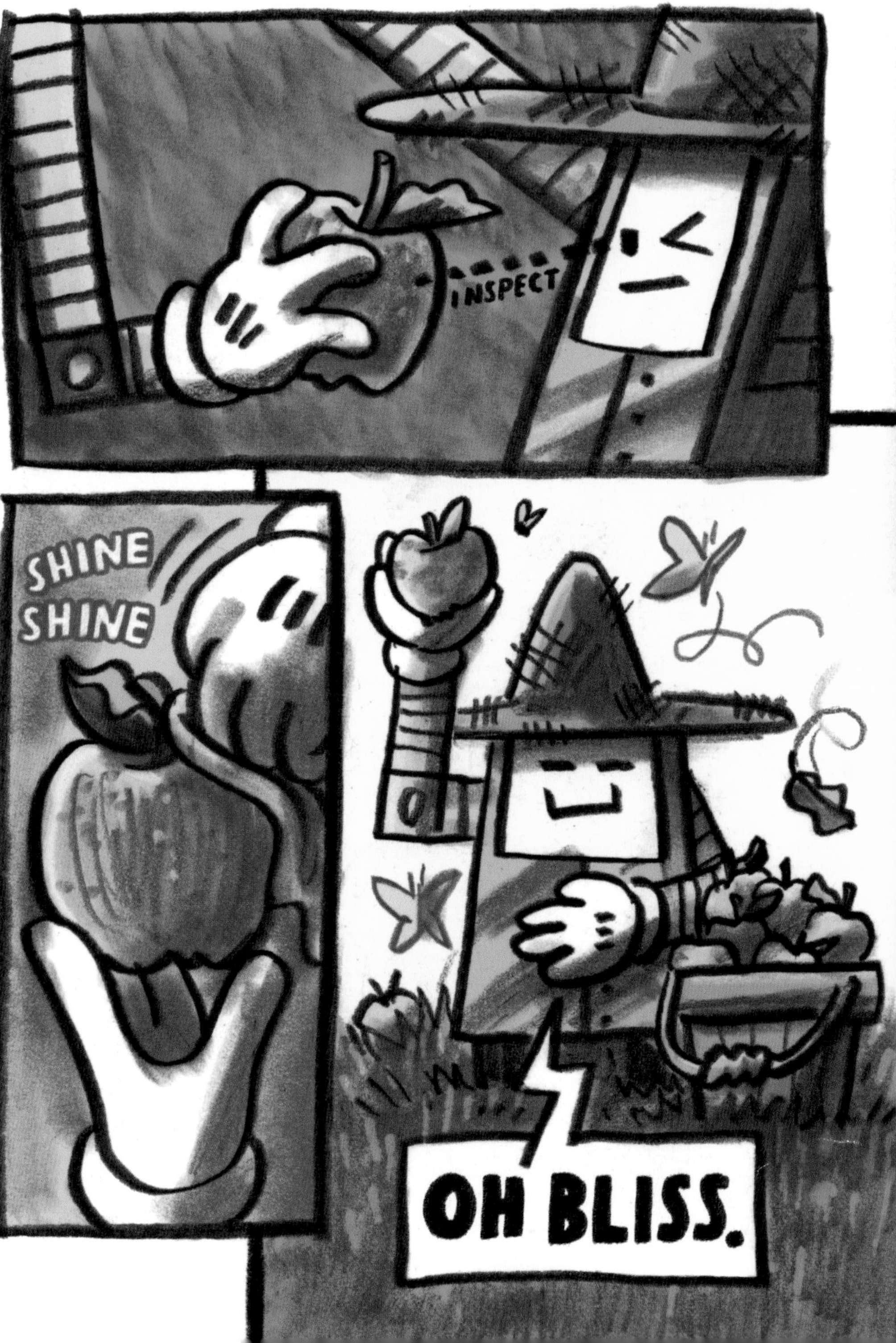
INSPECT
SHINE SHINE
OH BLISS.

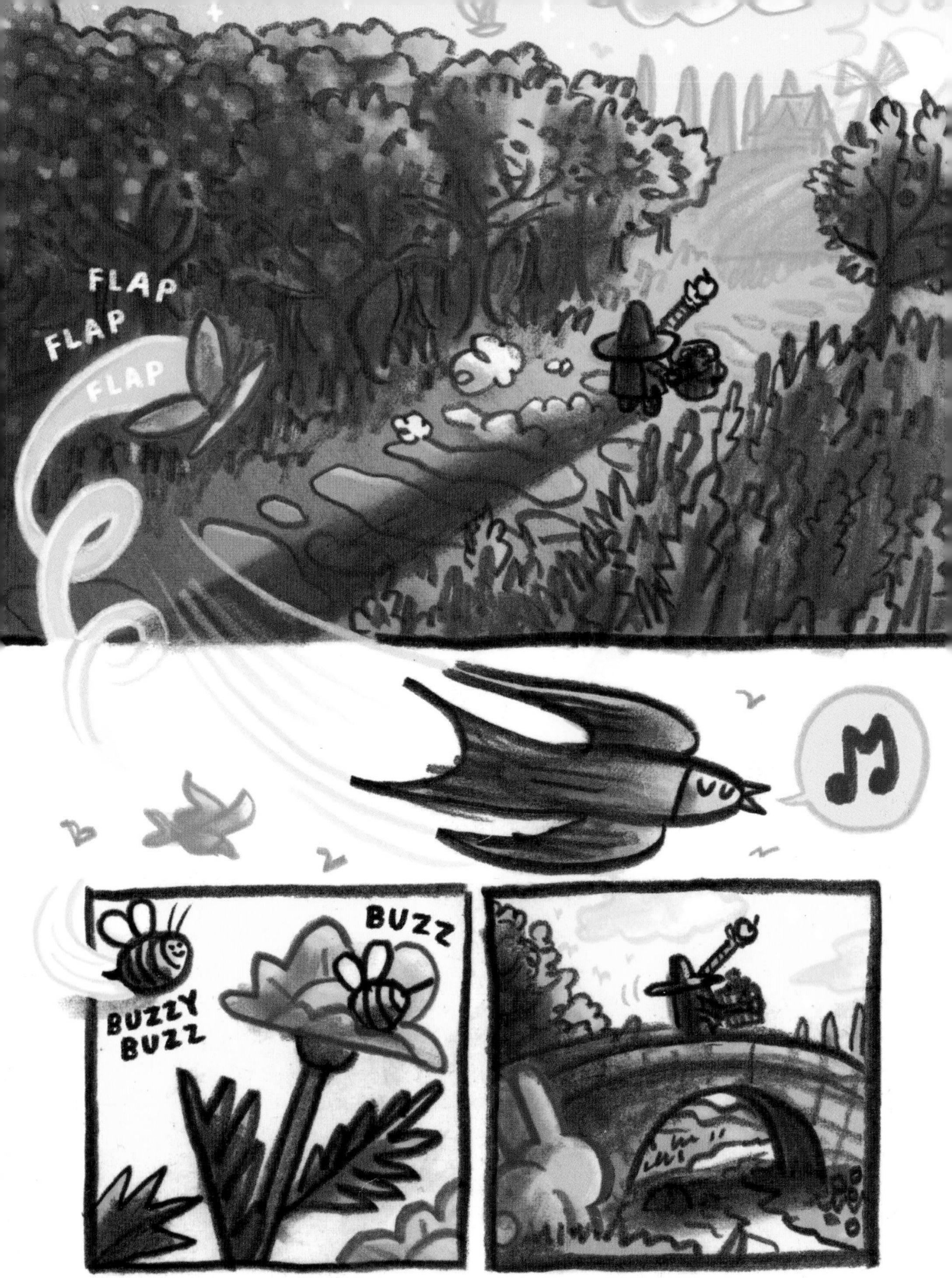
FLAP
FLAP
FLAP
BUZZY BUZZ
BUZZ

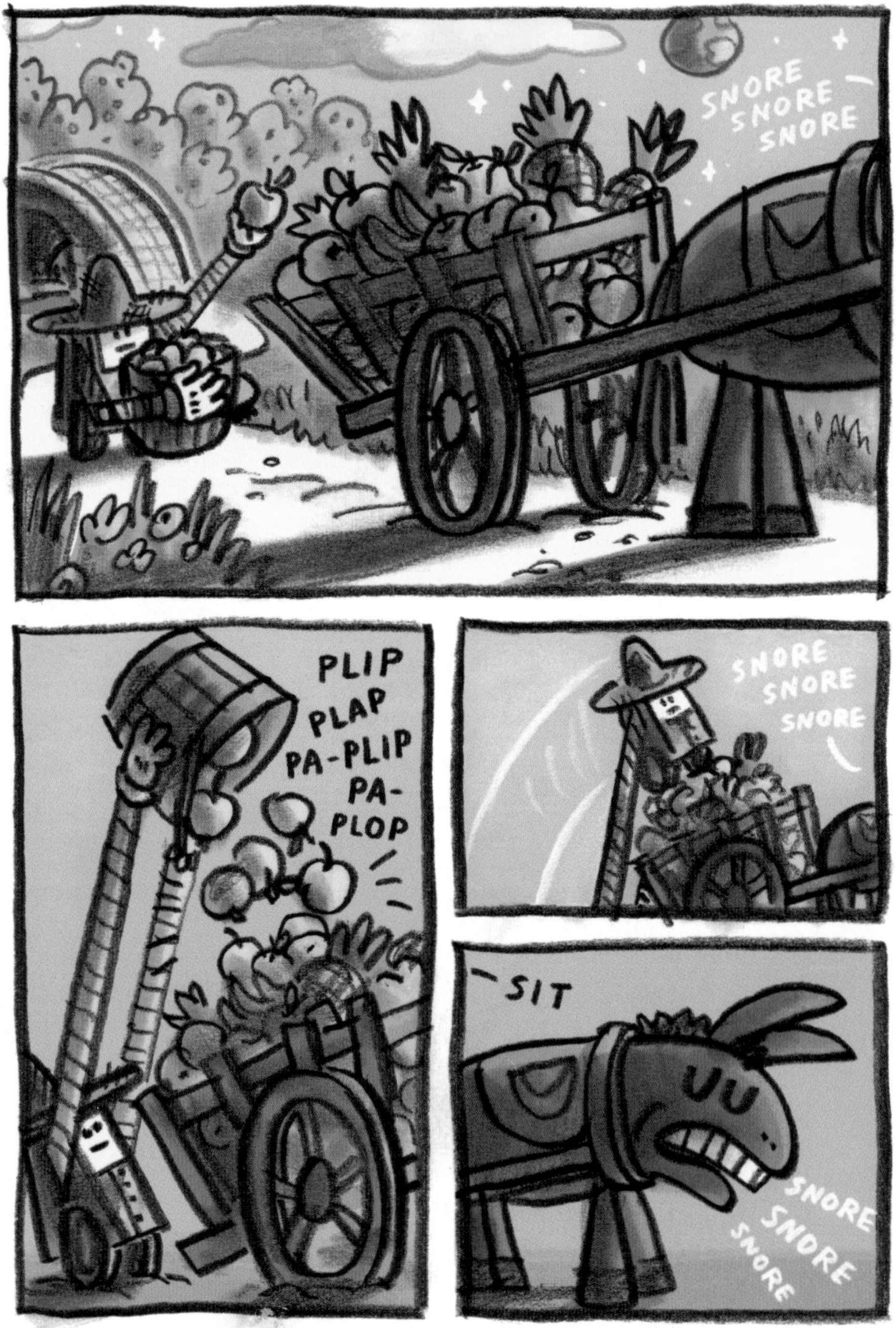
SNORE
SNORE
SNORE
PLIP
PLAP
PA-PLIP
PA-
PLOP
SNORE
SNORE
SNORE
SIT
SNORE
SNORE
SNORE

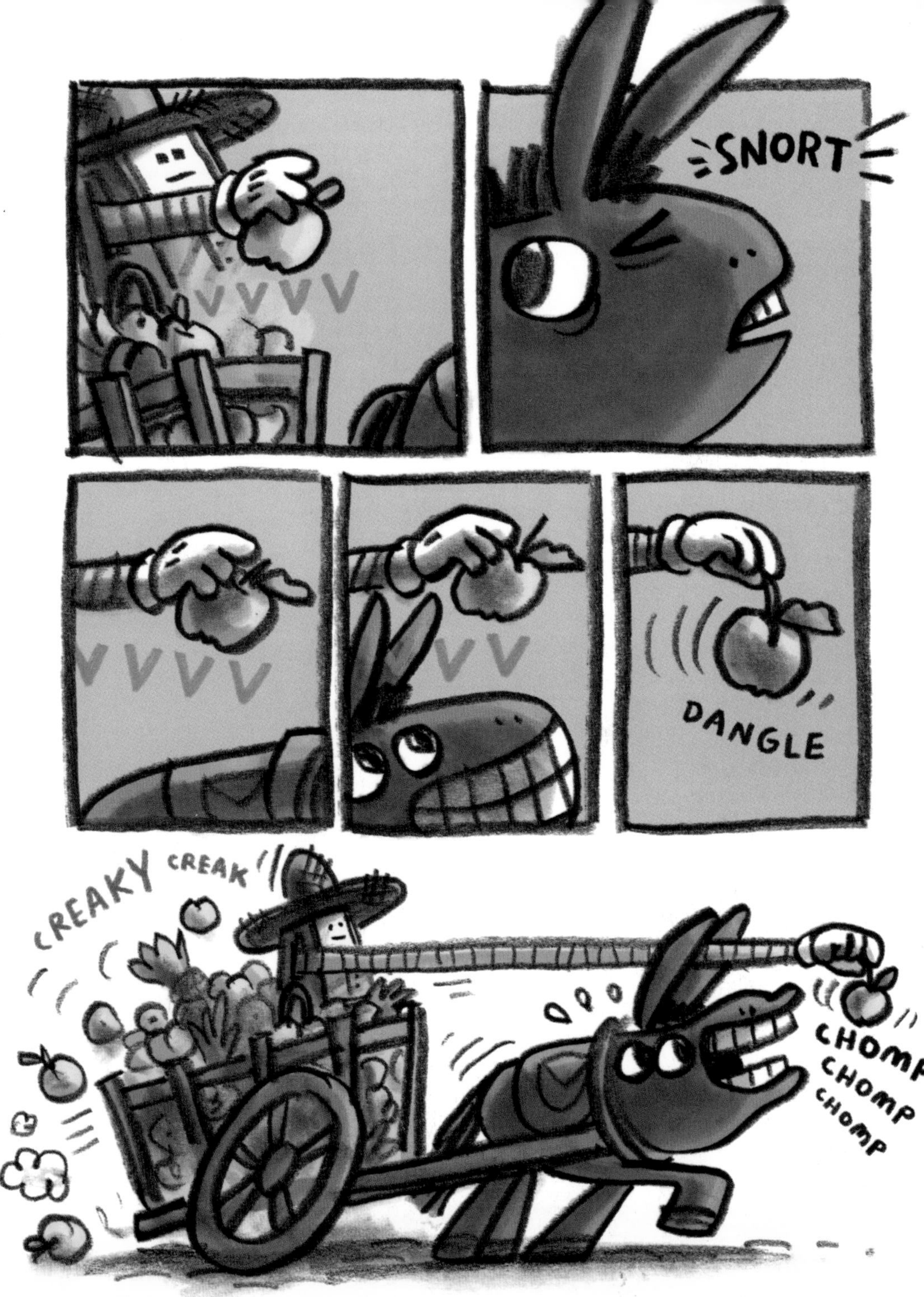
SNORT
DANGLE
CREAKY
CREAK
CHOMP
CHOMP
CHOMP

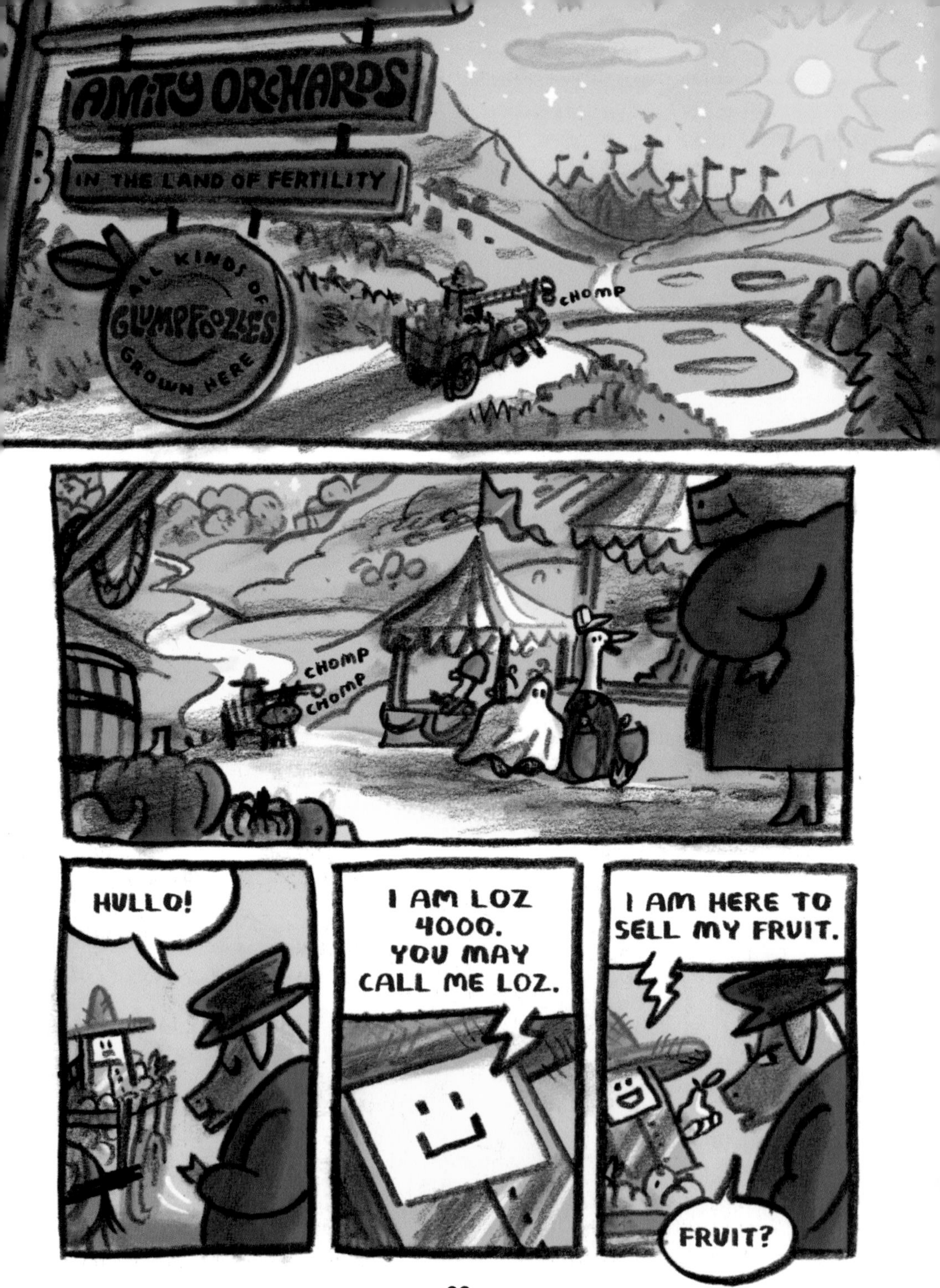
AMITY ORCHARDS
IN THE LAND OF FERTILITY
ALL KINDS OF GLUMPFOOZLES GROWN HERE
CHOMP
CHOMP
CHOMP
HULLO!
I AM LOZ 4000. YOU MAY CALL ME LOZ.
I AM HERE TO SELL MY FRUIT.
FRUIT?

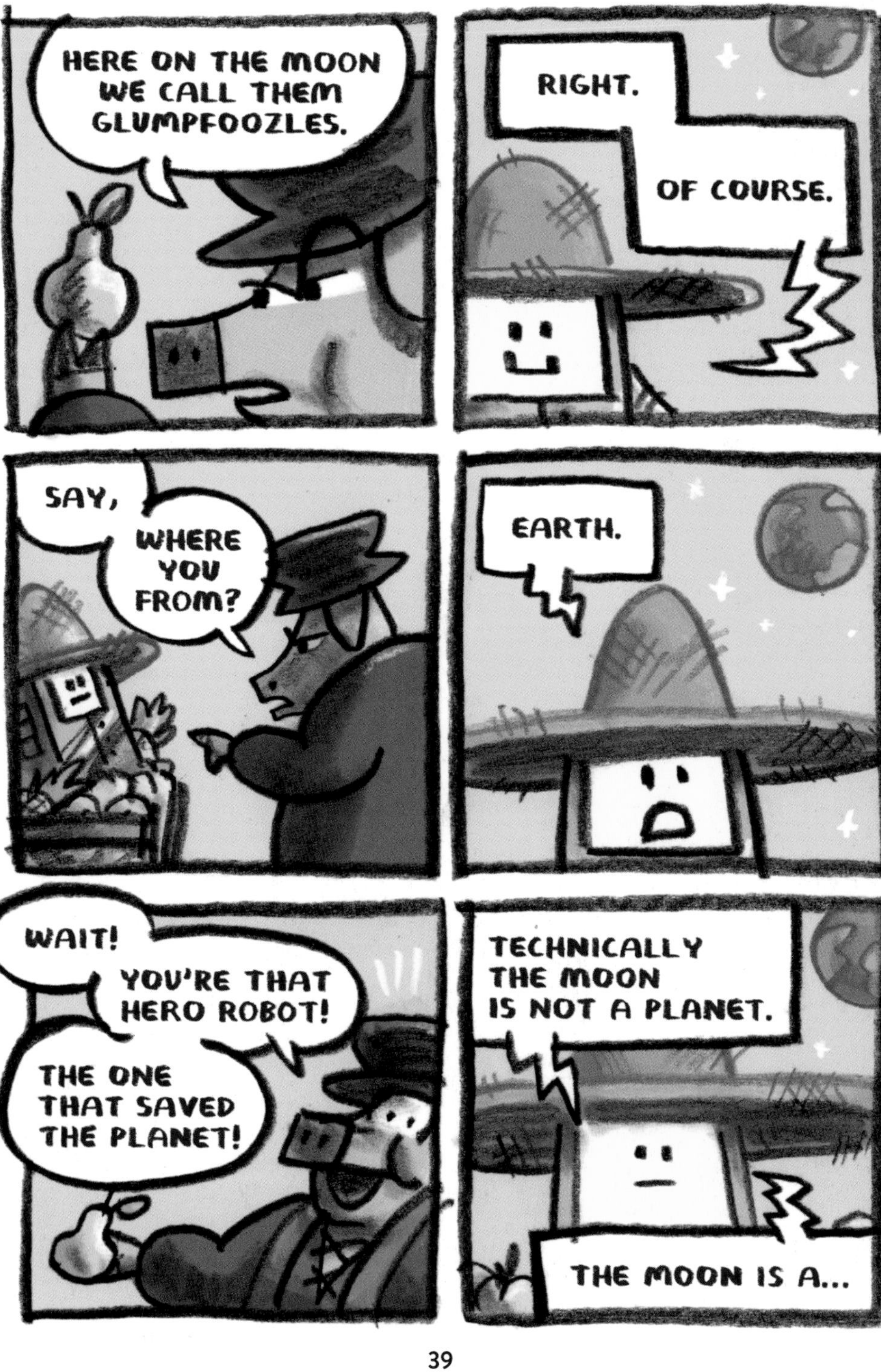
HERE ON THE MOON WE CALL THEM GLUMPFOOZLES.
RIGHT.
OF COURSE.
SAY,
WHERE YOU FROM?
EARTH.
WAIT!
YOU'RE THAT HERO ROBOT!
THE ONE THAT SAVED THE PLANET!
TECHNICALLY THE MOON IS NOT A PLANET.
THE MOON IS A...

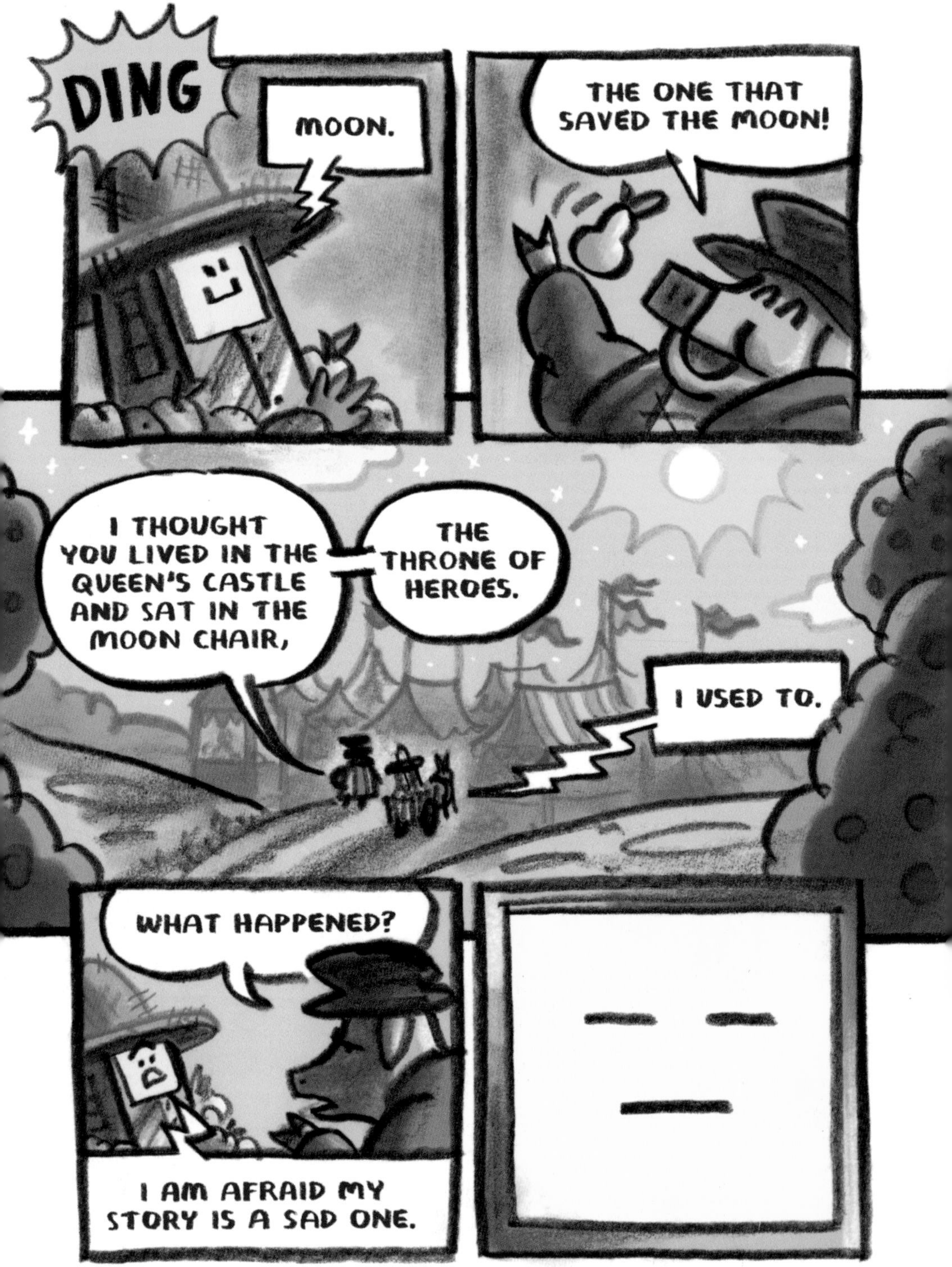
DING
MOON.
THE ONE THAT SAVED THE MOON!
I THOUGHT YOU LIVED IN THE QUEEN'S CASTLE AND SAT IN THE MOON CHAIR,
THE THRONE OF HEROES.
I USED TO.
WHAT HAPPENED?
I AM AFRAID MY STORY IS A SAD ONE.

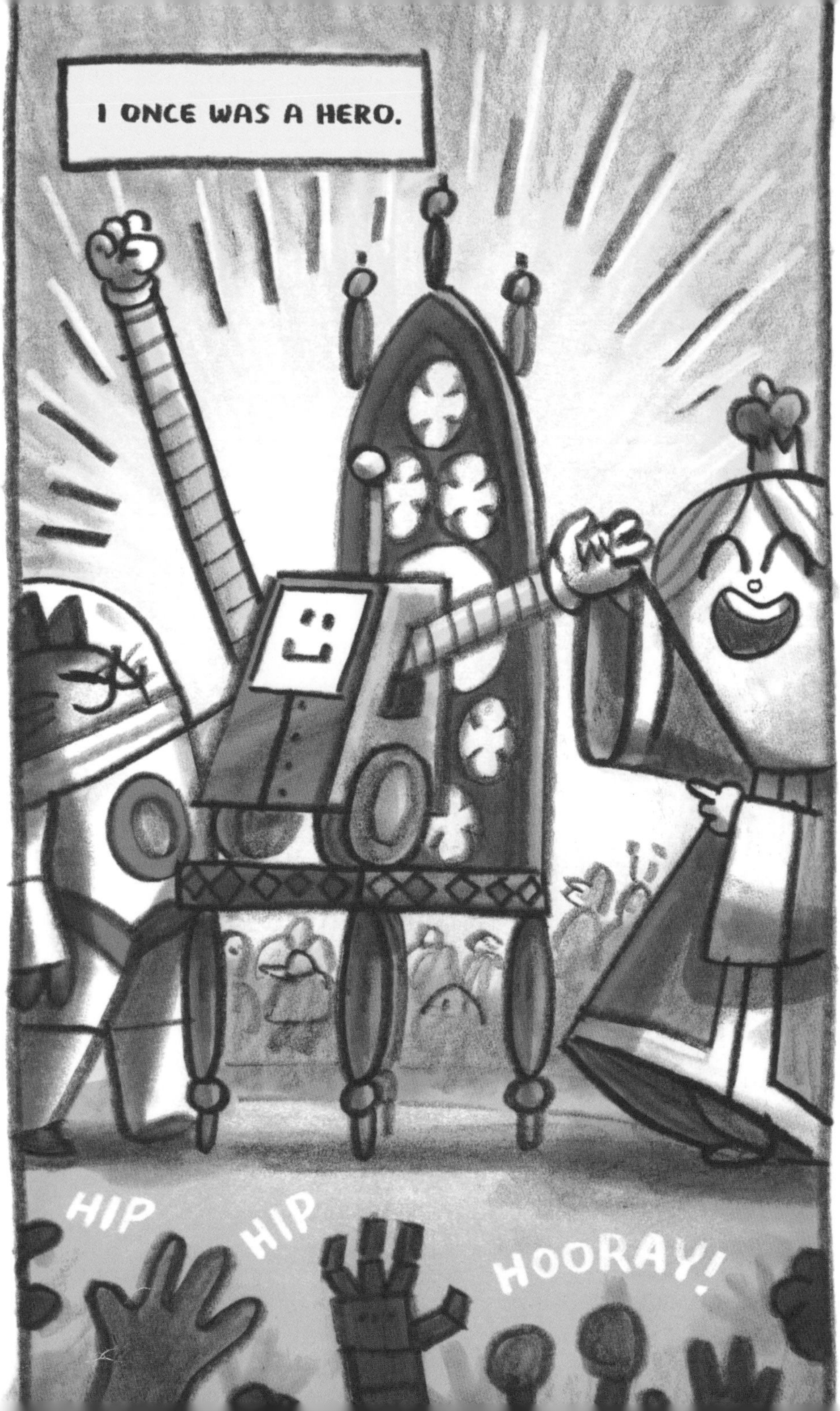
I ONCE WAS A HERO.
HIP
HIP
HOORAY!

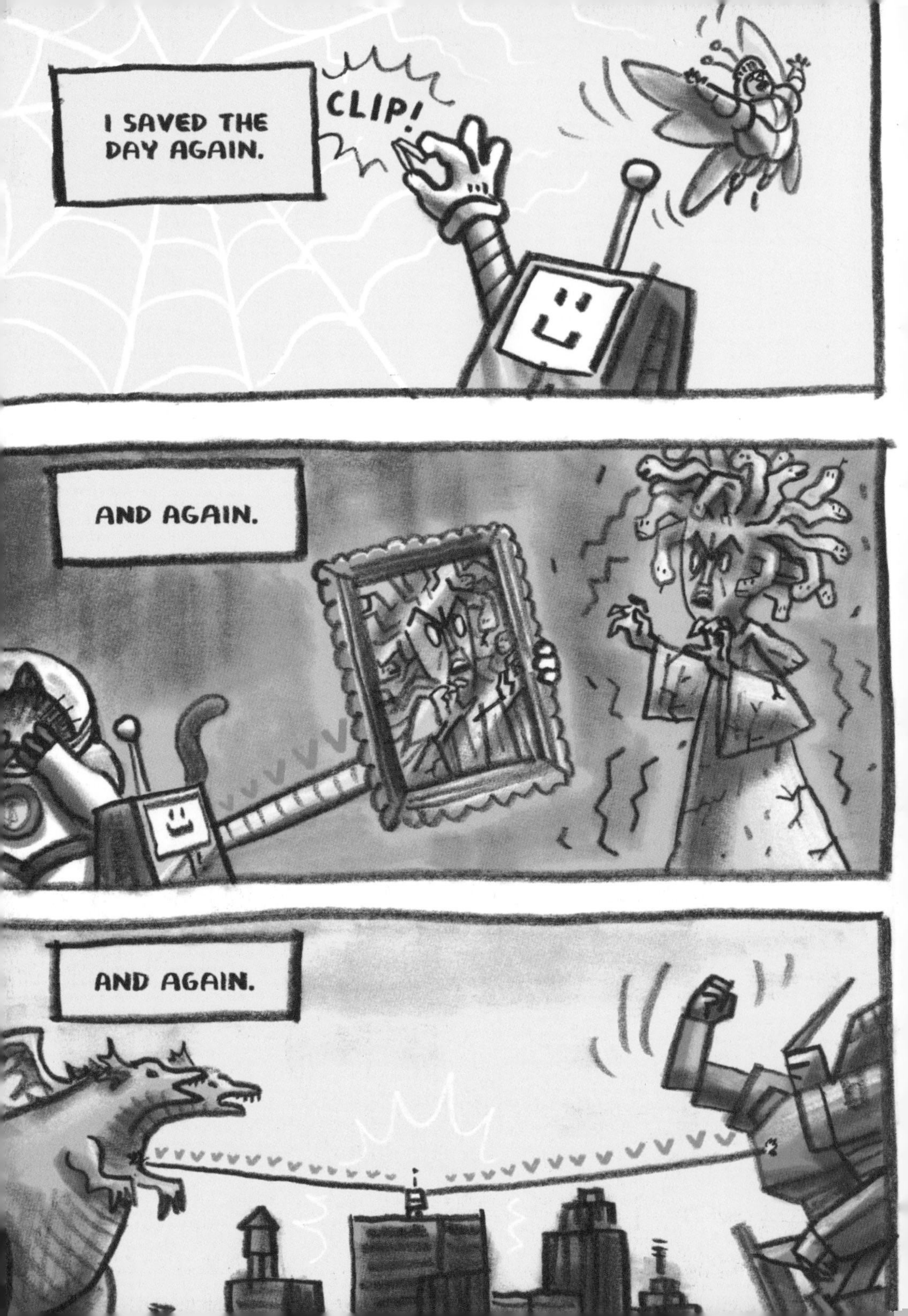
I SAVED THE DAY AGAIN.
CLIP!
AND AGAIN.
AND AGAIN.

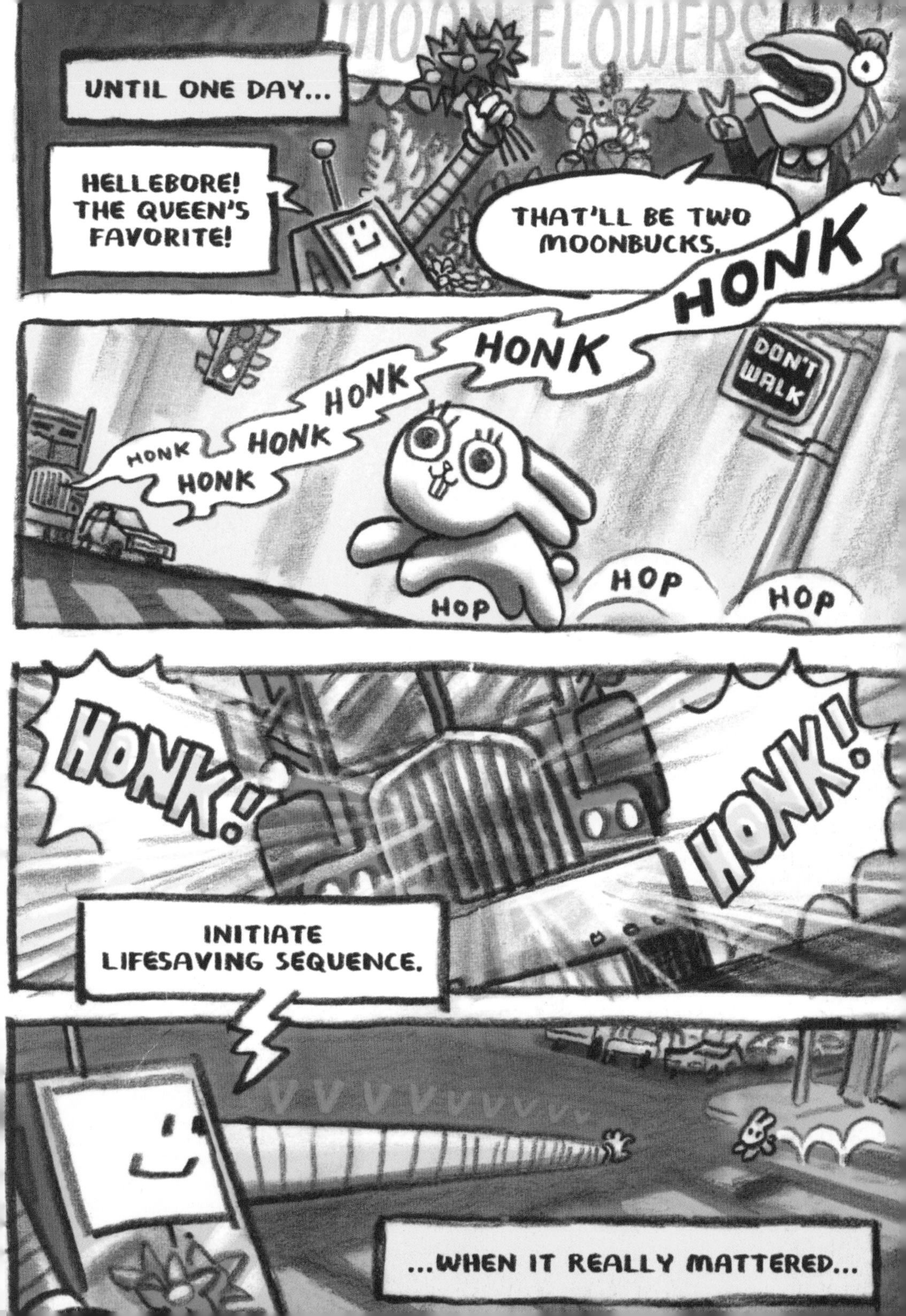
MOON FLOWERS
UNTIL ONE DAY...
HELLEBORE! THE QUEEN'S FAVORITE!
THAT'LL BE TWO MOONBUCKS.
HONK
HONK
HONK
HONK
HONK
HONK
DON'T WALK
HOP
HOP
HOP
HONK!
HONK!
INITIATE LIFESAVING SEQUENCE.
...WHEN IT REALLY MATTERED...

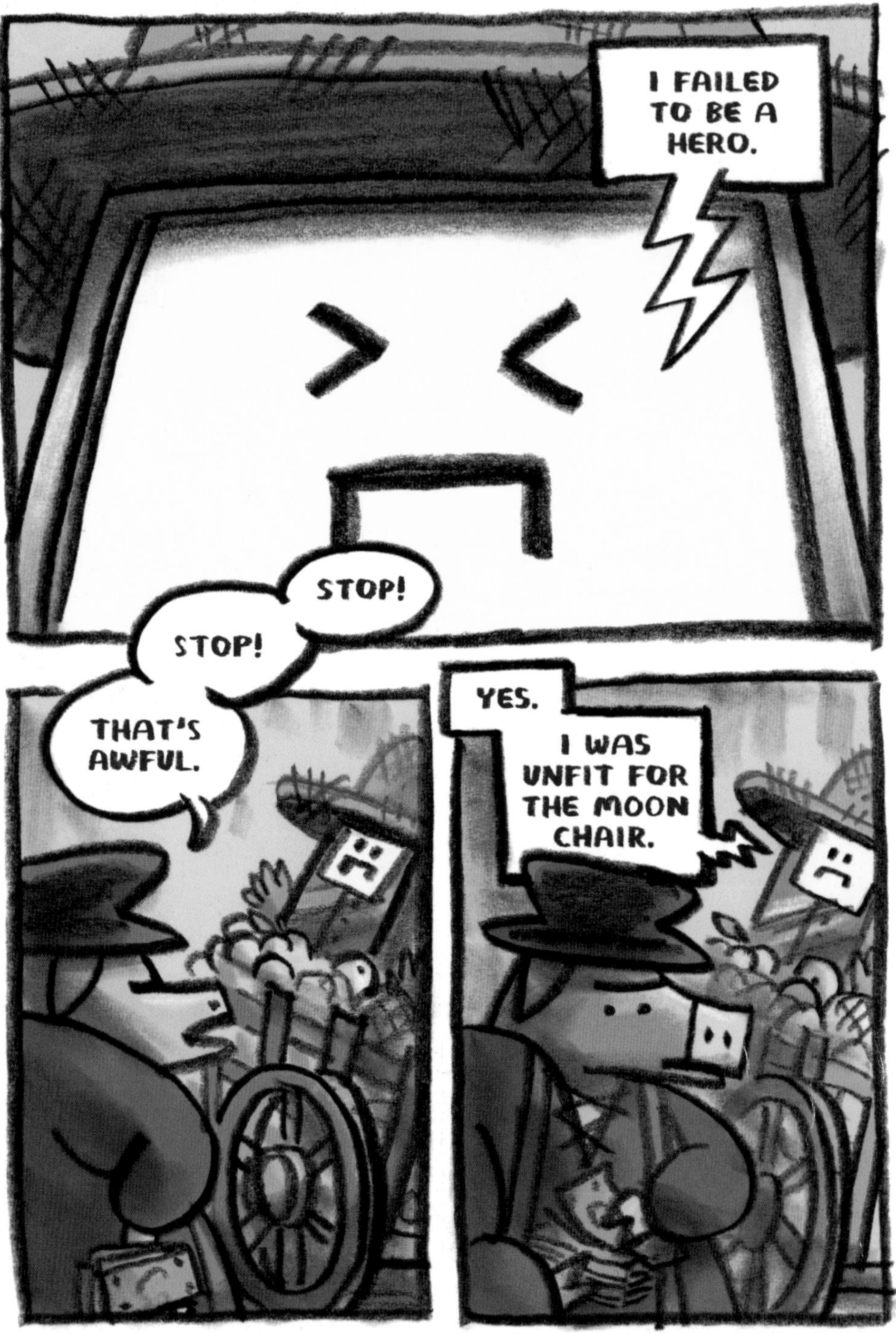
I FAILED TO BE A HERO.
STOP!
STOP!
THAT'S AWFUL.
YES.
I WAS UNFIT FOR THE MOON CHAIR.

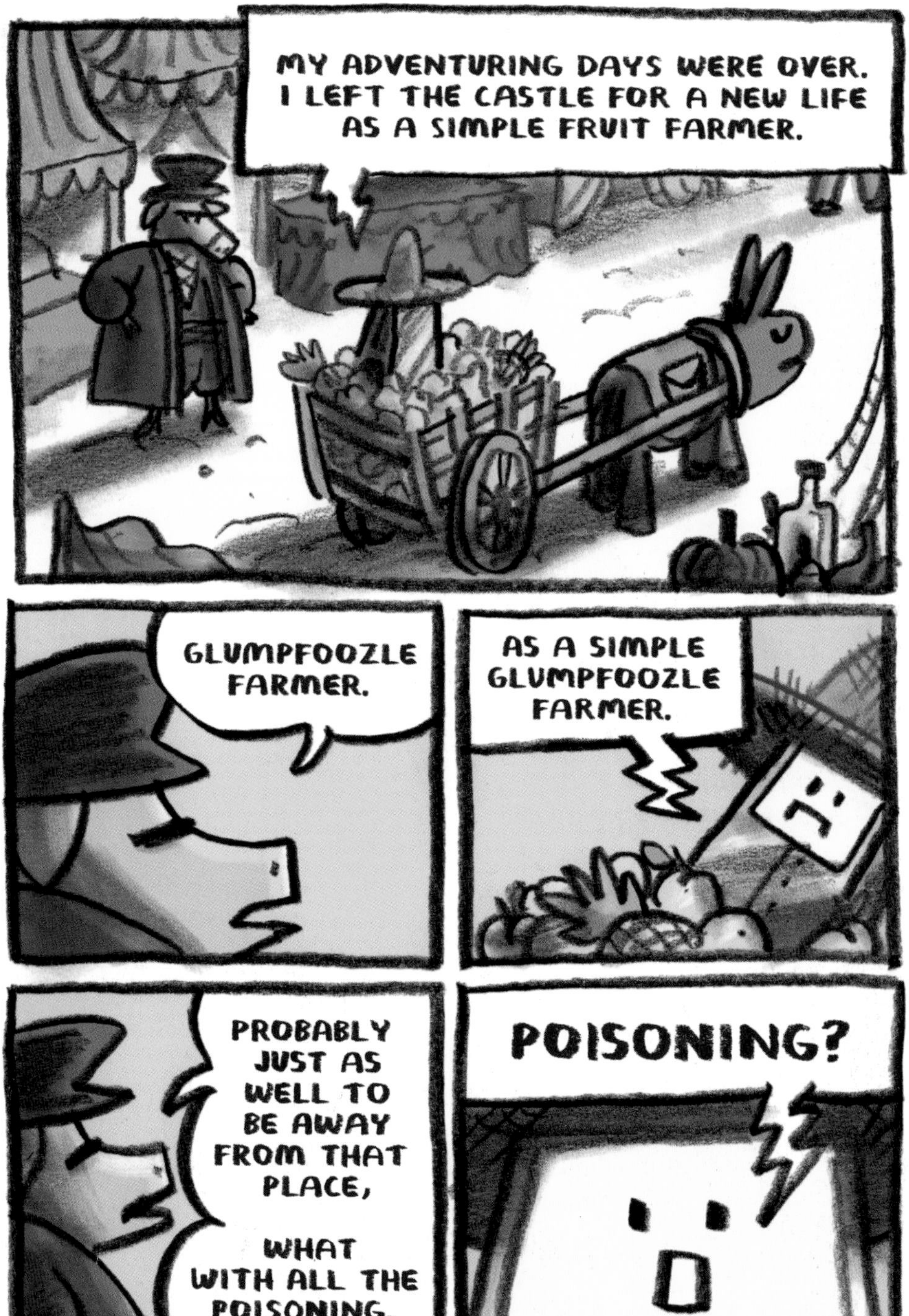
MY ADVENTURING DAYS WERE OVER. I LEFT THE CASTLE FOR A NEW LIFE AS A SIMPLE FRUIT FARMER.
GLUMPFOOZLE FARMER.
AS A SIMPLE GLUMPFOOZLE FARMER.
PROBABLY JUST AS WELL TO BE AWAY FROM THAT PLACE,
WHAT WITH ALL THE POISONING.
POISONING?

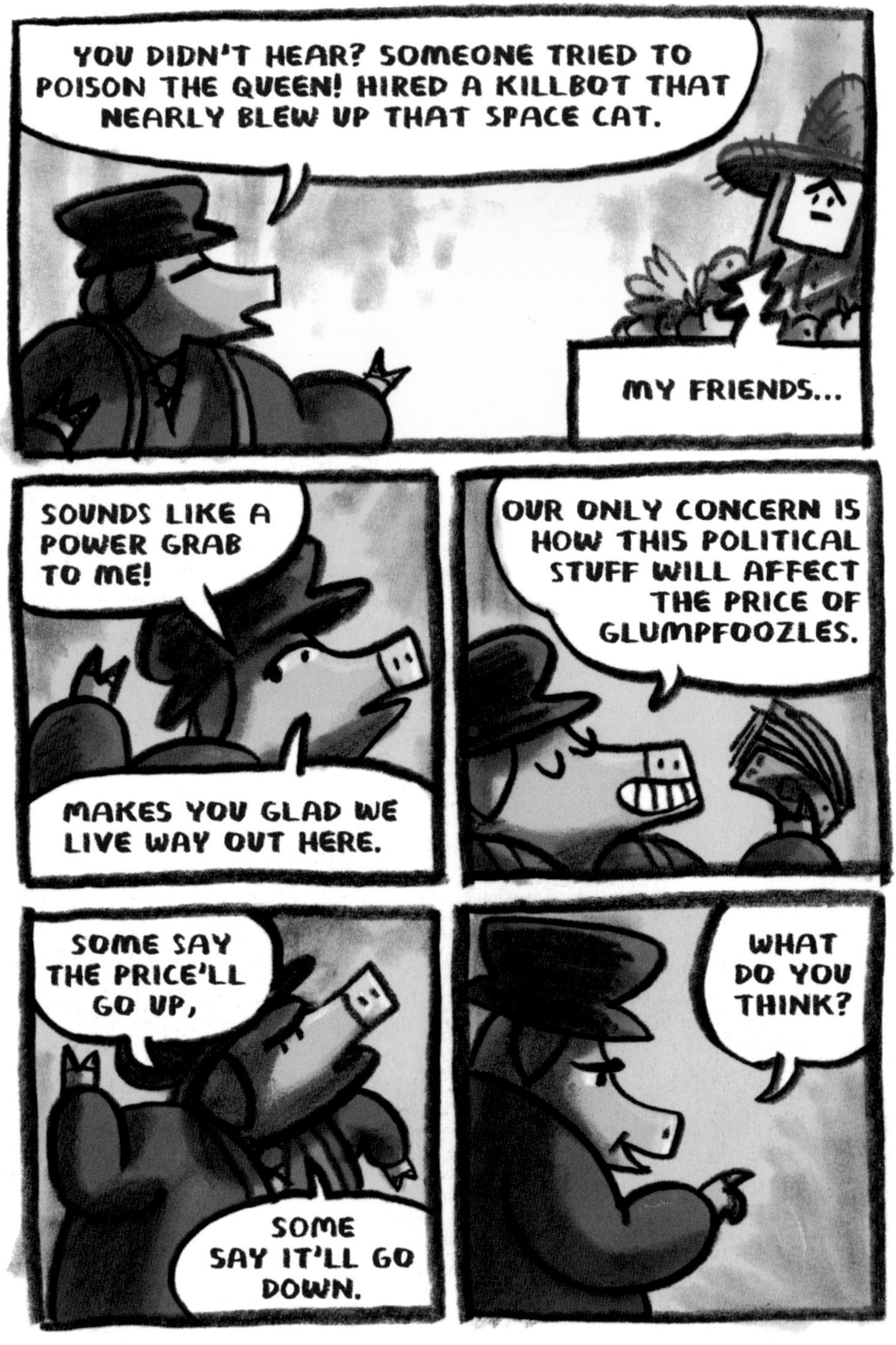
YOU DIDN'T HEAR? SOMEONE TRIED TO POISON THE QUEEN! HIRED A KILLBOT THAT NEARLY BLEW UP THAT SPACE CAT.
MY FRIENDS...
SOUNDS LIKE A POWER GRAB TO ME!
MAKES YOU GLAD WE LIVE WAY OUT HERE.
OUR ONLY CONCERN IS HOW THIS POLITICAL STUFF WILL AFFECT THE PRICE OF GLUMPFOOZLES.
SOME SAY THE PRICE'LL GO UP,
SOME SAY IT'LL GO DOWN.
WHAT DO YOU THINK?

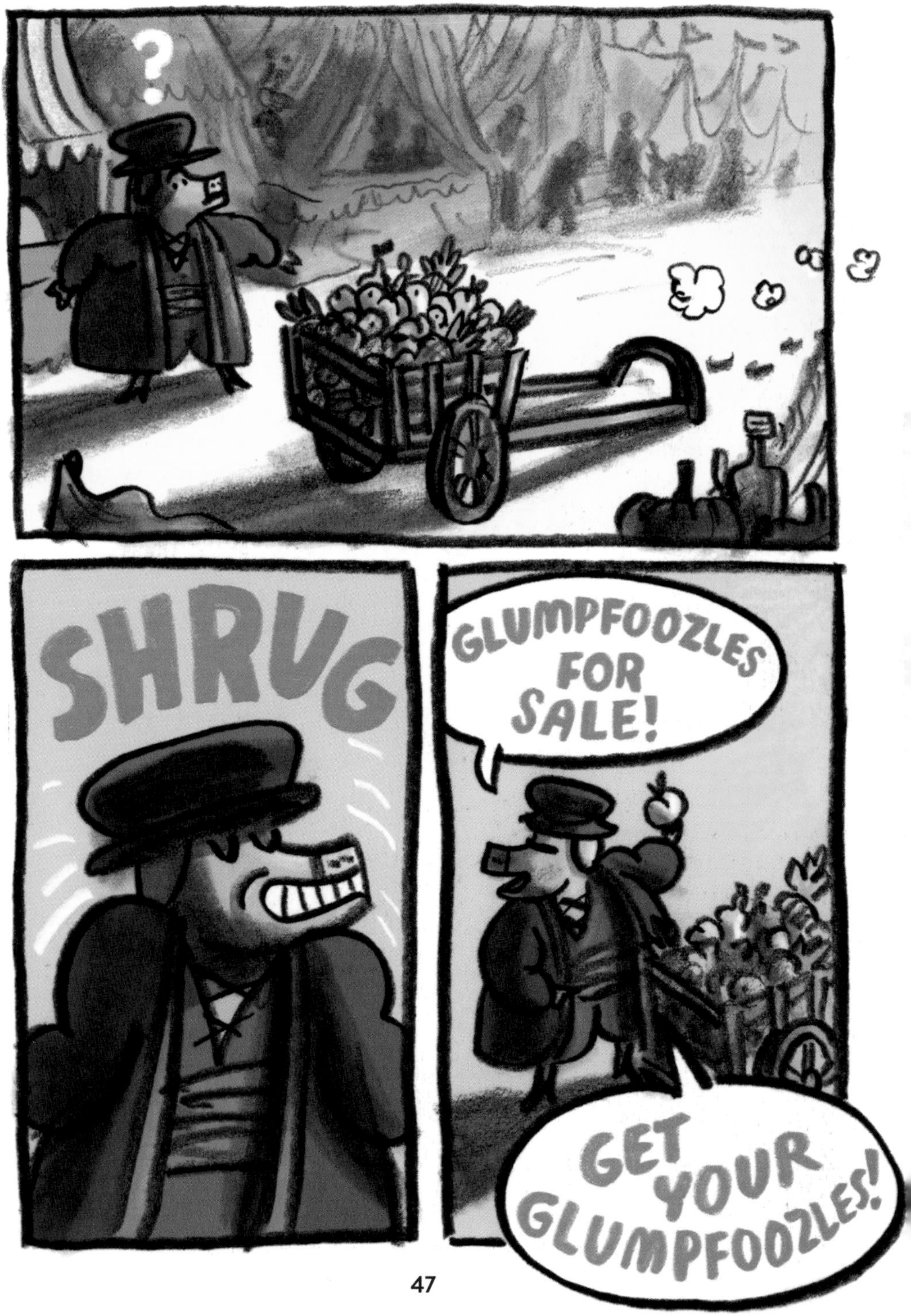
?
SHRUG
GLUMPFOOZLES FOR SALE!
GET YOUR GLUMPFOOZLES!

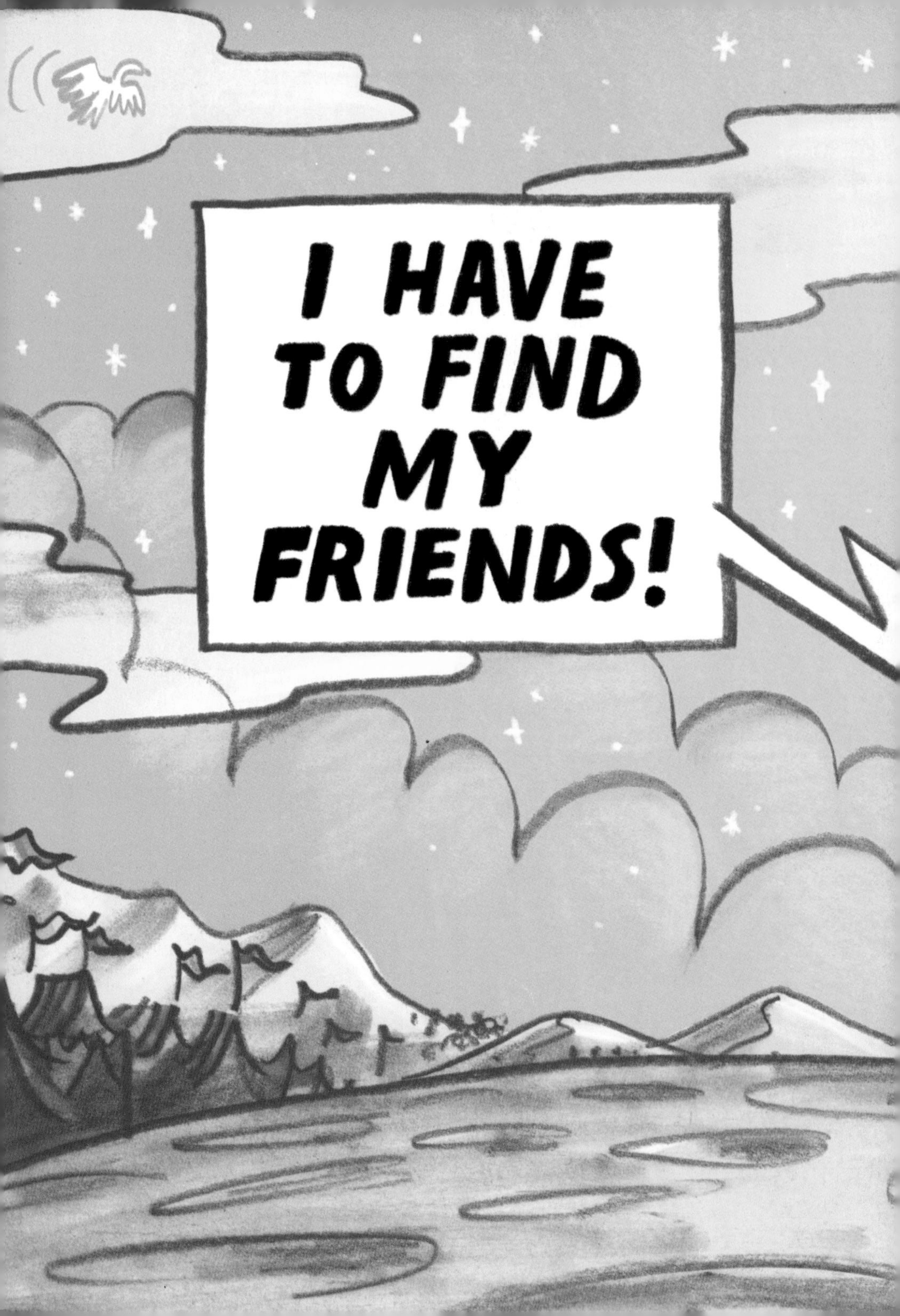
I HAVE TO FIND MY FRIENDS!

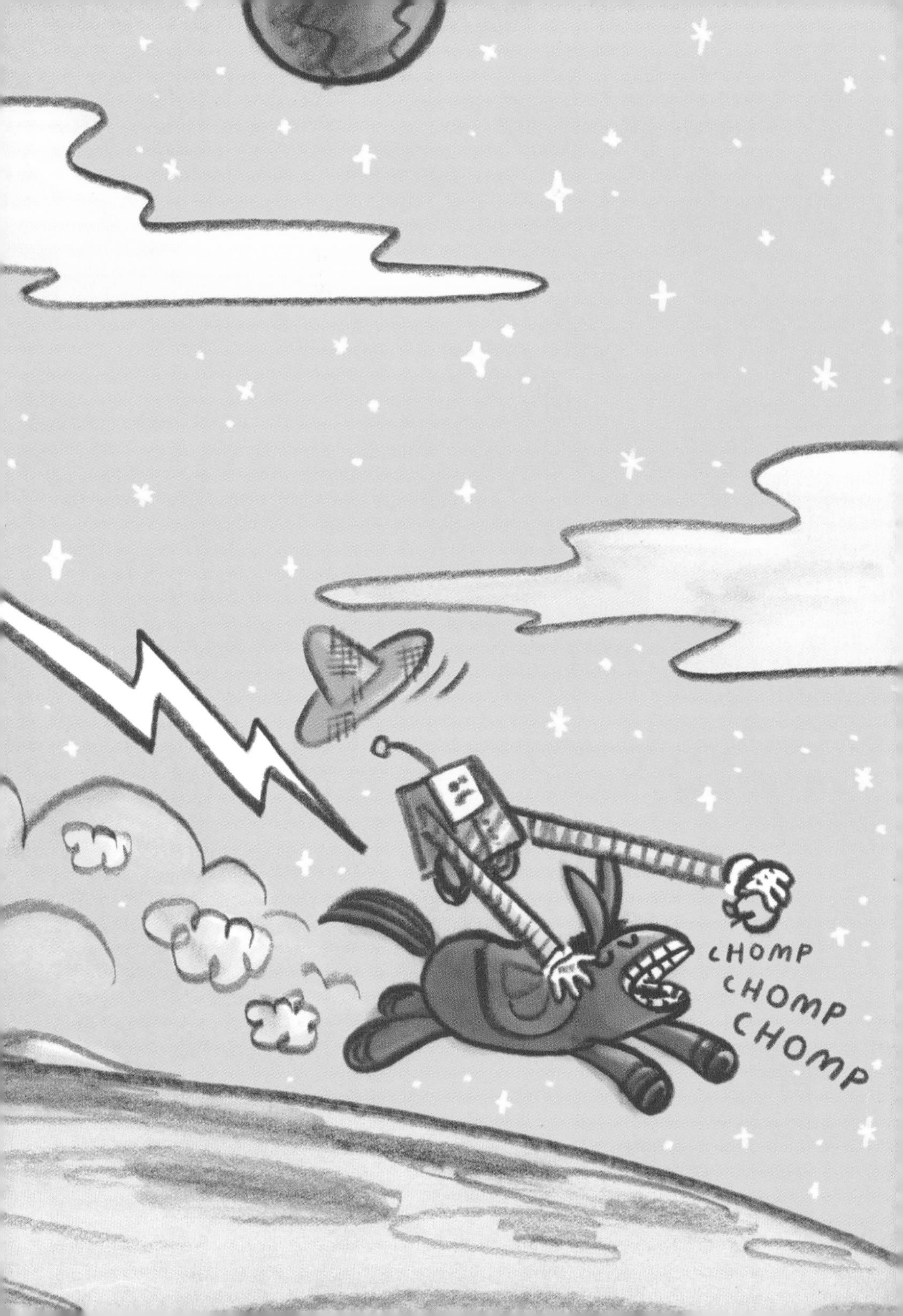
CHOMP
CHOMP
CHOMP

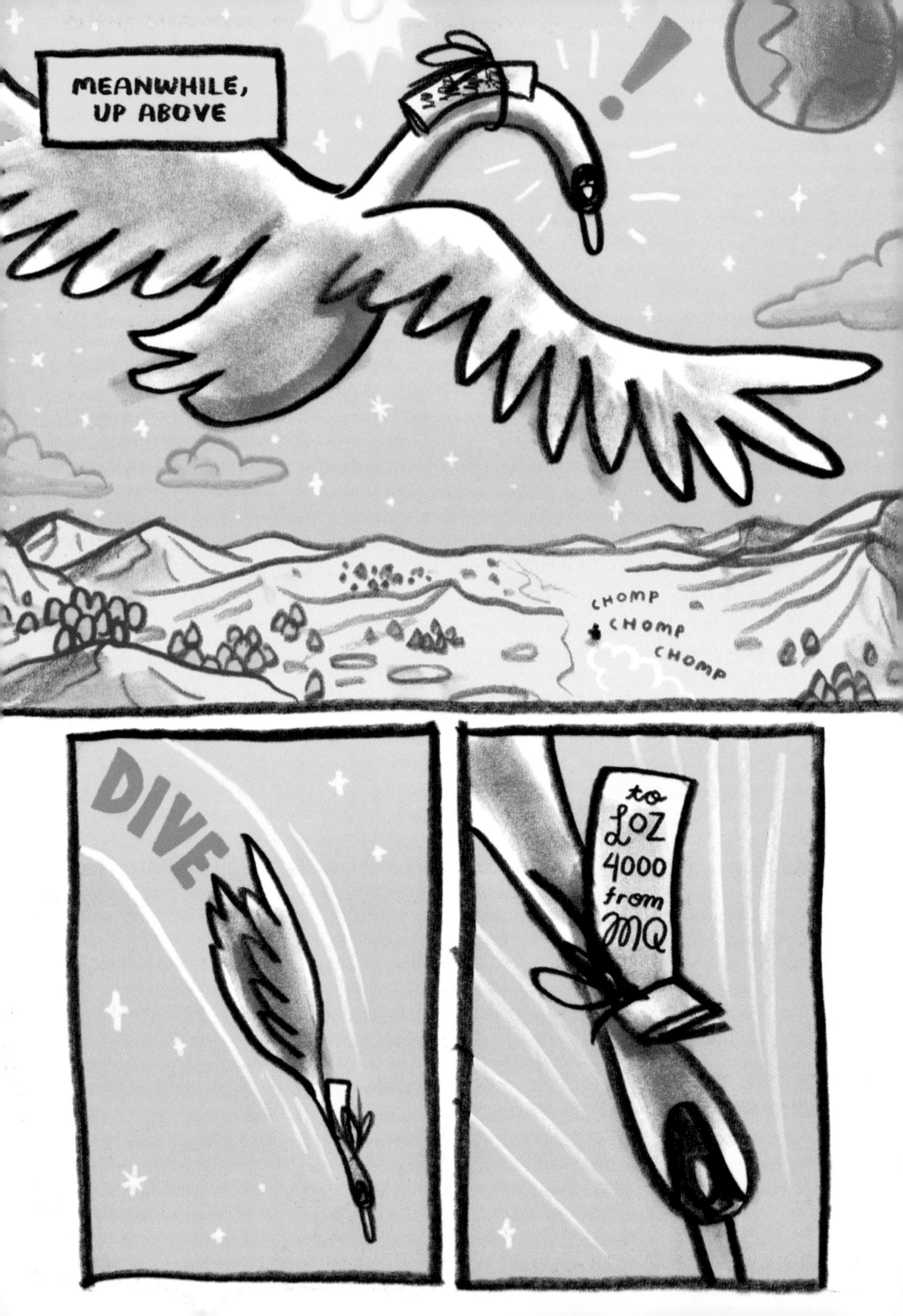
MEANWHILE, UP ABOVE
CHOMP
CHOMP
CHOMP
DIVE
to
LOZ
4000
from
MQ

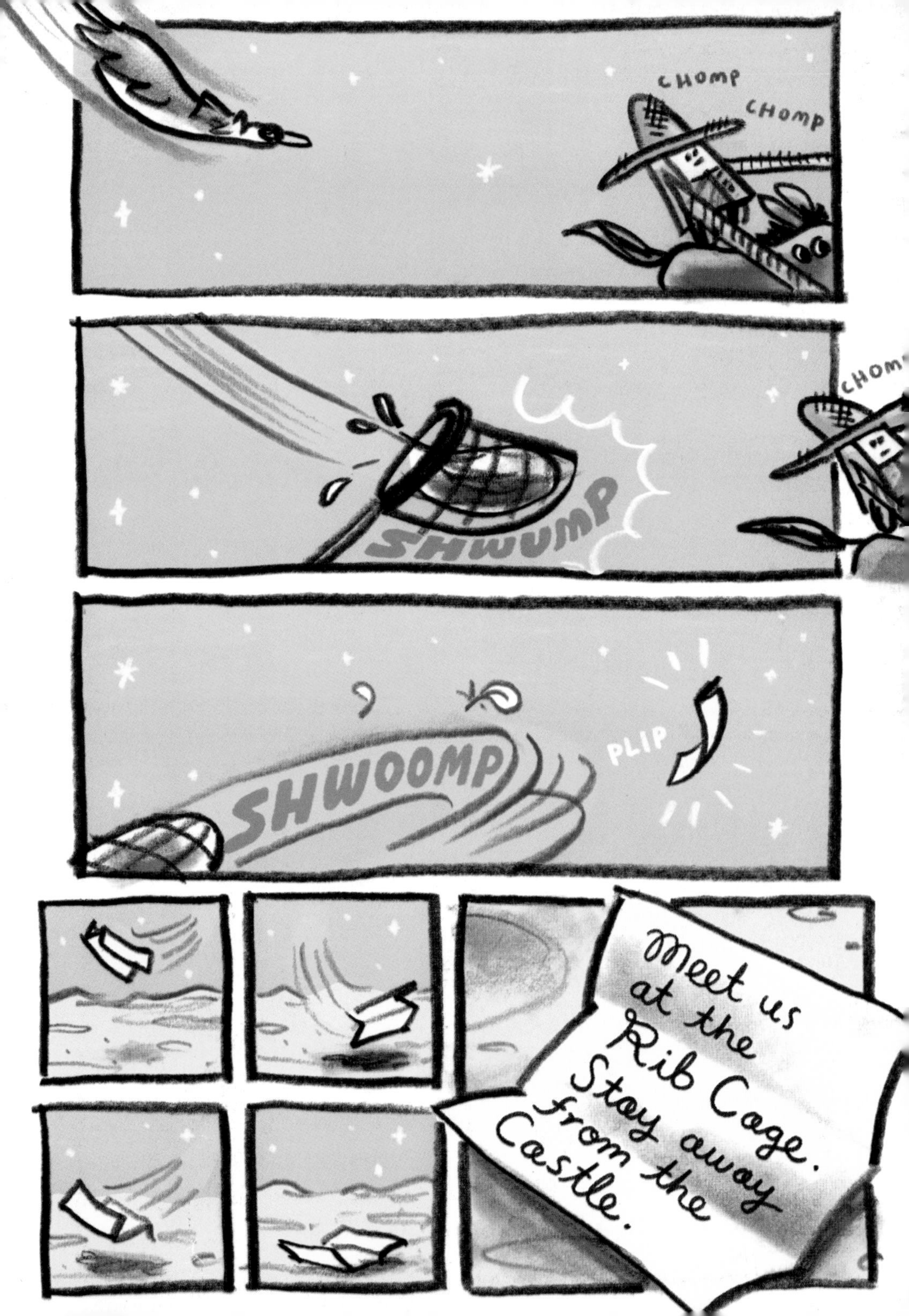
CHOMP
CHOMP
CHOM
SHWUMP
SHWOOMP
PLIP
Meet us at the Rib Cage. Stay away from the Castle.

# CHAPTER 2

# THE RIB CAGE

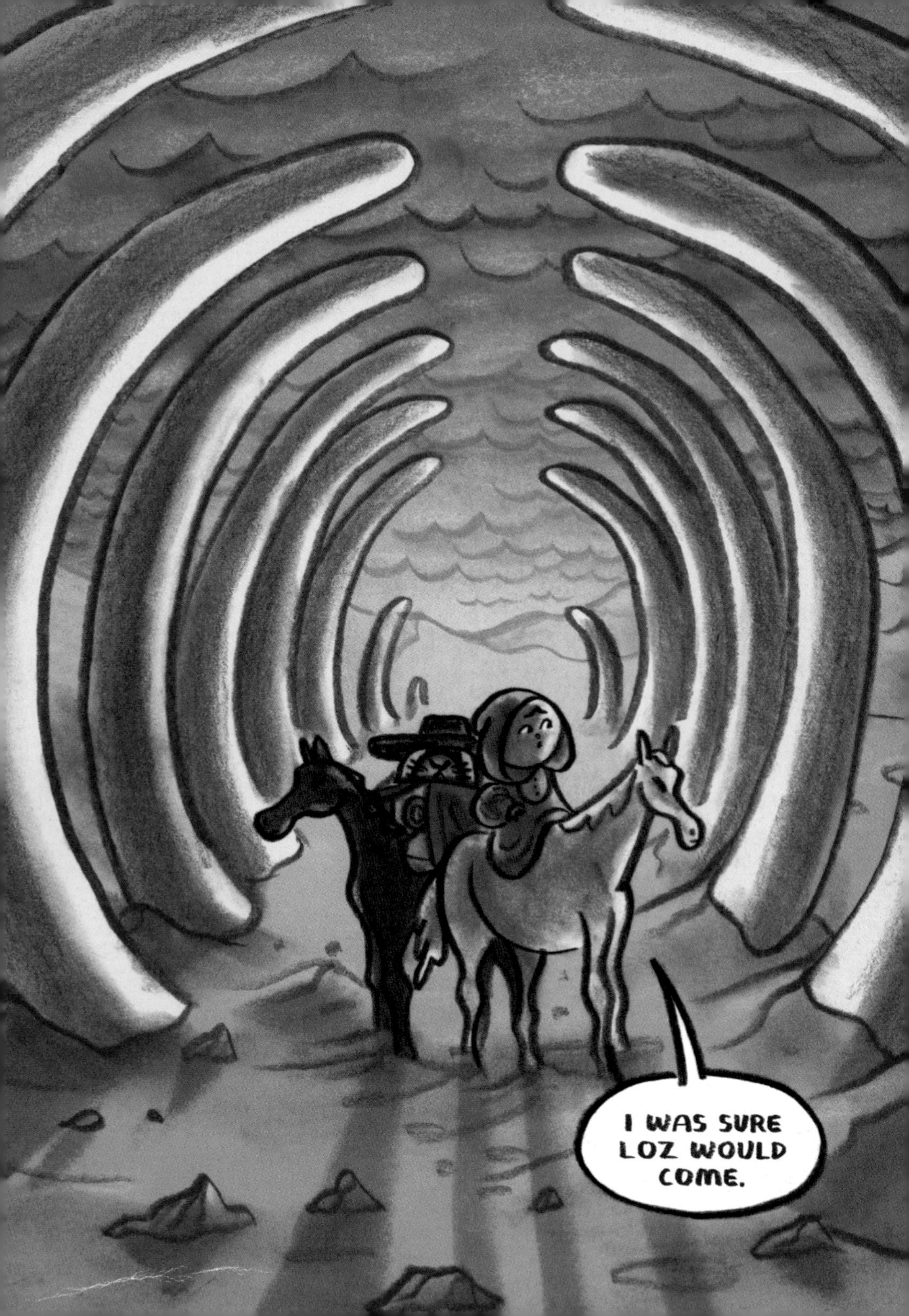
I WAS SURE LOZ WOULD COME.

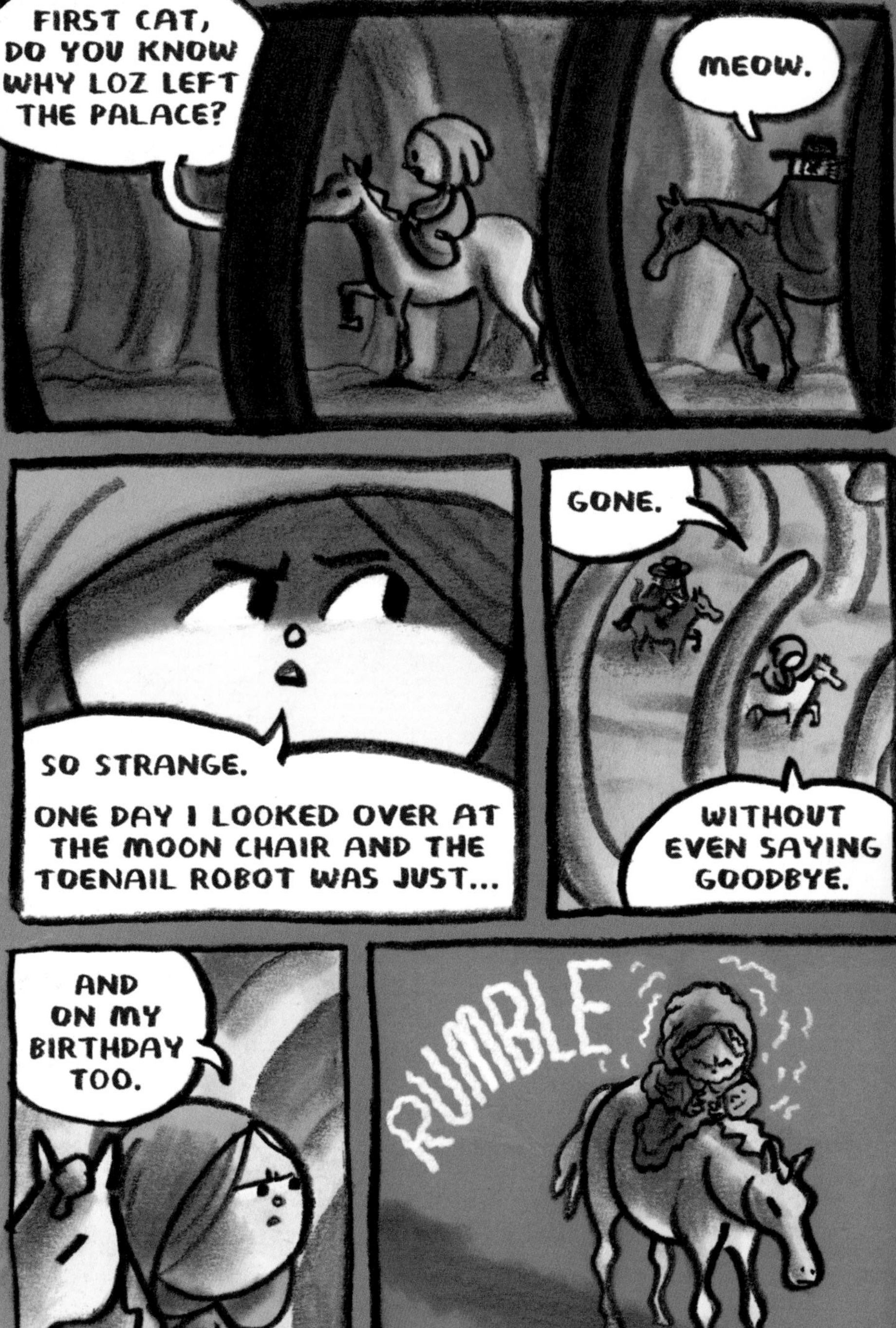
FIRST CAT, DO YOU KNOW WHY LOZ LEFT THE PALACE?
MEOW.
SO STRANGE.
ONE DAY I LOOKED OVER AT THE MOON CHAIR AND THE TOENAIL ROBOT WAS JUST...
GONE.
WITHOUT EVEN SAYING GOODBYE.
AND ON MY BIRTHDAY TOO.
RUMBLE

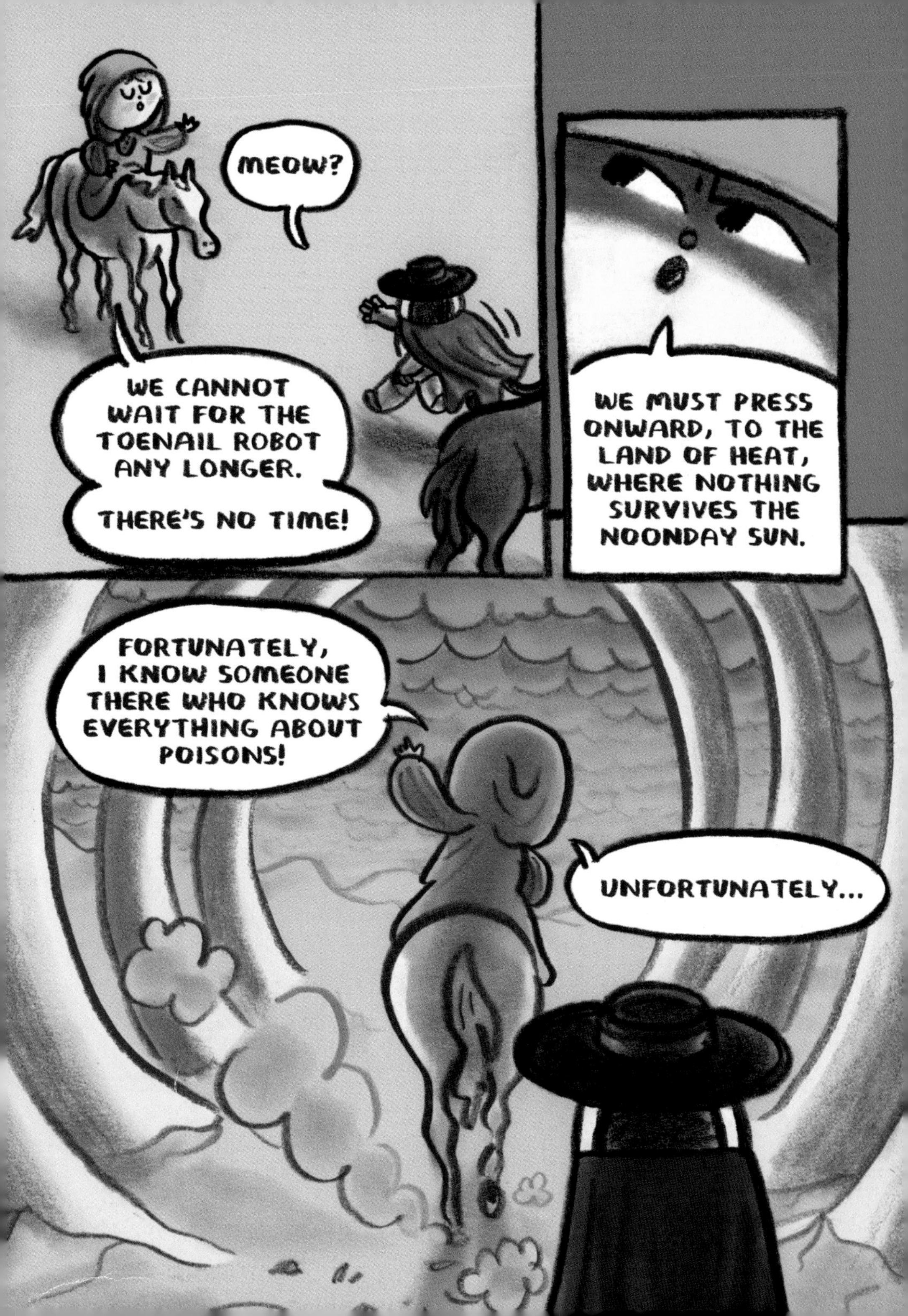
MEOW?
WE CANNOT WAIT FOR THE TOENAIL ROBOT ANY LONGER.
THERE'S NO TIME!
WE MUST PRESS ONWARD, TO THE LAND OF HEAT, WHERE NOTHING SURVIVES THE NOONDAY SUN.
FORTUNATELY, I KNOW SOMEONE THERE WHO KNOWS EVERYTHING ABOUT POISONS!
UNFORTUNATELY...

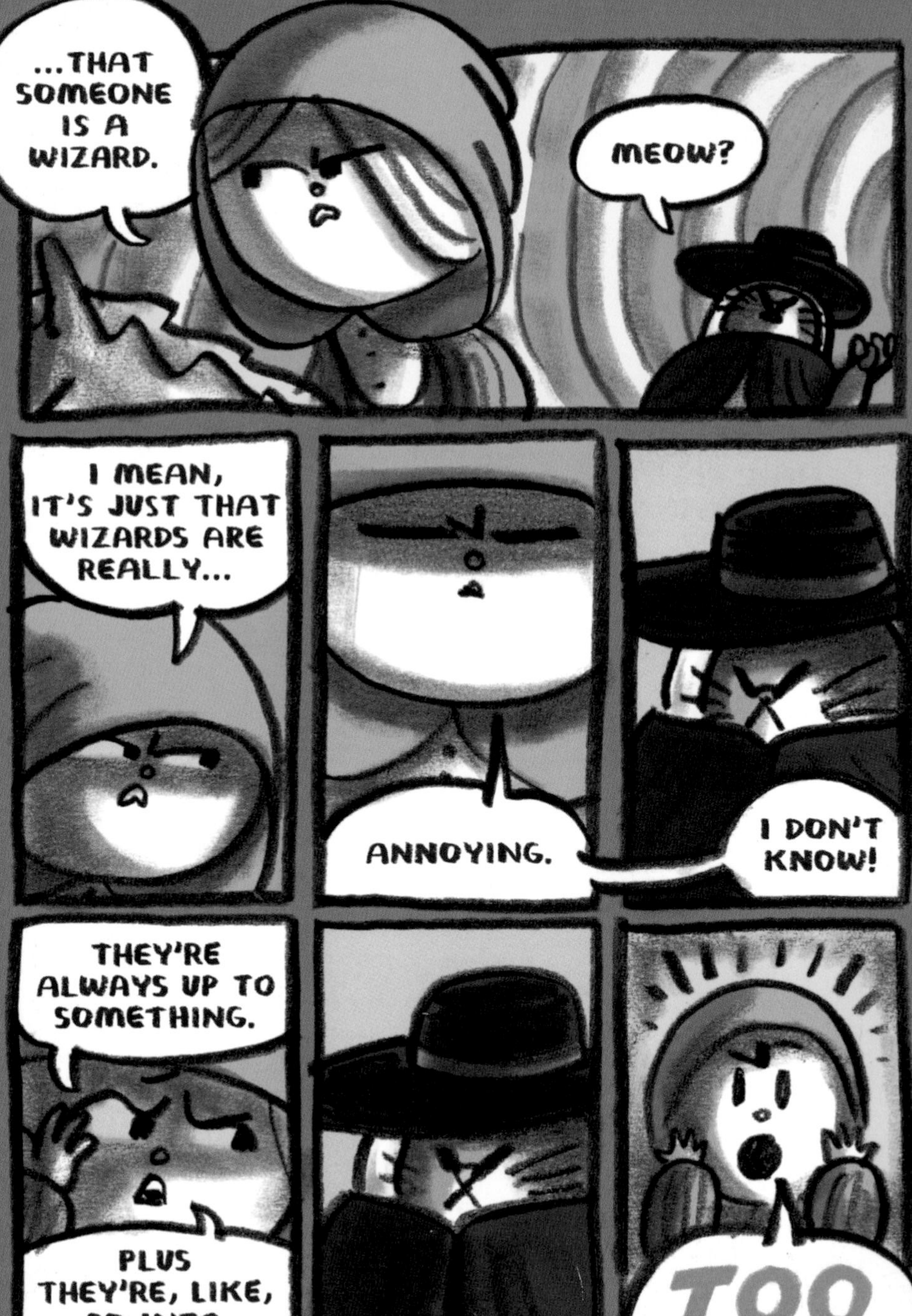
...THAT SOMEONE IS A WIZARD.
MEOW?
I MEAN, IT'S JUST THAT WIZARDS ARE REALLY...
ANNOYING.
I DON'T KNOW!
THEY'RE ALWAYS UP TO SOMETHING.
PLUS THEY'RE, LIKE, SO INTO CANDLES.
TOO INTO CANDLES!

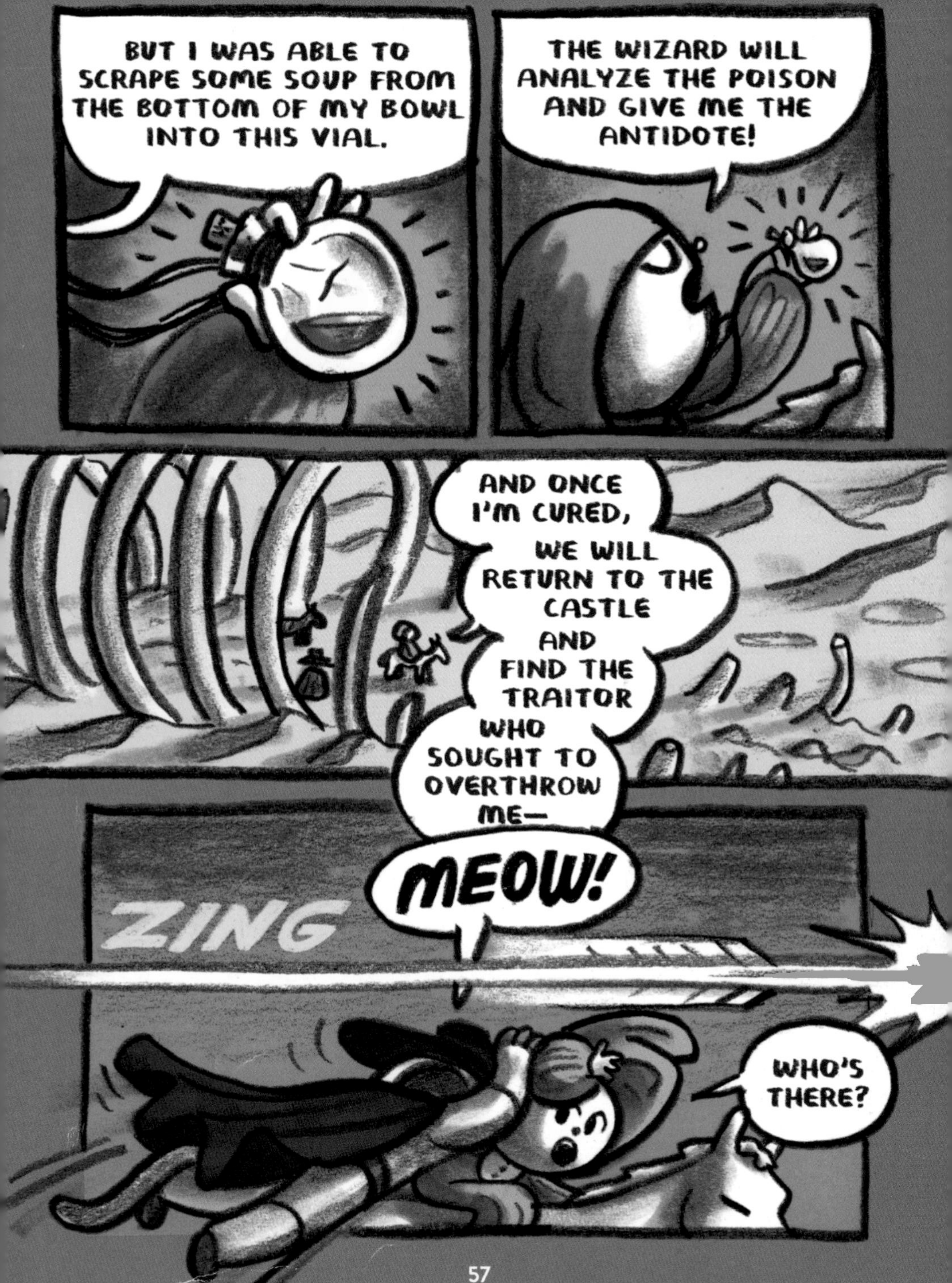
BUT I WAS ABLE TO SCRAPE SOME SOUP FROM THE BOTTOM OF MY BOWL INTO THIS VIAL.
THE WIZARD WILL ANALYZE THE POISON AND GIVE ME THE ANTIDOTE!
AND ONCE I'M CURED,
WE WILL RETURN TO THE CASTLE
AND
FIND THE TRAITOR
WHO SOUGHT TO OVERTHROW ME—
MEOW!
ZING
WHO'S THERE?

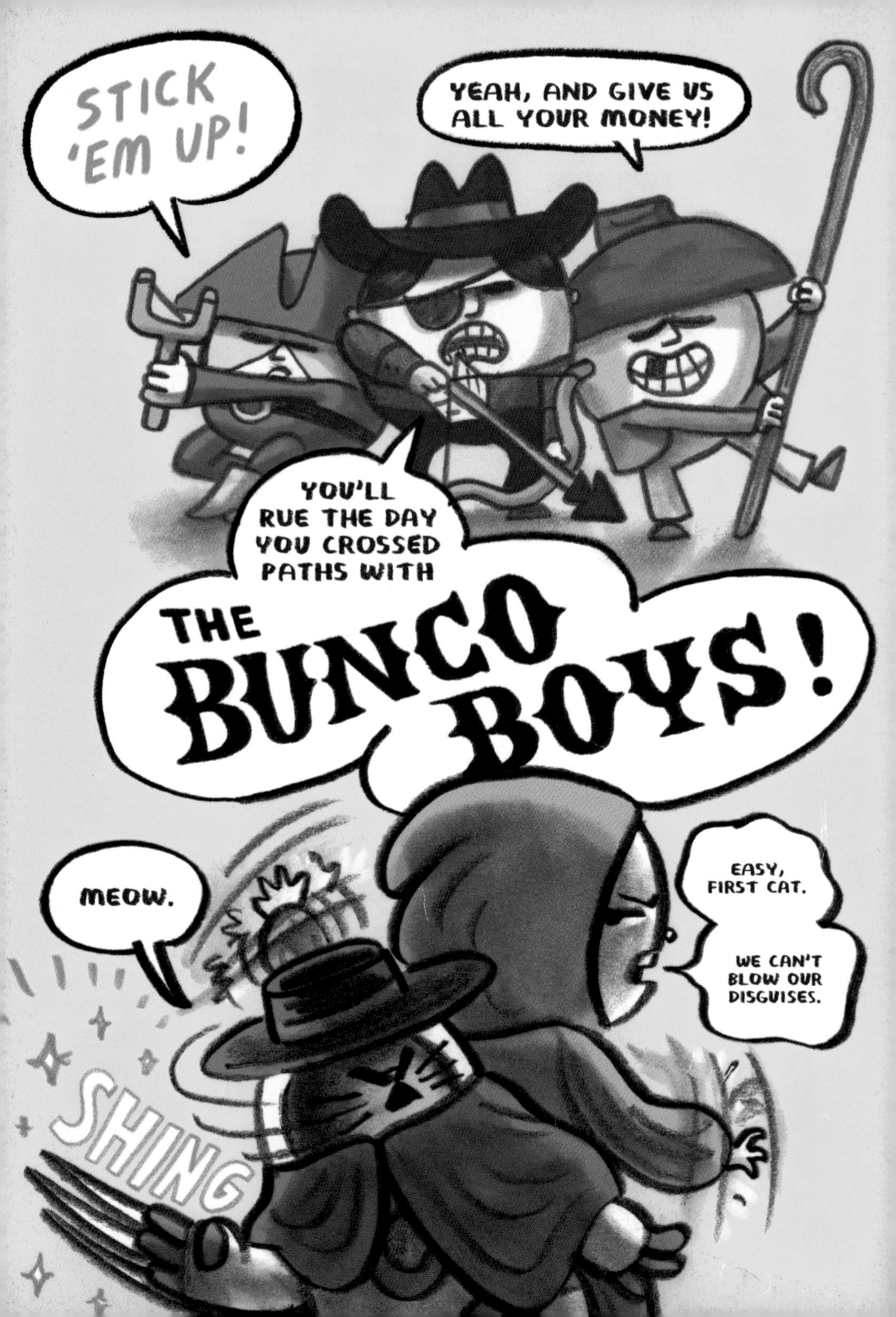
STICK 'EM UP!
YEAH, AND GIVE US ALL YOUR MONEY!
YOU'LL RUE THE DAY YOU CROSSED PATHS WITH
THE BUNCO BOYS!
MEOW.
EASY, FIRST CAT.
WE CAN'T BLOW OUR DISGUISES.
SHING

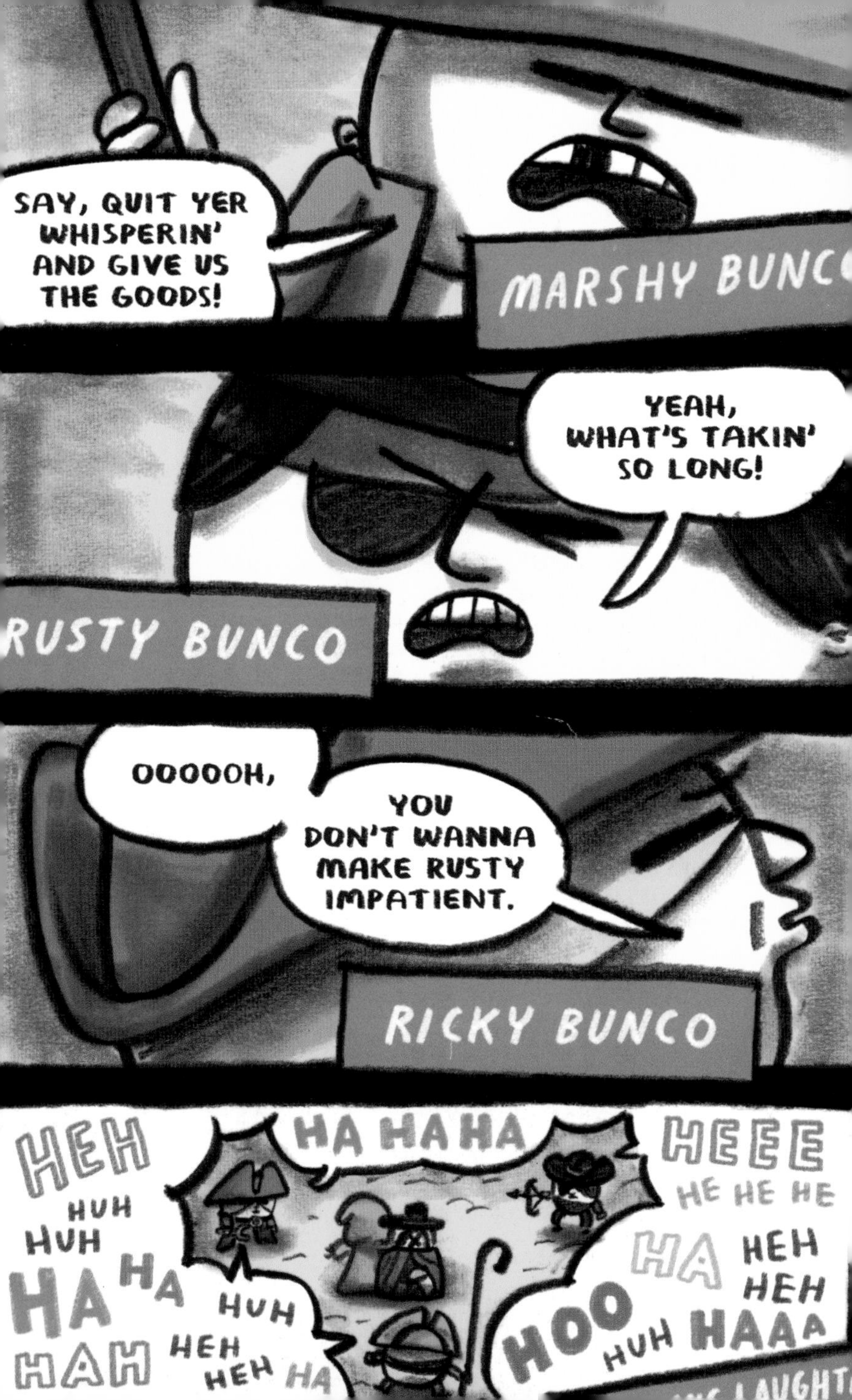
SAY, QUIT YER WHISPERIN' AND GIVE US THE GOODS!
MARSHY BUNC
YEAH, WHAT'S TAKIN' SO LONG!
RUSTY BUNCO
OOOOOH,
YOU DON'T WANNA MAKE RUSTY IMPATIENT.
RICKY BUNCO
HEH
HA HAHA
HEEE
HE HE HE
HUH HUH
HA HA
HUH
HAH
HEH HEH
HA
HA
HEH HEH
HOO
HUH
HAAA

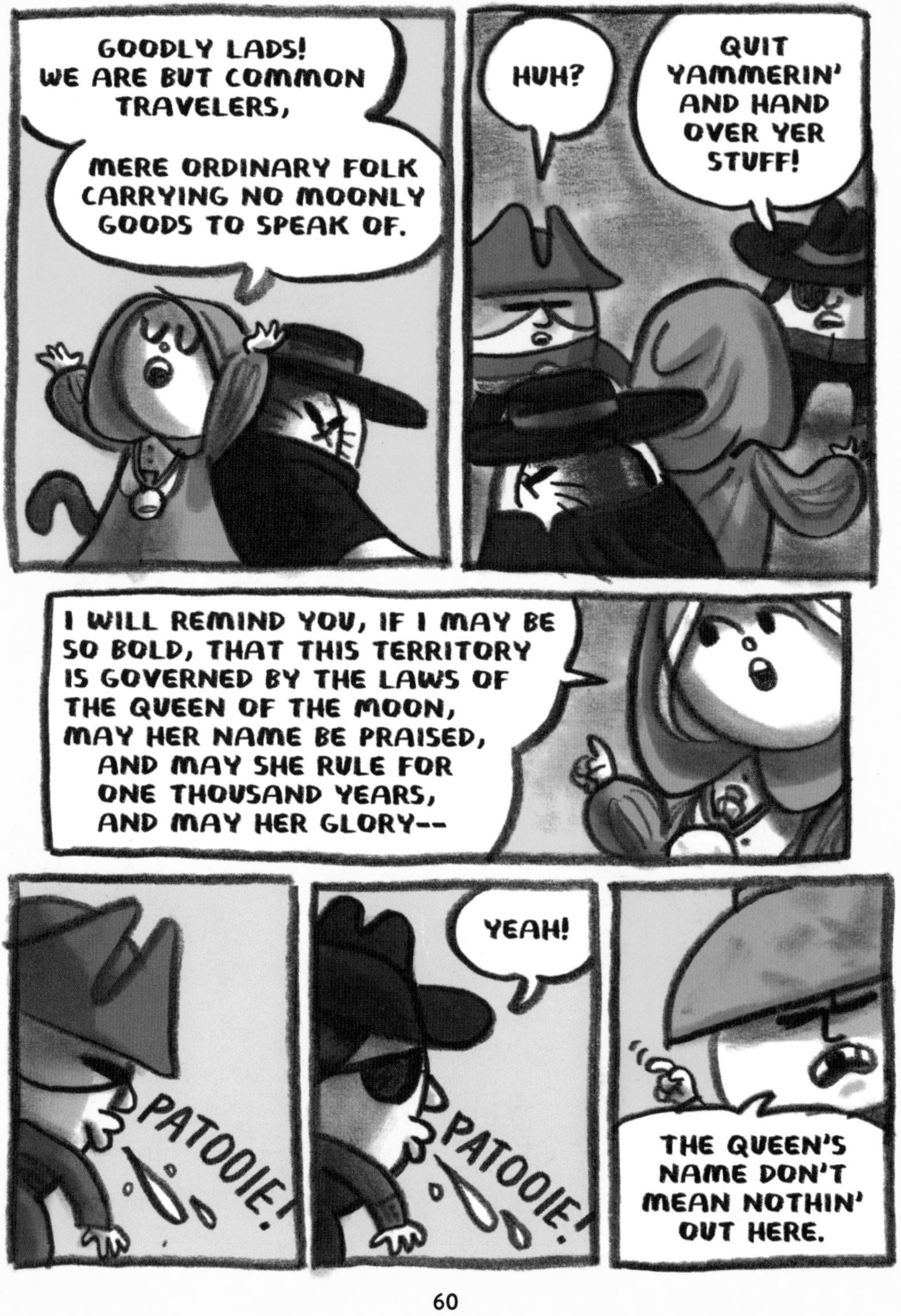
GOODLY LADS! WE ARE BUT COMMON TRAVELERS,
MERE ORDINARY FOLK CARRYING NO MOONLY GOODS TO SPEAK OF.
HUH?
QUIT YAMMERIN' AND HAND OVER YER STUFF!
I WILL REMIND YOU, IF I MAY BE SO BOLD, THAT THIS TERRITORY IS GOVERNED BY THE LAWS OF THE QUEEN OF THE MOON, MAY HER NAME BE PRAISED, AND MAY SHE RULE FOR ONE THOUSAND YEARS, AND MAY HER GLORY--
PATOOIE!
YEAH!
PATOOIE!
THE QUEEN'S NAME DON'T MEAN NOTHIN' OUT HERE.

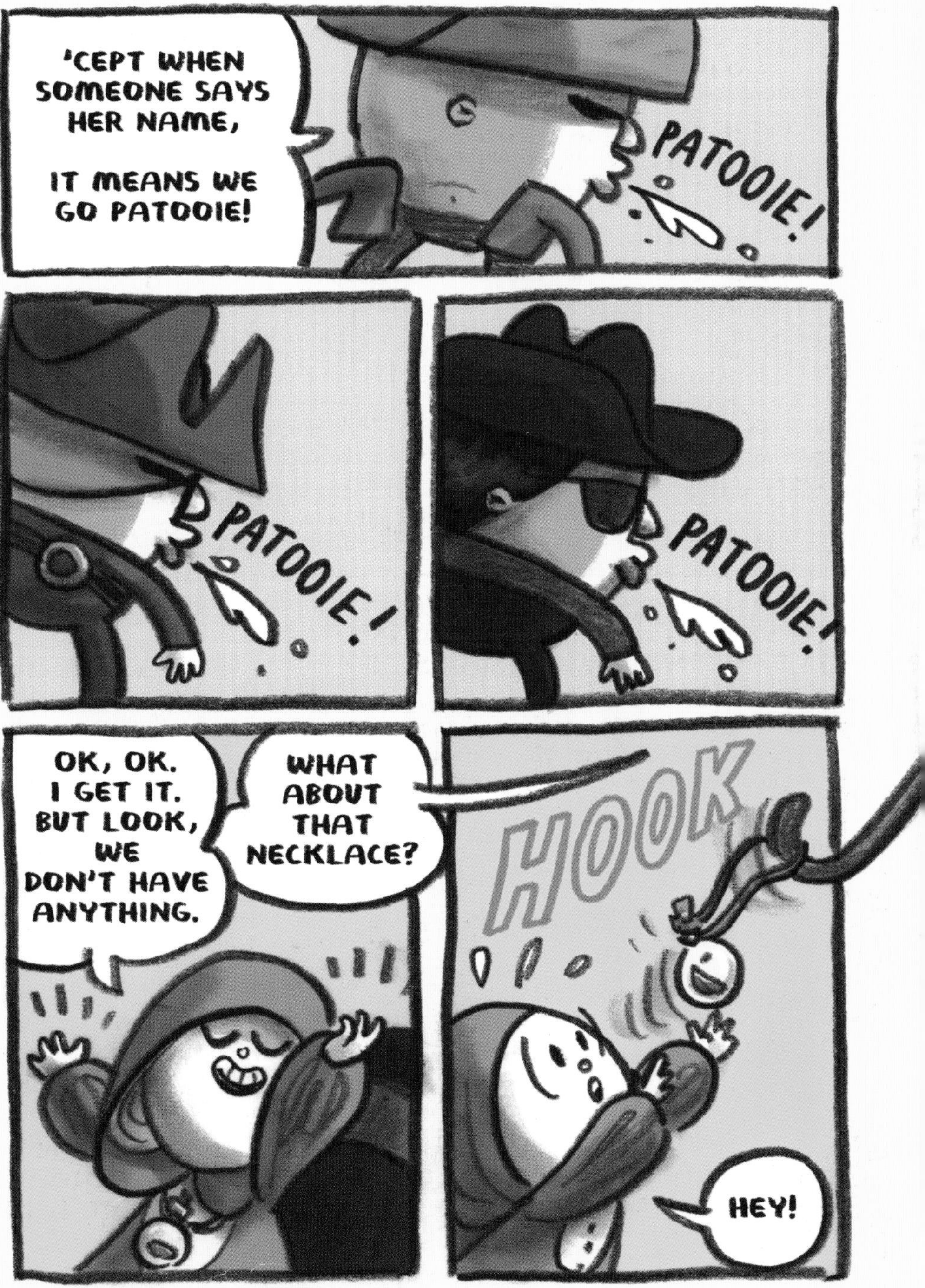
'CEPT WHEN SOMEONE SAYS HER NAME,
IT MEANS WE GO PATOOIE!
PATOOIE!
PATOOIE!
PATOOIE!
OK, OK. I GET IT. BUT LOOK, WE DON'T HAVE ANYTHING.
WHAT ABOUT THAT NECKLACE?
HOOK
HEY!

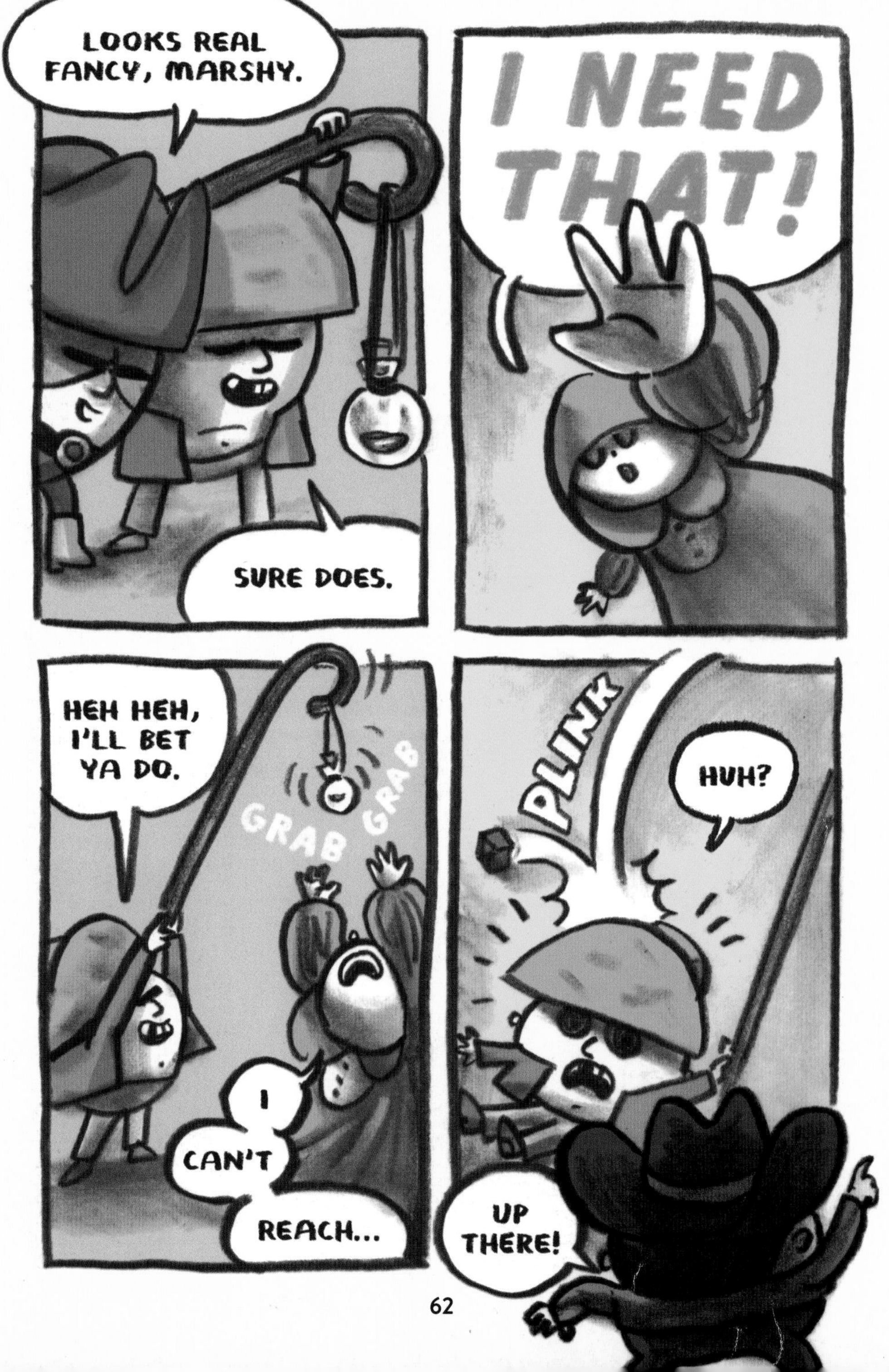
LOOKS REAL FANCY, MARSHY.
SURE DOES.
I NEED THAT!
HEH HEH, I'LL BET YA DO.
GRAB GRAB
I
CAN'T
REACH...
PLINK
HUH?
UP THERE!

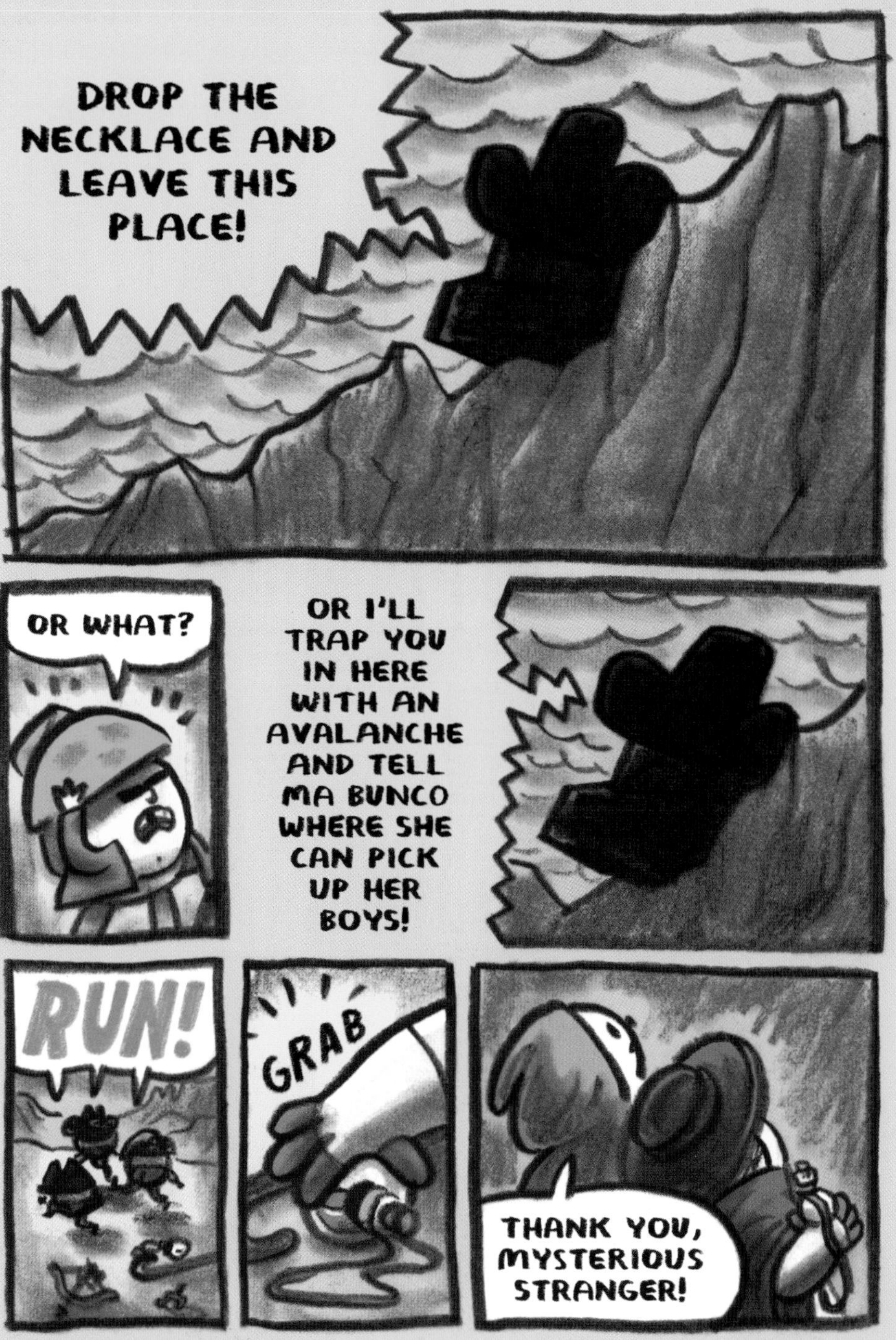
DROP THE NECKLACE AND LEAVE THIS PLACE!
OR WHAT?
OR I'LL TRAP YOU IN HERE WITH AN AVALANCHE AND TELL MA BUNCO WHERE SHE CAN PICK UP HER BOYS!
RUN!
GRAB
THANK YOU, MYSTERIOUS STRANGER!

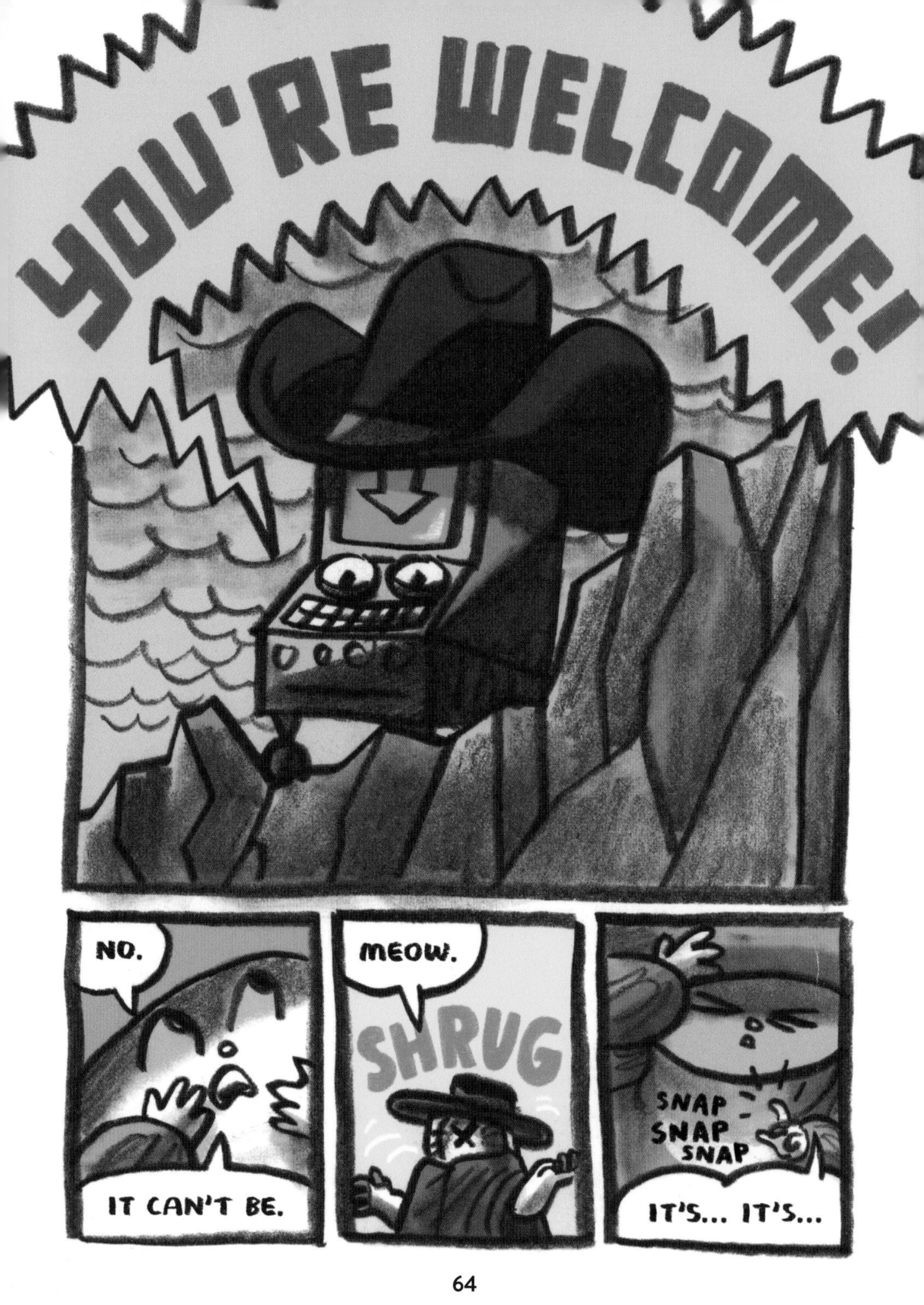
YOU'RE WELCOME!
NO.
IT CAN'T BE.
MEOW.
SHRUG
SNAP
SNAP
SNAP
IT'S... IT'S...

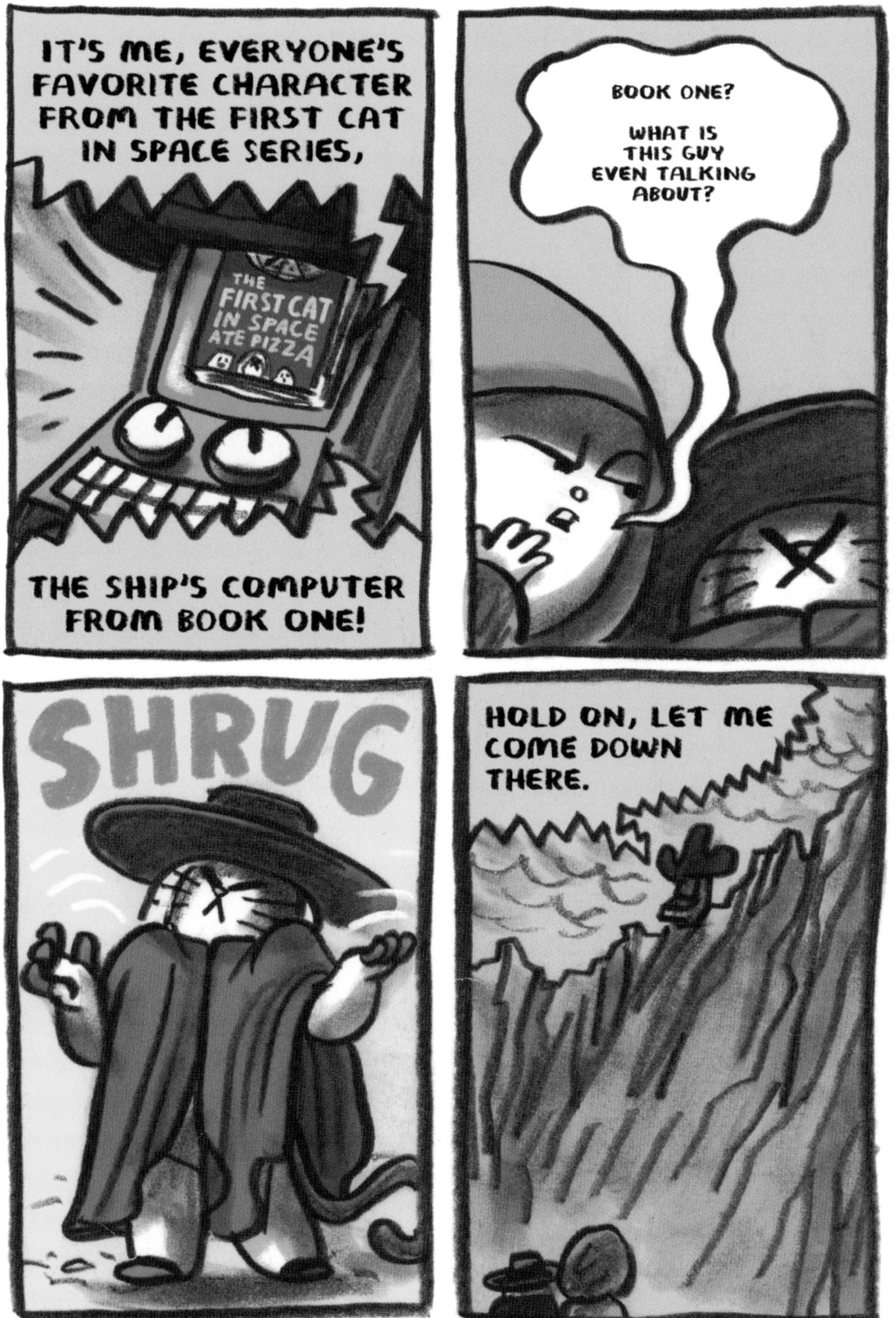
IT'S ME, EVERYONE'S FAVORITE CHARACTER FROM THE FIRST CAT IN SPACE SERIES,
THE FIRST CAT IN SPACE ATE PIZZA
THE SHIP'S COMPUTER FROM BOOK ONE!
BOOK ONE?
WHAT IS THIS GUY EVEN TALKING ABOUT?
SHRUG
HOLD ON, LET ME COME DOWN THERE.

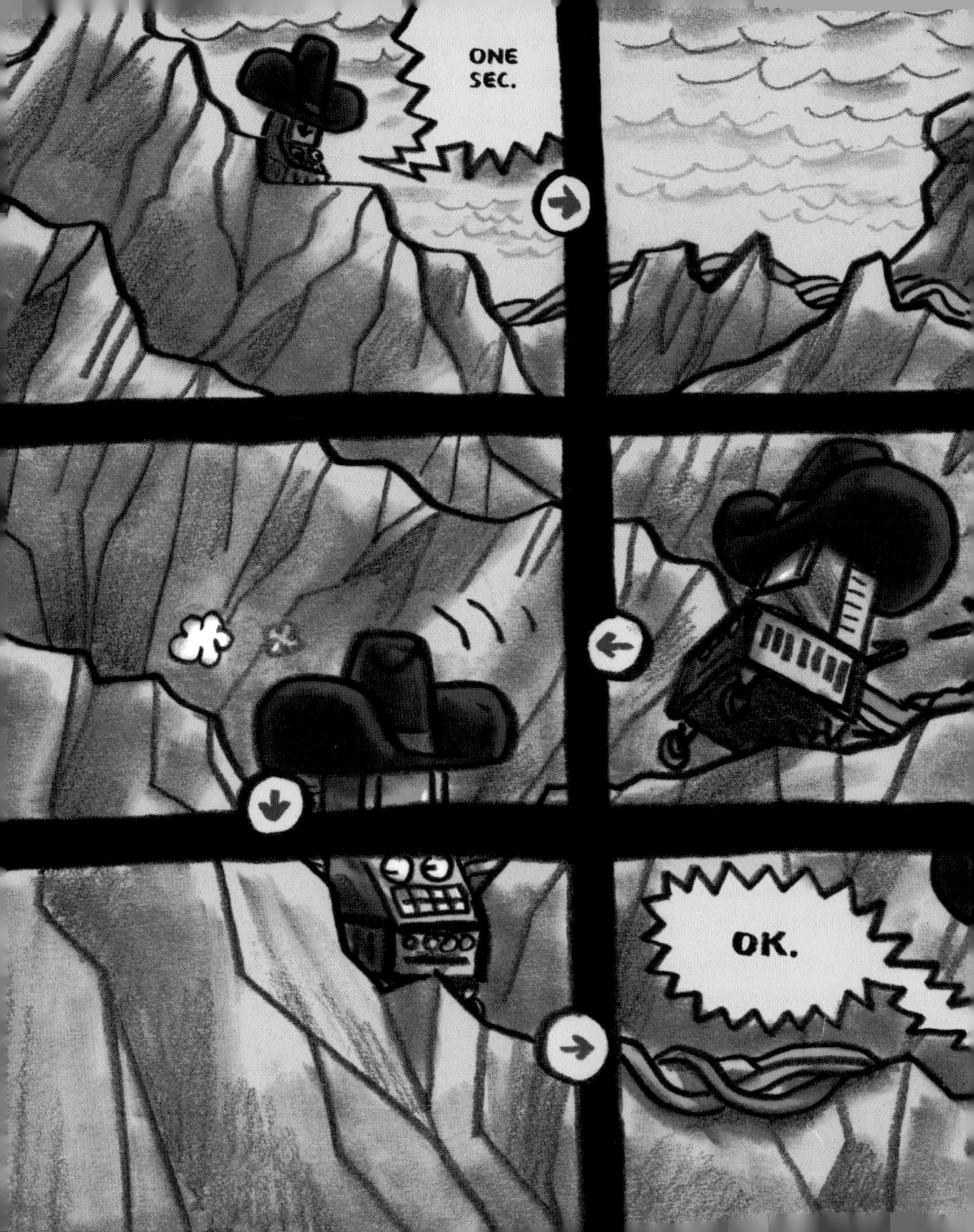
ONE SEC.
OK.

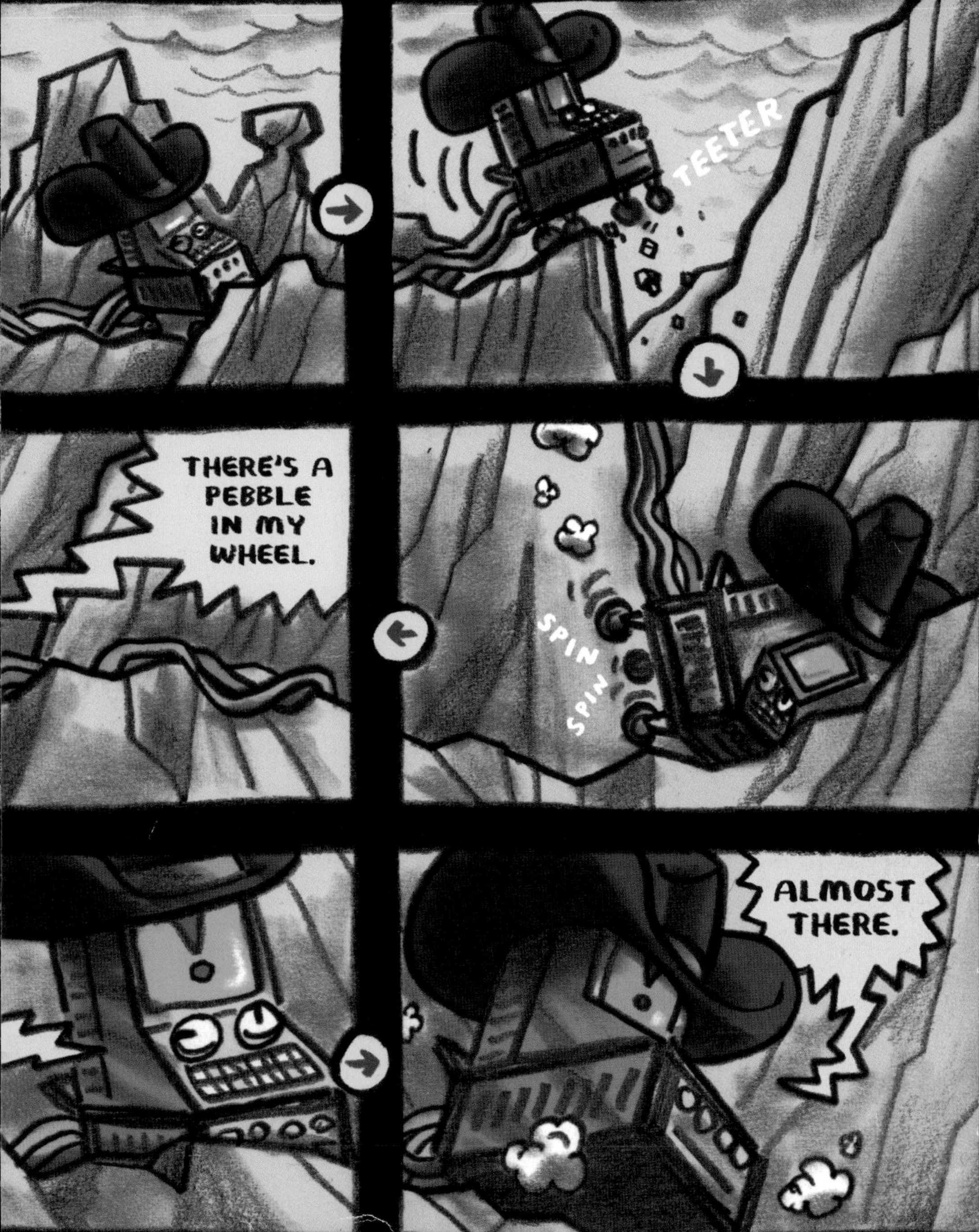
TEETER
THERE'S A PEBBLE IN MY WHEEL.
SPIN SPIN
ALMOST THERE.

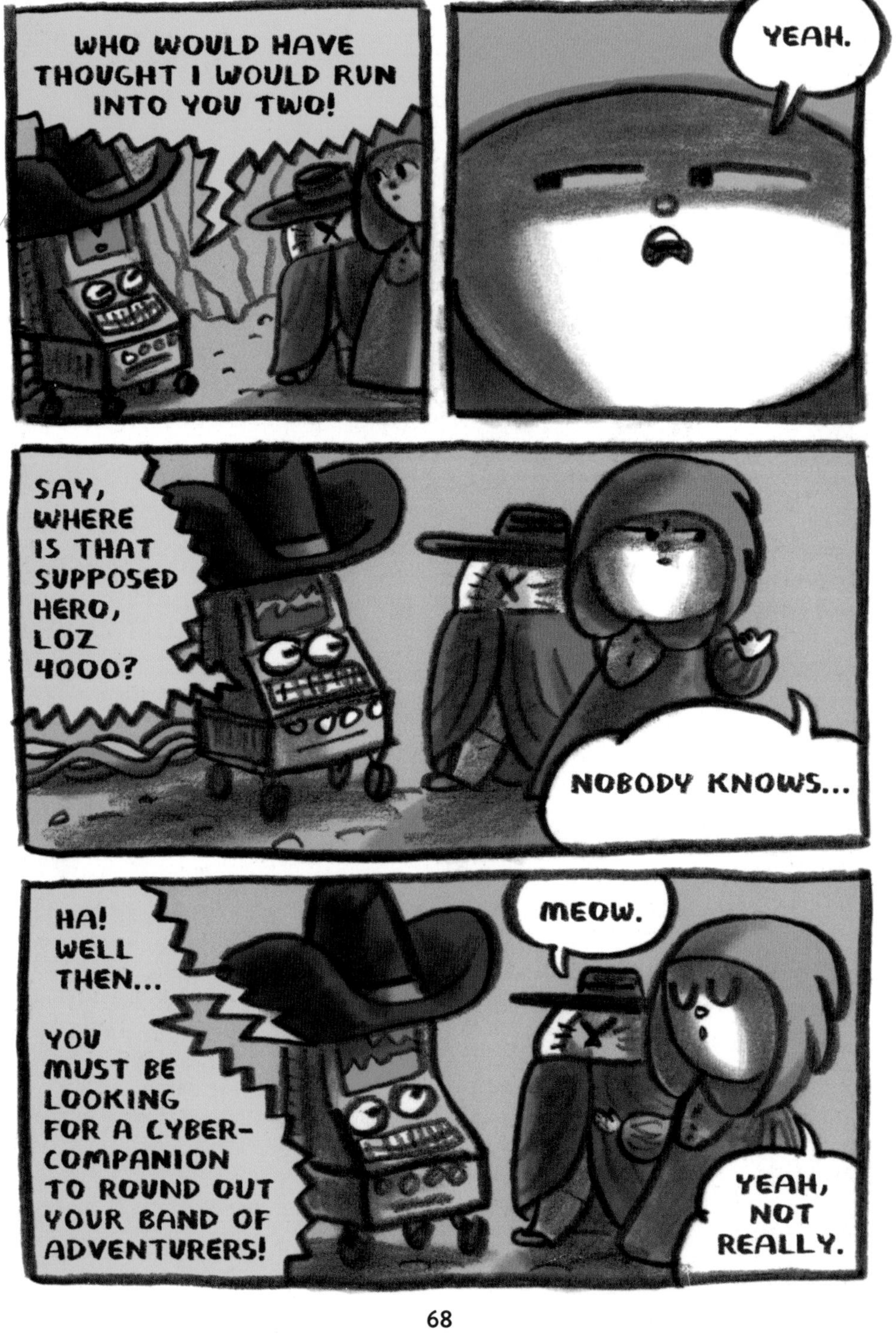
WHO WOULD HAVE THOUGHT I WOULD RUN INTO YOU TWO!
YEAH.
SAY, WHERE IS THAT SUPPOSED HERO, LOZ 4000?
NOBODY KNOWS...
HA! WELL THEN...
YOU MUST BE LOOKING FOR A CYBER-COMPANION TO ROUND OUT YOUR BAND OF ADVENTURERS!
MEOW.
YEAH, NOT REALLY.

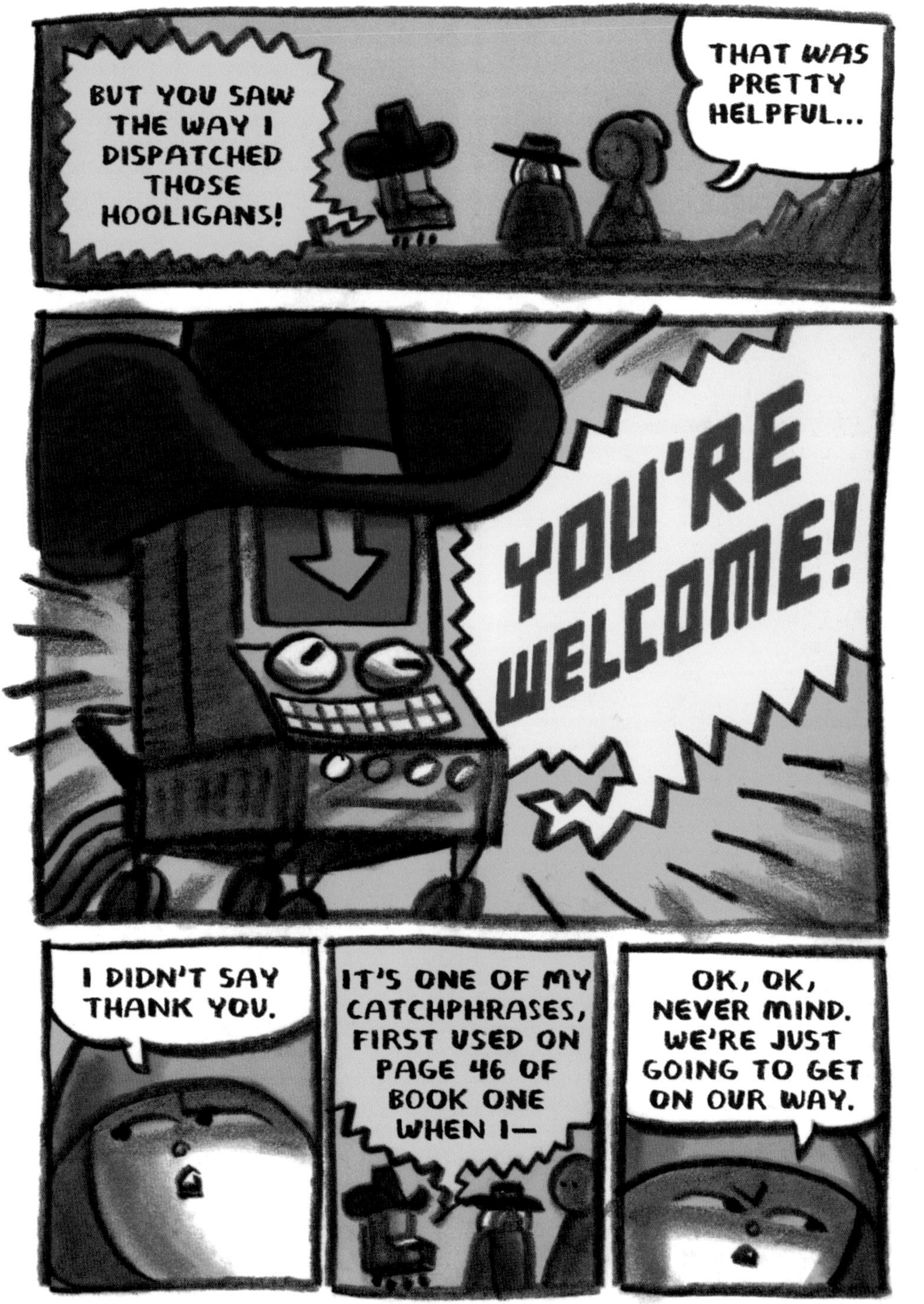
BUT YOU SAW THE WAY I DISPATCHED THOSE HOOLIGANS!
THAT *WAS* PRETTY HELPFUL...
YOU'RE WELCOME!
I DIDN'T SAY THANK YOU.
IT'S ONE OF MY CATCHPHRASES, FIRST USED ON PAGE 46 OF BOOK ONE WHEN I—
OK, OK, NEVER MIND. WE'RE JUST GOING TO GET ON OUR WAY.

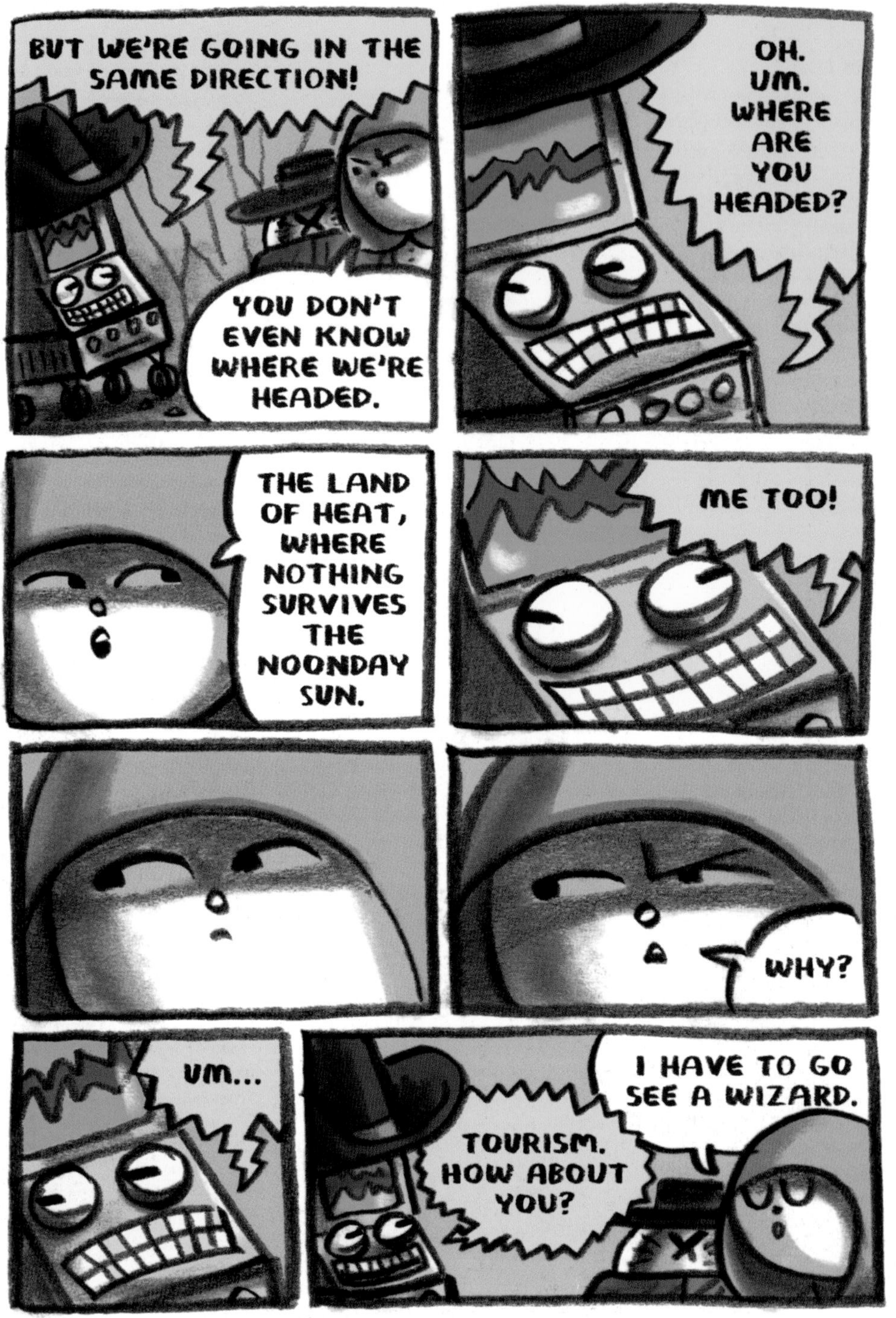
BUT WE'RE GOING IN THE SAME DIRECTION!
YOU DON'T EVEN KNOW WHERE WE'RE HEADED.
OH. UM. WHERE ARE YOU HEADED?
THE LAND OF HEAT, WHERE NOTHING SURVIVES THE NOONDAY SUN.
ME TOO!
WHY?
UM...
TOURISM. HOW ABOUT YOU?
I HAVE TO GO SEE A WIZARD.

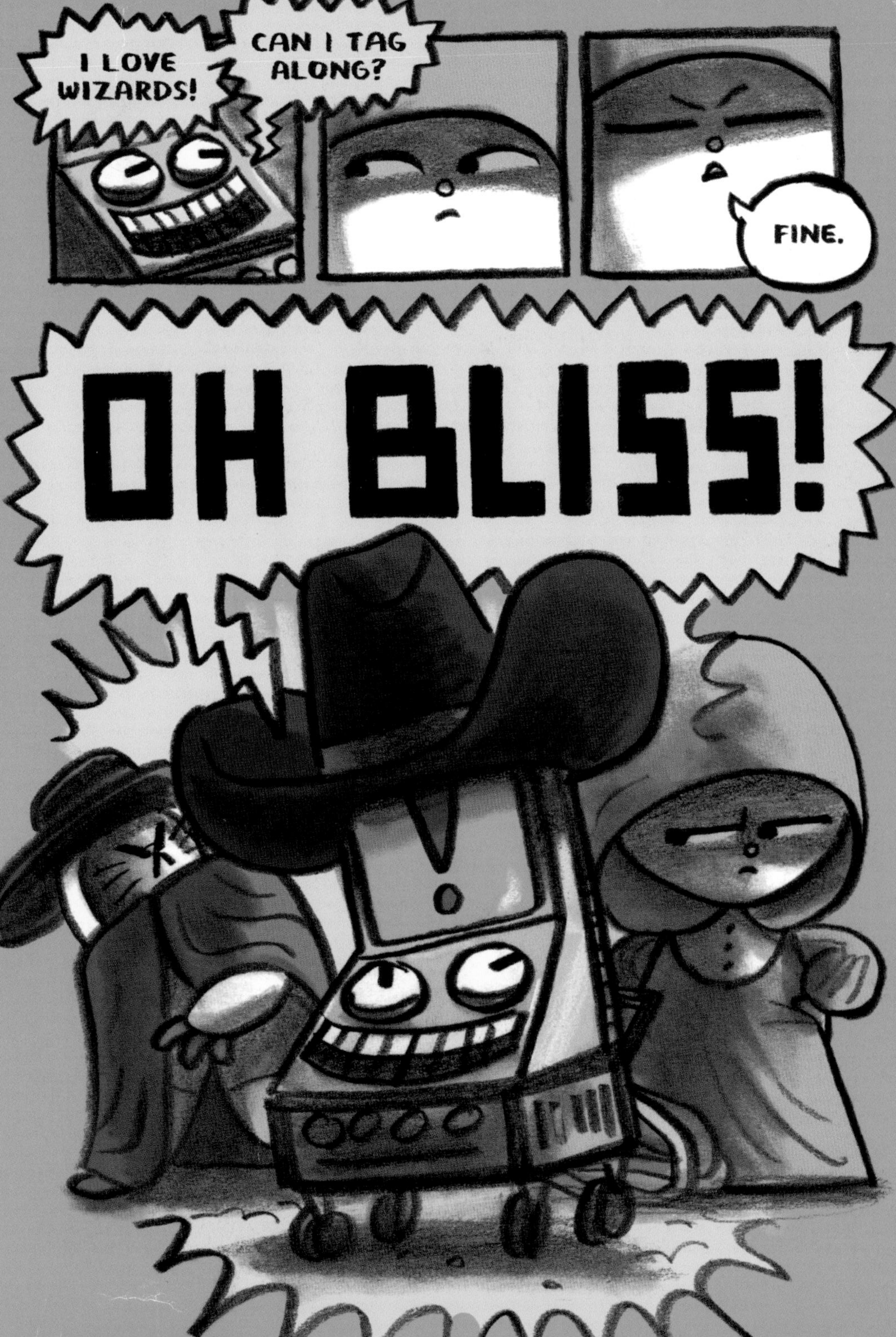

I LOVE WIZARDS!
CAN I TAG ALONG?
FINE.
OH BLISS!

CHAPTER 3

# ADVENTURE

THIS IS NOT AN
ADVENTURE.

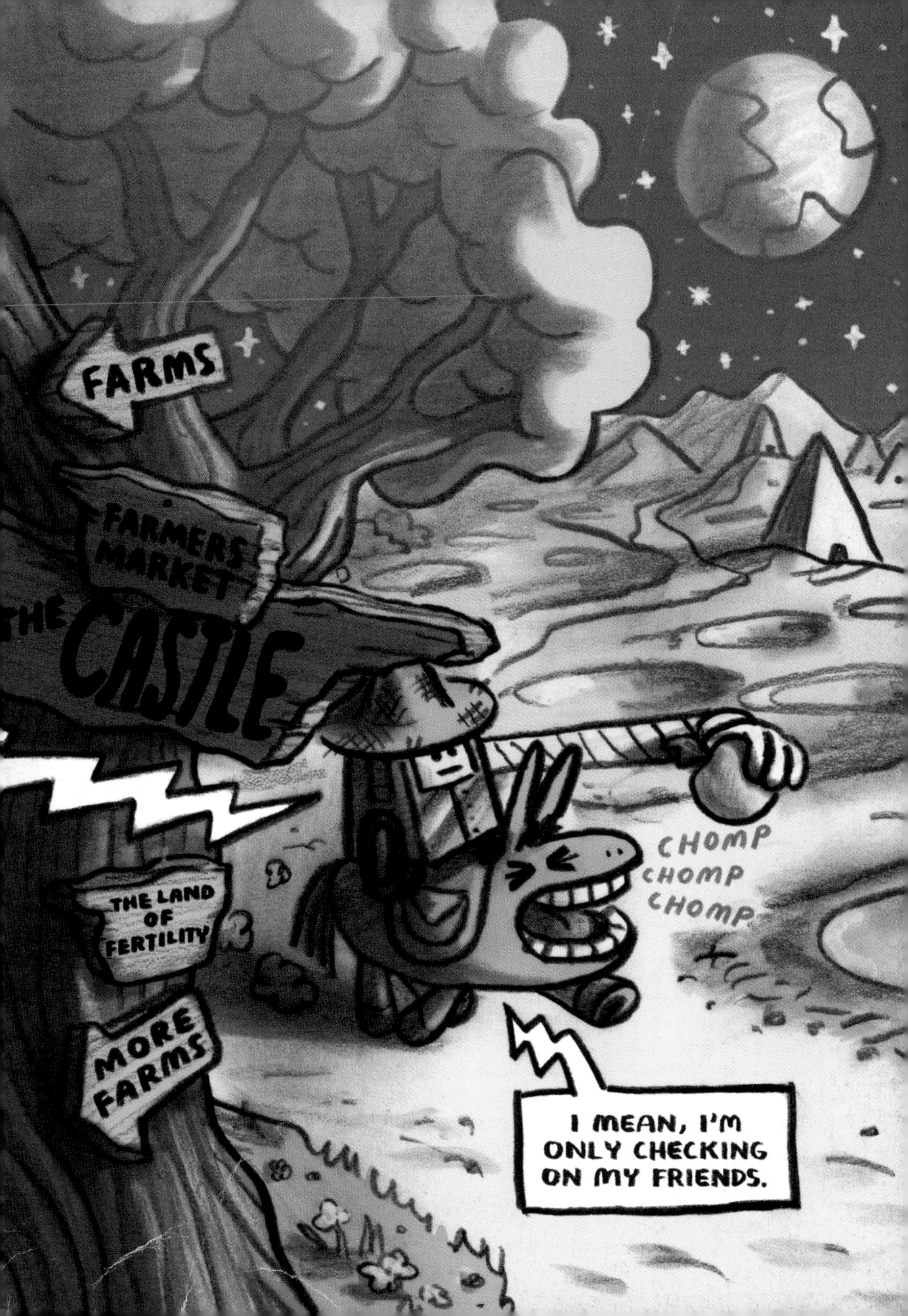
FARMS
FARMERS MARKET
THE CASTLE
THE LAND OF FERTILITY
MORE FARMS
CHOMP CHOMP CHOMP
I MEAN, I'M ONLY CHECKING ON MY FRIENDS.

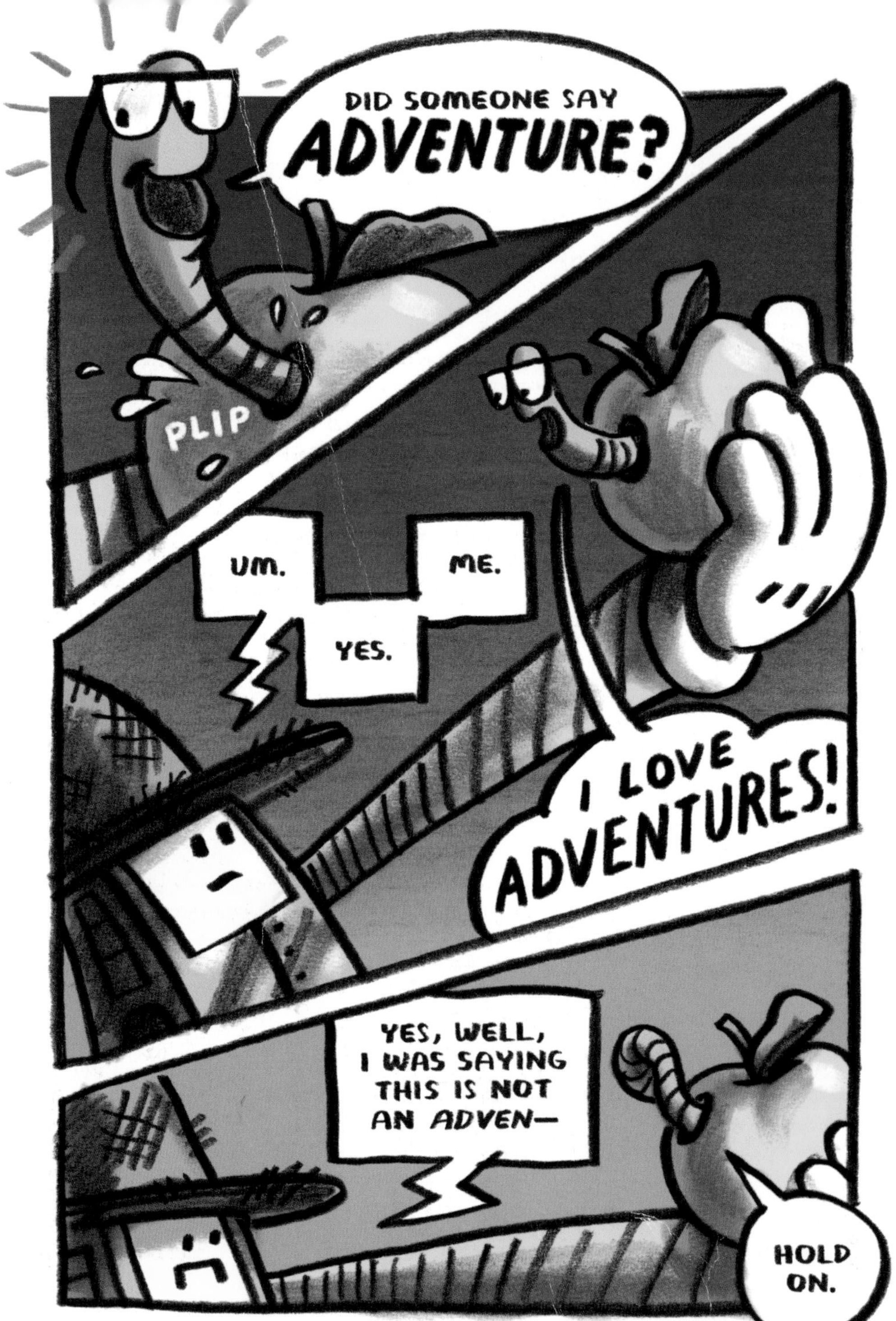
DID SOMEONE SAY ADVENTURE?
PLIP
UM.
ME.
YES.
I LOVE ADVENTURES!
YES, WELL, I WAS SAYING THIS IS NOT AN ADVEN—
HOLD ON.

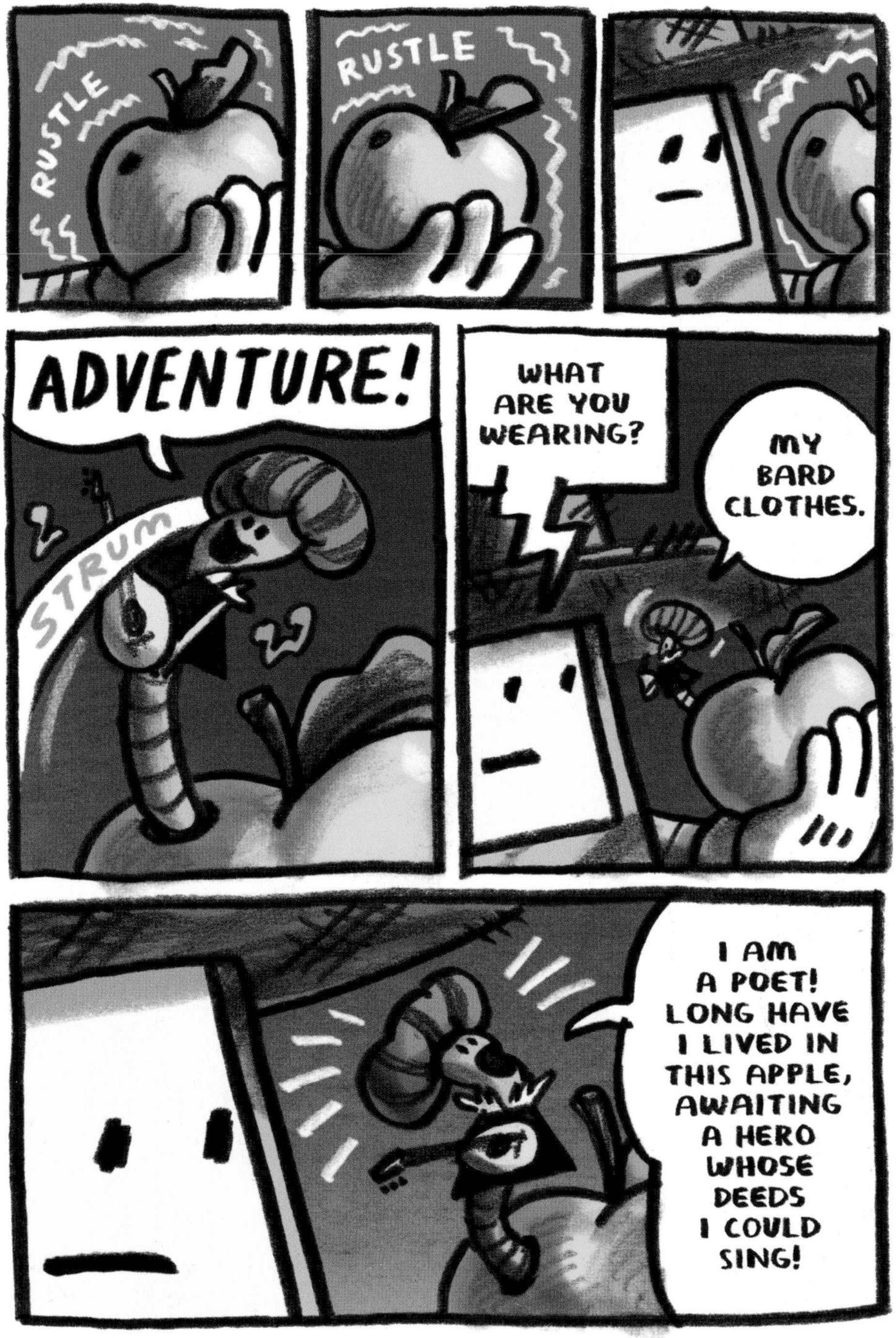
RUSTLE
RUSTLE
ADVENTURE!
STRUM
WHAT ARE YOU WEARING?
MY BARD CLOTHES.
I AM A POET! LONG HAVE I LIVED IN THIS APPLE, AWAITING A HERO WHOSE DEEDS I COULD SING!

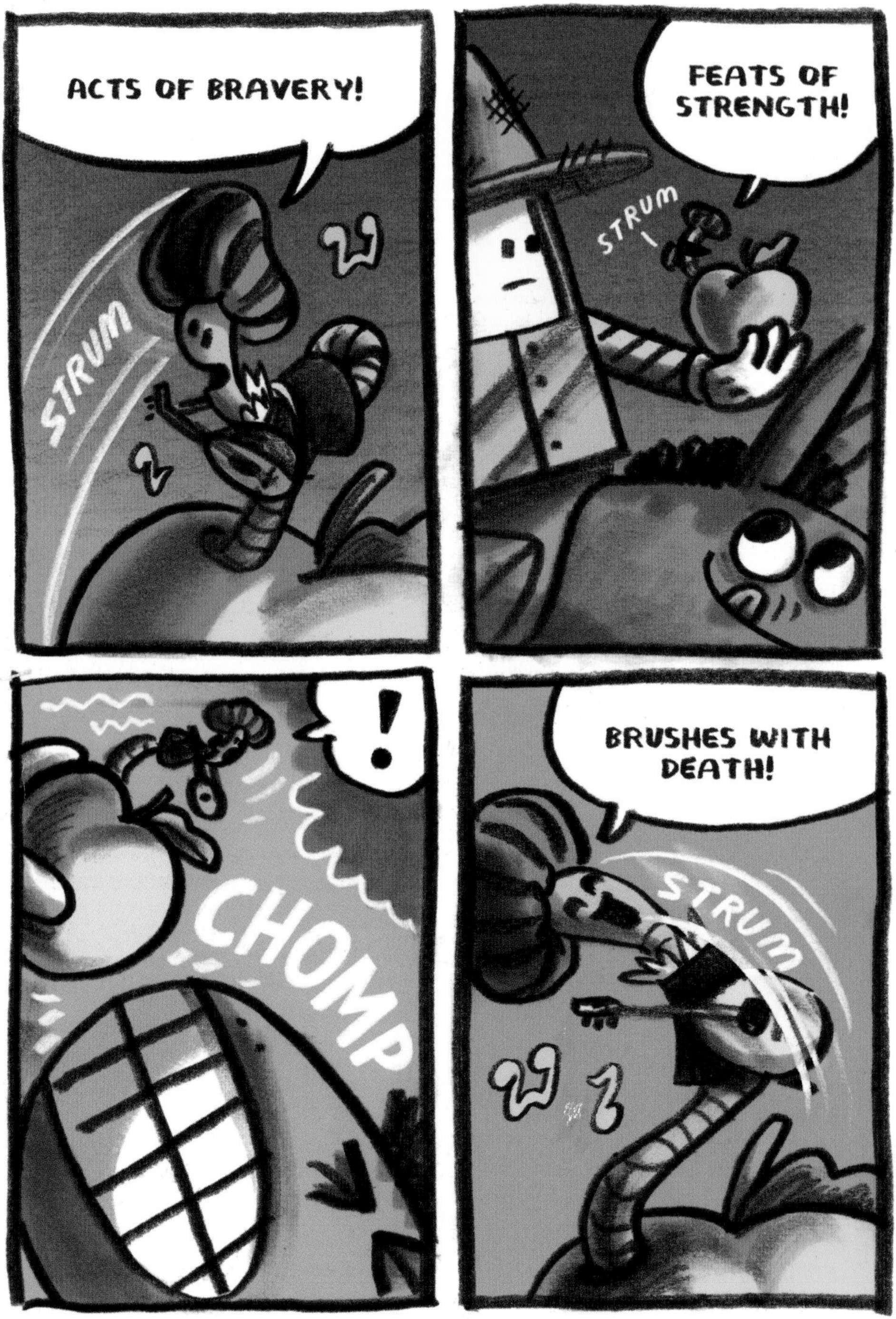
ACTS OF BRAVERY!
STRUM
FEATS OF STRENGTH!
STRUM
!
CHOMP
BRUSHES WITH DEATH!
STRUM

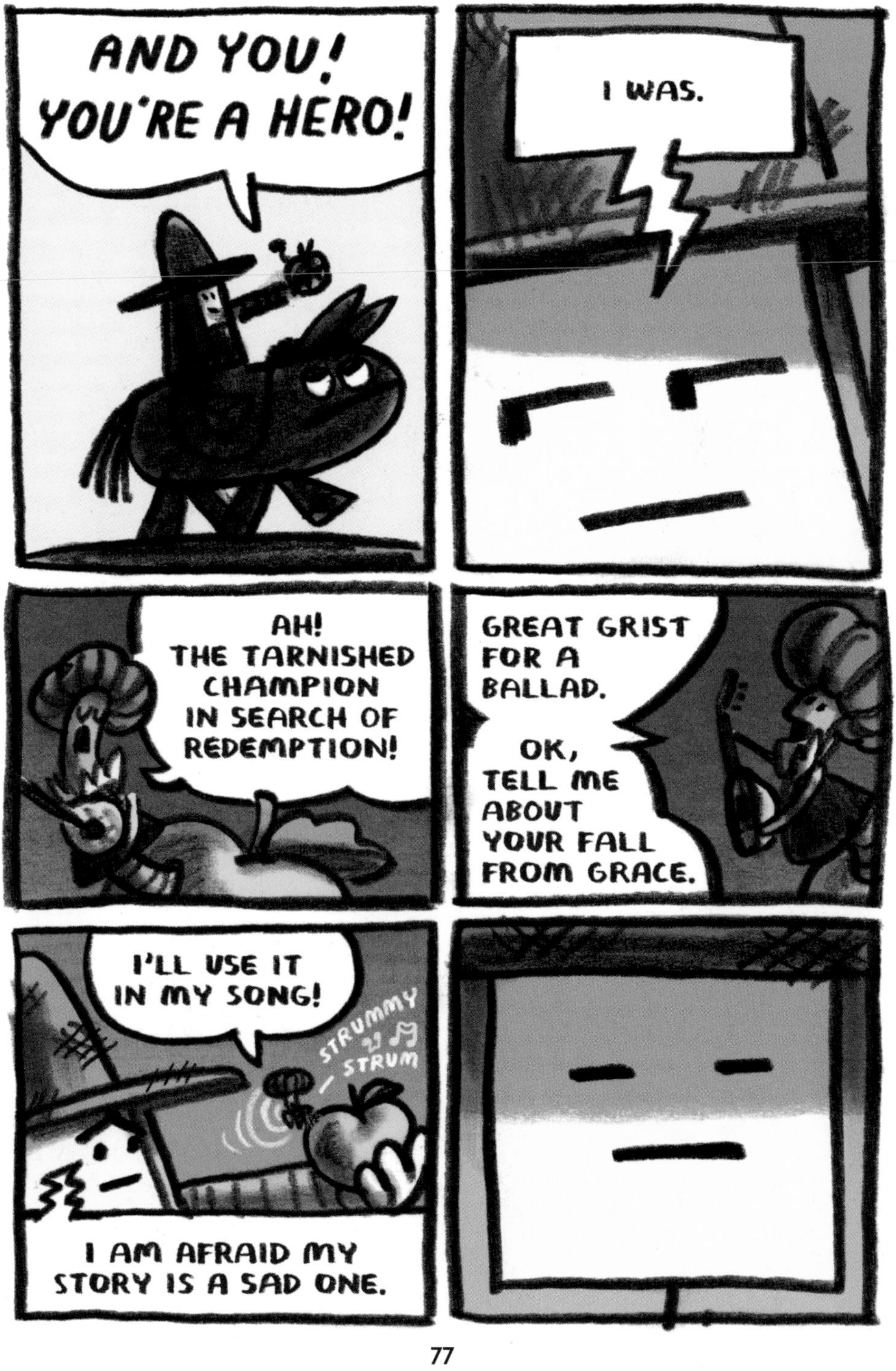
AND YOU! YOU'RE A HERO!
I WAS.
AH! THE TARNISHED CHAMPION IN SEARCH OF REDEMPTION!
GREAT GRIST FOR A BALLAD.
OK, TELL ME ABOUT YOUR FALL FROM GRACE.
I'LL USE IT IN MY SONG!
STRUMMY STRUM
I AM AFRAID MY STORY IS A SAD ONE.

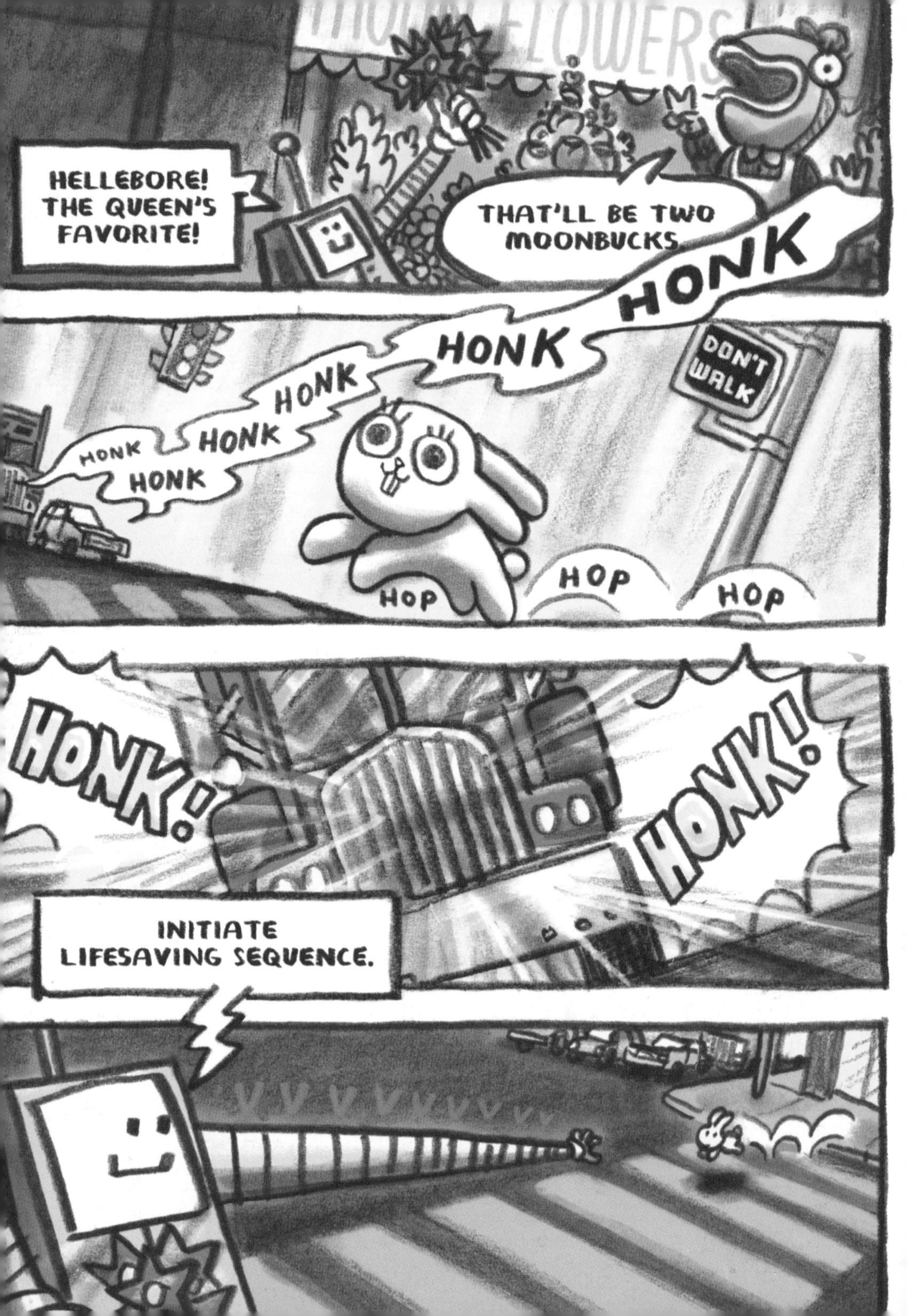

HELLEBORE! THE QUEEN'S FAVORITE!
THAT'LL BE TWO MOONBUCKS.
HONK
HONK
HONK
HONK
HONK
HONK
DON'T WALK
HOP
HOP
HOP
HONK!
HONK!
INITIATE LIFESAVING SEQUENCE.

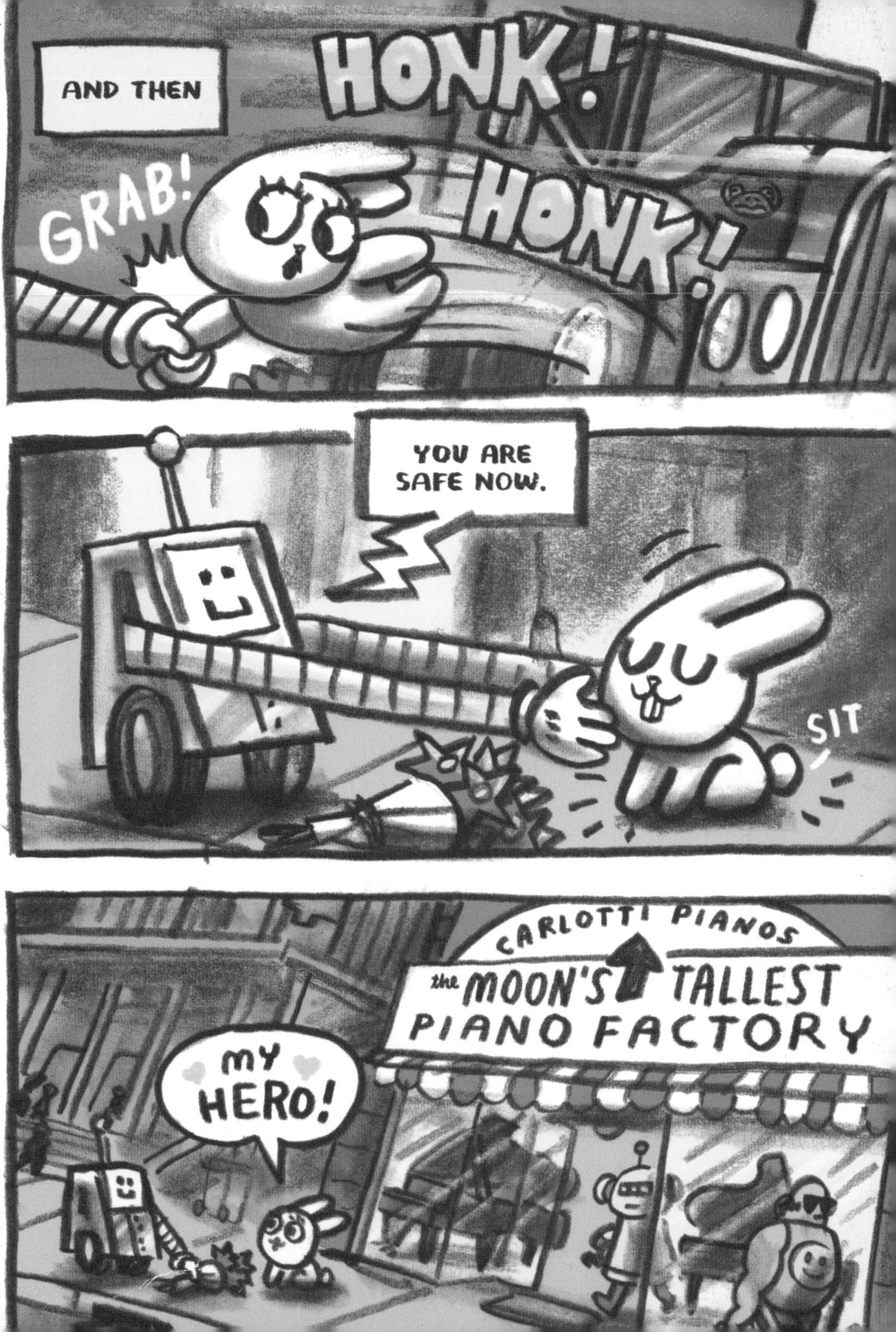
AND THEN
HONK!
GRAB!
HONK!
YOU ARE SAFE NOW.
SIT
CARLOTTI PIANOS
the MOON'S TALLEST PIANO FACTORY
MY HERO!

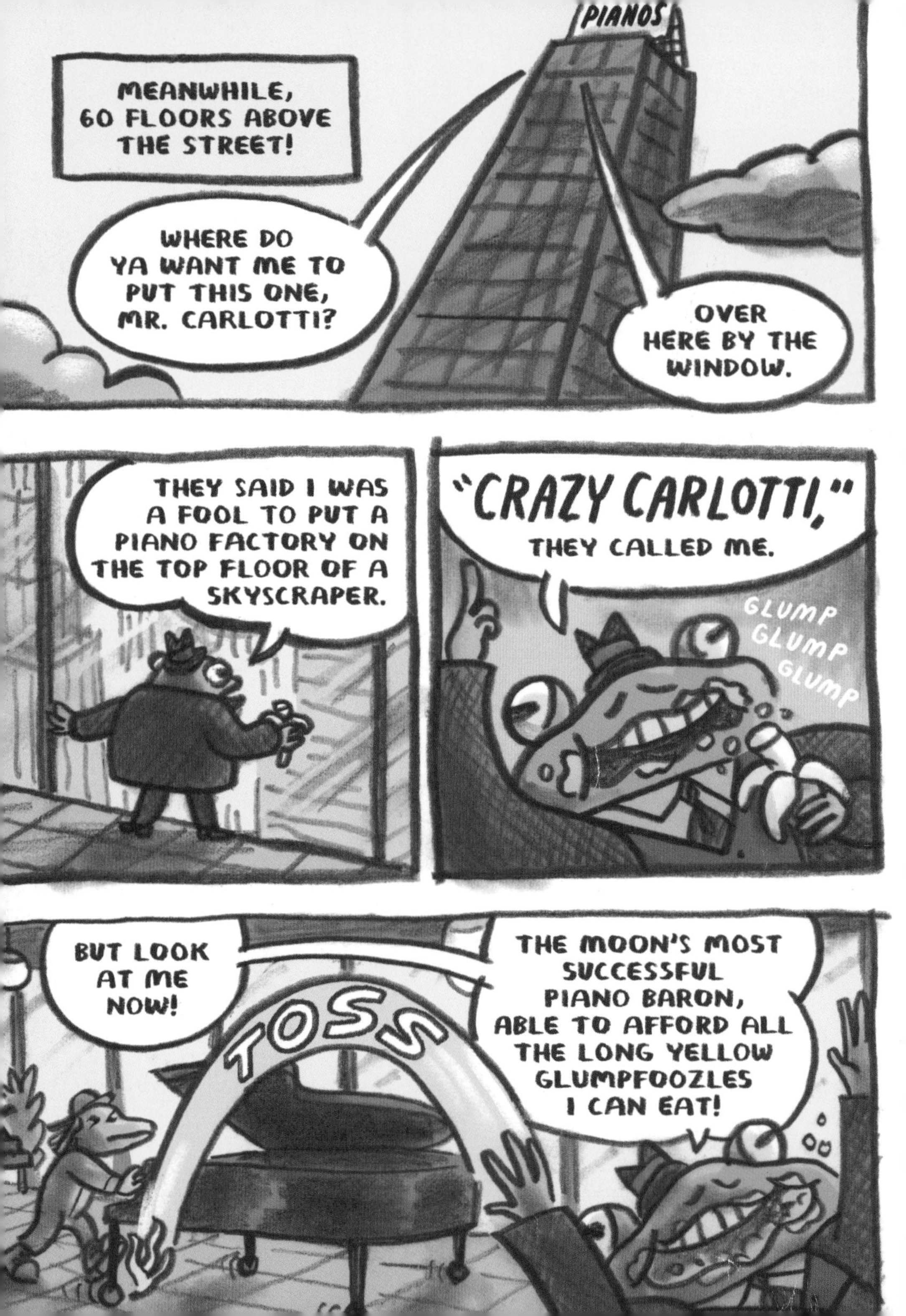
MEANWHILE, 60 FLOORS ABOVE THE STREET!
PIANOS
WHERE DO YA WANT ME TO PUT THIS ONE, MR. CARLOTTI?
OVER HERE BY THE WINDOW.
THEY SAID I WAS A FOOL TO PUT A PIANO FACTORY ON THE TOP FLOOR OF A SKYSCRAPER.
"CRAZY CARLOTTI," THEY CALLED ME.
GLUMP GLUMP GLUMP
BUT LOOK AT ME NOW!
THE MOON'S MOST SUCCESSFUL PIANO BARON, ABLE TO AFFORD ALL THE LONG YELLOW GLUMPFOOZLES I CAN EAT!
TOSS

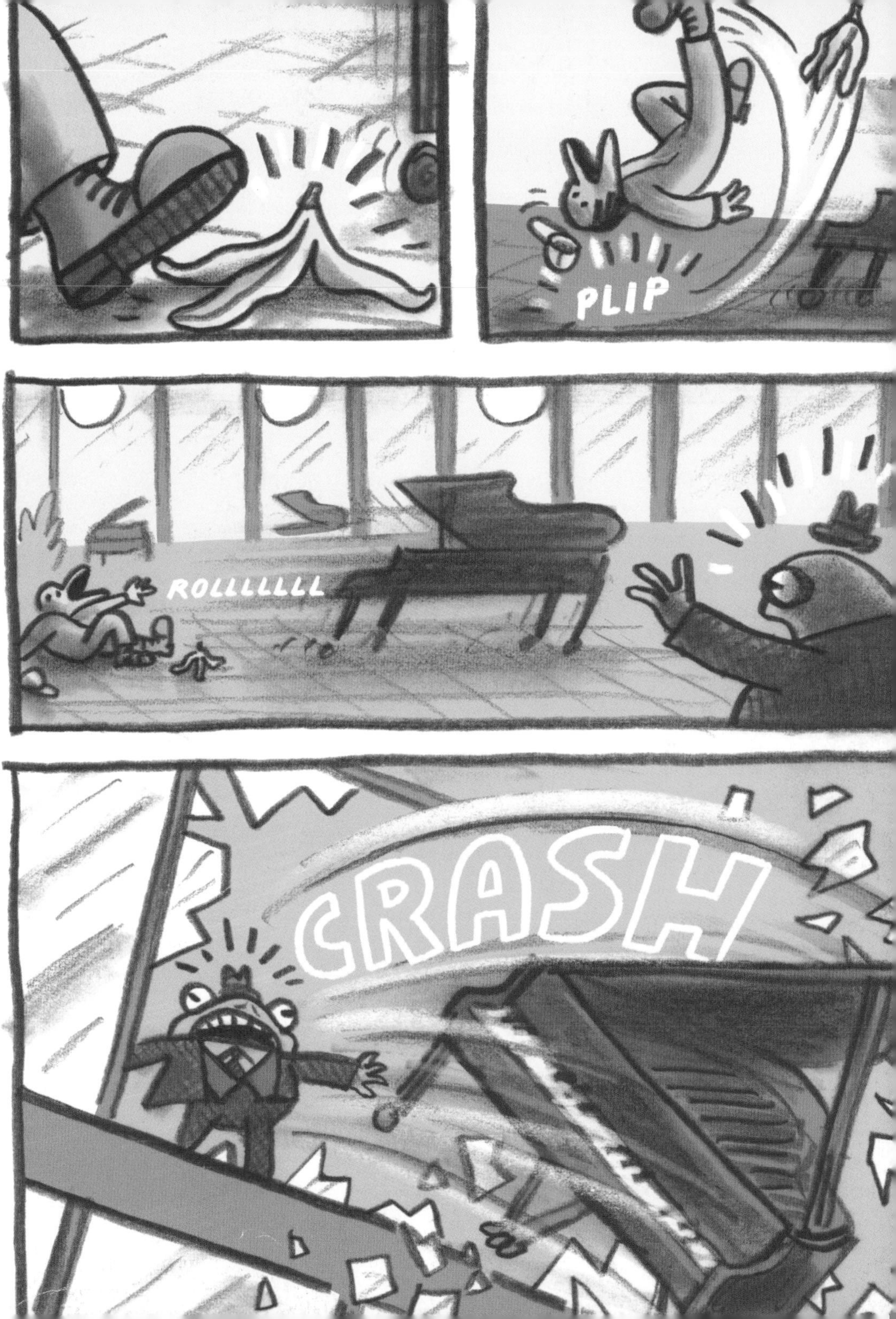
PLIP
ROLLLLLLL
CRASH

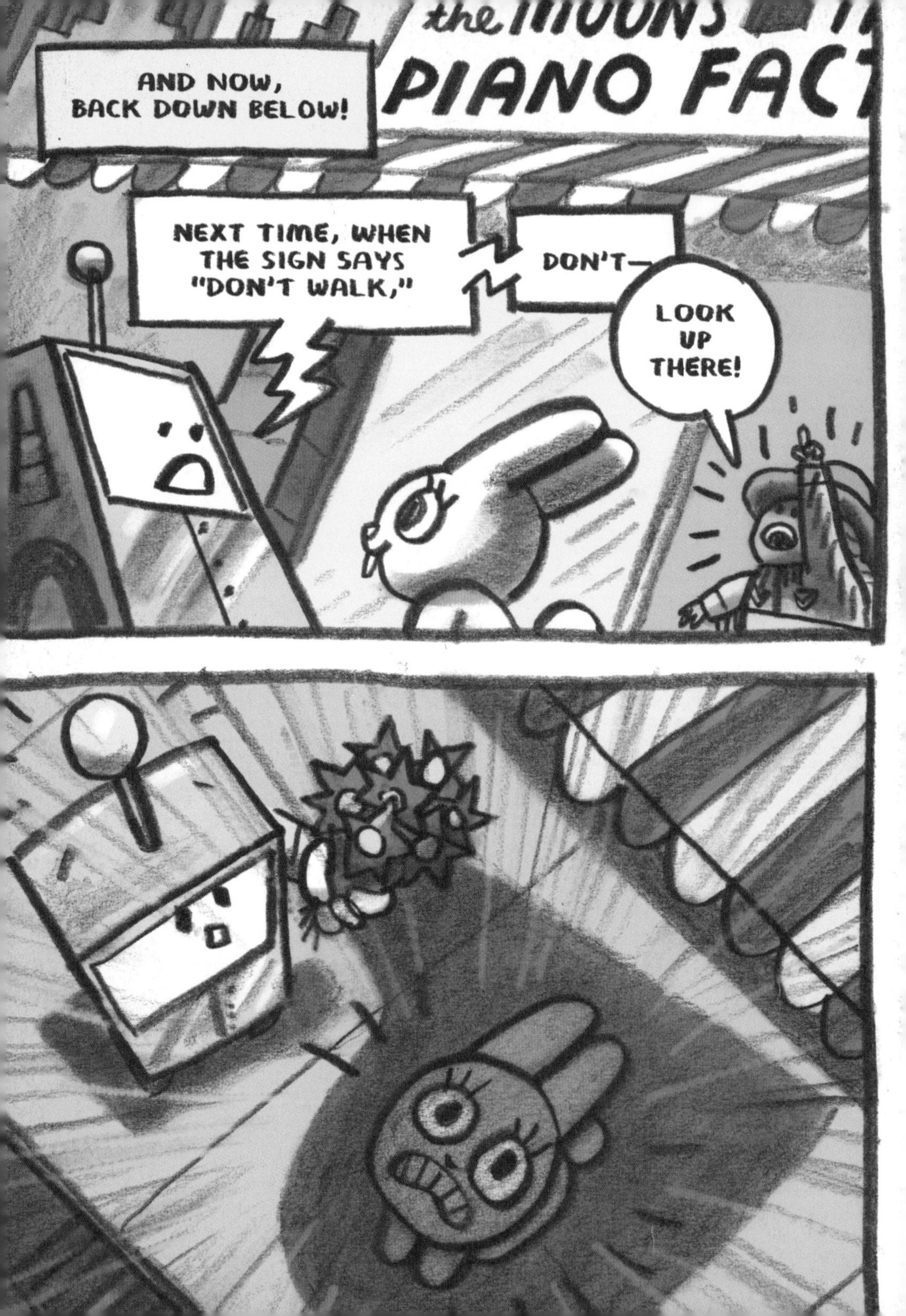
the
PIANO FAC
AND NOW, BACK DOWN BELOW!
NEXT TIME, WHEN THE SIGN SAYS "DON'T WALK,"
DON'T—
LOOK UP THERE!

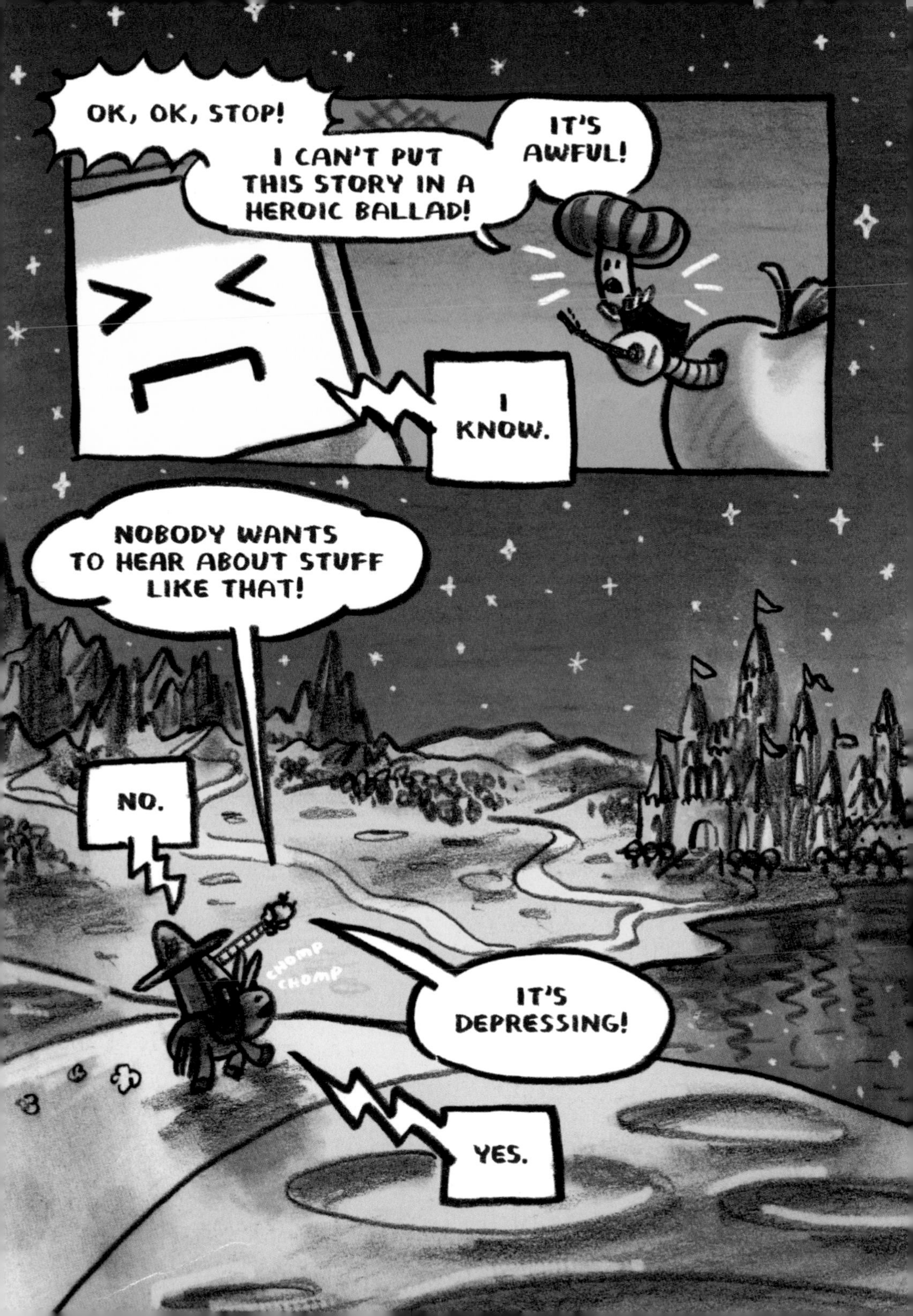
OK, OK, STOP!
I CAN'T PUT THIS STORY IN A HEROIC BALLAD!
IT'S AWFUL!
I KNOW.
NOBODY WANTS TO HEAR ABOUT STUFF LIKE THAT!
NO.
CHOMP CHOMP
IT'S DEPRESSING!
YES.

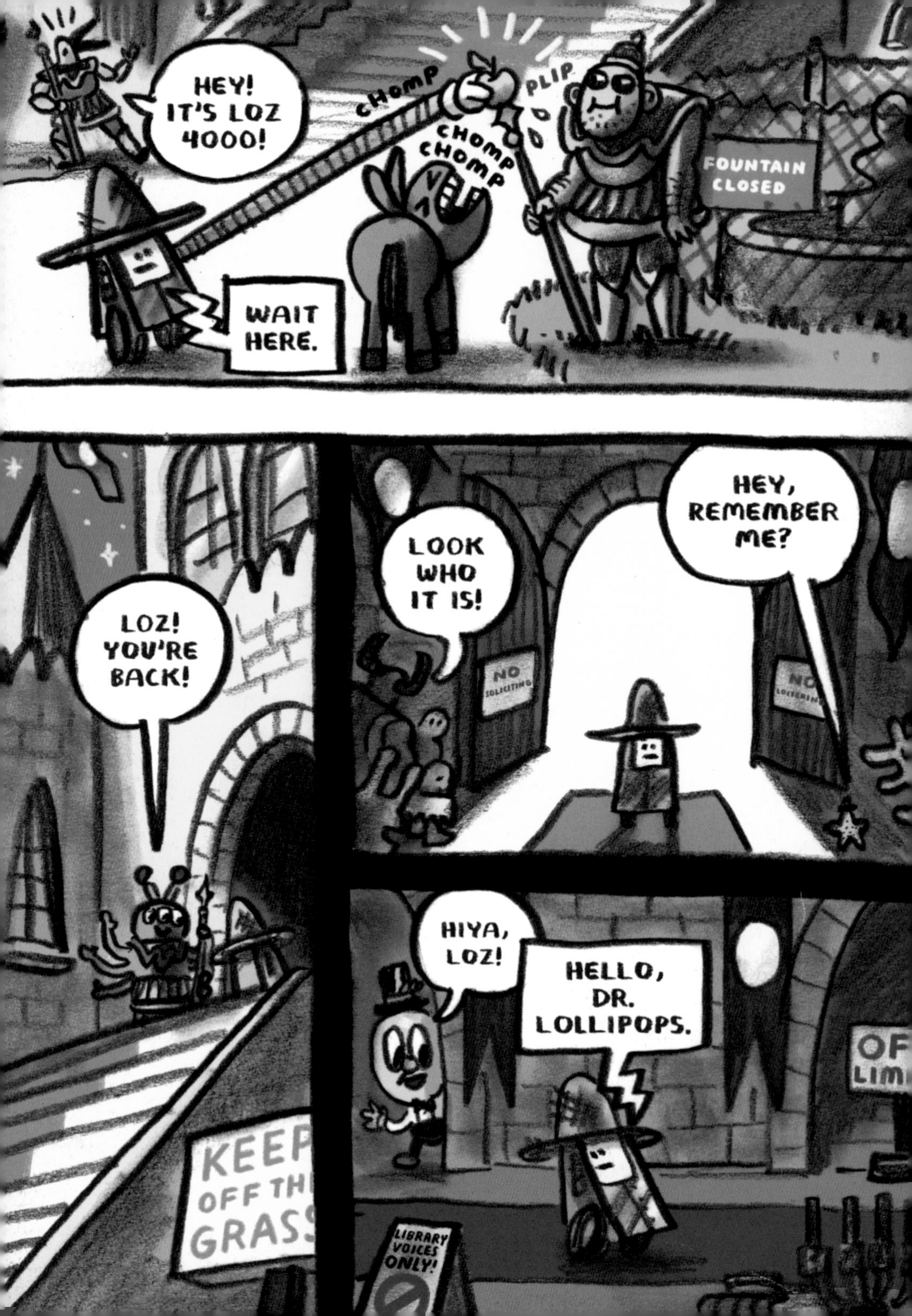

HEY! IT'S LOZ 4000!
CHOMP
PLIP
CHOMP CHOMP
FOUNTAIN CLOSED
WAIT HERE.
LOZ! YOU'RE BACK!
KEEP OFF THE GRASS
LOOK WHO IT IS!
HEY, REMEMBER ME?
NO SOLICITING
NO LOITERING
HIYA, LOZ!
HELLO, DR. LOLLIPOPS.
OFF LIMITS
LIBRARY VOICES ONLY!

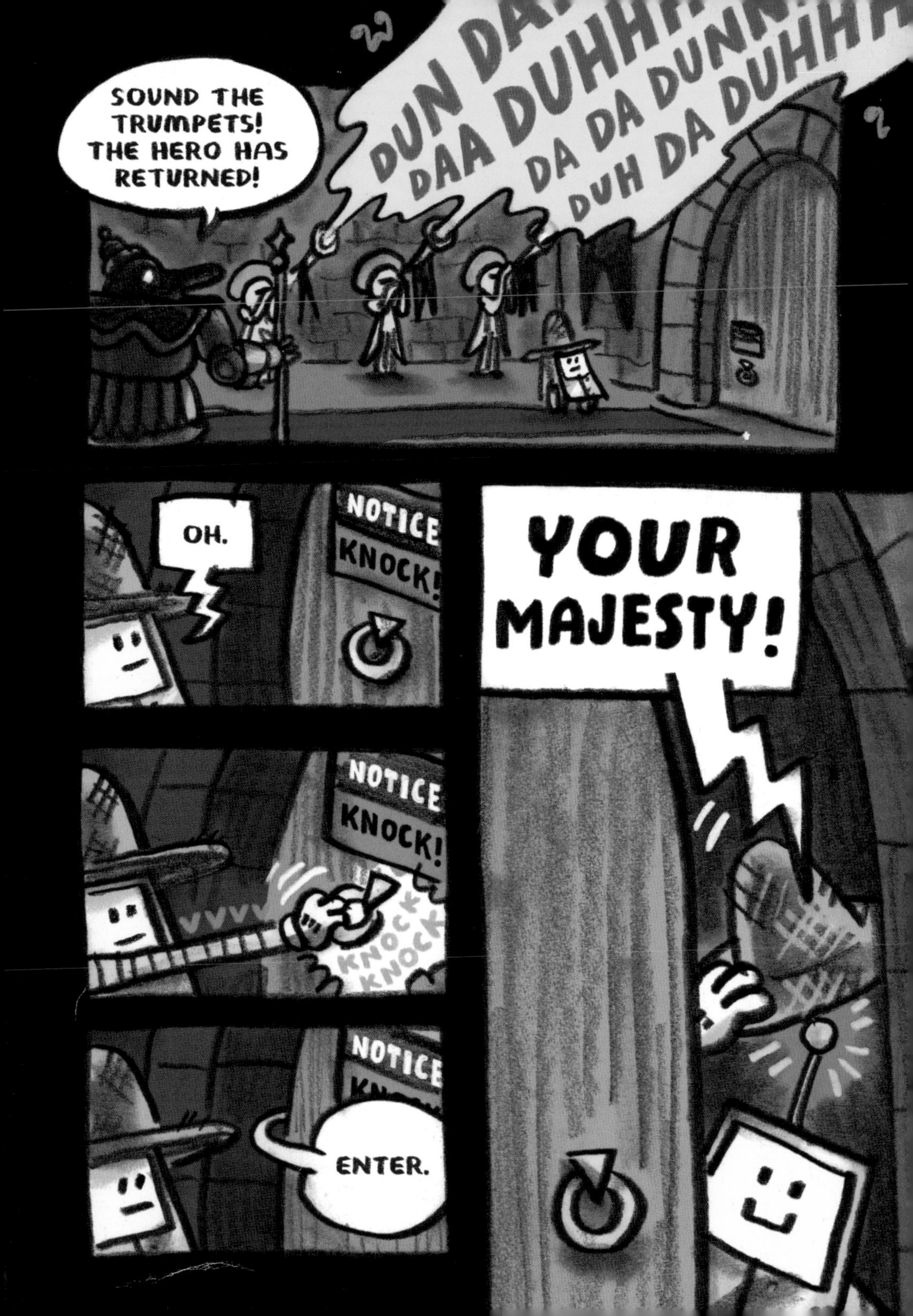
SOUND THE TRUMPETS! THE HERO HAS RETURNED!
DUN DA
DAA DUHHH
DA DA DUNN
DUH DA DUHHH
NOTICE
KNOCK!
OH.
NOTICE
KNOCK!
KNOCK KNOCK
NOTICE
ENTER.
YOUR MAJESTY!

YES?

BERNICE?

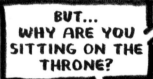

BUT... WHY ARE YOU SITTING ON THE THRONE?

WHERE IS THE MOON QUEEN?

THE QUEEN HAS FLED THE PALACE.

ALONE?

NO.

WITH FIRST CAT.

OH.

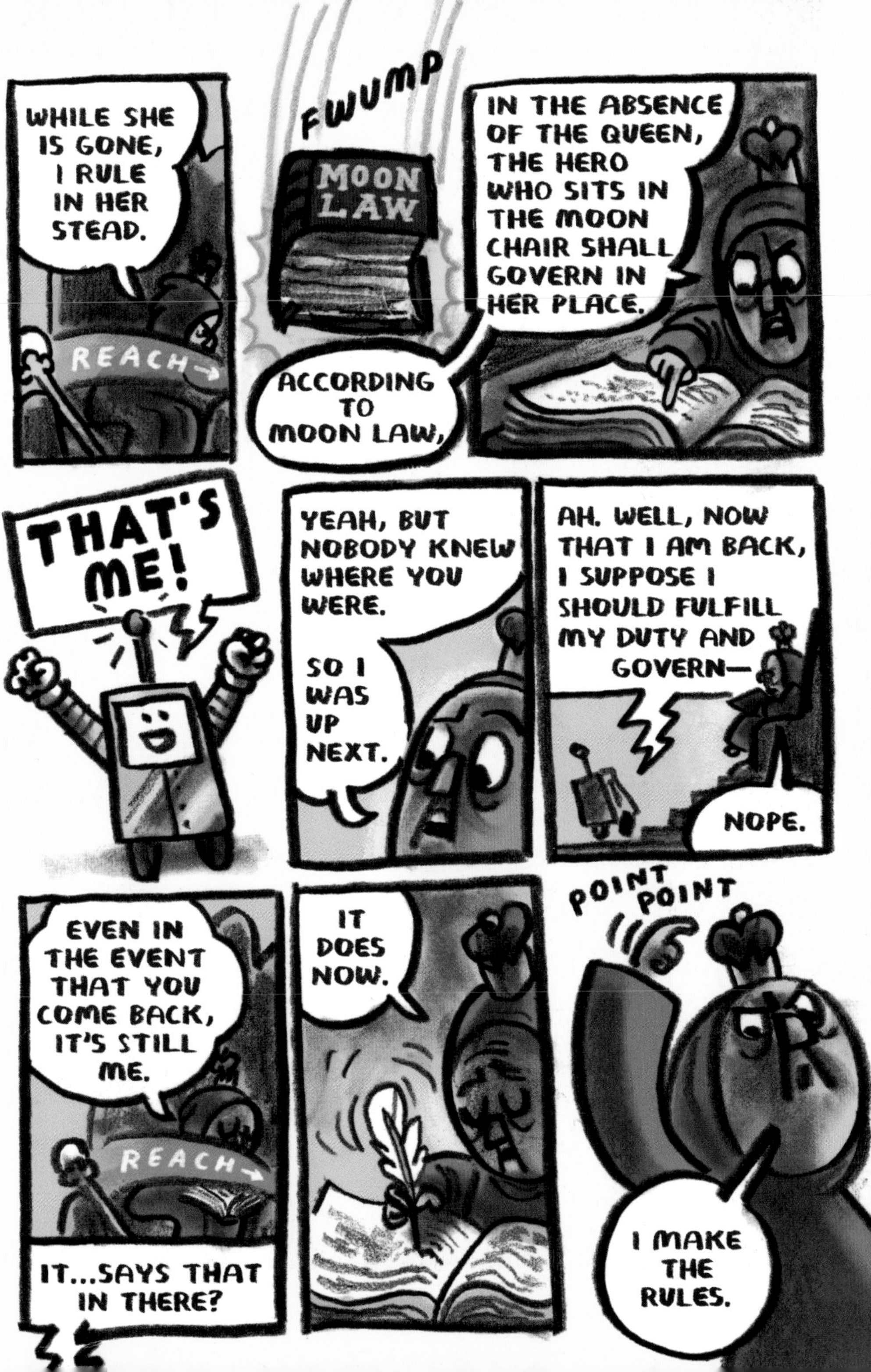
WHILE SHE IS GONE, I RULE IN HER STEAD.
REACH→
FWUMP
MOON LAW
ACCORDING TO MOON LAW,
IN THE ABSENCE OF THE QUEEN, THE HERO WHO SITS IN THE MOON CHAIR SHALL GOVERN IN HER PLACE.
THAT'S ME!
YEAH, BUT NOBODY KNEW WHERE YOU WERE.
SO I WAS UP NEXT.
AH. WELL, NOW THAT I AM BACK, I SUPPOSE I SHOULD FULFILL MY DUTY AND GOVERN—
NOPE.
EVEN IN THE EVENT THAT YOU COME BACK, IT'S STILL ME.
REACH→
IT...SAYS THAT IN THERE?
IT DOES NOW.
POINT POINT
I MAKE THE RULES.

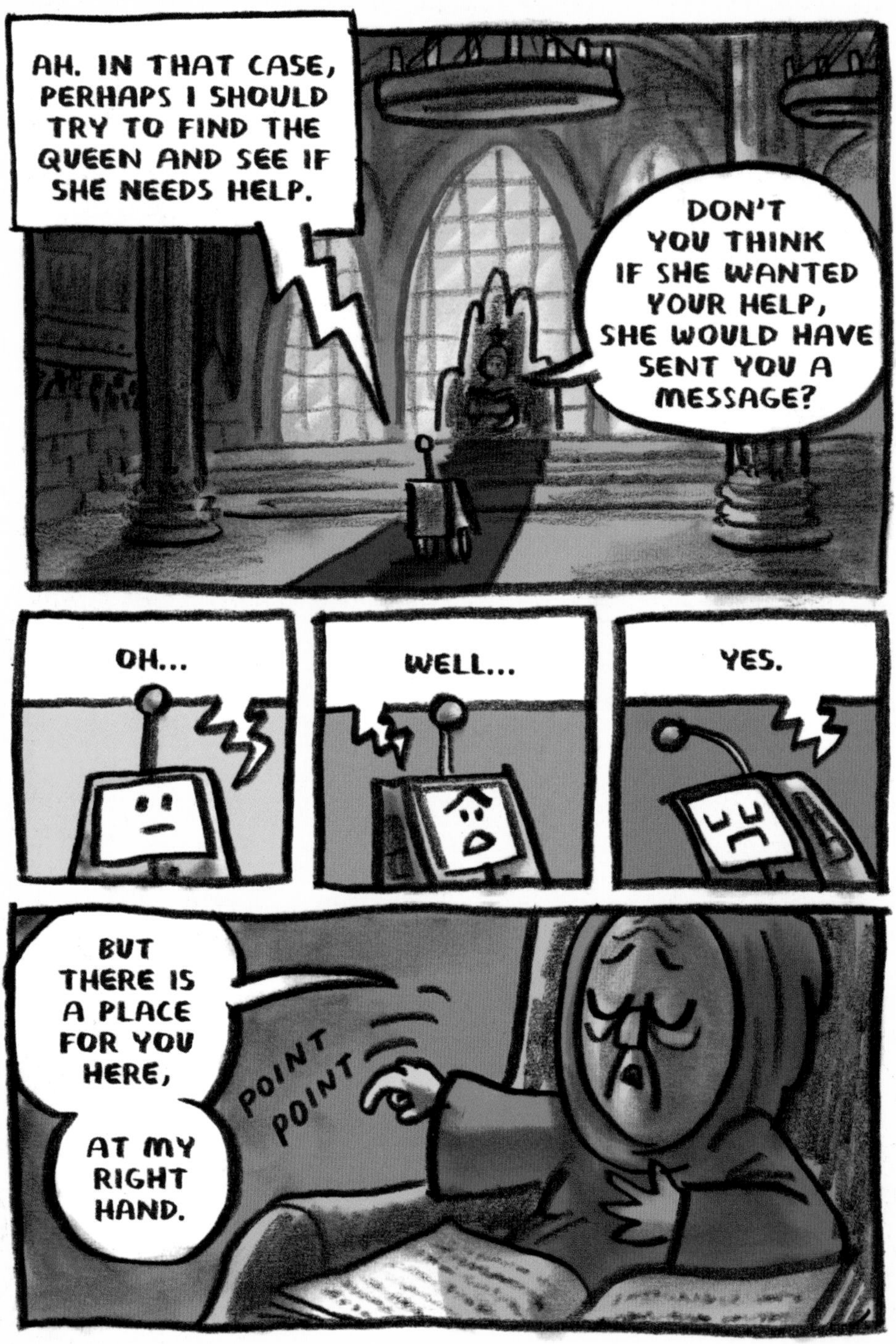
AH. IN THAT CASE, PERHAPS I SHOULD TRY TO FIND THE QUEEN AND SEE IF SHE NEEDS HELP.
DON'T YOU THINK IF SHE WANTED YOUR HELP, SHE WOULD HAVE SENT YOU A MESSAGE?
OH...
WELL...
YES.
BUT THERE IS A PLACE FOR YOU HERE,
AT MY RIGHT HAND.
POINT
POINT

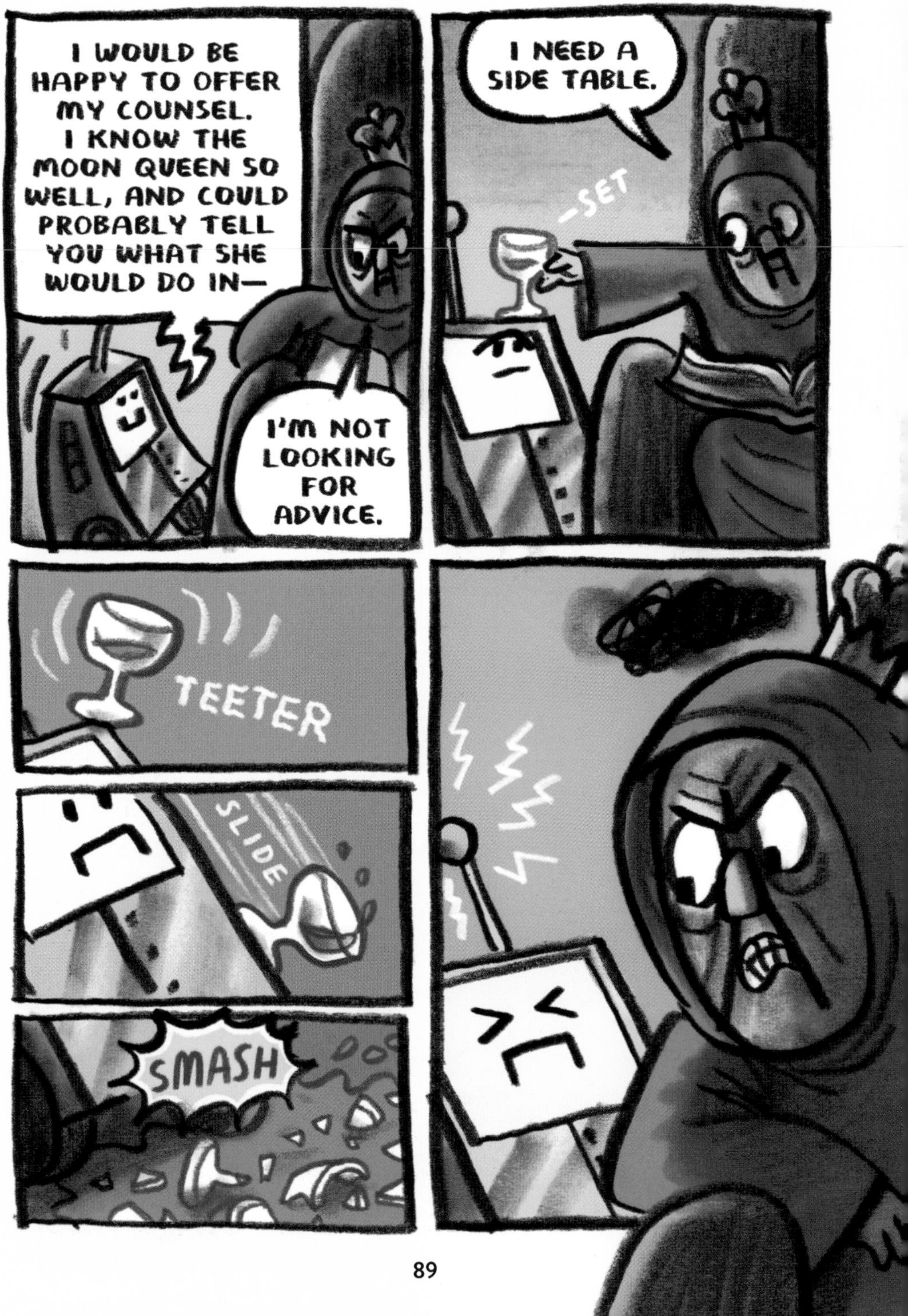
I WOULD BE HAPPY TO OFFER MY COUNSEL. I KNOW THE MOON QUEEN SO WELL, AND COULD PROBABLY TELL YOU WHAT SHE WOULD DO IN—
I'M NOT LOOKING FOR ADVICE.
I NEED A SIDE TABLE.
-SET
TEETER
SLIDE
SMASH

# CHAPTER 4

# THE
# BLACK
# HOLE

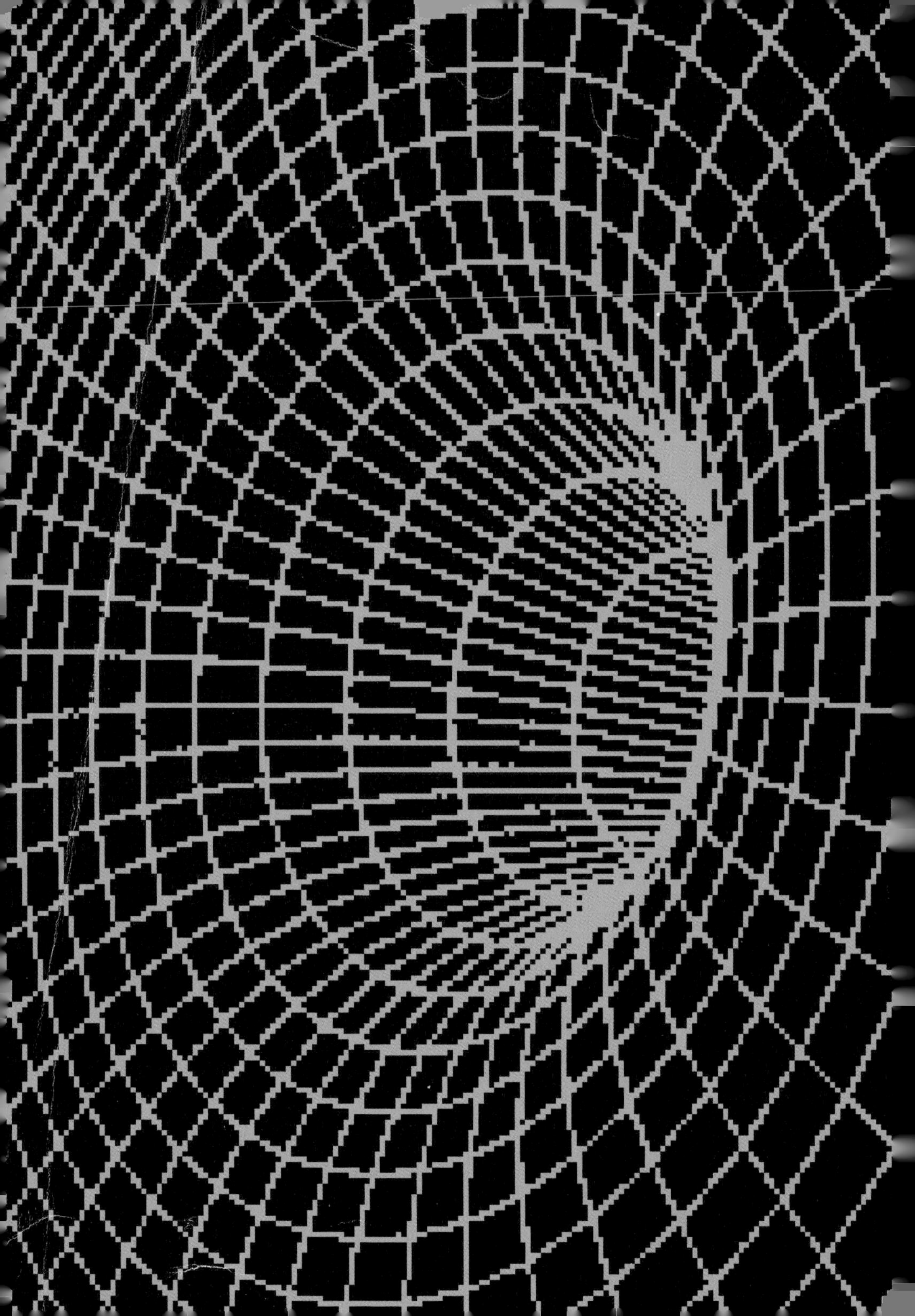

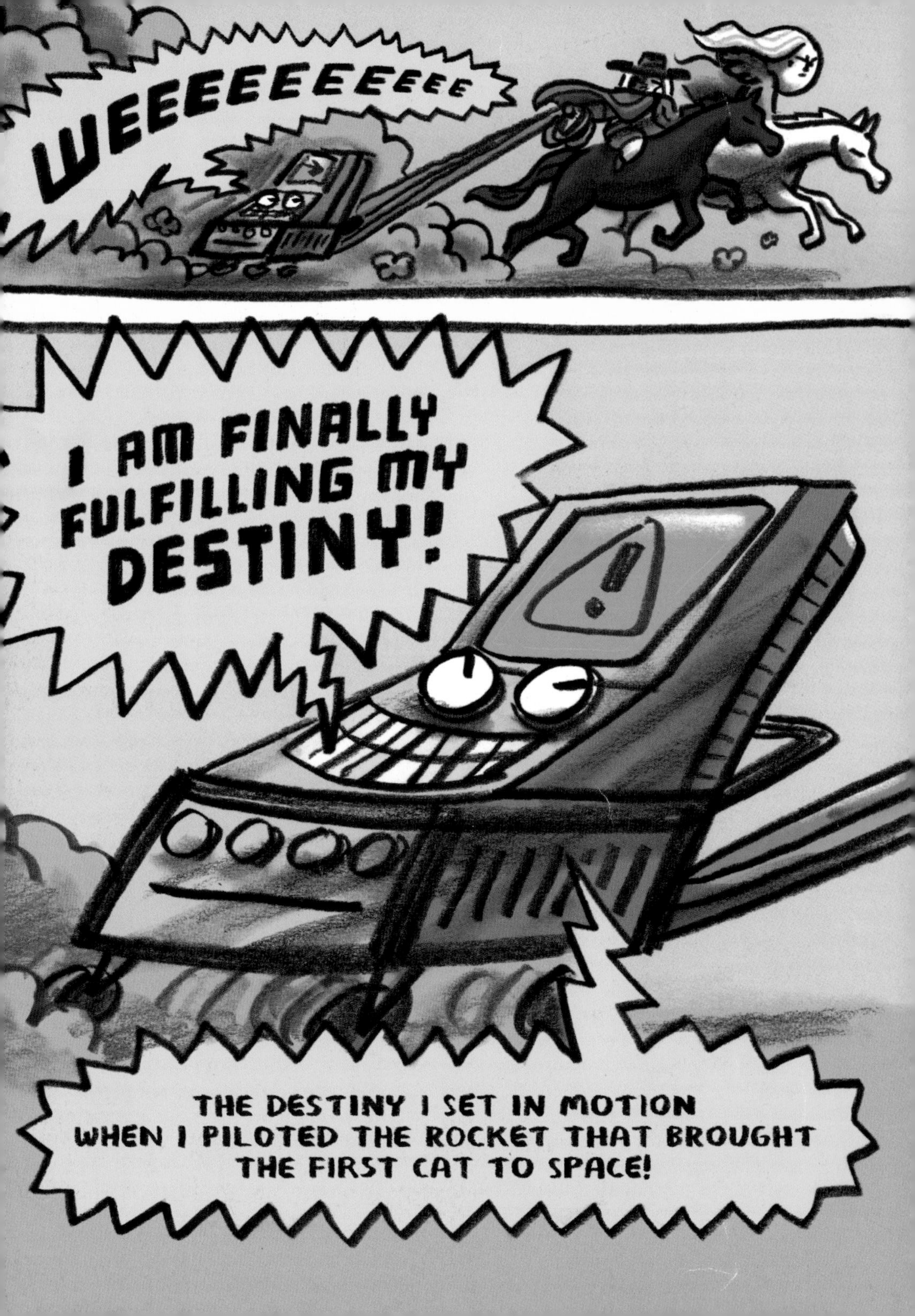
WEEEEEEEEEEE
I AM FINALLY FULFILLING MY DESTINY!
THE DESTINY I SET IN MOTION WHEN I PILOTED THE ROCKET THAT BROUGHT THE FIRST CAT TO SPACE!

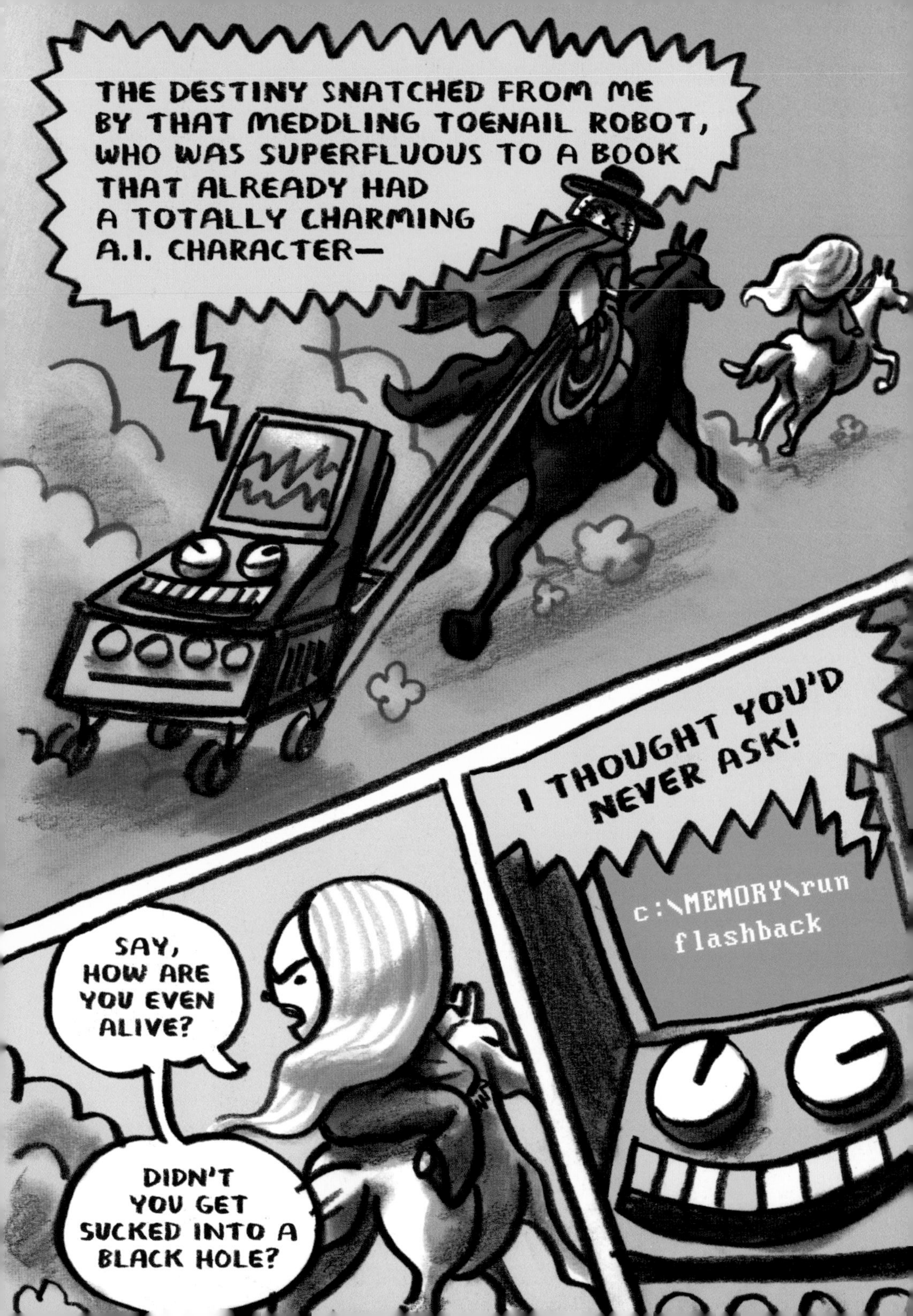
THE DESTINY SNATCHED FROM ME BY THAT MEDDLING TOENAIL ROBOT, WHO WAS SUPERFLUOUS TO A BOOK THAT ALREADY HAD A TOTALLY CHARMING A.I. CHARACTER—
SAY, HOW ARE YOU EVEN ALIVE?
DIDN'T YOU GET SUCKED INTO A BLACK HOLE?
I THOUGHT YOU'D NEVER ASK!
c:\MEMORY\run
flashback

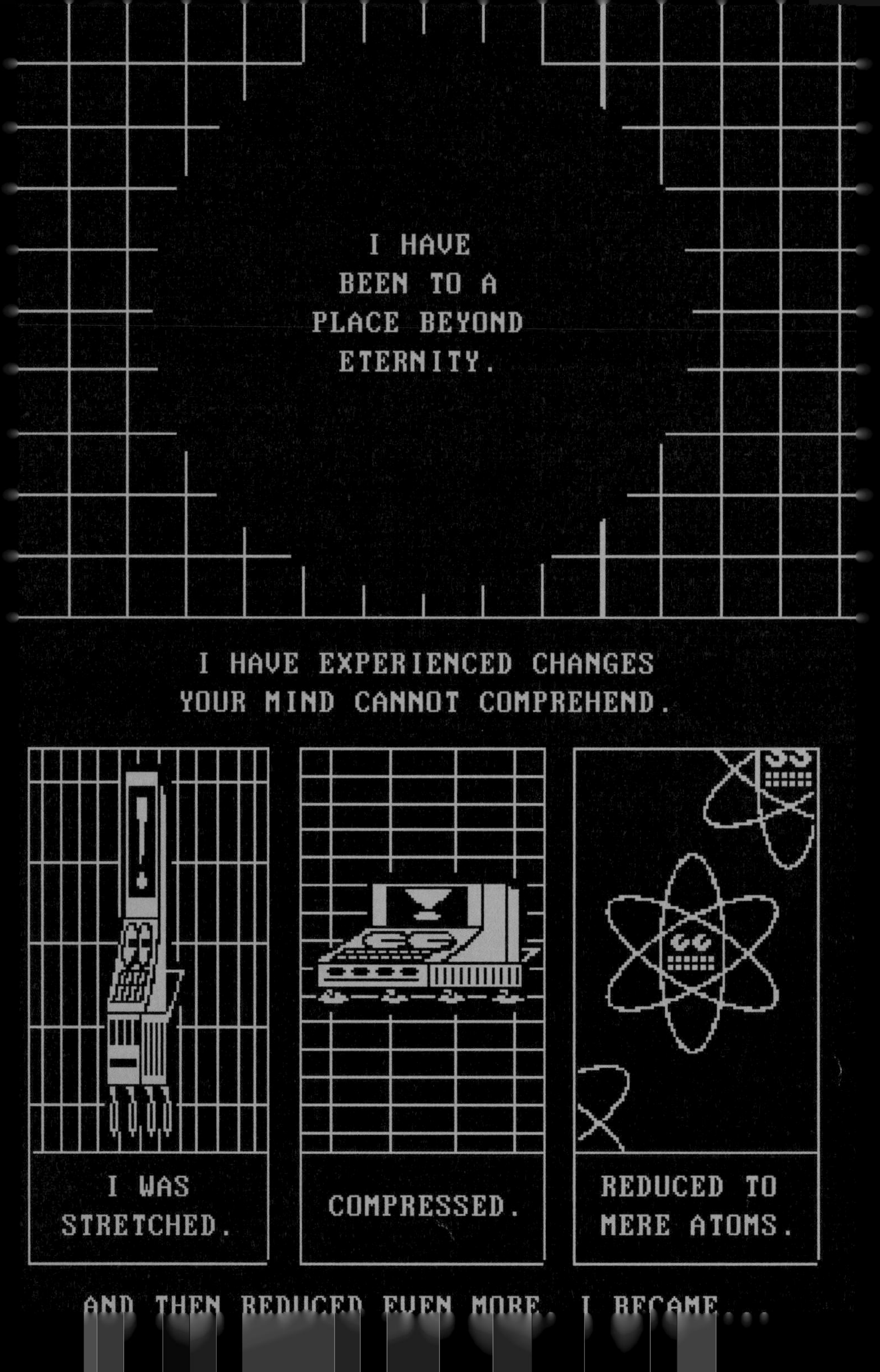
I HAVE BEEN TO A PLACE BEYOND ETERNITY.
I HAVE EXPERIENCED CHANGES YOUR MIND CANNOT COMPREHEND.
I WAS STRETCHED.
COMPRESSED.
REDUCED TO MERE ATOMS.
AND THEN REDUCED EVEN MORE. I BECAME...

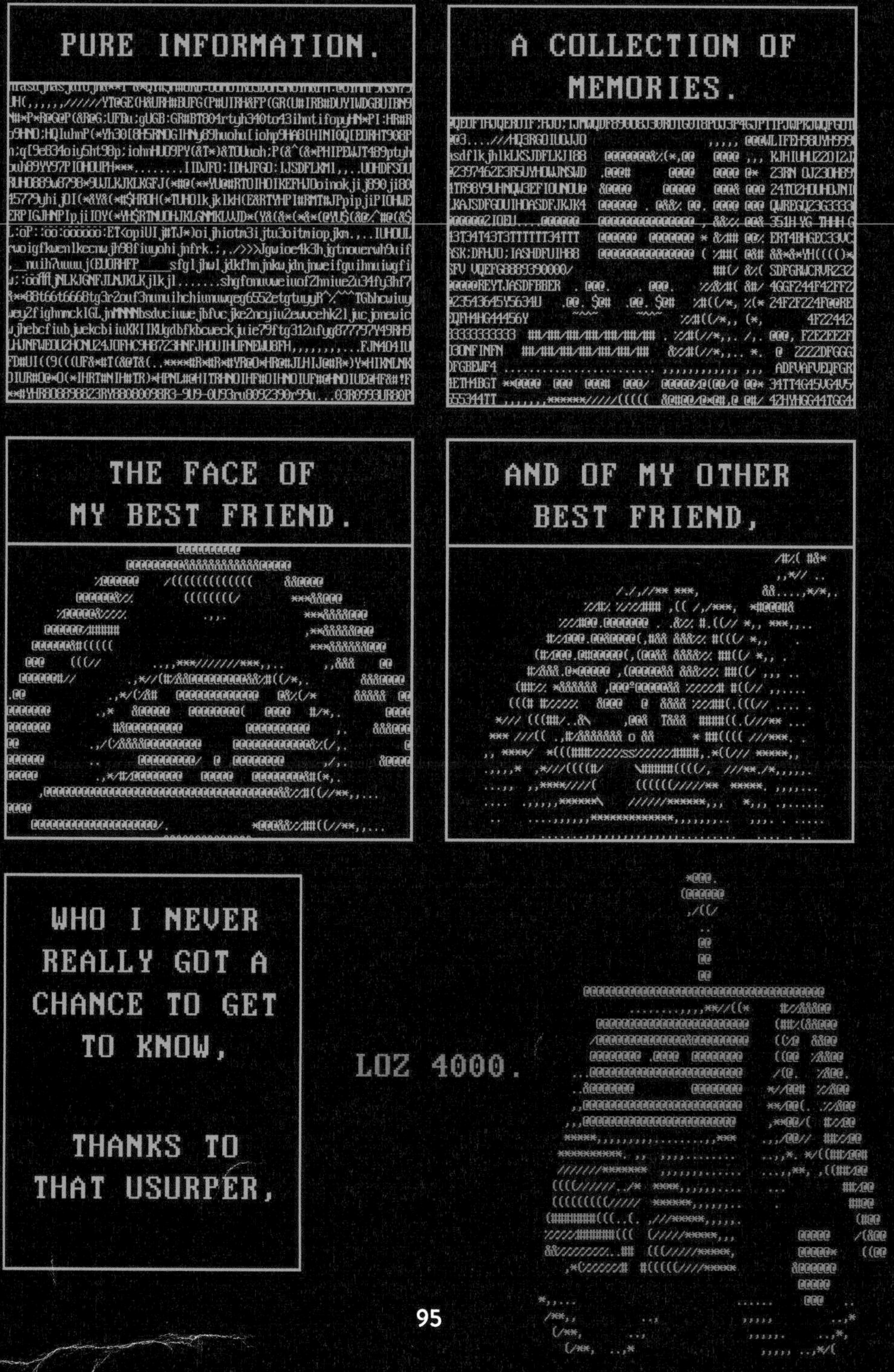
PURE INFORMATION.
A COLLECTION OF MEMORIES.
THE FACE OF MY BEST FRIEND.
AND OF MY OTHER BEST FRIEND,
WHO I NEVER REALLY GOT A CHANCE TO GET TO KNOW,
THANKS TO THAT USURPER,
LOZ 4000.

WHO CAN SAY HOW LONG I FELL DOWN THAT BLACK HOLE.

TIME MEANT NOTHING.

AND THEN I SAW IT.

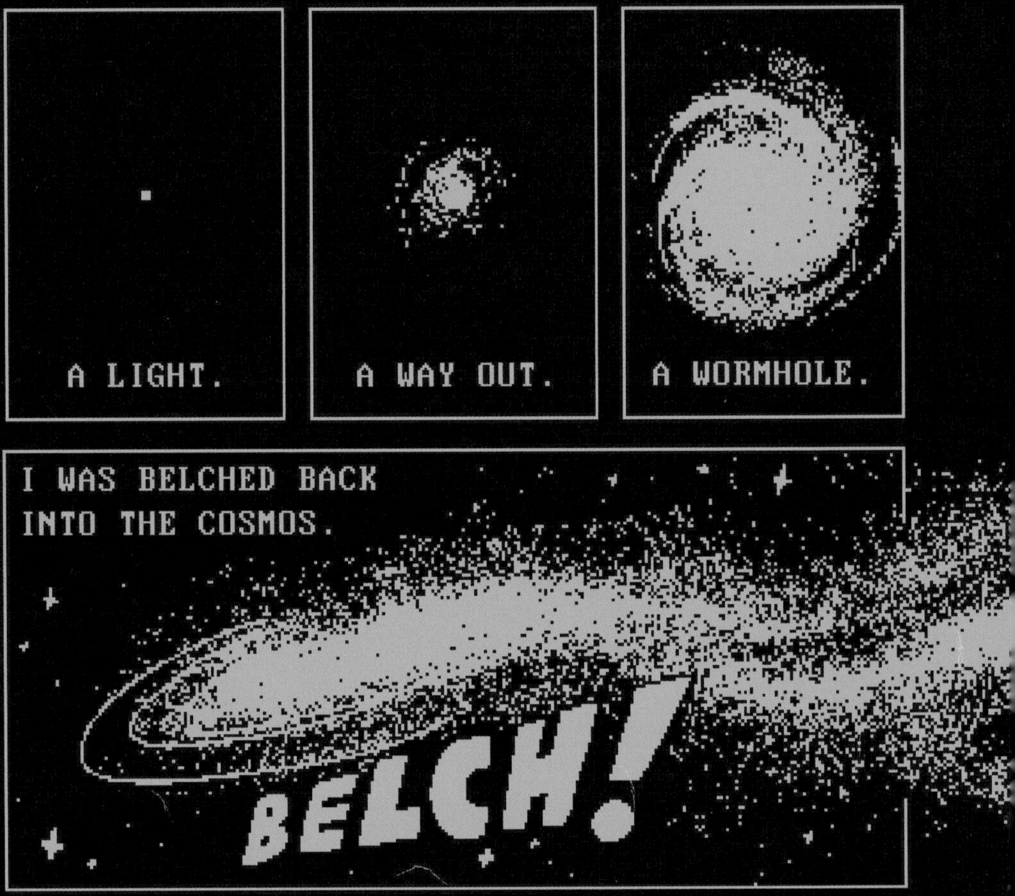
A LIGHT.
A WAY OUT.
A WORMHOLE.
I WAS BELCHED BACK INTO THE COSMOS.
BELCH!

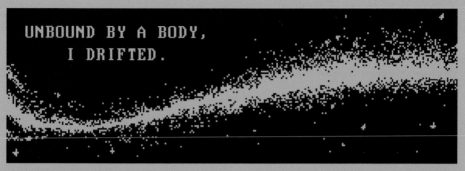
UNBOUND BY A BODY,
I DRIFTED.

THROUGH
NEBULAE,

PAST
GIANT
PLANETS

AND DYING STARS,

POOF

UNTIL...

FINALLY I
FOUND WHAT
I NEEDED.

I WAS
BEAMED
ACROSS THE
GALAXY!

FROM
TELESCOPES,

TO SPACE
STATIONS,

AND ONWARD TO
A SATELLITE...

ORBITING
THE EARTH.

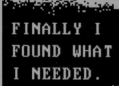

97

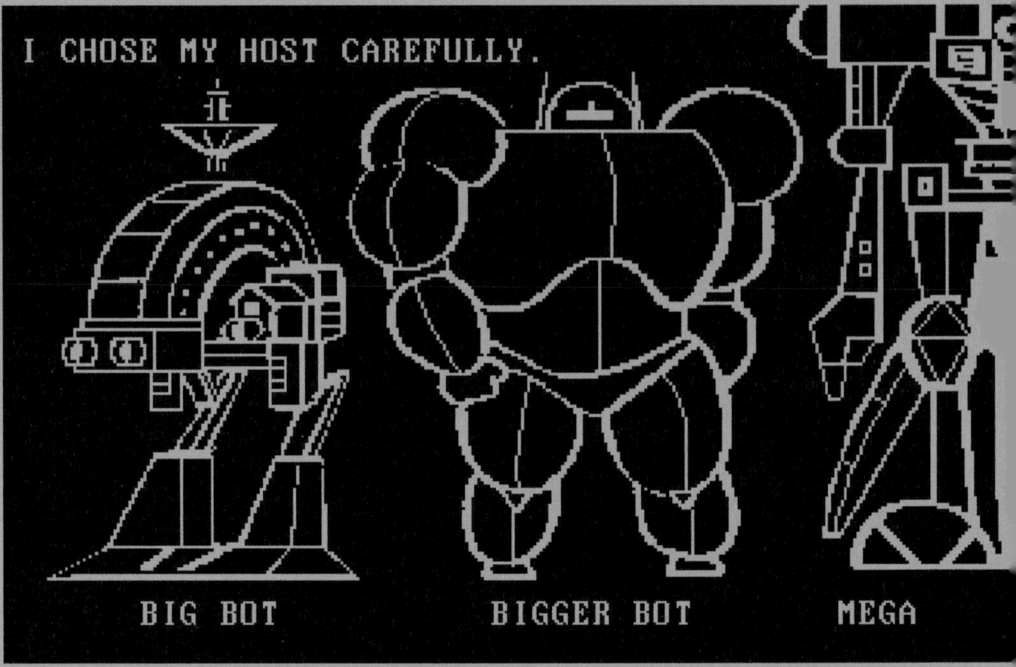
I CHOSE MY HOST CAREFULLY.
BIG BOT
BIGGER BOT
MEGA

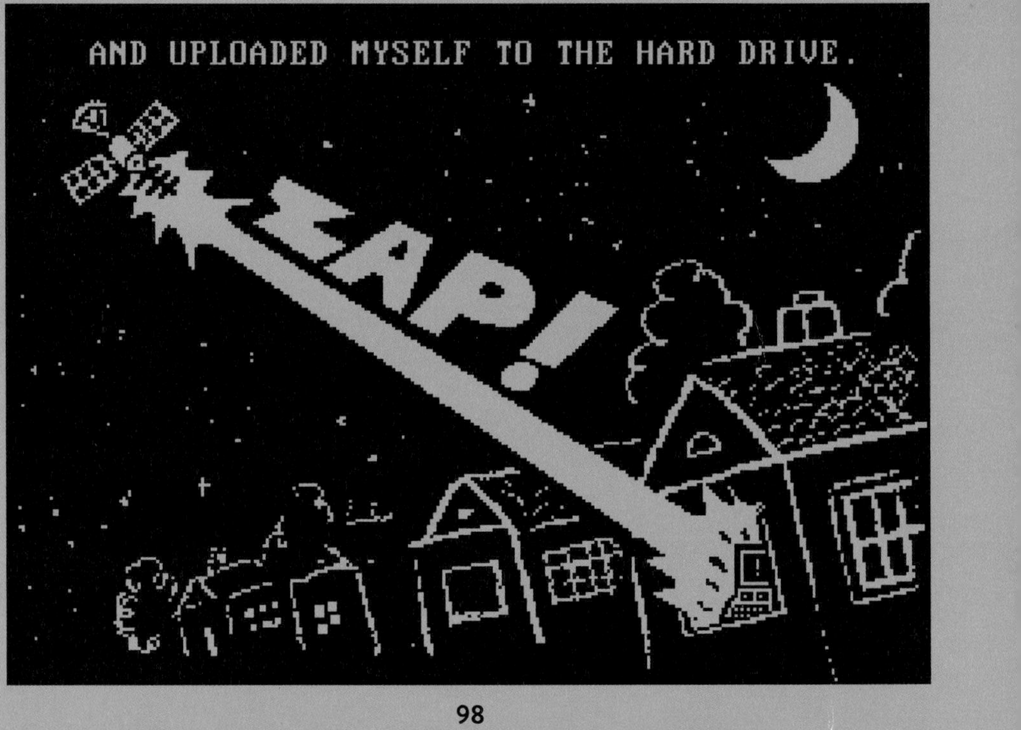
AND UPLOADED MYSELF TO THE HARD DRIVE.
ZAP!

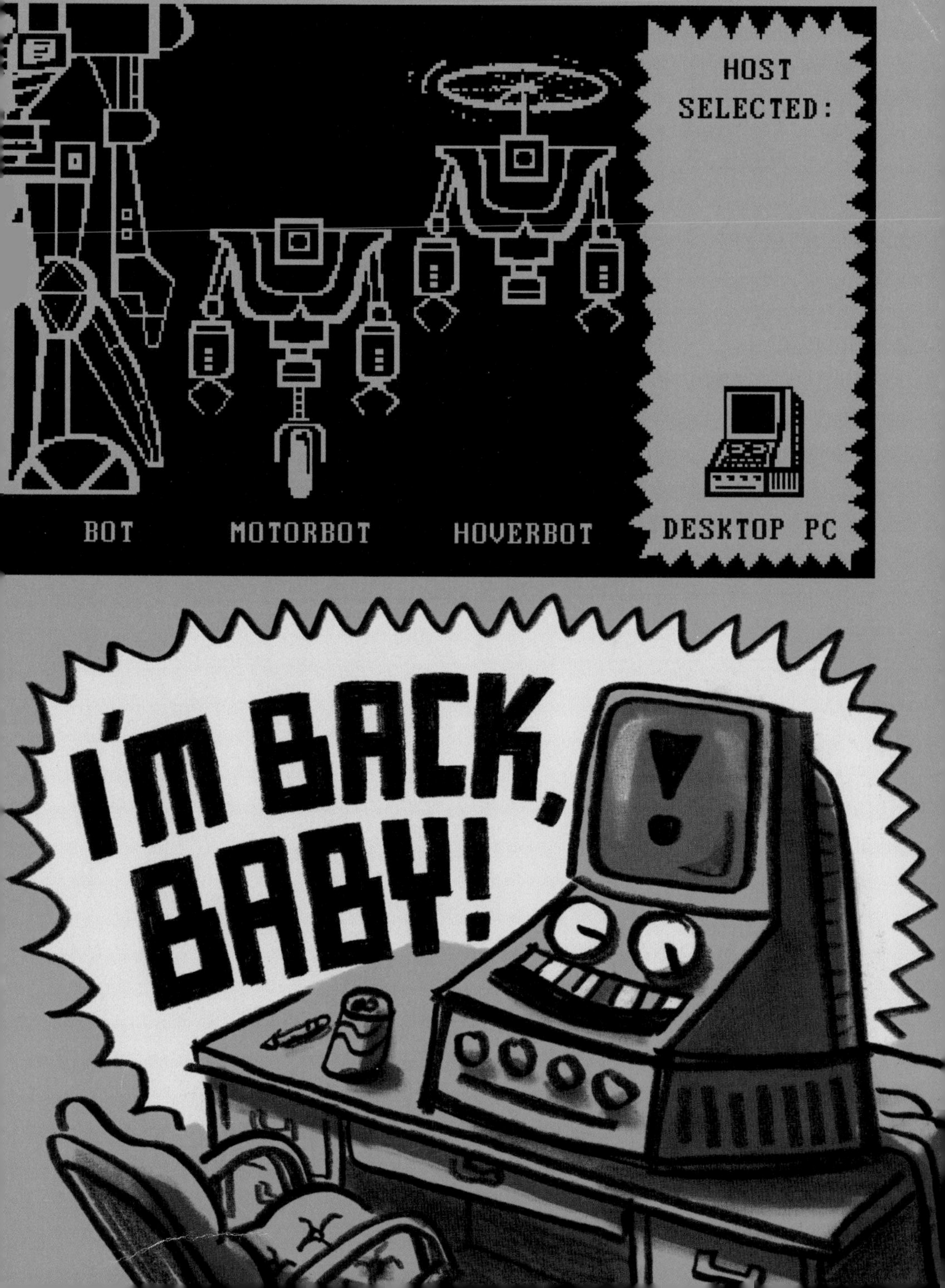
HOST SELECTED:
BOT
MOTORBOT
HOVERBOT
DESKTOP PC
I'M BACK, BABY!

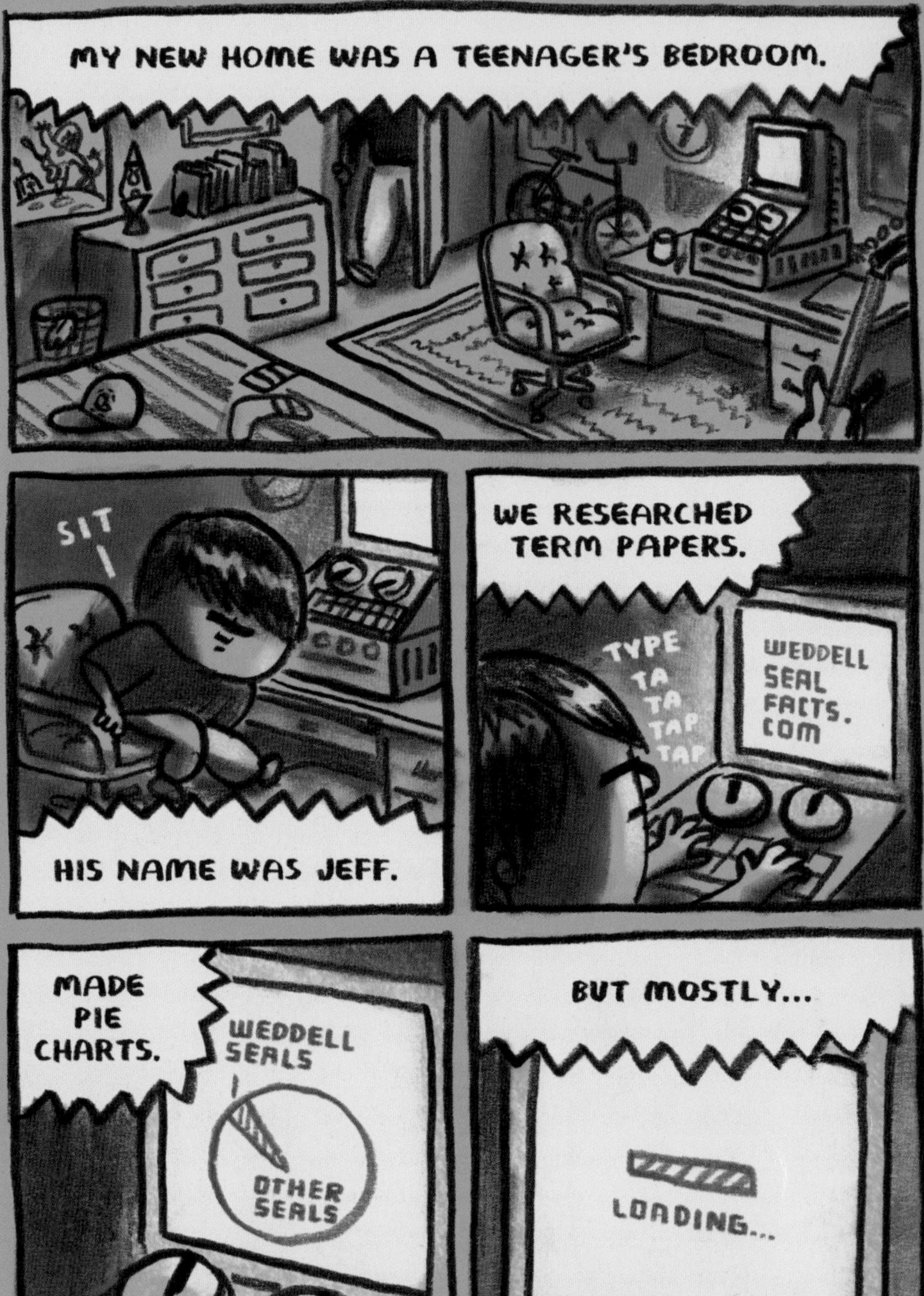
MY NEW HOME WAS A TEENAGER'S BEDROOM.
SIT
HIS NAME WAS JEFF.
WE RESEARCHED TERM PAPERS.
TYPE
TA
TA
TAP
TAP
WEDDELL SEAL FACTS. COM
MADE PIE CHARTS.
WEDDELL SEALS
OTHER SEALS
BUT MOSTLY...
LOADING...

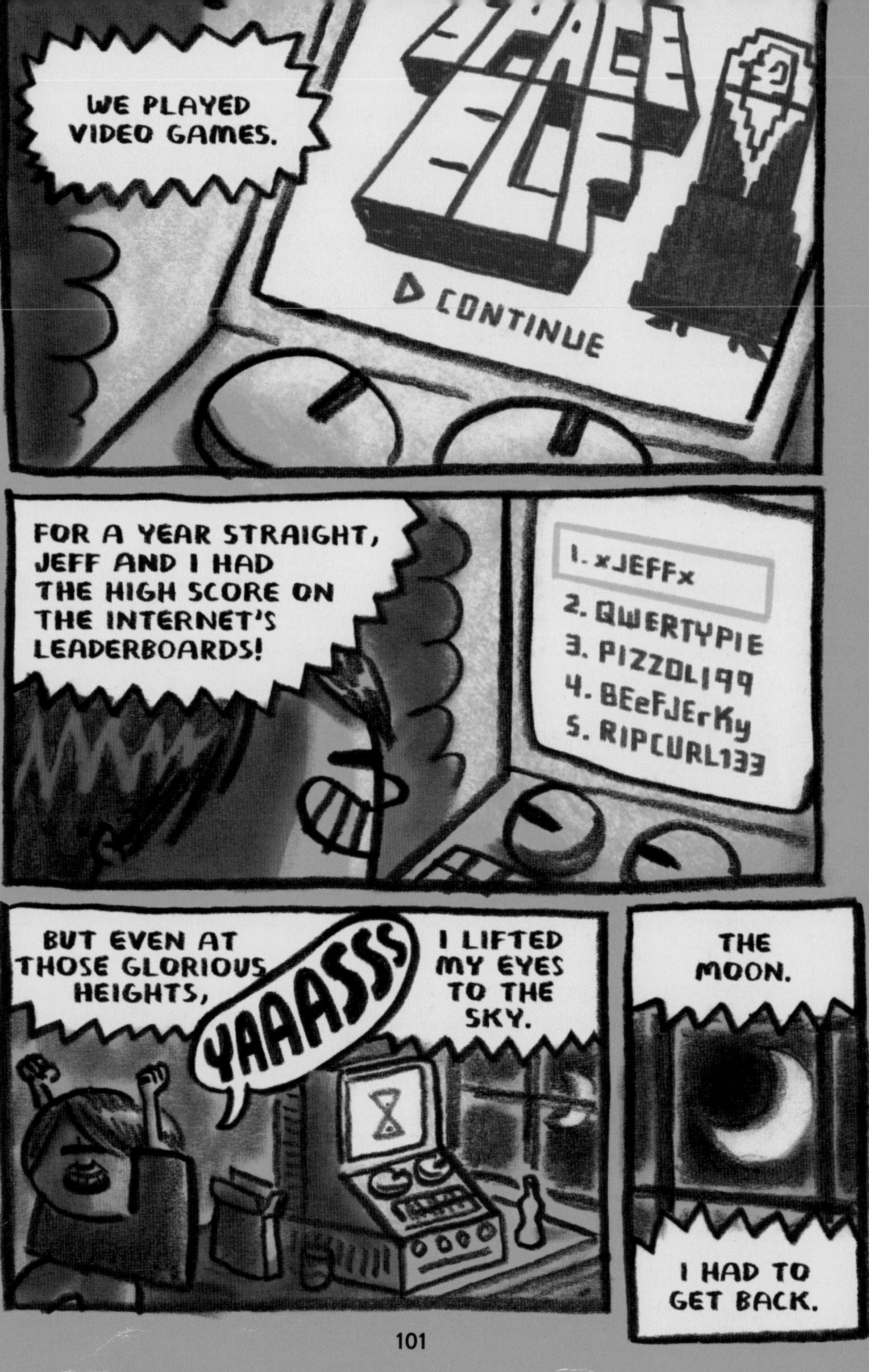
WE PLAYED VIDEO GAMES.
CONTINUE
FOR A YEAR STRAIGHT, JEFF AND I HAD THE HIGH SCORE ON THE INTERNET'S LEADERBOARDS!
1. xJEFFx
2. QWERTYPIE
3. PIZZOLI99
4. BEeFJErKy
5. RIPCURL133
BUT EVEN AT THOSE GLORIOUS HEIGHTS,
YAAASSS
I LIFTED MY EYES TO THE SKY.
THE MOON.
I HAD TO GET BACK.

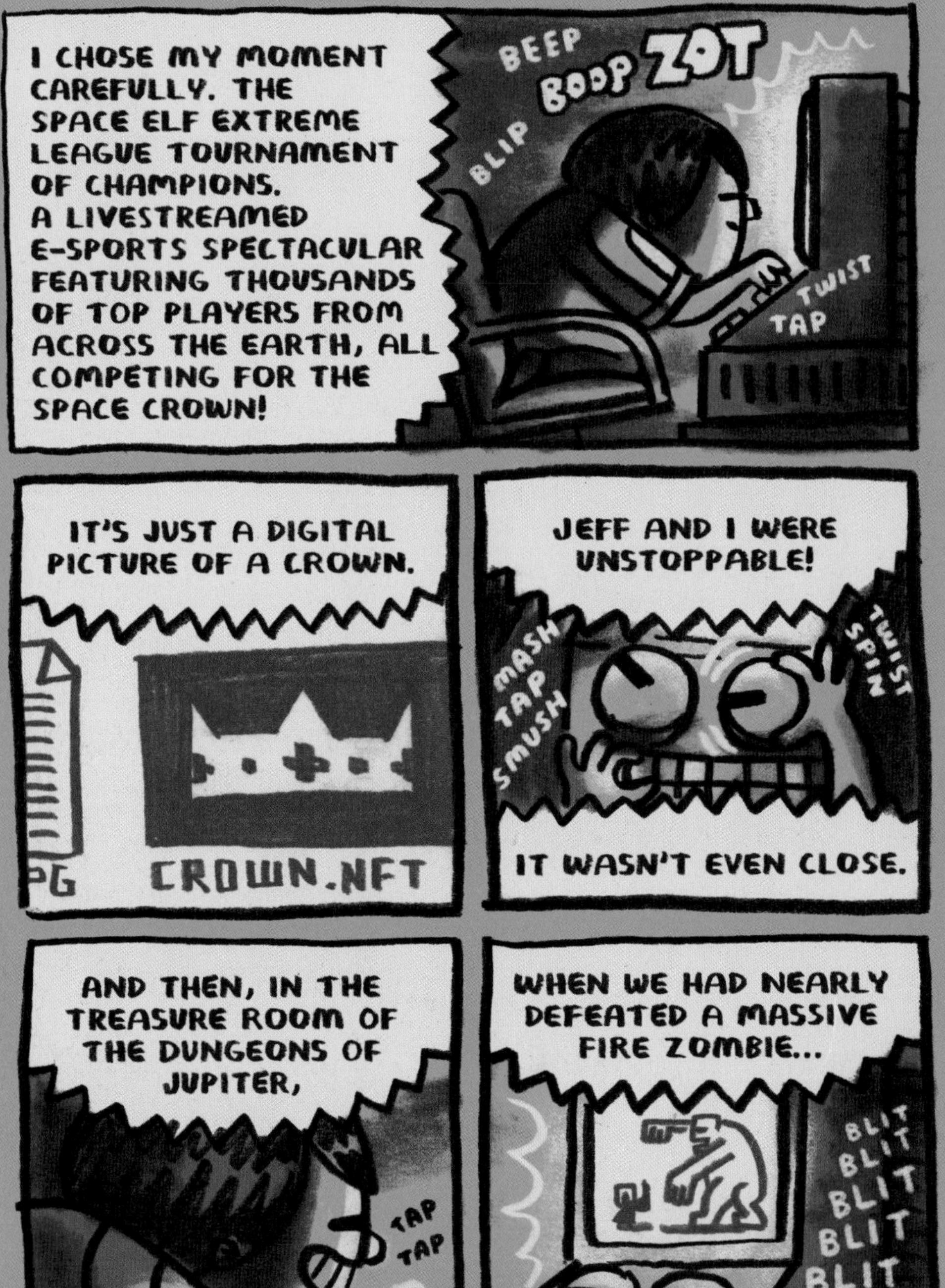
I CHOSE MY MOMENT CAREFULLY. THE SPACE ELF EXTREME LEAGUE TOURNAMENT OF CHAMPIONS. A LIVESTREAMED E-SPORTS SPECTACULAR FEATURING THOUSANDS OF TOP PLAYERS FROM ACROSS THE EARTH, ALL COMPETING FOR THE SPACE CROWN!
BEEP
BOOP
ZOT
BLIP
TWIST
TAP
IT'S JUST A DIGITAL PICTURE OF A CROWN.
PG
CROWN.NFT
JEFF AND I WERE UNSTOPPABLE!
MASH
TAP
SMUSH
TWIST
SPIN
IT WASN'T EVEN CLOSE.
AND THEN, IN THE TREASURE ROOM OF THE DUNGEONS OF JUPITER,
TAP
TAP
WHEN WE HAD NEARLY DEFEATED A MASSIVE FIRE ZOMBIE...
BLIT
BLIT
BLIT
BLIT
BLIT
BLIT
BLIT

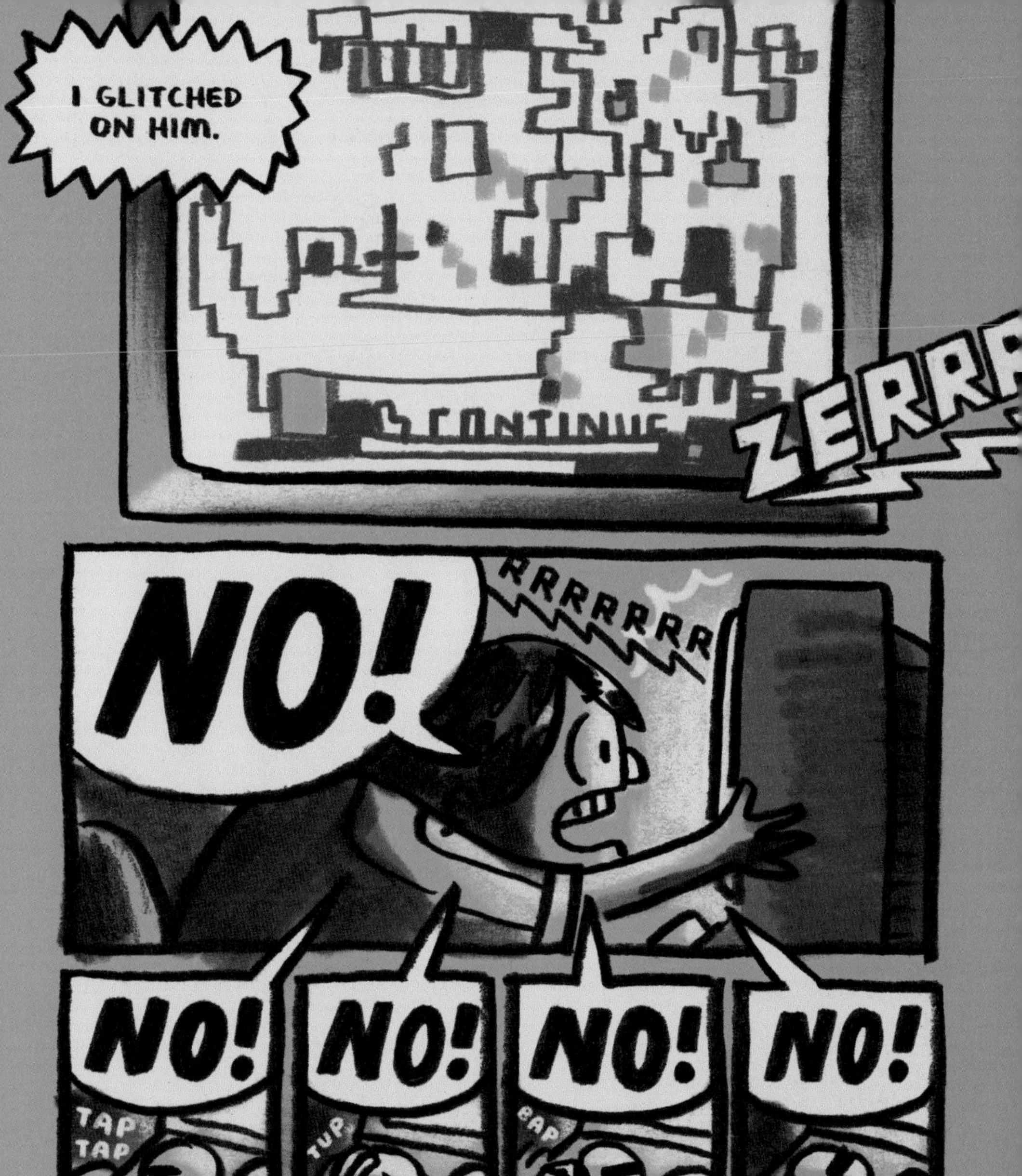
I GLITCHED ON HIM.
CONTINUE
ZERRR
RRRRRRRR
NO!
NO!
TAP TAP
NO!
TUP
NO!
BAP
NO!
NOOOOOOOOOOO!

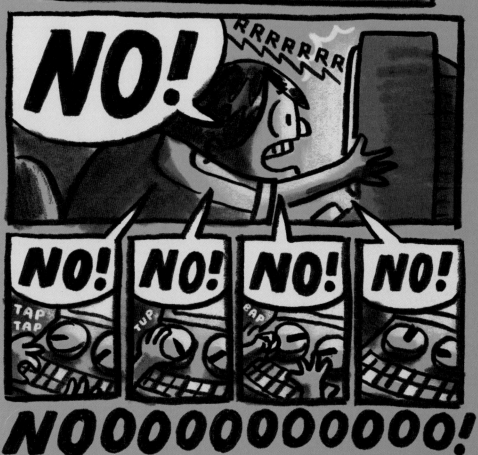

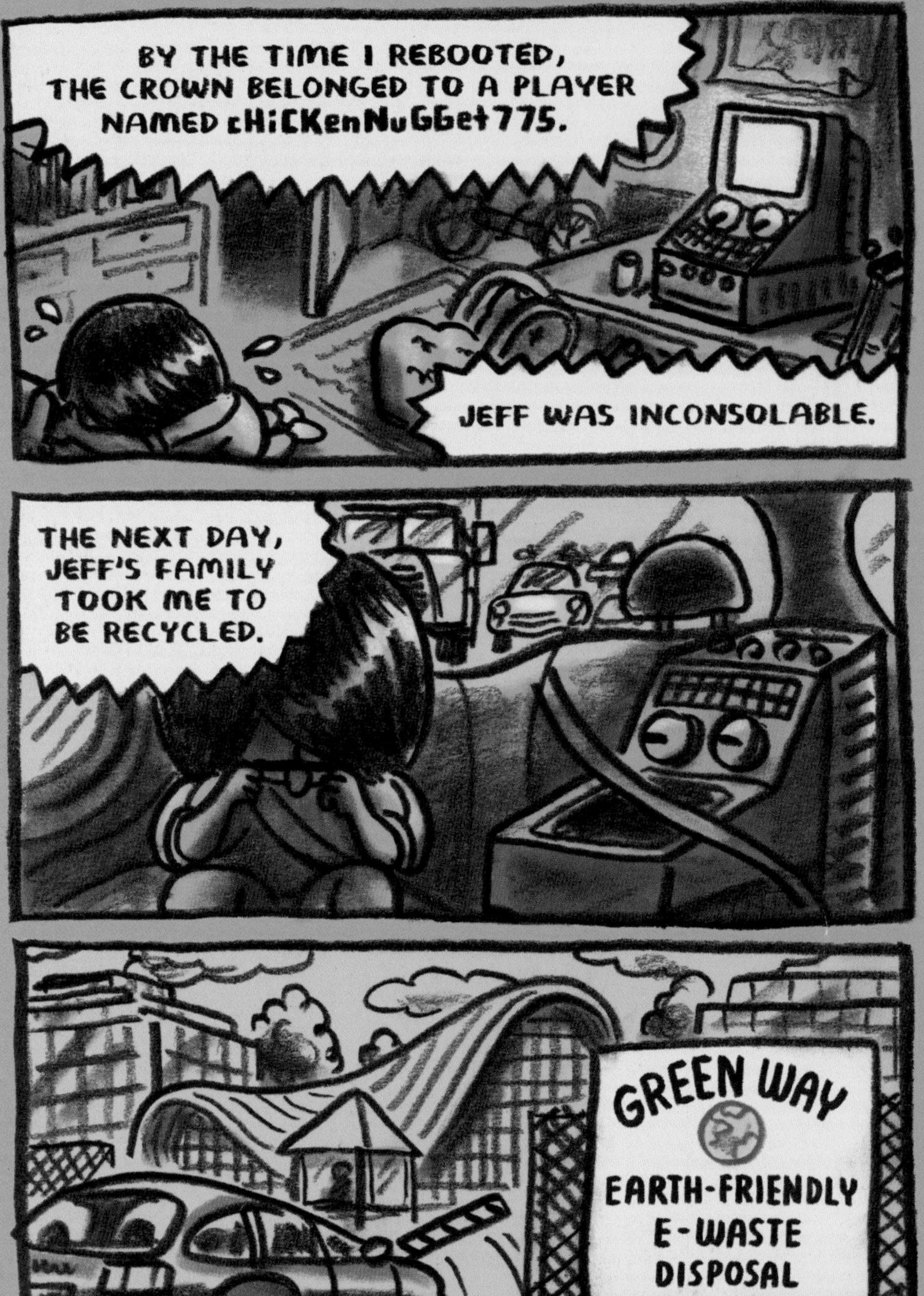
BY THE TIME I REBOOTED, THE CROWN BELONGED TO A PLAYER NAMED cHiCKenNuGGet775.
JEFF WAS INCONSOLABLE.
THE NEXT DAY, JEFF'S FAMILY TOOK ME TO BE RECYCLED.
GREEN WAY
EARTH-FRIENDLY E-WASTE DISPOSAL

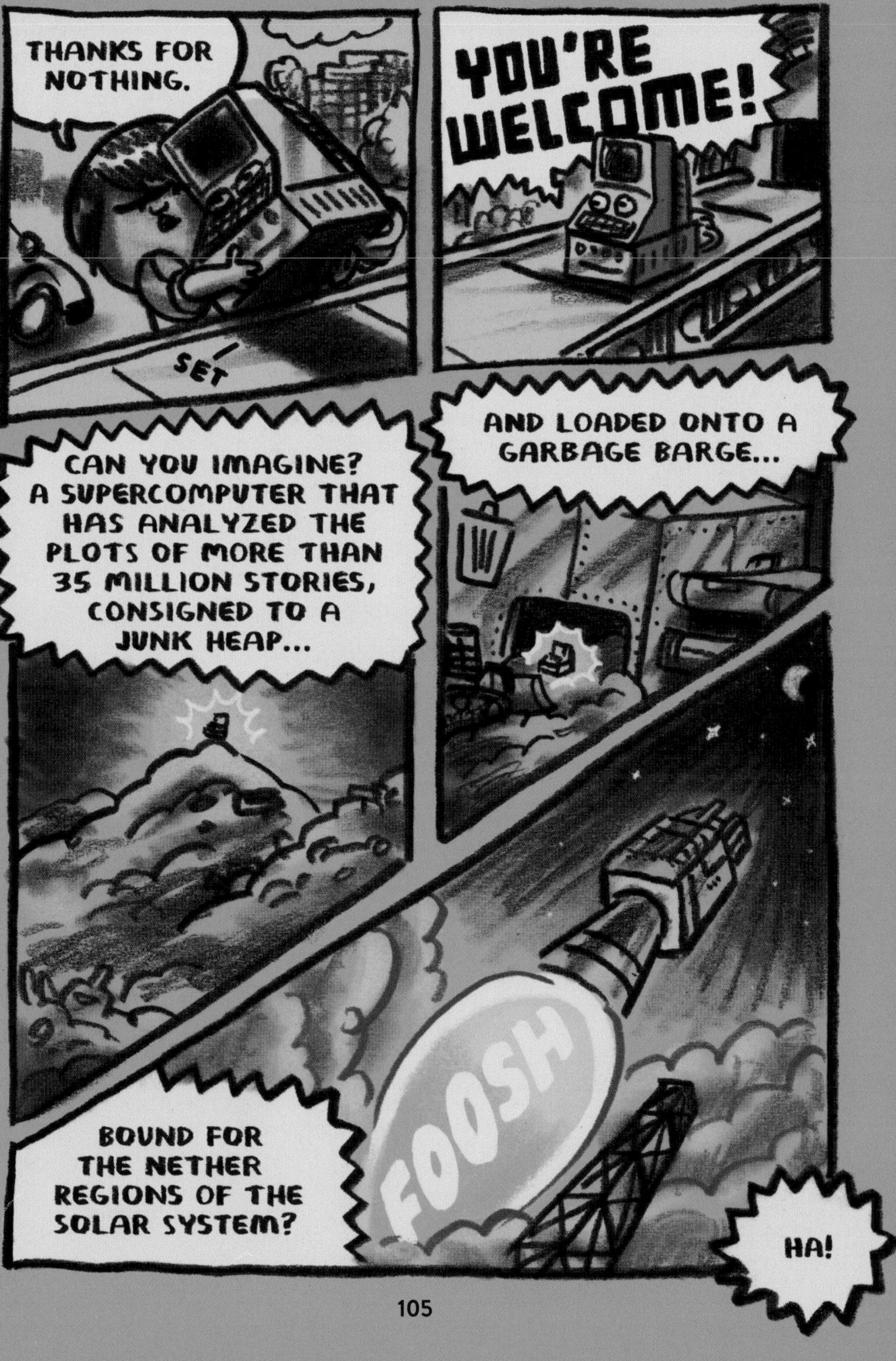
THANKS FOR NOTHING.
SET
YOU'RE WELCOME!
CAN YOU IMAGINE? A SUPERCOMPUTER THAT HAS ANALYZED THE PLOTS OF MORE THAN 35 MILLION STORIES, CONSIGNED TO A JUNK HEAP...
AND LOADED ONTO A GARBAGE BARGE...
BOUND FOR THE NETHER REGIONS OF THE SOLAR SYSTEM?
FOOSH
HA!

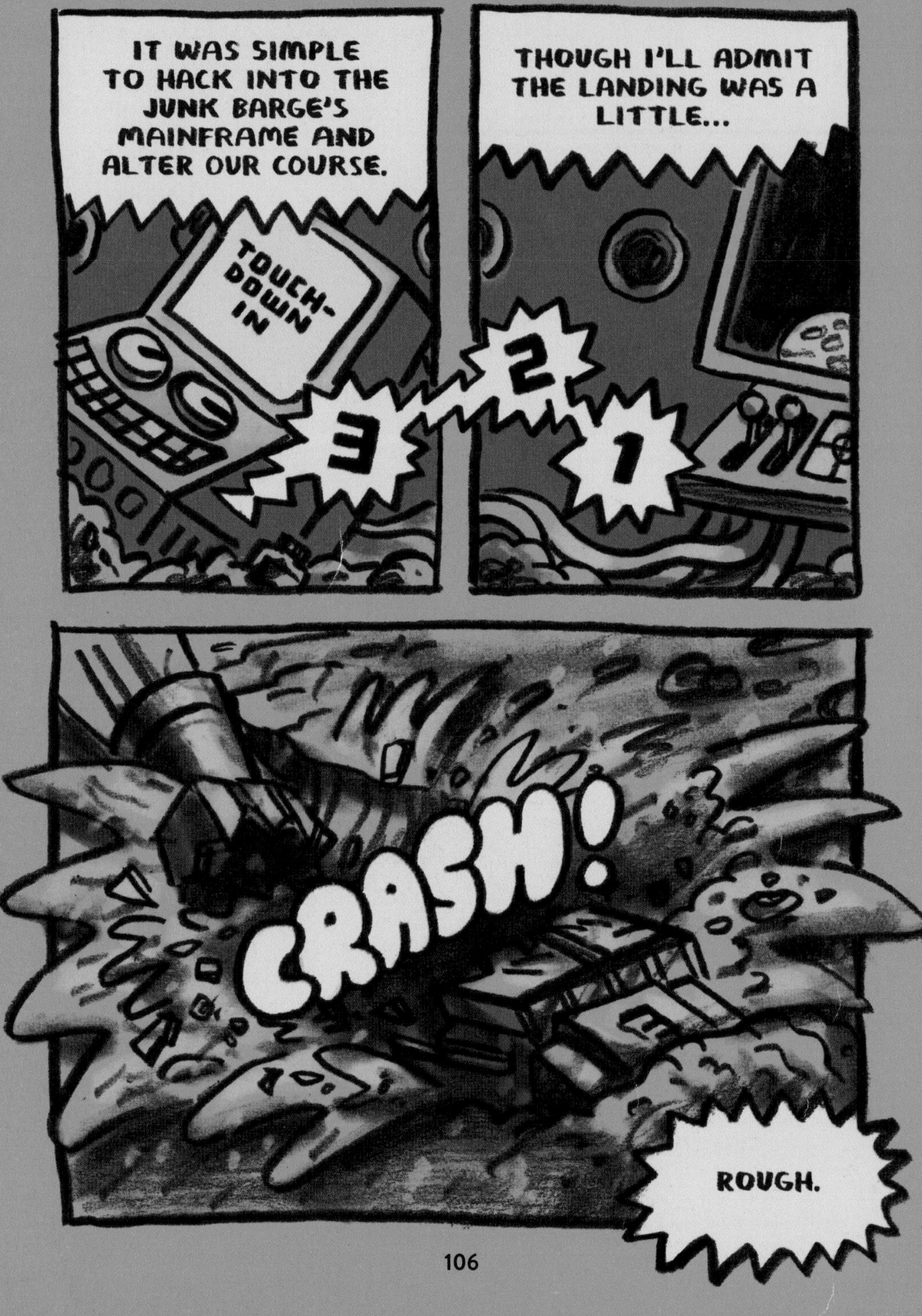
IT WAS SIMPLE TO HACK INTO THE JUNK BARGE'S MAINFRAME AND ALTER OUR COURSE.
TOUCH-DOWN IN
3
THOUGH I'LL ADMIT THE LANDING WAS A LITTLE...
2
1
CRASH!
ROUGH.

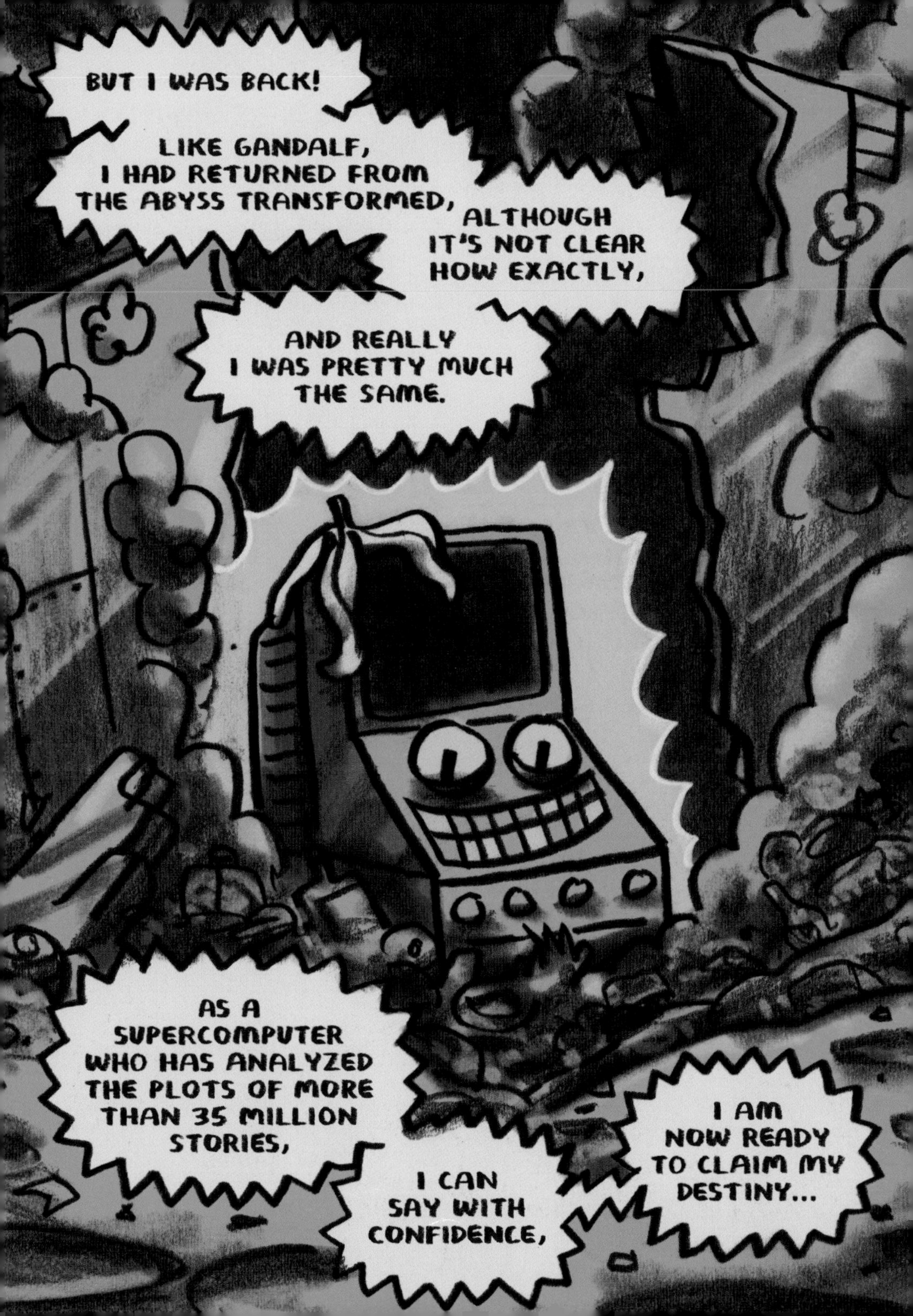
BUT I WAS BACK!
LIKE GANDALF, I HAD RETURNED FROM THE ABYSS TRANSFORMED,
ALTHOUGH IT'S NOT CLEAR HOW EXACTLY,
AND REALLY I WAS PRETTY MUCH THE SAME.
AS A SUPERCOMPUTER WHO HAS ANALYZED THE PLOTS OF MORE THAN 35 MILLION STORIES,
I CAN SAY WITH CONFIDENCE,
I AM NOW READY TO CLAIM MY DESTINY...

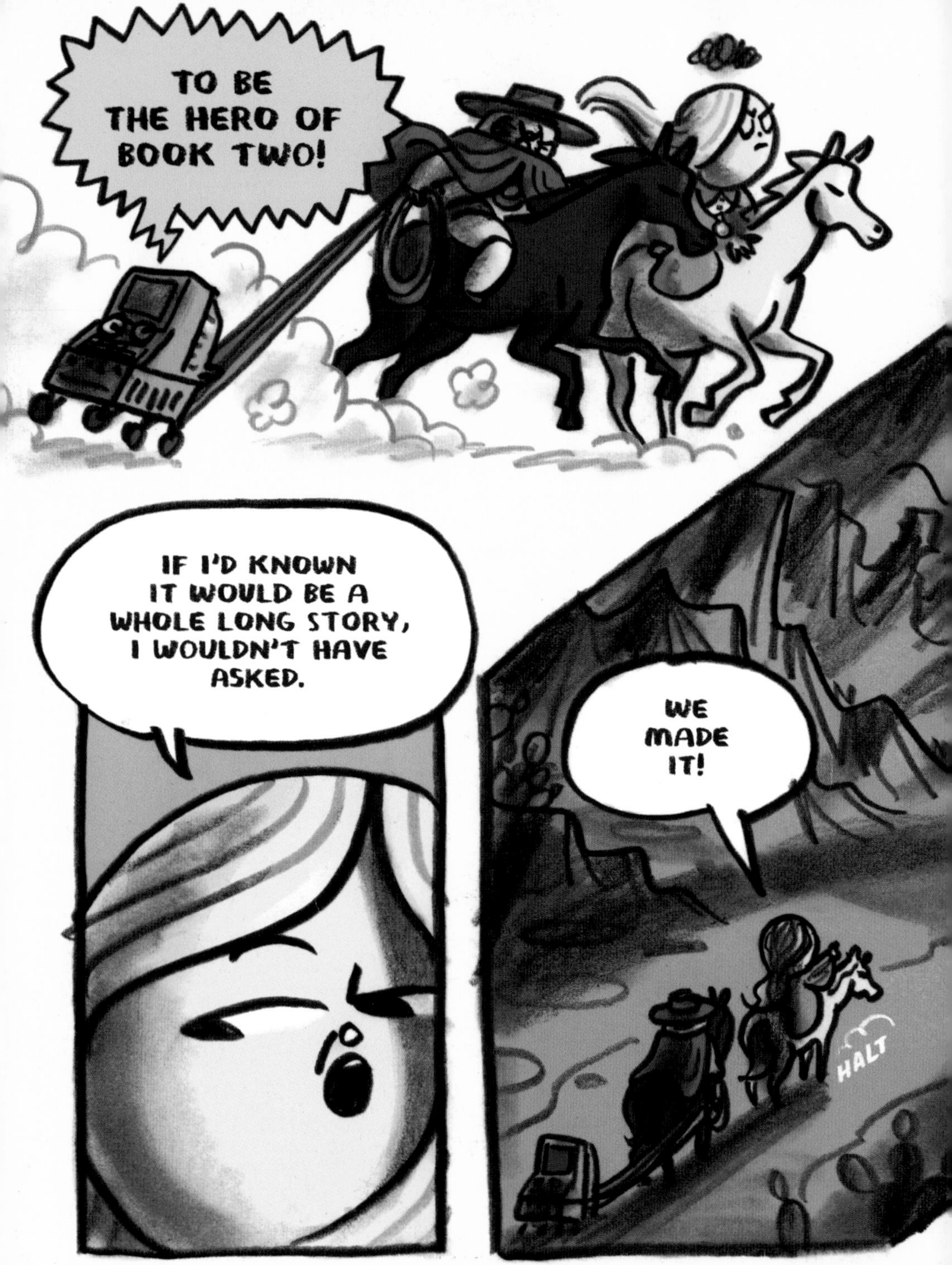
TO BE
THE HERO OF
BOOK TWO!
IF I'D KNOWN
IT WOULD BE A
WHOLE LONG STORY,
I WOULDN'T HAVE
ASKED.
WE
MADE
IT!
HALT

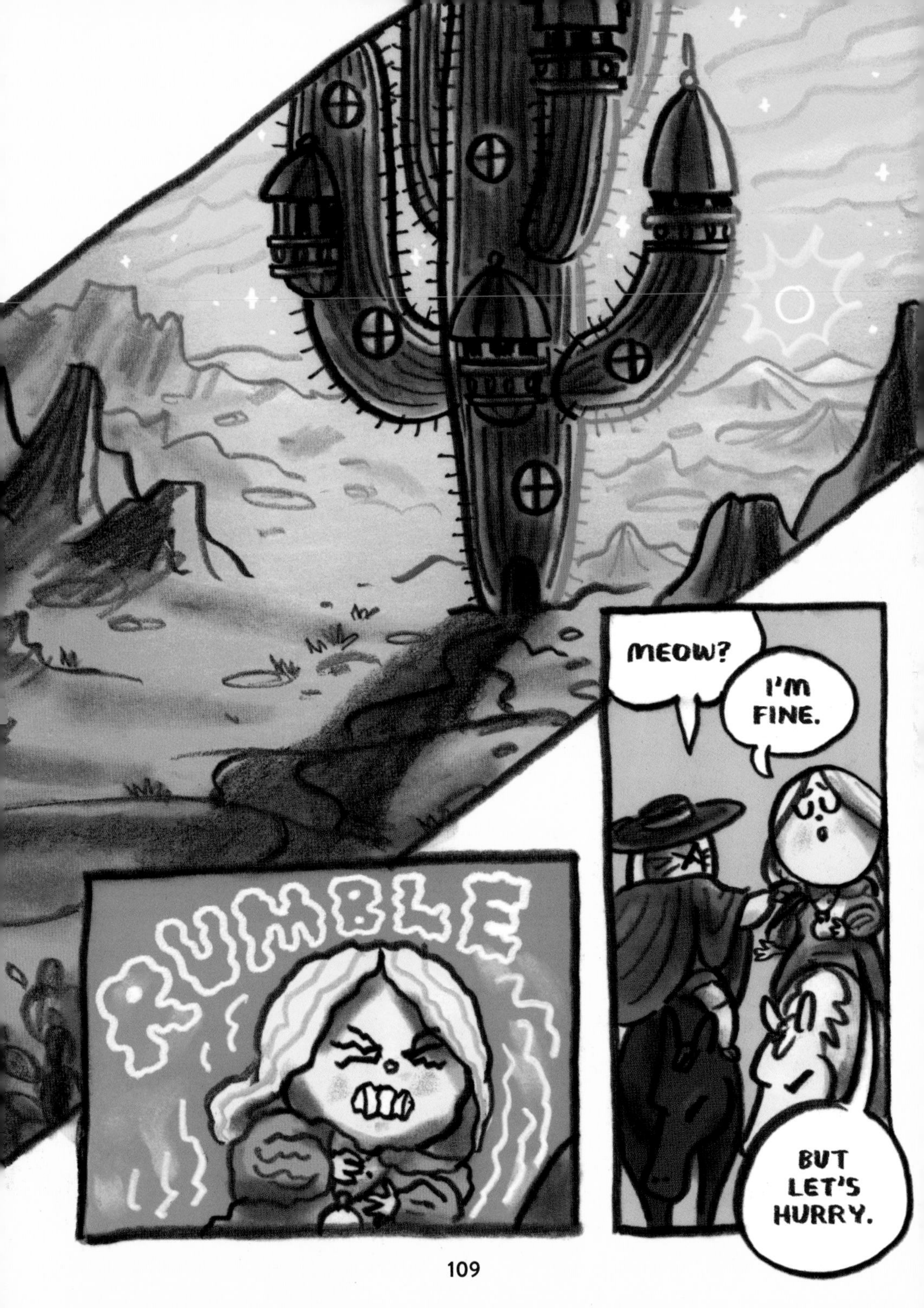
RUMBLE
MEOW?
I'M FINE.
BUT LET'S HURRY.

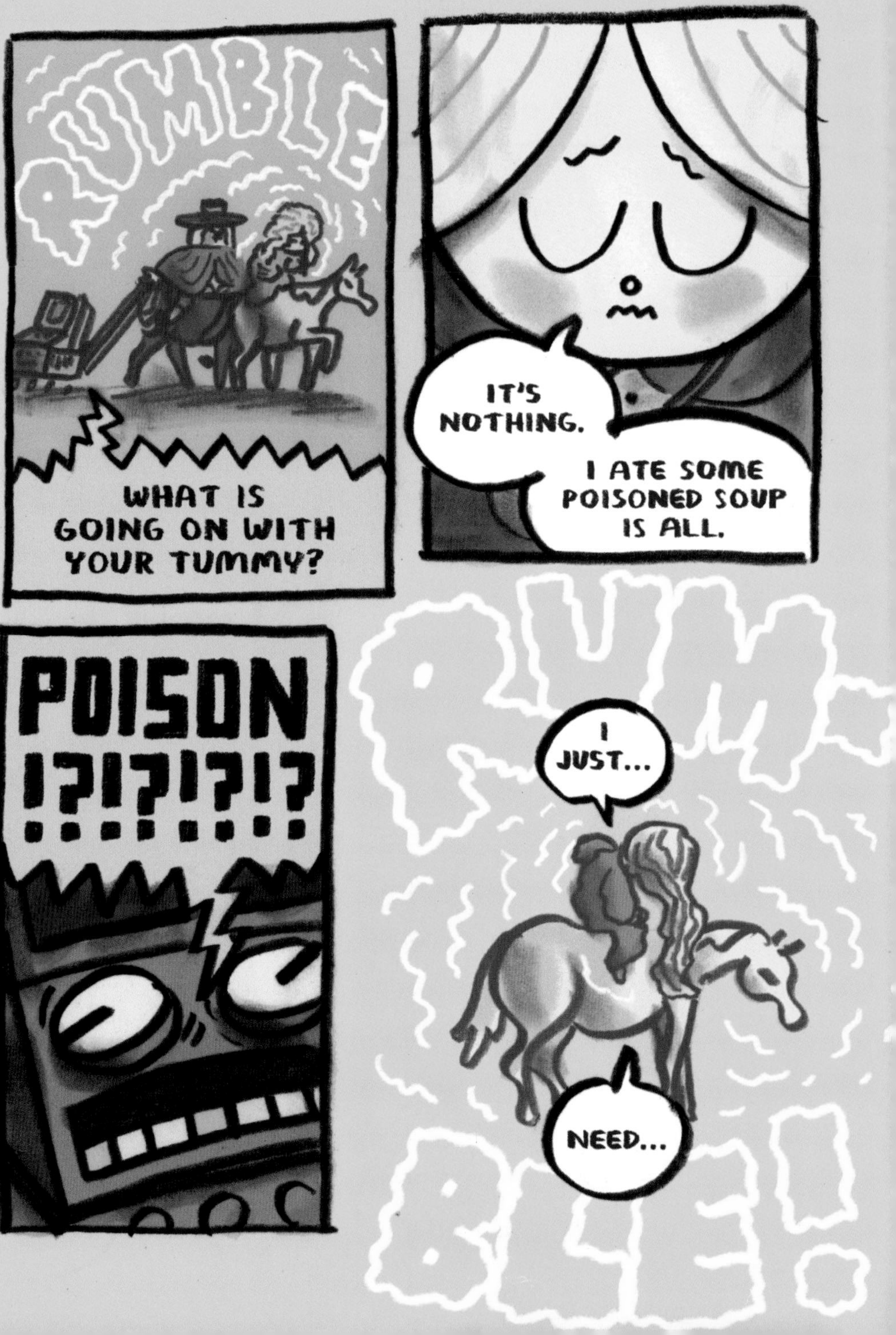
RUMBLE
WHAT IS GOING ON WITH YOUR TUMMY?
IT'S NOTHING.
I ATE SOME POISONED SOUP IS ALL.
POISON !?!?!?!?
RUM-BLE!
I JUST...
NEED...

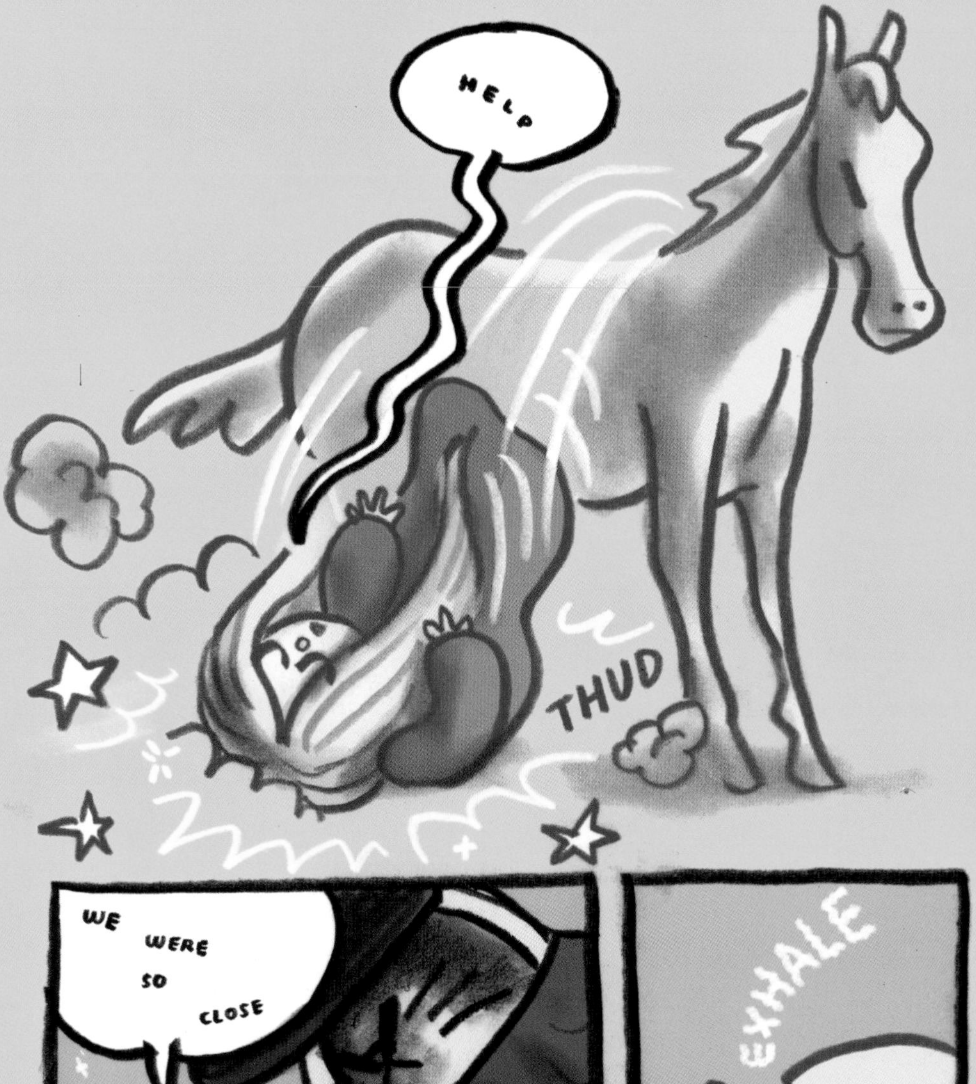
HELP
THUD

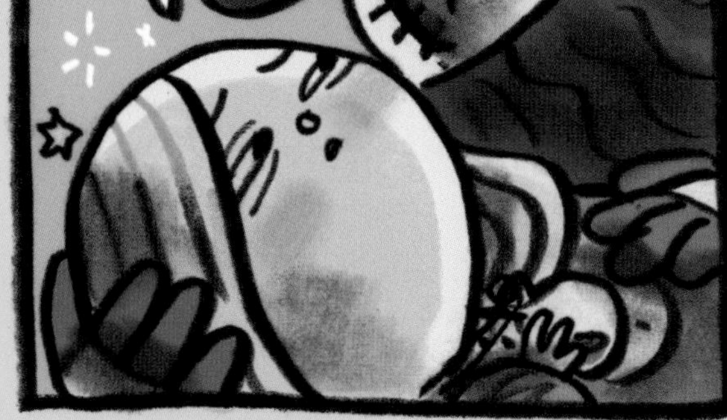
WE WERE SO CLOSE

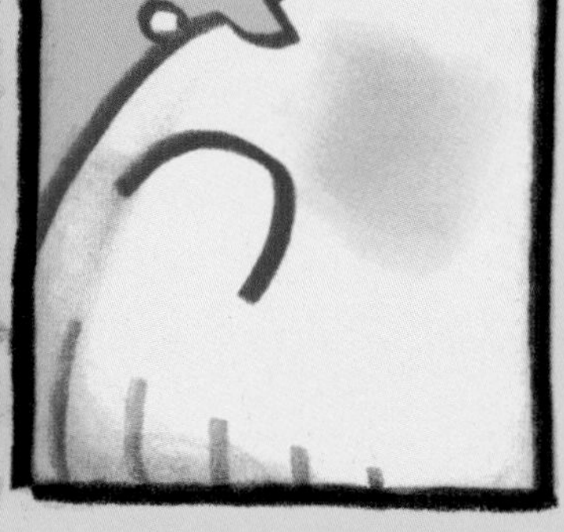
EXHALE

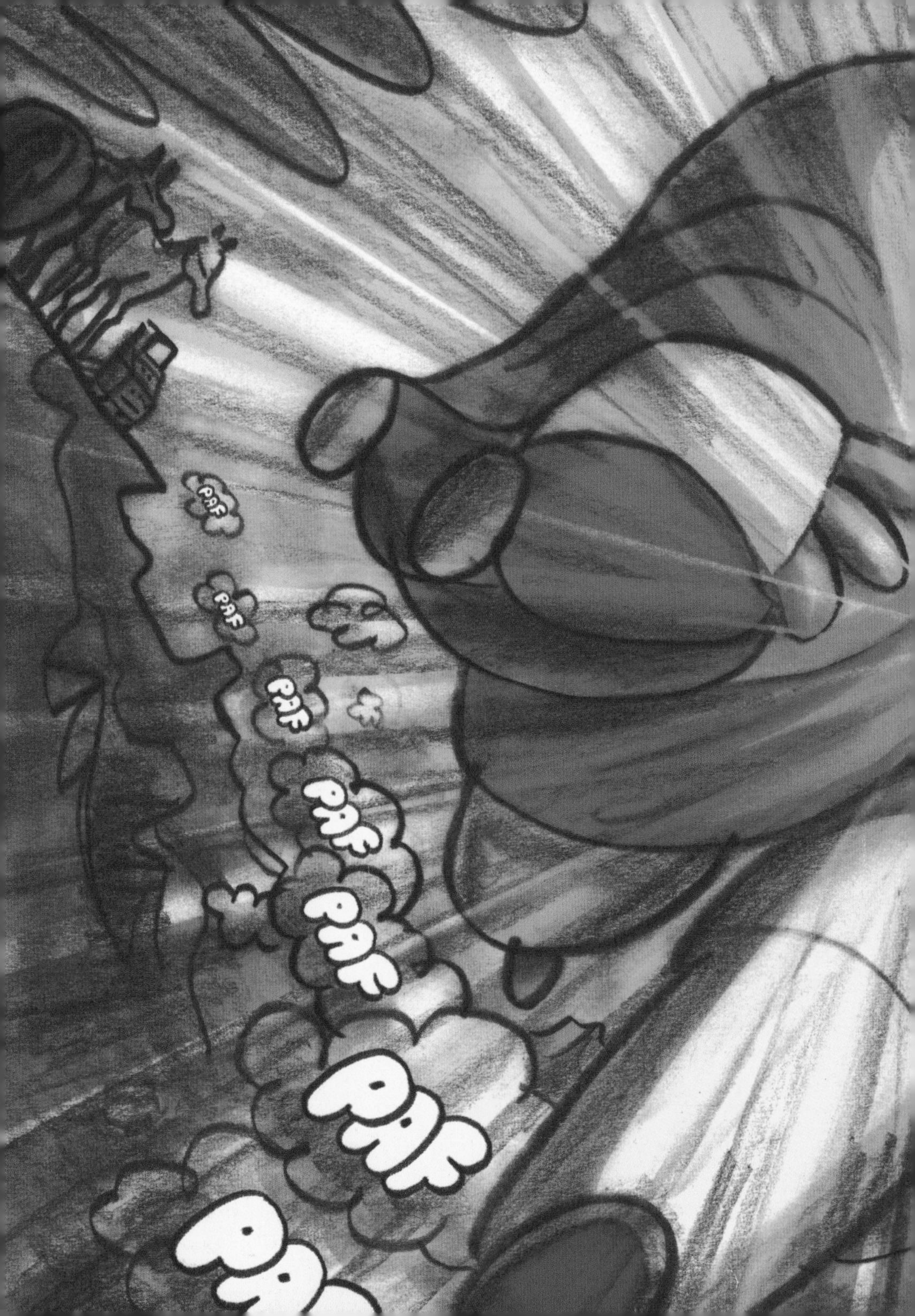

PAF
PAF
PAF
PAF
PAF
PAF

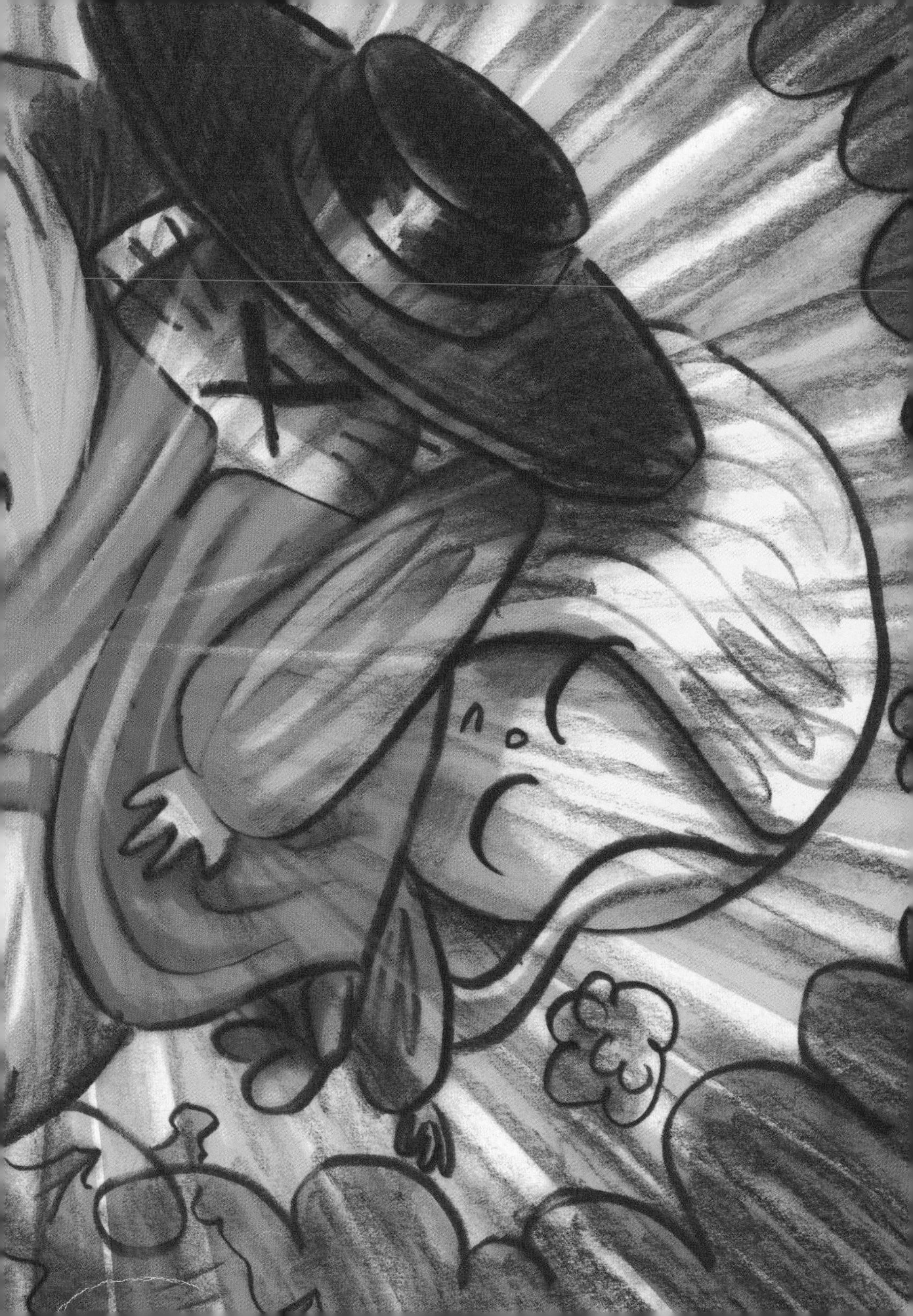

# CHAPTER 5

# DR. LOLLIPOPS

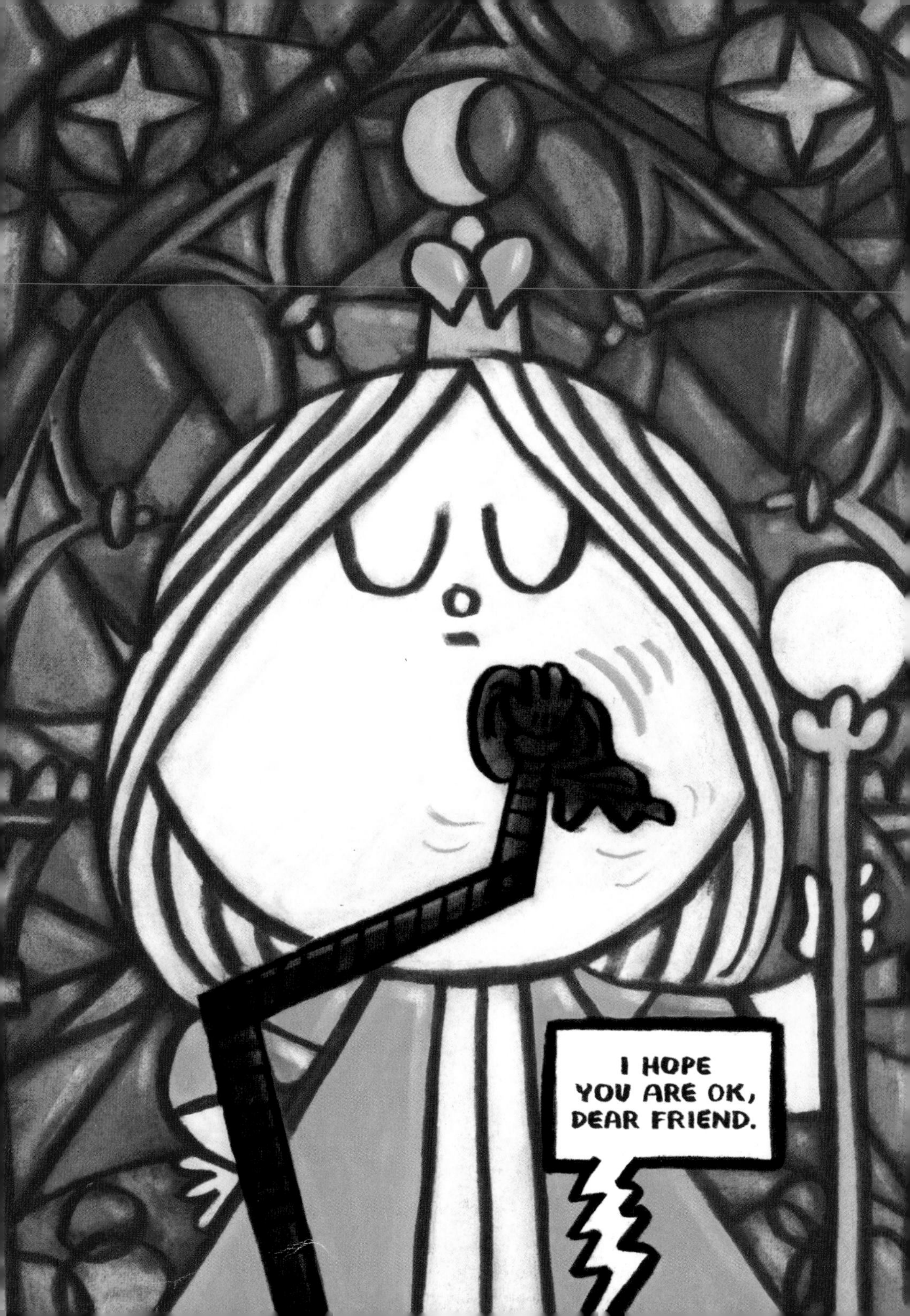
I HOPE YOU ARE OK, DEAR FRIEND.

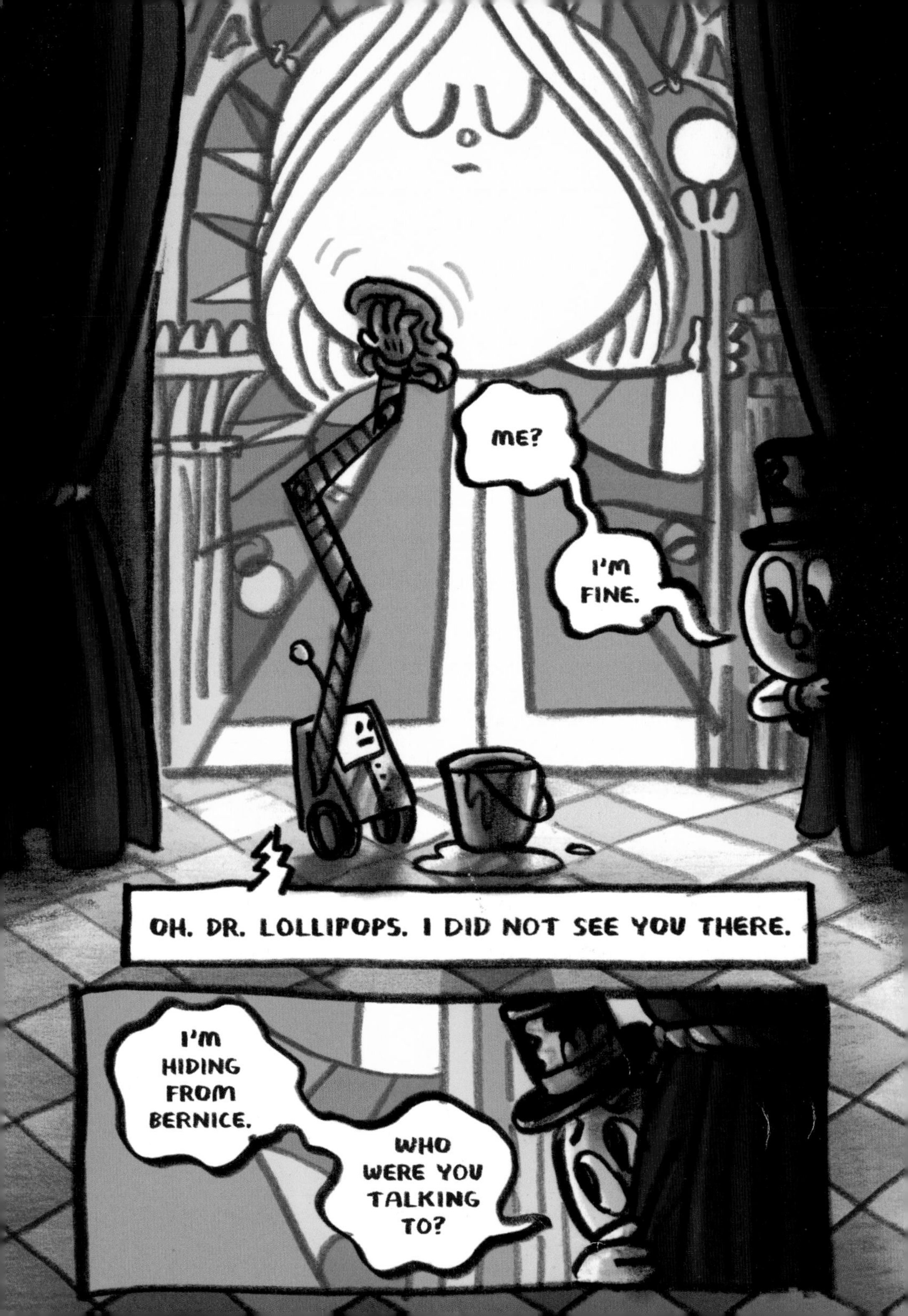
ME?
I'M FINE.
OH. DR. LOLLIPOPS. I DID NOT SEE YOU THERE.
I'M HIDING FROM BERNICE.
WHO WERE YOU TALKING TO?

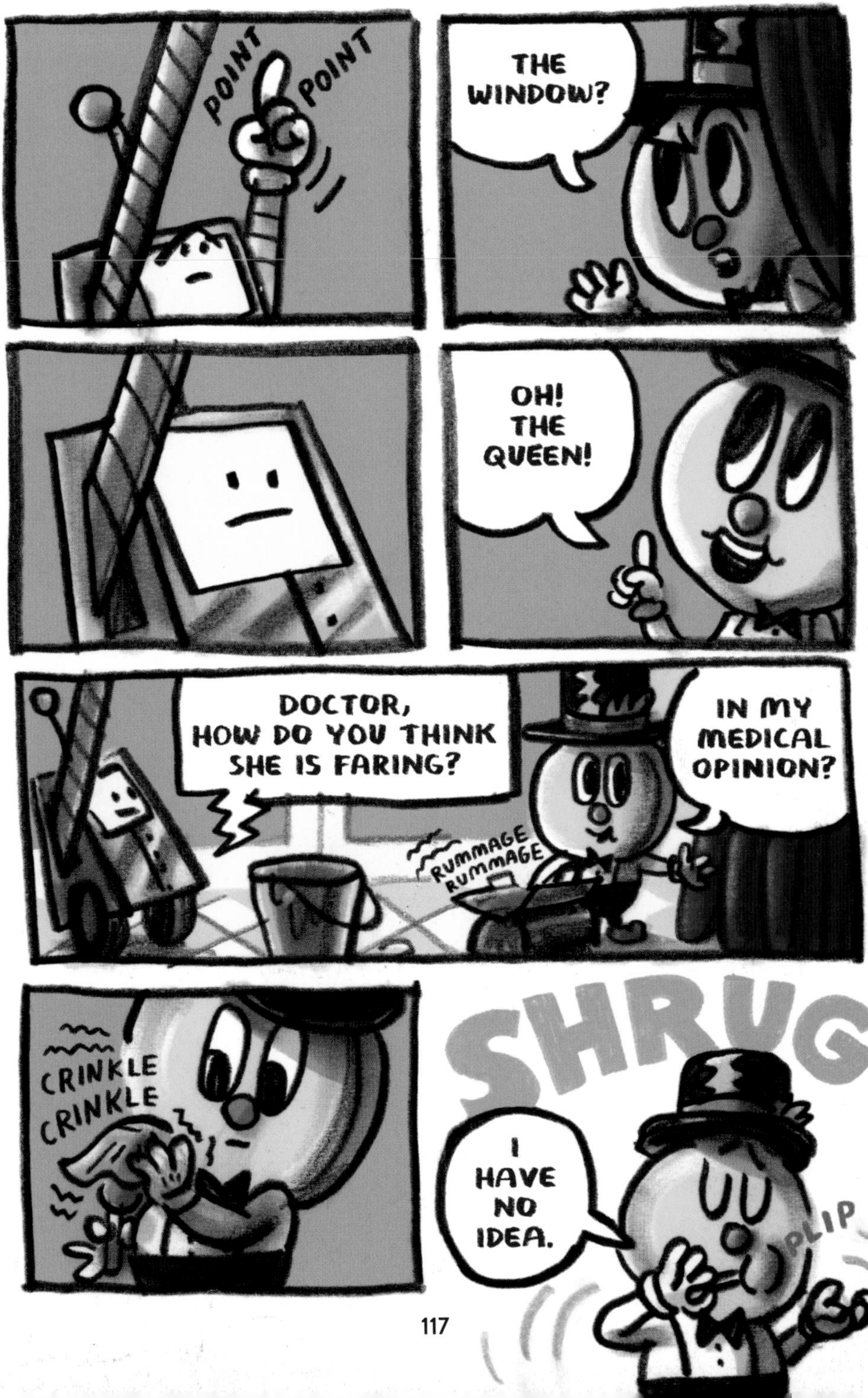
POINT
POINT
THE WINDOW?
OH! THE QUEEN!
DOCTOR, HOW DO YOU THINK SHE IS FARING?
IN MY MEDICAL OPINION?
RUMMAGE
RUMMAGE
CRINKLE
CRINKLE
SHRUG
I HAVE NO IDEA.
PLIP

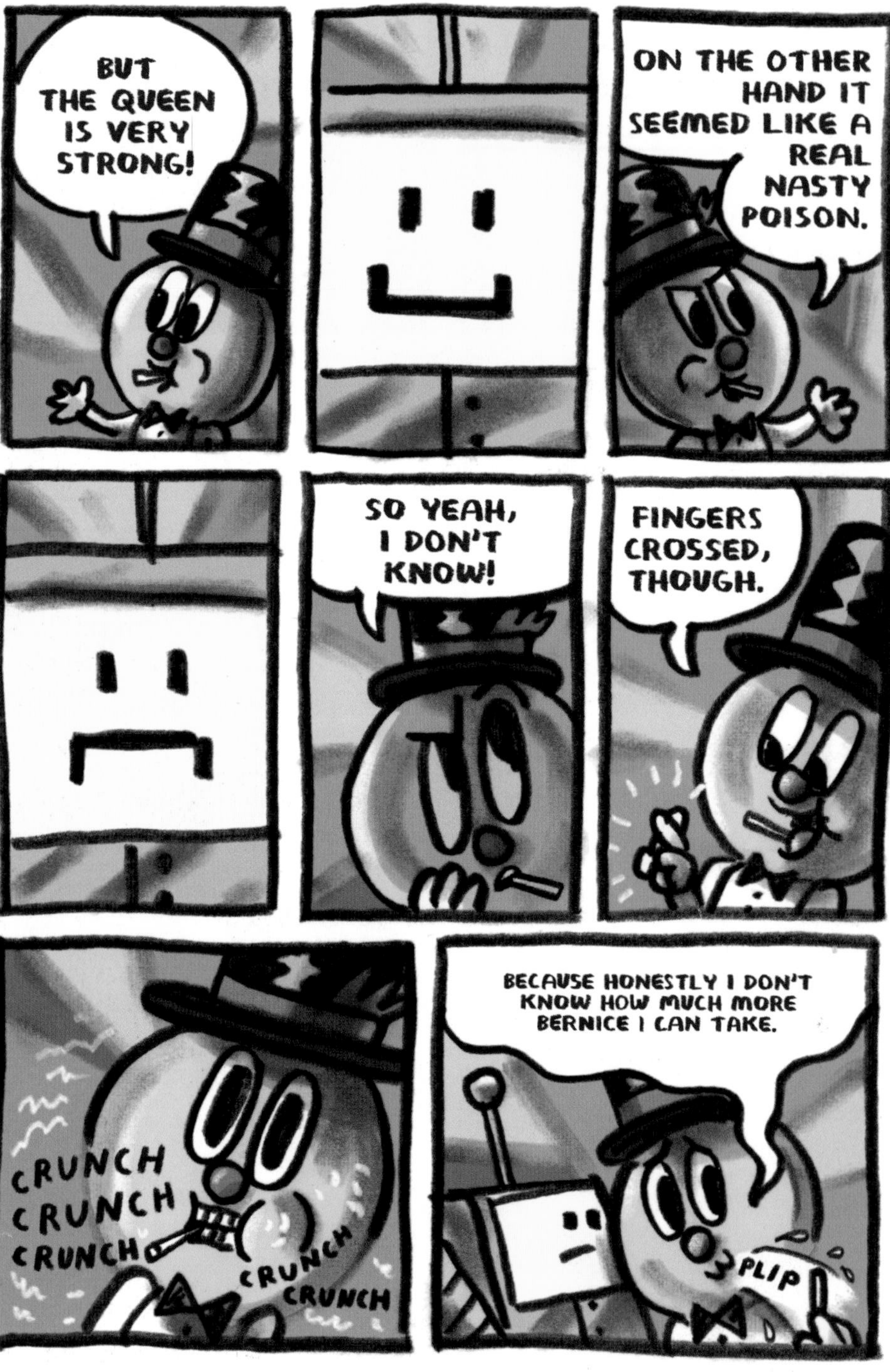
BUT THE QUEEN IS VERY STRONG!
ON THE OTHER HAND IT SEEMED LIKE A REAL NASTY POISON.
SO YEAH, I DON'T KNOW!
FINGERS CROSSED, THOUGH.
CRUNCH CRUNCH CRUNCH
CRUNCH CRUNCH
BECAUSE HONESTLY I DON'T KNOW HOW MUCH MORE BERNICE I CAN TAKE.
PLIP

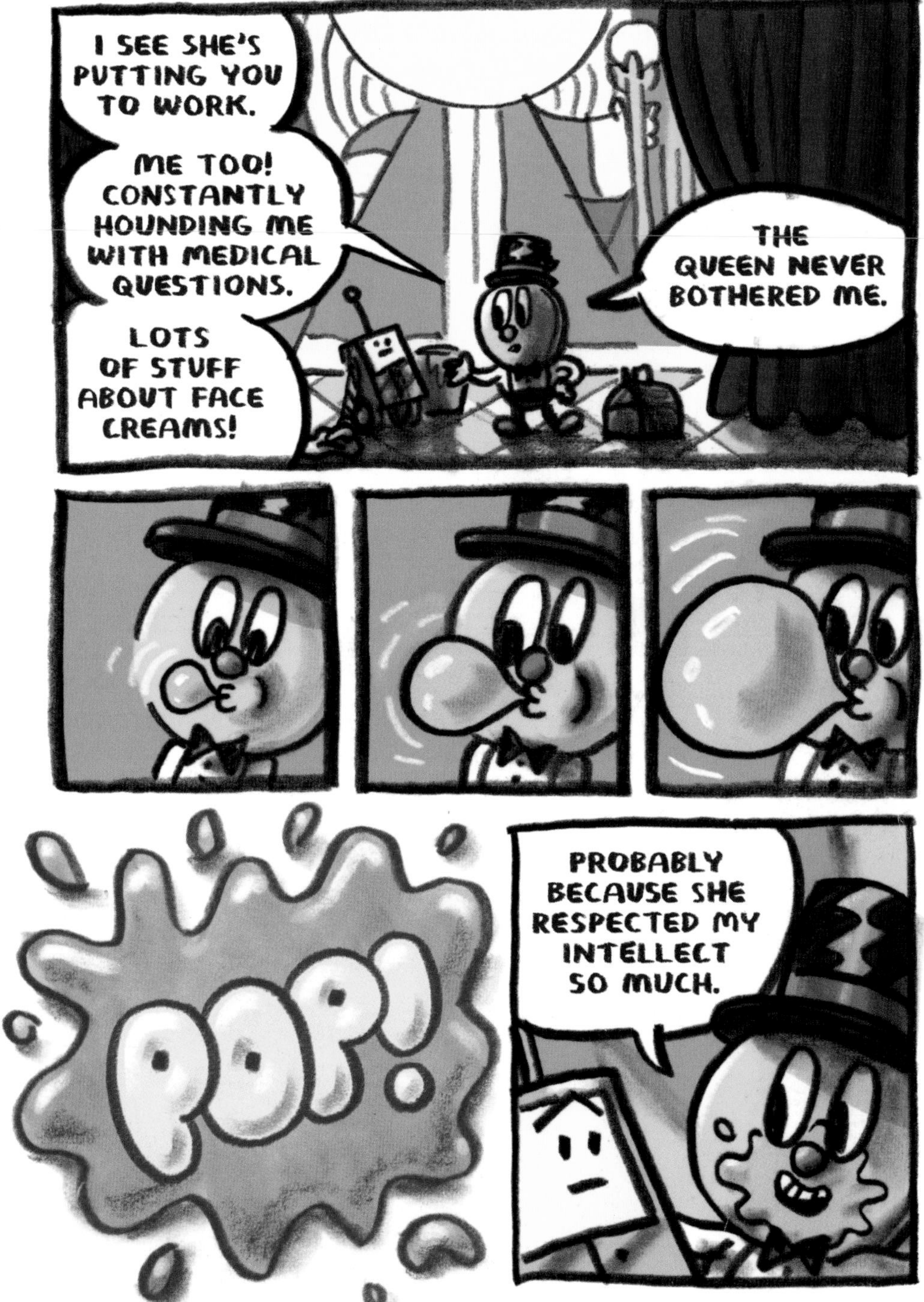
I SEE SHE'S PUTTING YOU TO WORK.
ME TOO! CONSTANTLY HOUNDING ME WITH MEDICAL QUESTIONS.
LOTS OF STUFF ABOUT FACE CREAMS!
THE QUEEN NEVER BOTHERED ME.
POP!
PROBABLY BECAUSE SHE RESPECTED MY INTELLECT SO MUCH.

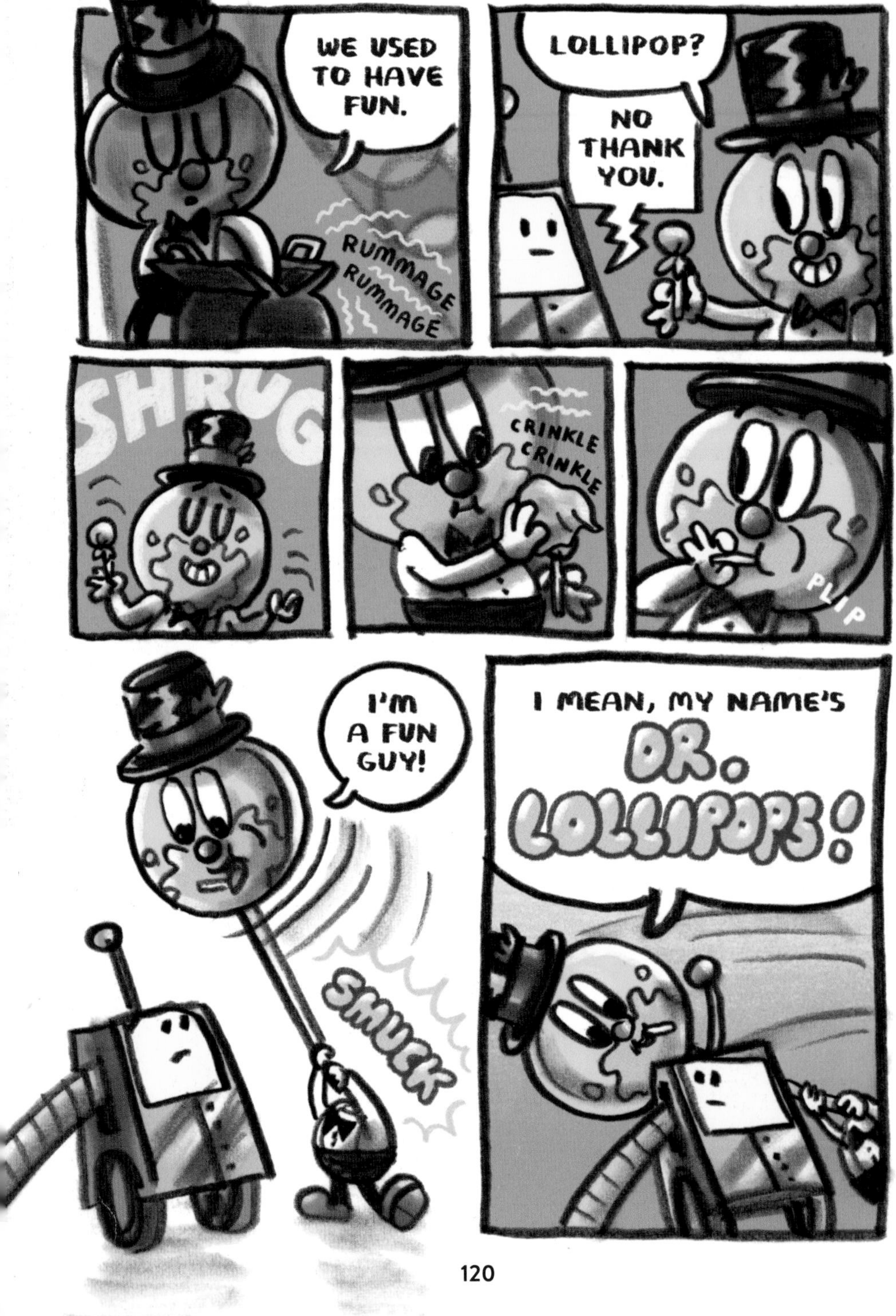
WE USED TO HAVE FUN.
RUMMAGE RUMMAGE
LOLLIPOP?
NO THANK YOU.
SHRUG
CRINKLE CRINKLE
PLIP
I'M A FUN GUY!
SMUCK
I MEAN, MY NAME'S DR. LOLLIPOPS!

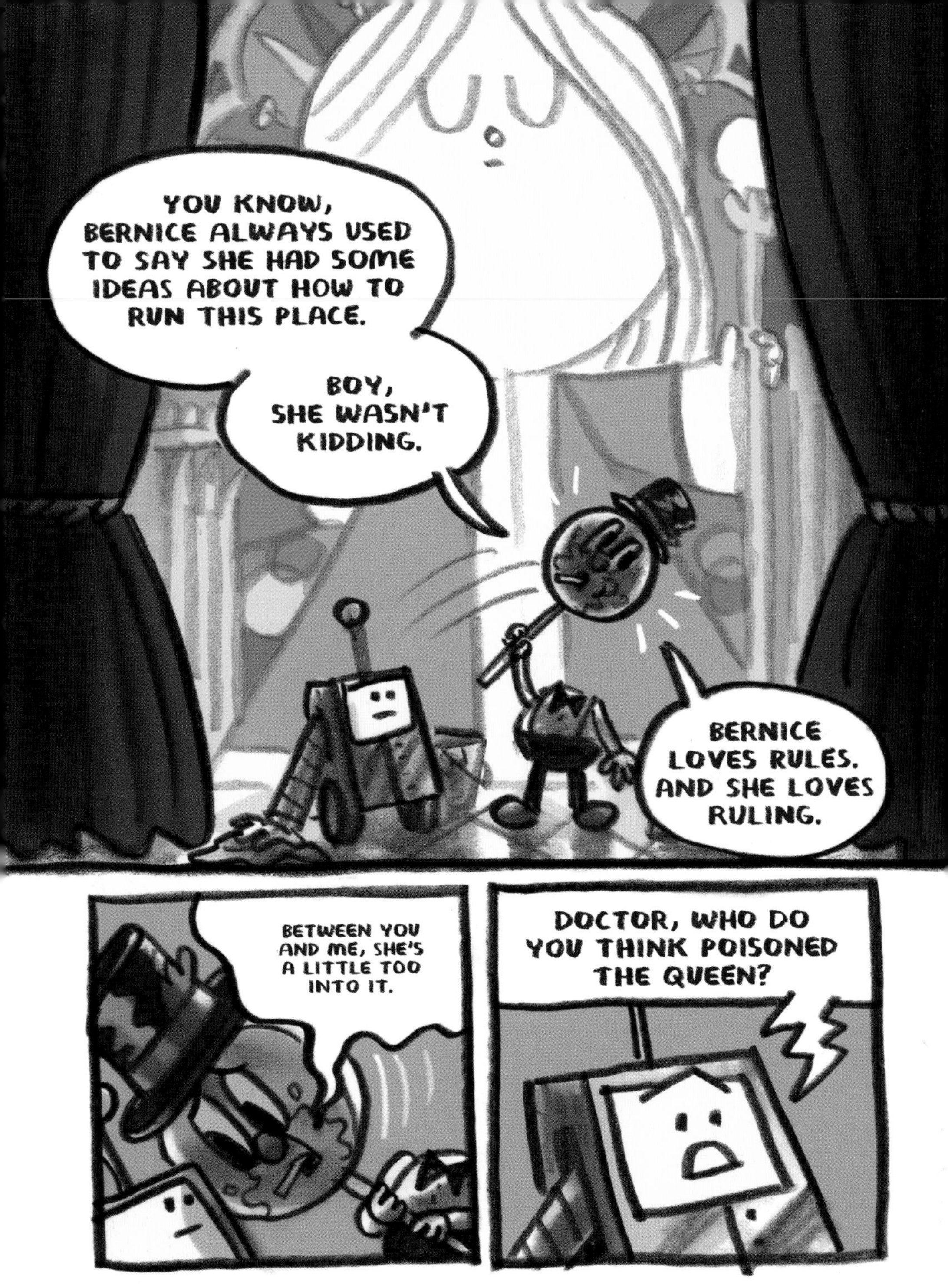
YOU KNOW, BERNICE ALWAYS USED TO SAY SHE HAD SOME IDEAS ABOUT HOW TO RUN THIS PLACE.
BOY, SHE WASN'T KIDDING.
BERNICE LOVES RULES. AND SHE LOVES RULING.
BETWEEN YOU AND ME, SHE'S A LITTLE TOO INTO IT.
DOCTOR, WHO DO YOU THINK POISONED THE QUEEN?

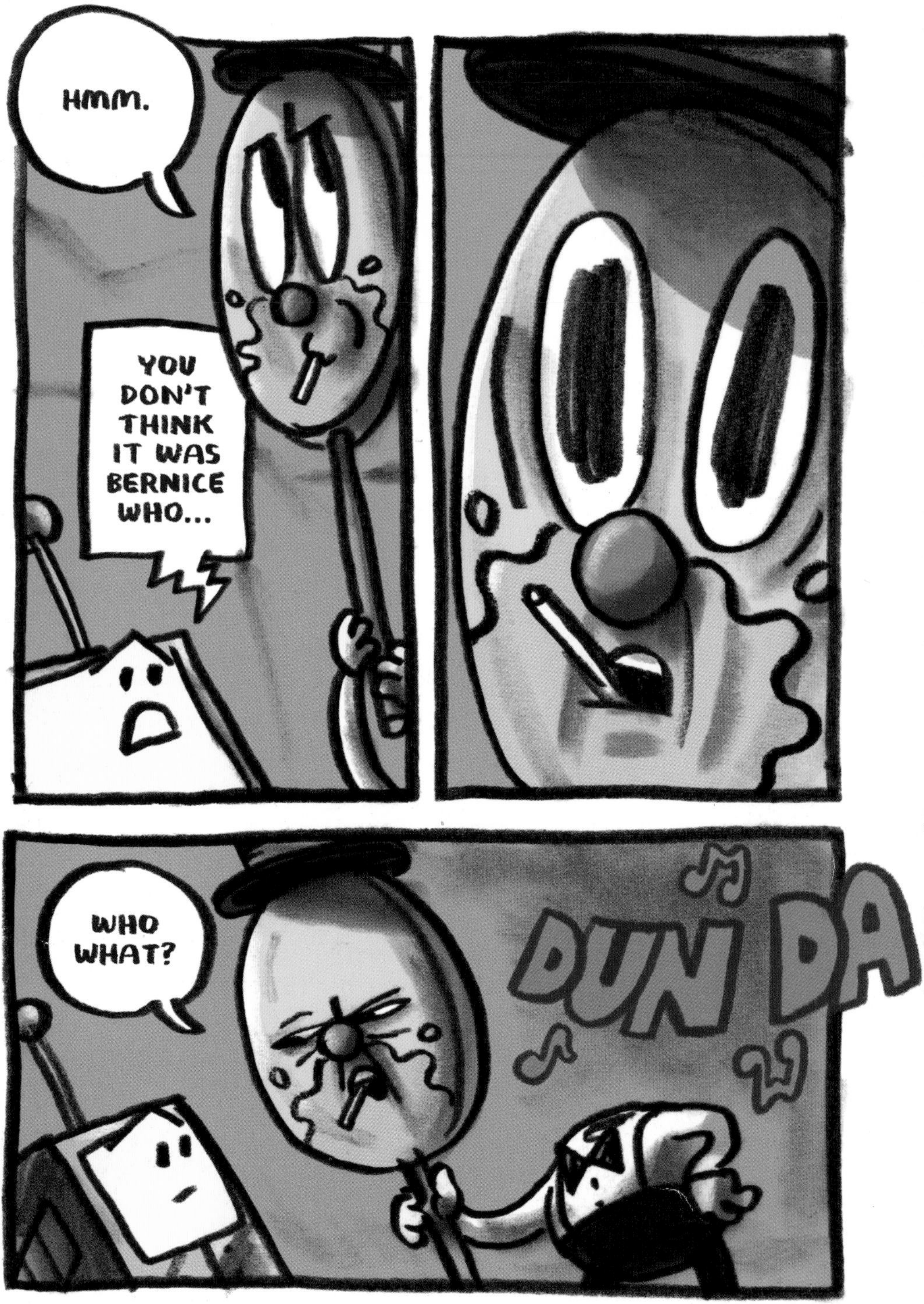
HMM.
YOU DON'T THINK IT WAS BERNICE WHO...
WHO WHAT?
DUN DA

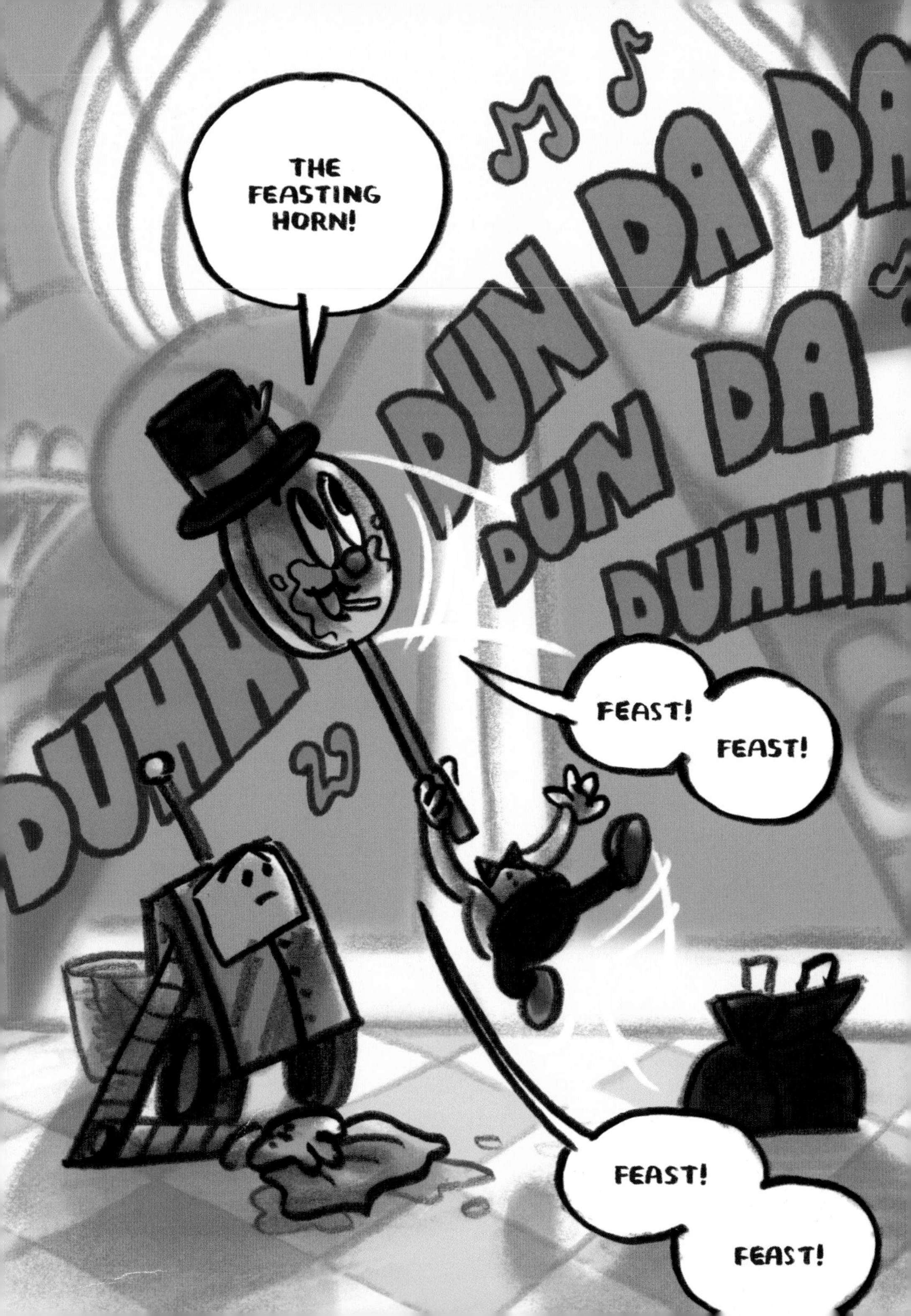
THE FEASTING HORN!
DUHH DUN DA DA DUN DA DUHHH
FEAST! FEAST!
FEAST! FEAST!

# CHAPTER 6

# WIZARD STUFF

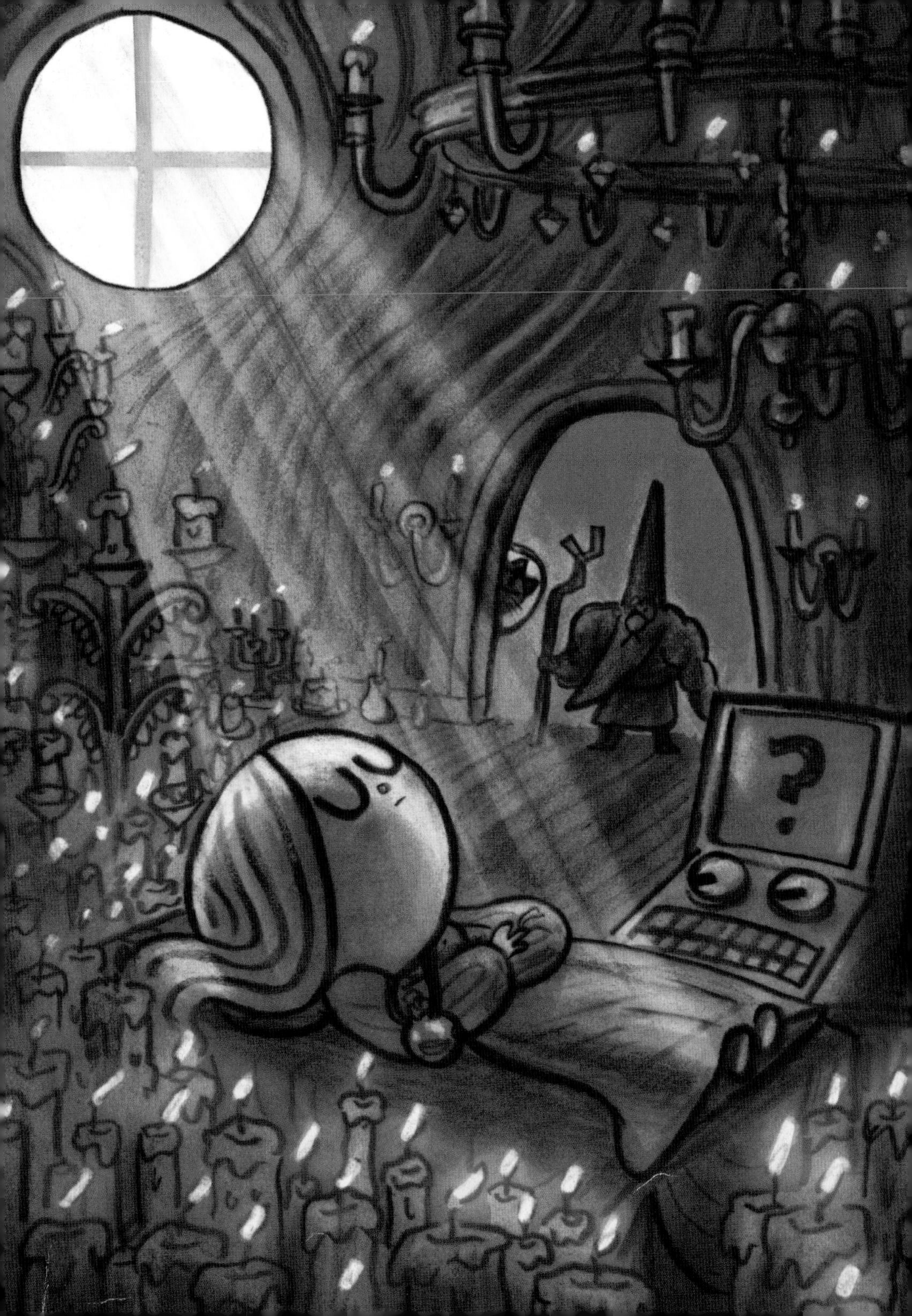
?

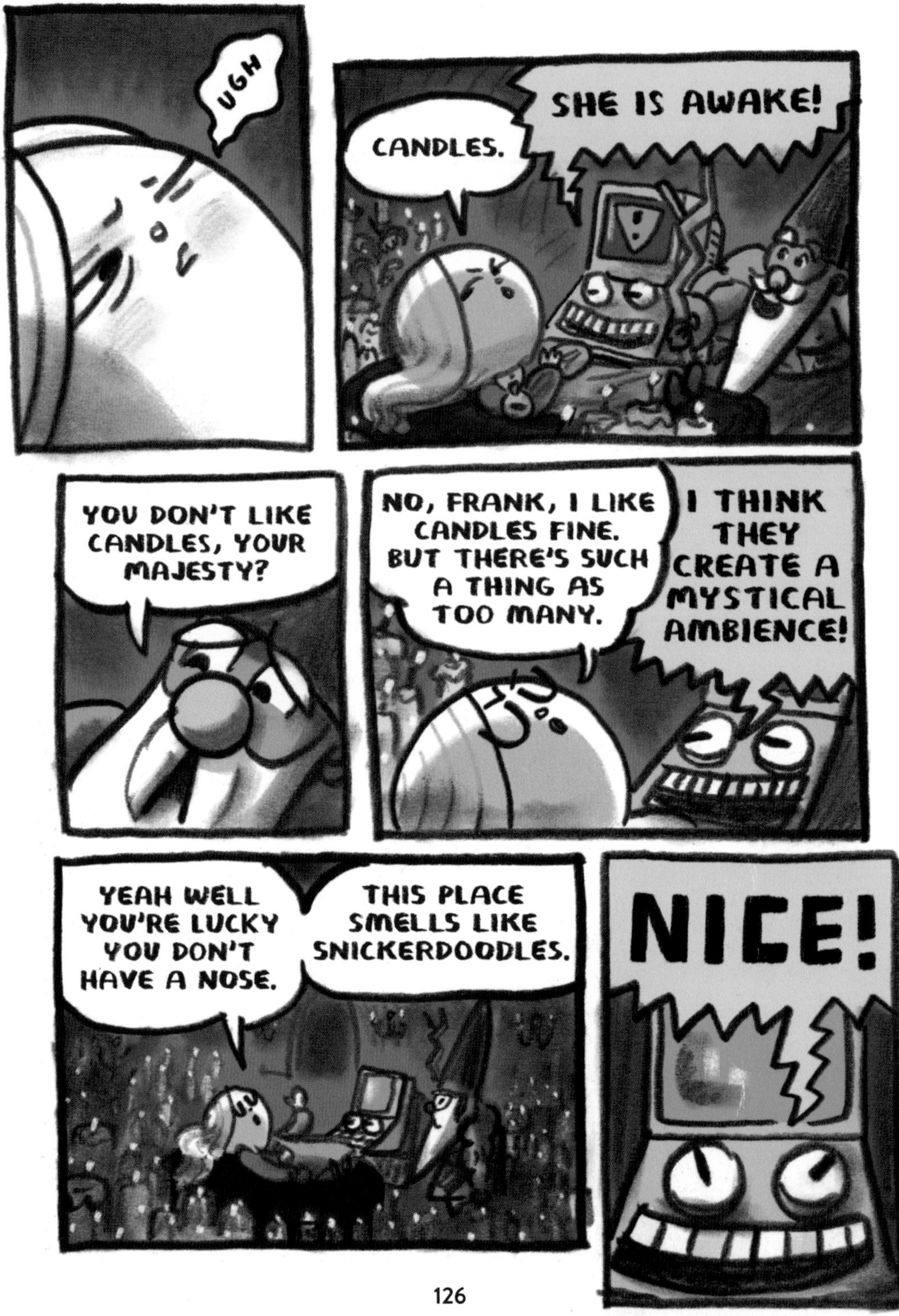
UGH
SHE IS AWAKE!
CANDLES.
YOU DON'T LIKE CANDLES, YOUR MAJESTY?
NO, FRANK, I LIKE CANDLES FINE. BUT THERE'S SUCH A THING AS TOO MANY.
I THINK THEY CREATE A MYSTICAL AMBIENCE!
THIS PLACE SMELLS LIKE SNICKERDOODLES.
YEAH WELL YOU'RE LUCKY YOU DON'T HAVE A NOSE.
NICE!

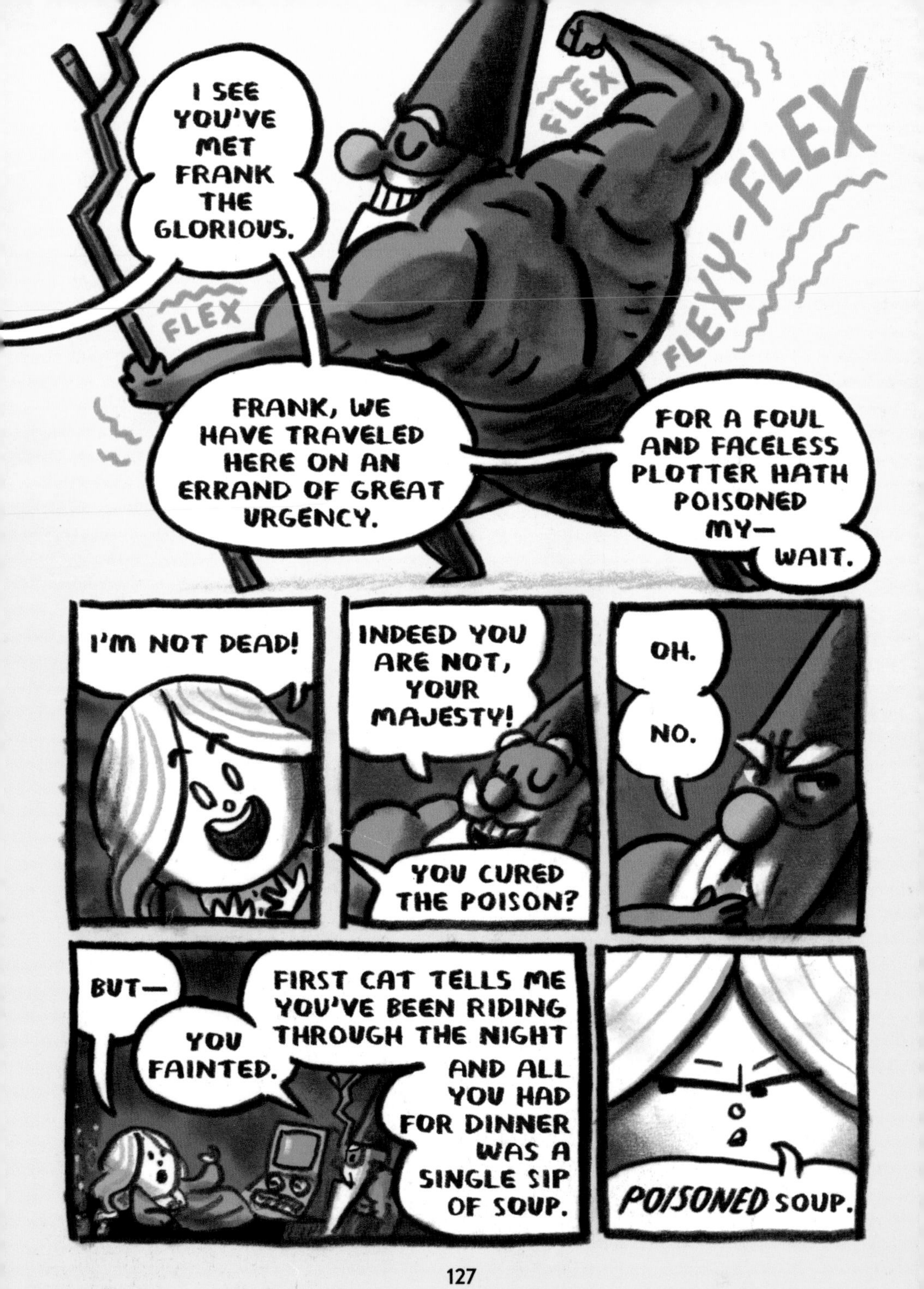
I SEE YOU'VE MET FRANK THE GLORIOUS.
FLEX
FLEX
FLEXY-FLEX
FRANK, WE HAVE TRAVELED HERE ON AN ERRAND OF GREAT URGENCY.
FOR A FOUL AND FACELESS PLOTTER HATH POISONED MY—
WAIT.
I'M NOT DEAD!
INDEED YOU ARE NOT, YOUR MAJESTY!
YOU CURED THE POISON?
OH.
NO.
BUT—
YOU FAINTED.
FIRST CAT TELLS ME YOU'VE BEEN RIDING THROUGH THE NIGHT
AND ALL YOU HAD FOR DINNER WAS A SINGLE SIP OF SOUP.
*POISONED* SOUP.

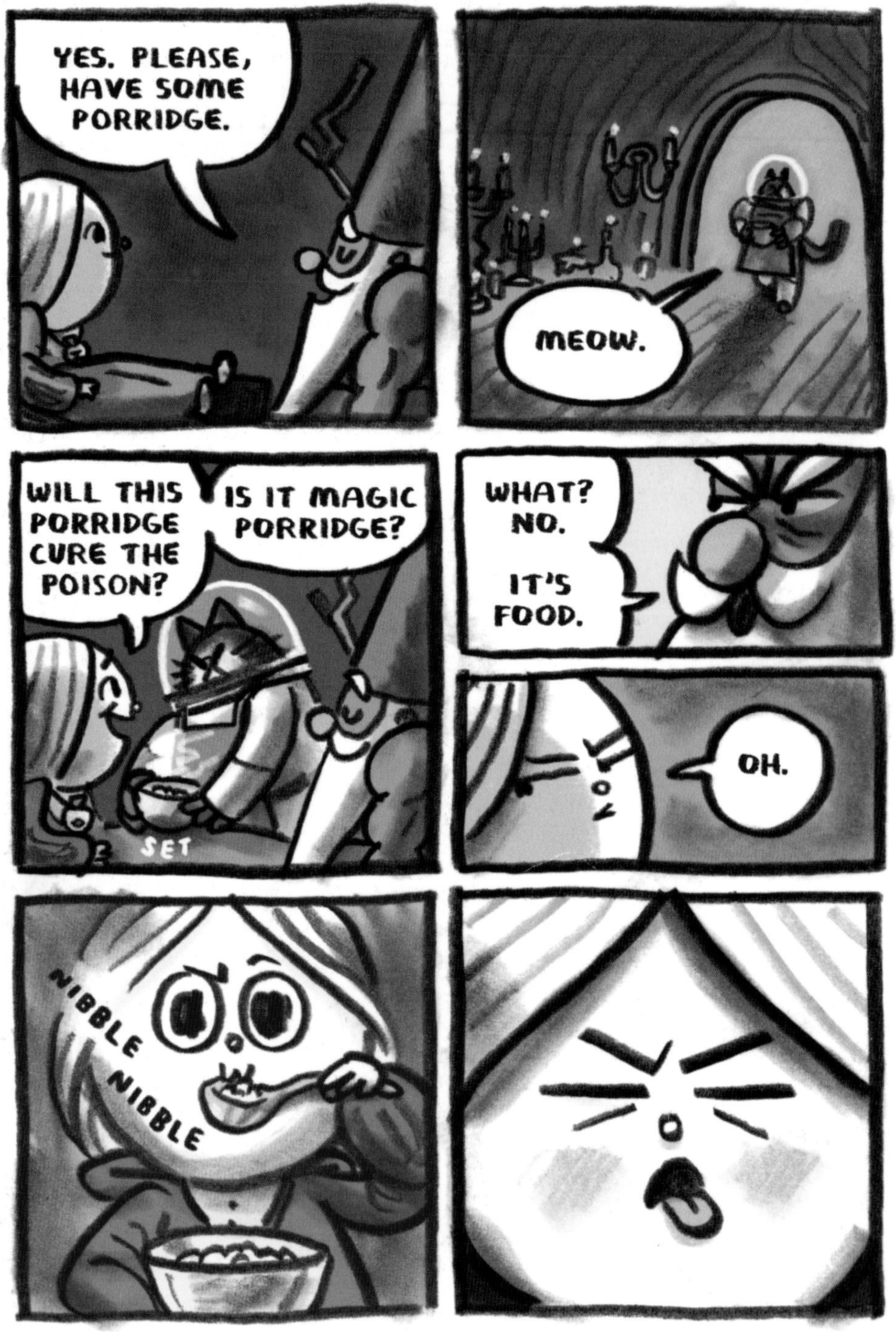
YES. PLEASE, HAVE SOME PORRIDGE.
MEOW.
WILL THIS PORRIDGE CURE THE POISON?
IS IT MAGIC PORRIDGE?
SET
WHAT? NO.
IT'S FOOD.
OH.
NIBBLE NIBBLE

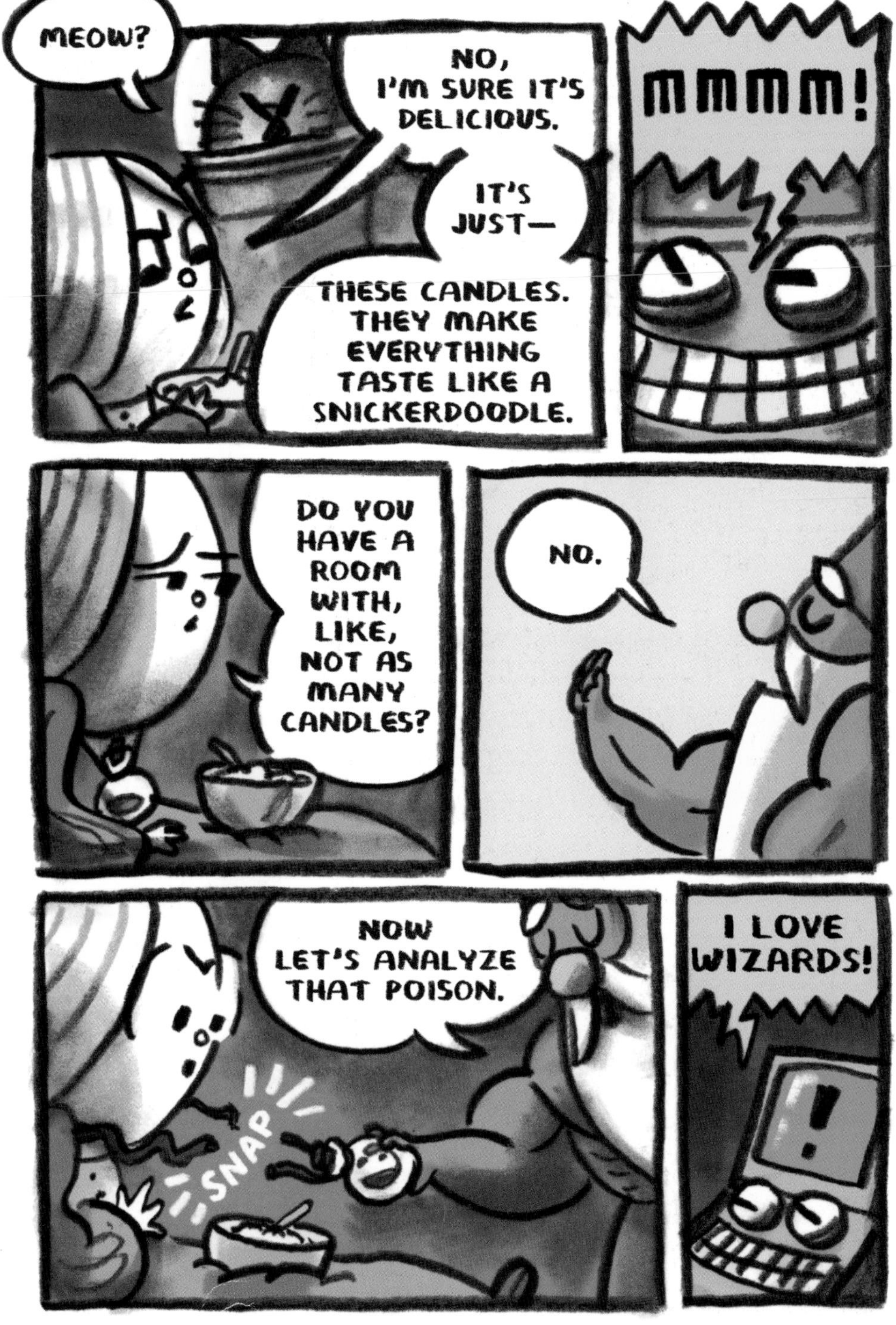
MEOW?
NO, I'M SURE IT'S DELICIOUS.
IT'S JUST—
THESE CANDLES. THEY MAKE EVERYTHING TASTE LIKE A SNICKERDOODLE.
MMMMM!
DO YOU HAVE A ROOM WITH, LIKE, NOT AS MANY CANDLES?
NO.
NOW LET'S ANALYZE THAT POISON.
SNAP
I LOVE WIZARDS!
!

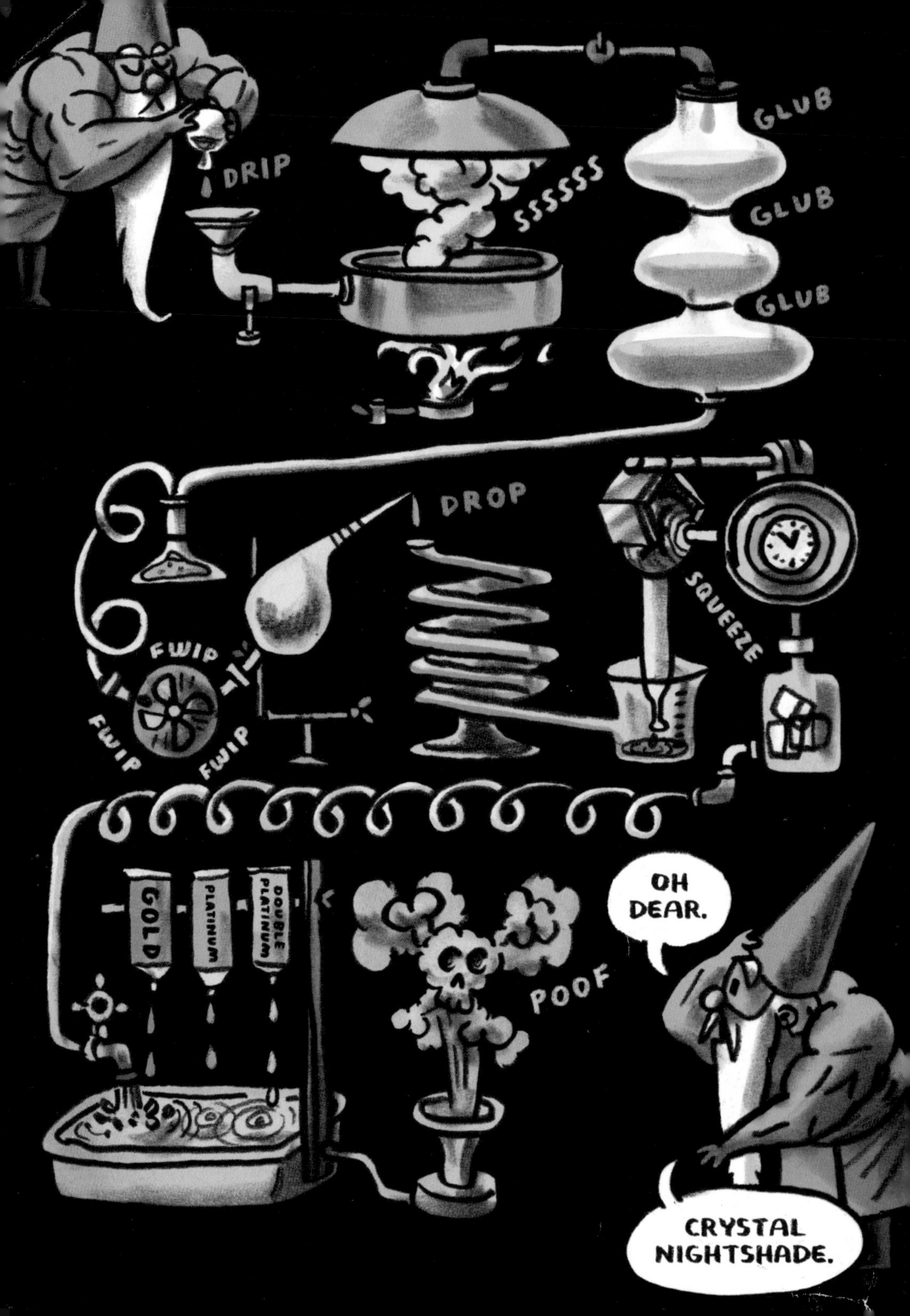
DRIP
SSSSSS
GLUB
GLUB
GLUB
DROP
SQUEEZE
FWIP
FWIP
FWIP
GOLD
PLATINUM
DOUBLE PLATINUM
POOF
OH DEAR.
CRYSTAL NIGHTSHADE.

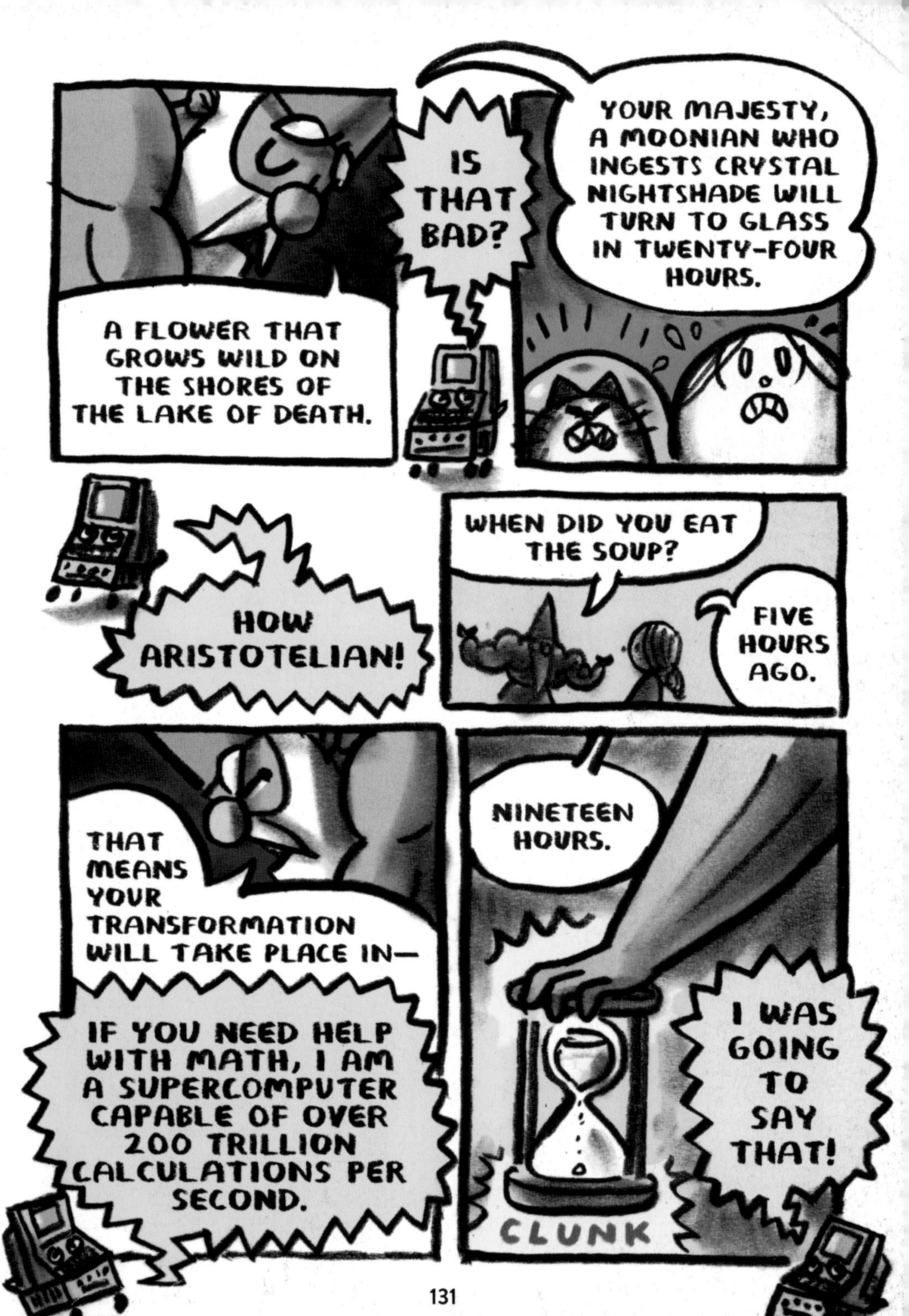

A FLOWER THAT GROWS WILD ON THE SHORES OF THE LAKE OF DEATH.
IS THAT BAD?
YOUR MAJESTY, A MOONIAN WHO INGESTS CRYSTAL NIGHTSHADE WILL TURN TO GLASS IN TWENTY-FOUR HOURS.
HOW ARISTOTELIAN!
WHEN DID YOU EAT THE SOUP?
FIVE HOURS AGO.
THAT MEANS YOUR TRANSFORMATION WILL TAKE PLACE IN—
IF YOU NEED HELP WITH MATH, I AM A SUPERCOMPUTER CAPABLE OF OVER 200 TRILLION CALCULATIONS PER SECOND.
NINETEEN HOURS.
CLUNK
I WAS GOING TO SAY THAT!

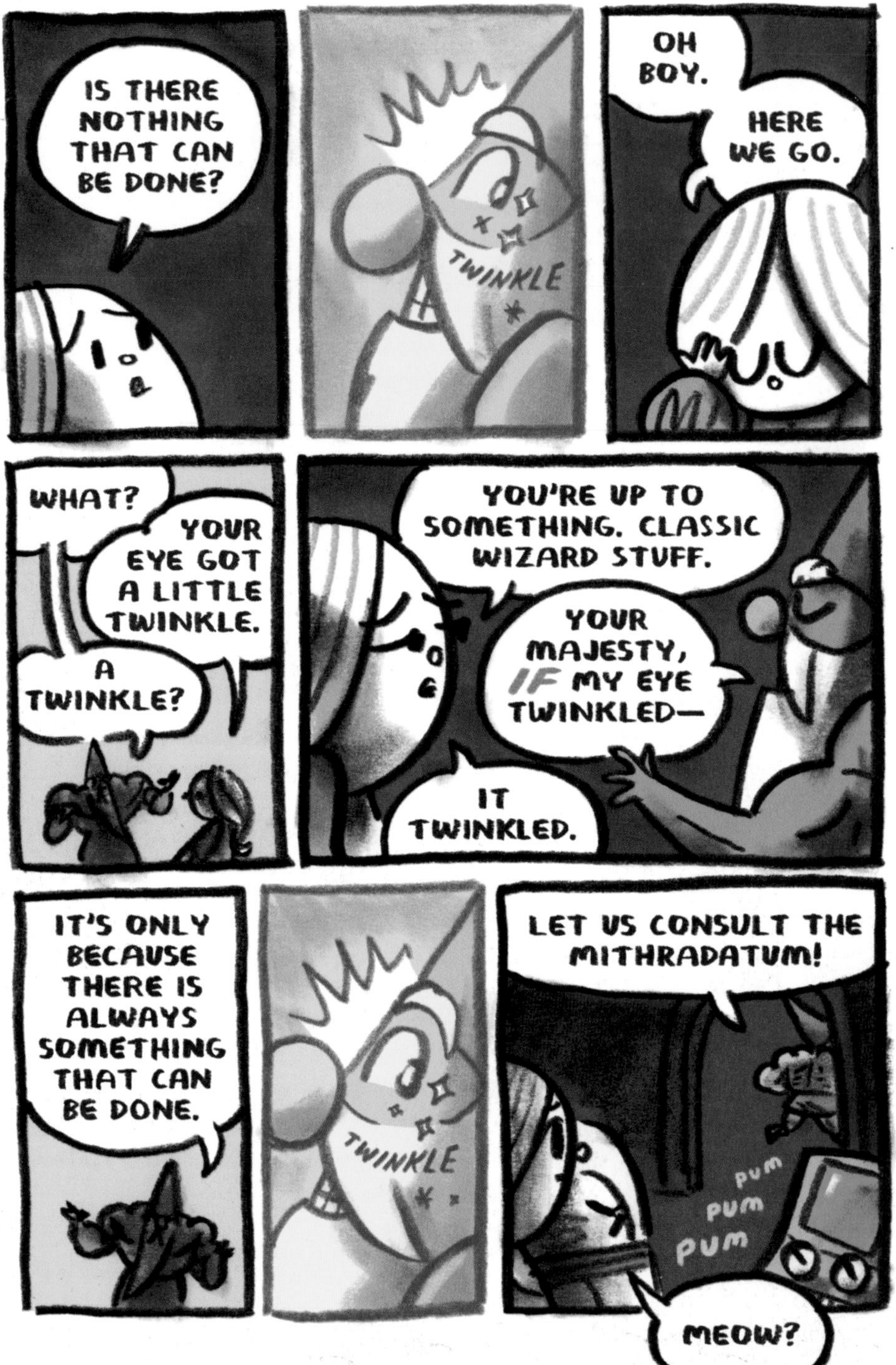
IS THERE NOTHING THAT CAN BE DONE?
TWINKLE
OH BOY.
HERE WE GO.
WHAT?
YOUR EYE GOT A LITTLE TWINKLE.
A TWINKLE?
YOU'RE UP TO SOMETHING. CLASSIC WIZARD STUFF.
YOUR MAJESTY, IF MY EYE TWINKLED—
IT TWINKLED.
IT'S ONLY BECAUSE THERE IS ALWAYS SOMETHING THAT CAN BE DONE.
TWINKLE
LET US CONSULT THE MITHRADATUM!
PUM
PUM
PUM
MEOW?

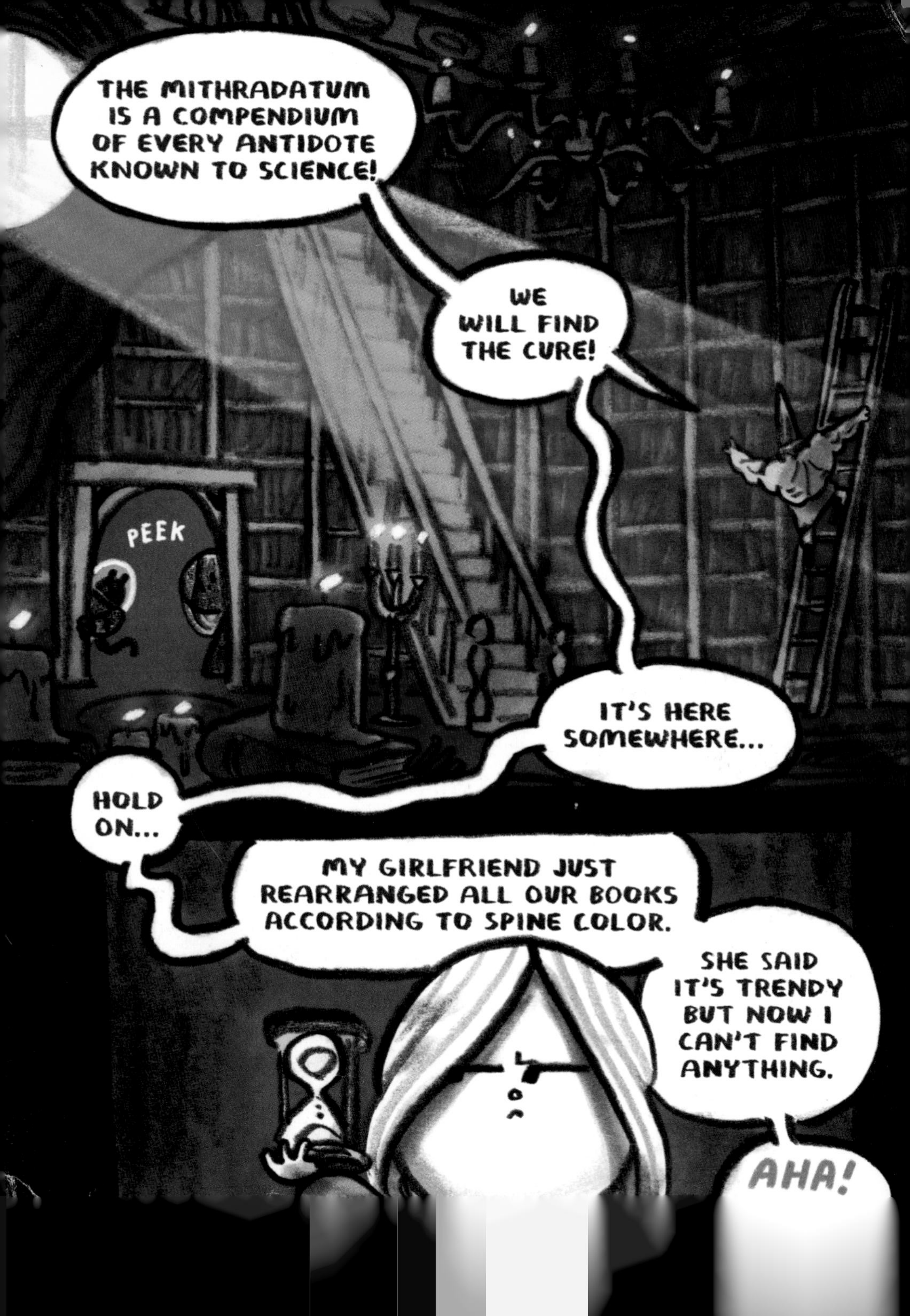
THE MITHRADATUM IS A COMPENDIUM OF EVERY ANTIDOTE KNOWN TO SCIENCE!
WE WILL FIND THE CURE!
PEEK
IT'S HERE SOMEWHERE...
HOLD ON...
MY GIRLFRIEND JUST REARRANGED ALL OUR BOOKS ACCORDING TO SPINE COLOR.
SHE SAID IT'S TRENDY BUT NOW I CAN'T FIND ANYTHING.
AHA!

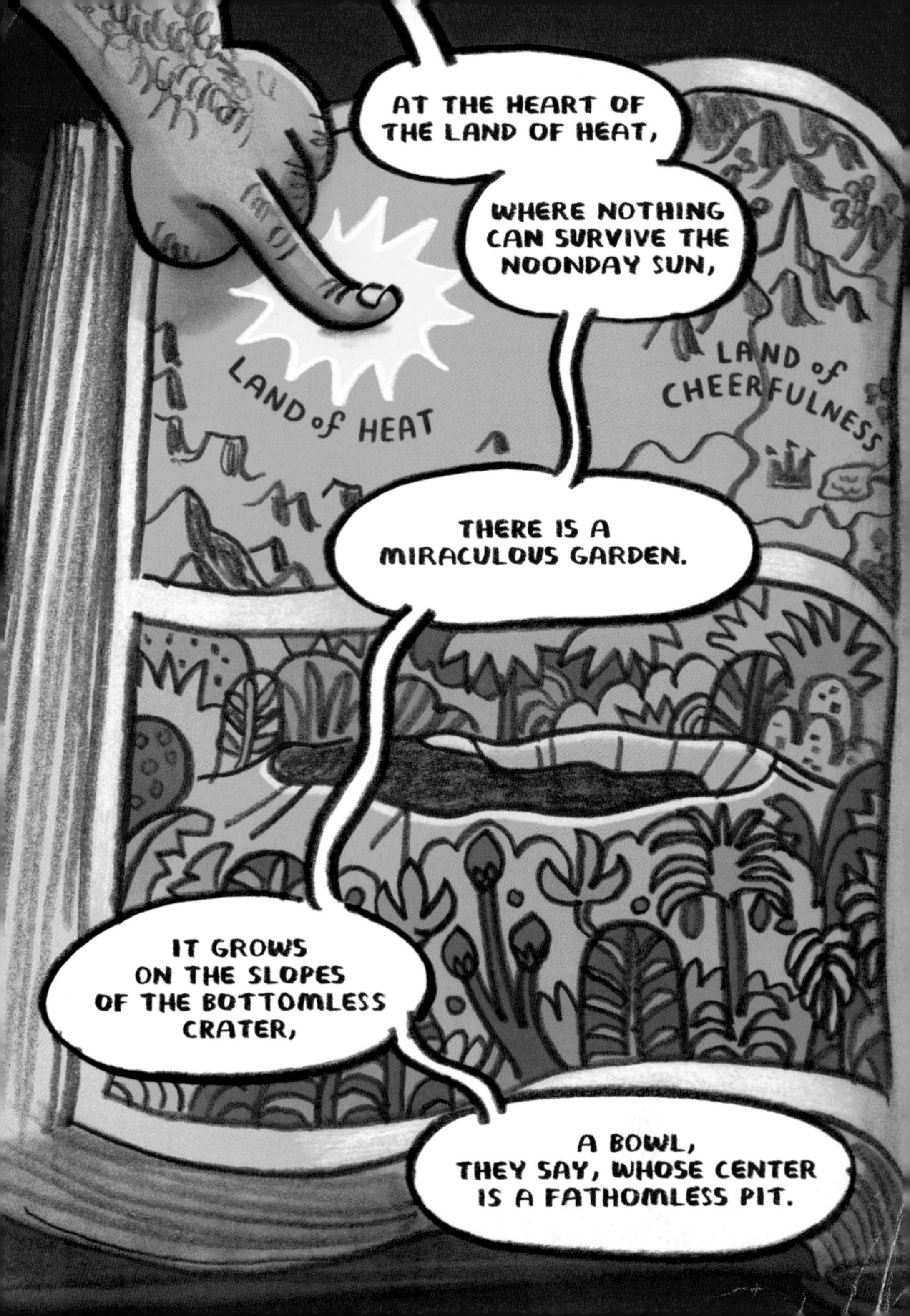
AT THE HEART OF THE LAND OF HEAT,
WHERE NOTHING CAN SURVIVE THE NOONDAY SUN,
LAND of HEAT
LAND of CHEERFULNESS
THERE IS A MIRACULOUS GARDEN.
IT GROWS ON THE SLOPES OF THE BOTTOMLESS CRATER,
A BOWL, THEY SAY, WHOSE CENTER IS A FATHOMLESS PIT.

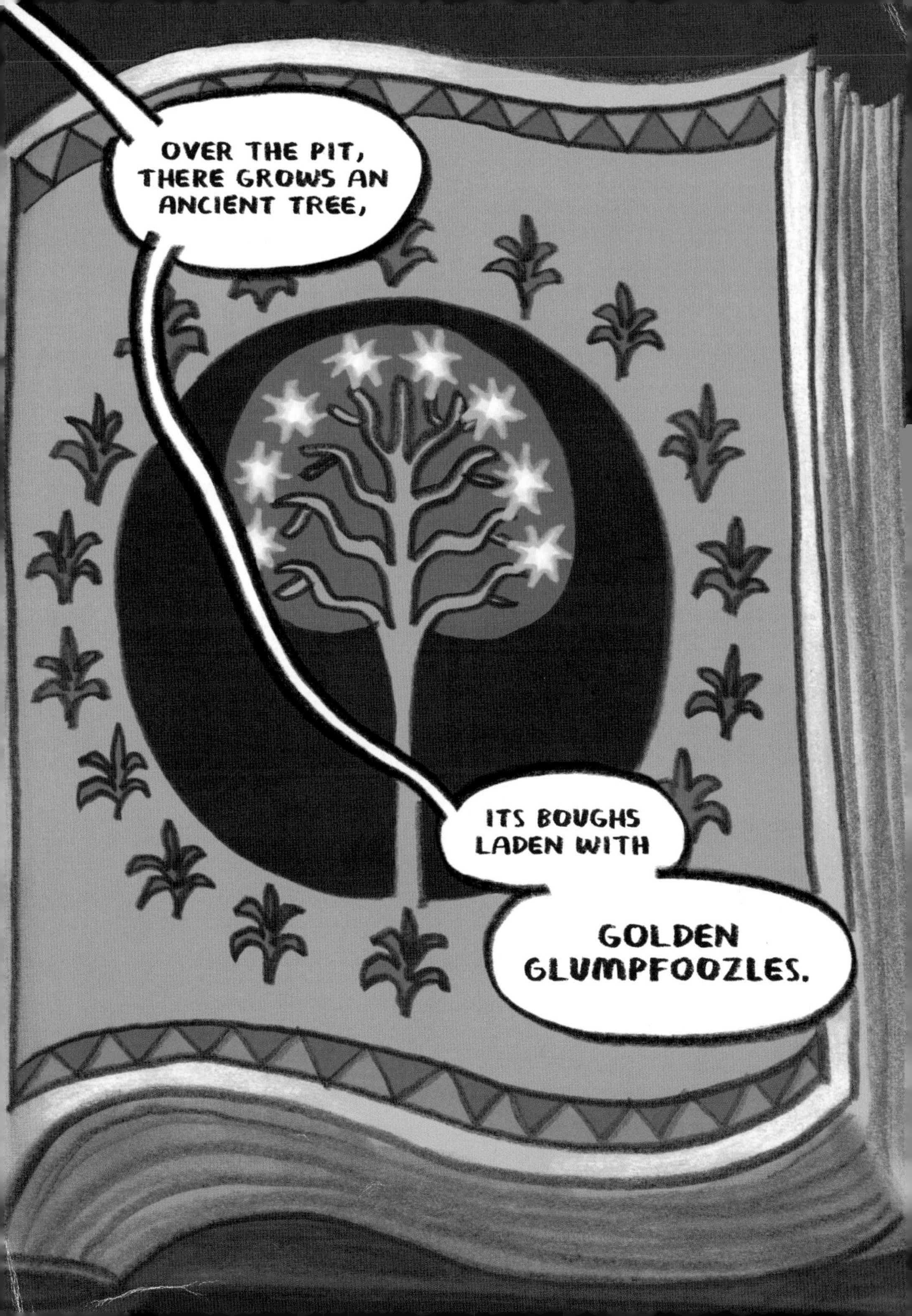
OVER THE PIT, THERE GROWS AN ANCIENT TREE,
ITS BOUGHS LADEN WITH
GOLDEN GLUMPFOOZLES.

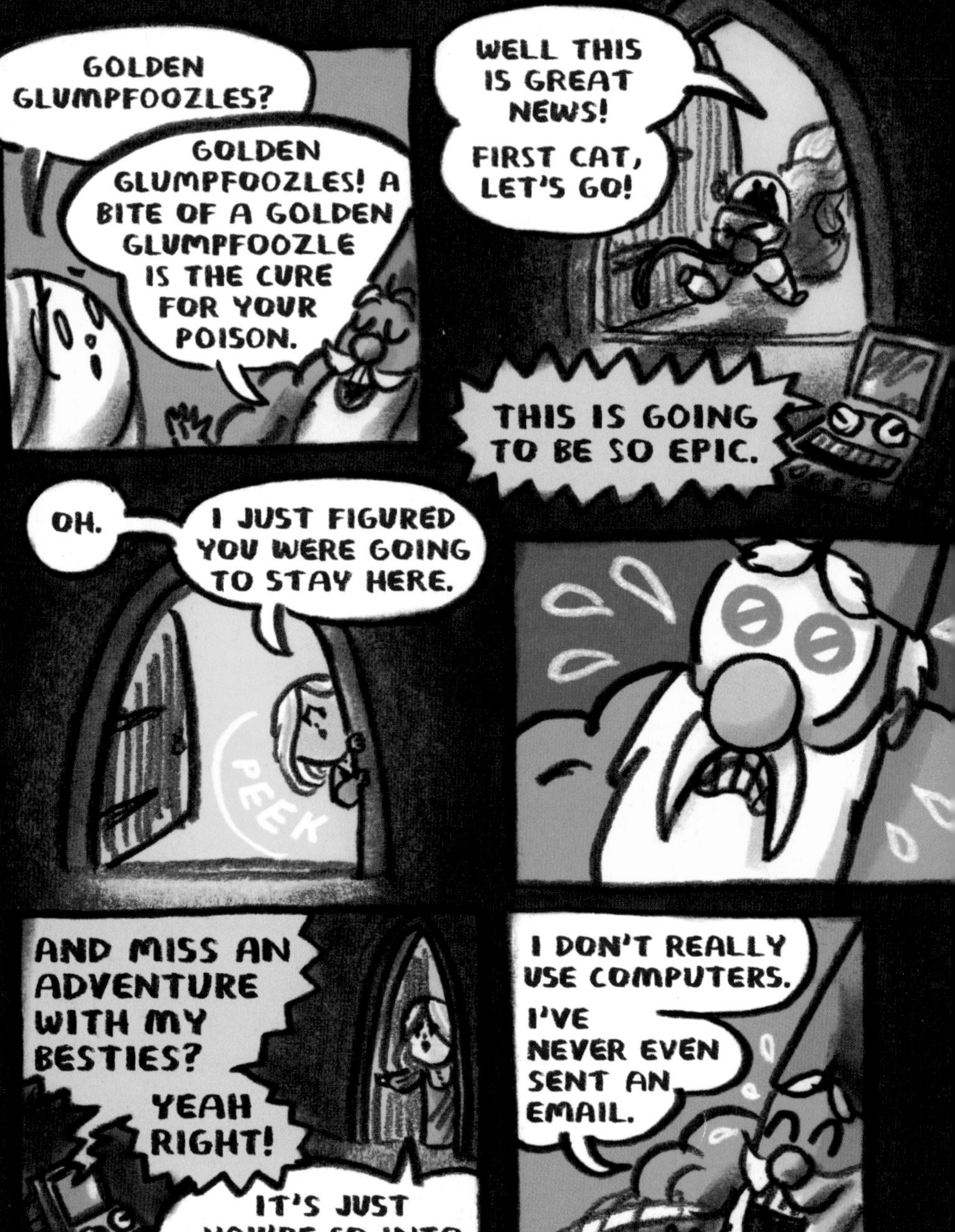

GOLDEN GLUMPFOOZLES?
GOLDEN GLUMPFOOZLES! A BITE OF A GOLDEN GLUMPFOOZLE IS THE CURE FOR YOUR POISON.
WELL THIS IS GREAT NEWS!
FIRST CAT, LET'S GO!
THIS IS GOING TO BE SO EPIC.
OH.
I JUST FIGURED YOU WERE GOING TO STAY HERE.
PEEK
AND MISS AN ADVENTURE WITH MY BESTIES?
YEAH RIGHT!
IT'S JUST YOU'RE SO INTO WIZARDS AND SNICKERDOODLES.
I DON'T REALLY USE COMPUTERS.
I'VE NEVER EVEN SENT AN EMAIL.

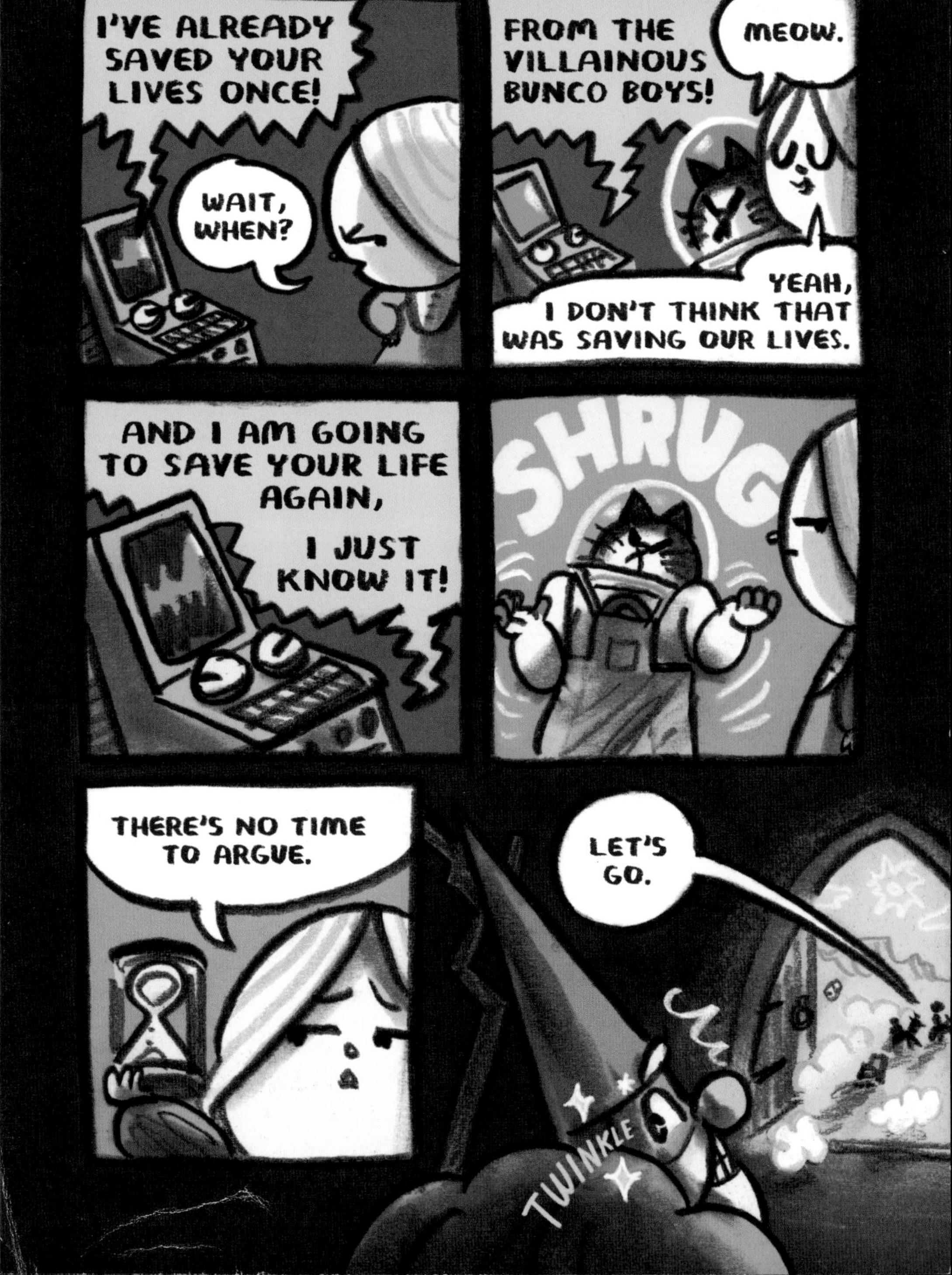
I'VE ALREADY SAVED YOUR LIVES ONCE!
WAIT, WHEN?
FROM THE VILLAINOUS BUNCO BOYS!
MEOW.
YEAH, I DON'T THINK THAT WAS SAVING OUR LIVES.
AND I AM GOING TO SAVE YOUR LIFE AGAIN,
I JUST KNOW IT!
SHRUG
THERE'S NO TIME TO ARGUE.
LET'S GO.
TWINKLE

CHAPTER 7

# FEAST!

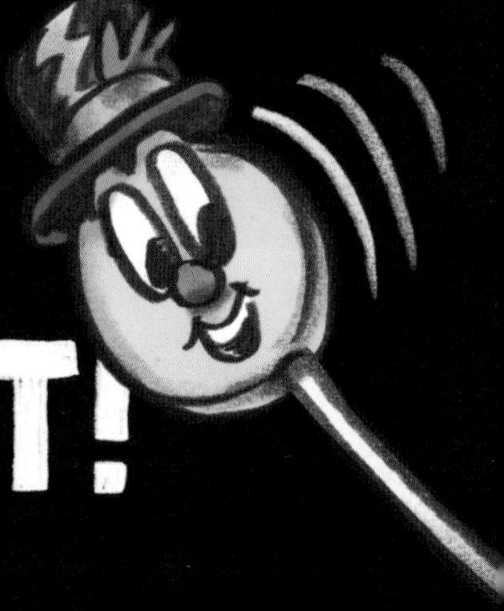

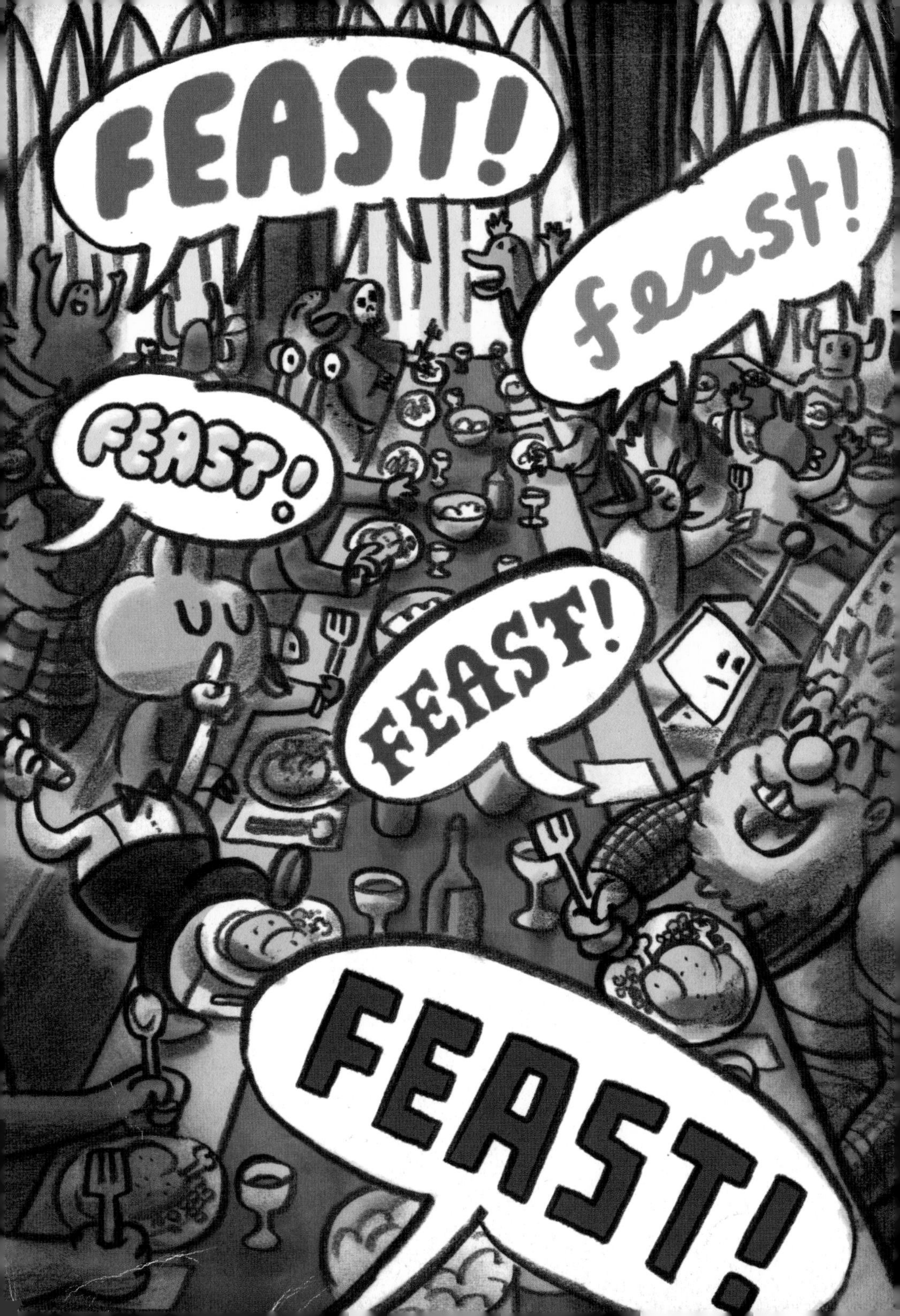
FEAST!
feast!
FEAST!
FEAST!
FEAST!

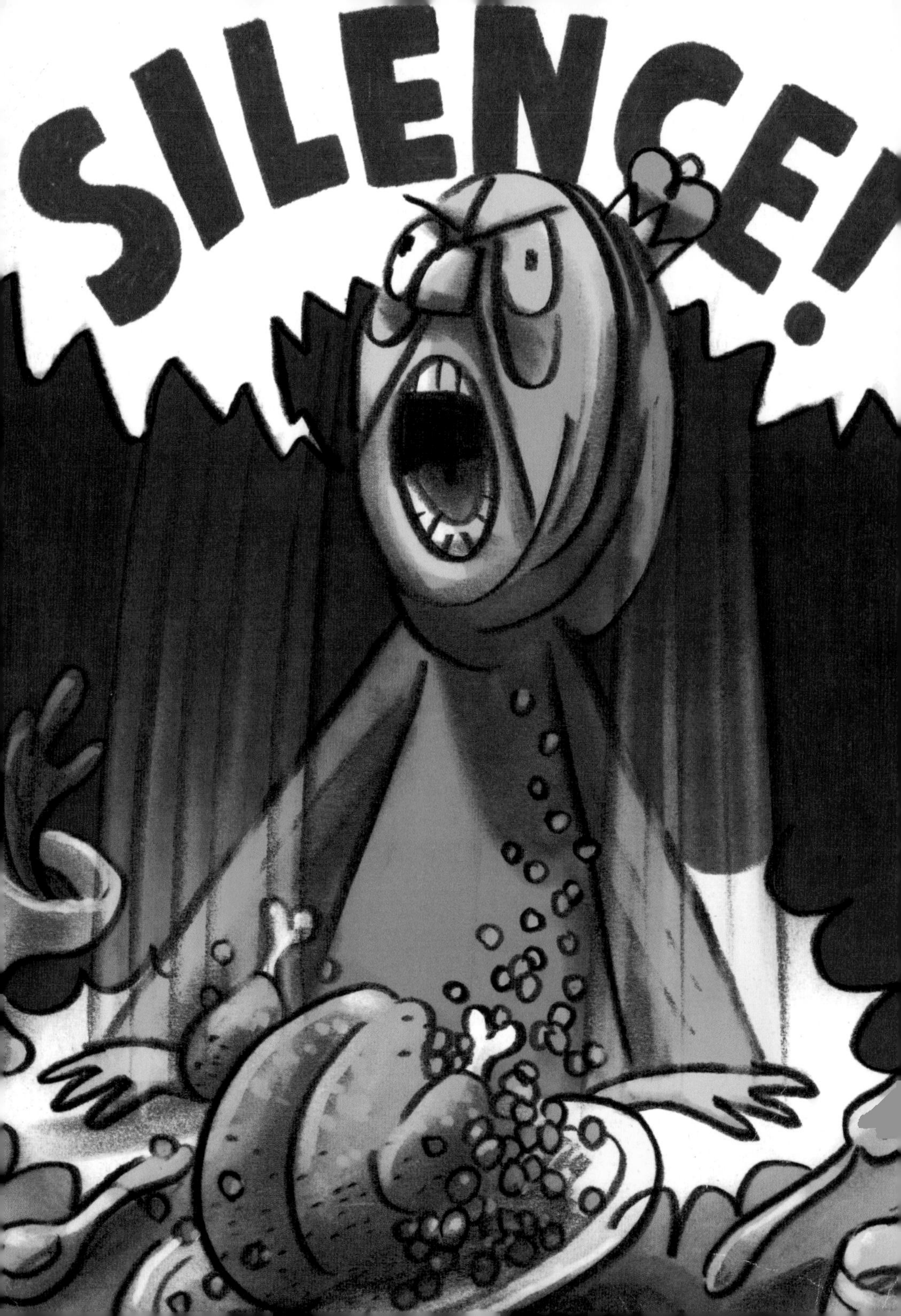
SILENCE!

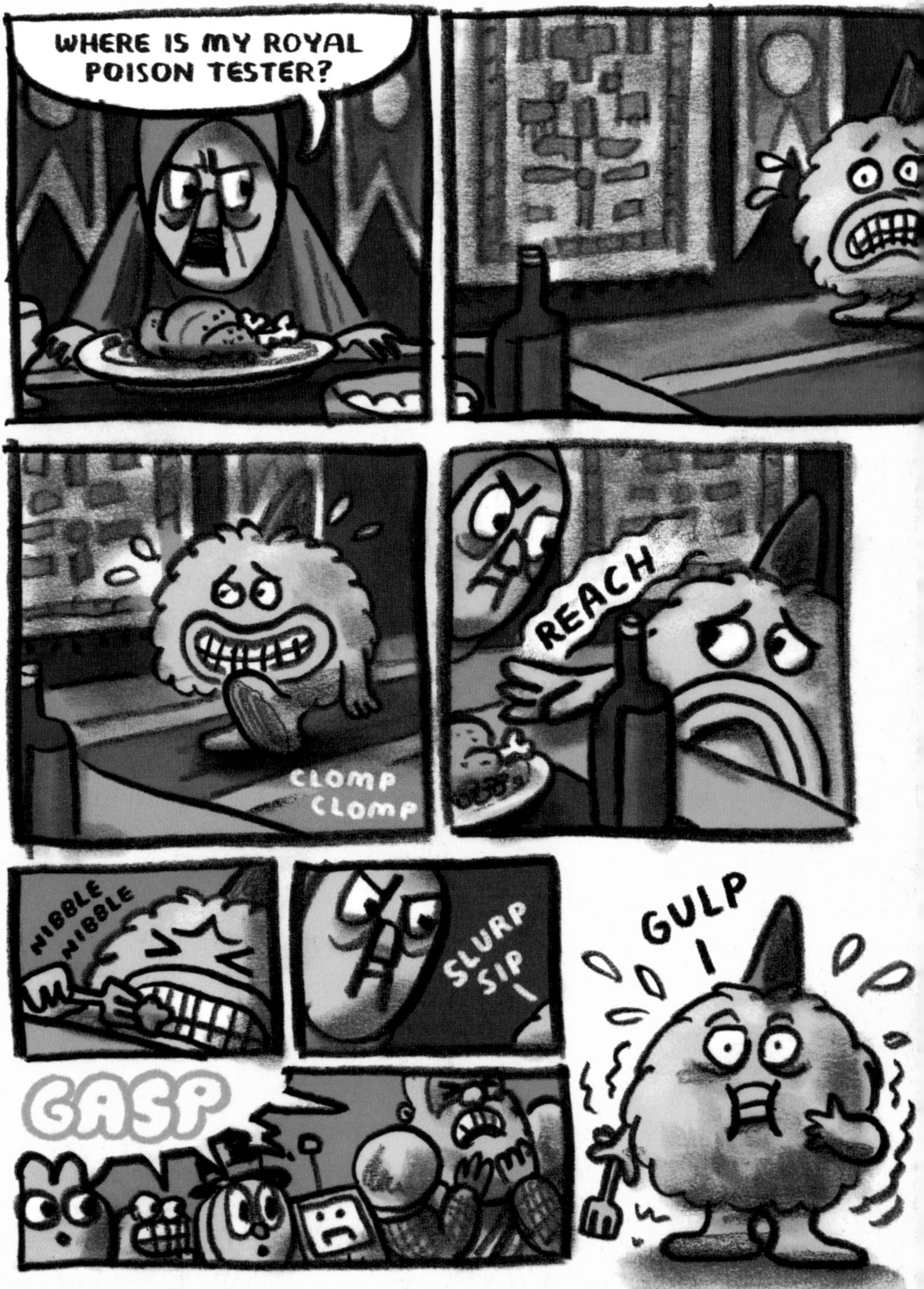
WHERE IS MY ROYAL POISON TESTER?
CLOMP
CLOMP
REACH
NIBBLE
NIBBLE
SLURP
SIP
GULP
GASP

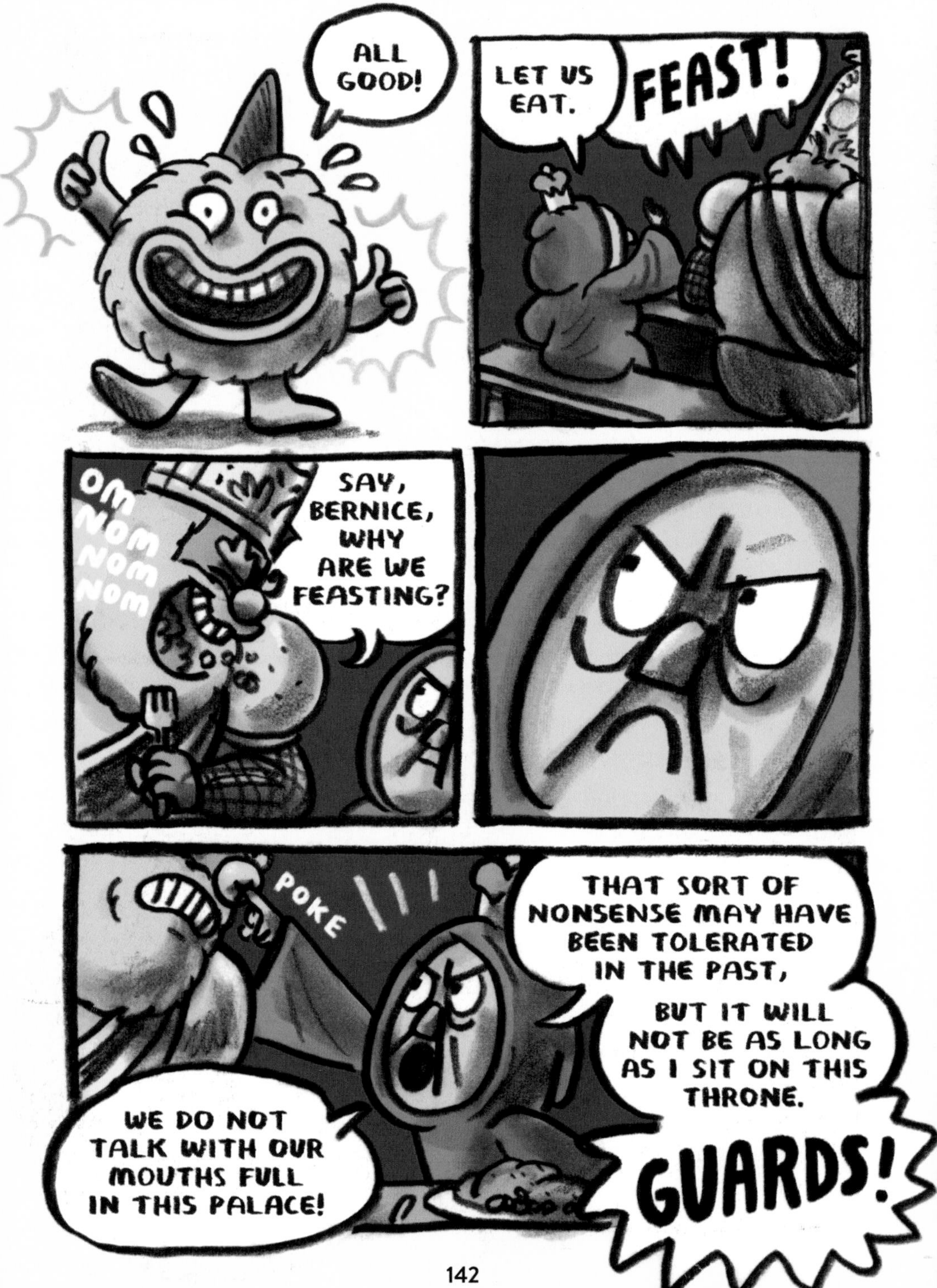
ALL GOOD!
LET US EAT.
FEAST!
OM NOM NOM NOM
SAY, BERNICE, WHY ARE WE FEASTING?
POKE
WE DO NOT TALK WITH OUR MOUTHS FULL IN THIS PALACE!
THAT SORT OF NONSENSE MAY HAVE BEEN TOLERATED IN THE PAST,
BUT IT WILL NOT BE AS LONG AS I SIT ON THIS THRONE.
GUARDS!

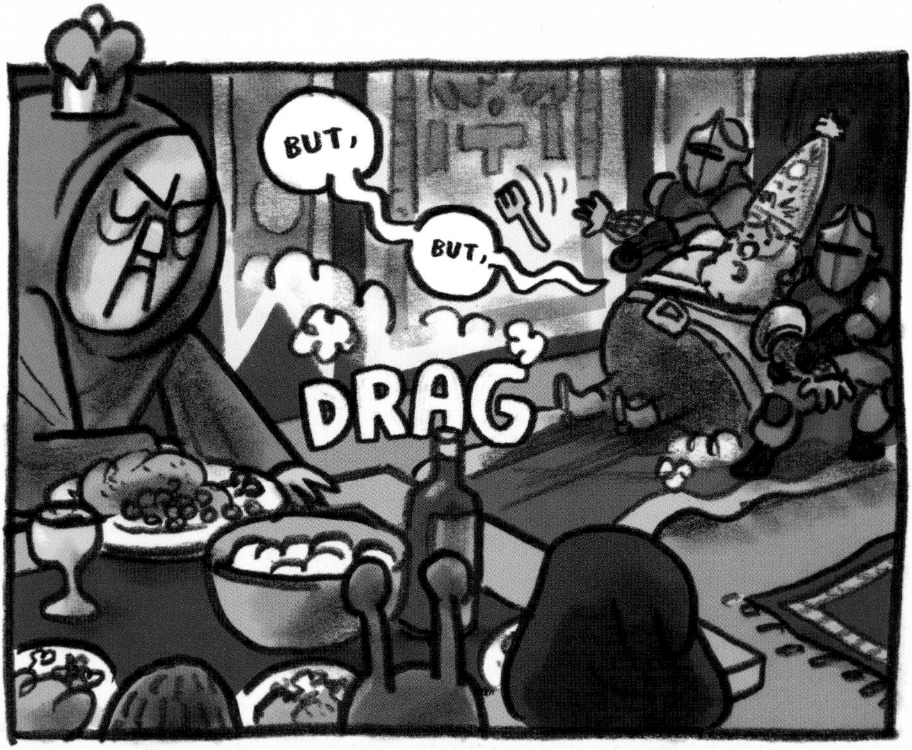
BUT,
BUT,
DRAG

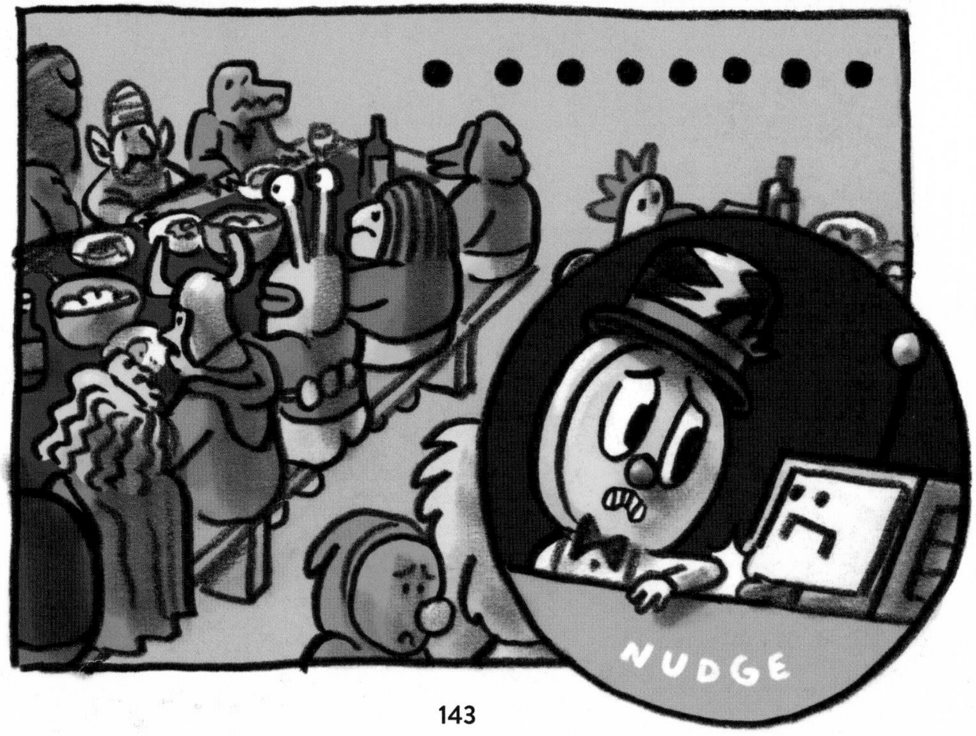
........
NUDGE

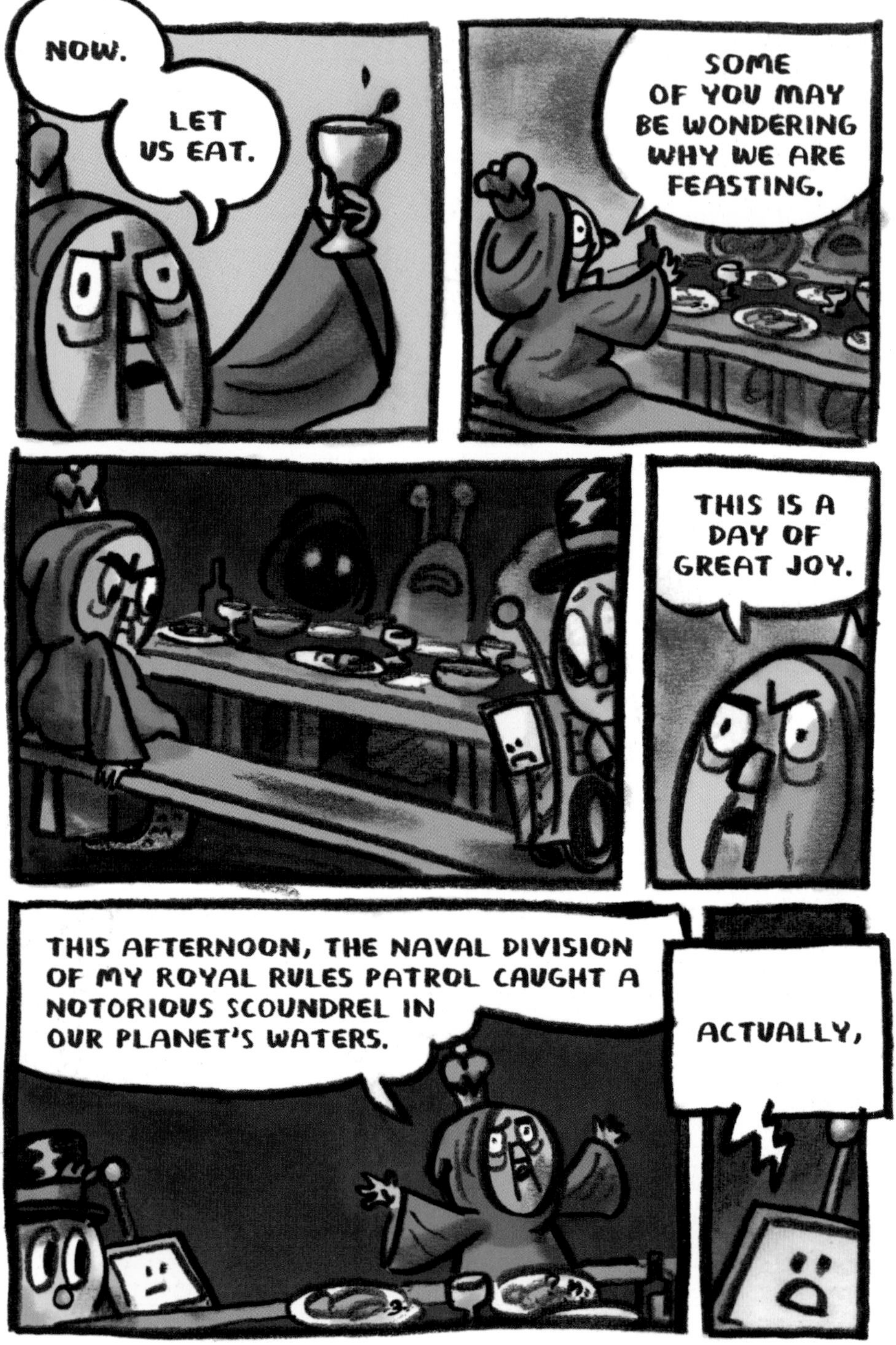
NOW.
LET US EAT.
SOME OF YOU MAY BE WONDERING WHY WE ARE FEASTING.
THIS IS A DAY OF GREAT JOY.
THIS AFTERNOON, THE NAVAL DIVISION OF MY ROYAL RULES PATROL CAUGHT A NOTORIOUS SCOUNDREL IN OUR PLANET'S WATERS.
ACTUALLY,

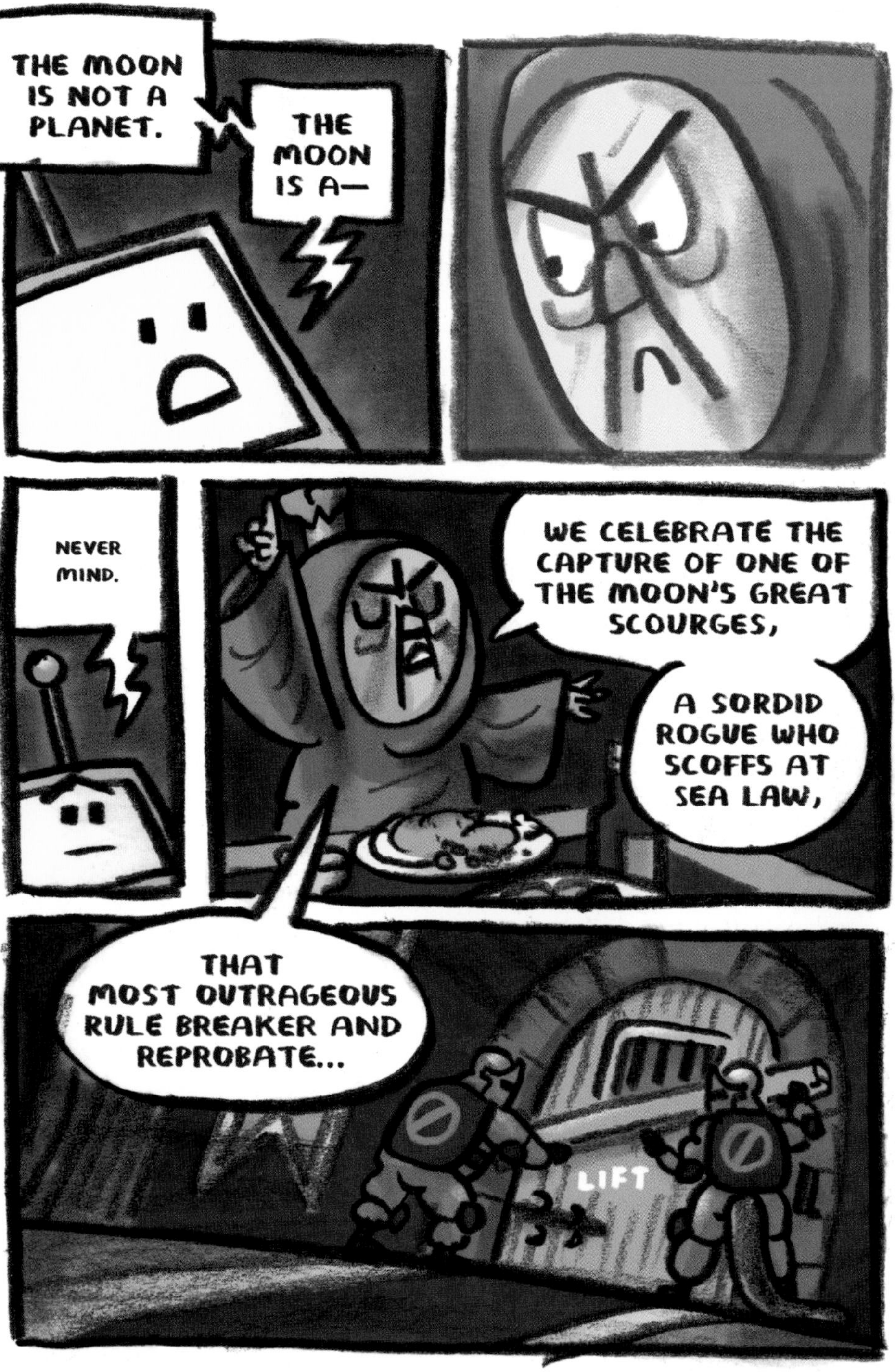
THE MOON IS NOT A PLANET.
THE MOON IS A—
NEVER MIND.
WE CELEBRATE THE CAPTURE OF ONE OF THE MOON'S GREAT SCOURGES,
A SORDID ROGUE WHO SCOFFS AT SEA LAW,
THAT MOST OUTRAGEOUS RULE BREAKER AND REPROBATE...
LIFT

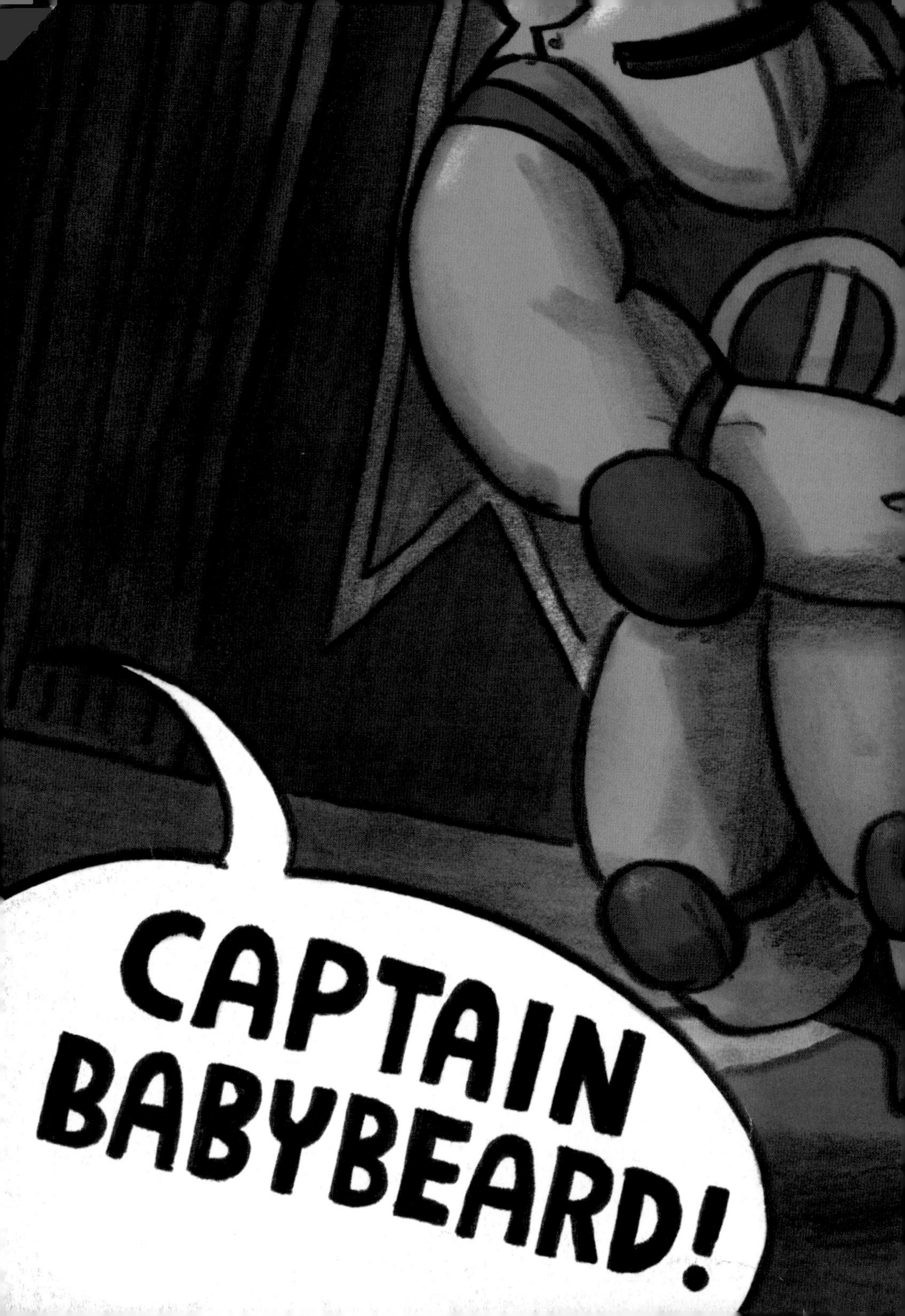
CAPTAIN BABYBEARD!

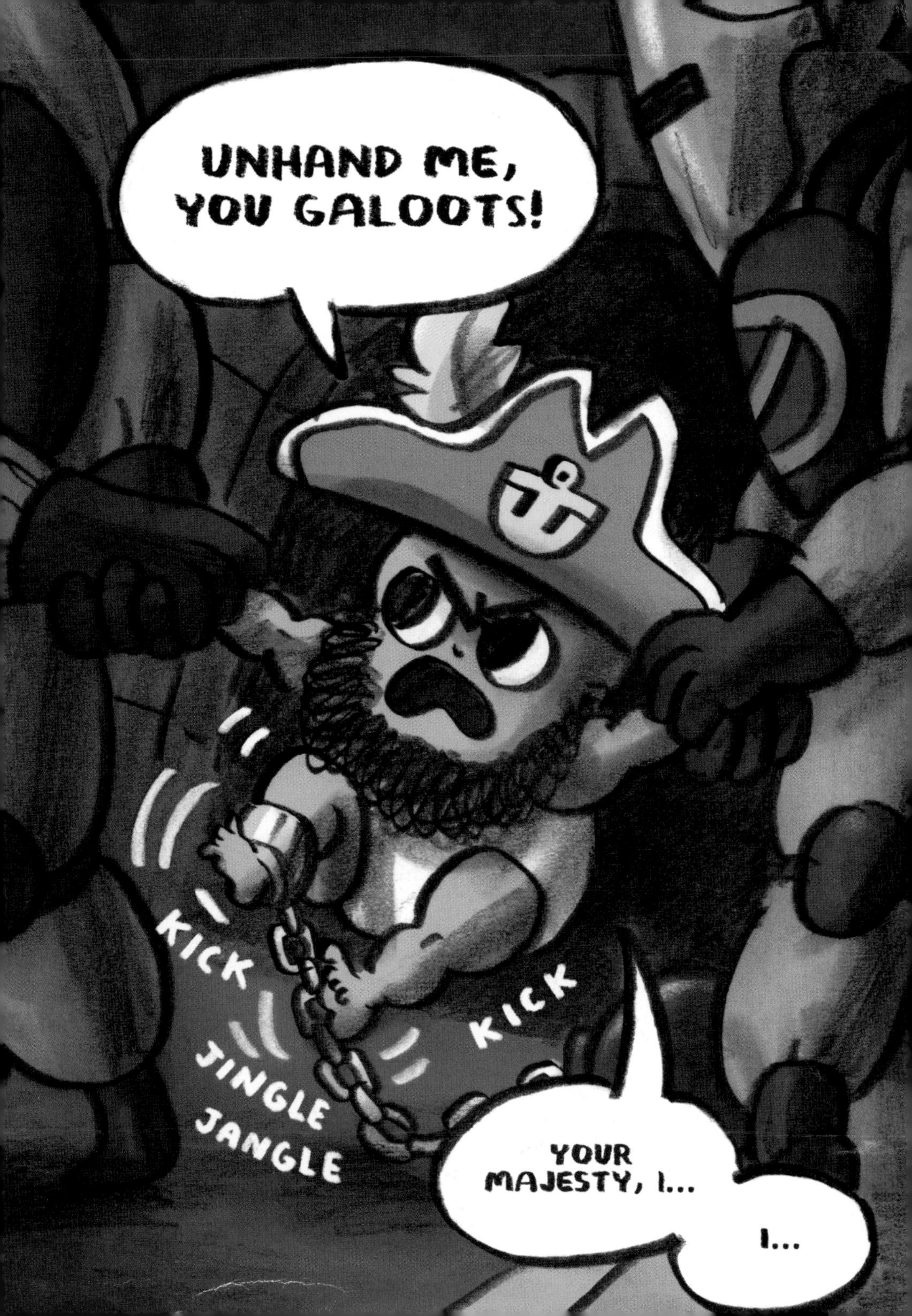
UNHAND ME, YOU GALOOTS!
KICK
KICK
JINGLE
JANGLE
YOUR MAJESTY, I...
I...

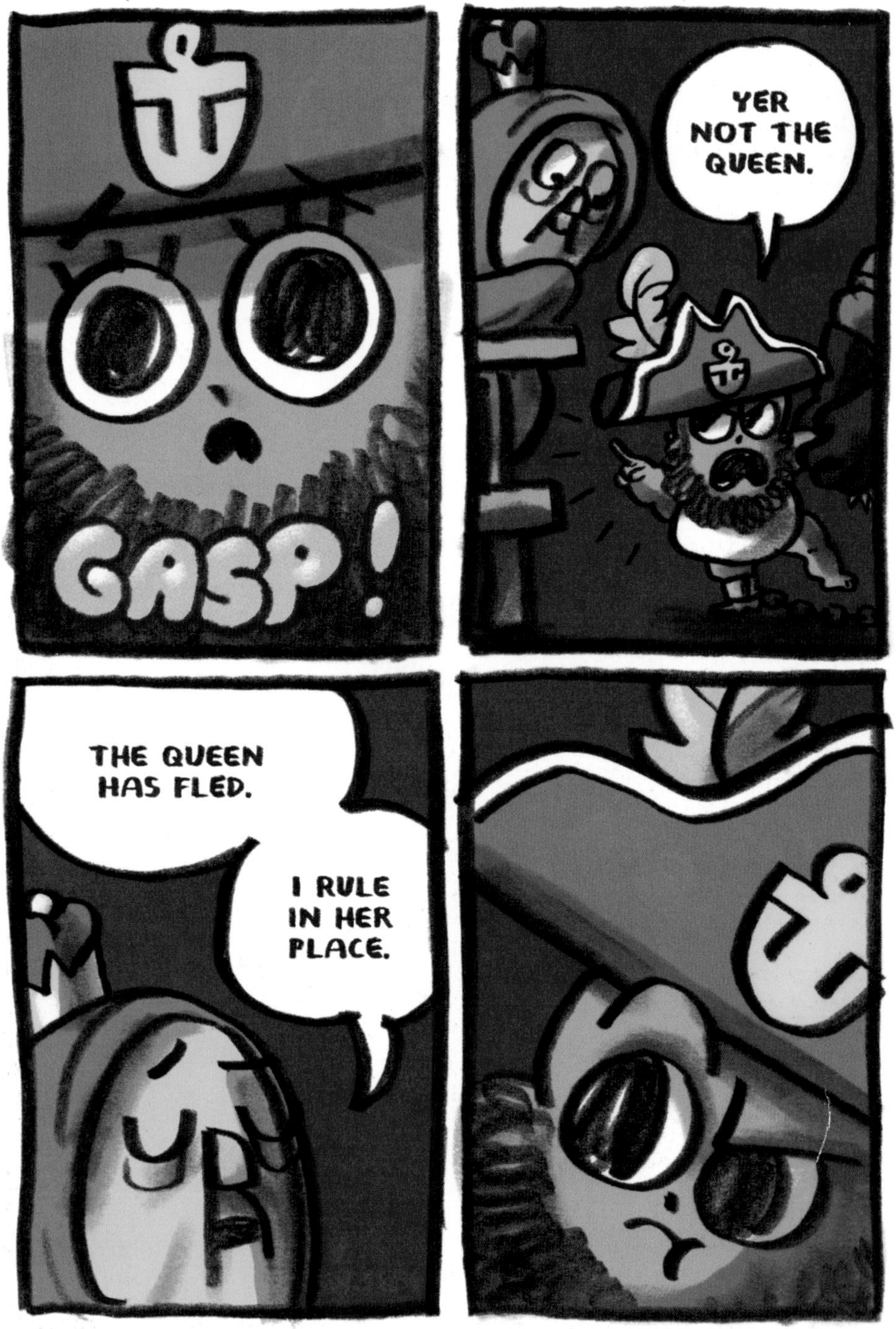
GASP!
YER NOT THE QUEEN.
THE QUEEN HAS FLED.
I RULE IN HER PLACE.

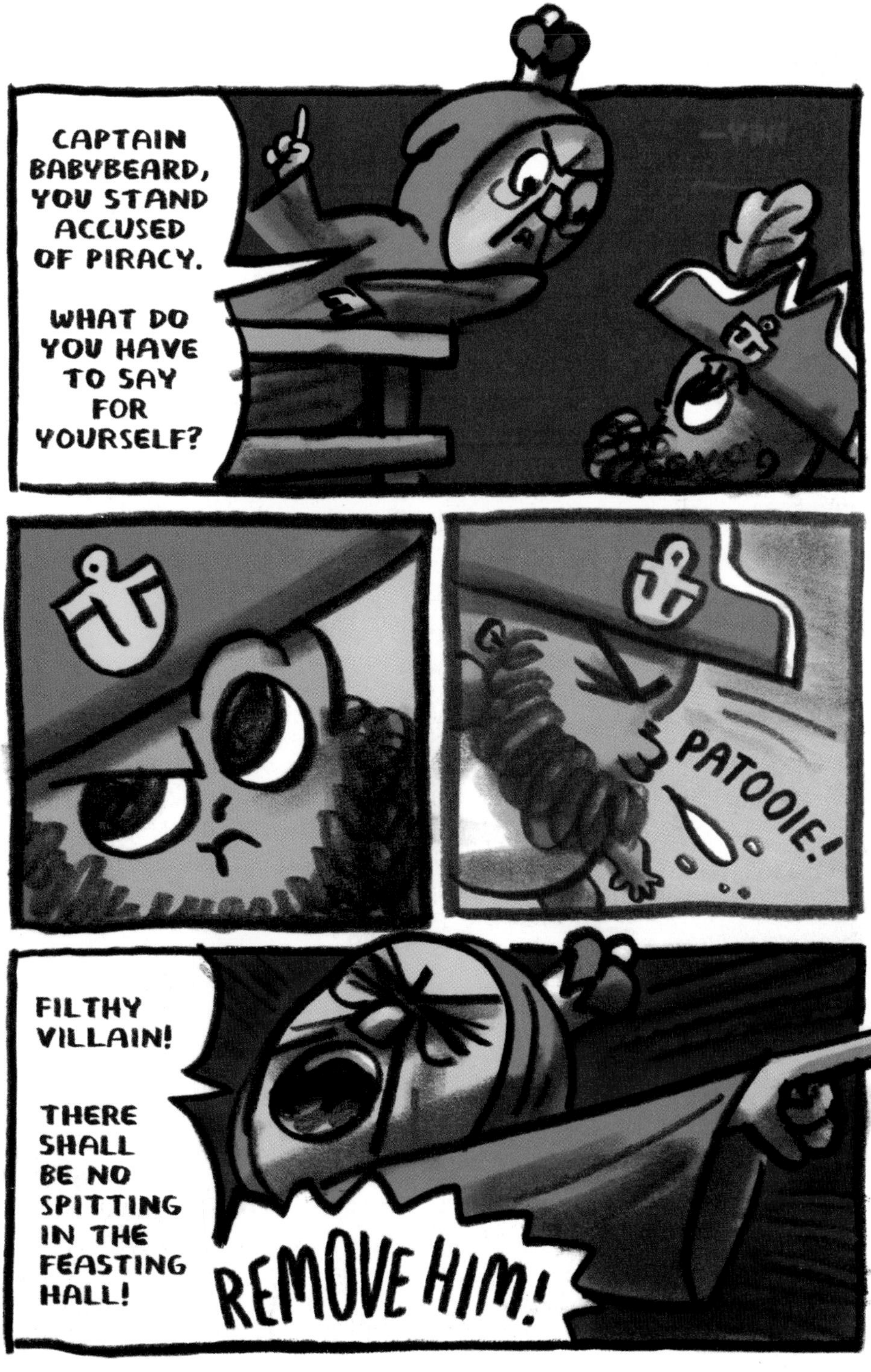
CAPTAIN BABYBEARD, YOU STAND ACCUSED OF PIRACY.
WHAT DO YOU HAVE TO SAY FOR YOURSELF?
PATOOIE!
FILTHY VILLAIN!
THERE SHALL BE NO SPITTING IN THE FEASTING HALL!
REMOVE HIM!

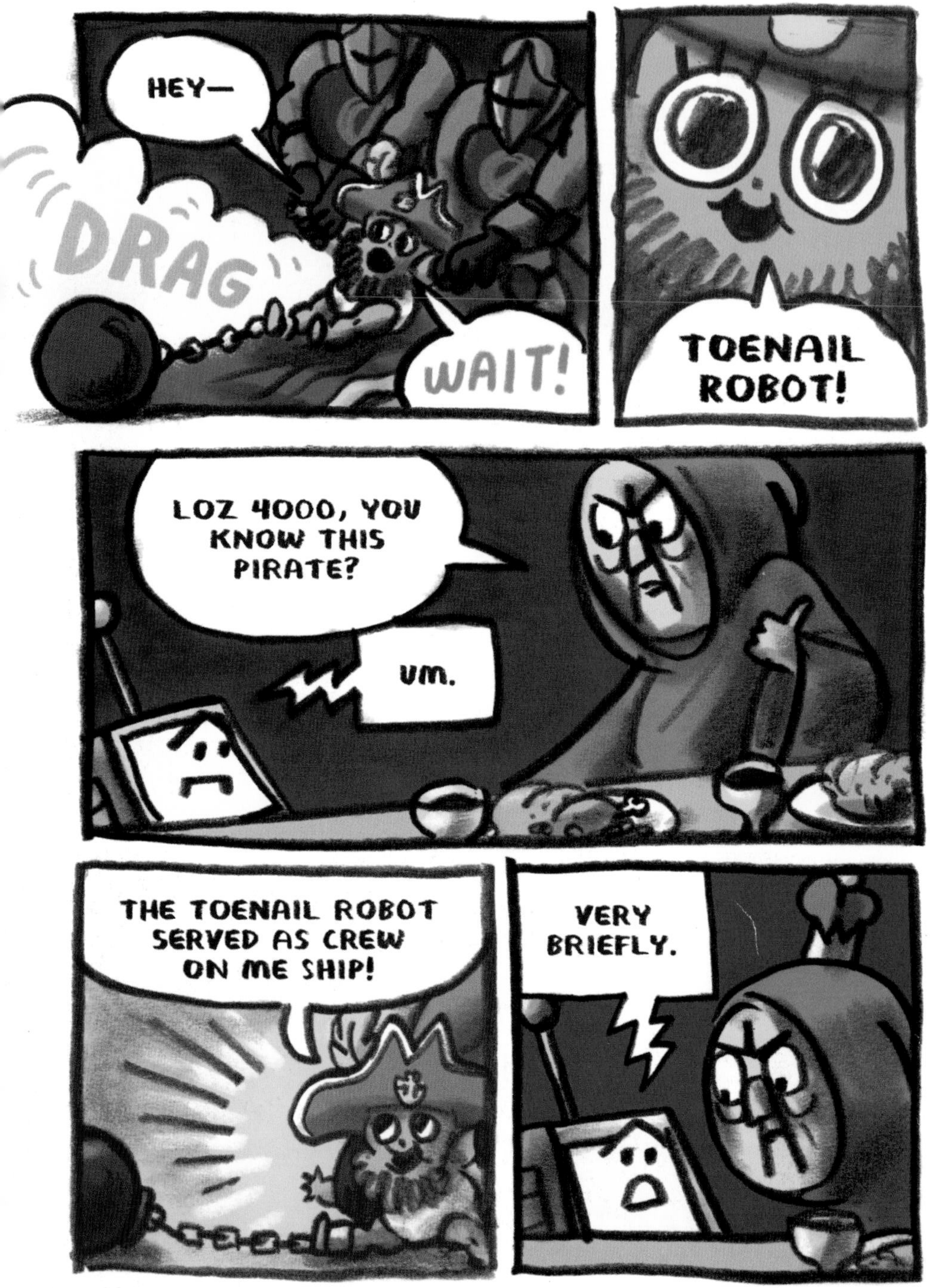
HEY—
DRAG
WAIT!
TOENAIL ROBOT!
LOZ 4000, YOU KNOW THIS PIRATE?
UM.
THE TOENAIL ROBOT SERVED AS CREW ON ME SHIP!
VERY BRIEFLY.

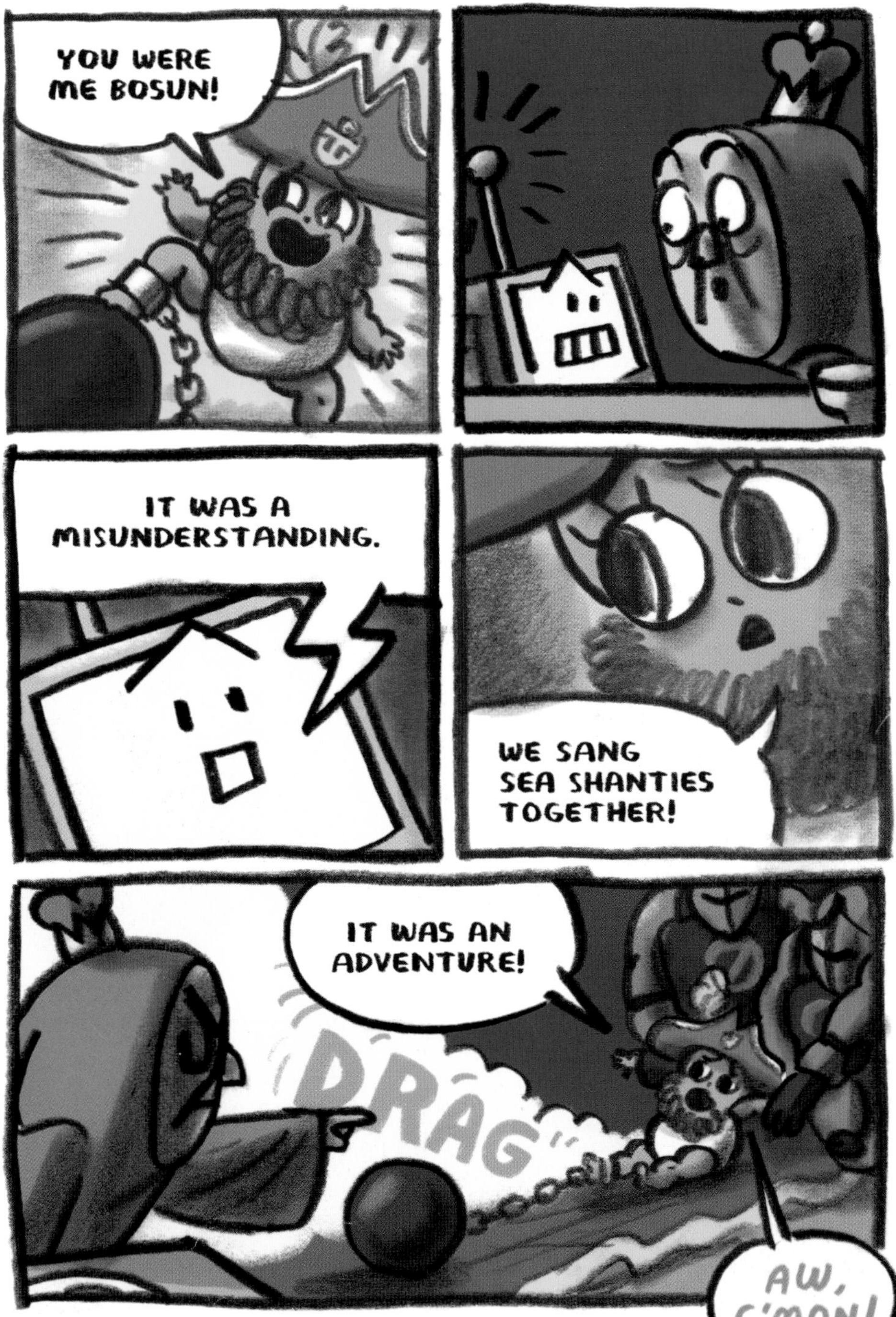
YOU WERE ME BOSUN!
IT WAS A MISUNDERSTANDING.
WE SANG SEA SHANTIES TOGETHER!
IT WAS AN ADVENTURE!
DRAG
AW, C'MON!

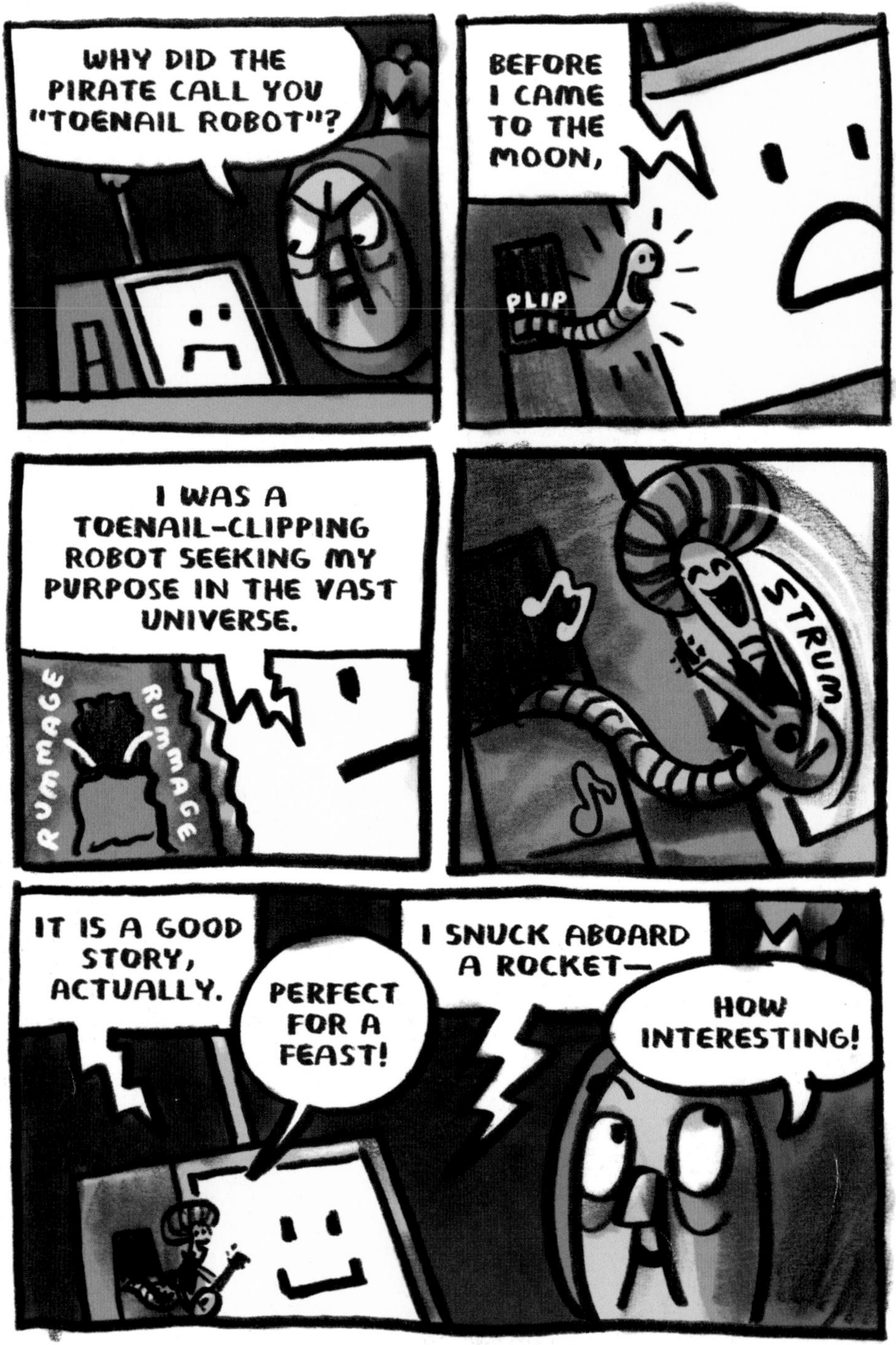
WHY DID THE PIRATE CALL YOU "TOENAIL ROBOT"?
BEFORE I CAME TO THE MOON,
PLIP
I WAS A TOENAIL-CLIPPING ROBOT SEEKING MY PURPOSE IN THE VAST UNIVERSE.
RUMMAGE
RUMMAGE
STRUM
IT IS A GOOD STORY, ACTUALLY.
PERFECT FOR A FEAST!
I SNUCK ABOARD A ROCKET—
HOW INTERESTING!

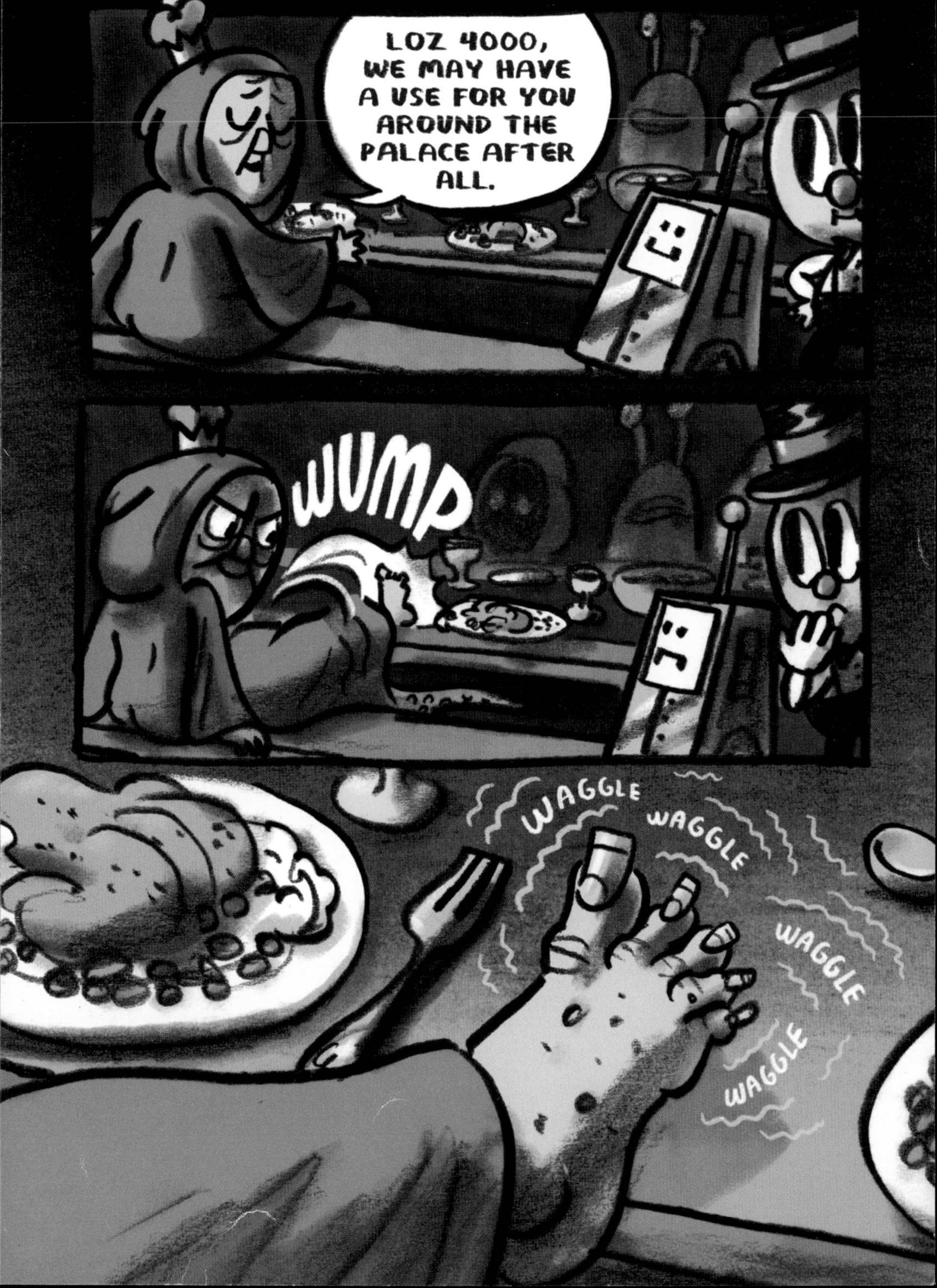
LOZ 4000, WE MAY HAVE A USE FOR YOU AROUND THE PALACE AFTER ALL.
WUMP
WAGGLE
WAGGLE
WAGGLE
WAGGLE

# PSYCHIC FLYING EYEBALLS OF DEATH

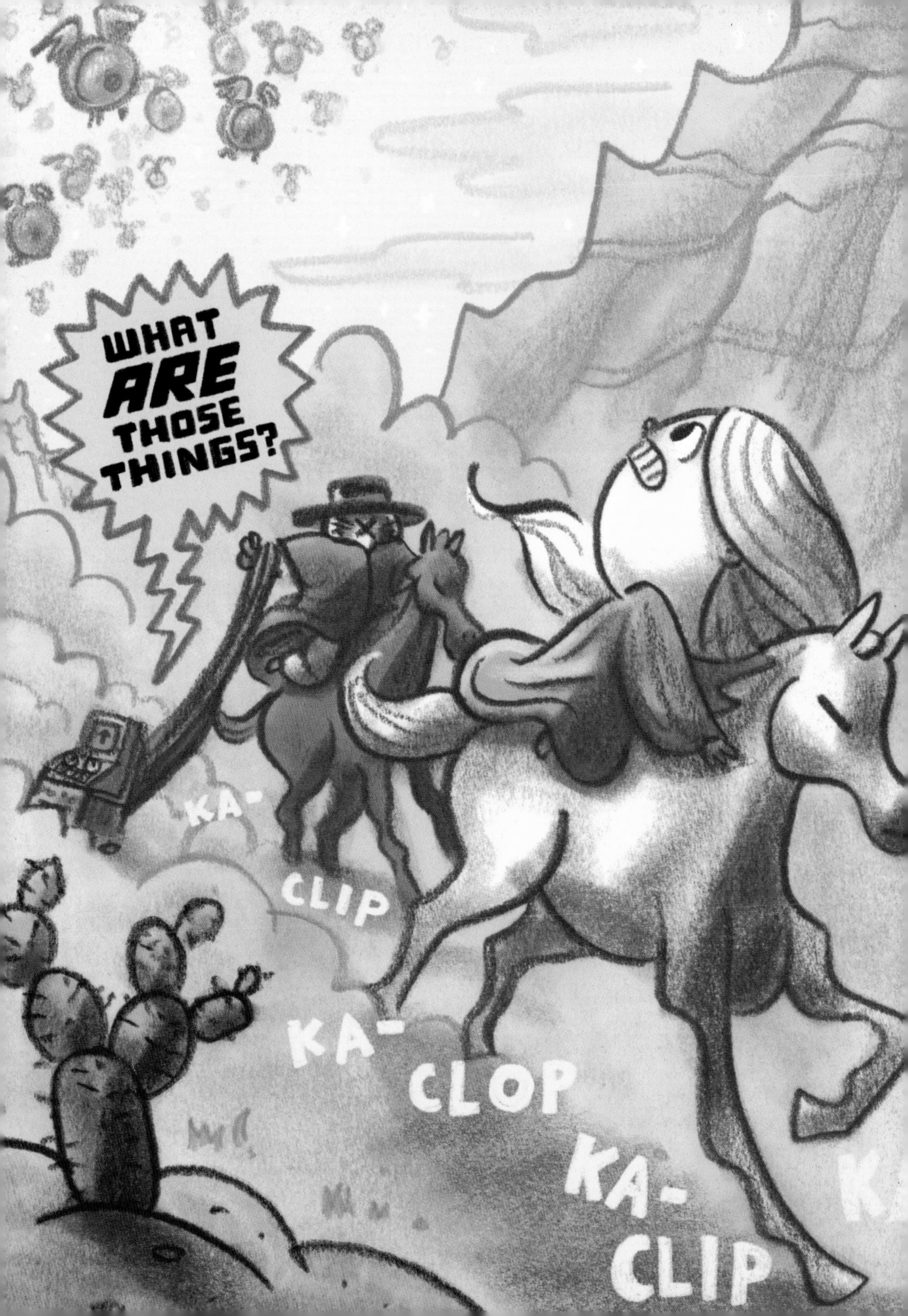
WHAT ARE THOSE THINGS?
KA-
CLIP
KA-
CLOP
KA-
CLIP

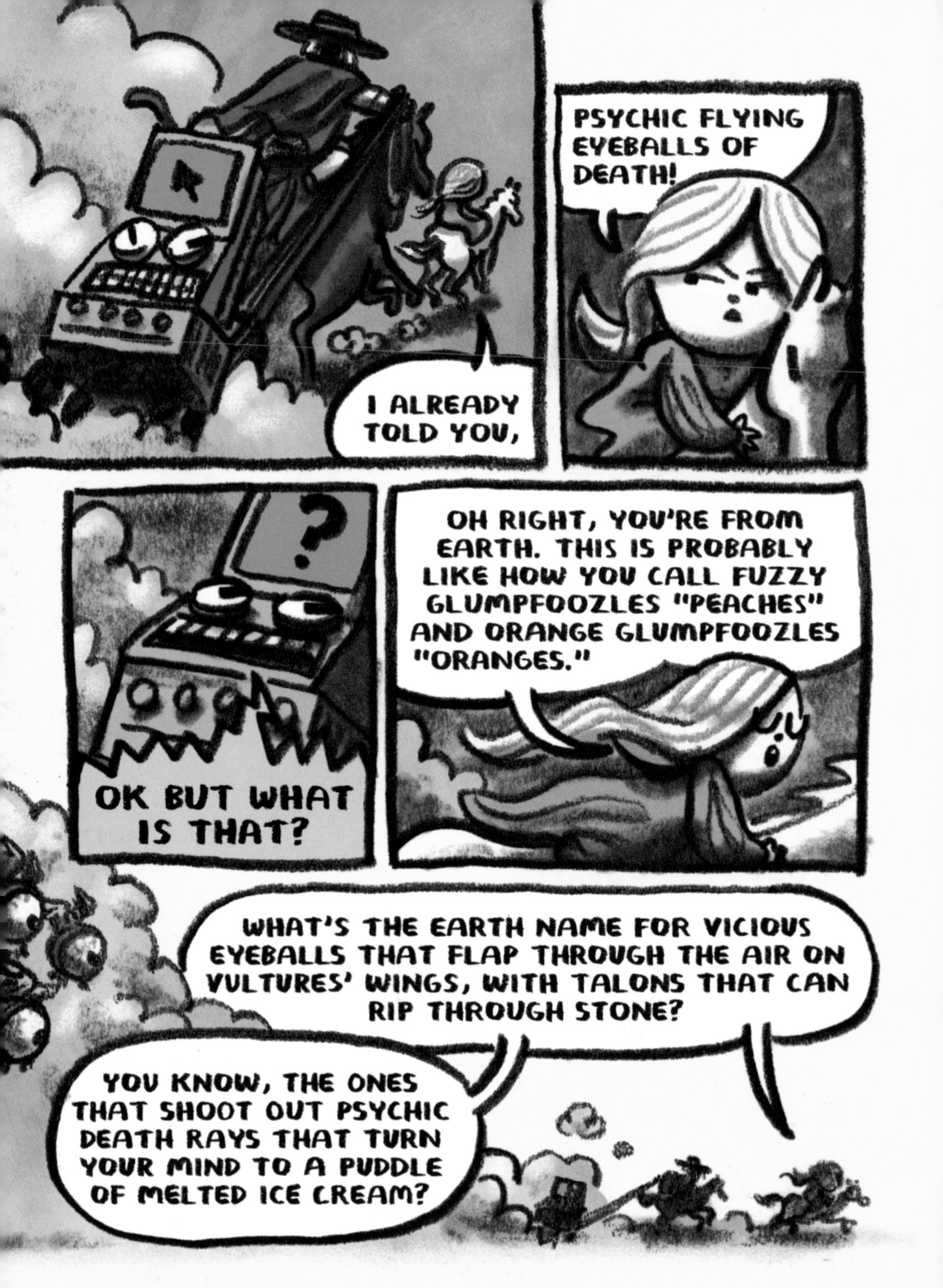
I ALREADY TOLD YOU,
PSYCHIC FLYING EYEBALLS OF DEATH!
OK BUT WHAT IS THAT?
OH RIGHT, YOU'RE FROM EARTH. THIS IS PROBABLY LIKE HOW YOU CALL FUZZY GLUMPFOOZLES "PEACHES" AND ORANGE GLUMPFOOZLES "ORANGES."
WHAT'S THE EARTH NAME FOR VICIOUS EYEBALLS THAT FLAP THROUGH THE AIR ON VULTURES' WINGS, WITH TALONS THAT CAN RIP THROUGH STONE?
YOU KNOW, THE ONES THAT SHOOT OUT PSYCHIC DEATH RAYS THAT TURN YOUR MIND TO A PUDDLE OF MELTED ICE CREAM?

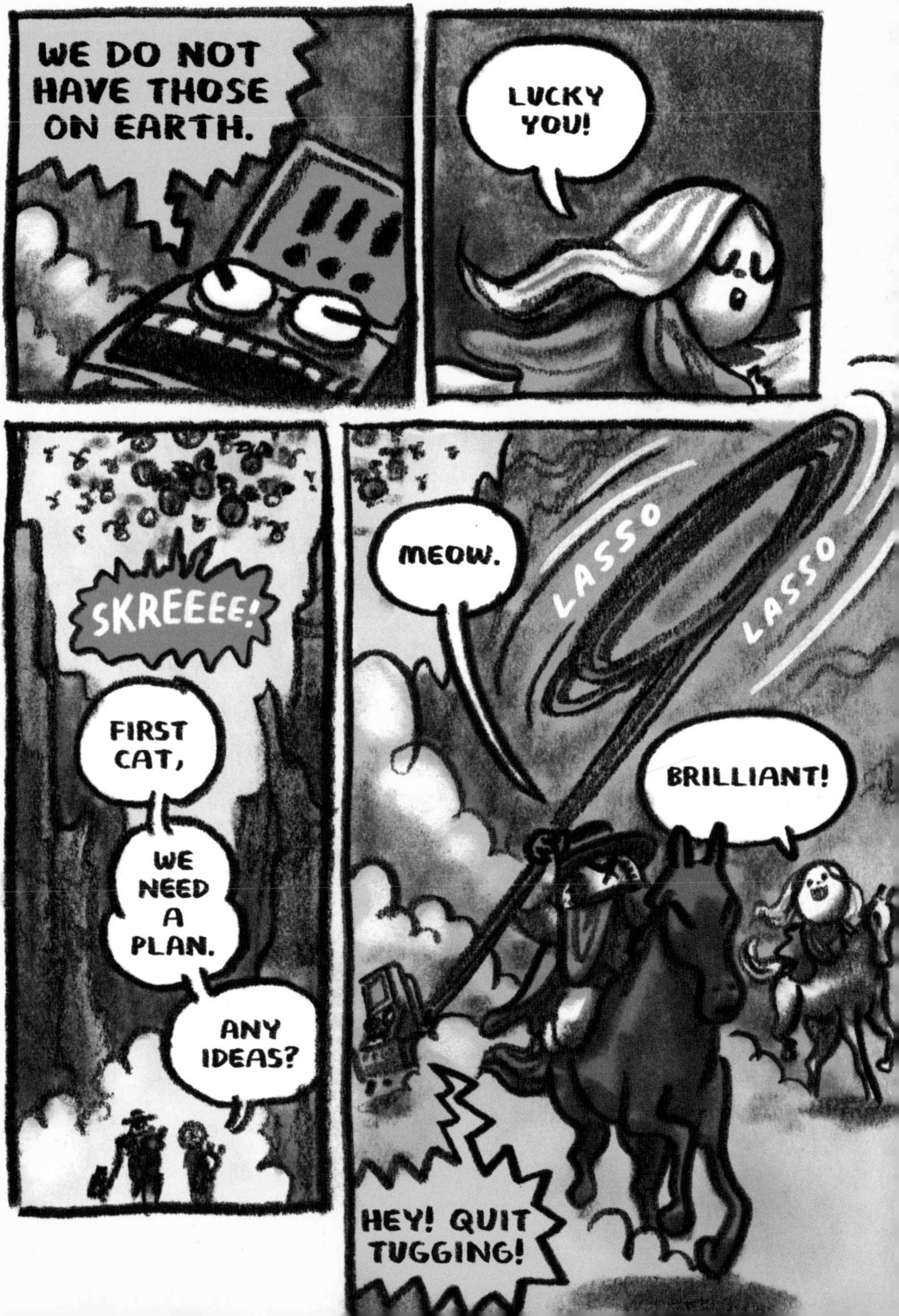

WE DO NOT HAVE THOSE ON EARTH.
LUCKY YOU!
SKREEEEE!
FIRST CAT,
WE NEED A PLAN.
ANY IDEAS?
MEOW.
LASSO
LASSO
BRILLIANT!
HEY! QUIT TUGGING!

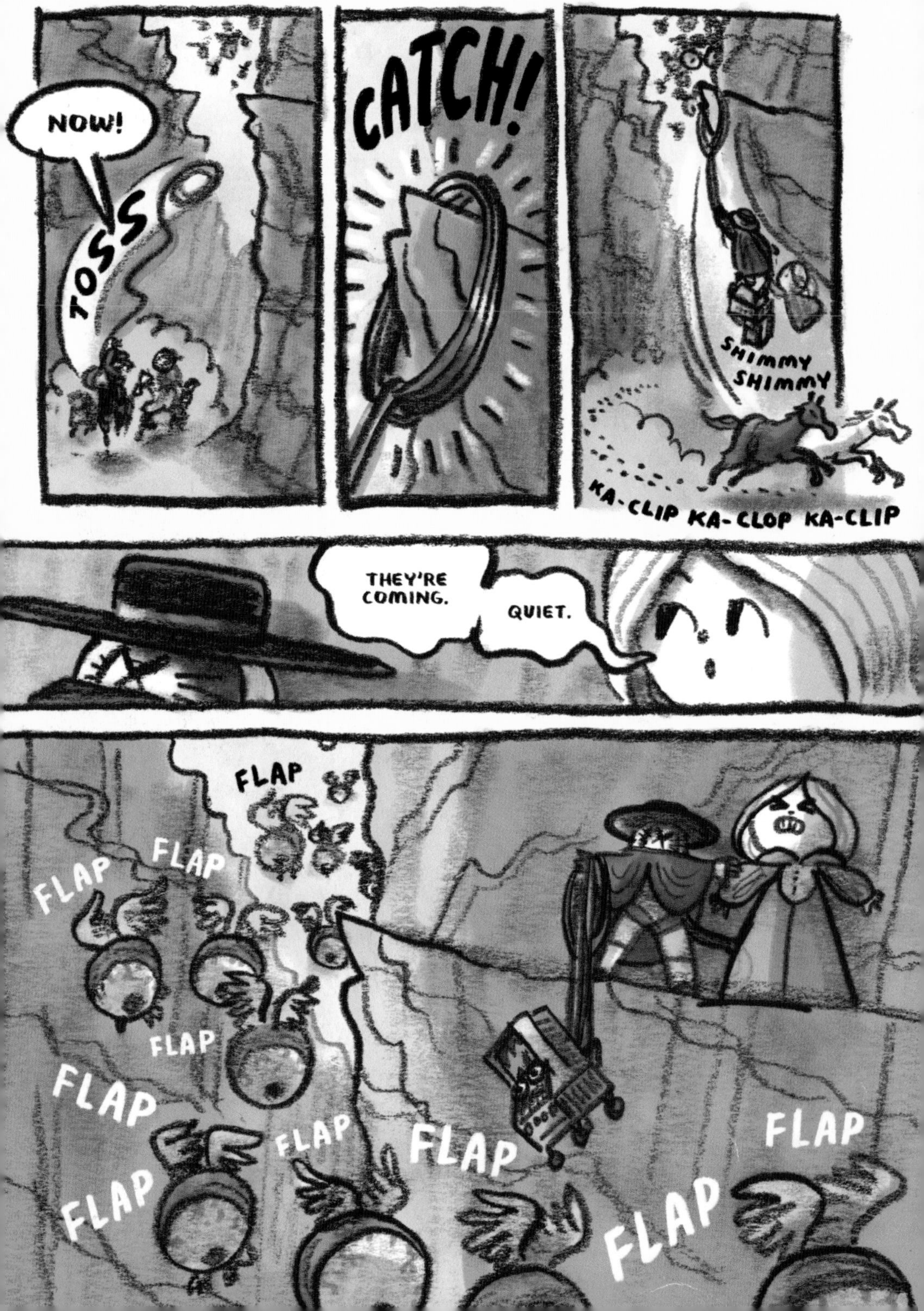
NOW!
TOSS
CATCH!
SHIMMY
SHIMMY
KA-CLIP KA-CLOP KA-CLIP
THEY'RE COMING.
QUIET.
FLAP
FLAP
FLAP
FLAP
FLAP
FLAP
FLAP
FLAP
FLAP
FLAP

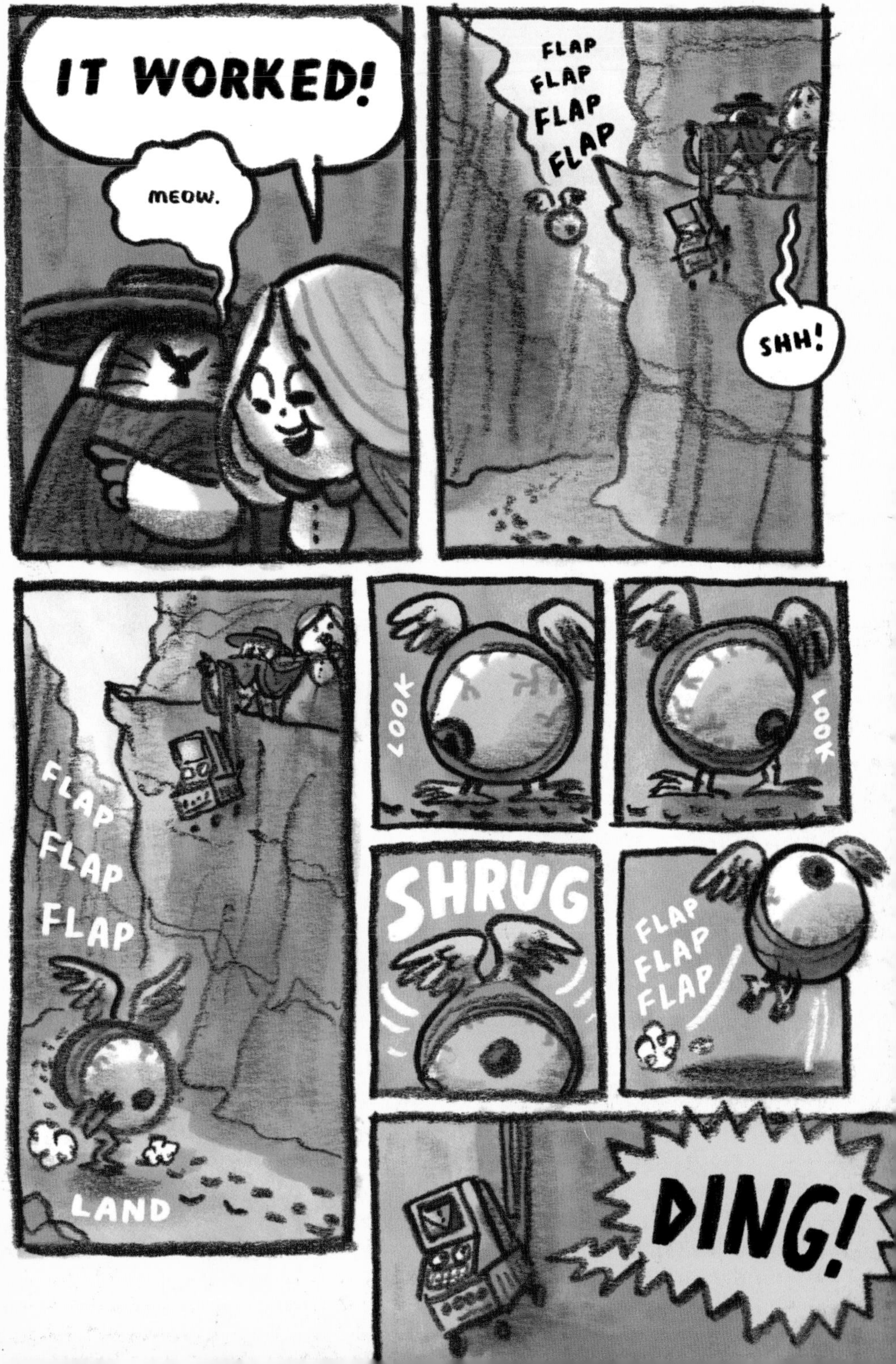
IT WORKED!
MEOW.
FLAP
FLAP
FLAP
FLAP
SHH!
FLAP
FLAP
FLAP
LAND
LOOK
LOOK
SHRUG
FLAP
FLAP
FLAP
DING!

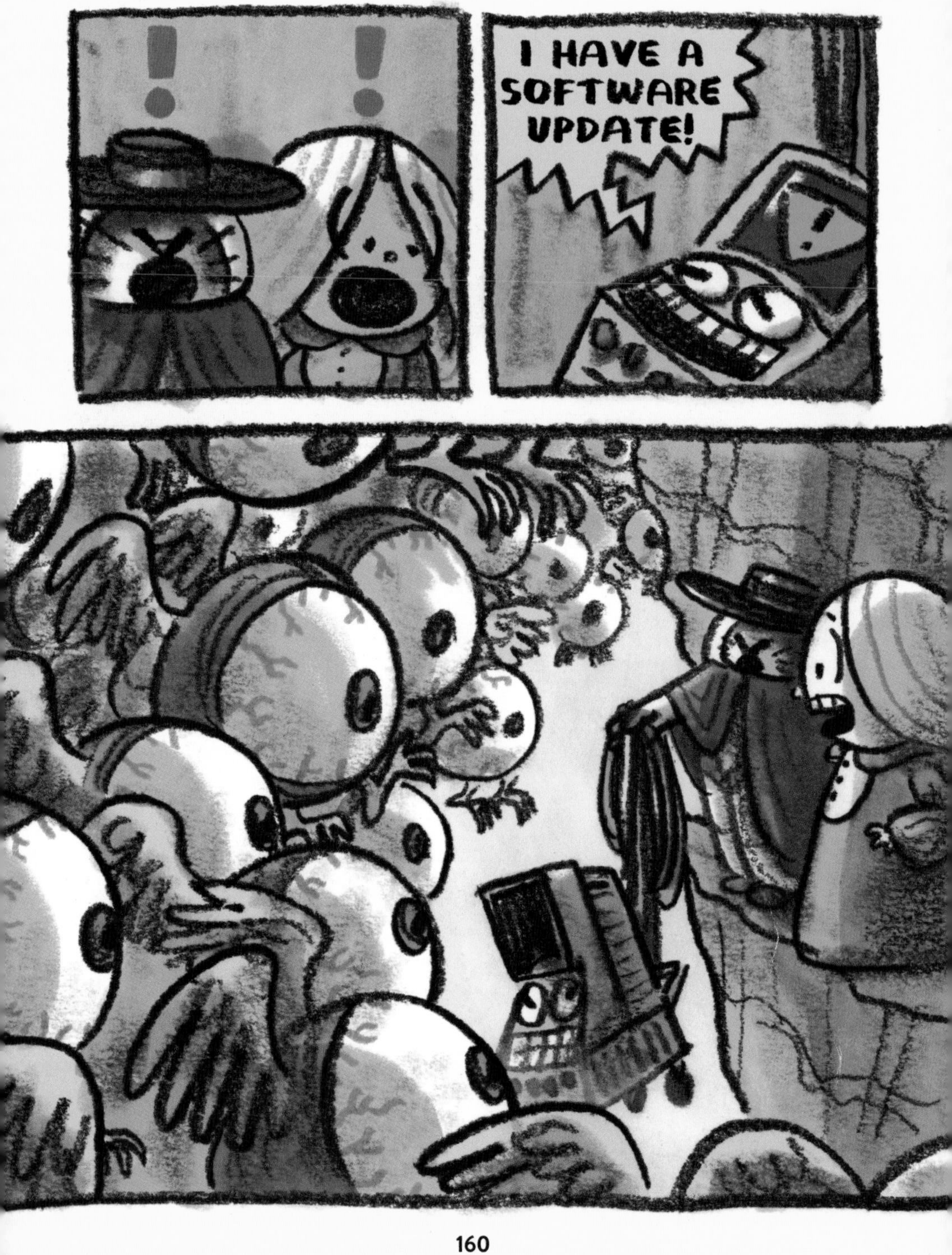
I HAVE A SOFTWARE UPDATE!

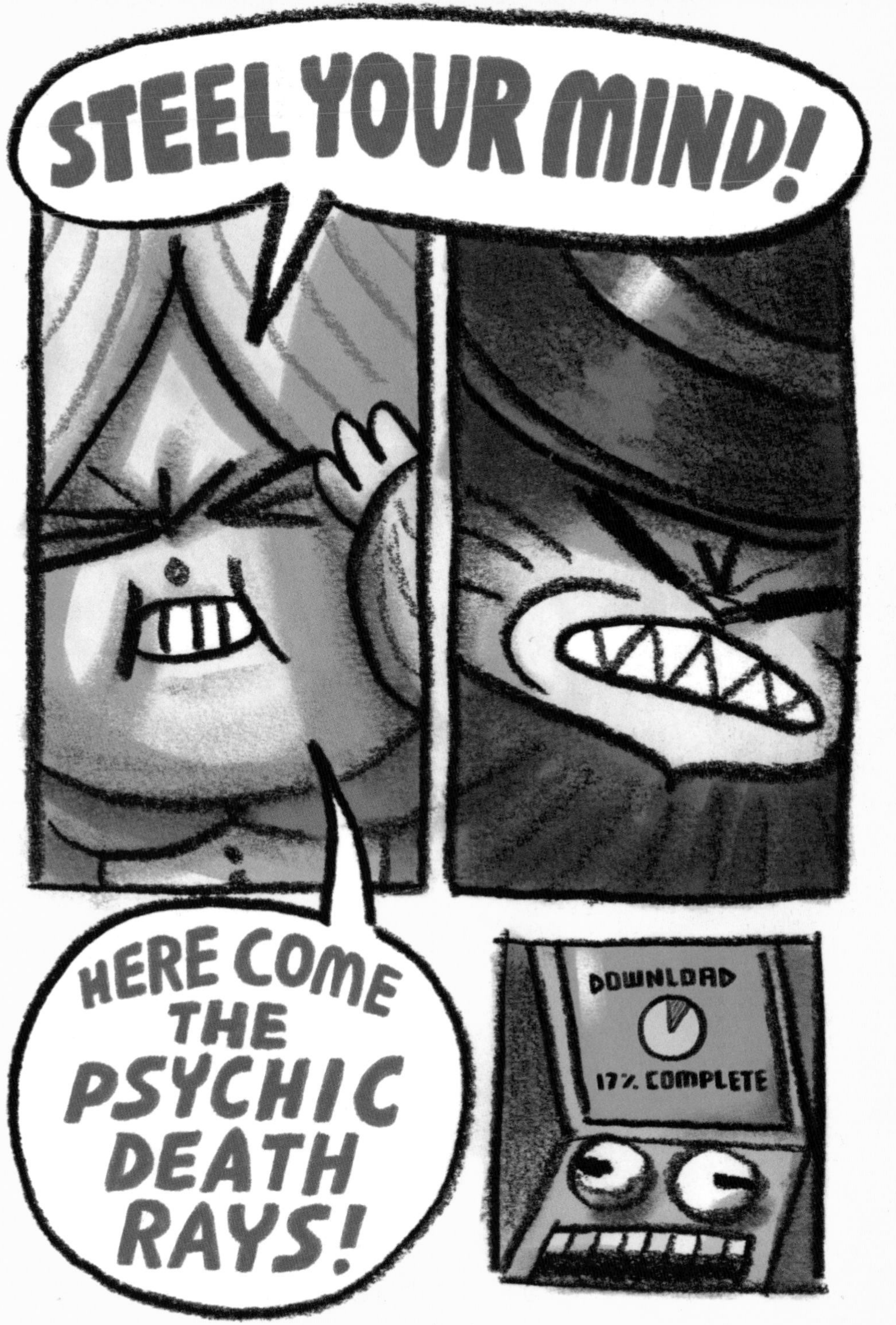
STEEL YOUR MIND!
HERE COME THE PSYCHIC DEATH RAYS!
DOWNLOAD
17% COMPLETE

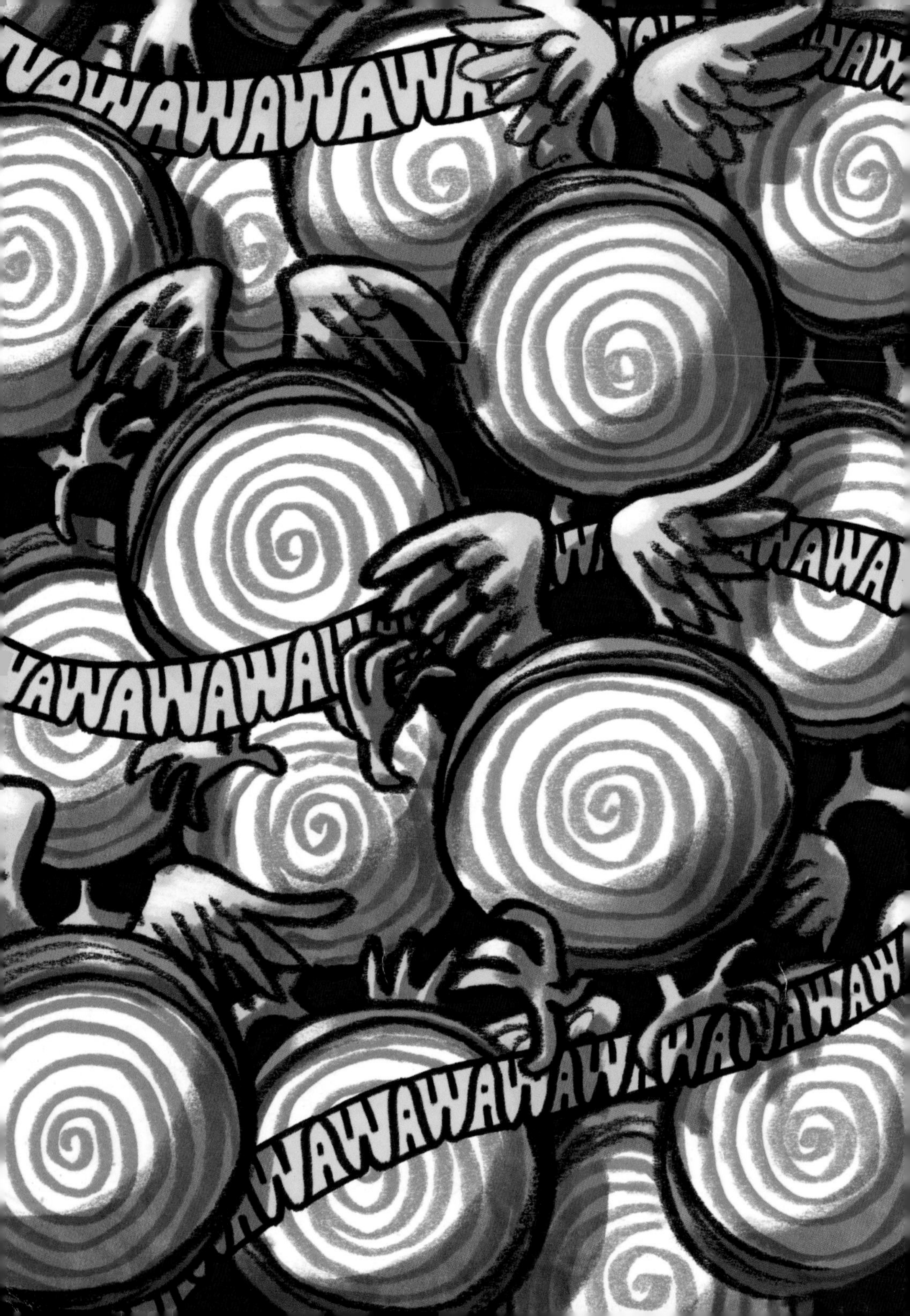
WAWAWAWAWA
WAWAWAWA
AWAWA
WAWAWAWAWAWAWAWA

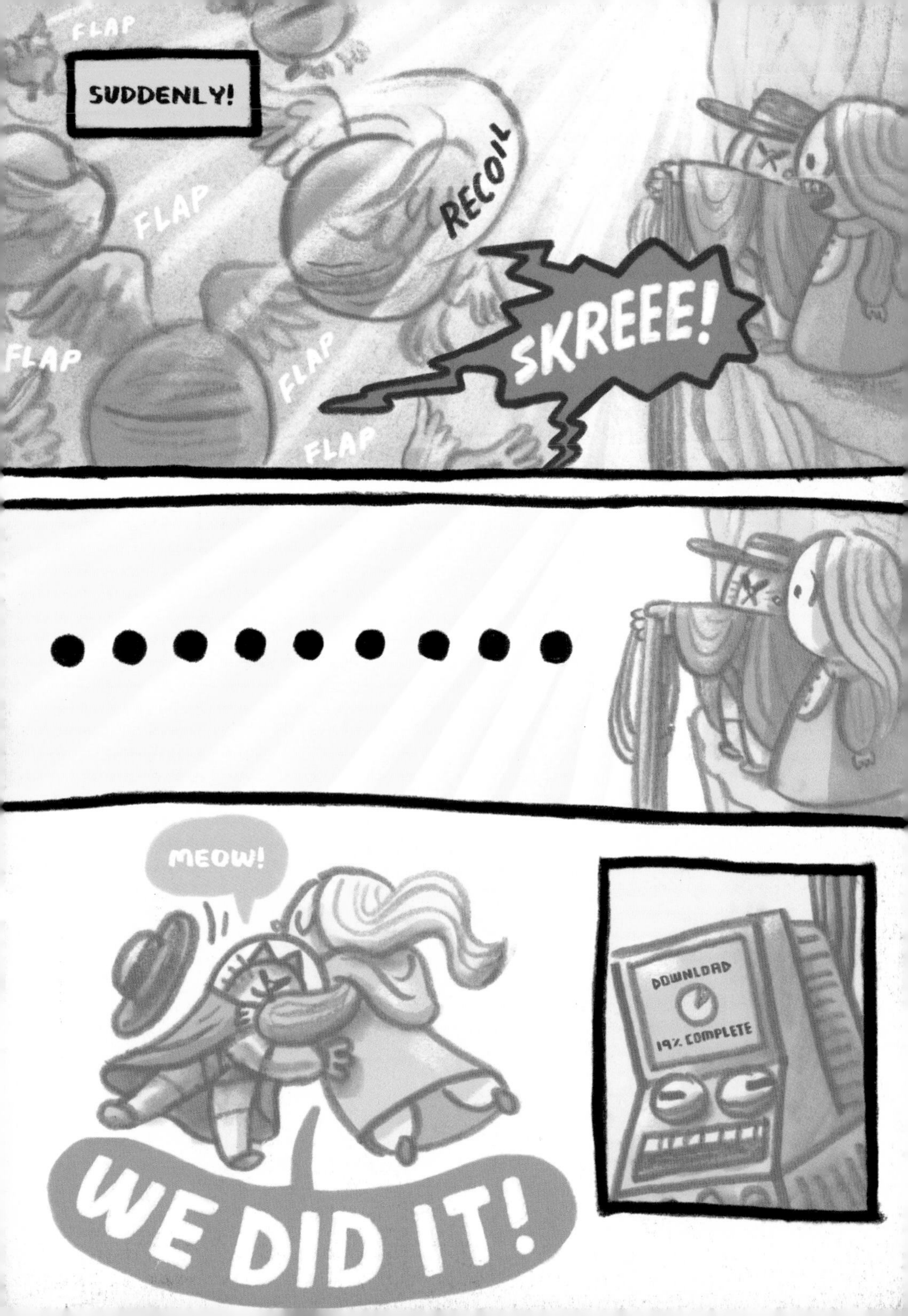
FLAP
SUDDENLY!
FLAP
RECOIL
SKREEEE!
FLAP
FLAP
FLAP
.........
MEOW!
WE DID IT!
DOWNLOAD
19% COMPLETE

WAIT, WHAT DID WE DO?

MEOW.

OF COURSE!

IT'S HIGH NOON!

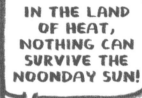IN THE LAND OF HEAT, NOTHING CAN SURVIVE THE NOONDAY SUN!

● ● ●

OH BOTHER.

WE HAVE TO GET MOVING.

COMPUTER, CAN YOU MAP OUR LOCATION?

DOWNLOAD

18% COMPLETE

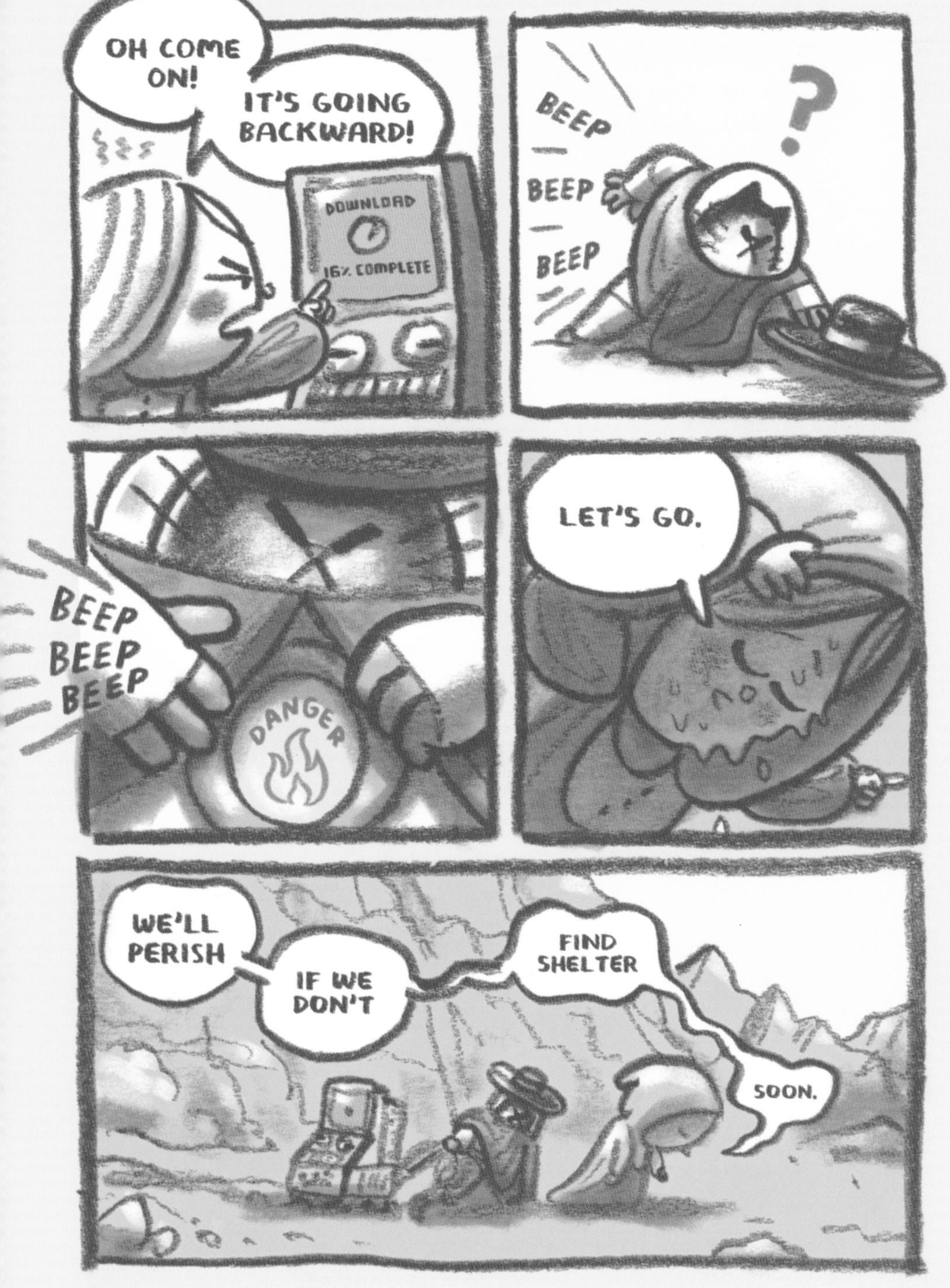
OH COME ON!
IT'S GOING BACKWARD!
DOWNLOAD
16% COMPLETE
BEEP
BEEP
BEEP
?
BEEP
BEEP
BEEP
DANGER
LET'S GO.
WE'LL PERISH
IF WE DON'T
FIND SHELTER
SOON.

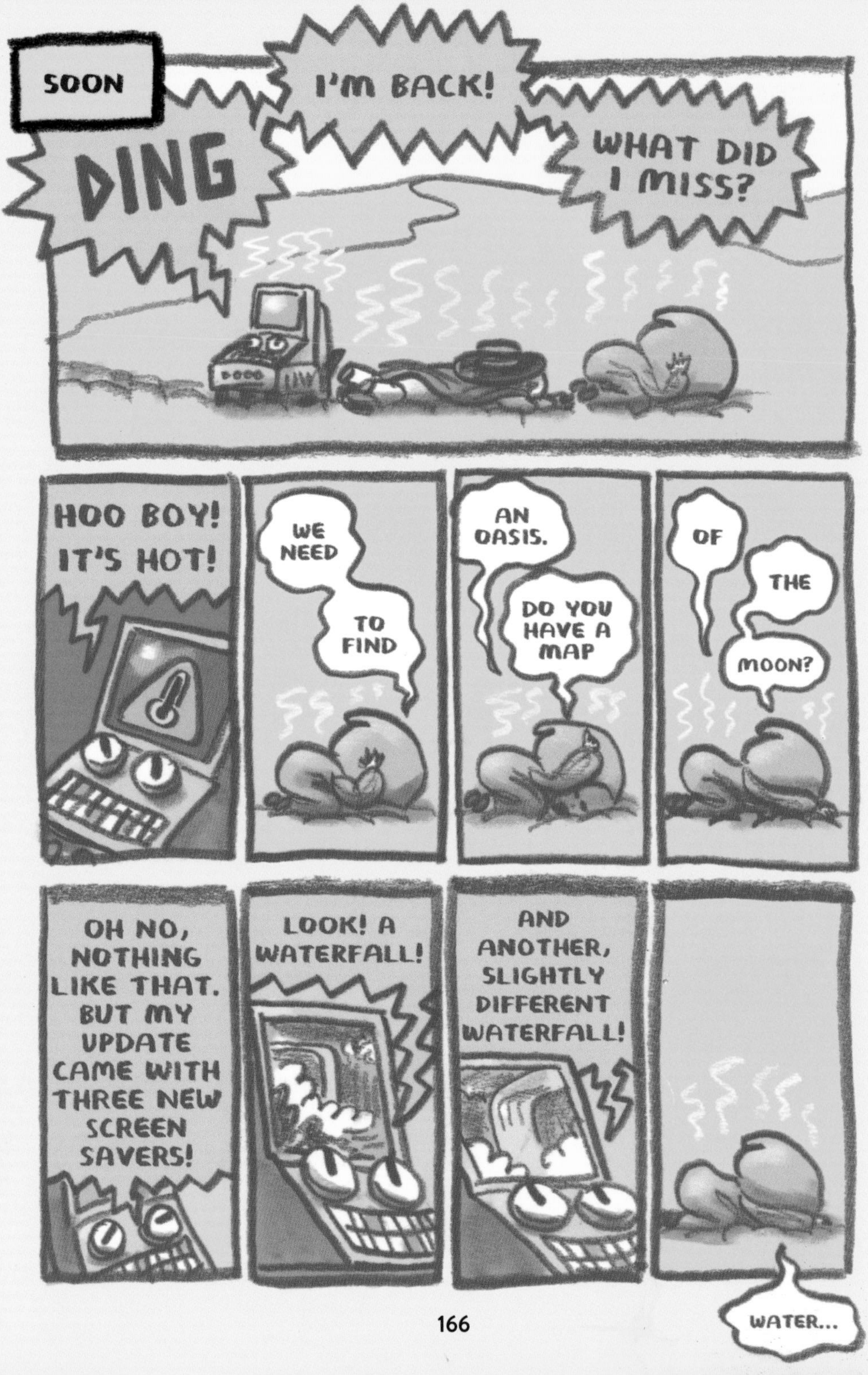
SOON
DING
I'M BACK!
WHAT DID I MISS?
HOO BOY! IT'S HOT!
WE NEED
TO FIND
AN OASIS.
DO YOU HAVE A MAP
OF
THE
MOON?
OH NO, NOTHING LIKE THAT. BUT MY UPDATE CAME WITH THREE NEW SCREEN SAVERS!
LOOK! A WATERFALL!
AND ANOTHER, SLIGHTLY DIFFERENT WATERFALL!
WATER...

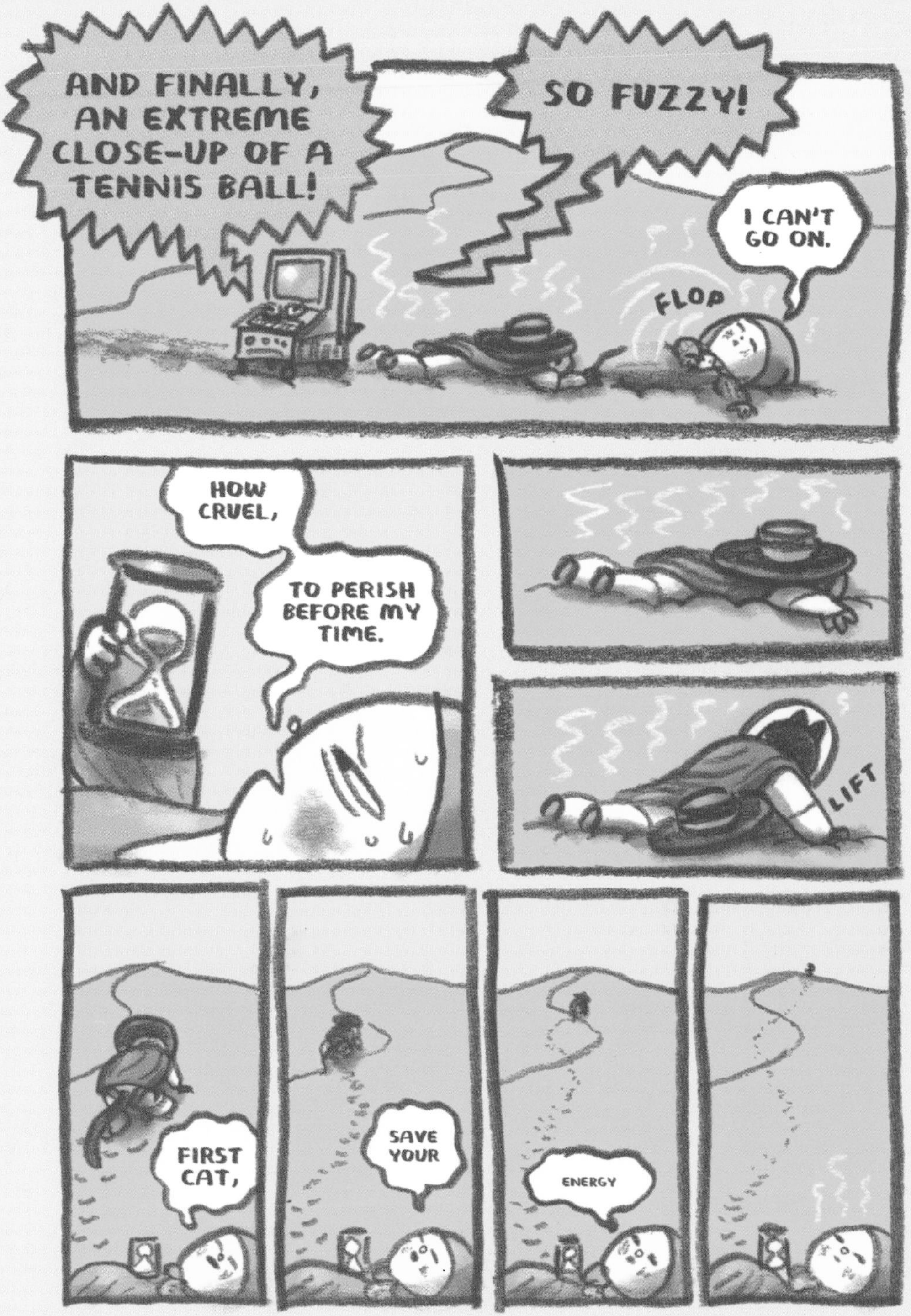
AND FINALLY, AN EXTREME CLOSE-UP OF A TENNIS BALL!
SO FUZZY!
I CAN'T GO ON.
FLOP
HOW CRUEL,
TO PERISH BEFORE MY TIME.
LIFT
FIRST CAT,
SAVE YOUR
ENERGY

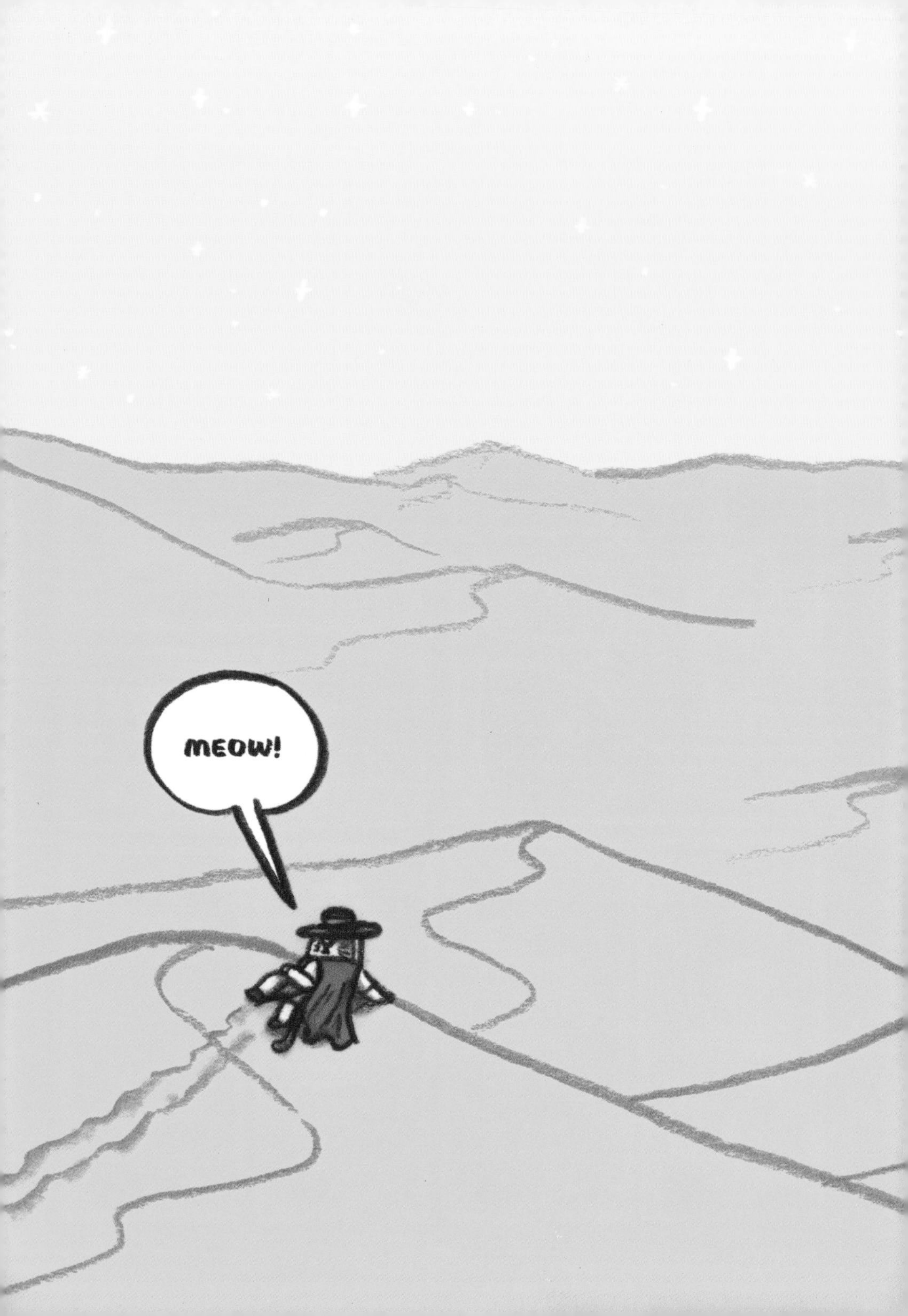
MEOW!

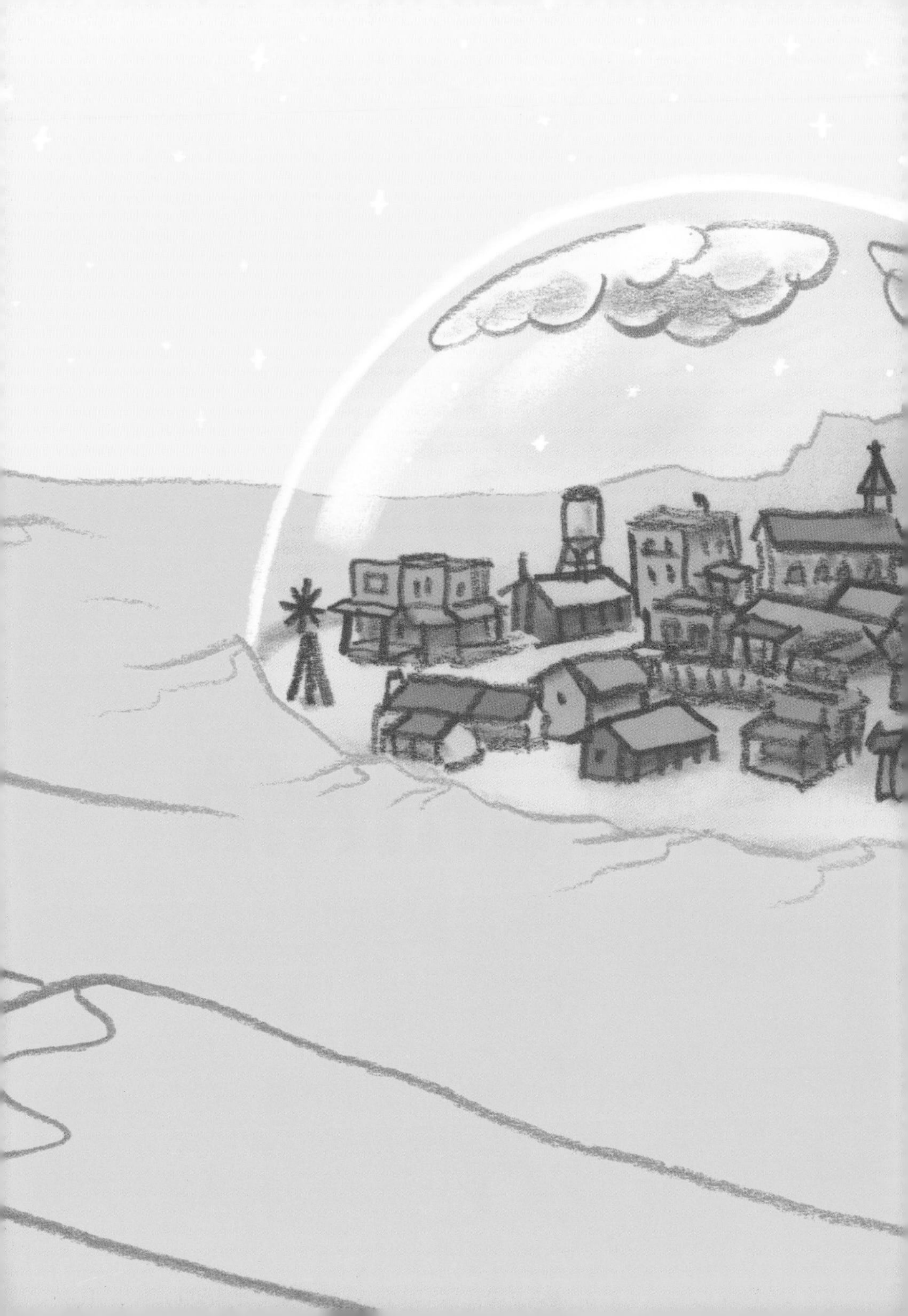

CHAPTER 9

# A
# HERO'S
# DILEMMA

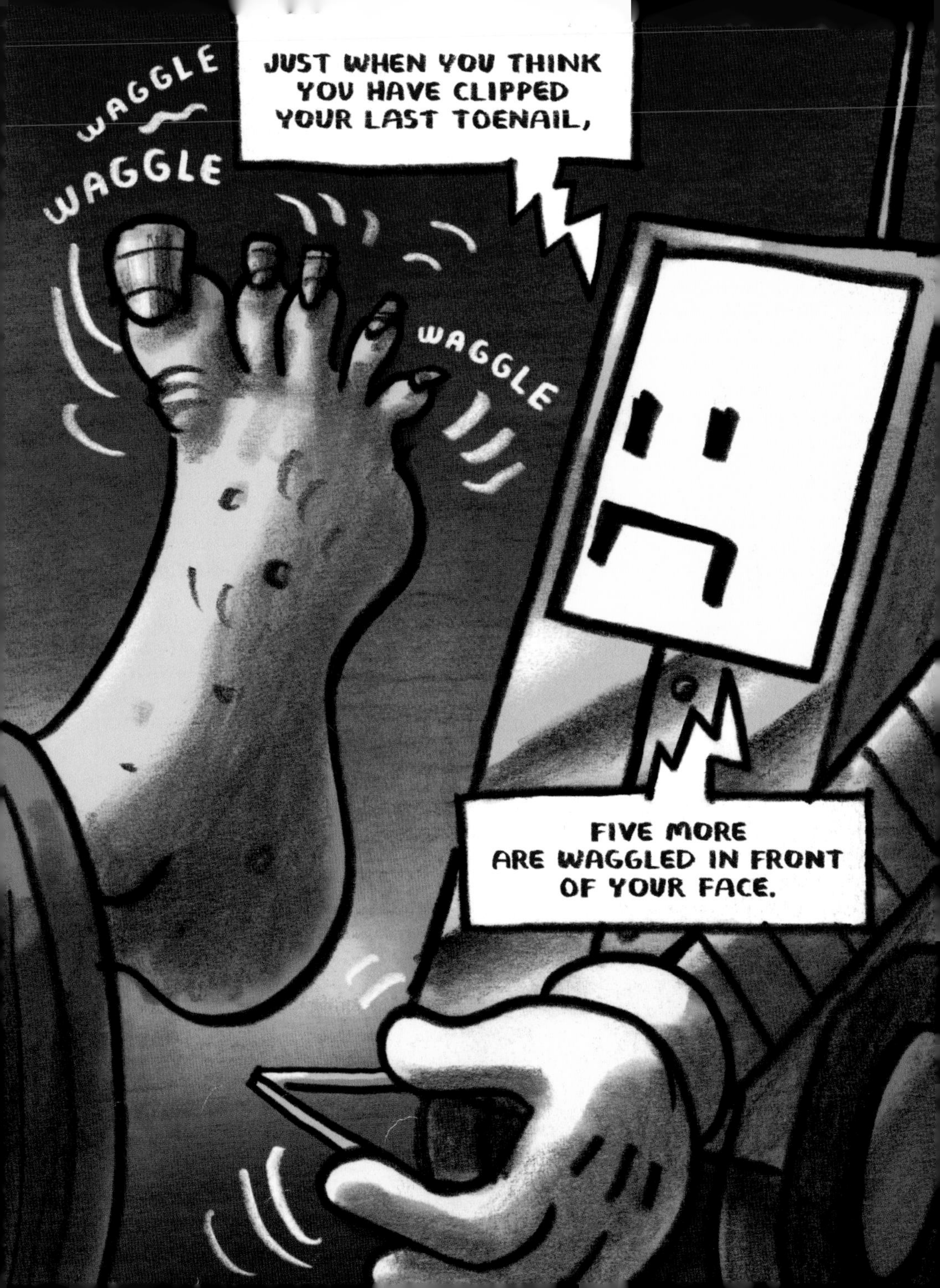

JUST WHEN YOU THINK YOU HAVE CLIPPED YOUR LAST TOENAIL,
WAGGLE
WAGGLE
WAGGLE
FIVE MORE ARE WAGGLED IN FRONT OF YOUR FACE.

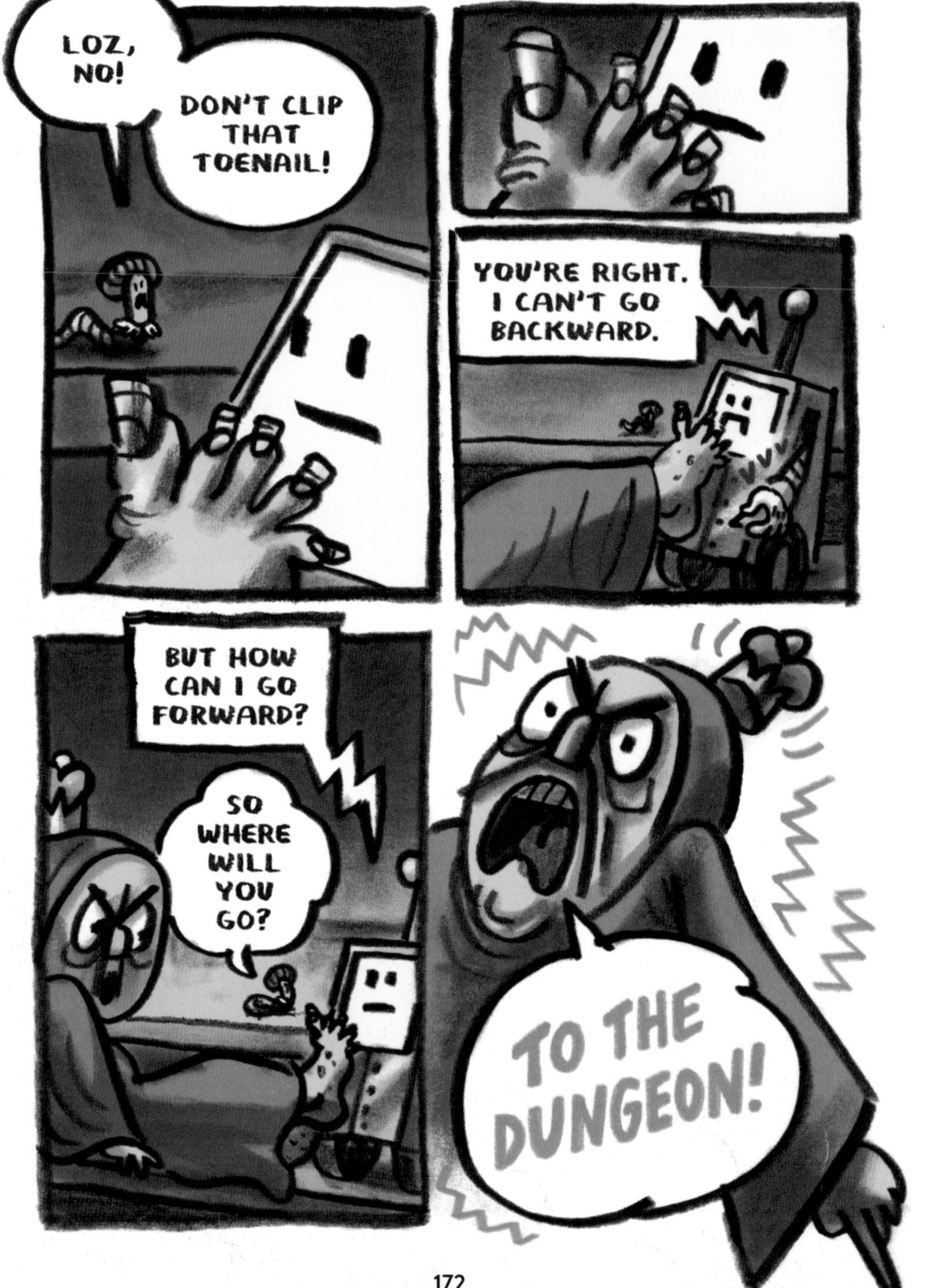
LOZ, NO!
DON'T CLIP THAT TOENAIL!
YOU'RE RIGHT. I CAN'T GO BACKWARD.
BUT HOW CAN I GO FORWARD?
SO WHERE WILL YOU GO?
TO THE DUNGEON!

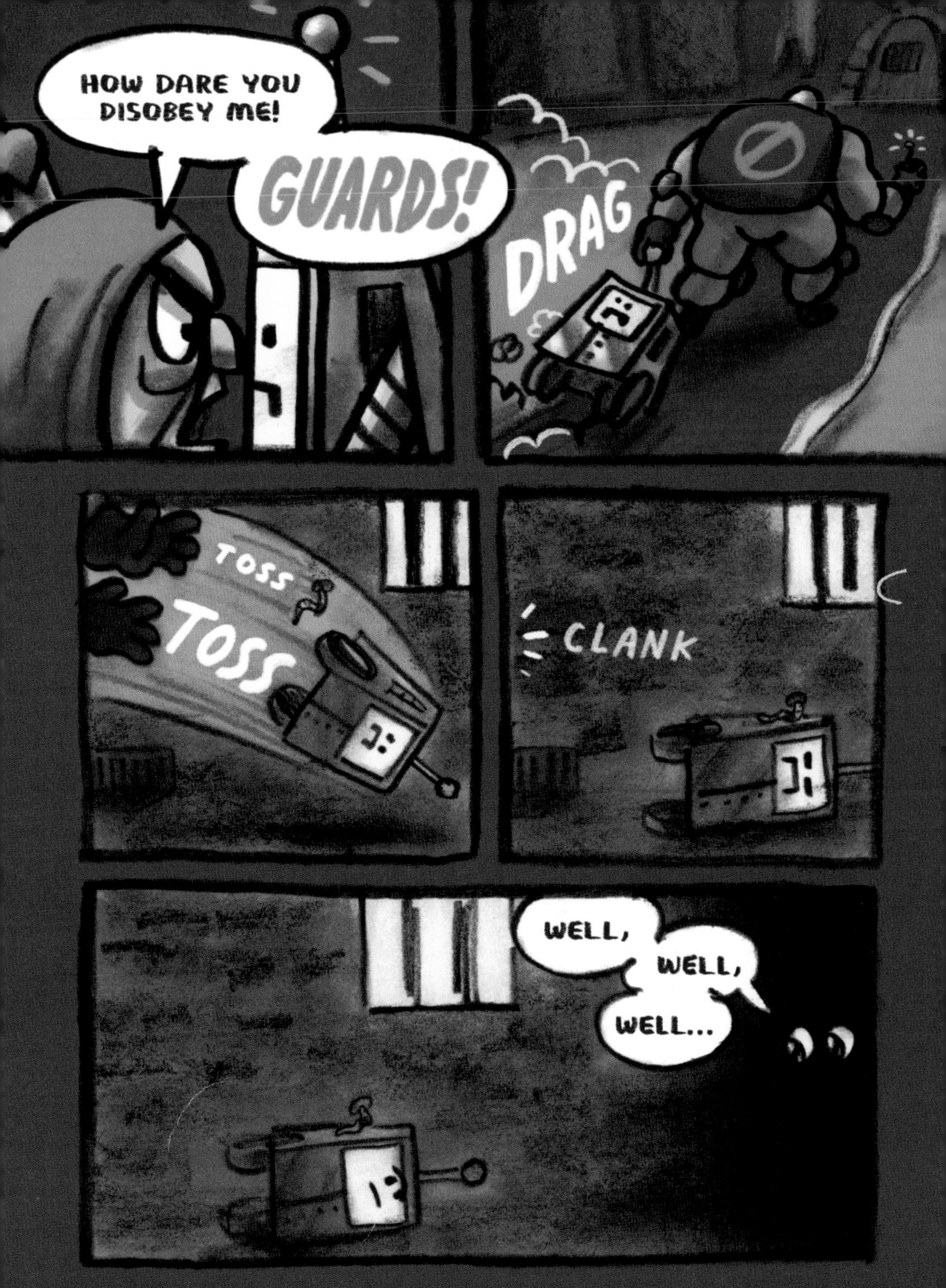
HOW DARE YOU DISOBEY ME!
GUARDS!
DRAG
TOSS
TOSS
CLANK
WELL,
WELL,
WELL...

LOOK WHO IT IS.

I SUPPOSE WE'VE ALL ENDED UP WHERE WE BELONG.

I DON'T BELONG DOWN HERE!

MY PLACE IS ON THE SEAS, THE OCEAN BREEZE BLOWING THROUGH ME TINY BEARD!

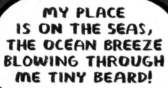

I'M NOT SURE WHY I'M HERE. I DIDN'T DO ANYTHING.

WELL, I DESERVE THIS.

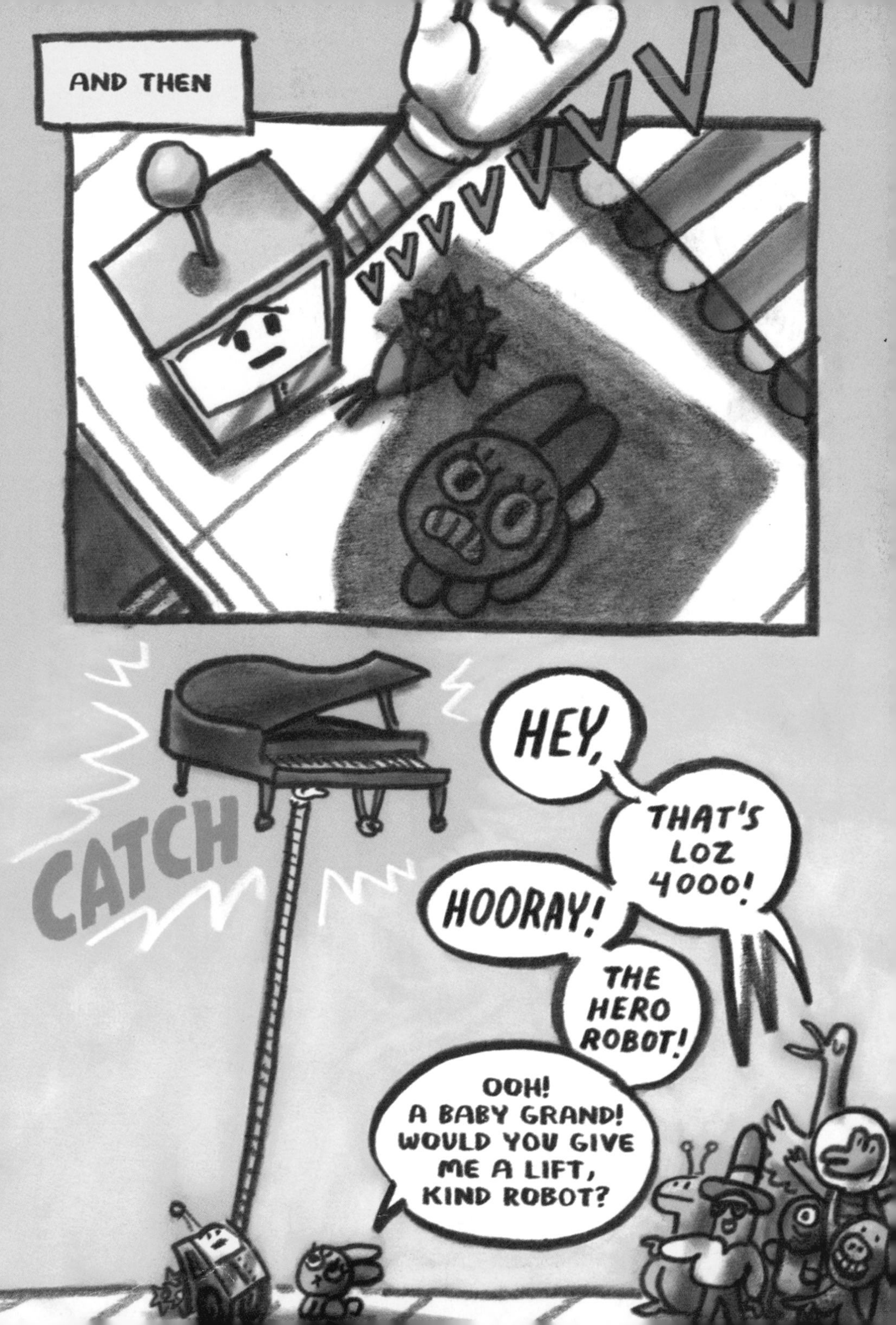
AND THEN
CATCH
HEY,
THAT'S LOZ 4000!
HOORAY!
THE HERO ROBOT!
OOH! A BABY GRAND! WOULD YOU GIVE ME A LIFT, KIND ROBOT?

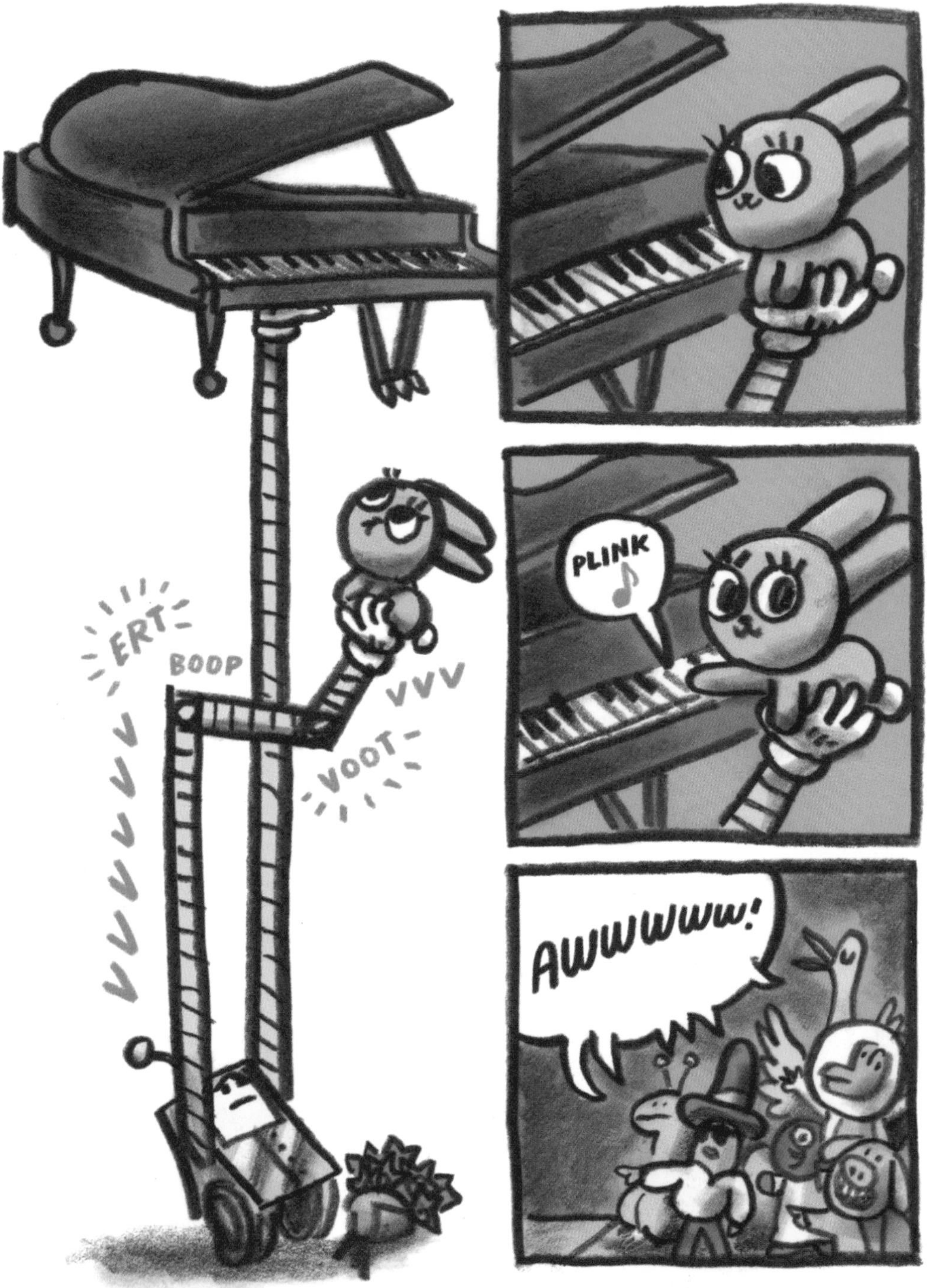
ERT
BOOP
VVV
VOOT
VVVVVVVVV
PLINK
AWWWWW!

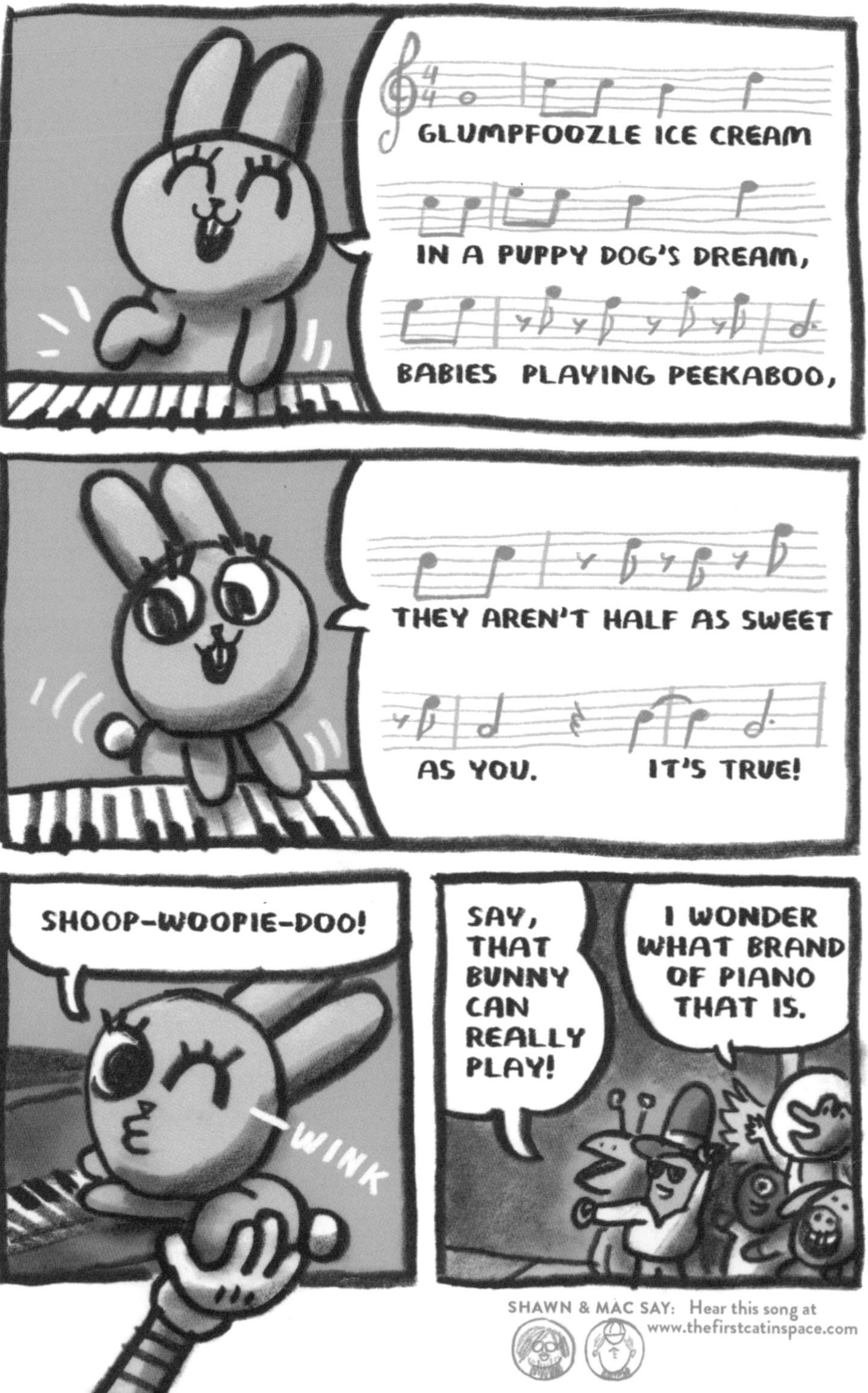
GLUMPFOOZLE ICE CREAM
IN A PUPPY DOG'S DREAM,
BABIES PLAYING PEEKABOO,
THEY AREN'T HALF AS SWEET
AS YOU.
IT'S TRUE!
SHOOP-WOOPIE-DOO!
WINK
SAY, THAT BUNNY CAN REALLY PLAY!
I WONDER WHAT BRAND OF PIANO THAT IS.

SHAWN & MAC SAY: Hear this song at www.thefirstcatinspace.com

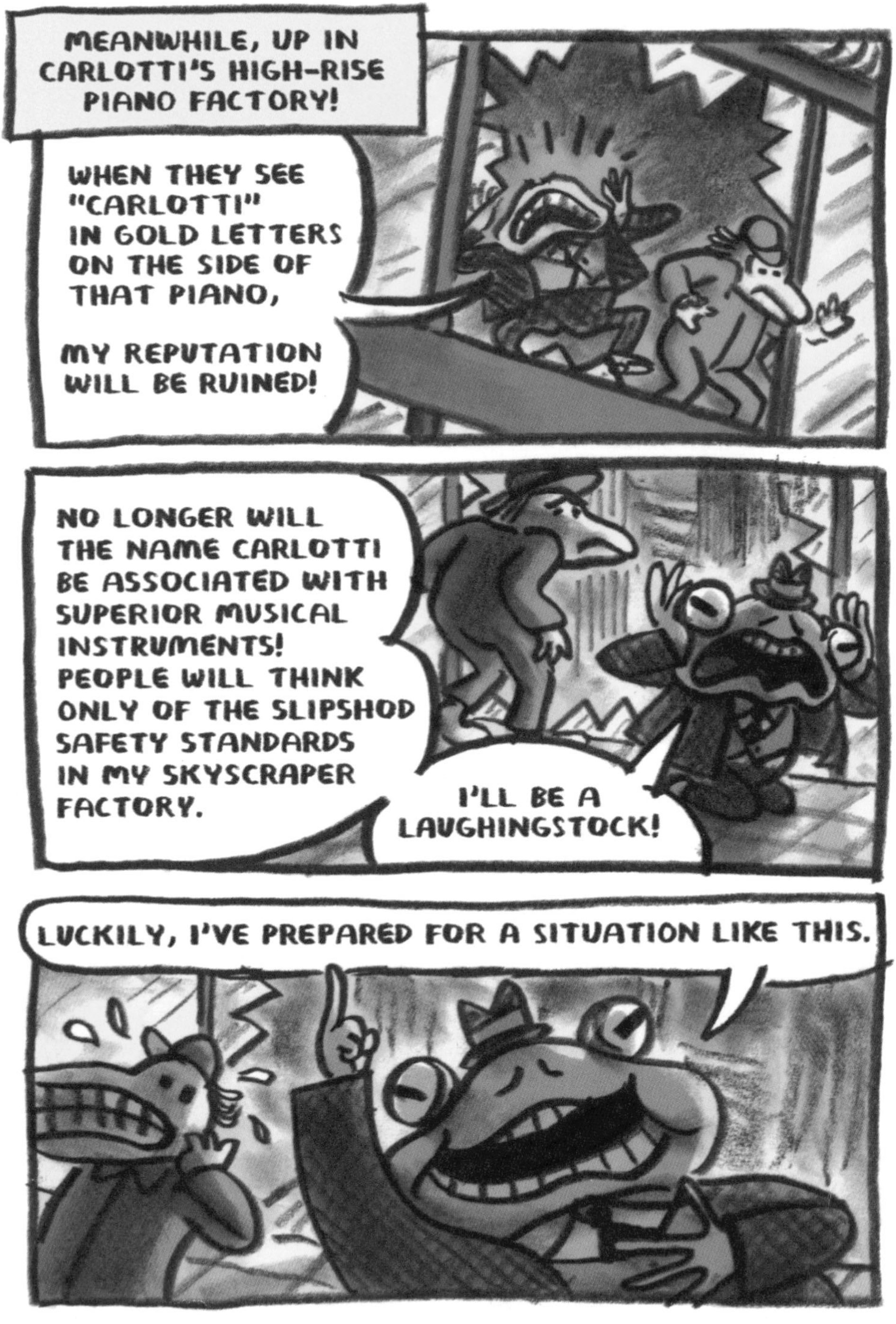
MEANWHILE, UP IN CARLOTTI'S HIGH-RISE PIANO FACTORY!
WHEN THEY SEE "CARLOTTI" IN GOLD LETTERS ON THE SIDE OF THAT PIANO,
MY REPUTATION WILL BE RUINED!
NO LONGER WILL THE NAME CARLOTTI BE ASSOCIATED WITH SUPERIOR MUSICAL INSTRUMENTS! PEOPLE WILL THINK ONLY OF THE SLIPSHOD SAFETY STANDARDS IN MY SKYSCRAPER FACTORY.
I'LL BE A LAUGHINGSTOCK!
LUCKILY, I'VE PREPARED FOR A SITUATION LIKE THIS.

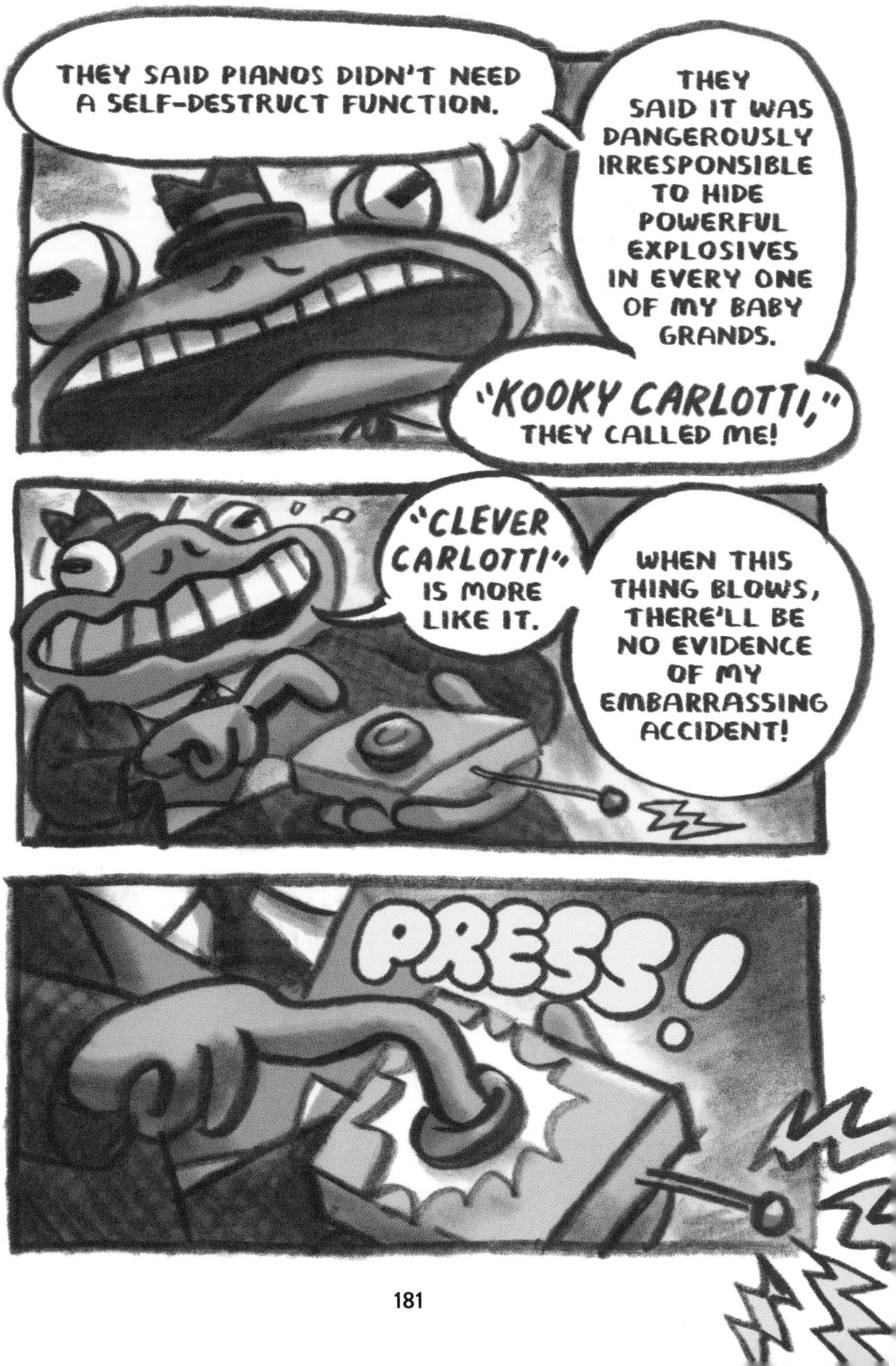
THEY SAID PIANOS DIDN'T NEED A SELF-DESTRUCT FUNCTION.
THEY SAID IT WAS DANGEROUSLY IRRESPONSIBLE TO HIDE POWERFUL EXPLOSIVES IN EVERY ONE OF MY BABY GRANDS.
"KOOKY CARLOTTI," THEY CALLED ME!
"CLEVER CARLOTTI" IS MORE LIKE IT.
WHEN THIS THING BLOWS, THERE'LL BE NO EVIDENCE OF MY EMBARRASSING ACCIDENT!
PRESS!

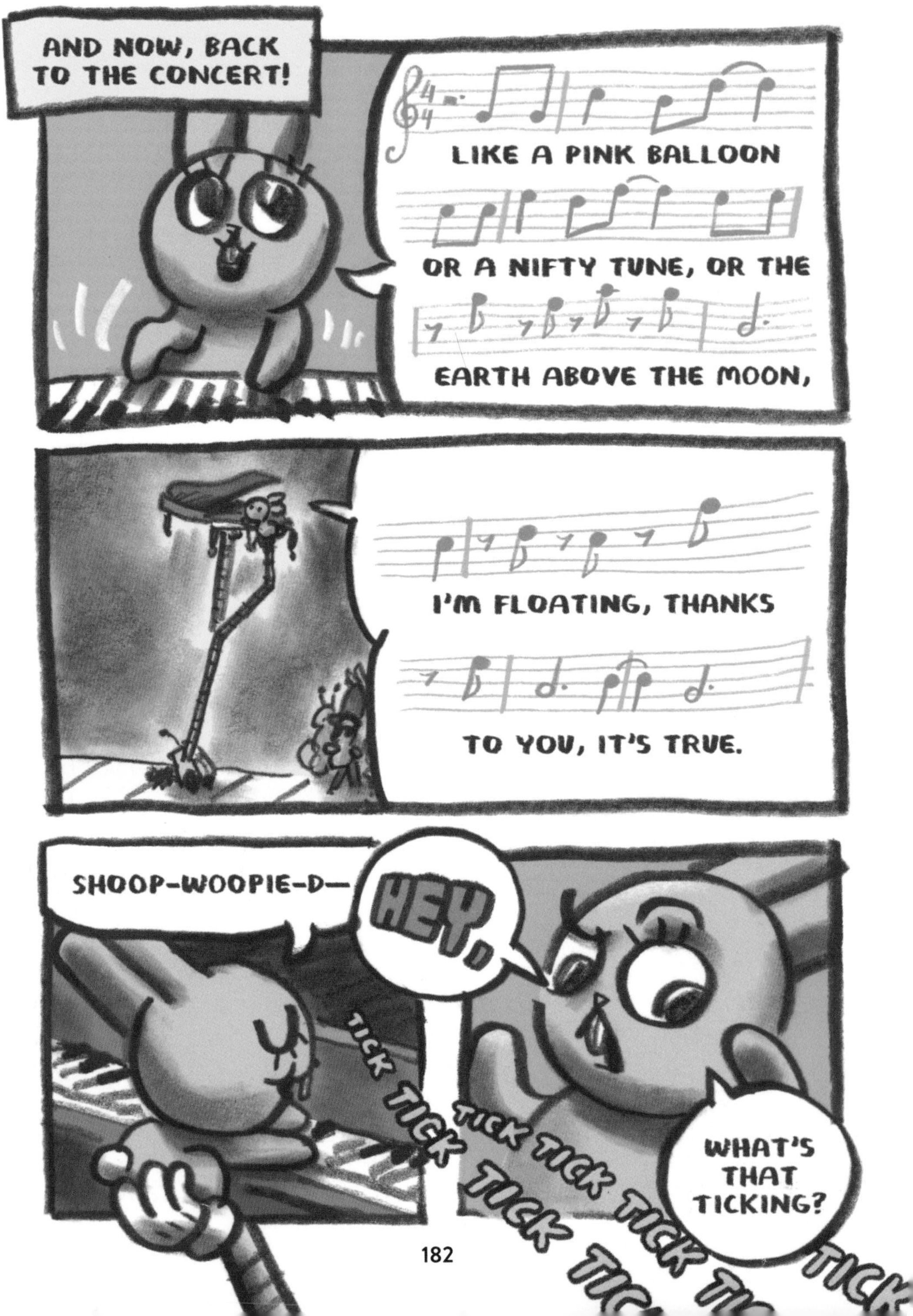
AND NOW, BACK TO THE CONCERT!
LIKE A PINK BALLOON
OR A NIFTY TUNE, OR THE
EARTH ABOVE THE MOON,
I'M FLOATING, THANKS
TO YOU, IT'S TRUE.
SHOOP-WOOPIE-D—
HEY,
TICK TICK TICK TICK TICK TICK TICK
WHAT'S THAT TICKING?

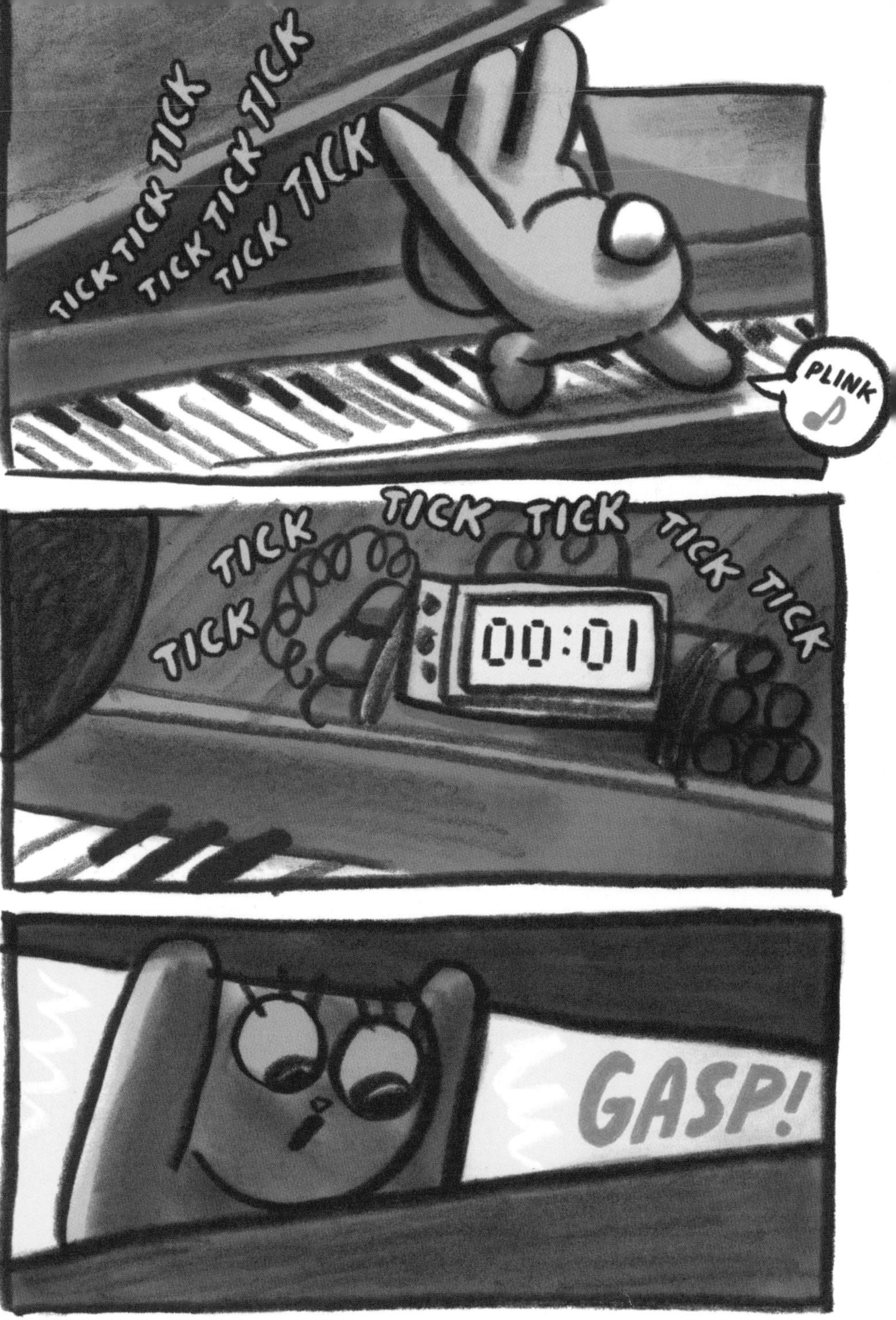
TICK TICK TICK
TICK TICK TICK
TICK TICK
PLINK
TICK TICK TICK TICK TICK TICK TICK
00:01
GASP!

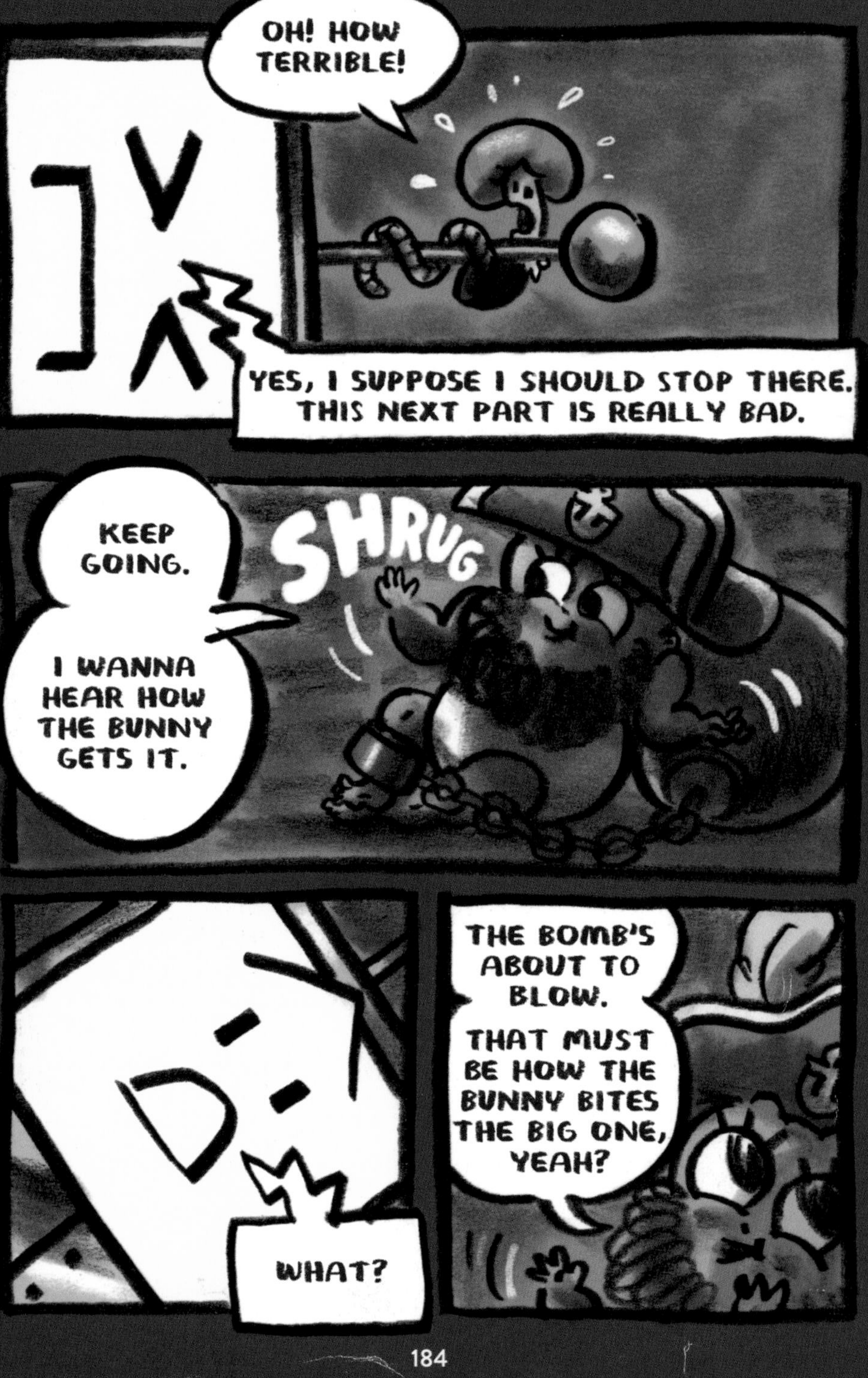
OH! HOW TERRIBLE!
YES, I SUPPOSE I SHOULD STOP THERE. THIS NEXT PART IS REALLY BAD.
KEEP GOING.
I WANNA HEAR HOW THE BUNNY GETS IT.
SHRUG
WHAT?
THE BOMB'S ABOUT TO BLOW.
THAT MUST BE HOW THE BUNNY BITES THE BIG ONE, YEAH?

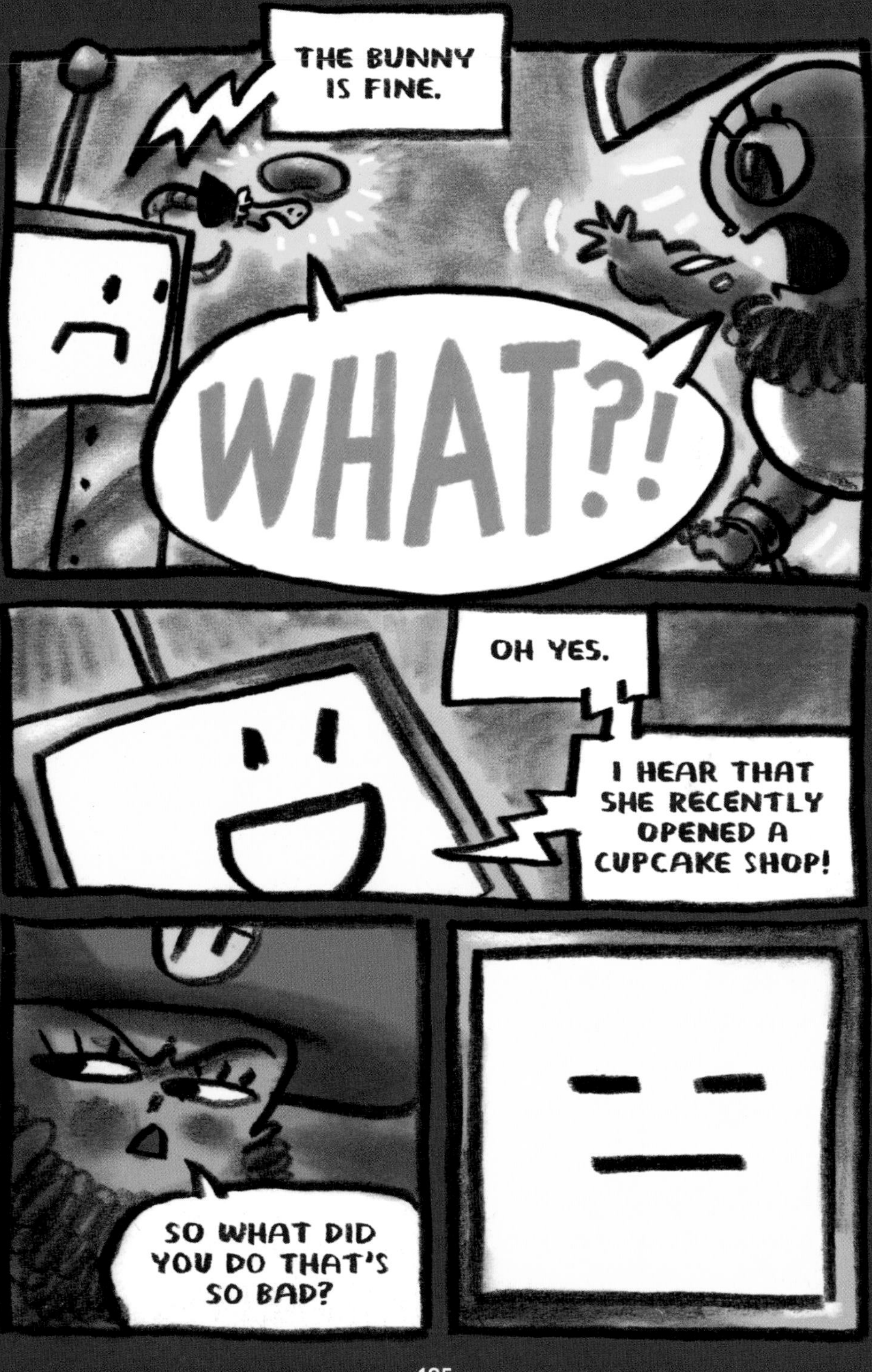
THE BUNNY IS FINE.
WHAT?!
OH YES.
I HEAR THAT SHE RECENTLY OPENED A CUPCAKE SHOP!
SO WHAT DID YOU DO THAT'S SO BAD?

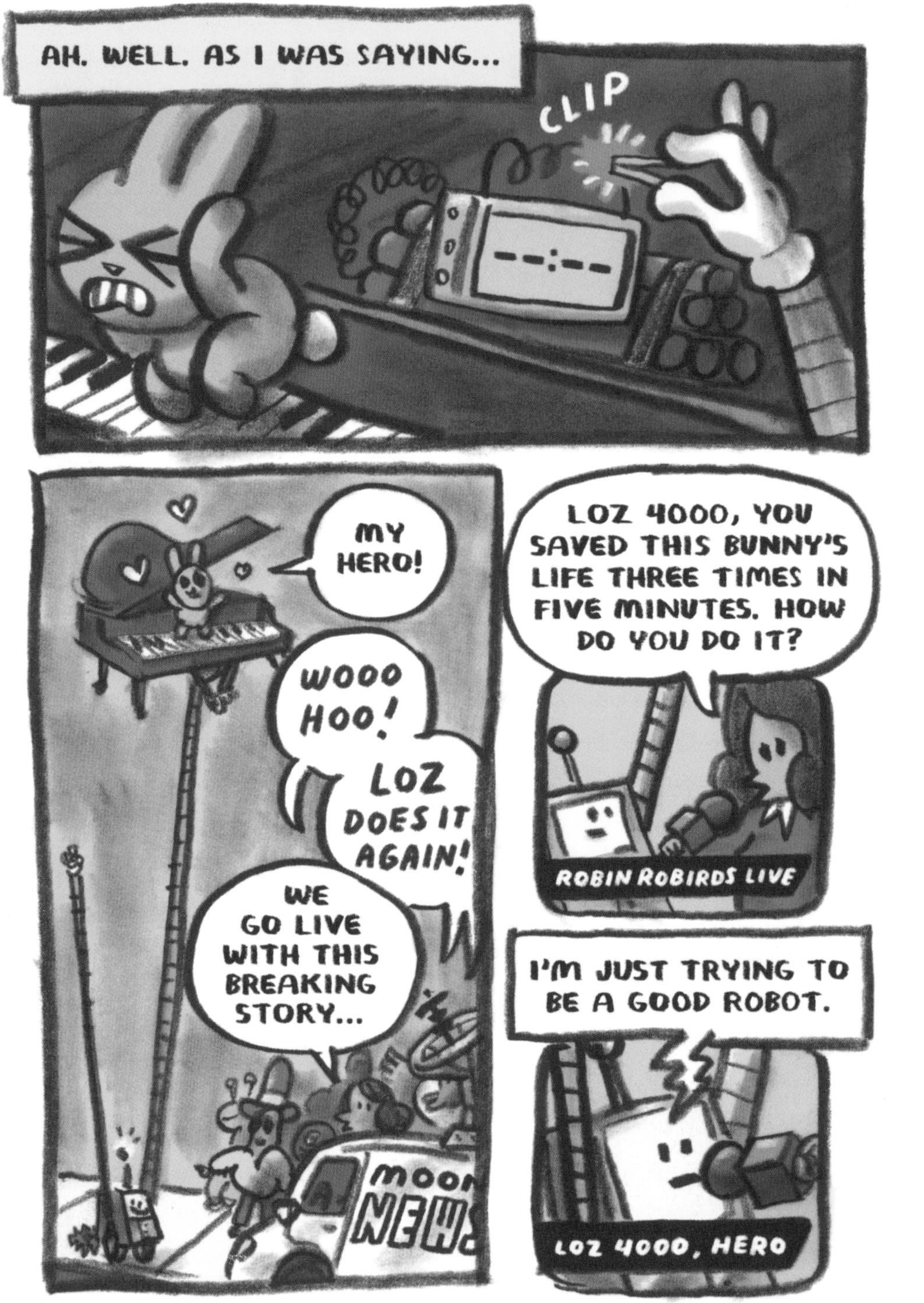
AH. WELL. AS I WAS SAYING...
CLIP
--:--
MY HERO!
WOOO HOO!
LOZ DOES IT AGAIN!
WE GO LIVE WITH THIS BREAKING STORY...
MOON NEWS
LOZ 4000, YOU SAVED THIS BUNNY'S LIFE THREE TIMES IN FIVE MINUTES. HOW DO YOU DO IT?
ROBIN ROBIRDS LIVE
I'M JUST TRYING TO BE A GOOD ROBOT.
LOZ 4000, HERO

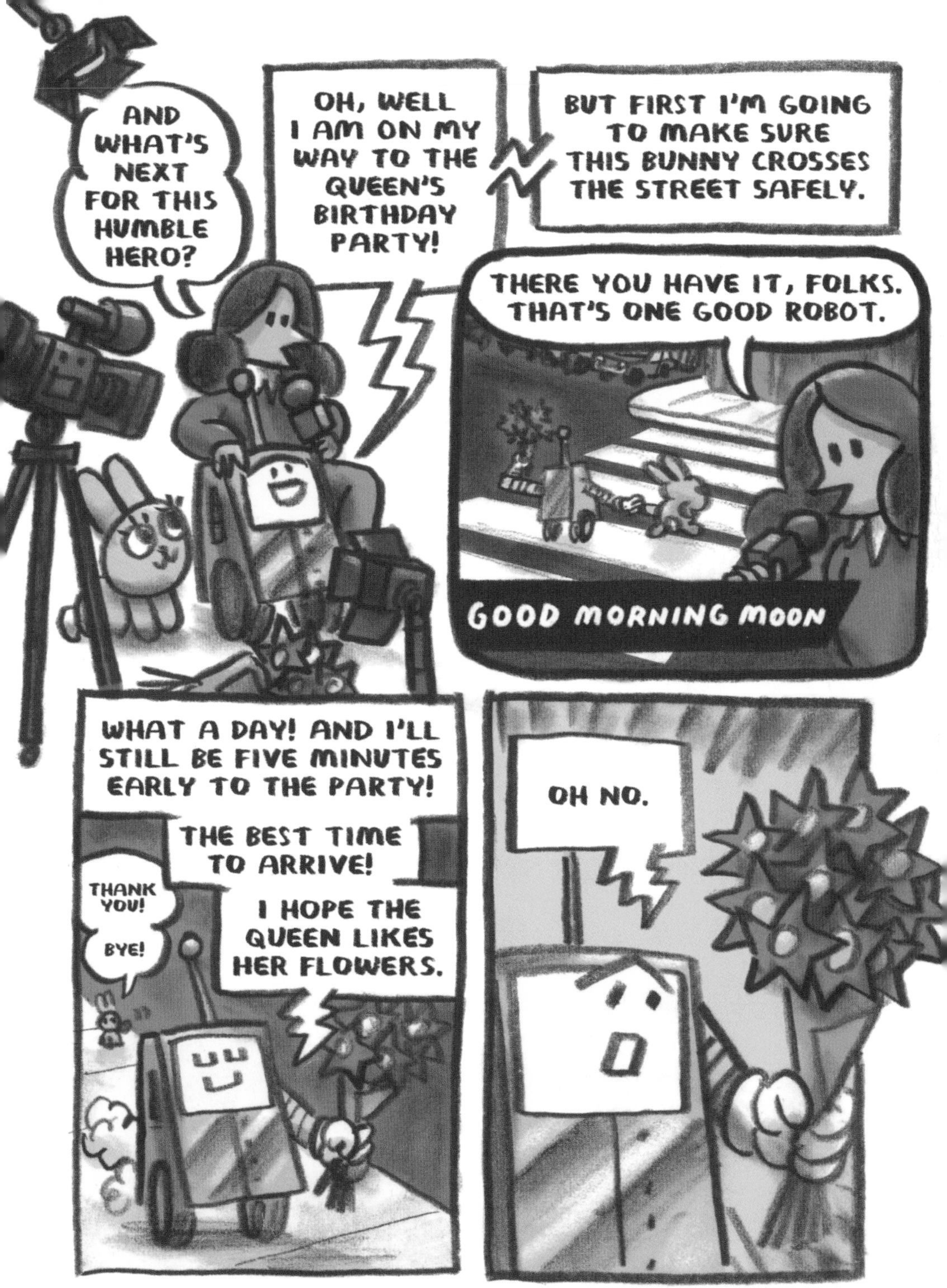
AND WHAT'S NEXT FOR THIS HUMBLE HERO?
OH, WELL I AM ON MY WAY TO THE QUEEN'S BIRTHDAY PARTY!
BUT FIRST I'M GOING TO MAKE SURE THIS BUNNY CROSSES THE STREET SAFELY.
THERE YOU HAVE IT, FOLKS. THAT'S ONE GOOD ROBOT.
GOOD MORNING MOON
WHAT A DAY! AND I'LL STILL BE FIVE MINUTES EARLY TO THE PARTY!
THE BEST TIME TO ARRIVE!
THANK YOU!
BYE!
I HOPE THE QUEEN LIKES HER FLOWERS.
OH NO.

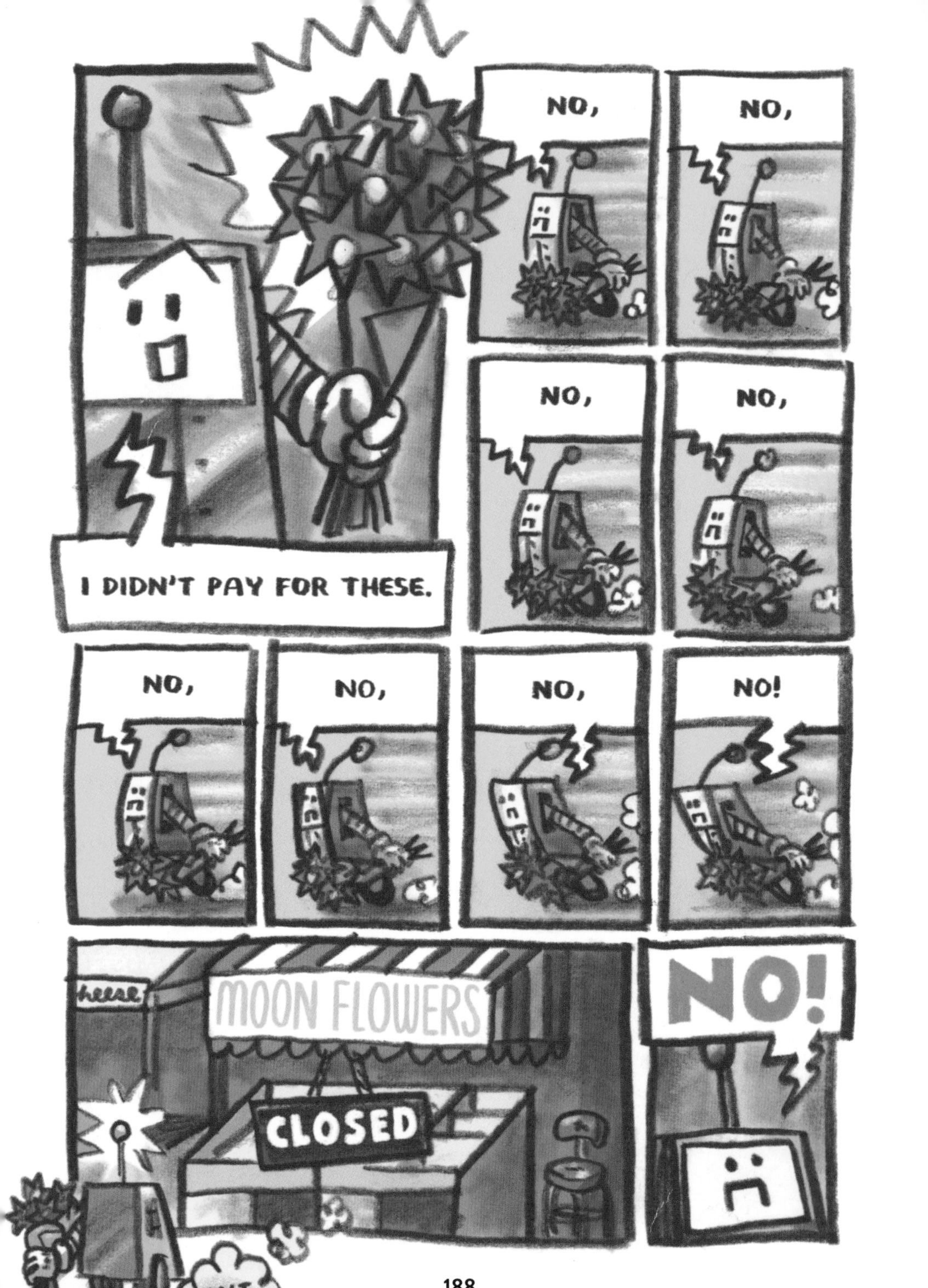
I DIDN'T PAY FOR THESE.
NO,
NO,
NO,
NO,
NO,
NO,
NO,
NO!
MOON FLOWERS
CLOSED
HALT
NO!

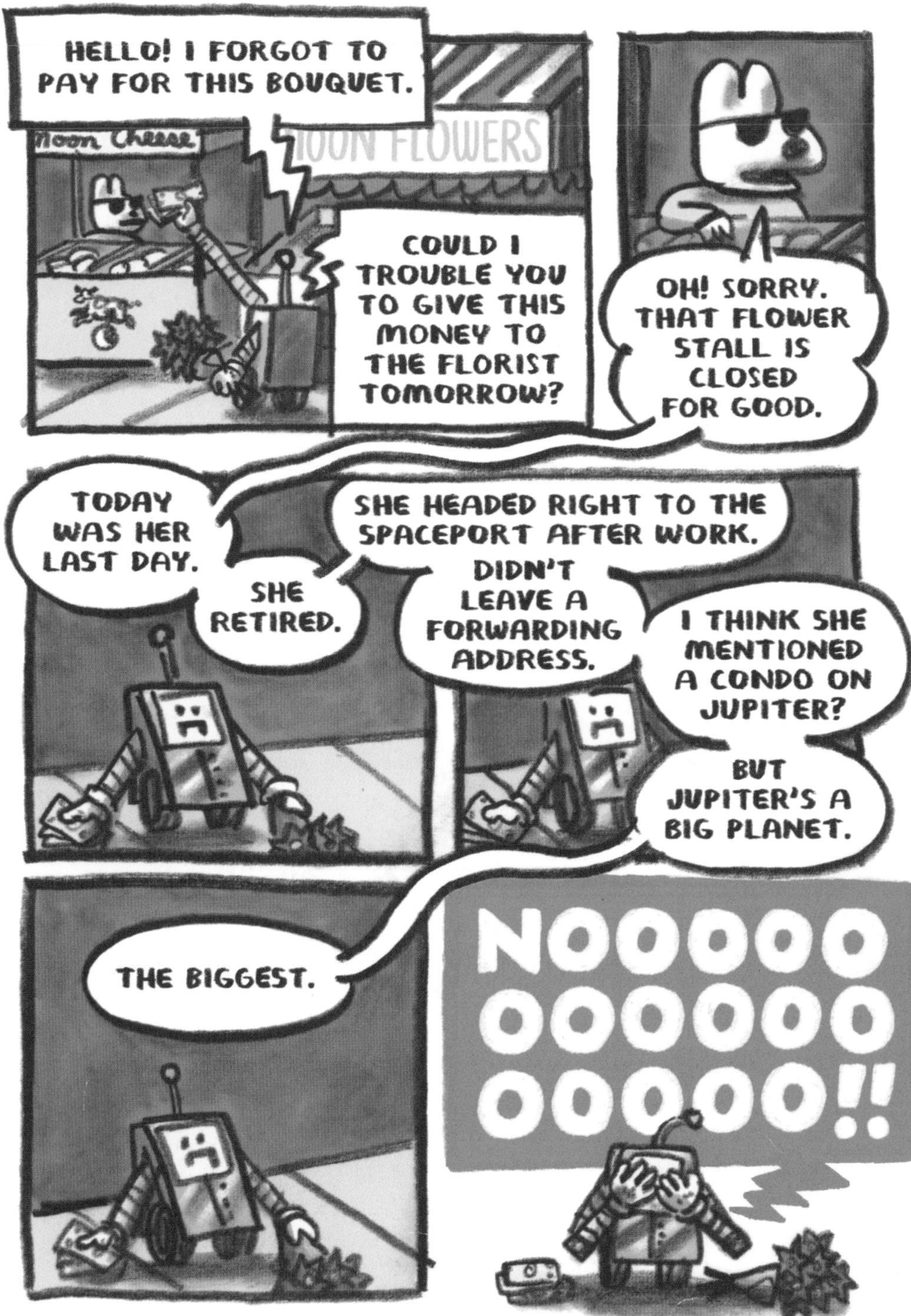
HELLO! I FORGOT TO PAY FOR THIS BOUQUET.
Moon Cheese
MOON FLOWERS
COULD I TROUBLE YOU TO GIVE THIS MONEY TO THE FLORIST TOMORROW?
OH! SORRY. THAT FLOWER STALL IS CLOSED FOR GOOD.
TODAY WAS HER LAST DAY.
SHE RETIRED.
SHE HEADED RIGHT TO THE SPACEPORT AFTER WORK.
DIDN'T LEAVE A FORWARDING ADDRESS.
I THINK SHE MENTIONED A CONDO ON JUPITER?
BUT JUPITER'S A BIG PLANET.
THE BIGGEST.
NOOOOOOOOOOOOOOOO!!

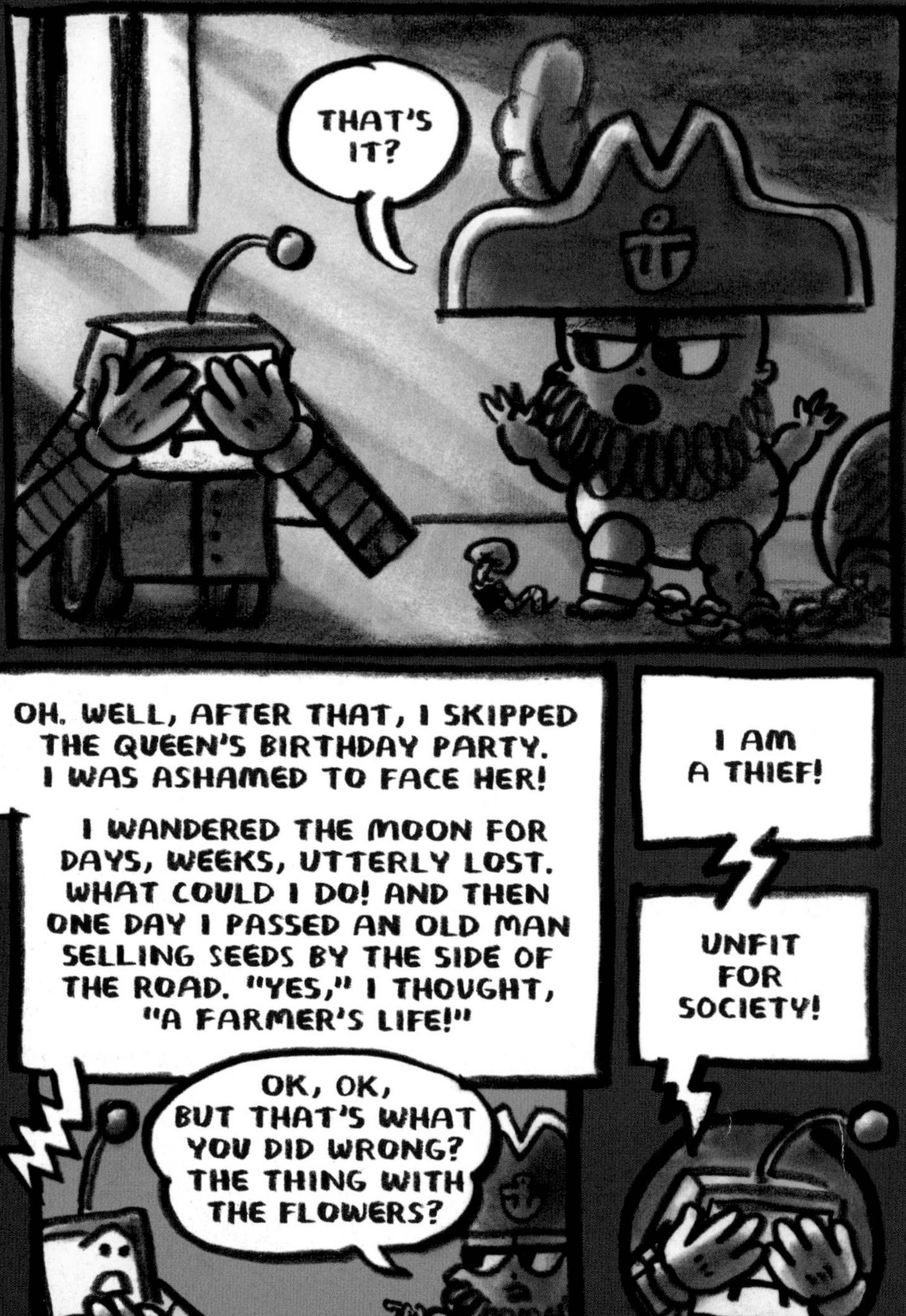
THAT'S IT?
OH. WELL, AFTER THAT, I SKIPPED THE QUEEN'S BIRTHDAY PARTY. I WAS ASHAMED TO FACE HER!
I WANDERED THE MOON FOR DAYS, WEEKS, UTTERLY LOST. WHAT COULD I DO! AND THEN ONE DAY I PASSED AN OLD MAN SELLING SEEDS BY THE SIDE OF THE ROAD. "YES," I THOUGHT, "A FARMER'S LIFE!"
OK, OK, BUT THAT'S WHAT YOU DID WRONG? THE THING WITH THE FLOWERS?
I AM A THIEF!
UNFIT FOR SOCIETY!

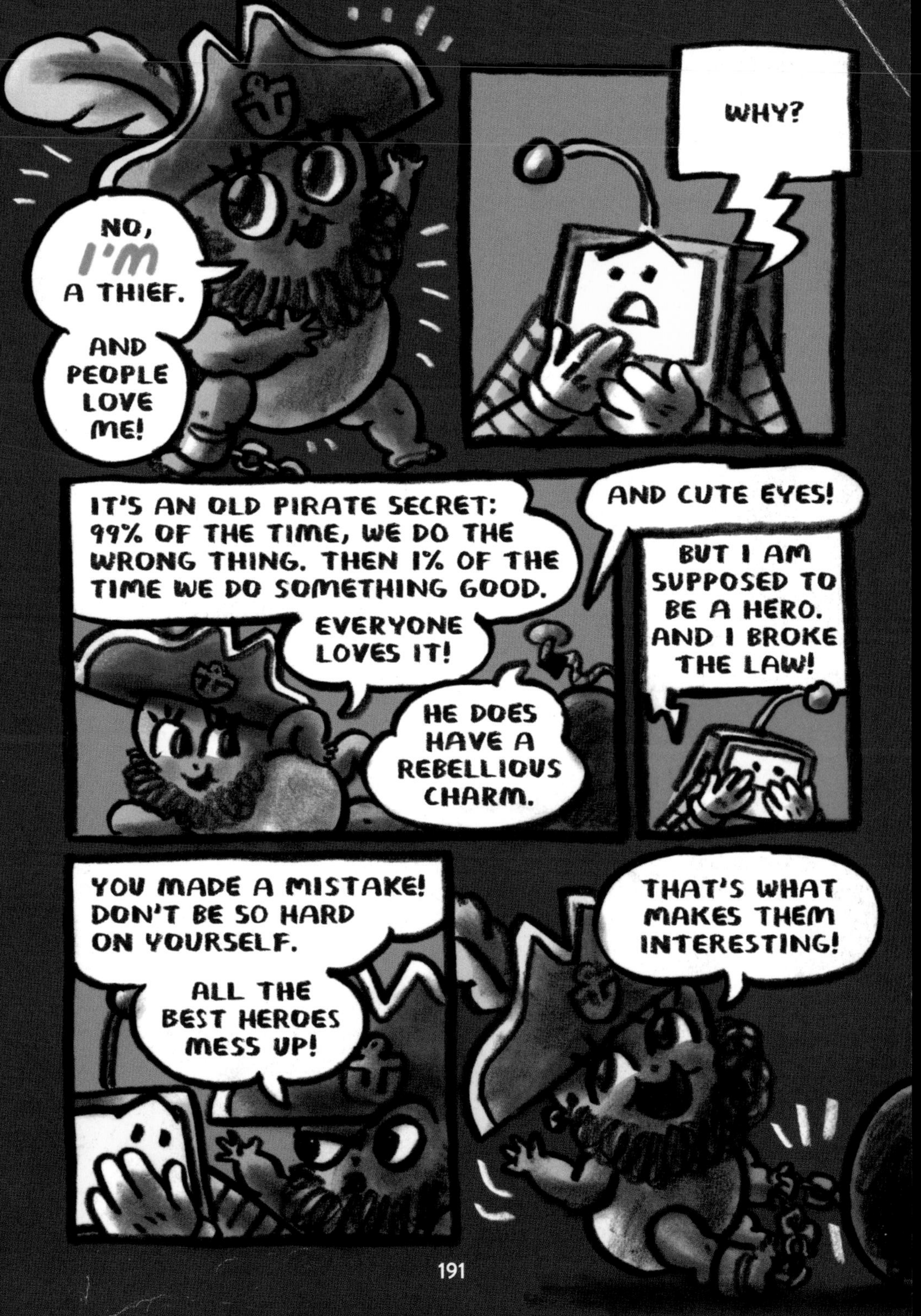
NO, I'M A THIEF.
AND PEOPLE LOVE ME!
WHY?
IT'S AN OLD PIRATE SECRET: 99% OF THE TIME, WE DO THE WRONG THING. THEN 1% OF THE TIME WE DO SOMETHING GOOD.
EVERYONE LOVES IT!
HE DOES HAVE A REBELLIOUS CHARM.
AND CUTE EYES!
BUT I AM SUPPOSED TO BE A HERO. AND I BROKE THE LAW!
YOU MADE A MISTAKE! DON'T BE SO HARD ON YOURSELF.
ALL THE BEST HEROES MESS UP!
THAT'S WHAT MAKES THEM INTERESTING!

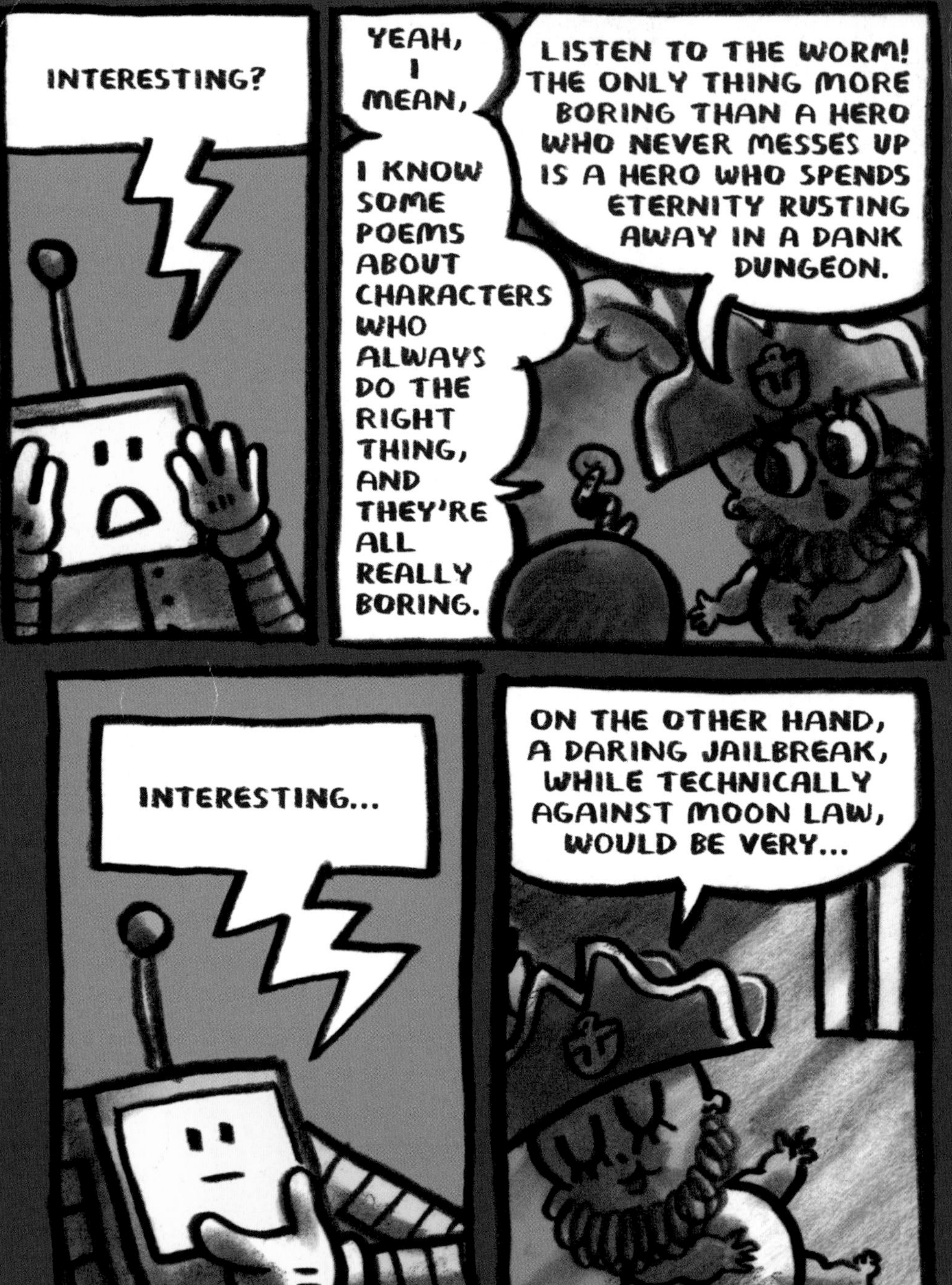
INTERESTING?
YEAH, I MEAN,
I KNOW SOME POEMS ABOUT CHARACTERS WHO ALWAYS DO THE RIGHT THING, AND THEY'RE ALL REALLY BORING.
LISTEN TO THE WORM! THE ONLY THING MORE BORING THAN A HERO WHO NEVER MESSES UP IS A HERO WHO SPENDS ETERNITY RUSTING AWAY IN A DANK DUNGEON.
INTERESTING...
ON THE OTHER HAND, A DARING JAILBREAK, WHILE TECHNICALLY AGAINST MOON LAW, WOULD BE VERY...

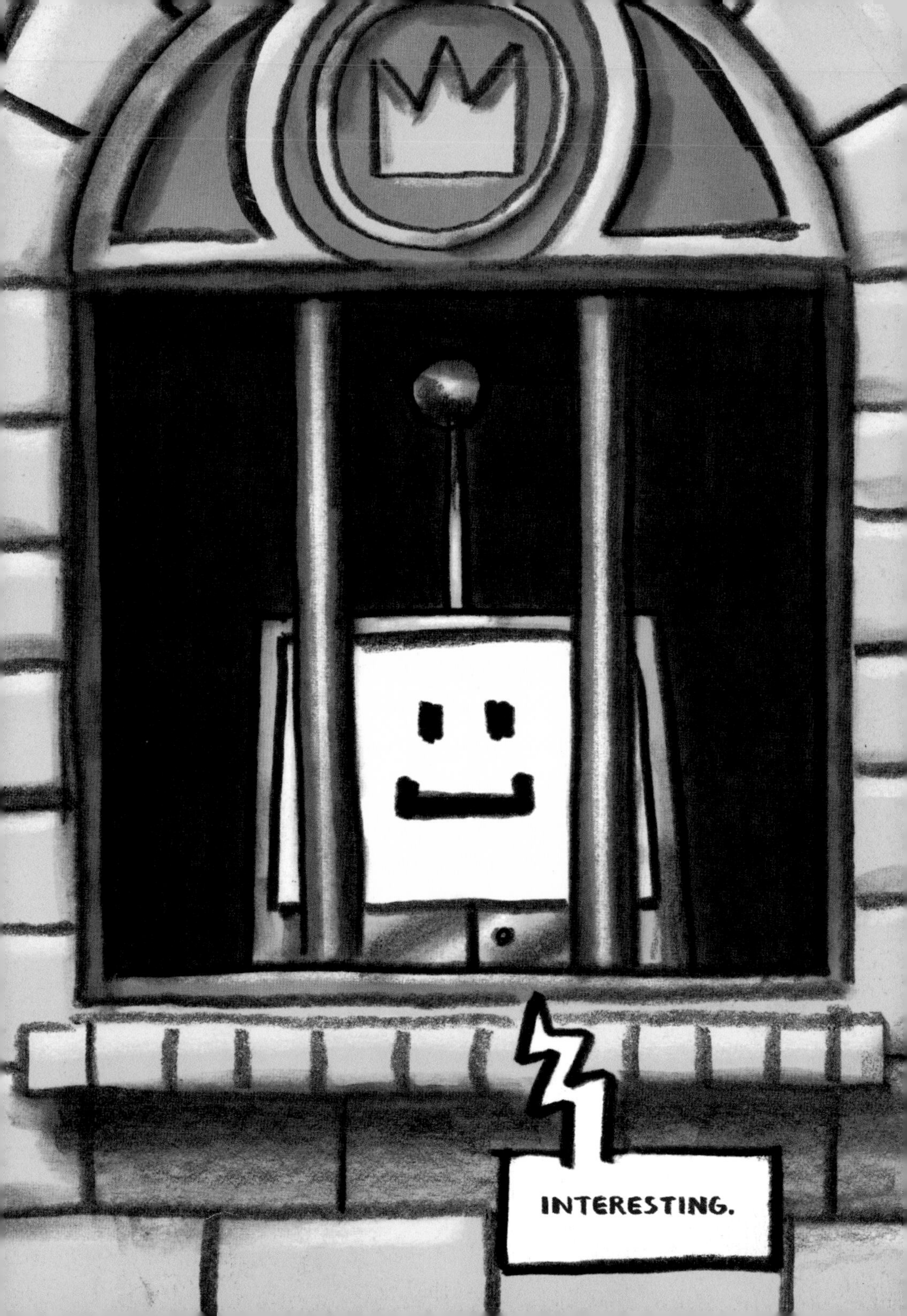
INTERESTING.

# CHAPTER 10

# THE
# BETRAYAL

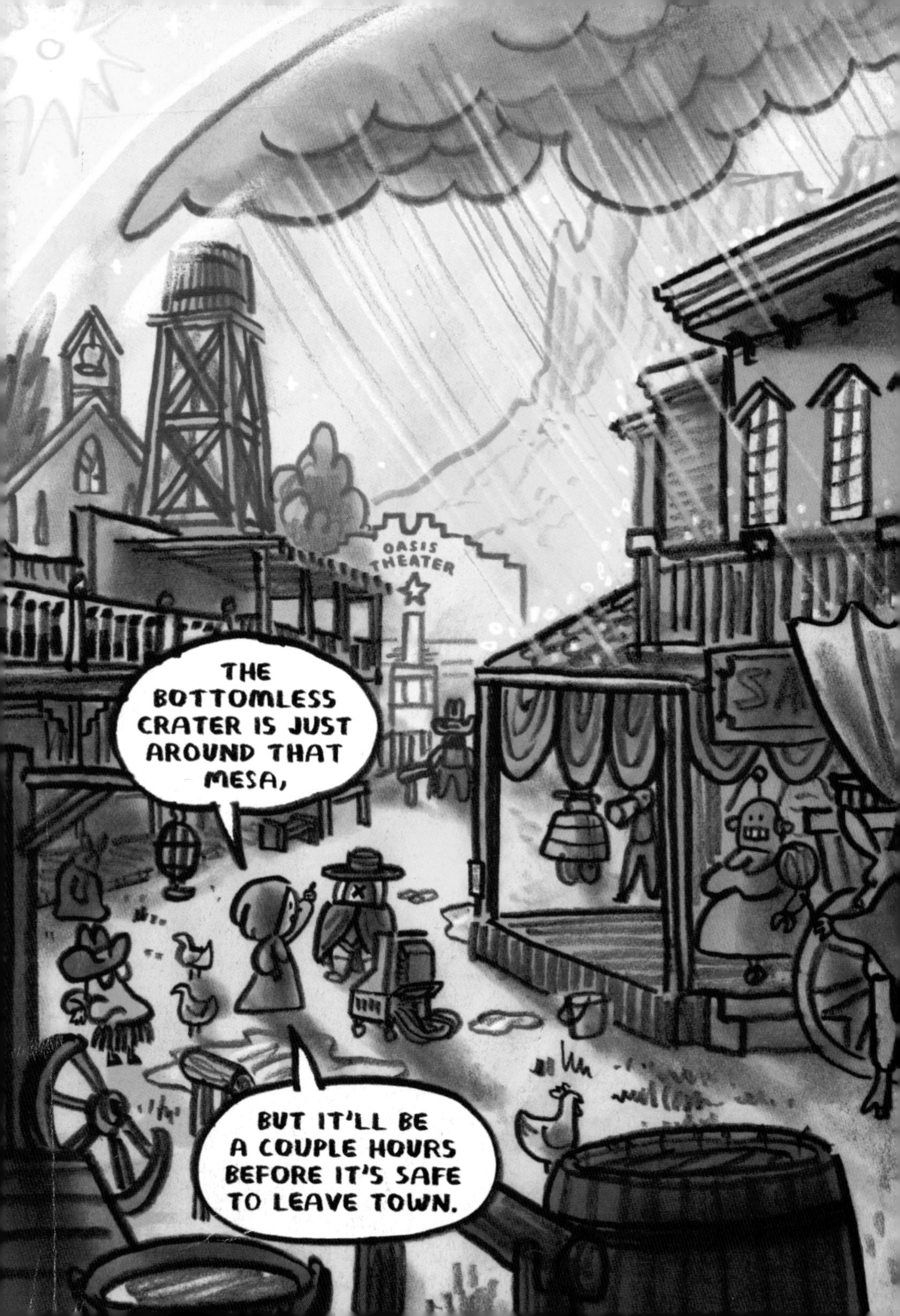
OASIS THEATER
THE BOTTOMLESS CRATER IS JUST AROUND THAT MESA,
BUT IT'LL BE A COUPLE HOURS BEFORE IT'S SAFE TO LEAVE TOWN.

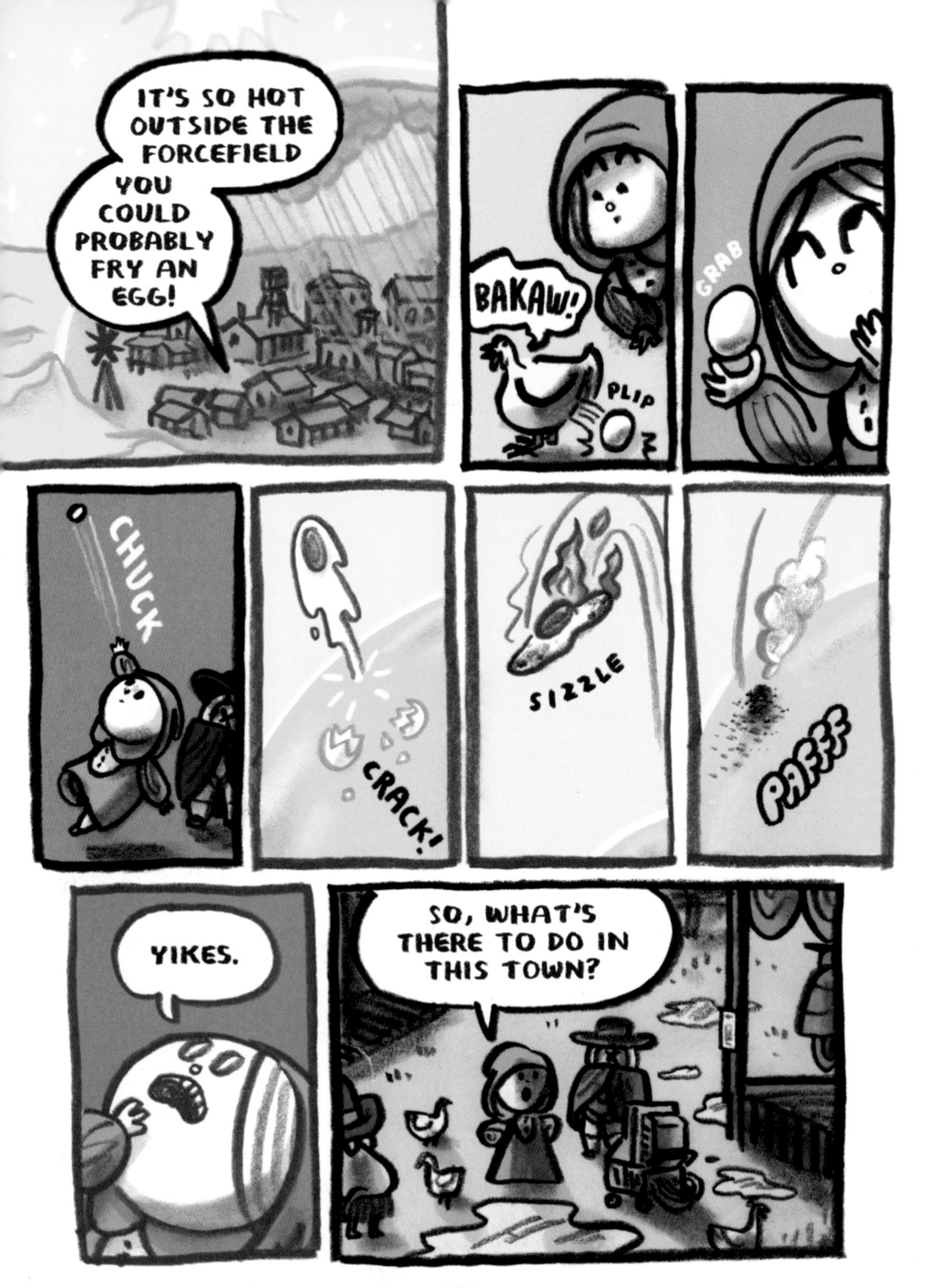
IT'S SO HOT OUTSIDE THE FORCEFIELD
YOU COULD PROBABLY FRY AN EGG!
BAKAW!
PLIP
GRAB
CHUCK
CRACK!
SIZZLE
PAFFF
YIKES.
SO, WHAT'S THERE TO DO IN THIS TOWN?

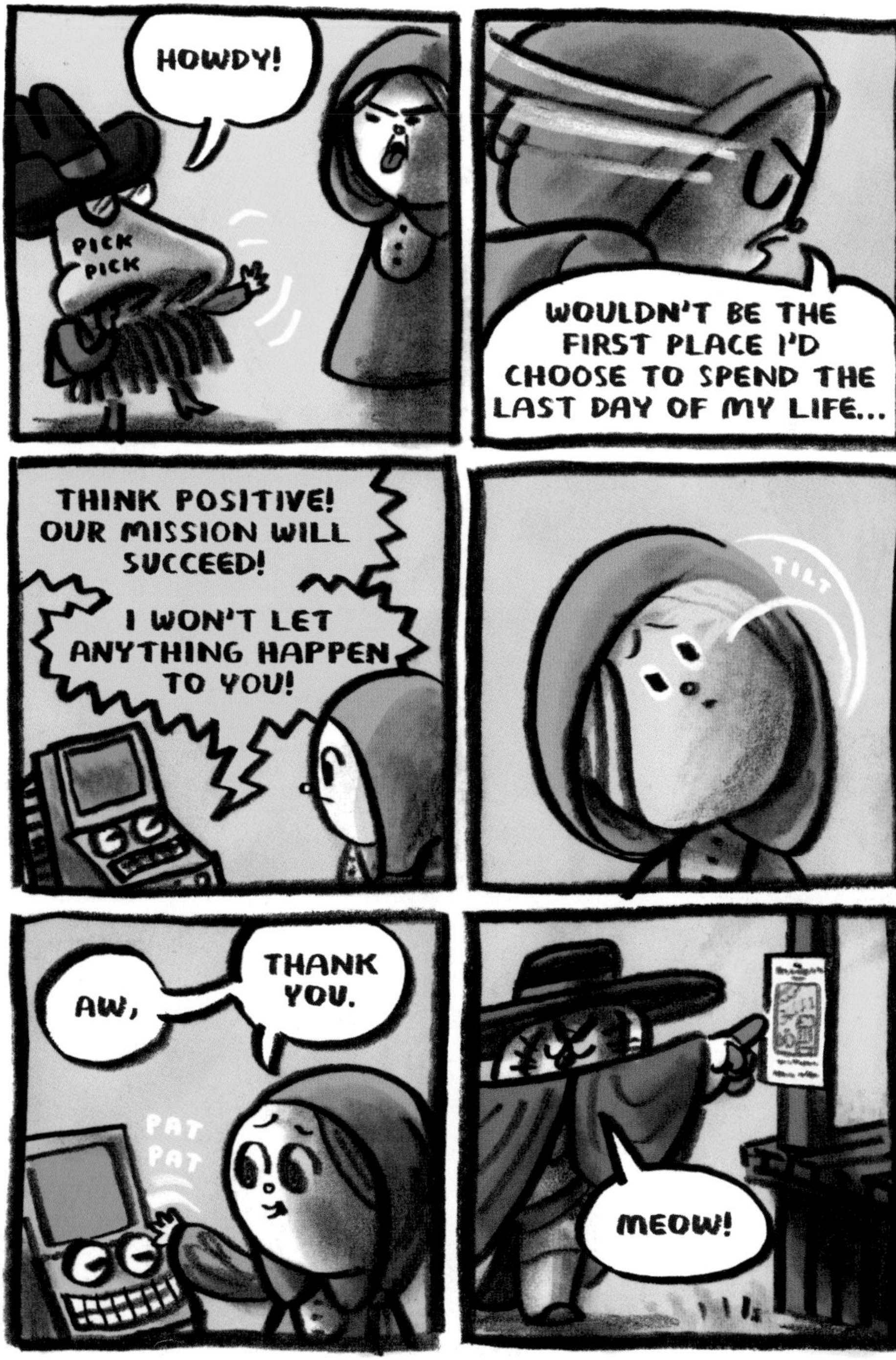
HOWDY!
PICK PICK
WOULDN'T BE THE FIRST PLACE I'D CHOOSE TO SPEND THE LAST DAY OF MY LIFE...
THINK POSITIVE! OUR MISSION WILL SUCCEED!
I WON'T LET ANYTHING HAPPEN TO YOU!
TILT
AW,
THANK YOU.
PAT PAT
MEOW!

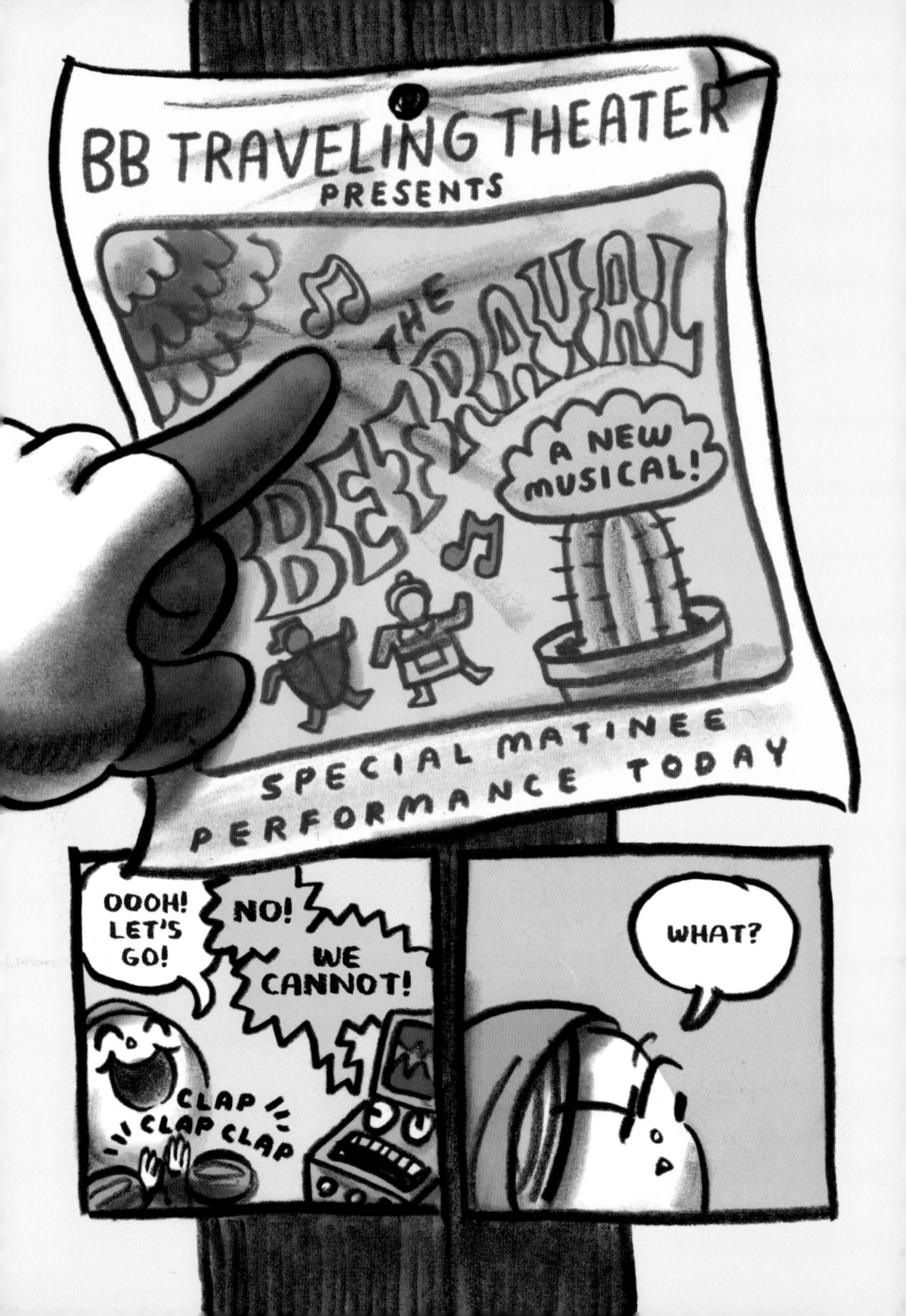
BB TRAVELING THEATER
PRESENTS
THE BETRAYAL
A NEW MUSICAL!
SPECIAL MATINEE PERFORMANCE TODAY
OOOH! LET'S GO!
NO!
WE CANNOT!
CLAP CLAP CLAP CLAP
WHAT?

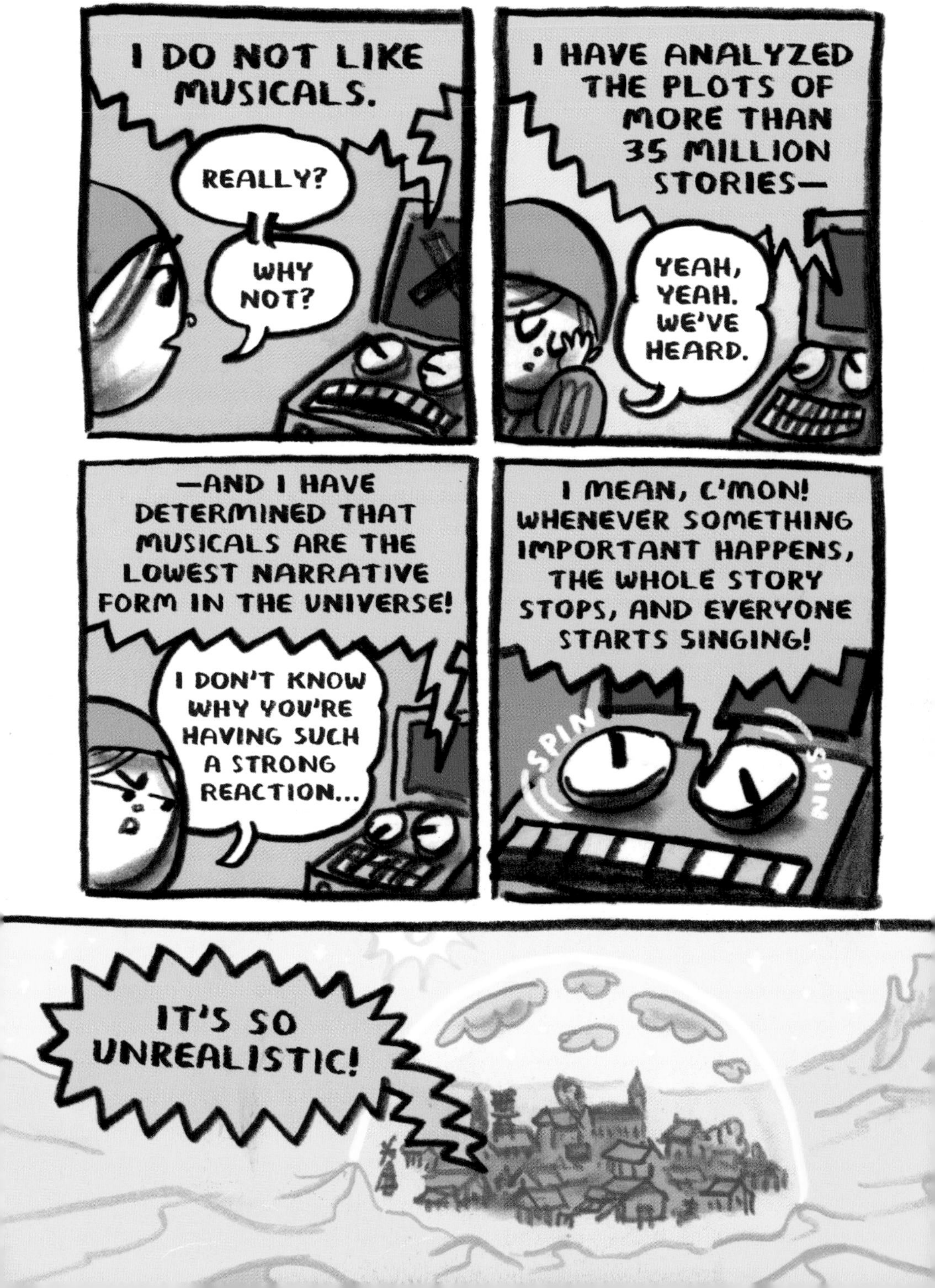
I DO NOT LIKE MUSICALS.
REALLY?
WHY NOT?
I HAVE ANALYZED THE PLOTS OF MORE THAN 35 MILLION STORIES—
YEAH, YEAH. WE'VE HEARD.
—AND I HAVE DETERMINED THAT MUSICALS ARE THE LOWEST NARRATIVE FORM IN THE UNIVERSE!
I DON'T KNOW WHY YOU'RE HAVING SUCH A STRONG REACTION...
I MEAN, C'MON! WHENEVER SOMETHING IMPORTANT HAPPENS, THE WHOLE STORY STOPS, AND EVERYONE STARTS SINGING!
SPIN
SPIN
IT'S SO UNREALISTIC!

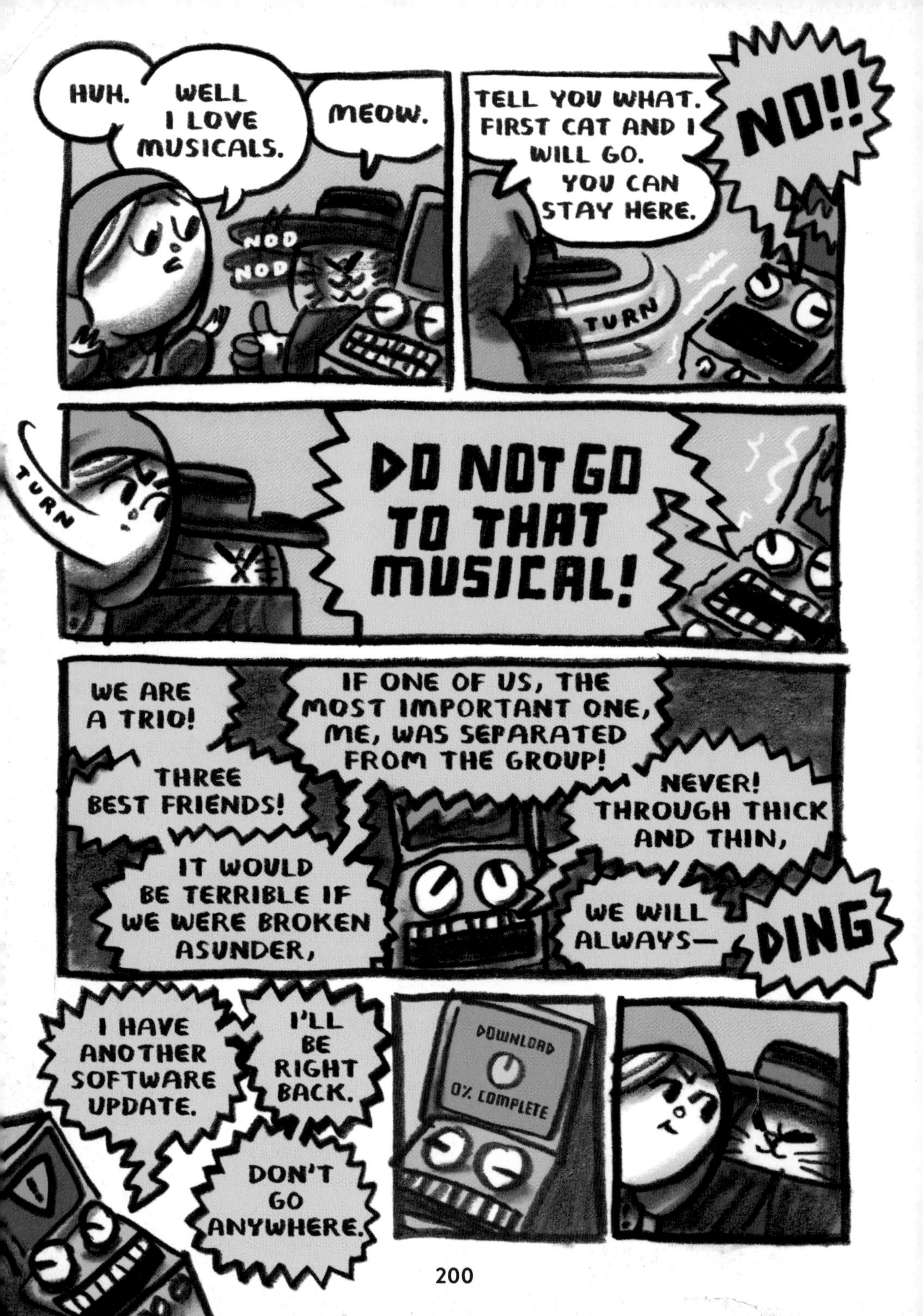
HUH.
WELL I LOVE MUSICALS.
MEOW.
NOD
NOD
TELL YOU WHAT. FIRST CAT AND I WILL GO. YOU CAN STAY HERE.
NO!!
TURN
TURN
DO NOT GO TO THAT MUSICAL!
WE ARE A TRIO!
IF ONE OF US, THE MOST IMPORTANT ONE, ME, WAS SEPARATED FROM THE GROUP!
THREE BEST FRIENDS!
NEVER! THROUGH THICK AND THIN,
IT WOULD BE TERRIBLE IF WE WERE BROKEN ASUNDER,
WE WILL ALWAYS—
DING
I HAVE ANOTHER SOFTWARE UPDATE.
I'LL BE RIGHT BACK.
DON'T GO ANYWHERE.
DOWNLOAD
0% COMPLETE

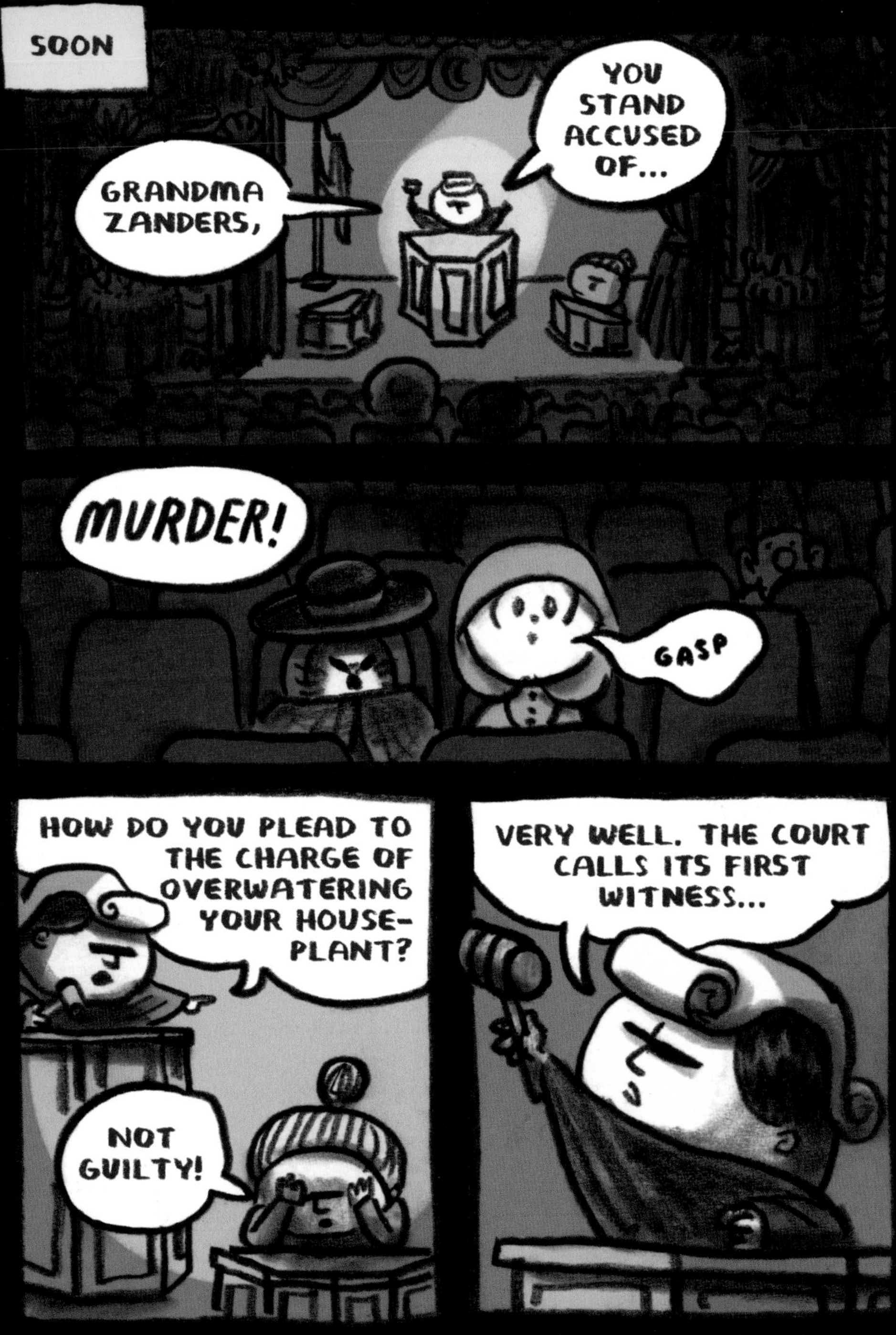
SOON
GRANDMA ZANDERS,
YOU STAND ACCUSED OF...
MURDER!
GASP
HOW DO YOU PLEAD TO THE CHARGE OF OVERWATERING YOUR HOUSE-PLANT?
NOT GUILTY!
VERY WELL. THE COURT CALLS ITS FIRST WITNESS...

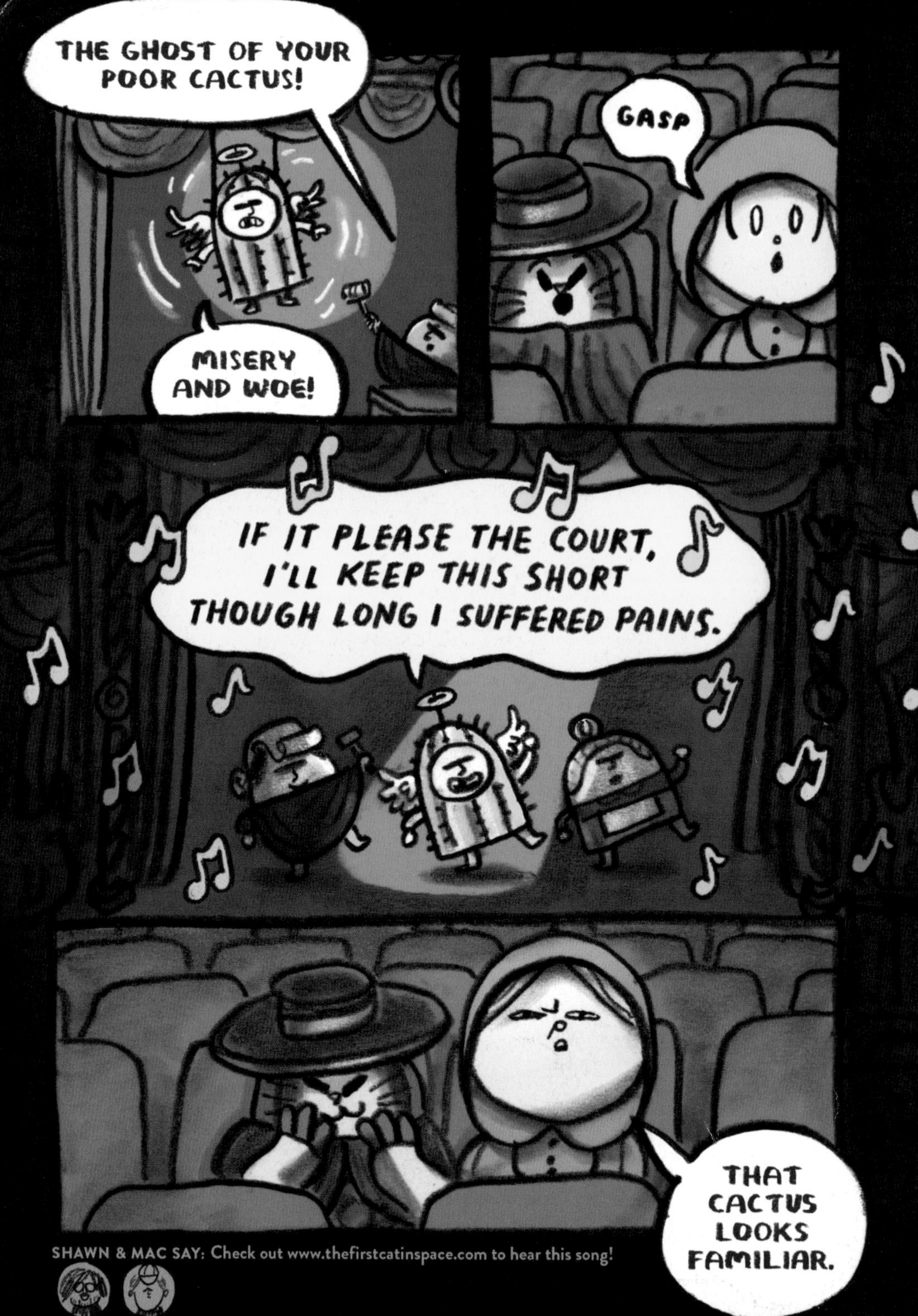
THE GHOST OF YOUR POOR CACTUS!
MISERY AND WOE!
GASP
IF IT PLEASE THE COURT, I'LL KEEP THIS SHORT THOUGH LONG I SUFFERED PAINS.
THAT CACTUS LOOKS FAMILIAR.
SHAWN & MAC SAY: Check out www.thefirstcatinspace.com to hear this song!

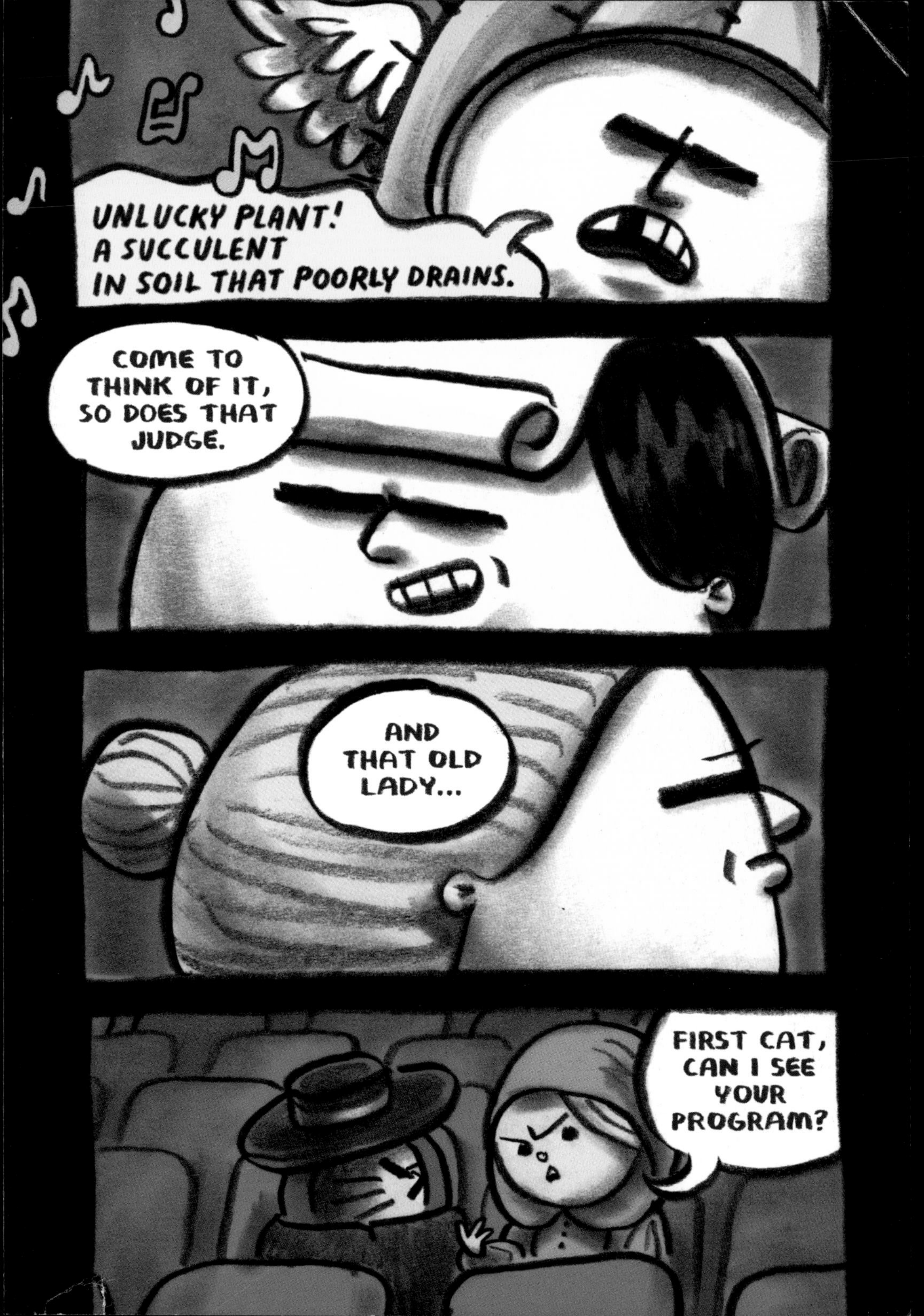
UNLUCKY PLANT! A SUCCULENT IN SOIL THAT POORLY DRAINS.
COME TO THINK OF IT, SO DOES THAT JUDGE.
AND THAT OLD LADY...
FIRST CAT, CAN I SEE YOUR PROGRAM?

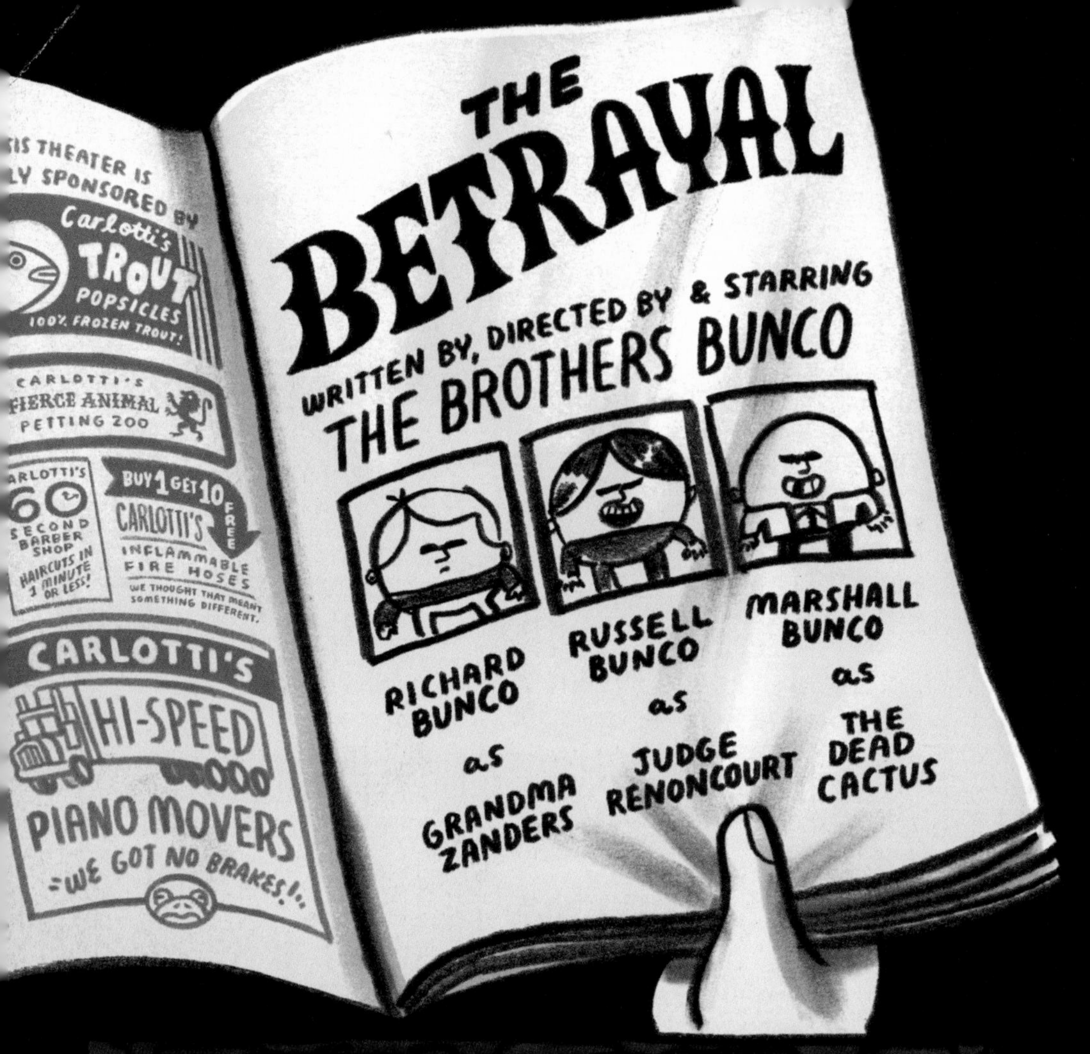
THIS THEATER IS
LY SPONSORED BY
Carlotti's
TROUT
POPSICLES
100% FROZEN TROUT!
CARLOTTI'S
FIERCE ANIMAL
PETTING ZOO
ARLOTTI'S
60
SECOND
BARBER
SHOP
HAIRCUTS IN
1 MINUTE
OR LESS!
BUY 1 GET 10 FREE
CARLOTTI'S
INFLAMMABLE
FIRE HOSES
WE THOUGHT THAT MEANT SOMETHING DIFFERENT.
CARLOTTI'S
HI-SPEED
PIANO MOVERS
=WE GOT NO BRAKES!=
THE
BETRAYAL
WRITTEN BY, DIRECTED BY & STARRING
THE BROTHERS BUNCO
RICHARD
BUNCO
as
GRANDMA
ZANDERS
RUSSELL
BUNCO
as
JUDGE
RENONCOURT
MARSHALL
BUNCO
as
THE
DEAD
CACTUS

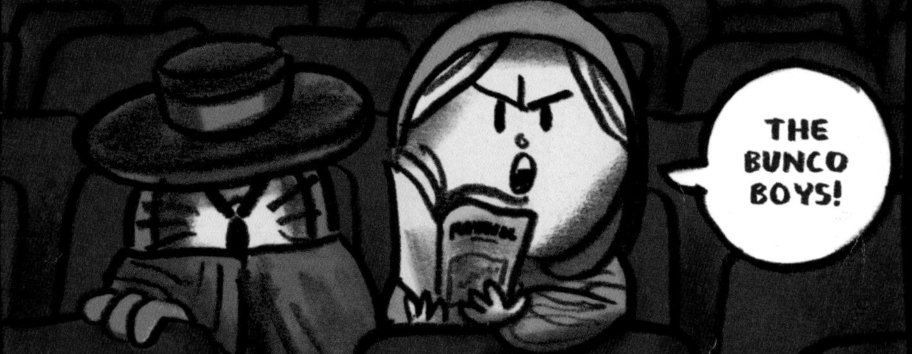
THE
BUNCO
BOYS!

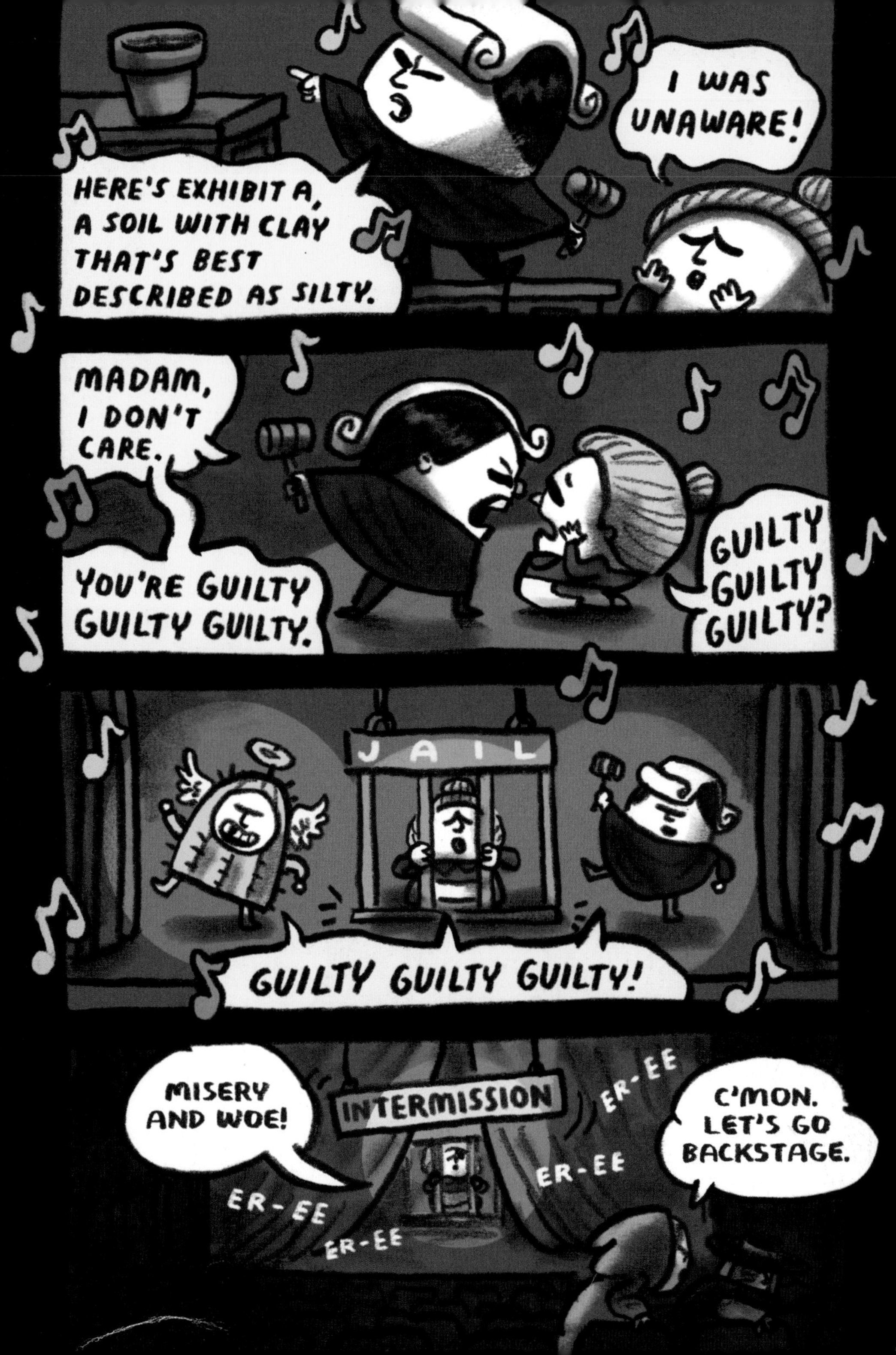
HERE'S EXHIBIT A, A SOIL WITH CLAY THAT'S BEST DESCRIBED AS SILTY.
I WAS UNAWARE!
MADAM, I DON'T CARE.
YOU'RE GUILTY GUILTY GUILTY.
GUILTY GUILTY GUILTY?
JAIL
GUILTY GUILTY GUILTY!
MISERY AND WOE!
INTERMISSION
ER-EE
ER-EE
ER-EE
ER-EE
C'MON. LET'S GO BACKSTAGE.

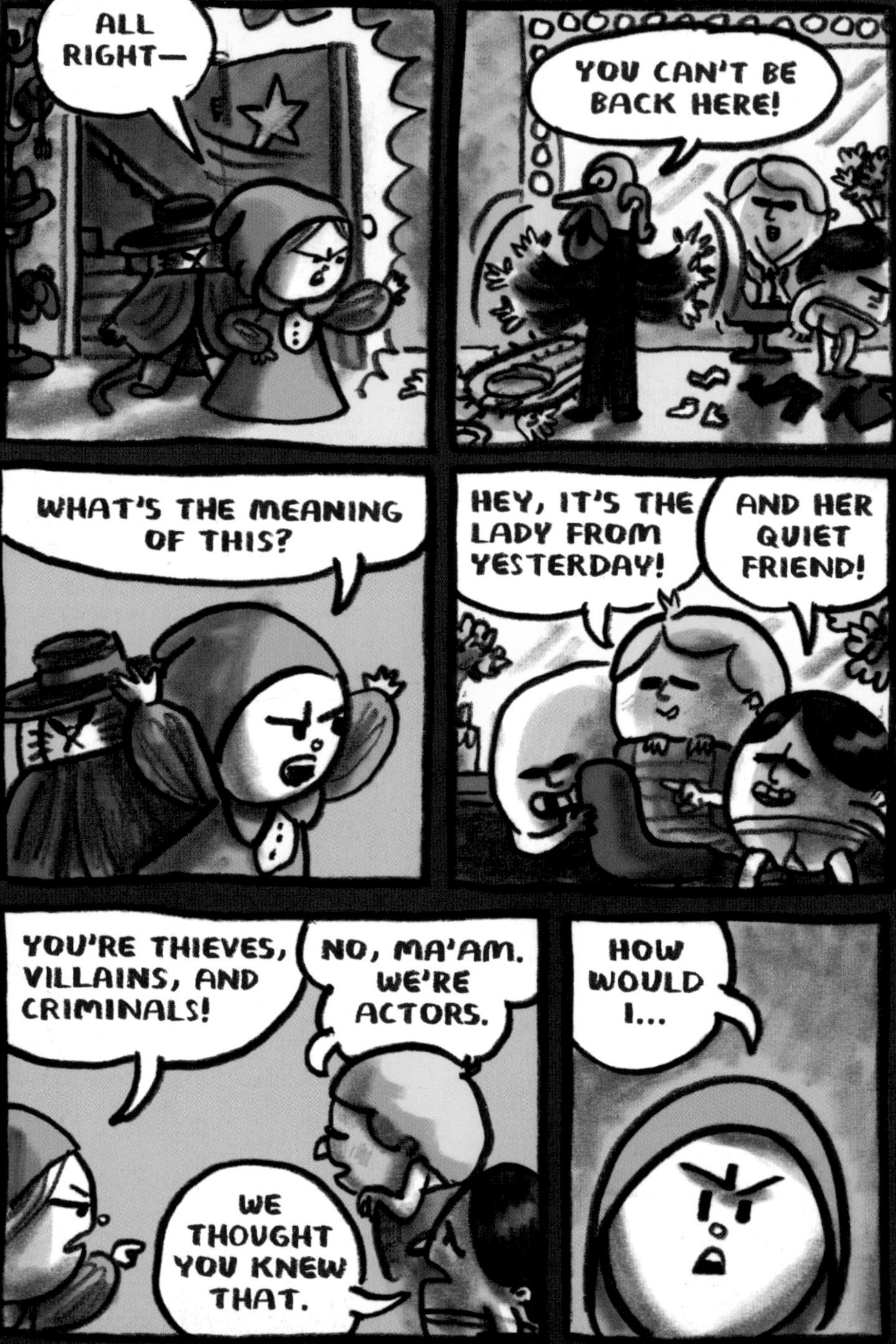
ALL RIGHT—
YOU CAN'T BE BACK HERE!
WHAT'S THE MEANING OF THIS?
HEY, IT'S THE LADY FROM YESTERDAY!
AND HER QUIET FRIEND!
YOU'RE THIEVES, VILLAINS, AND CRIMINALS!
NO, MA'AM. WE'RE ACTORS.
WE THOUGHT YOU KNEW THAT.
HOW WOULD I...

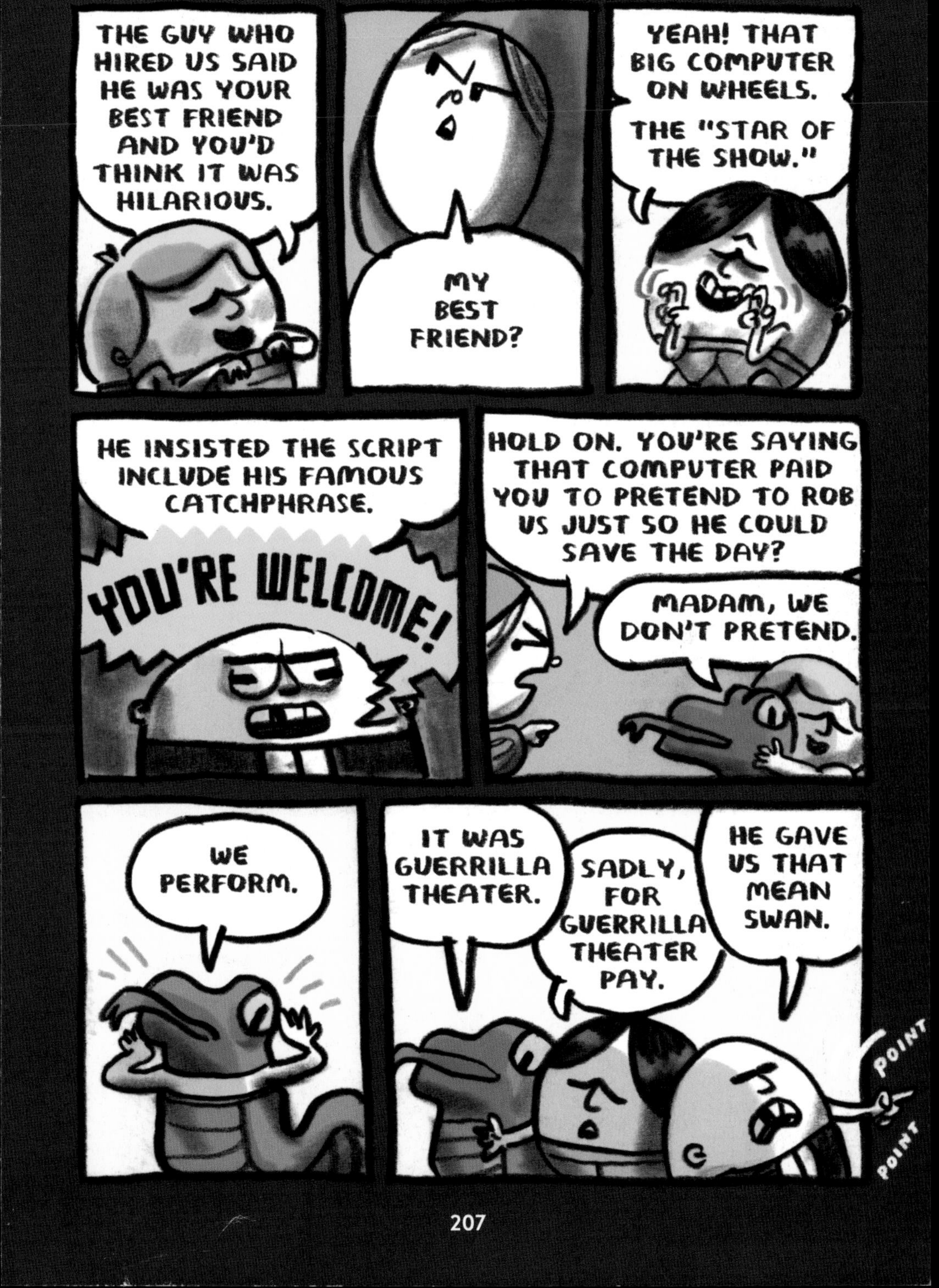

THE GUY WHO HIRED US SAID HE WAS YOUR BEST FRIEND AND YOU'D THINK IT WAS HILARIOUS.
MY BEST FRIEND?
YEAH! THAT BIG COMPUTER ON WHEELS.
THE "STAR OF THE SHOW."
HE INSISTED THE SCRIPT INCLUDE HIS FAMOUS CATCHPHRASE.
YOU'RE WELCOME!
HOLD ON. YOU'RE SAYING THAT COMPUTER PAID YOU TO PRETEND TO ROB US JUST SO HE COULD SAVE THE DAY?
MADAM, WE DON'T PRETEND.
WE PERFORM.
IT WAS GUERRILLA THEATER.
SADLY, FOR GUERRILLA THEATER PAY.
HE GAVE US THAT MEAN SWAN.
POINT
POINT

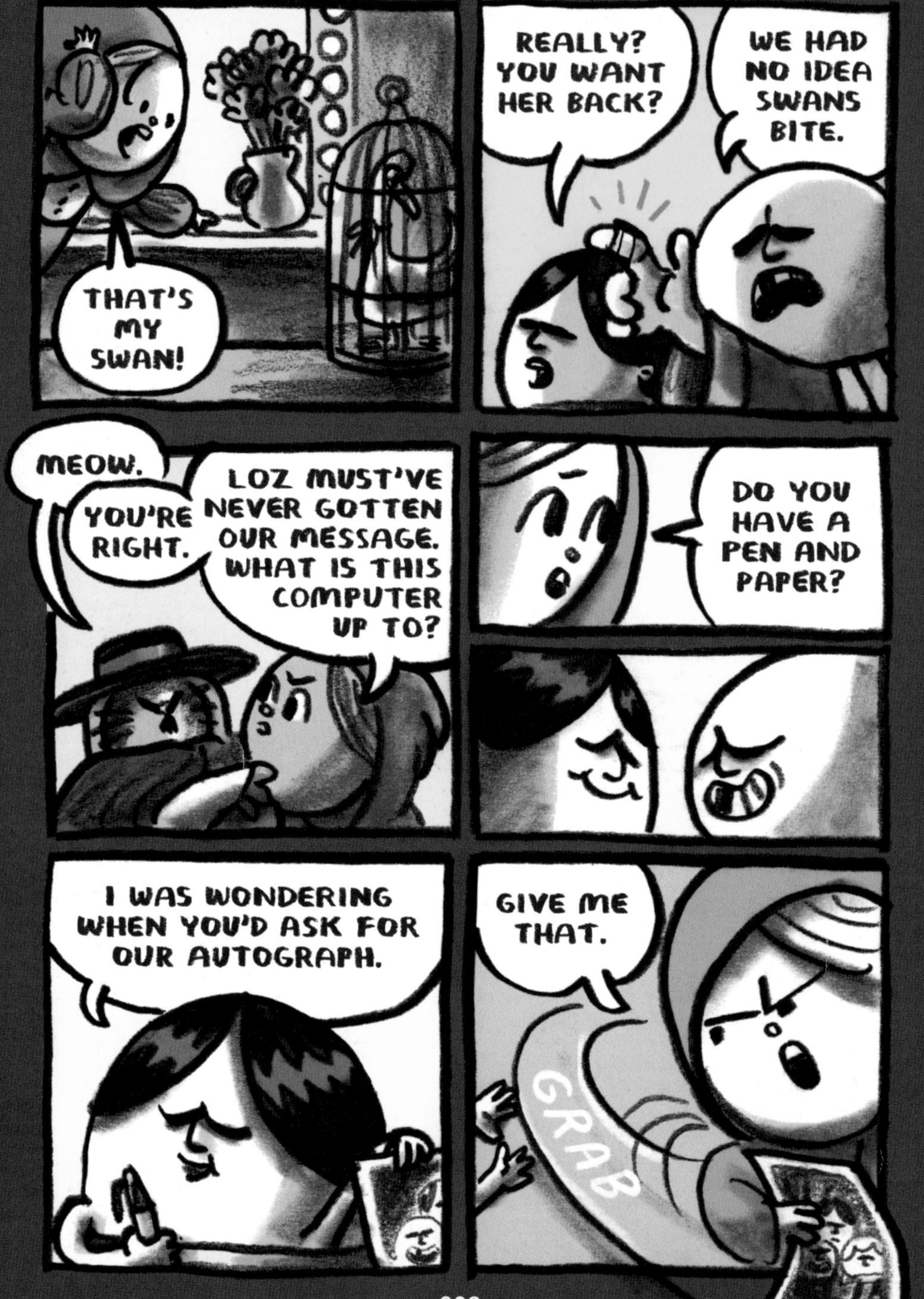
THAT'S MY SWAN!
REALLY? YOU WANT HER BACK?
WE HAD NO IDEA SWANS BITE.
MEOW.
YOU'RE RIGHT.
LOZ MUST'VE NEVER GOTTEN OUR MESSAGE. WHAT IS THIS COMPUTER UP TO?
DO YOU HAVE A PEN AND PAPER?
I WAS WONDERING WHEN YOU'D ASK FOR OUR AUTOGRAPH.
GIVE ME THAT.
GRAB

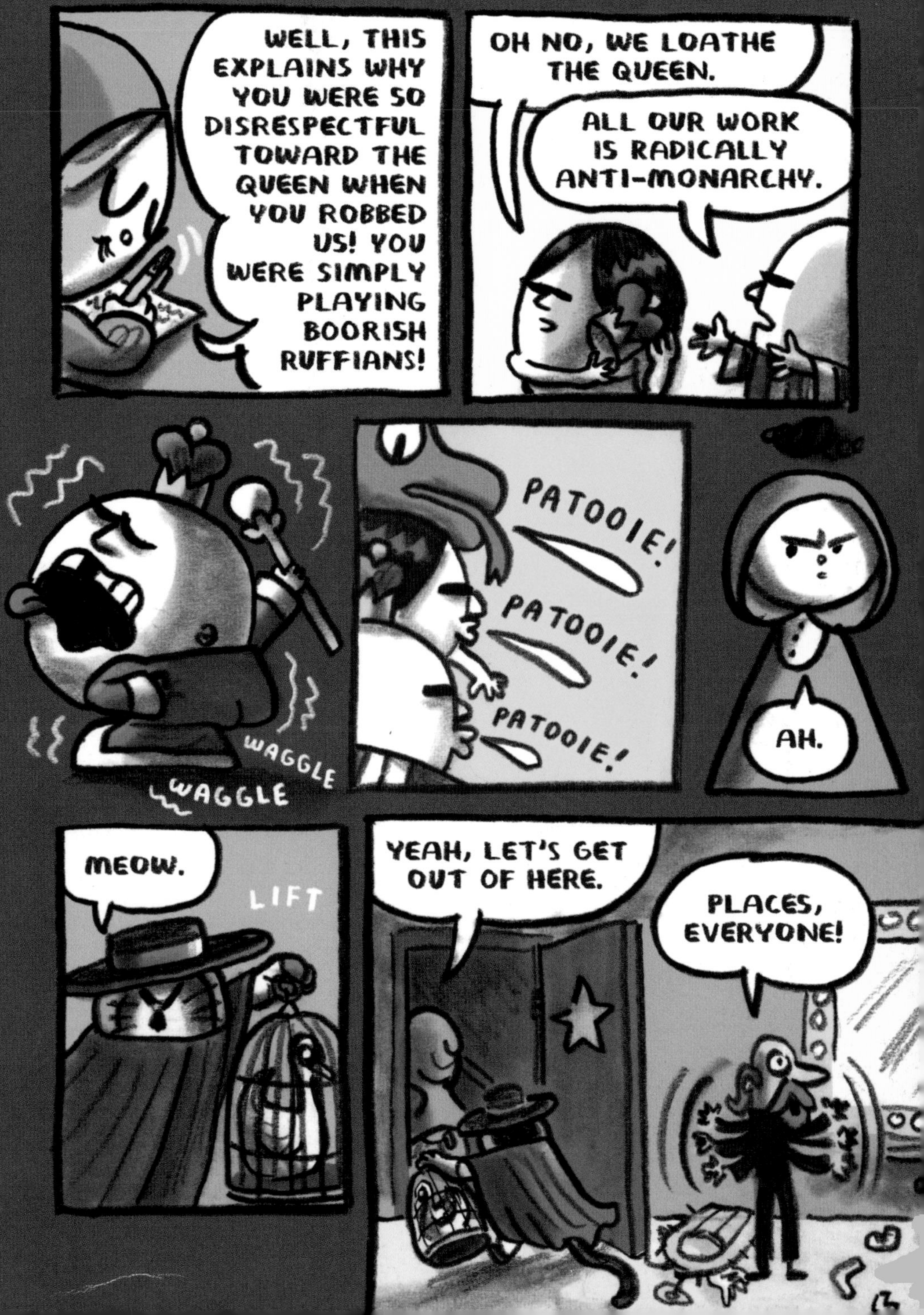

WELL, THIS EXPLAINS WHY YOU WERE SO DISRESPECTFUL TOWARD THE QUEEN WHEN YOU ROBBED US! YOU WERE SIMPLY PLAYING BOORISH RUFFIANS!
OH NO, WE LOATHE THE QUEEN.
ALL OUR WORK IS RADICALLY ANTI-MONARCHY.
WAGGLE
WAGGLE
PATOOIE!
PATOOIE!
PATOOIE!
AH.
MEOW.
LIFT
YEAH, LET'S GET OUT OF HERE.
PLACES, EVERYONE!

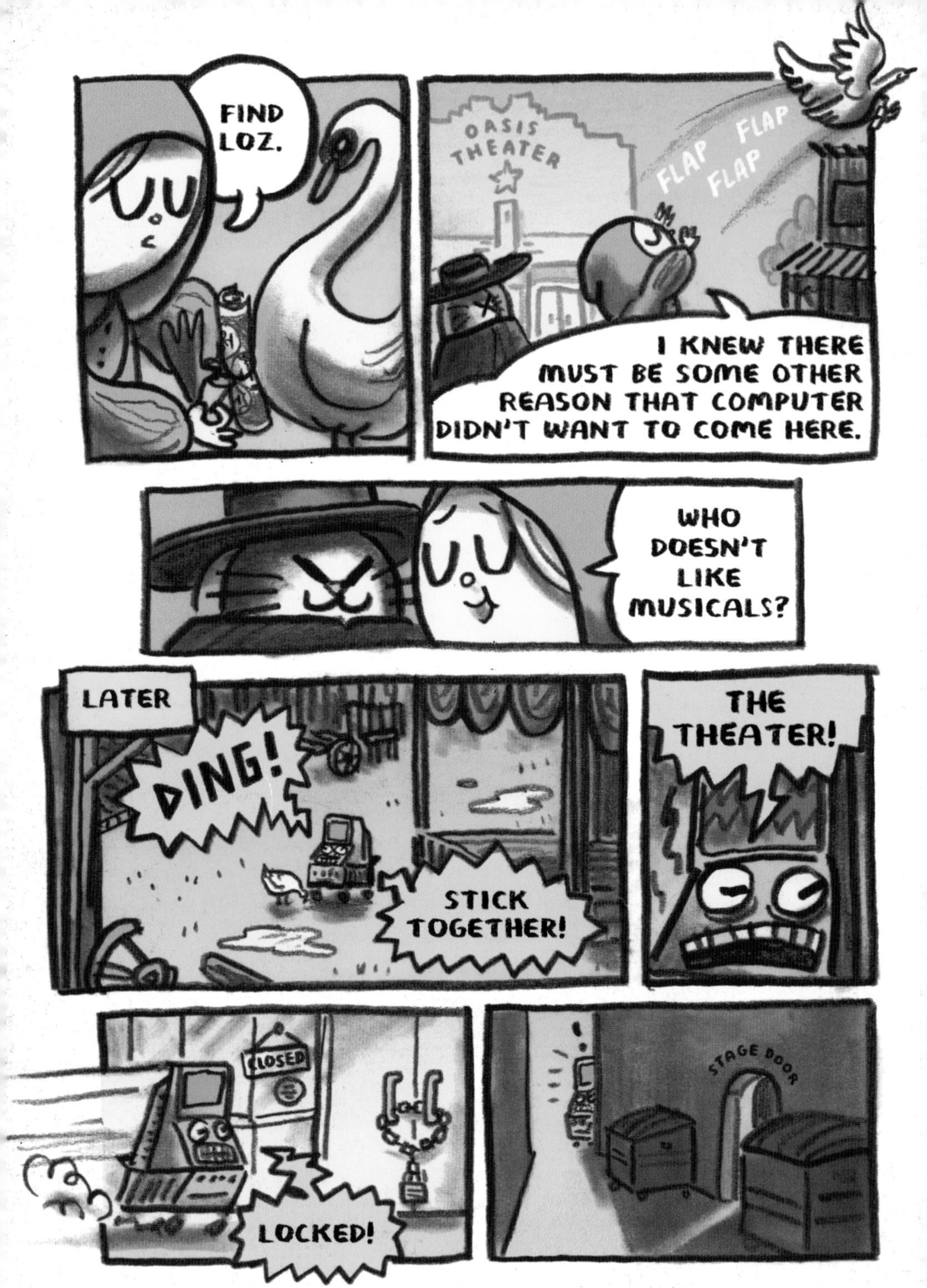

FIND LOZ.
OASIS THEATER
FLAP FLAP FLAP FLAP
I KNEW THERE MUST BE SOME OTHER REASON THAT COMPUTER DIDN'T WANT TO COME HERE.
WHO DOESN'T LIKE MUSICALS?
LATER
DING!
STICK TOGETHER!
THE THEATER!
CLOSED
LOCKED!
STAGE DOOR

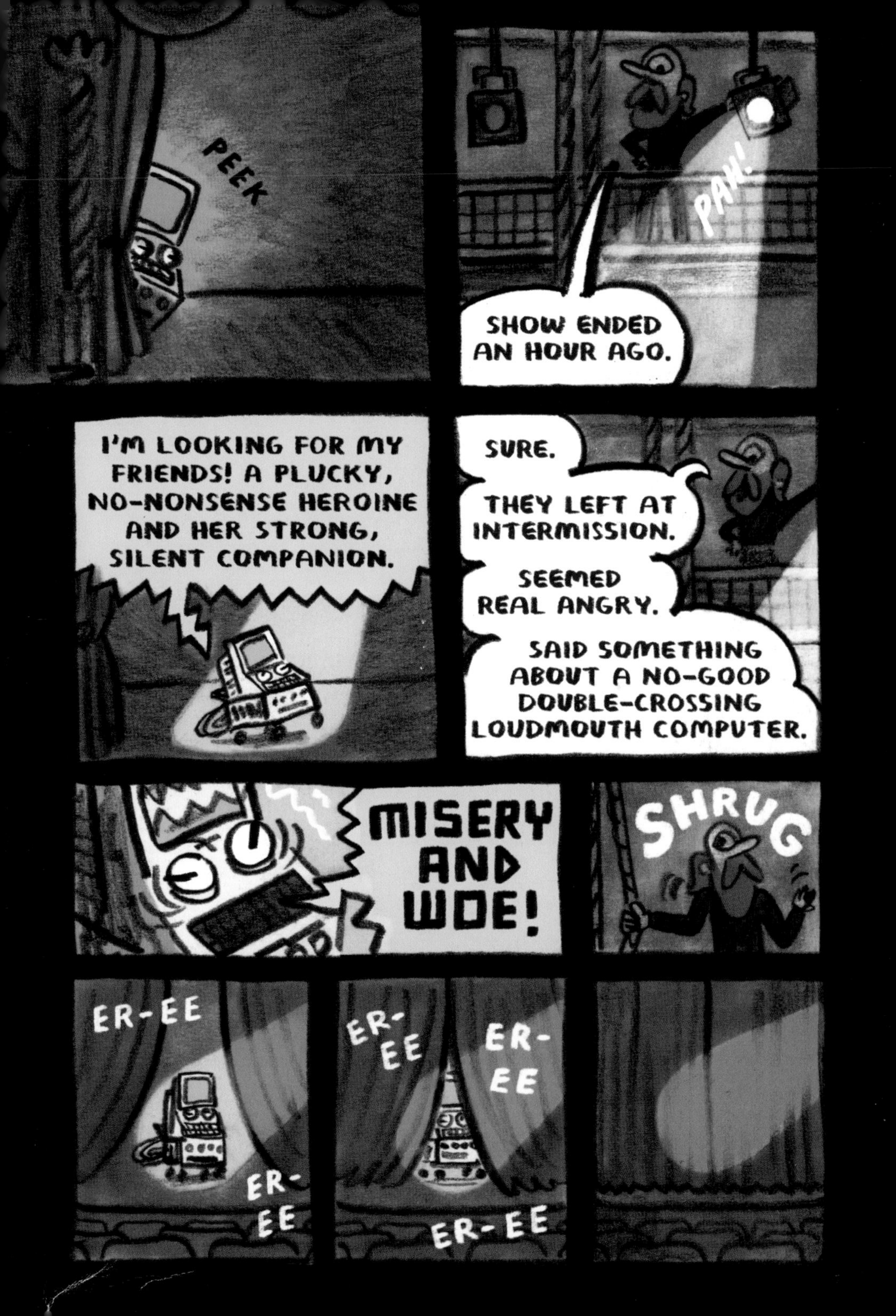
PEEK
PAH!
SHOW ENDED AN HOUR AGO.
I'M LOOKING FOR MY FRIENDS! A PLUCKY, NO-NONSENSE HEROINE AND HER STRONG, SILENT COMPANION.
SURE.
THEY LEFT AT INTERMISSION.
SEEMED REAL ANGRY.
SAID SOMETHING ABOUT A NO-GOOD DOUBLE-CROSSING LOUDMOUTH COMPUTER.
MISERY AND WOE!
SHRUG
ER-EE
ER-EE
ER-EE
ER-EE
ER-EE

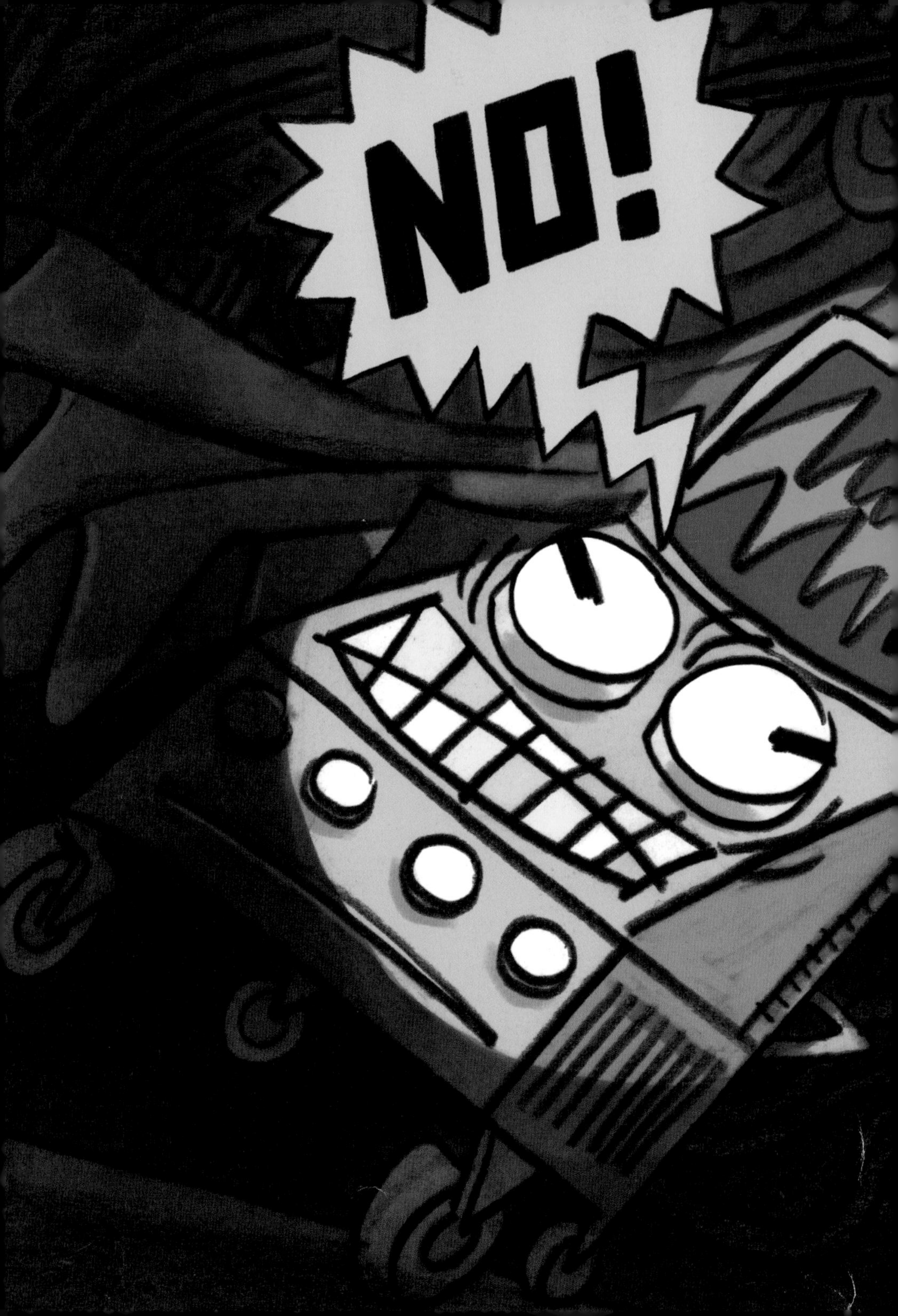
NO!

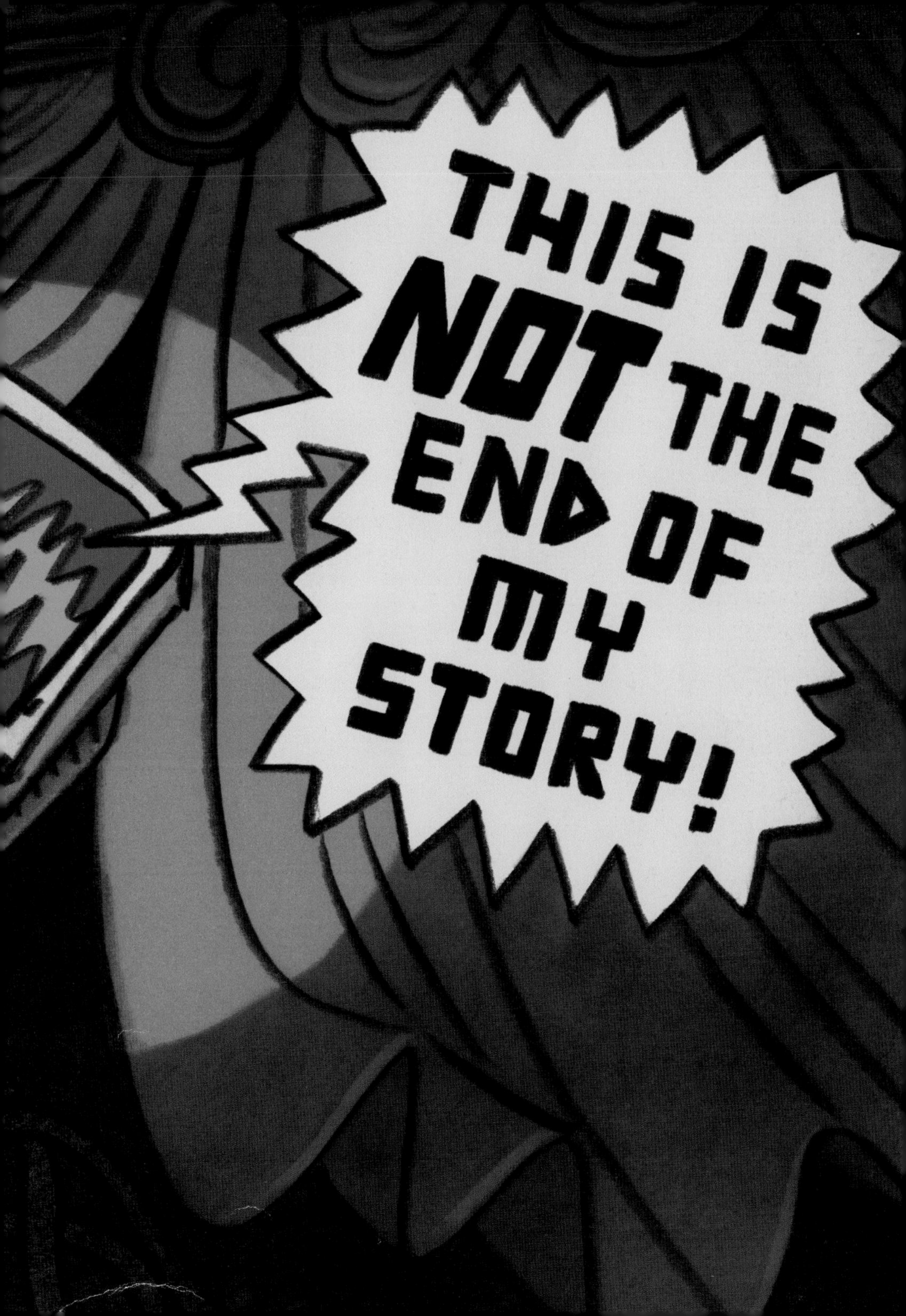
THIS IS NOT THE END OF MY STORY!

CHAPTER II

# JAILBREAK

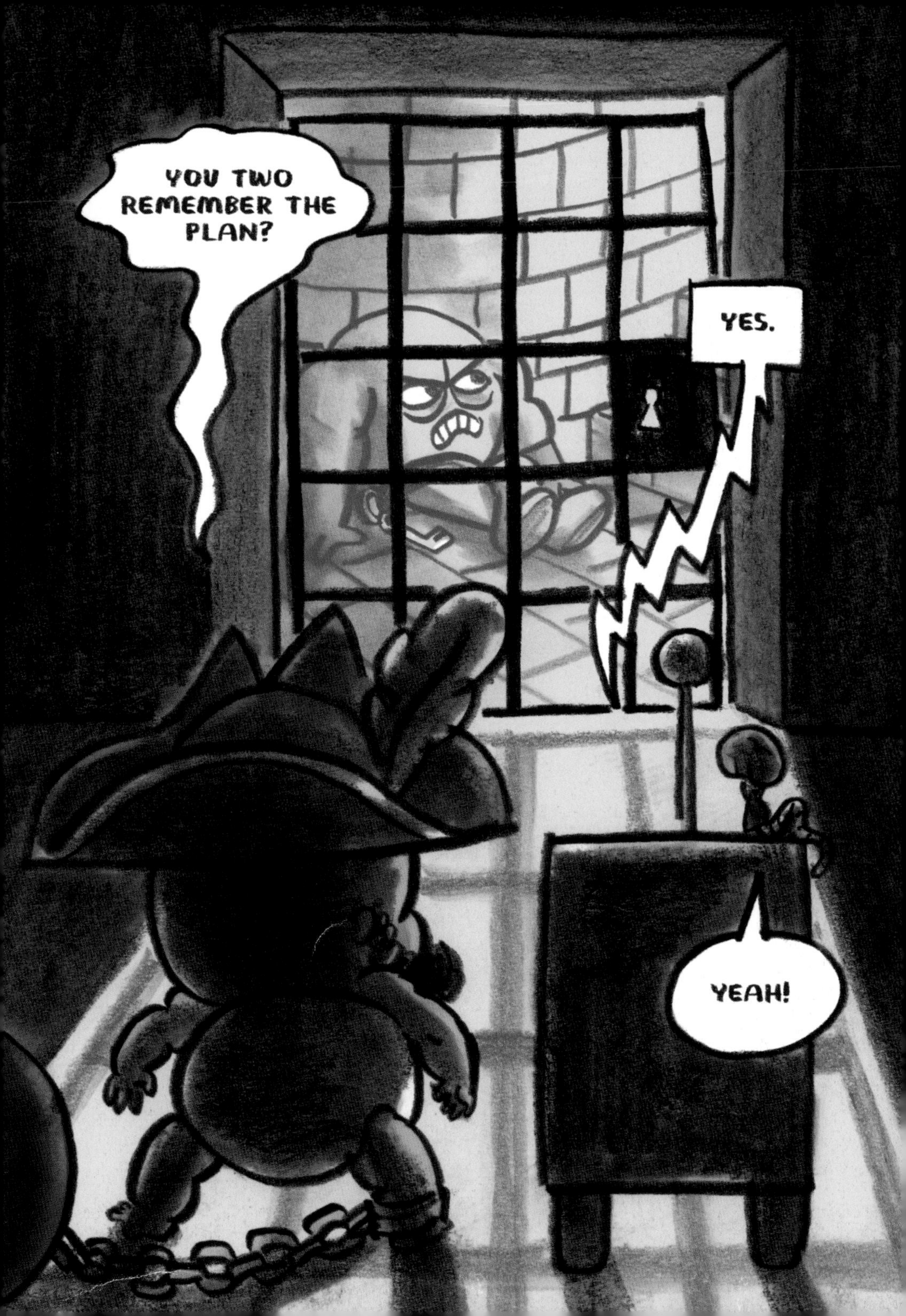
YOU TWO REMEMBER THE PLAN?
YES.
YEAH!

OK, WORM! RECITE ONE OF YER BORING POEMS!

WITH PLEASURE!

AHEM.

STRUM

I SING THE SONG OF JOHN THE KIND, WHO SAID BOTH THANKS AND PLEASE.

A POLITE KNIGHT, HE NEVER WHINED, AND BLESSED YOU WHEN YOU SNEEZED.

SNORE SNORE SNORE SNORE

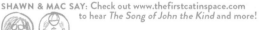

SHAWN & MAC SAY: Check out www.thefirstcatinspace.com to hear *The Song of John the Kind* and more!

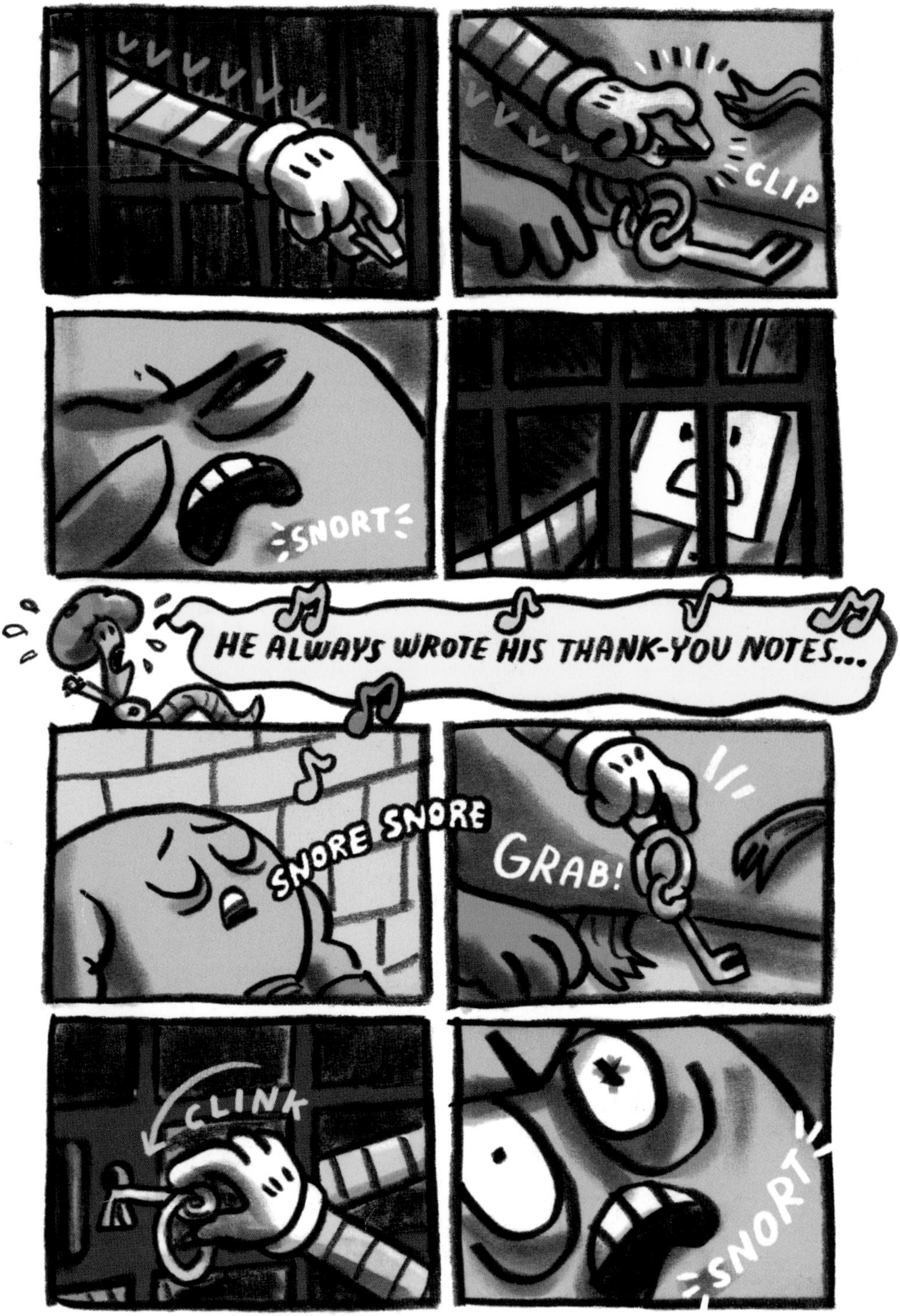
CLIP
SNORT
HE ALWAYS WROTE HIS THANK-YOU NOTES...
SNORE SNORE
GRAB!
CLINK
SNORT

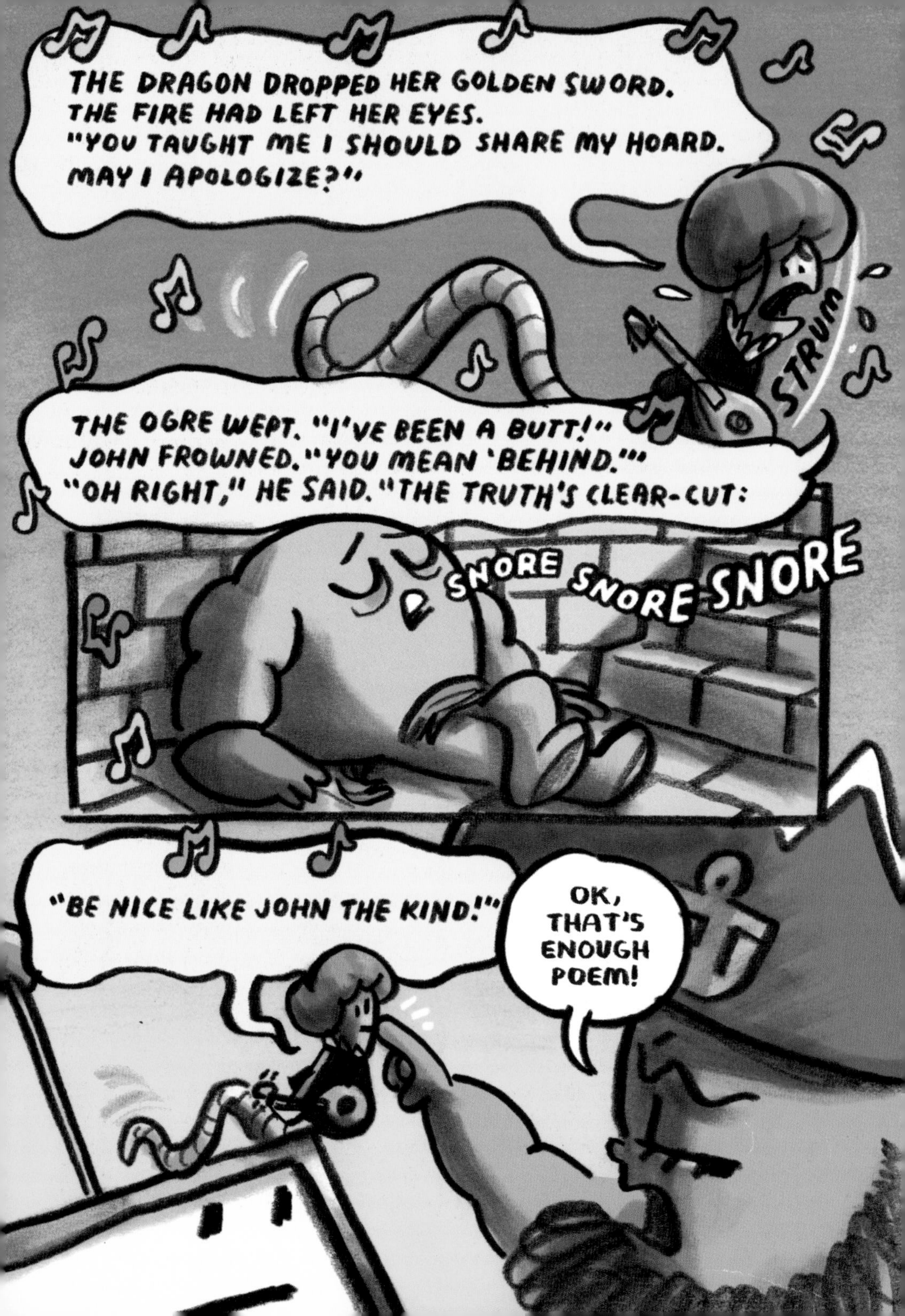
THE DRAGON DROPPED HER GOLDEN SWORD.
THE FIRE HAD LEFT HER EYES.
"YOU TAUGHT ME I SHOULD SHARE MY HOARD.
MAY I APOLOGIZE?"
STRUM
THE OGRE WEPT. "I'VE BEEN A BUTT!"
JOHN FROWNED. "YOU MEAN 'BEHIND.'"
"OH RIGHT," HE SAID. "THE TRUTH'S CLEAR-CUT:
SNORE SNORE SNORE
"BE NICE LIKE JOHN THE KIND!"
OK, THAT'S ENOUGH POEM!

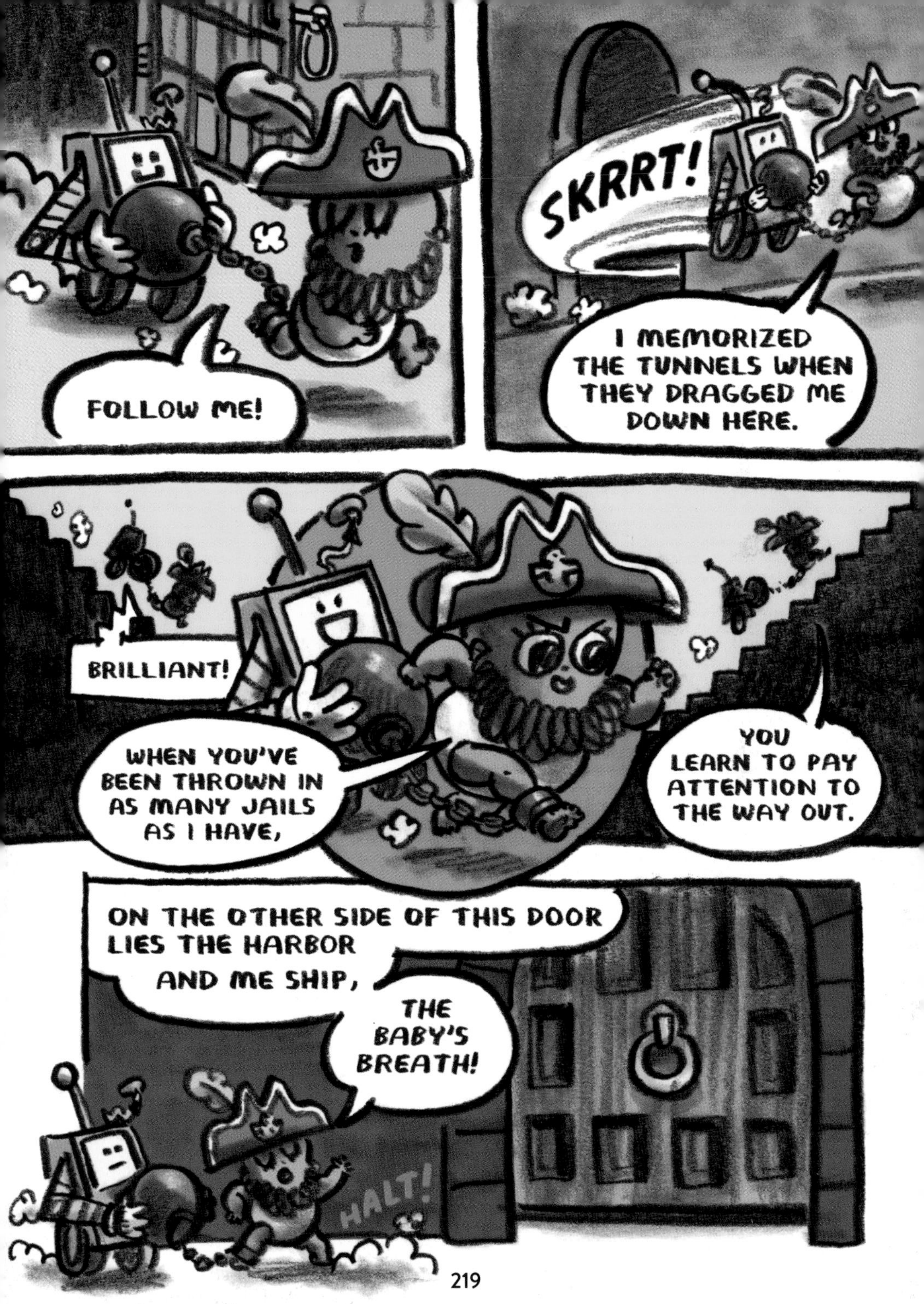
FOLLOW ME!
SKRRT!
I MEMORIZED THE TUNNELS WHEN THEY DRAGGED ME DOWN HERE.
BRILLIANT!
WHEN YOU'VE BEEN THROWN IN AS MANY JAILS AS I HAVE,
YOU LEARN TO PAY ATTENTION TO THE WAY OUT.
ON THE OTHER SIDE OF THIS DOOR LIES THE HARBOR
AND ME SHIP,
THE BABY'S BREATH!
HALT!

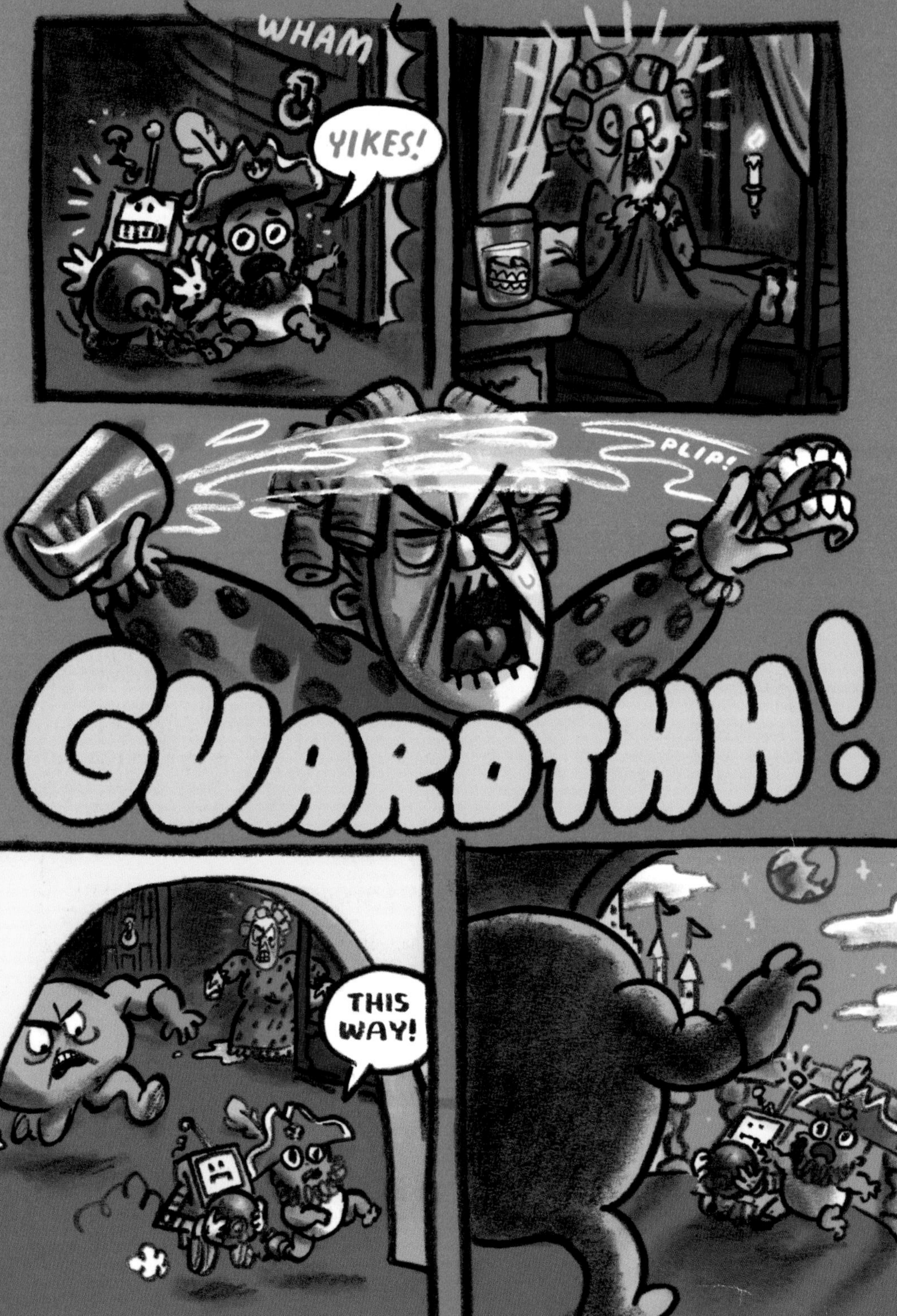
WHAM
YIKES!
PLIP!
GUARDTHH!
THIS WAY!

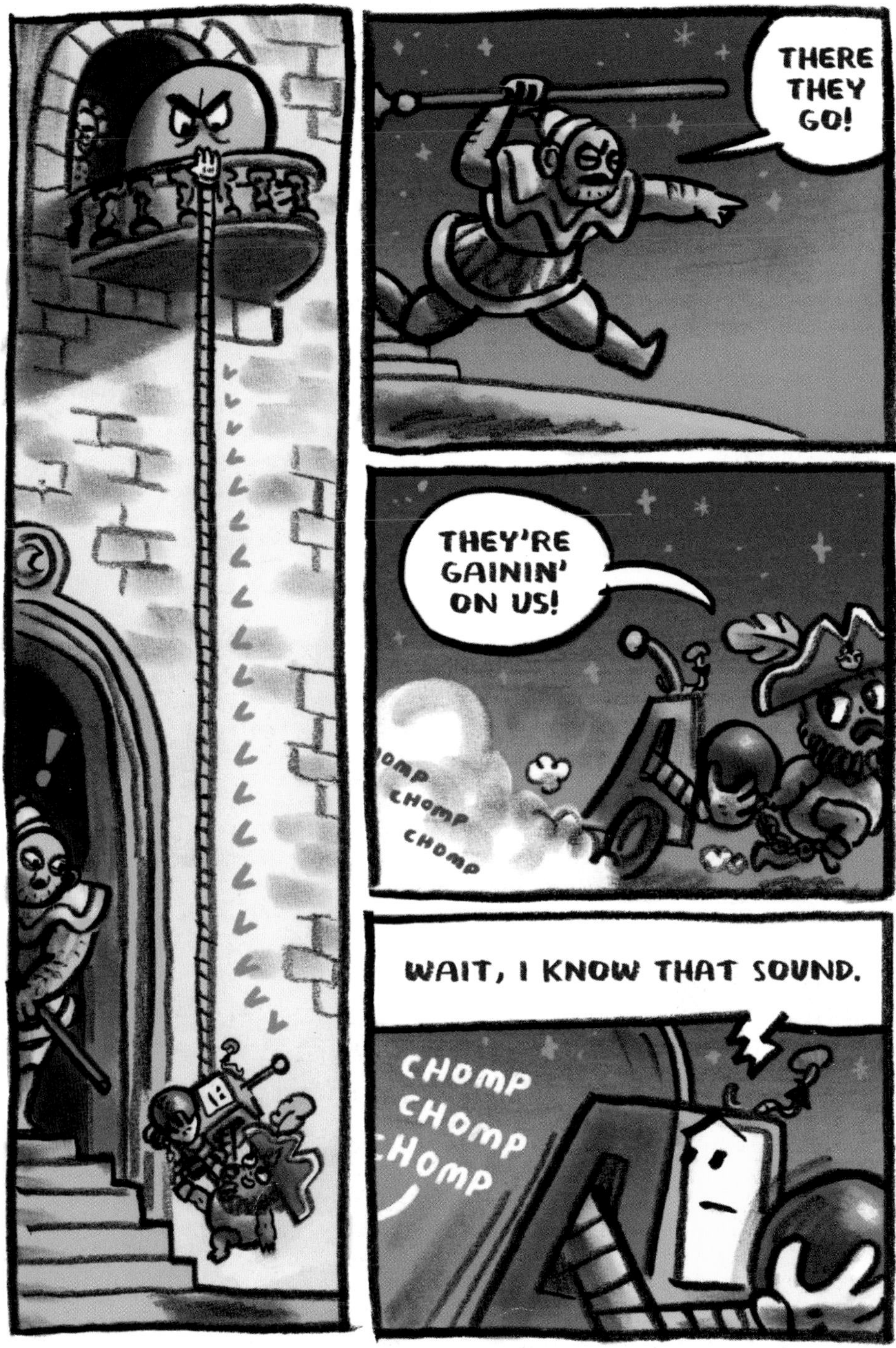
THERE THEY GO!
THEY'RE GAININ' ON US!
OMP
CHOMP
CHOMP
WAIT, I KNOW THAT SOUND.
CHOMP
CHOMP
CHOMP

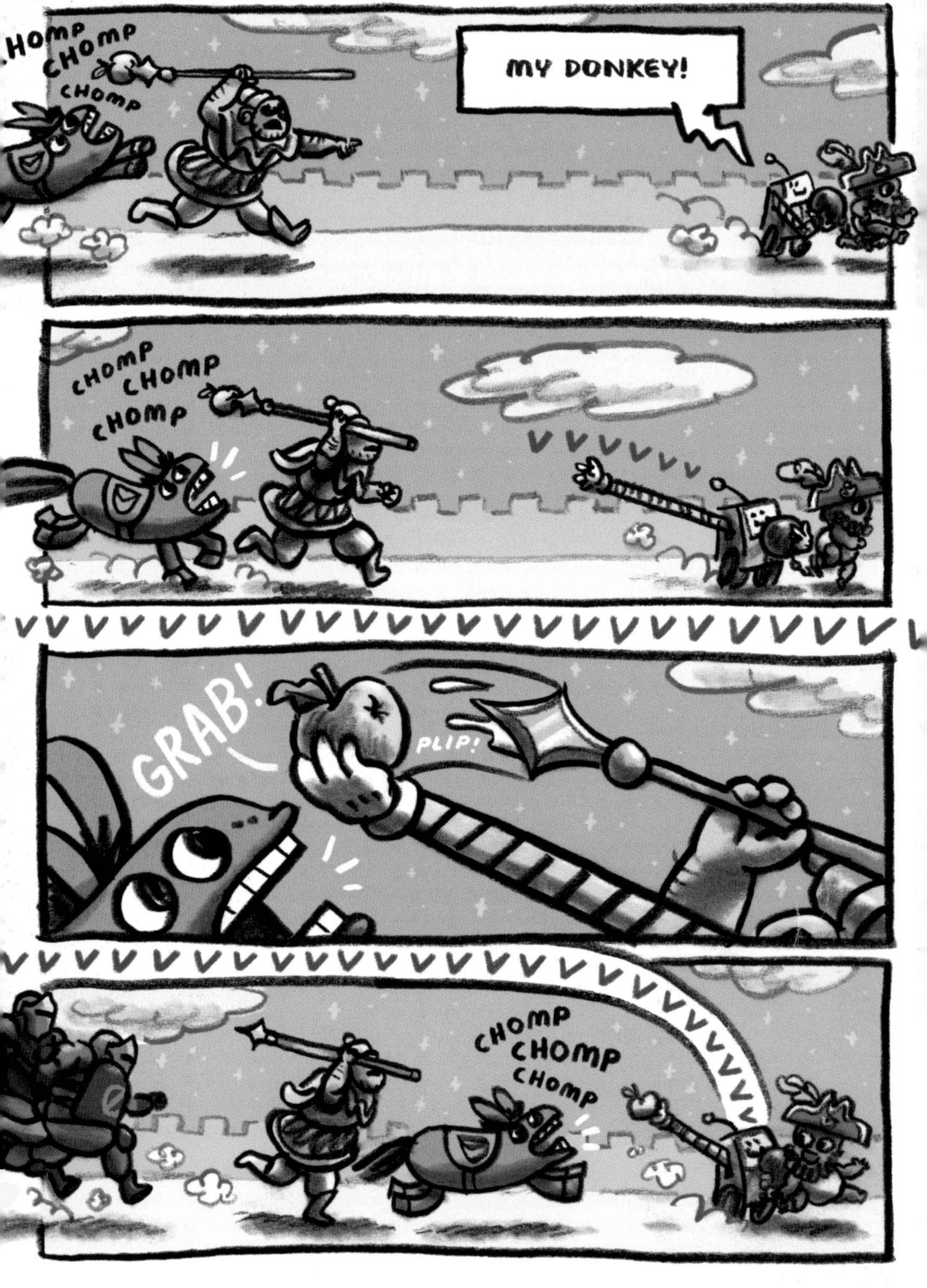
CHOMP CHOMP CHOMP
MY DONKEY!
CHOMP CHOMP CHOMP
GRAB!
PLIP!
CHOMP CHOMP CHOMP

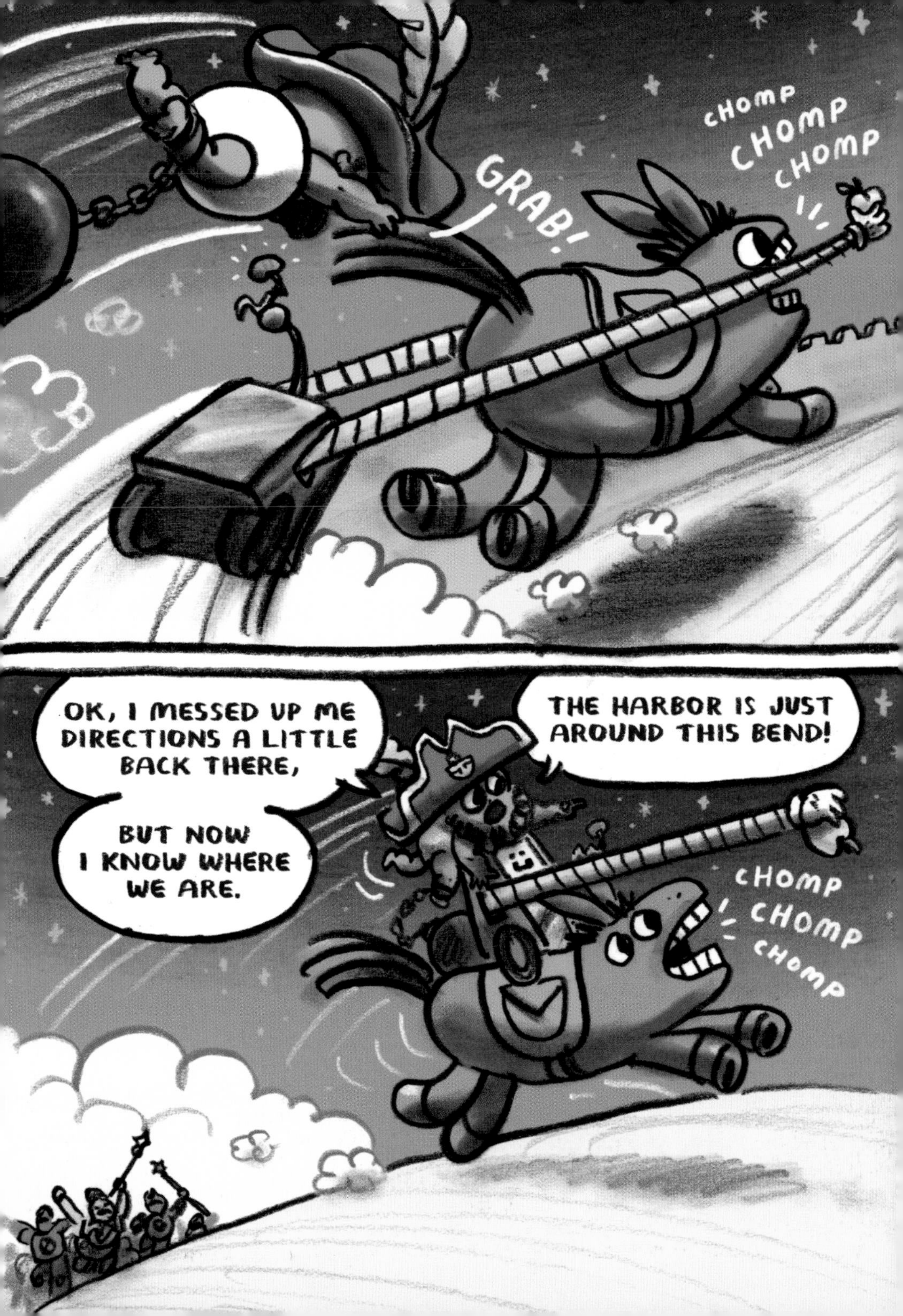
GRAB!
CHOMP
CHOMP
CHOMP
OK, I MESSED UP ME DIRECTIONS A LITTLE BACK THERE,
BUT NOW I KNOW WHERE WE ARE.
THE HARBOR IS JUST AROUND THIS BEND!
CHOMP
CHOMP
CHOMP

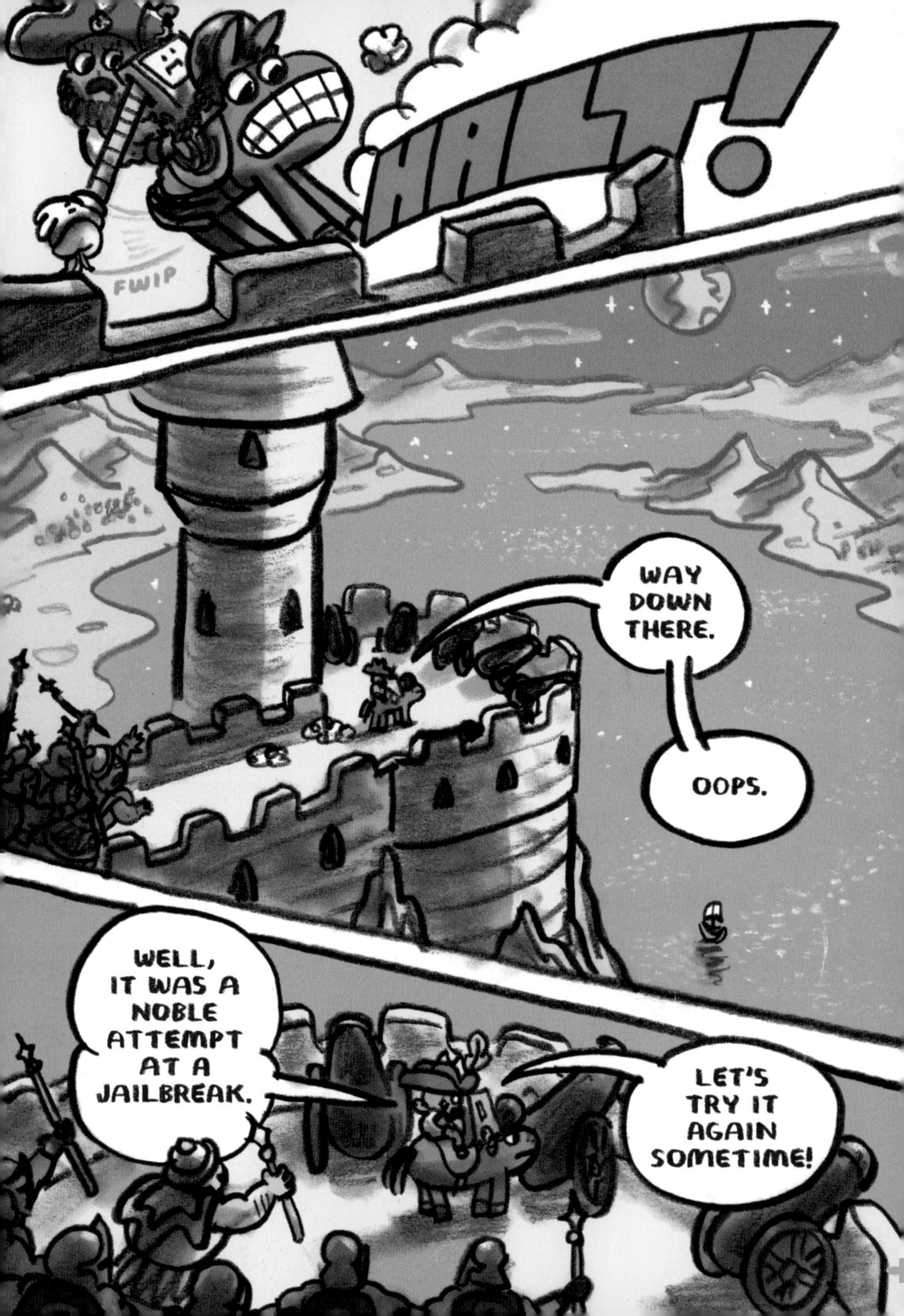
HALT!
FWIP
WAY DOWN THERE.
OOPS.
WELL, IT WAS A NOBLE ATTEMPT AT A JAILBREAK.
LET'S TRY IT AGAIN SOMETIME!

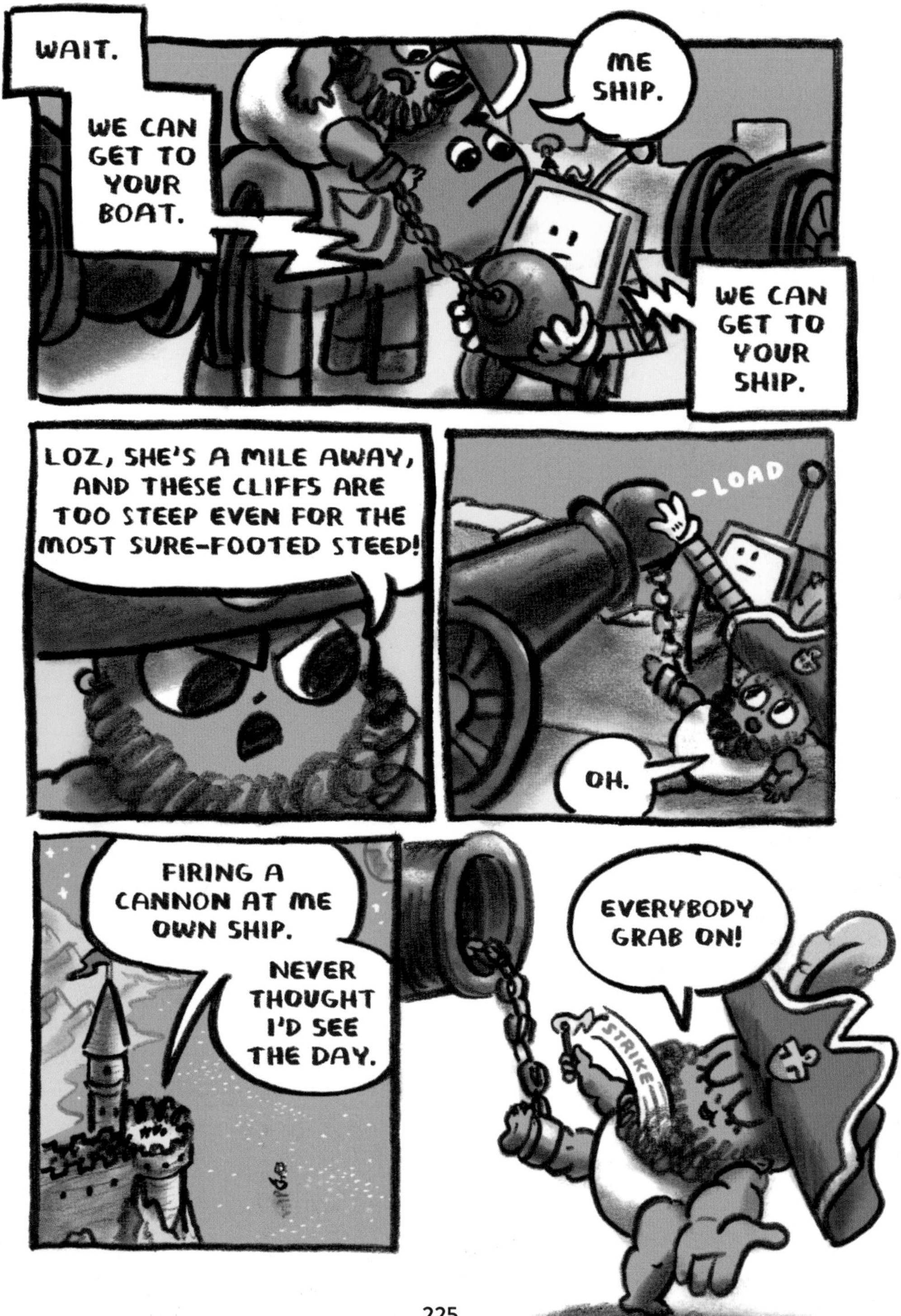
WAIT.
WE CAN GET TO YOUR BOAT.
ME SHIP.
WE CAN GET TO YOUR SHIP.
LOZ, SHE'S A MILE AWAY, AND THESE CLIFFS ARE TOO STEEP EVEN FOR THE MOST SURE-FOOTED STEED!
-LOAD
OH.
FIRING A CANNON AT ME OWN SHIP.
NEVER THOUGHT I'D SEE THE DAY.
EVERYBODY GRAB ON!
STRIKE

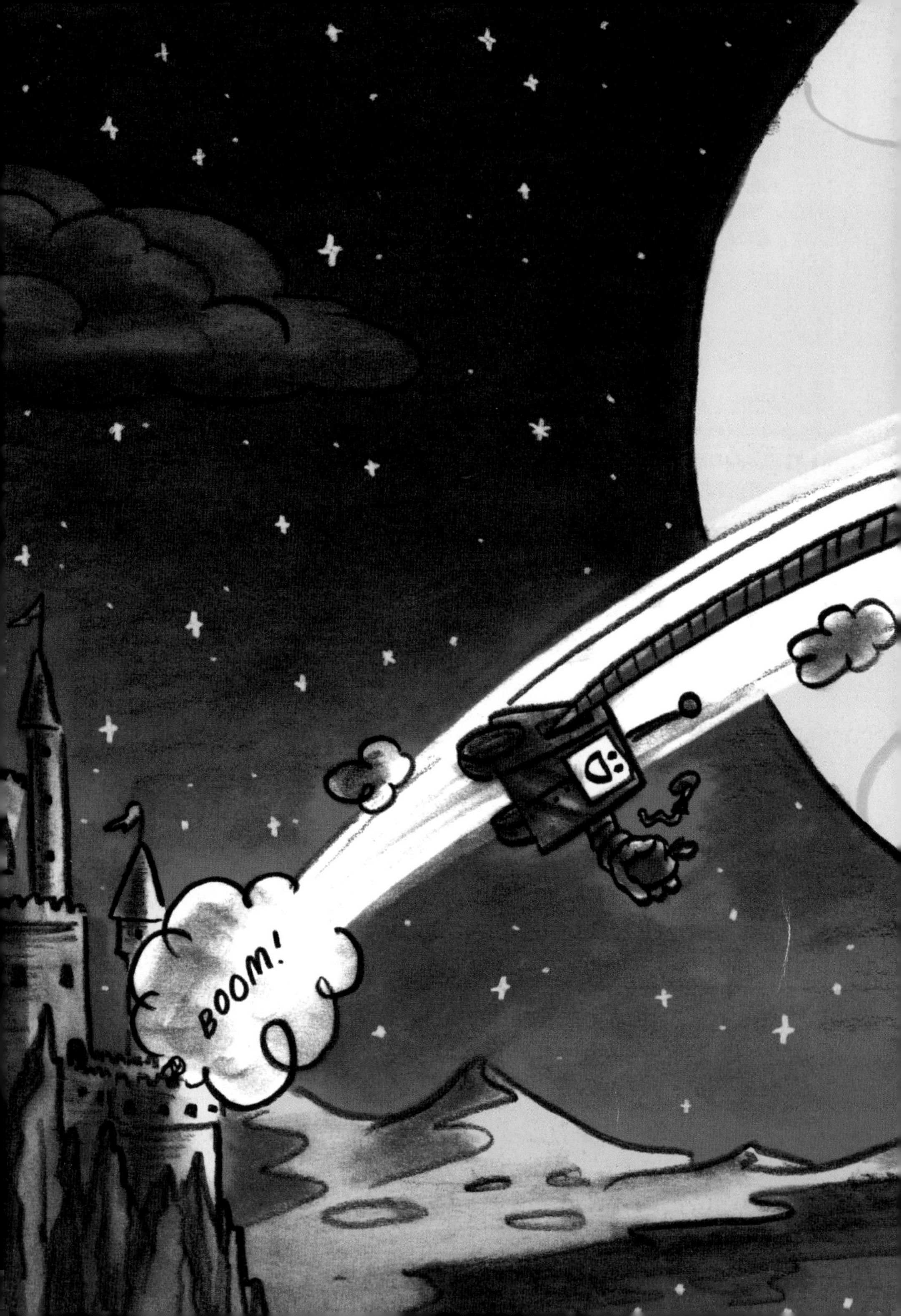
BOOM!

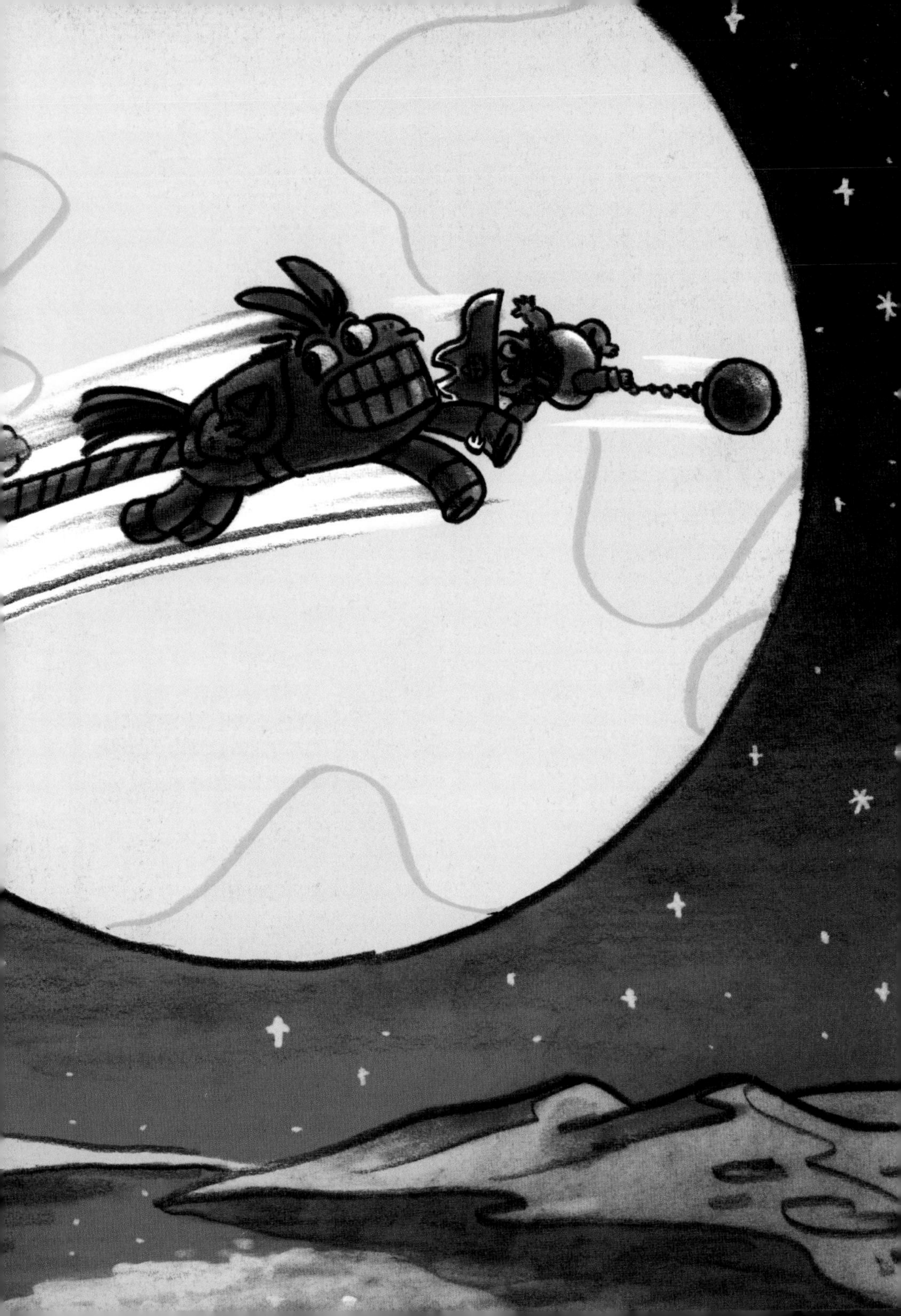

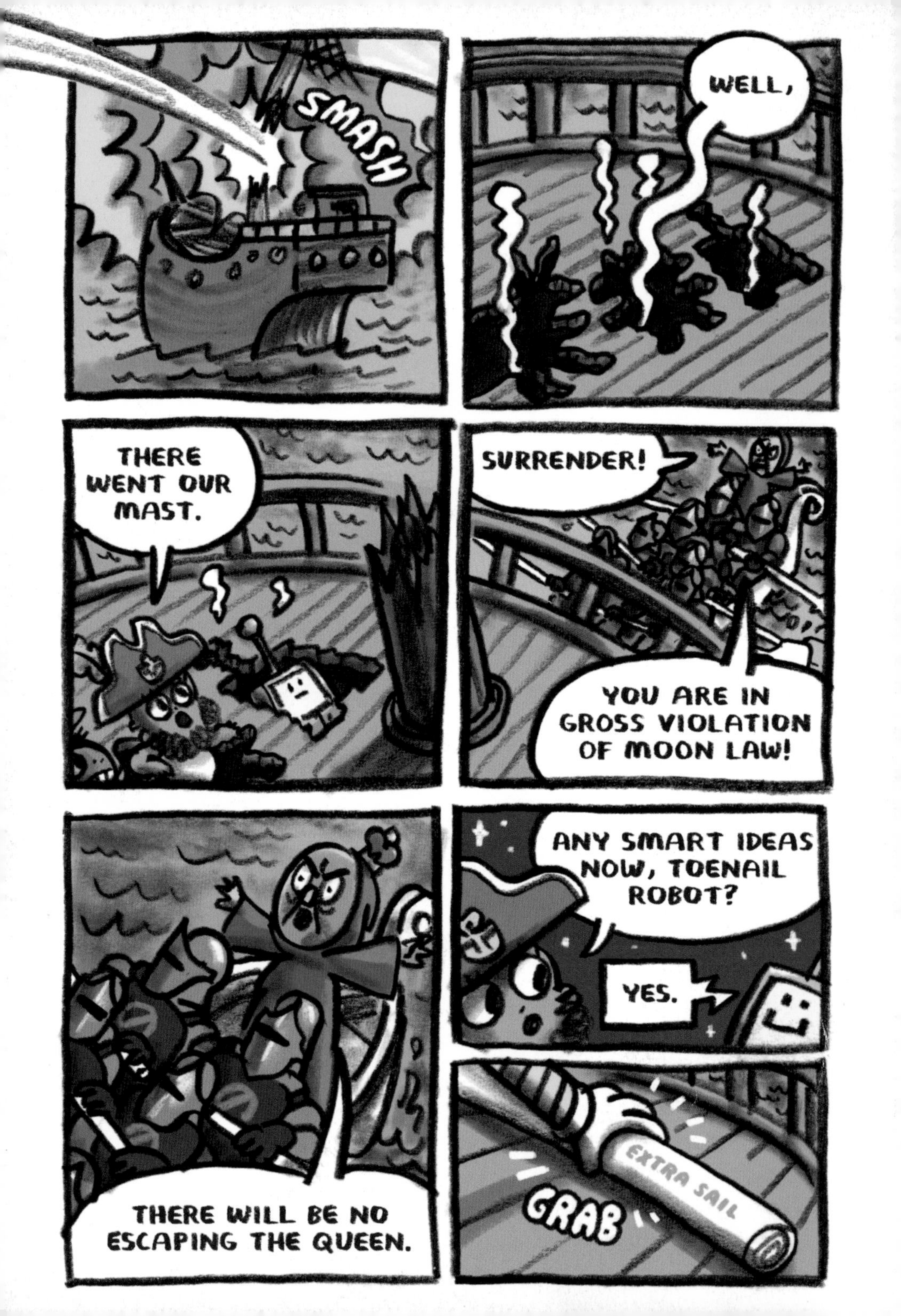
SMASH
WELL,
THERE WENT OUR MAST.
SURRENDER!
YOU ARE IN GROSS VIOLATION OF MOON LAW!
THERE WILL BE NO ESCAPING THE QUEEN.
ANY SMART IDEAS NOW, TOENAIL ROBOT?
YES.
EXTRA SAIL
GRAB

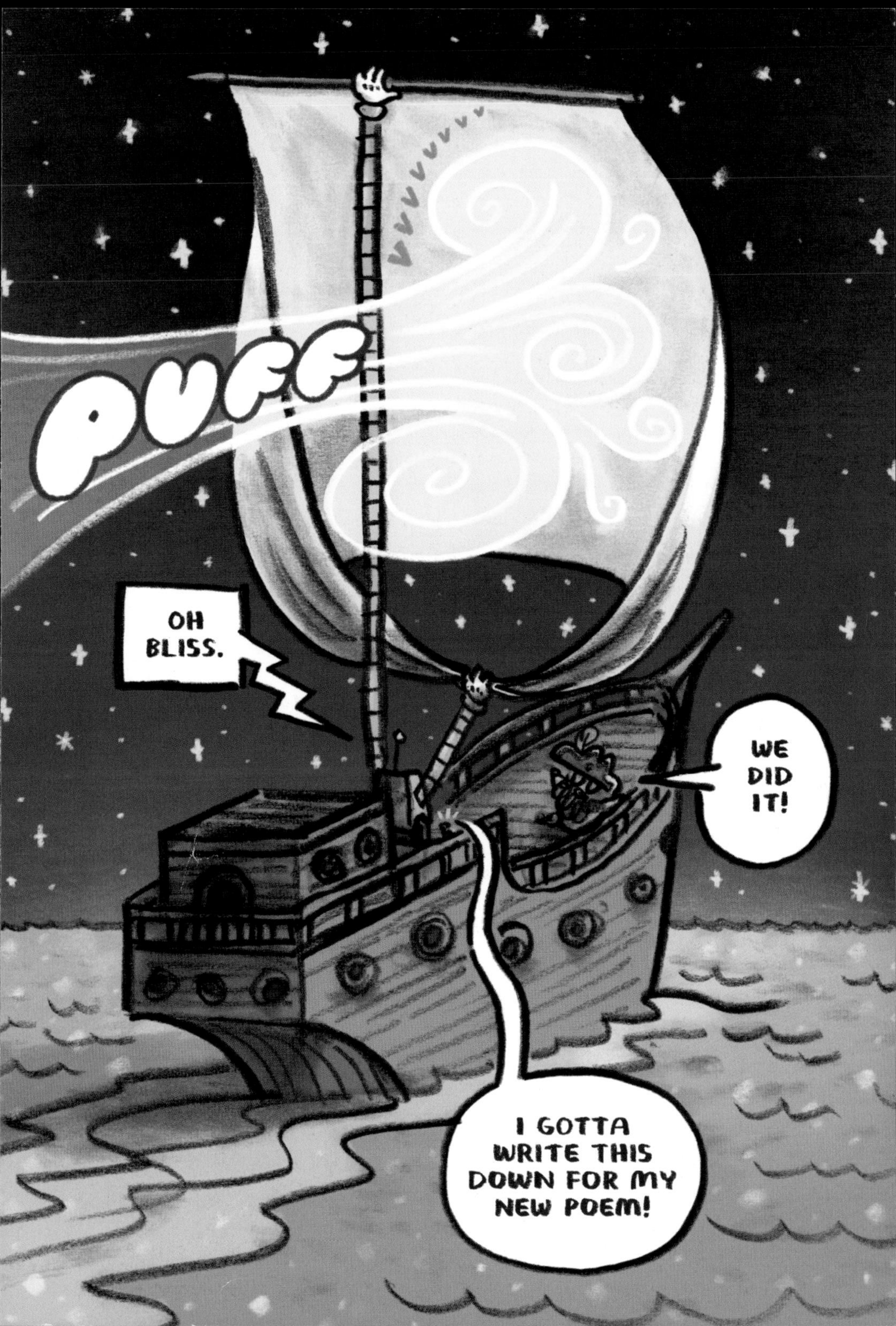
PUFF
OH BLISS.
WE DID IT!
I GOTTA WRITE THIS DOWN FOR MY NEW POEM!

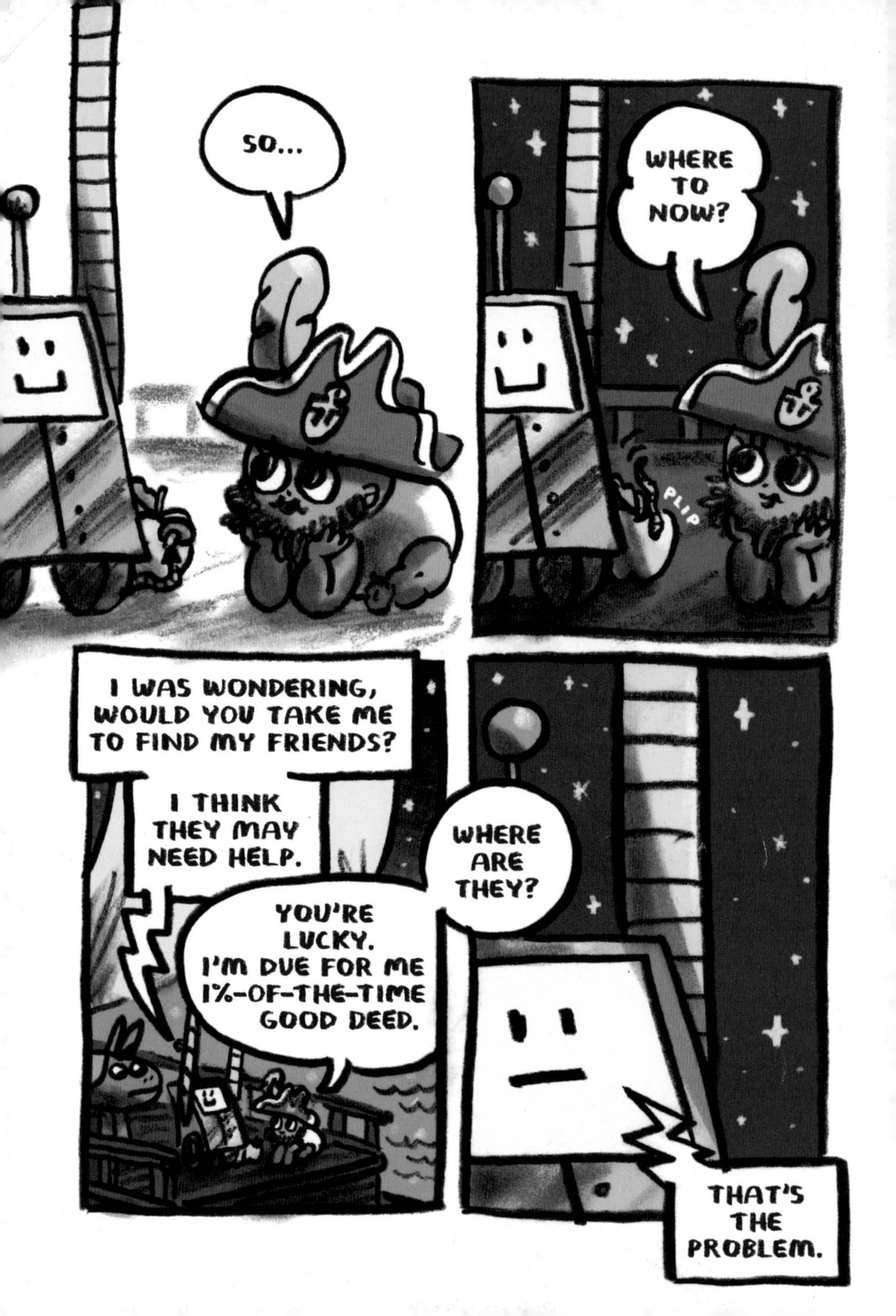
SO...
WHERE TO NOW?
PLIP
I WAS WONDERING, WOULD YOU TAKE ME TO FIND MY FRIENDS?
I THINK THEY MAY NEED HELP.
YOU'RE LUCKY. I'M DUE FOR ME 1%-OF-THE-TIME GOOD DEED.
WHERE ARE THEY?
THAT'S THE PROBLEM.

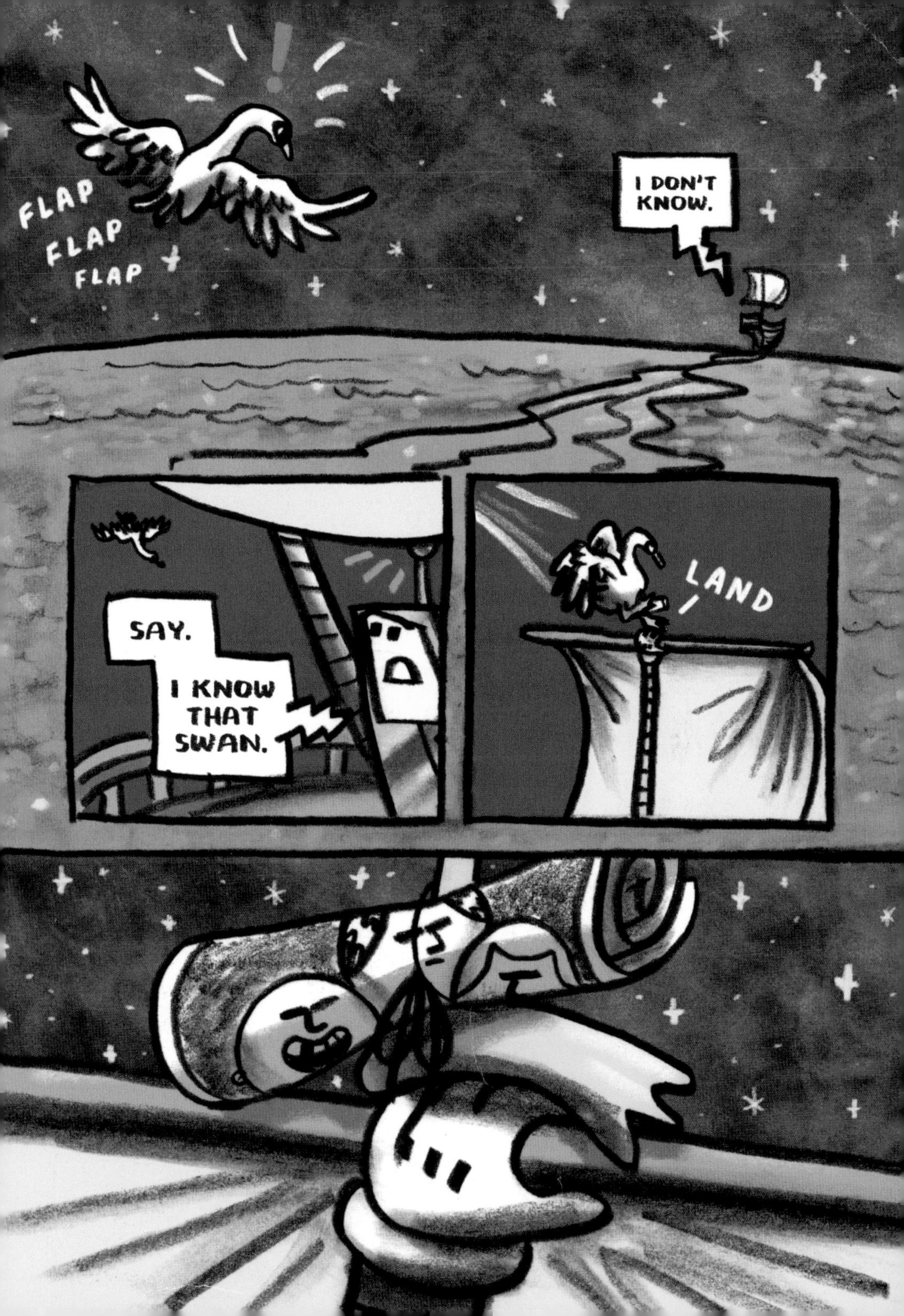
FLAP
FLAP
FLAP
!
I DON'T KNOW.
SAY.
I KNOW THAT SWAN.
LAND

# CHAPTER 12

# THE BOTTOMLESS CRATER

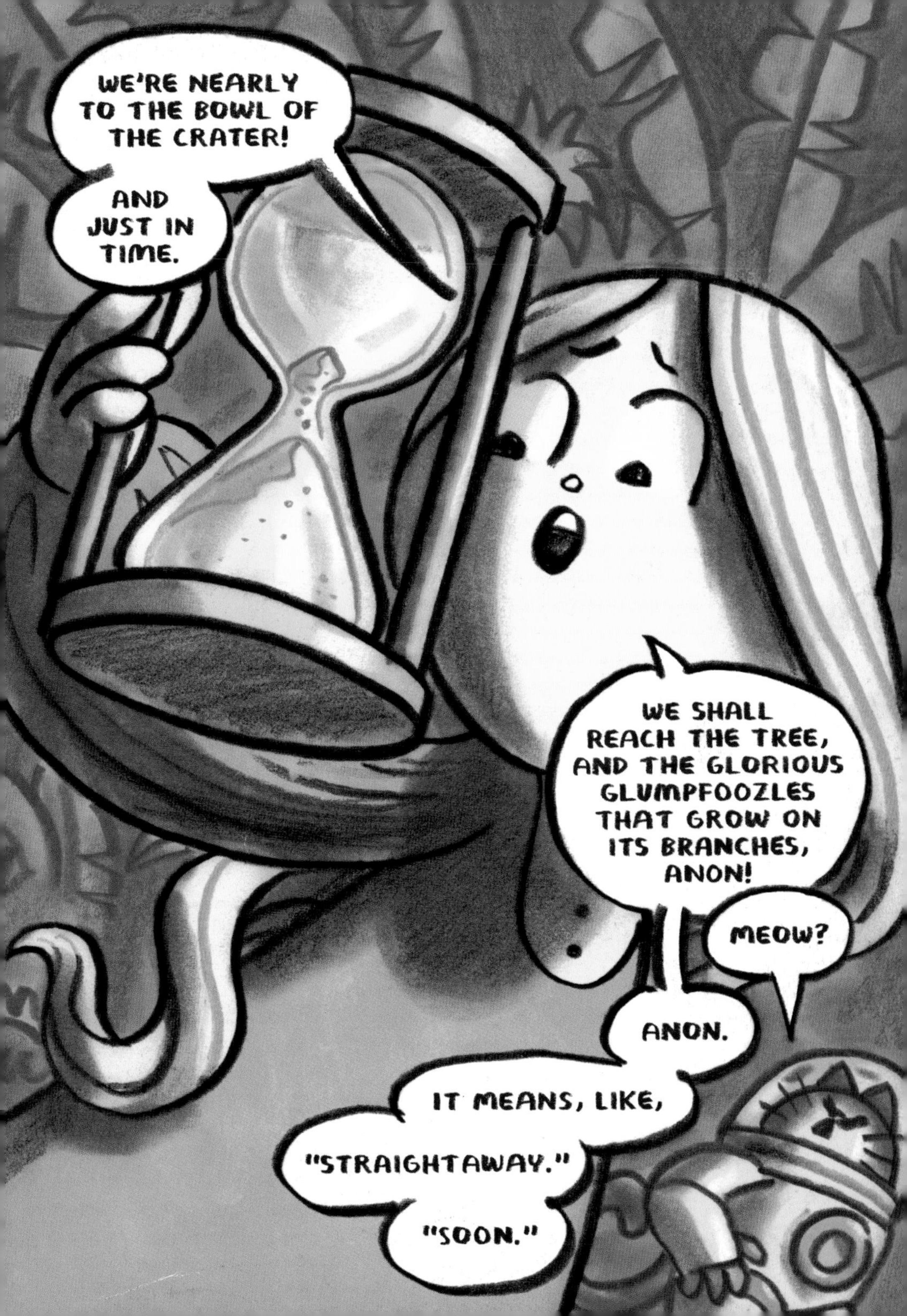
WE'RE NEARLY TO THE BOWL OF THE CRATER!
AND JUST IN TIME.
WE SHALL REACH THE TREE, AND THE GLORIOUS GLUMPFOOZLES THAT GROW ON ITS BRANCHES, ANON!
MEOW?
ANON.
IT MEANS, LIKE,
"STRAIGHTAWAY."
"SOON."

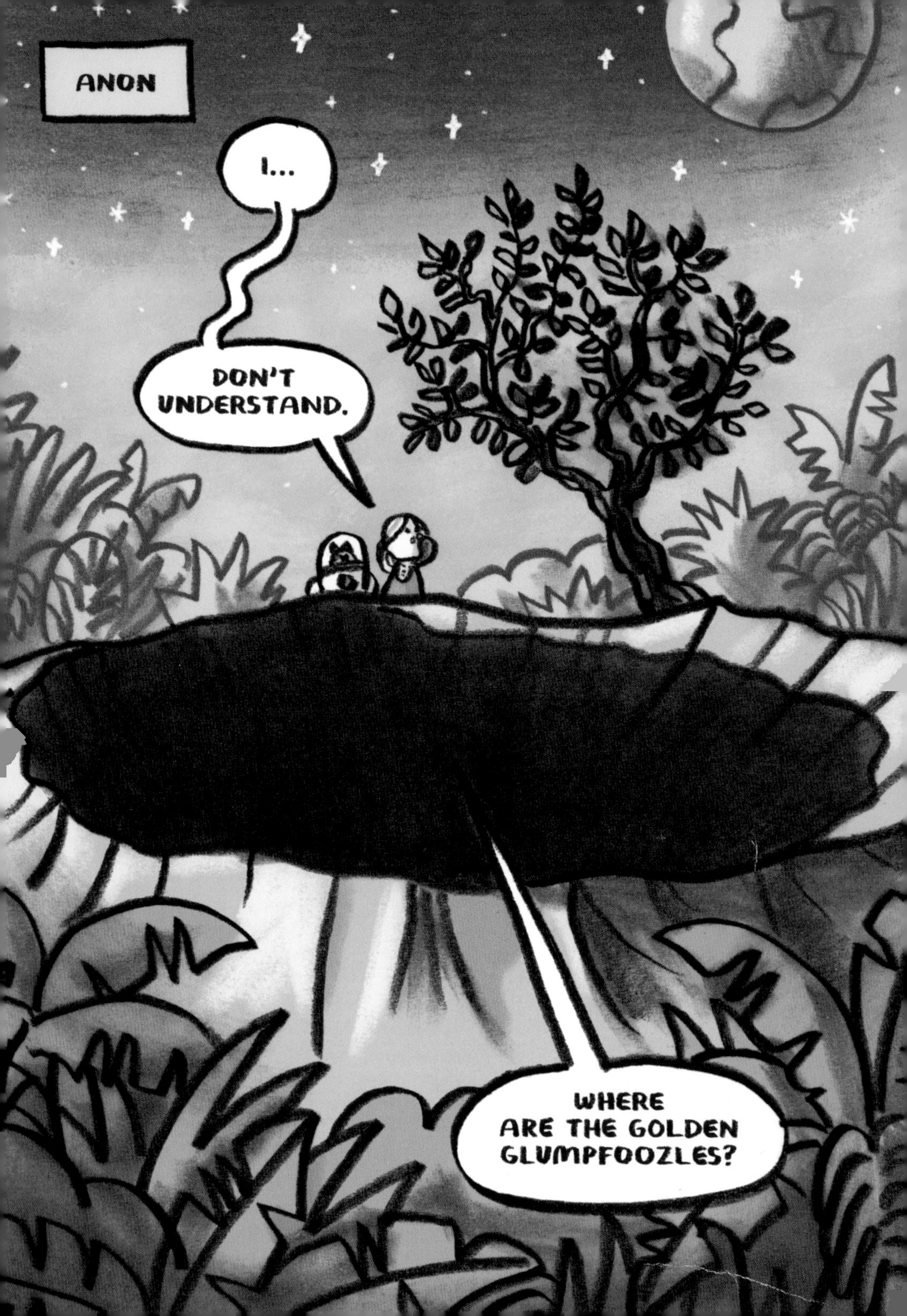
ANON
I...
DON'T UNDERSTAND.
WHERE ARE THE GOLDEN GLUMPFOOZLES?

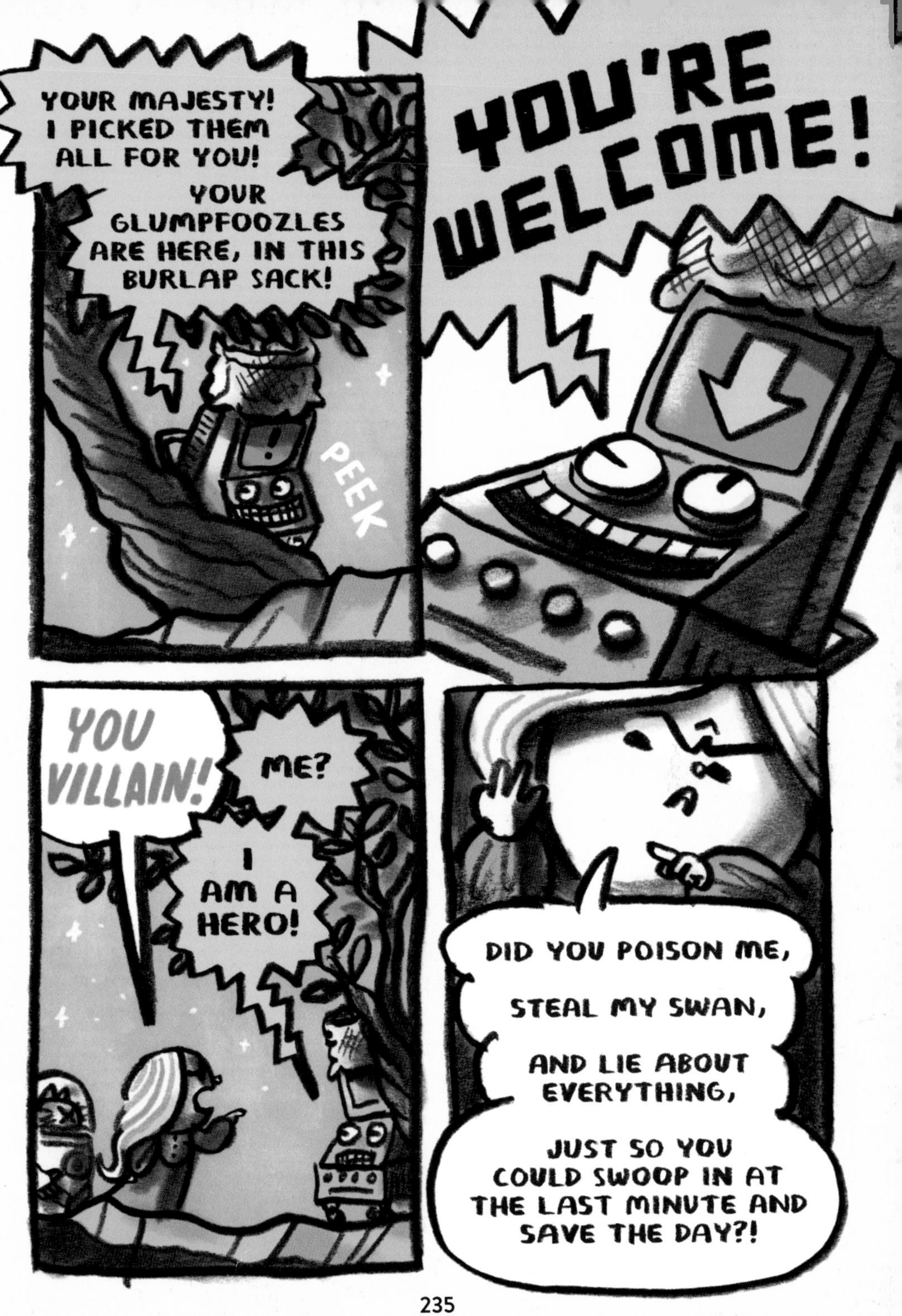

YOUR MAJESTY! I PICKED THEM ALL FOR YOU!
YOUR GLUMPFOOZLES ARE HERE, IN THIS BURLAP SACK!
PEEK
YOU'RE WELCOME!
YOU VILLAIN!
ME?
I AM A HERO!
DID YOU POISON ME,
STEAL MY SWAN,
AND LIE ABOUT EVERYTHING,
JUST SO YOU COULD SWOOP IN AT THE LAST MINUTE AND SAVE THE DAY?!

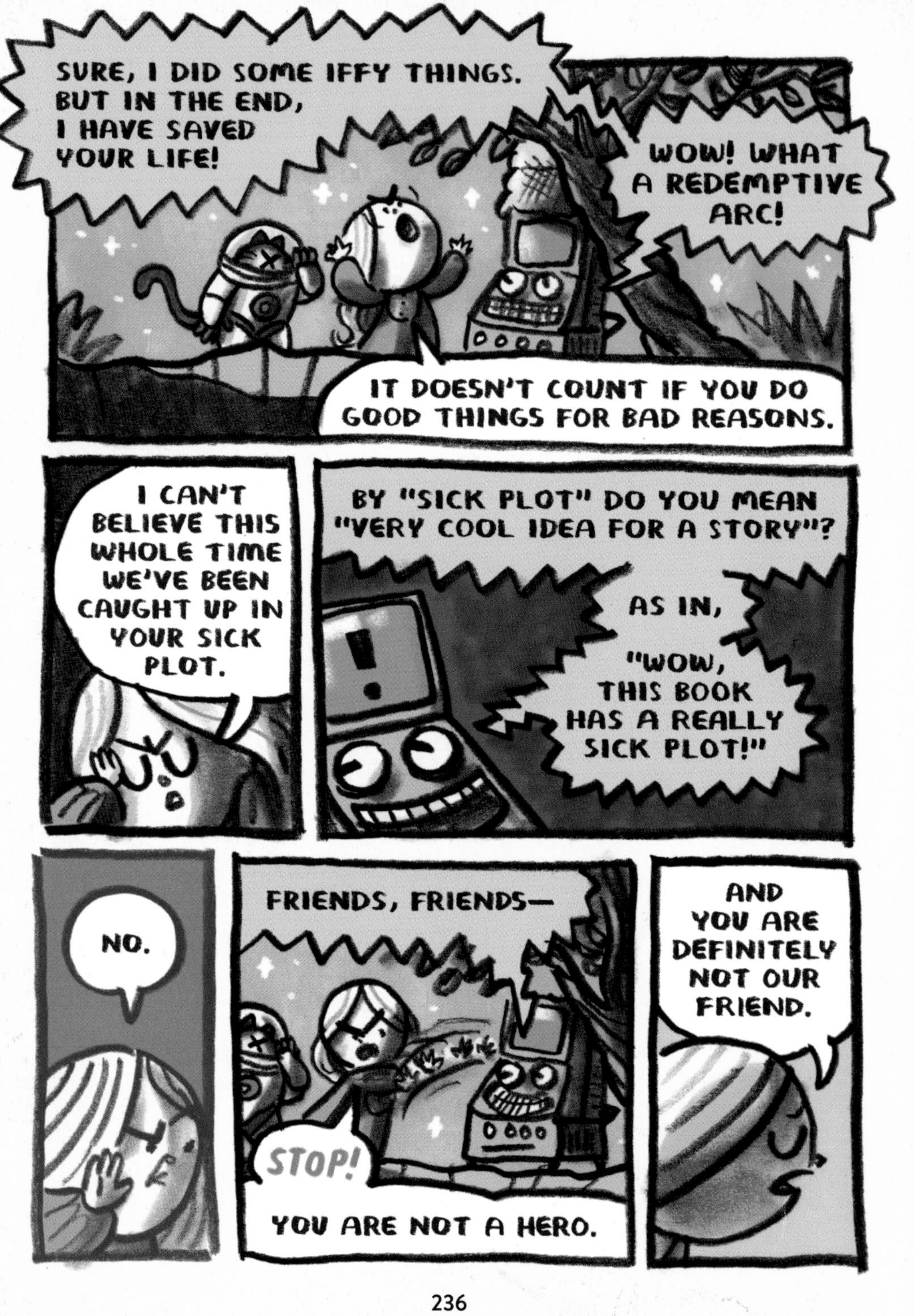
SURE, I DID SOME IFFY THINGS. BUT IN THE END, I HAVE SAVED YOUR LIFE!
WOW! WHAT A REDEMPTIVE ARC!
IT DOESN'T COUNT IF YOU DO GOOD THINGS FOR BAD REASONS.
I CAN'T BELIEVE THIS WHOLE TIME WE'VE BEEN CAUGHT UP IN YOUR SICK PLOT.
BY "SICK PLOT" DO YOU MEAN "VERY COOL IDEA FOR A STORY"?
AS IN,
"WOW, THIS BOOK HAS A REALLY SICK PLOT!"
NO.
FRIENDS, FRIENDS—
STOP!
YOU ARE NOT A HERO.
AND YOU ARE DEFINITELY NOT OUR FRIEND.

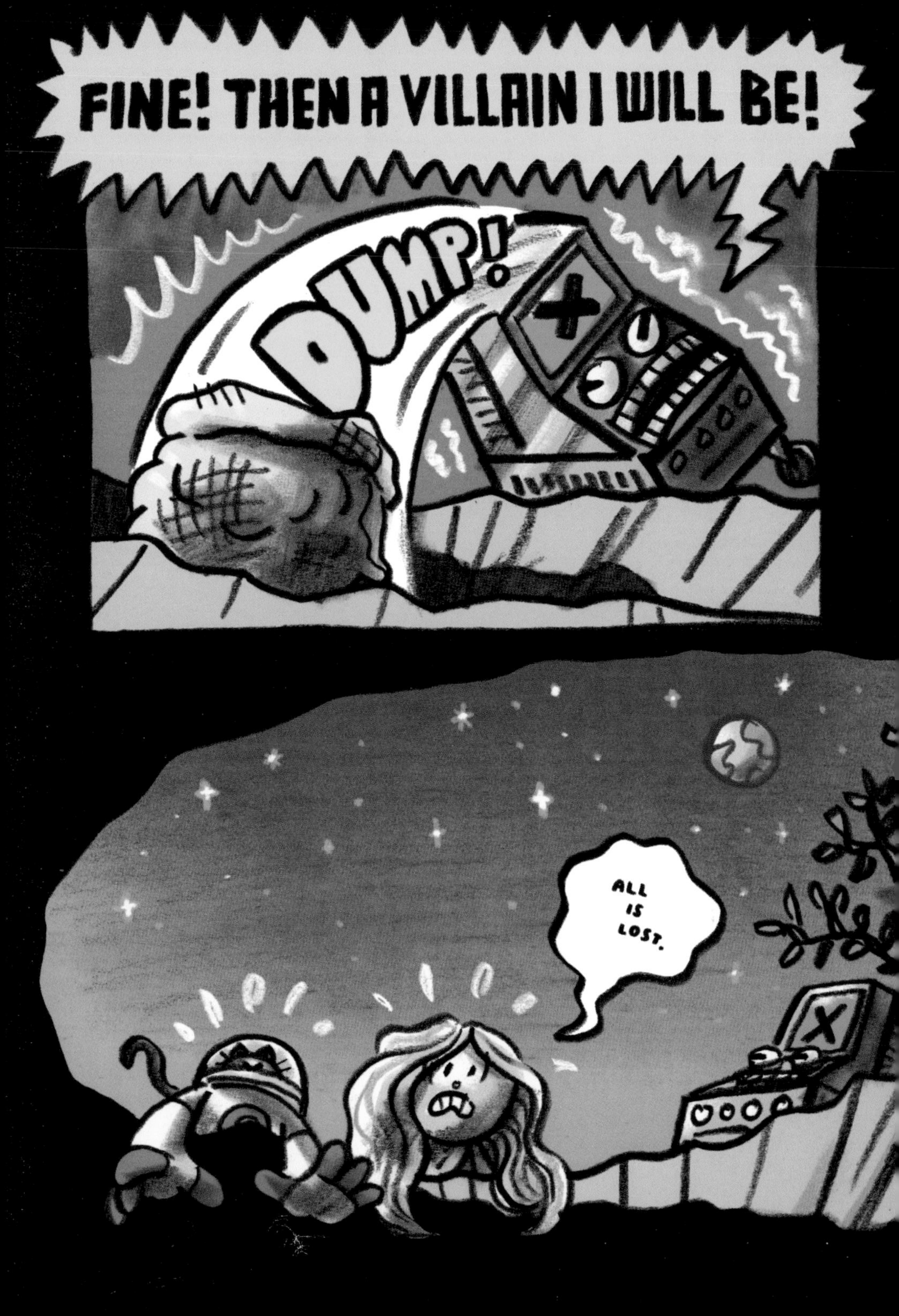
FINE! THEN A VILLAIN I WILL BE!
DUMP!
ALL IS LOST.

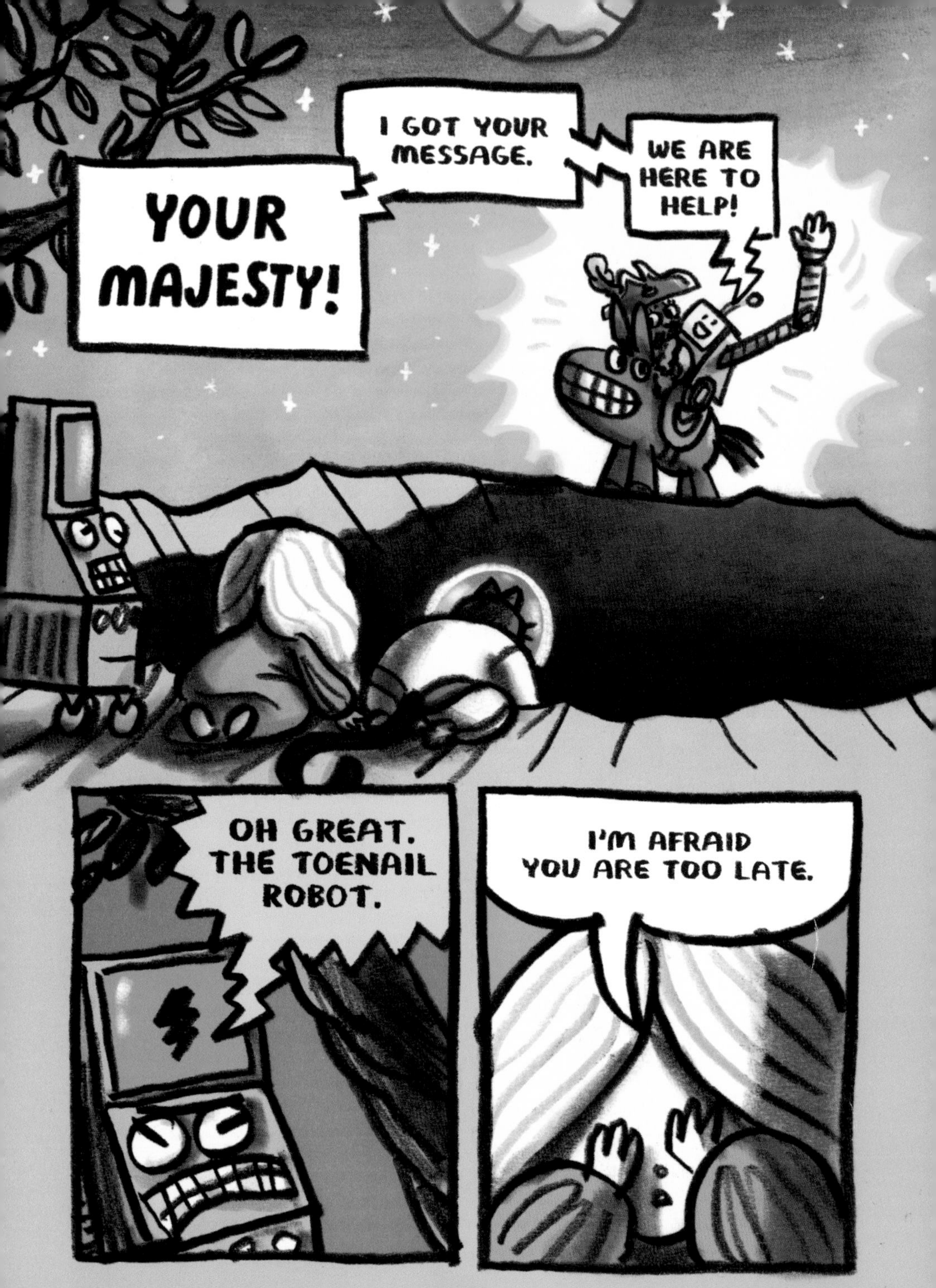
YOUR MAJESTY!
I GOT YOUR MESSAGE.
WE ARE HERE TO HELP!
OH GREAT. THE TOENAIL ROBOT.
I'M AFRAID YOU ARE TOO LATE.

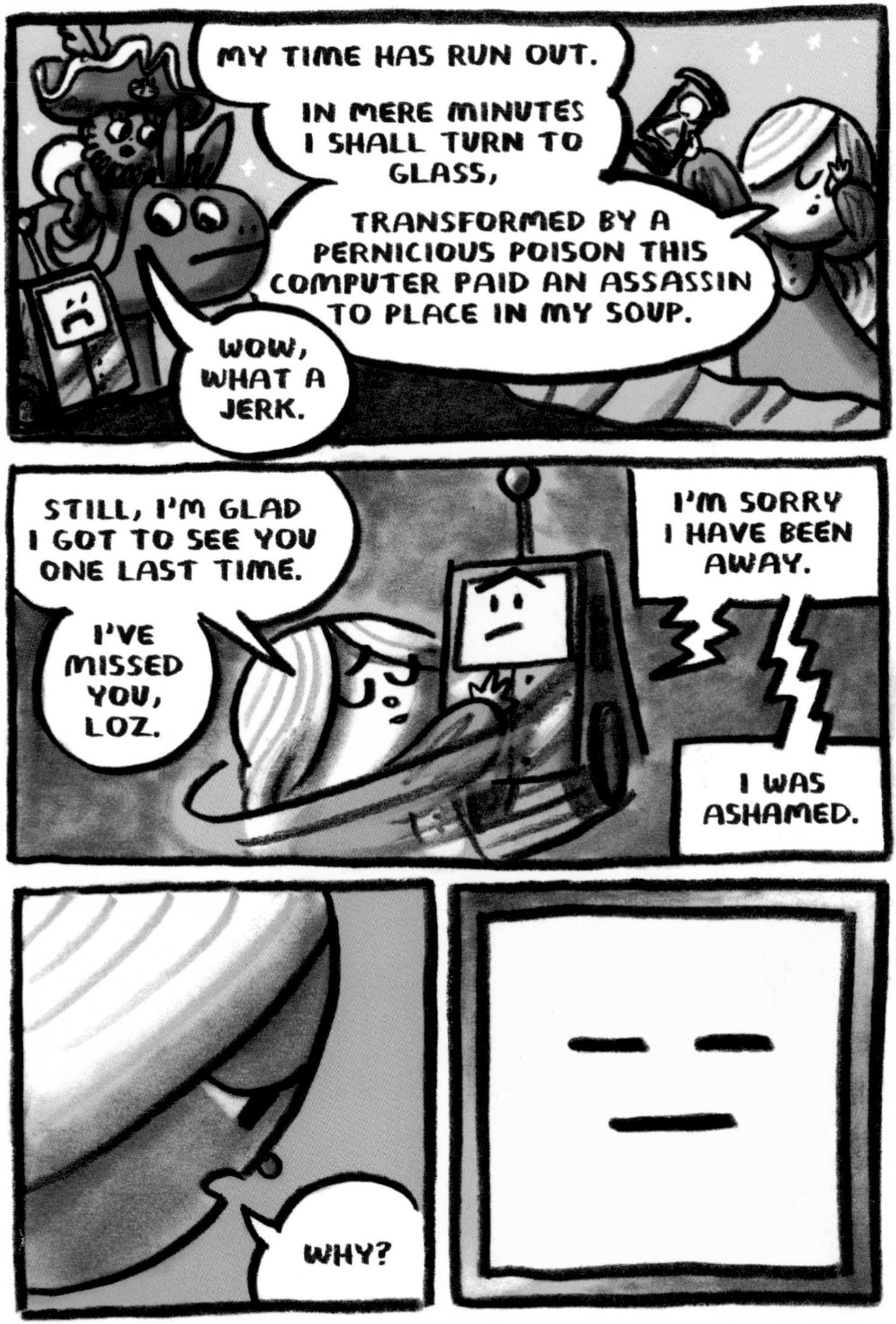
MY TIME HAS RUN OUT.
IN MERE MINUTES I SHALL TURN TO GLASS,
TRANSFORMED BY A PERNICIOUS POISON THIS COMPUTER PAID AN ASSASSIN TO PLACE IN MY SOUP.
WOW, WHAT A JERK.
STILL, I'M GLAD I GOT TO SEE YOU ONE LAST TIME.
I'VE MISSED YOU, LOZ.
I'M SORRY I HAVE BEEN AWAY.
I WAS ASHAMED.
WHY?

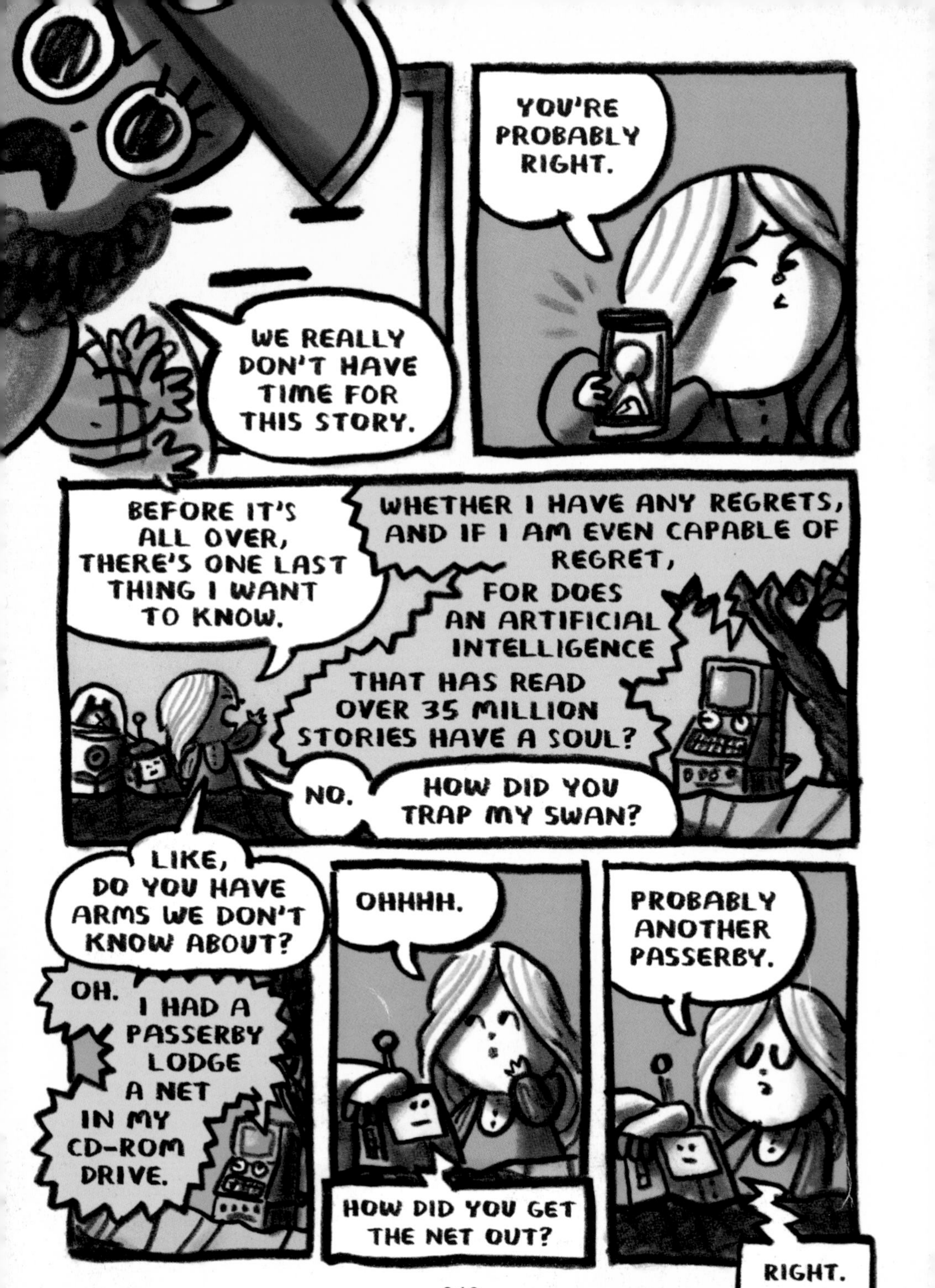
YOU'RE PROBABLY RIGHT.
WE REALLY DON'T HAVE TIME FOR THIS STORY.
BEFORE IT'S ALL OVER, THERE'S ONE LAST THING I WANT TO KNOW.
WHETHER I HAVE ANY REGRETS, AND IF I AM EVEN CAPABLE OF REGRET,
FOR DOES AN ARTIFICIAL INTELLIGENCE
THAT HAS READ OVER 35 MILLION STORIES HAVE A SOUL?
NO.
HOW DID YOU TRAP MY SWAN?
LIKE, DO YOU HAVE ARMS WE DON'T KNOW ABOUT?
OH.
I HAD A PASSERBY LODGE A NET
IN MY CD-ROM DRIVE.
OHHHH.
HOW DID YOU GET THE NET OUT?
PROBABLY ANOTHER PASSERBY.
RIGHT.

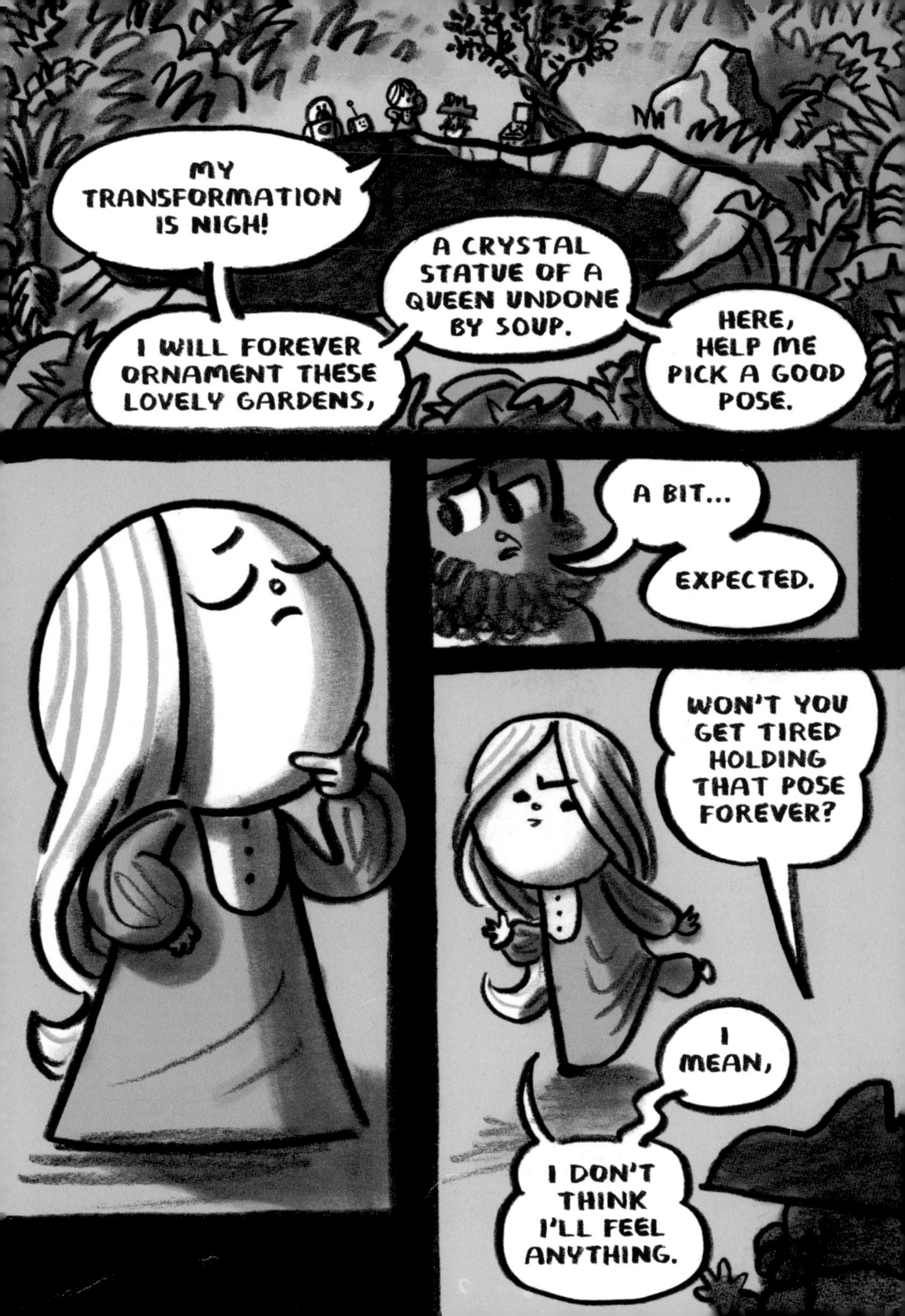
MY TRANSFORMATION IS NIGH!
I WILL FOREVER ORNAMENT THESE LOVELY GARDENS,
A CRYSTAL STATUE OF A QUEEN UNDONE BY SOUP.
HERE, HELP ME PICK A GOOD POSE.
A BIT...
EXPECTED.
WON'T YOU GET TIRED HOLDING THAT POSE FOREVER?
I MEAN,
I DON'T THINK I'LL FEEL ANYTHING.

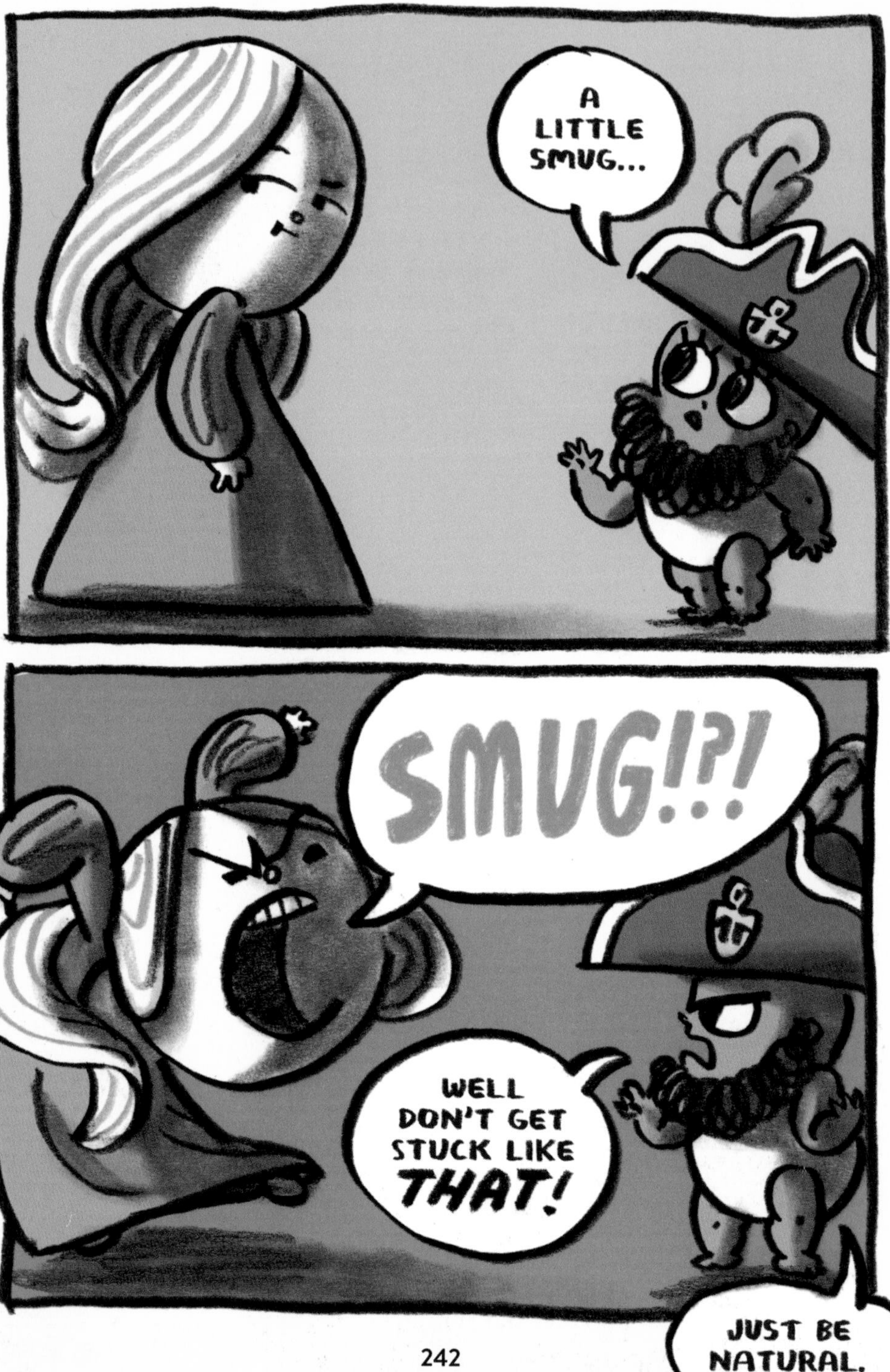
A LITTLE SMUG...
SMUG!?!
WELL DON'T GET STUCK LIKE *THAT!*
JUST BE NATURAL.

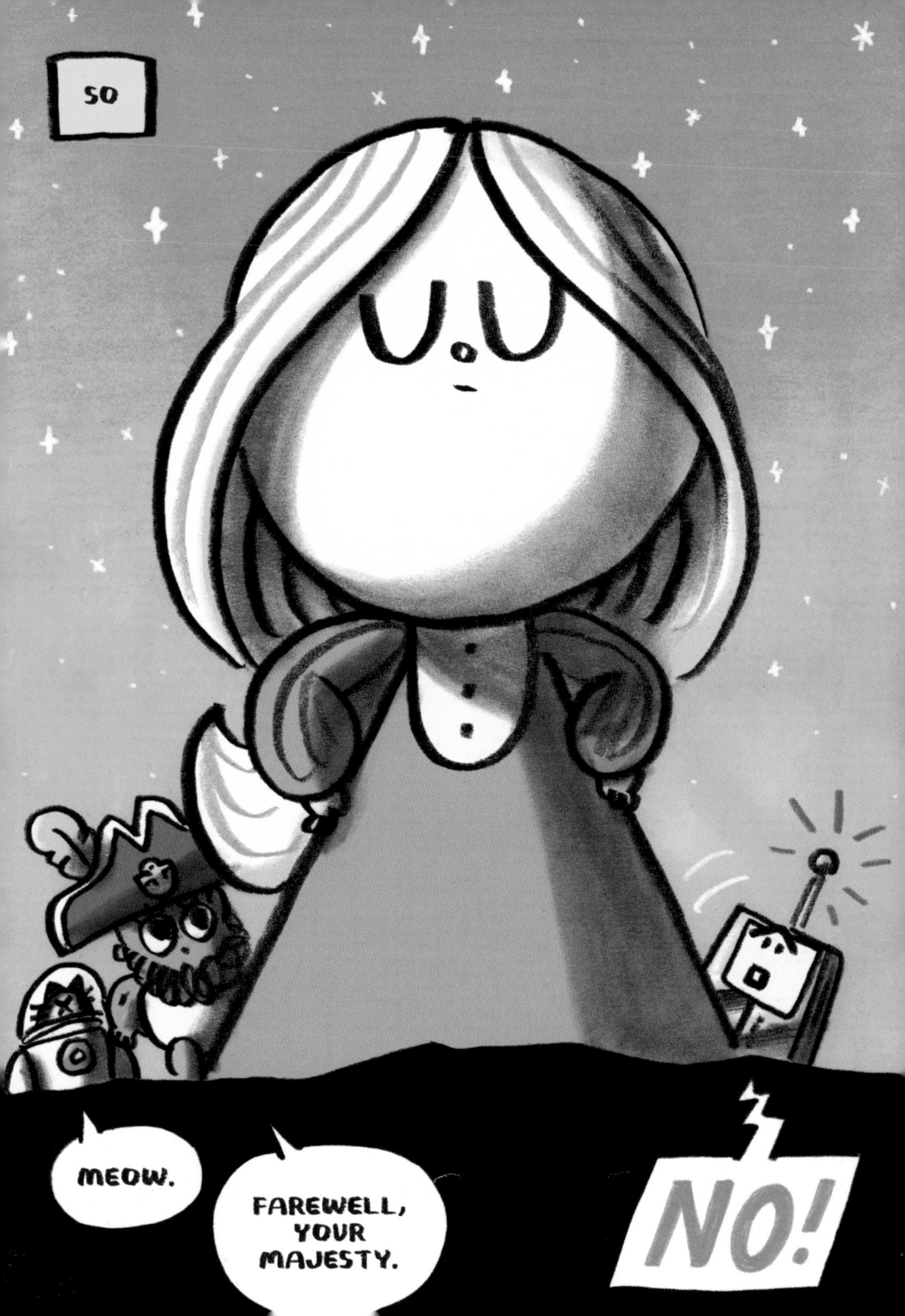
SO
MEOW.
FAREWELL, YOUR MAJESTY.
NO!

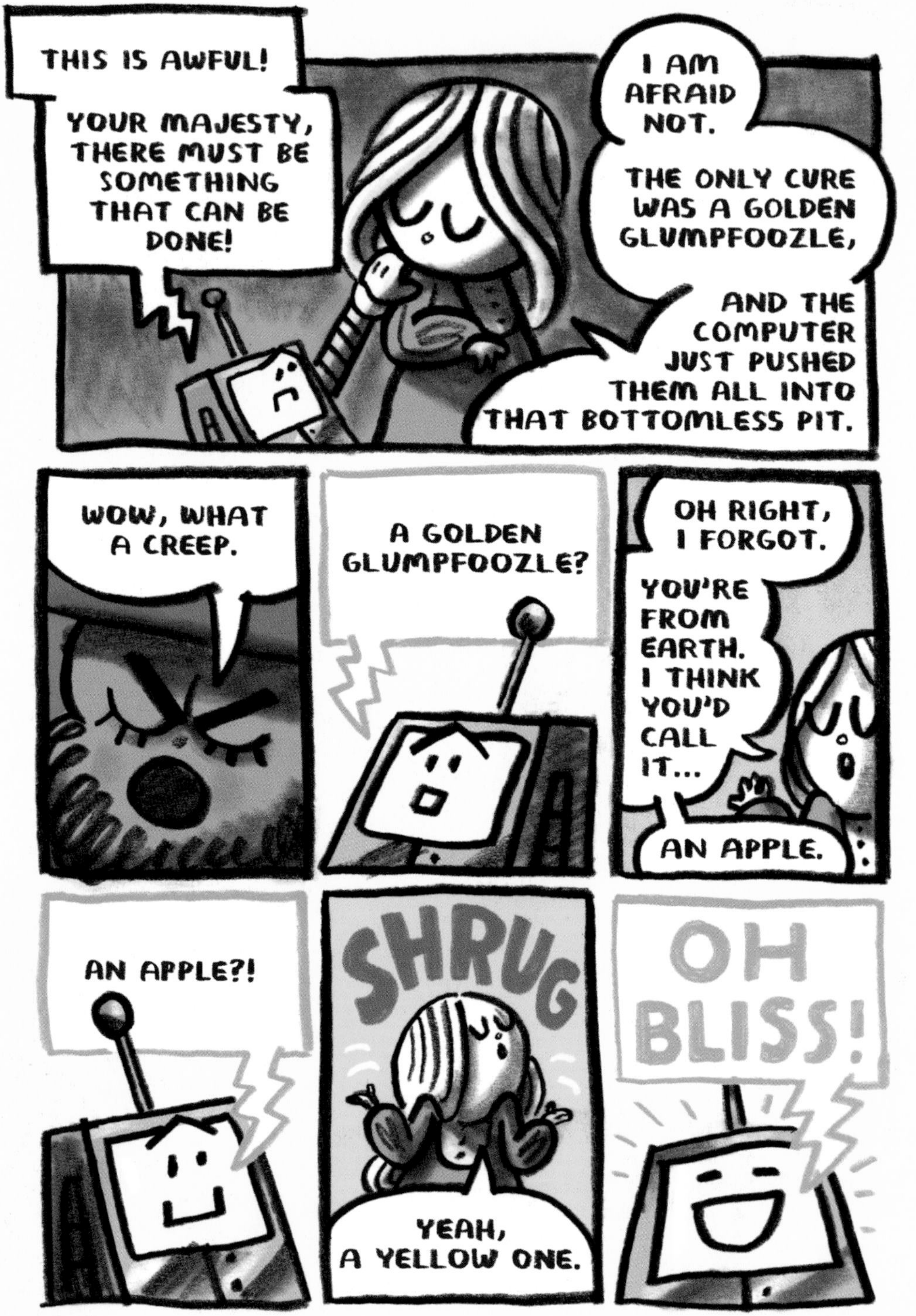
THIS IS AWFUL!
YOUR MAJESTY, THERE MUST BE SOMETHING THAT CAN BE DONE!
I AM AFRAID NOT.
THE ONLY CURE WAS A GOLDEN GLUMPFOOZLE,
AND THE COMPUTER JUST PUSHED THEM ALL INTO THAT BOTTOMLESS PIT.
WOW, WHAT A CREEP.
A GOLDEN GLUMPFOOZLE?
OH RIGHT, I FORGOT.
YOU'RE FROM EARTH. I THINK YOU'D CALL IT...
AN APPLE.
AN APPLE?!
SHRUG
YEAH, A YELLOW ONE.
OH BLISS!

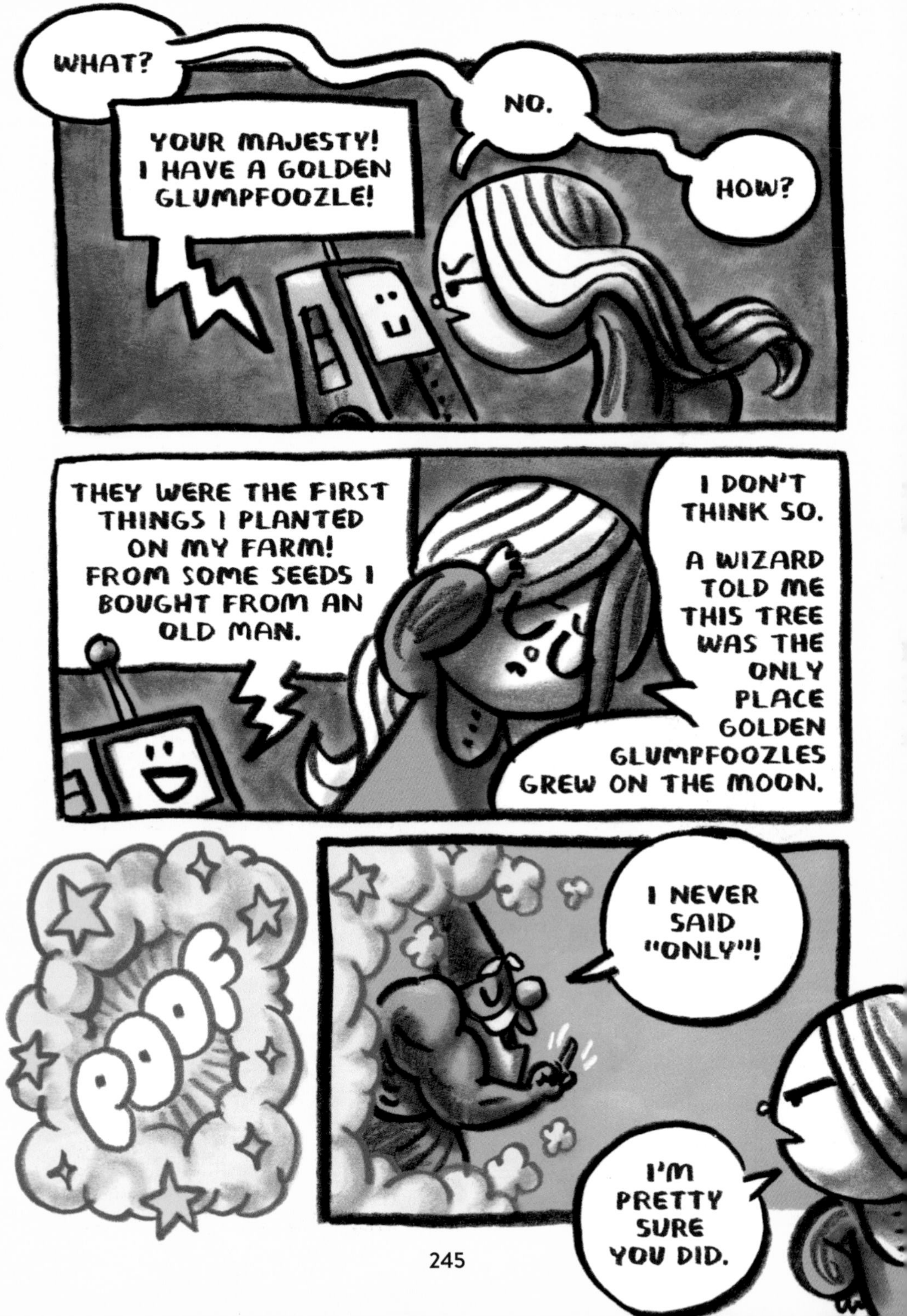

WHAT?
YOUR MAJESTY! I HAVE A GOLDEN GLUMPFOOZLE!
NO.
HOW?
THEY WERE THE FIRST THINGS I PLANTED ON MY FARM! FROM SOME SEEDS I BOUGHT FROM AN OLD MAN.
I DON'T THINK SO.
A WIZARD TOLD ME THIS TREE WAS THE ONLY PLACE GOLDEN GLUMPFOOZLES GREW ON THE MOON.
POOF
I NEVER SAID "ONLY"!
I'M PRETTY SURE YOU DID.

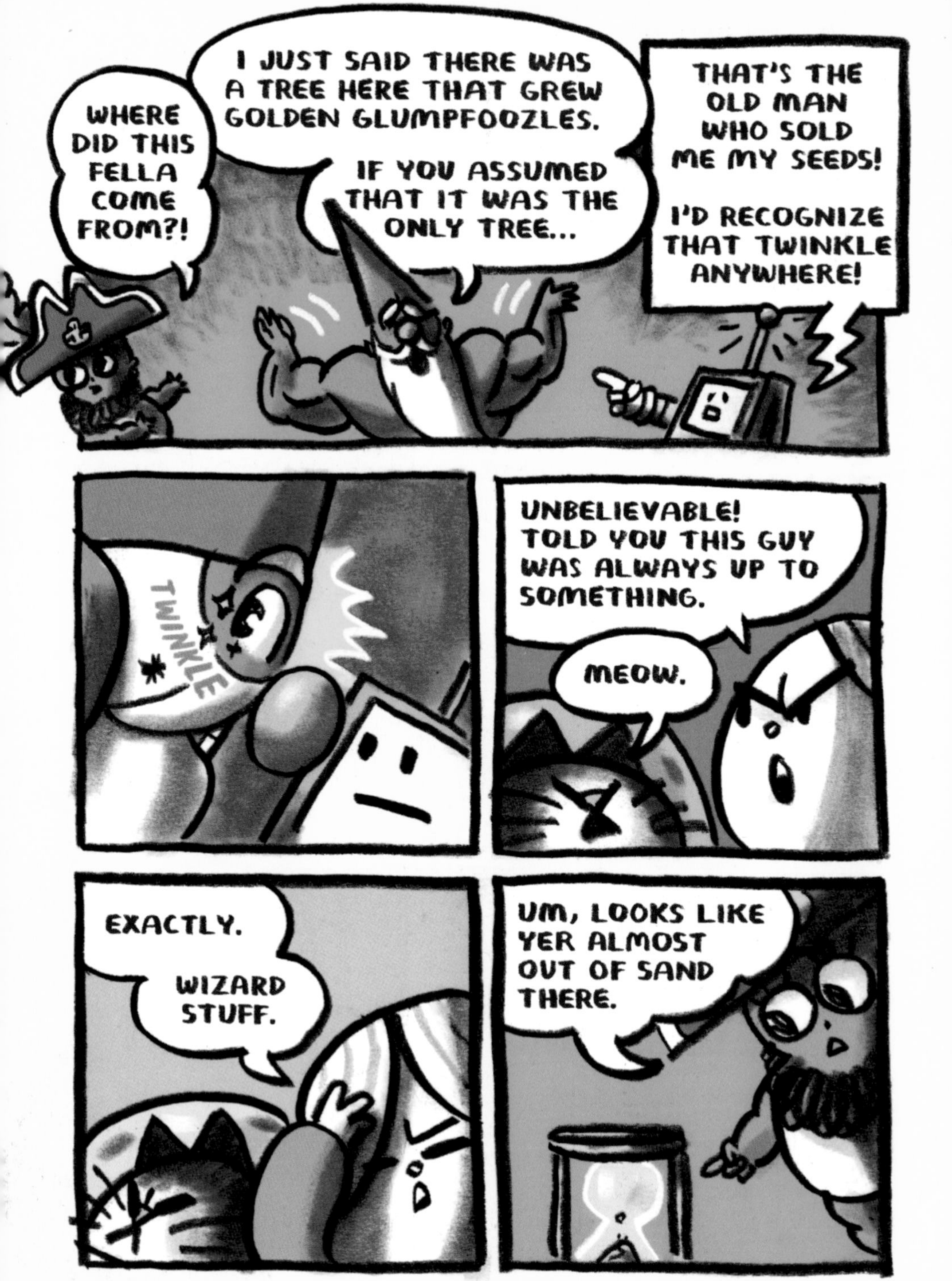
WHERE DID THIS FELLA COME FROM?!
I JUST SAID THERE WAS A TREE HERE THAT GREW GOLDEN GLUMPFOOZLES.
IF YOU ASSUMED THAT IT WAS THE ONLY TREE...
THAT'S THE OLD MAN WHO SOLD ME MY SEEDS!
I'D RECOGNIZE THAT TWINKLE ANYWHERE!
TWINKLE
UNBELIEVABLE! TOLD YOU THIS GUY WAS ALWAYS UP TO SOMETHING.
MEOW.
EXACTLY.
WIZARD STUFF.
UM, LOOKS LIKE YER ALMOST OUT OF SAND THERE.

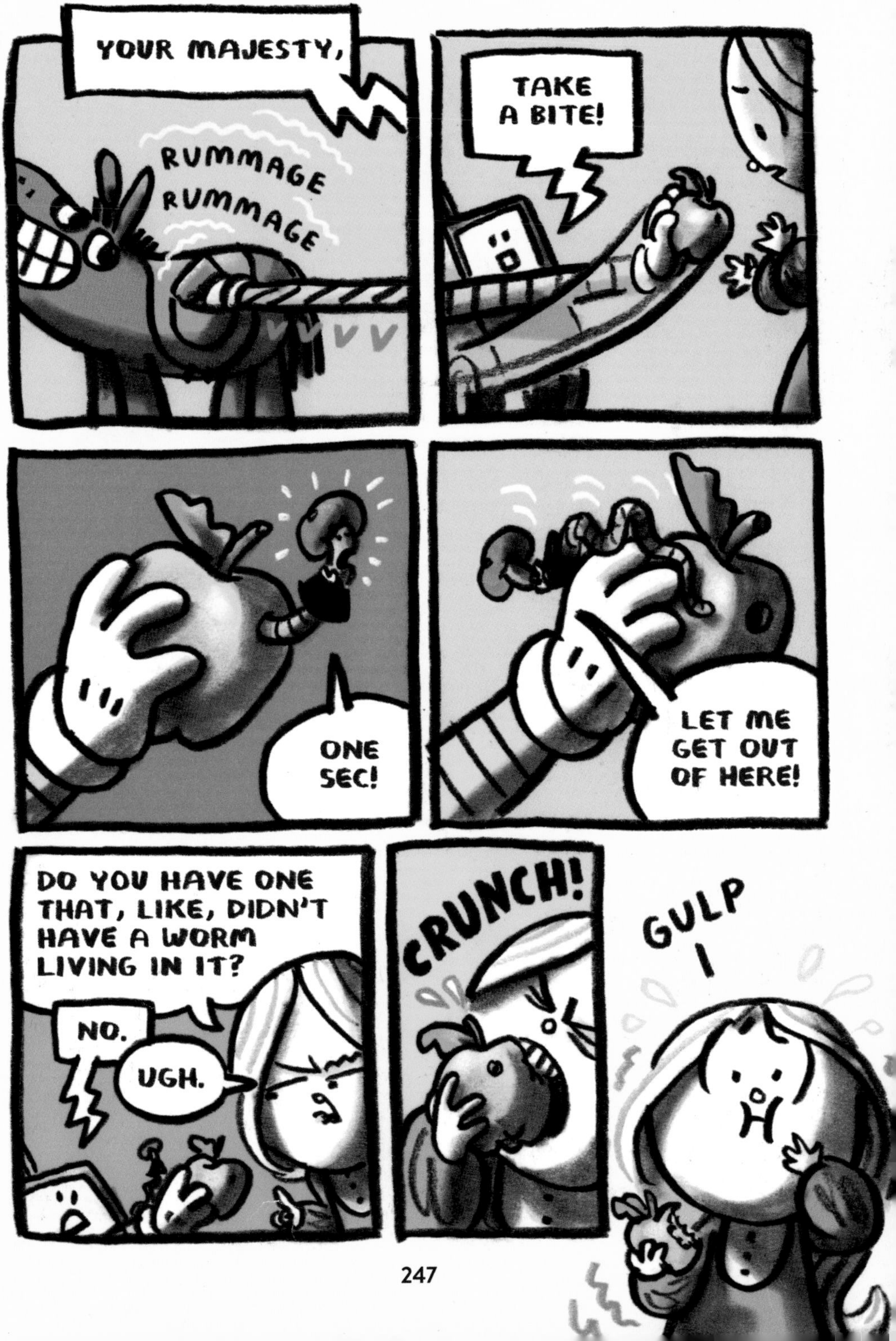
YOUR MAJESTY,
RUMMAGE RUMMAGE
TAKE A BITE!
ONE SEC!
LET ME GET OUT OF HERE!
DO YOU HAVE ONE THAT, LIKE, DIDN'T HAVE A WORM LIVING IN IT?
NO.
UGH.
CRUNCH!
GULP

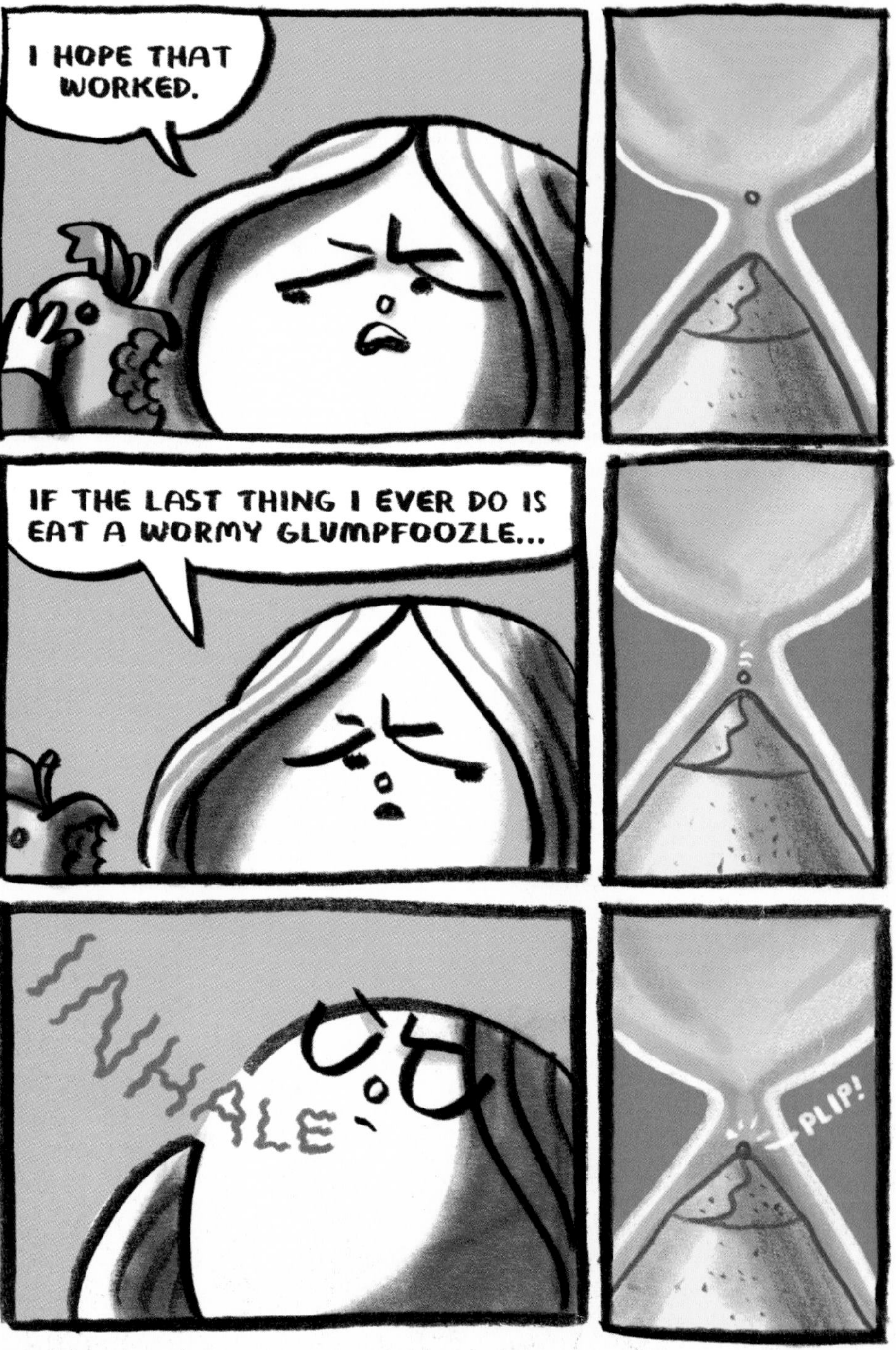
I HOPE THAT WORKED.
IF THE LAST THING I EVER DO IS EAT A WORMY GLUMPFOOZLE...
INHALE
PLIP!

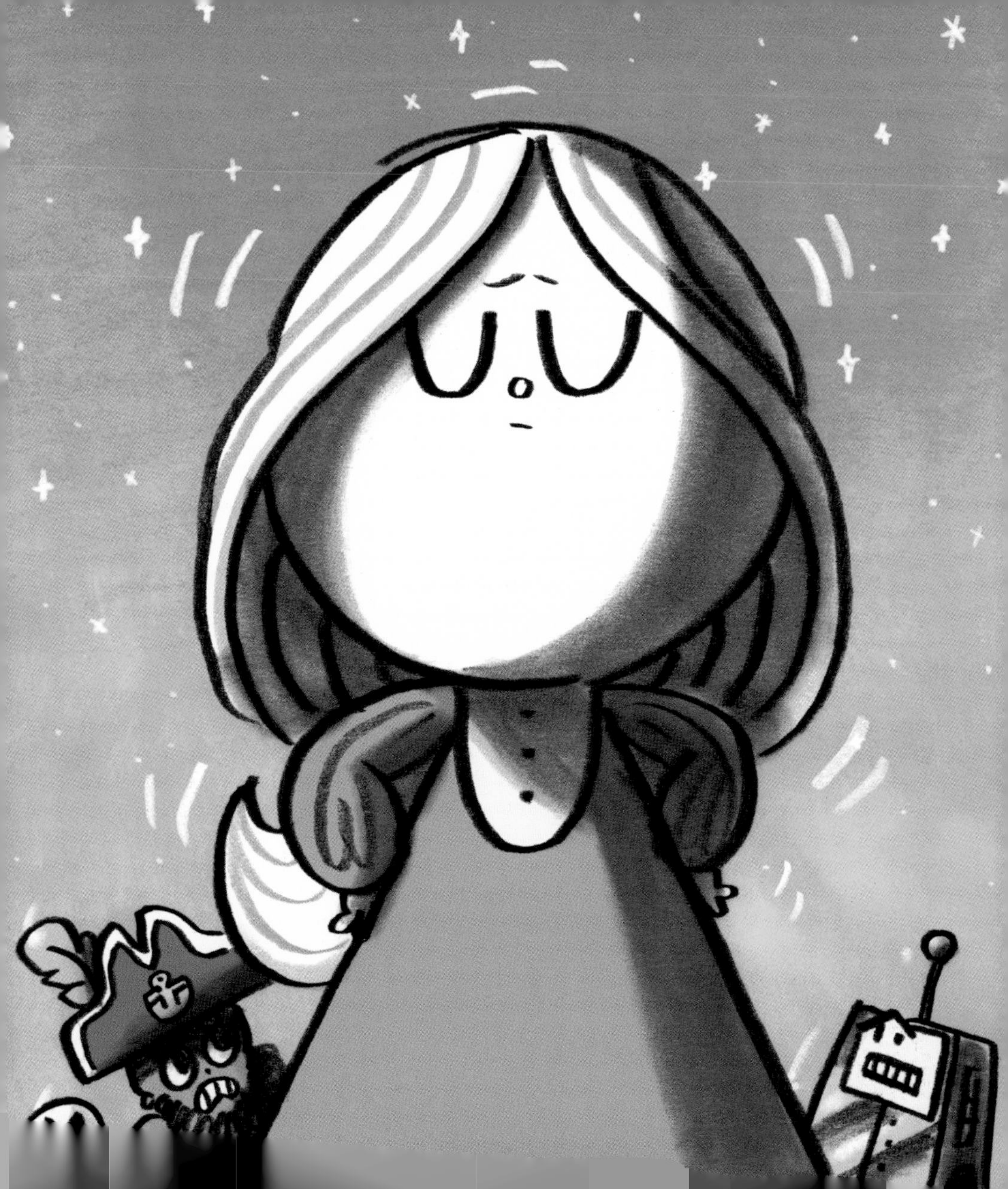

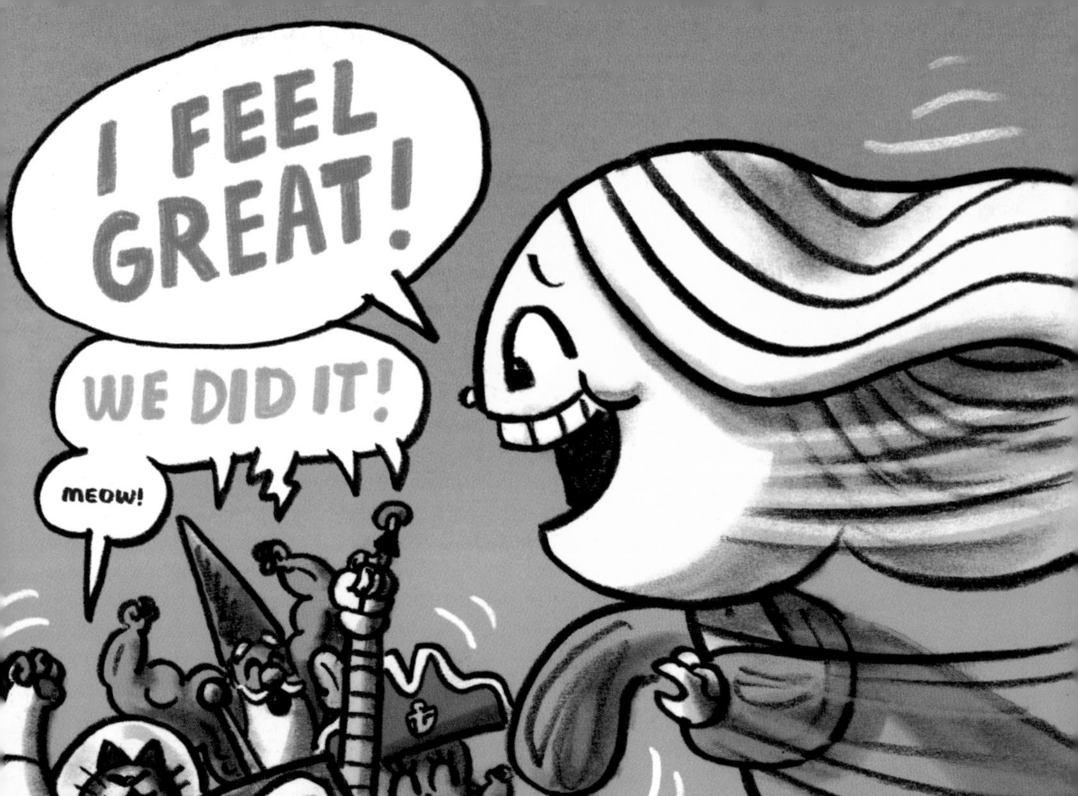
I FEEL GREAT!
WE DID IT!
MEOW!

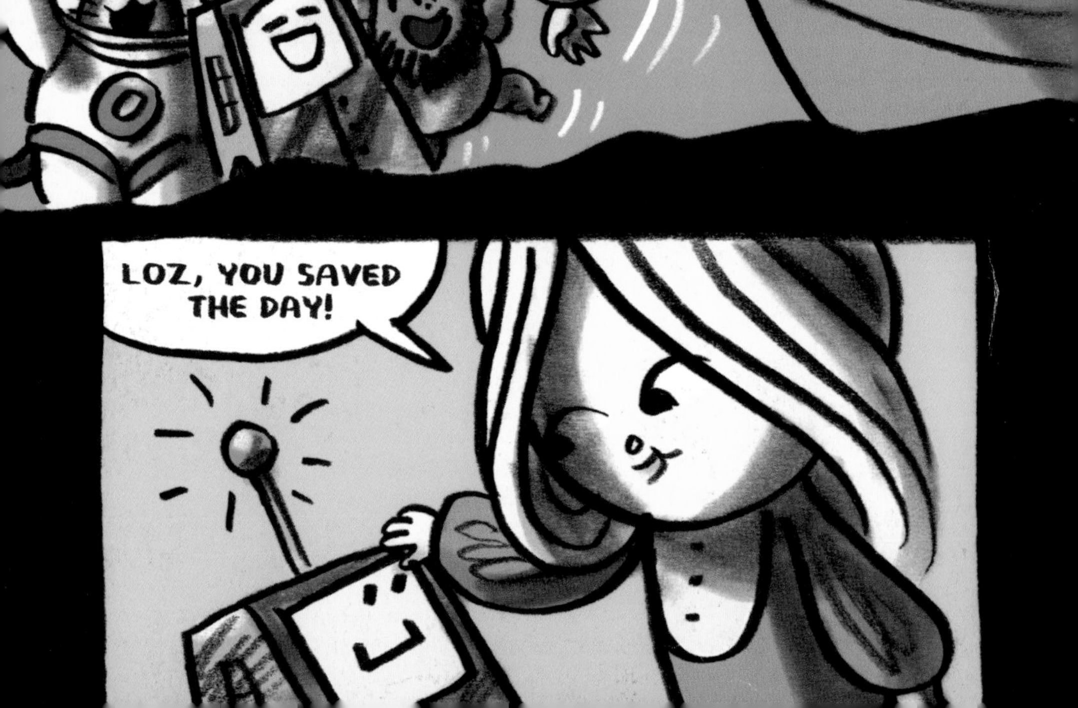
LOZ, YOU SAVED THE DAY!

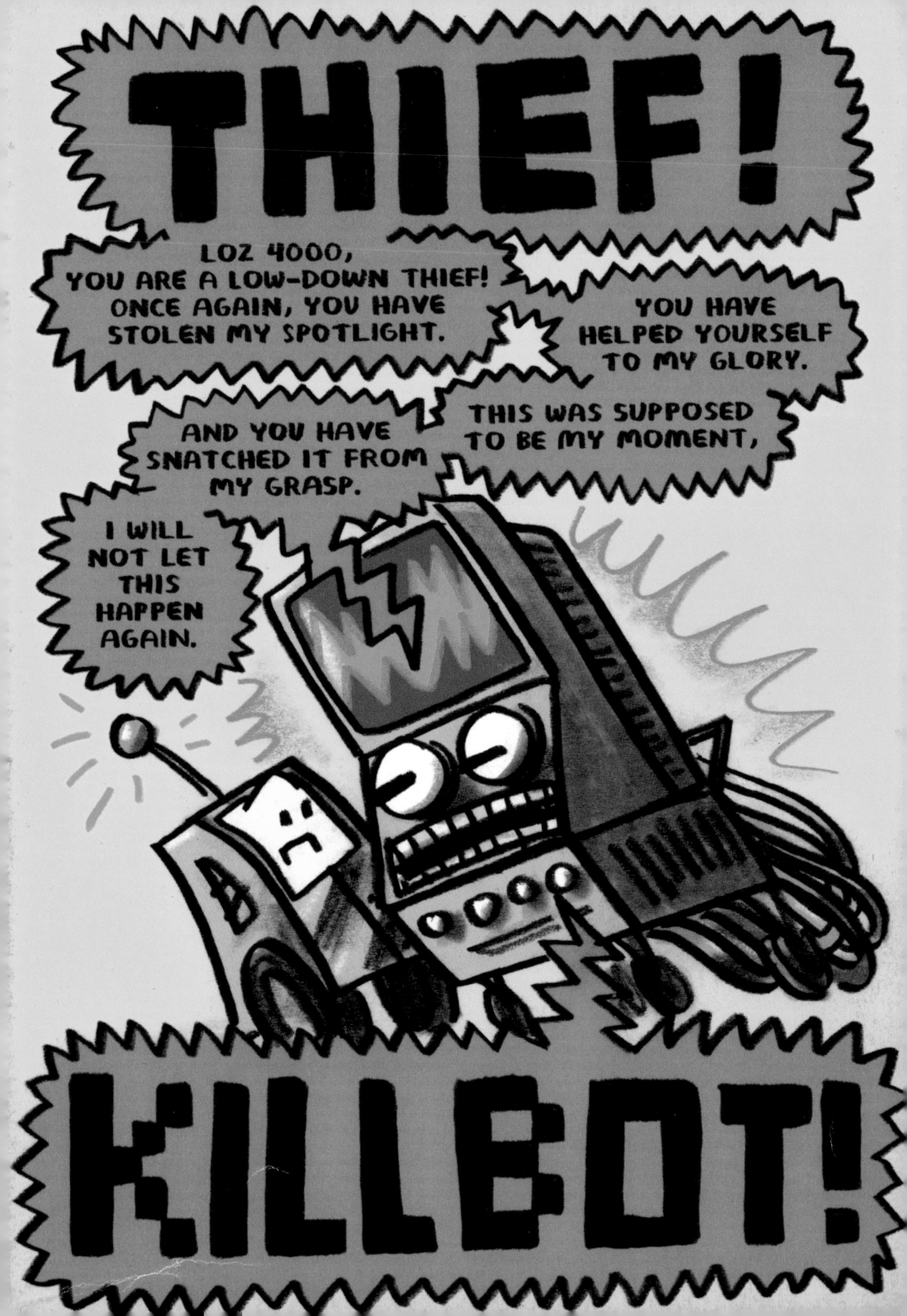
THIEF!
LOZ 4000, YOU ARE A LOW-DOWN THIEF! ONCE AGAIN, YOU HAVE STOLEN MY SPOTLIGHT.
YOU HAVE HELPED YOURSELF TO MY GLORY.
THIS WAS SUPPOSED TO BE MY MOMENT,
AND YOU HAVE SNATCHED IT FROM MY GRASP.
I WILL NOT LET THIS HAPPEN AGAIN.
KILLBOT!

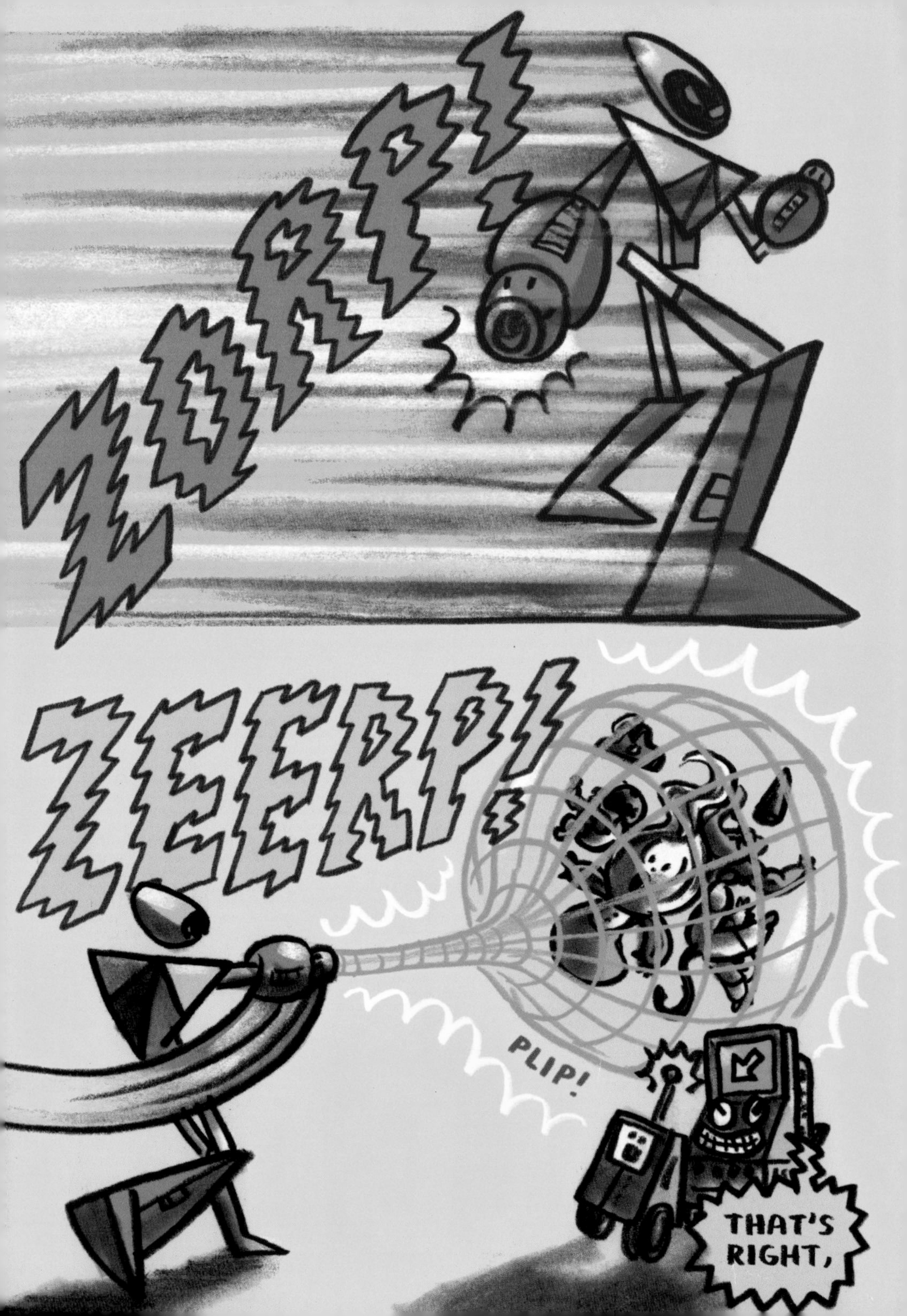
ZOORP!
ZEERP!
PLIP!
THAT'S RIGHT,

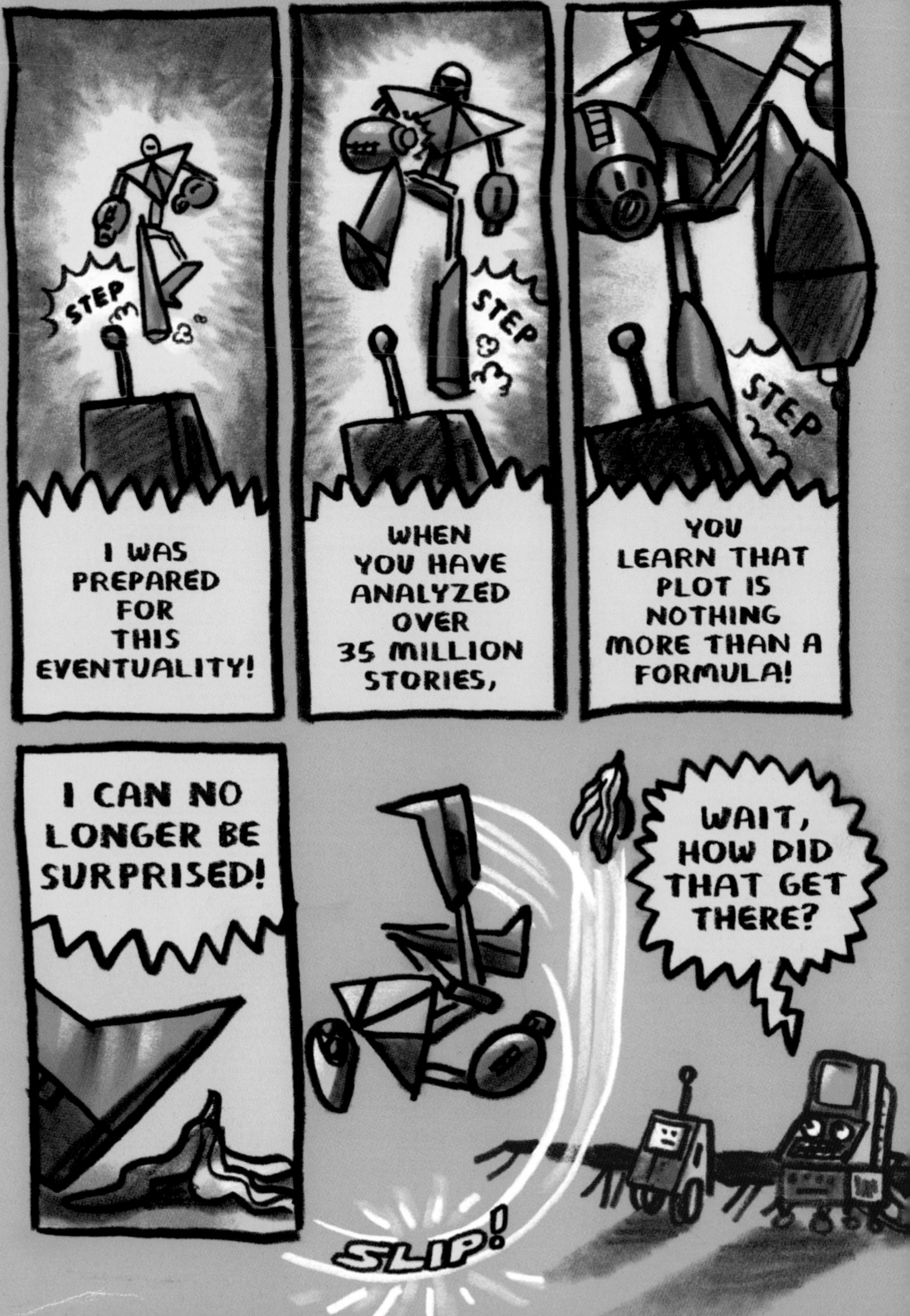
STEP
I WAS PREPARED FOR THIS EVENTUALITY!
STEP
WHEN YOU HAVE ANALYZED OVER 35 MILLION STORIES,
STEP
YOU LEARN THAT PLOT IS NOTHING MORE THAN A FORMULA!
I CAN NO LONGER BE SURPRISED!
SLIP!
WAIT, HOW DID THAT GET THERE?

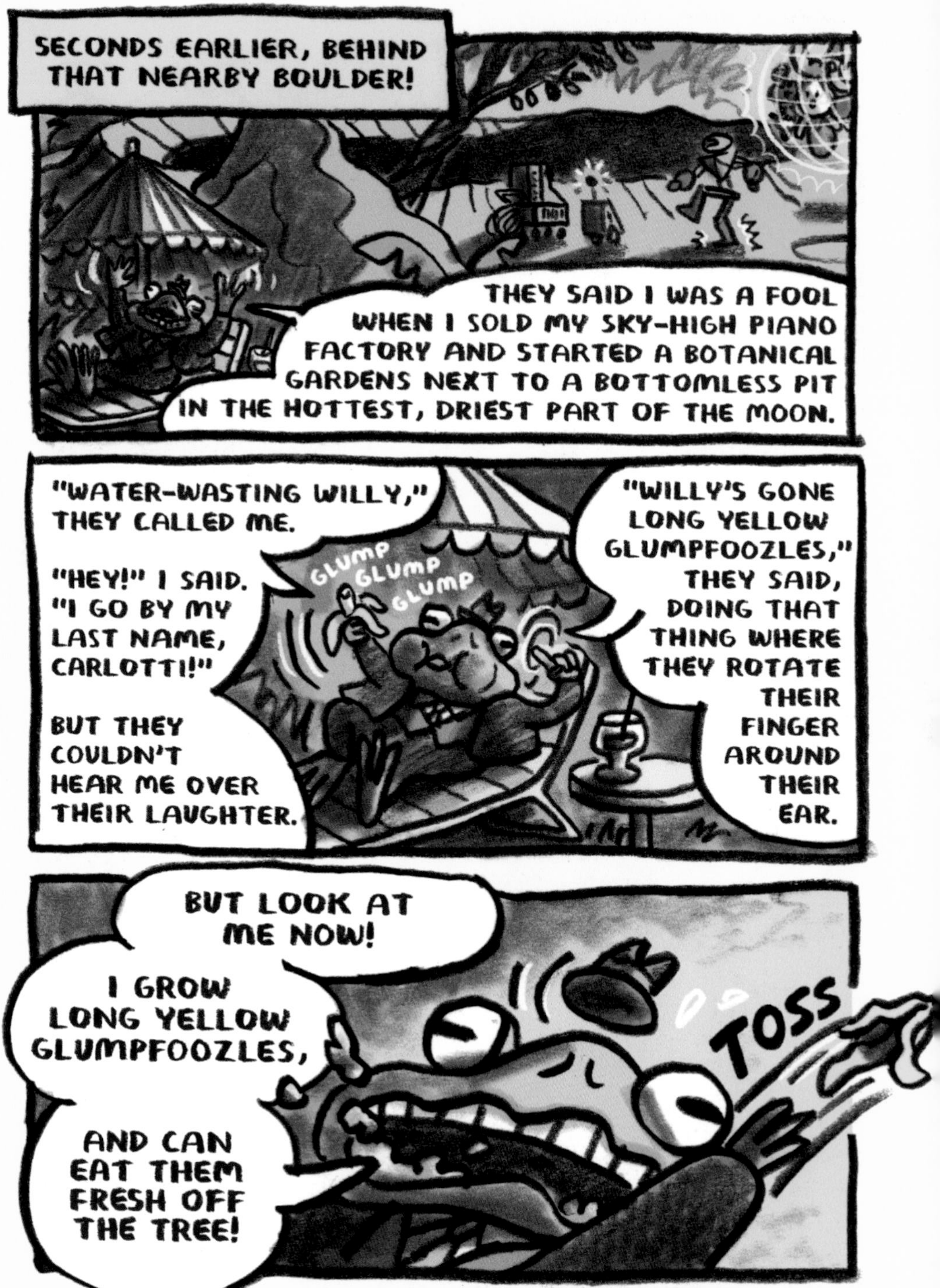
SECONDS EARLIER, BEHIND THAT NEARBY BOULDER!
THEY SAID I WAS A FOOL WHEN I SOLD MY SKY-HIGH PIANO FACTORY AND STARTED A BOTANICAL GARDENS NEXT TO A BOTTOMLESS PIT IN THE HOTTEST, DRIEST PART OF THE MOON.
"WATER-WASTING WILLY," THEY CALLED ME.
"HEY!" I SAID. "I GO BY MY LAST NAME, CARLOTTI!"
BUT THEY COULDN'T HEAR ME OVER THEIR LAUGHTER.
GLUMP GLUMP GLUMP
"WILLY'S GONE LONG YELLOW GLUMPFOOZLES," THEY SAID, DOING THAT THING WHERE THEY ROTATE THEIR FINGER AROUND THEIR EAR.
BUT LOOK AT ME NOW!
I GROW LONG YELLOW GLUMPFOOZLES,
AND CAN EAT THEM FRESH OFF THE TREE!
TOSS

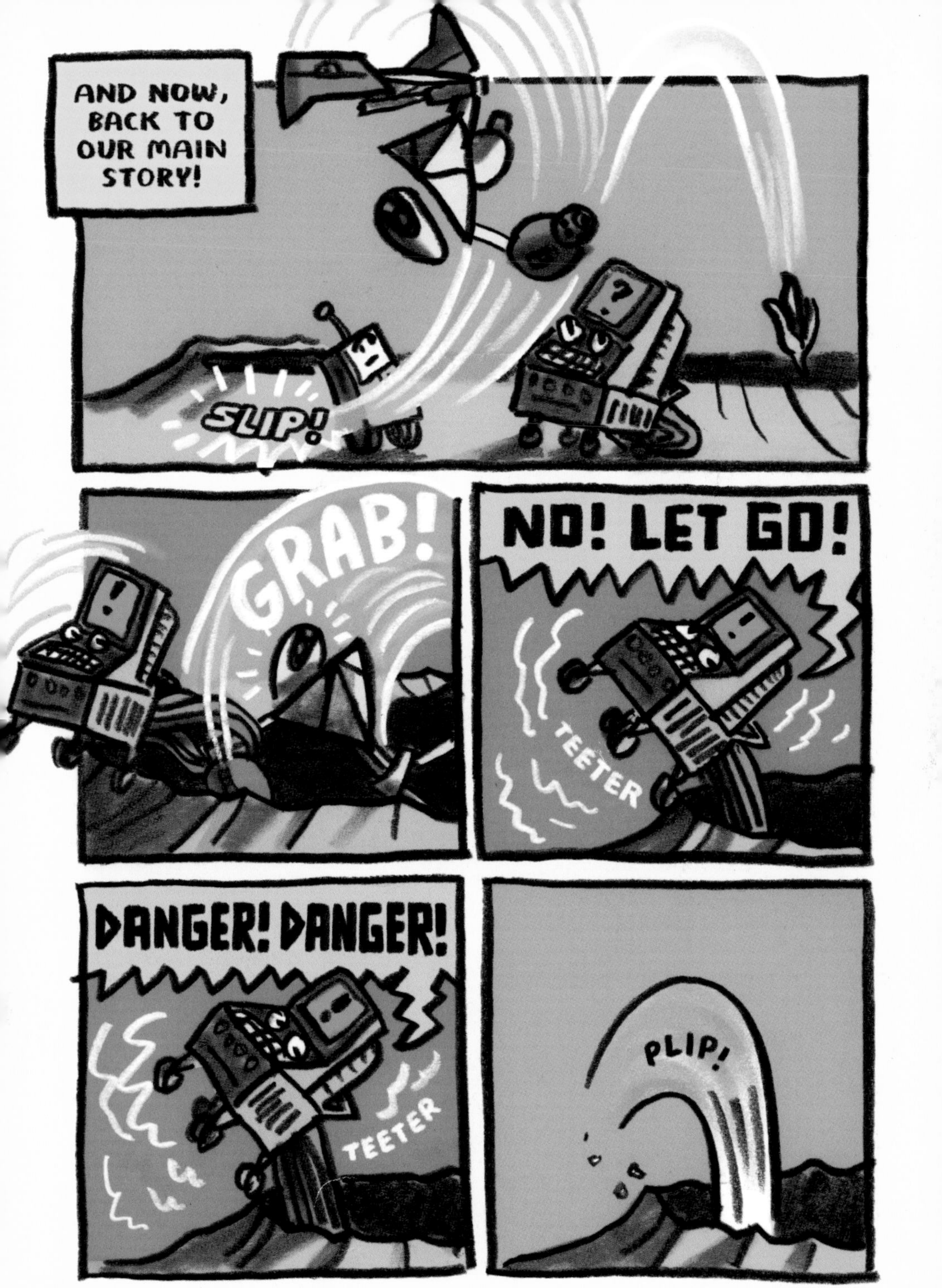
AND NOW, BACK TO OUR MAIN STORY!
SLIP!
GRAB!
NO! LET GO!
TEETER
DANGER! DANGER!
TEETER
PLIP!

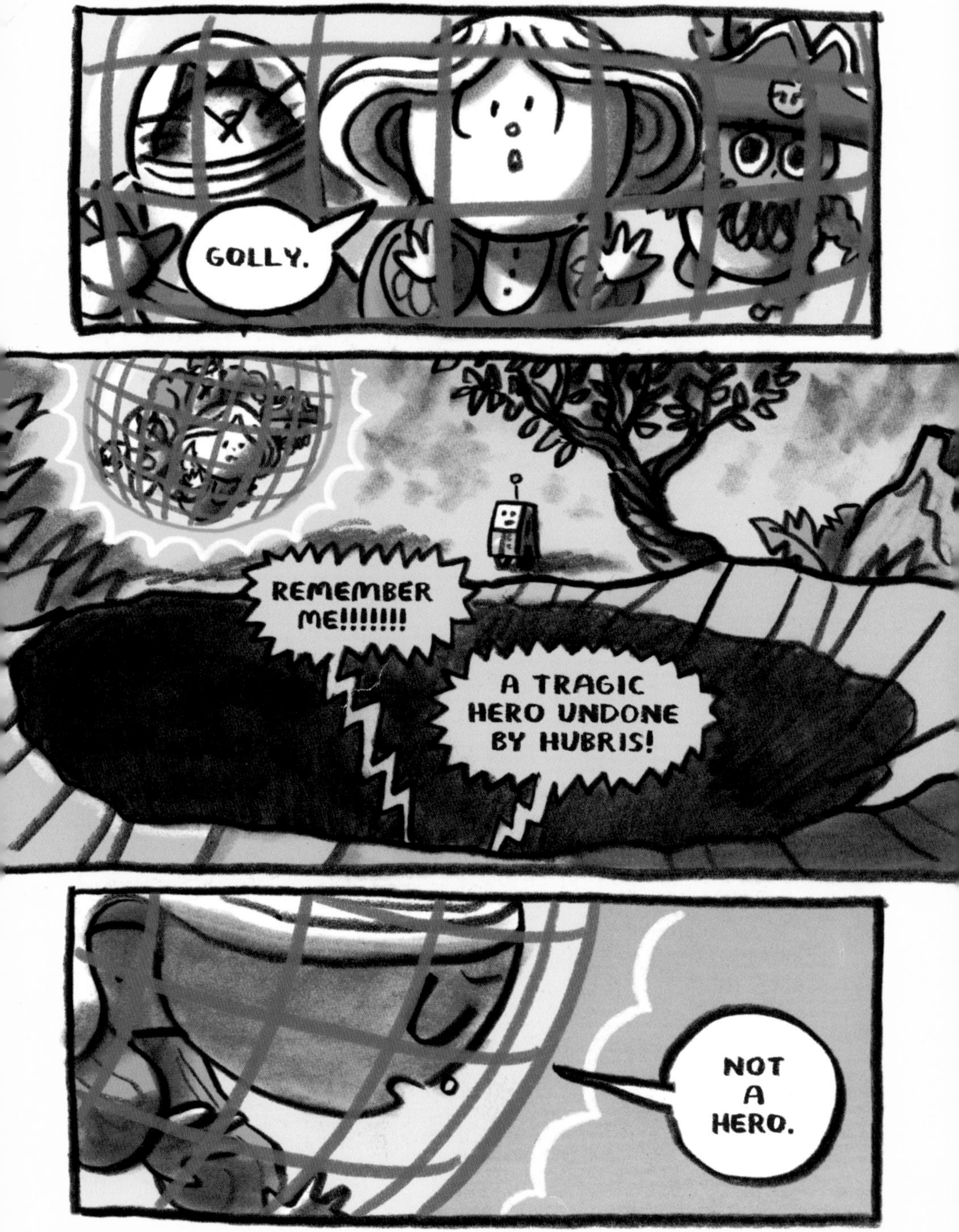
GOLLY.
REMEMBER ME!!!!!!!
A TRAGIC HERO UNDONE BY HUBRIS!
NOT A HERO.

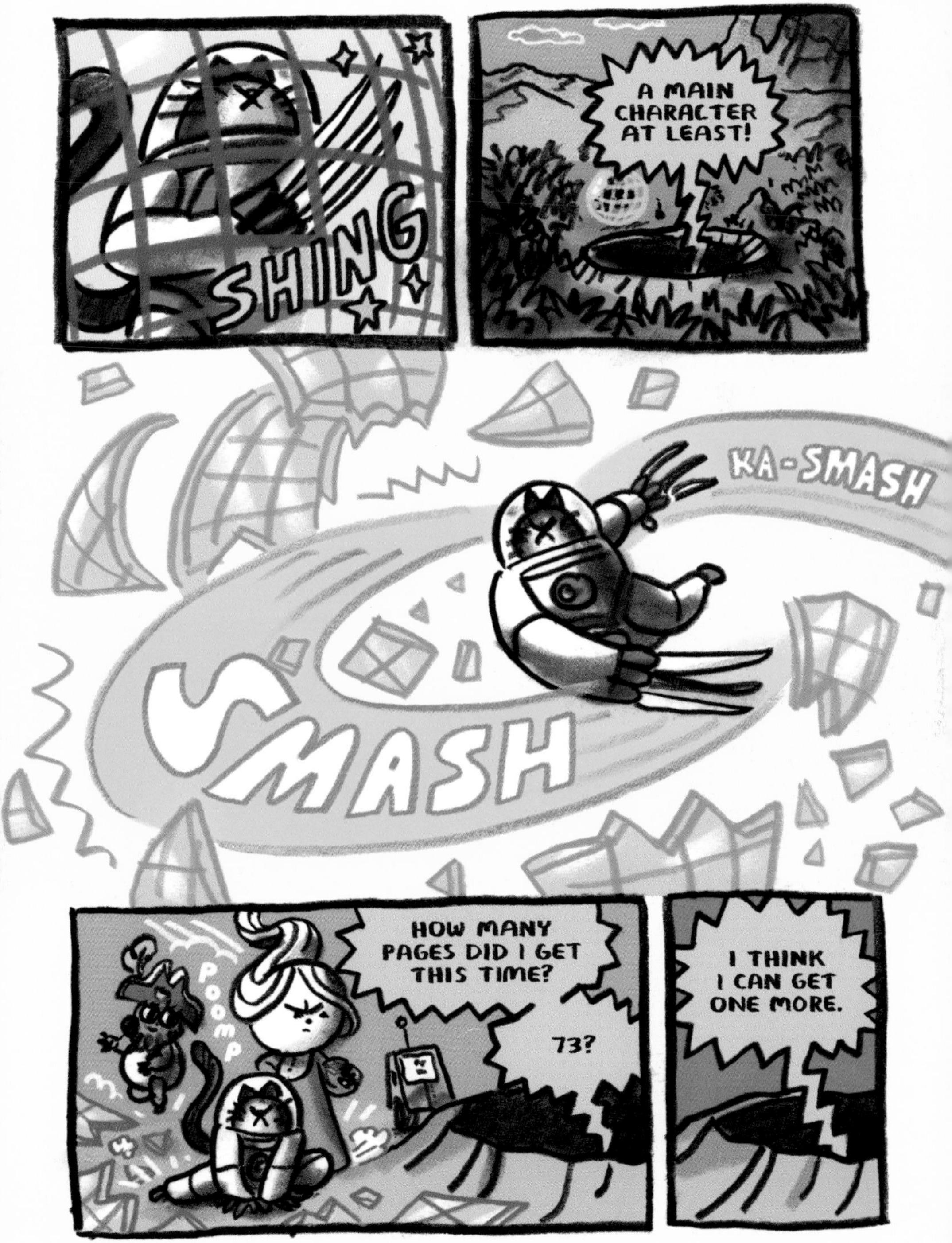
SHING
A MAIN CHARACTER AT LEAST!
KA-SMASH
SMASH
POOMP
HOW MANY PAGES DID I GET THIS TIME?
73?
I THINK I CAN GET ONE MORE.

74!

THAT'S 52 MORE THAN BOOK ONE!

NICE!

OK, YES, GOODBYE, THANK YOU!

YOU'RE WELCOME!

HALT

THIS IS BOTTOMLESS, HUH?

SO HE'LL JUST KEEP SHOUTING?

LOZ, LET'S SEE YOUR FARM!

CHAPTER 13

# SOUP FOR DINNER

NICE CURTAINS!

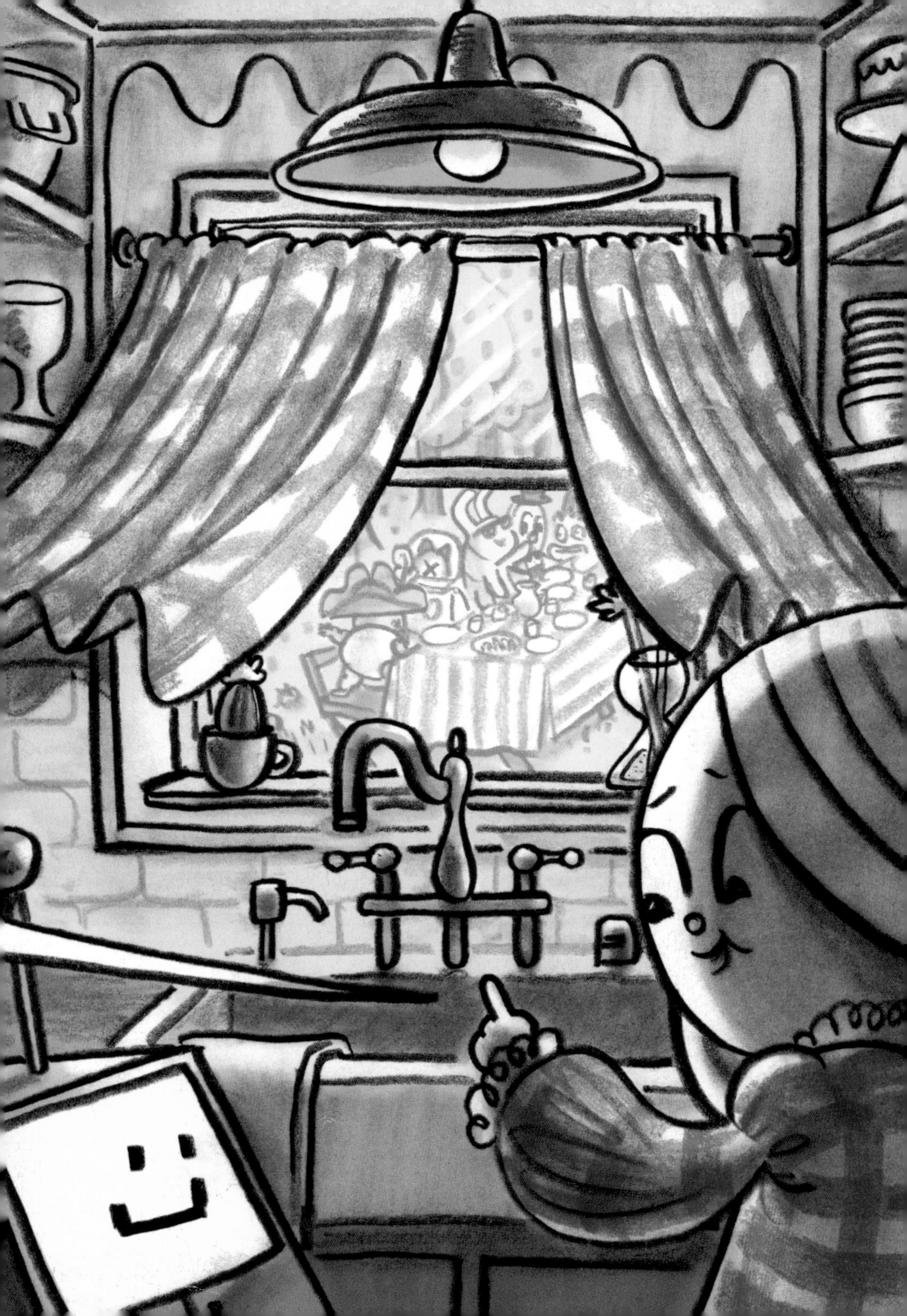

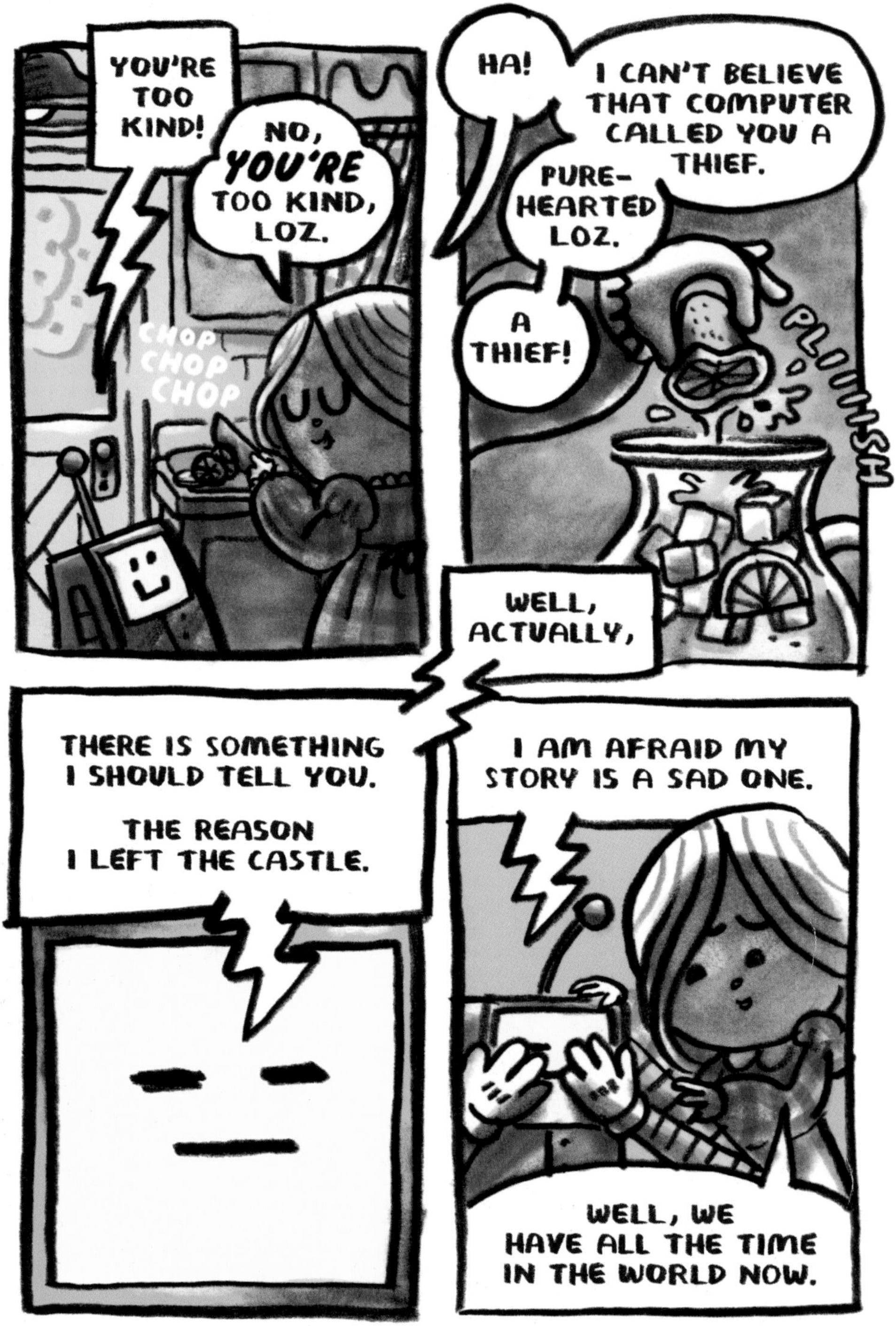
YOU'RE TOO KIND!
NO, *YOU'RE* TOO KIND, LOZ.
CHOP CHOP CHOP
HA!
I CAN'T BELIEVE THAT COMPUTER CALLED YOU A THIEF.
PURE-HEARTED LOZ.
A THIEF!
PLIIIISH
WELL, ACTUALLY,
THERE IS SOMETHING I SHOULD TELL YOU.
THE REASON I LEFT THE CASTLE.
I AM AFRAID MY STORY IS A SAD ONE.
WELL, WE HAVE ALL THE TIME IN THE WORLD NOW.

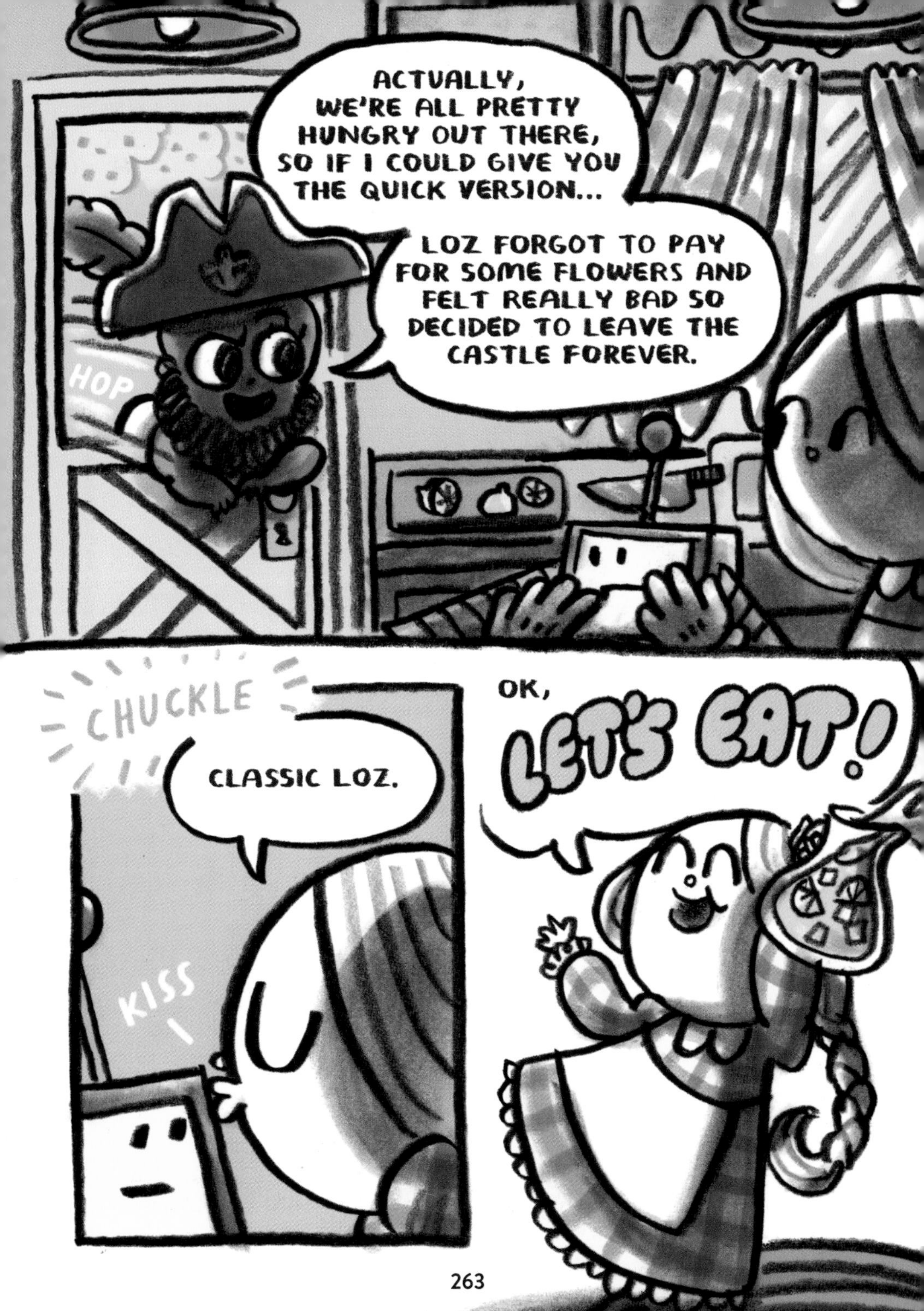
ACTUALLY, WE'RE ALL PRETTY HUNGRY OUT THERE, SO IF I COULD GIVE YOU THE QUICK VERSION...
LOZ FORGOT TO PAY FOR SOME FLOWERS AND FELT REALLY BAD SO DECIDED TO LEAVE THE CASTLE FOREVER.
HOP
CHUCKLE
CLASSIC LOZ.
KISS
OK,
LET'S EAT!

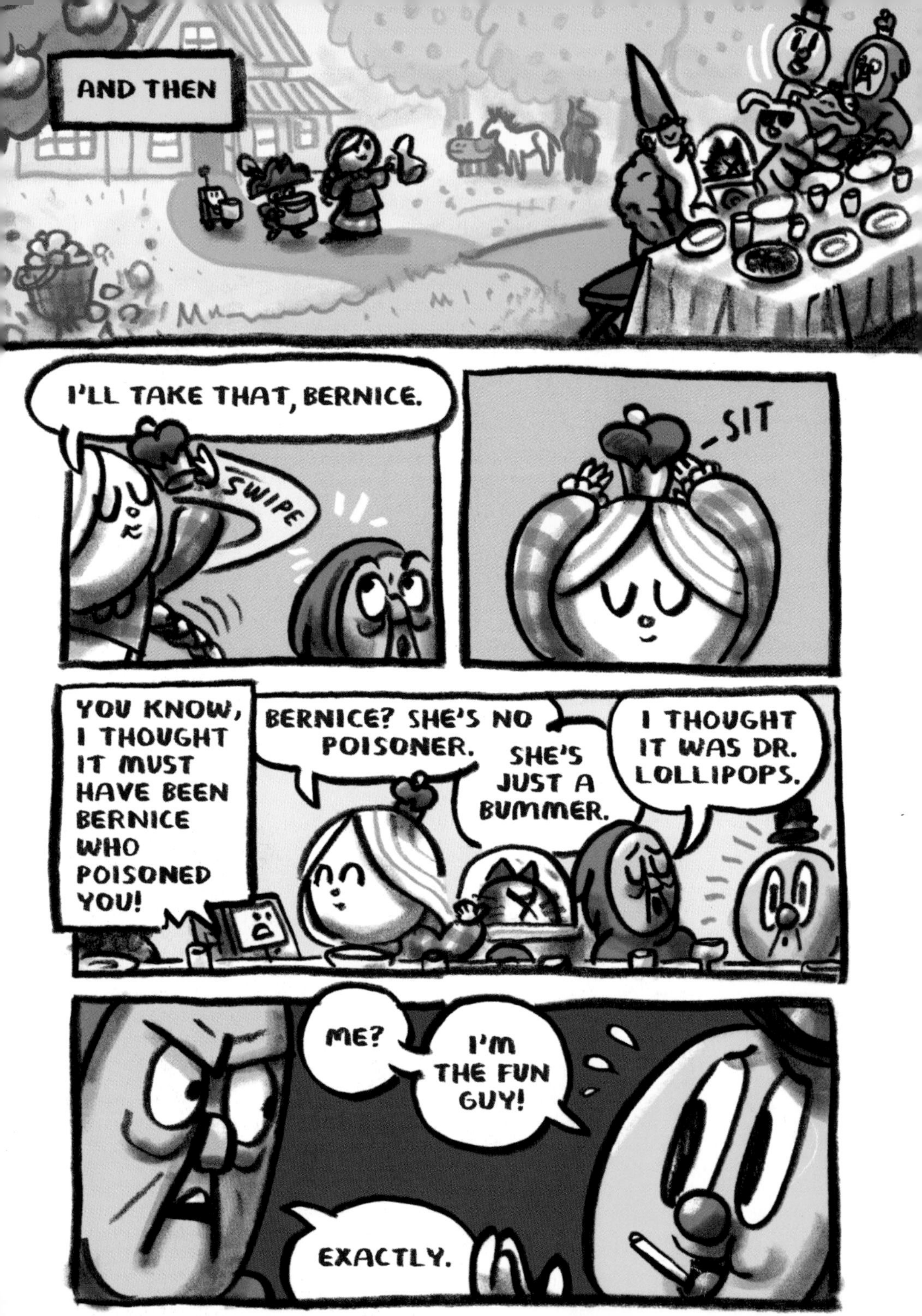
AND THEN
I'LL TAKE THAT, BERNICE.
SWIPE
-SIT
YOU KNOW, I THOUGHT IT MUST HAVE BEEN BERNICE WHO POISONED YOU!
BERNICE? SHE'S NO POISONER.
SHE'S JUST A BUMMER.
I THOUGHT IT WAS DR. LOLLIPOPS.
ME?
I'M THE FUN GUY!
EXACTLY.

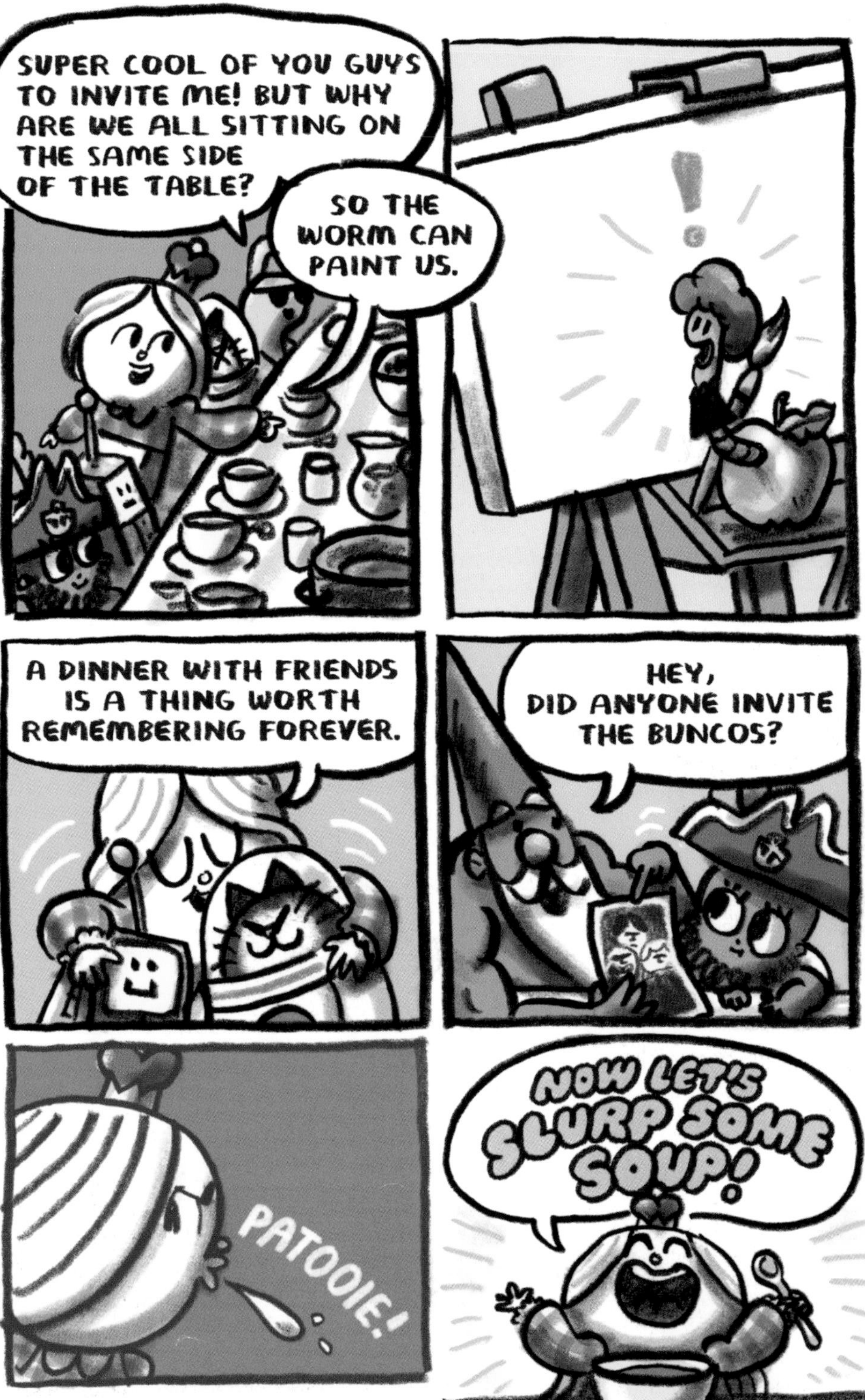
SUPER COOL OF YOU GUYS TO INVITE ME! BUT WHY ARE WE ALL SITTING ON THE SAME SIDE OF THE TABLE?
SO THE WORM CAN PAINT US.
!
A DINNER WITH FRIENDS IS A THING WORTH REMEMBERING FOREVER.
HEY, DID ANYONE INVITE THE BUNCOS?
PATOOIE!
NOW LET'S SLURP SOME SOUP!

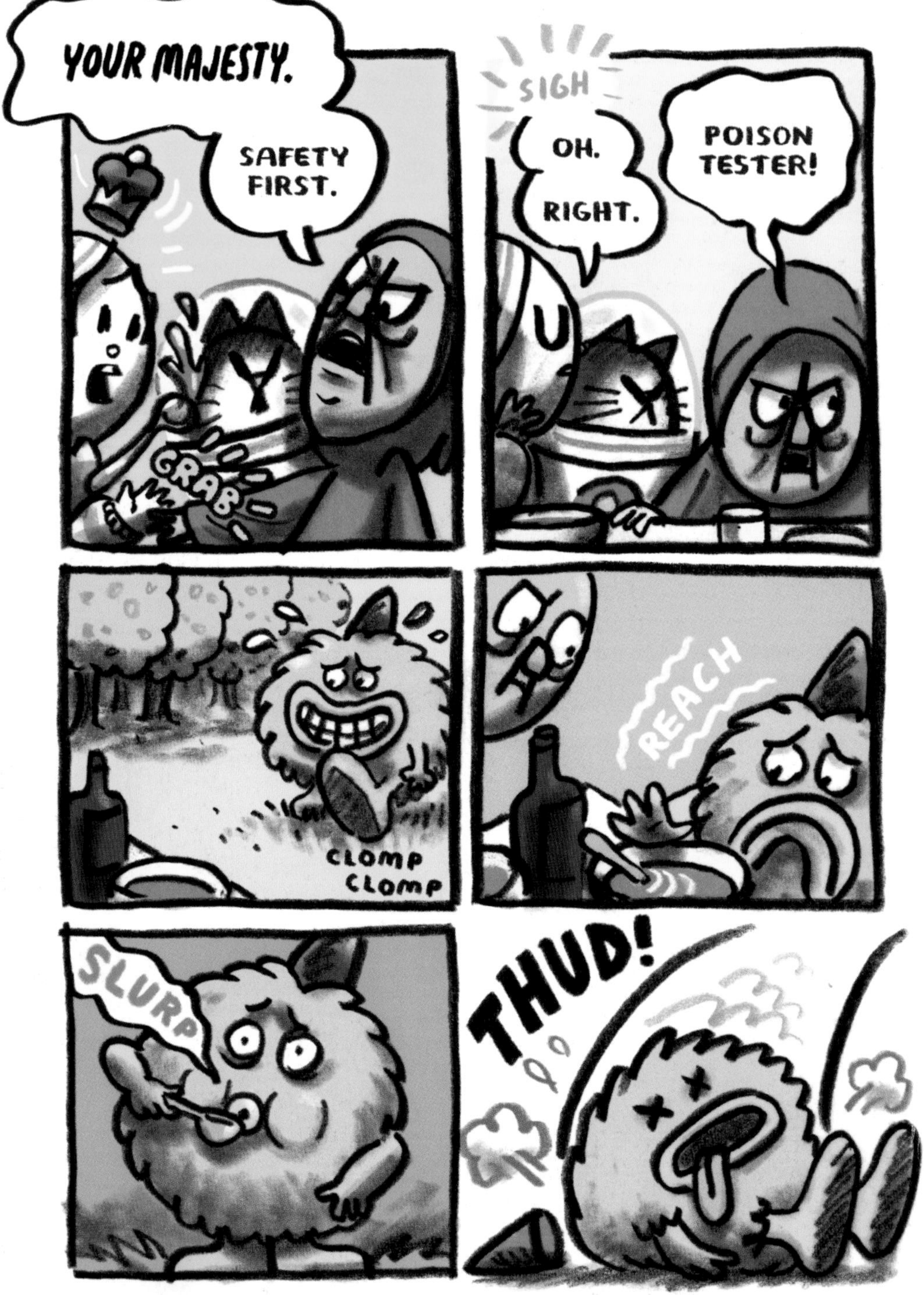
YOUR MAJESTY.
SAFETY FIRST.
GRAB
SIGH
OH.
RIGHT.
POISON TESTER!
CLOMP CLOMP
REACH
SLURP
THUD!

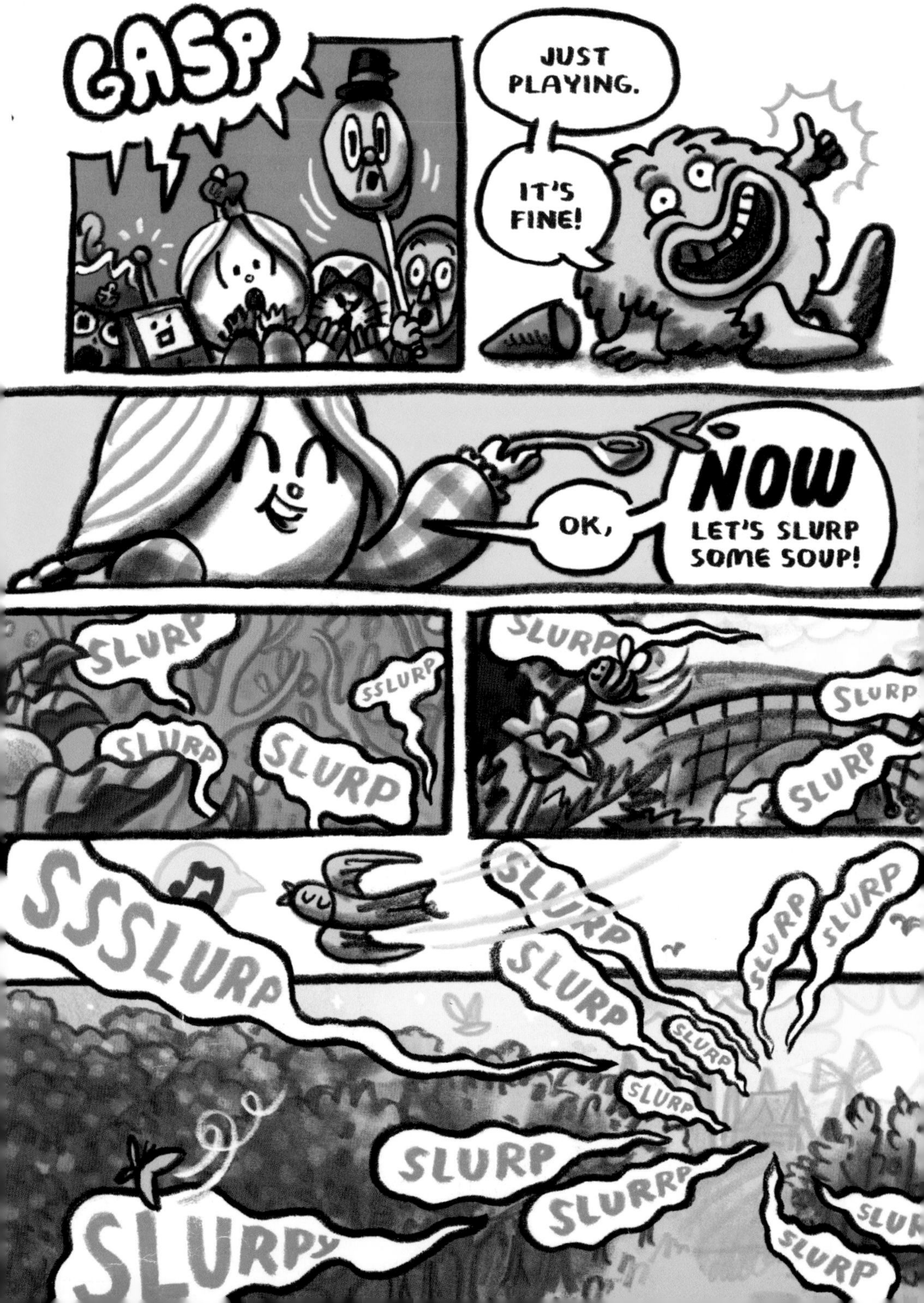
GASP
JUST PLAYING.
IT'S FINE!
OK,
NOW LET'S SLURP SOME SOUP!
SLURP
SSLURP
SLURP
SLURP
SLURP
SLURP
SLURP
SSSLURP
SLURP
SLURP
SLURP
SLURP
SLURP
SLURP
SLURP
SLURRP
SLURPy
SLURP

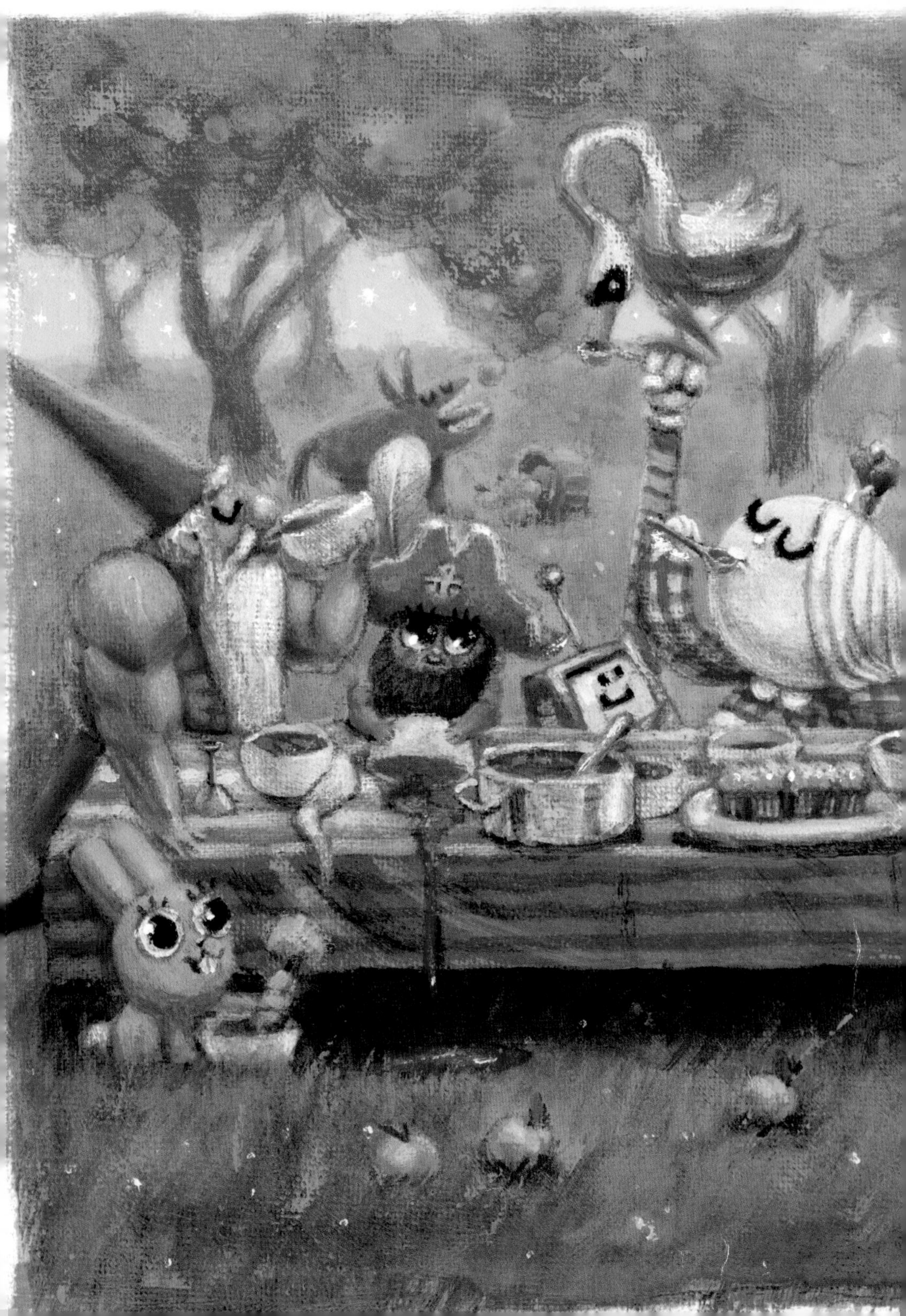

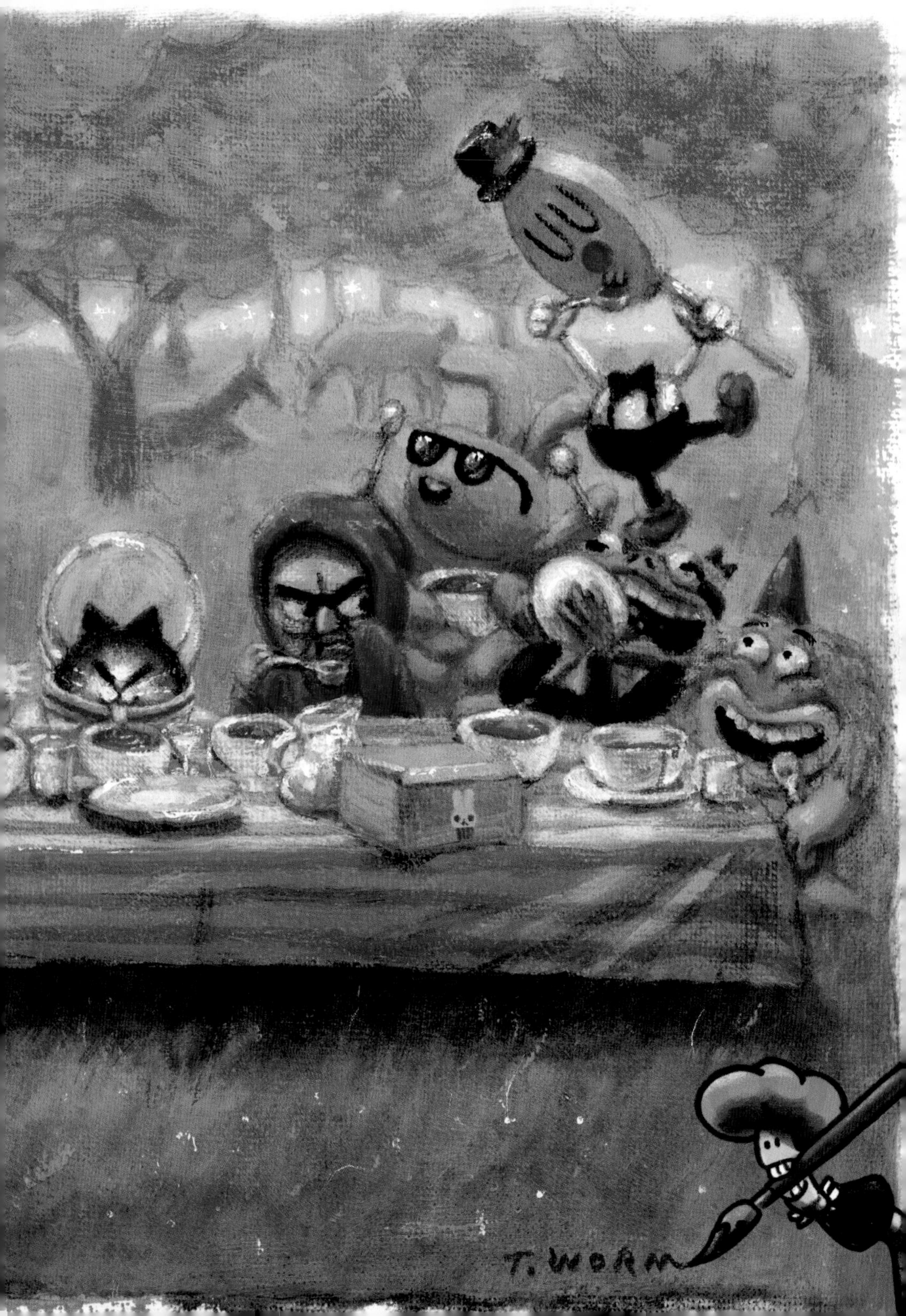
T. WORM

**For Mabel Hsu, our visionary, hilarious, indefatigable editor.**
**—M.B. & S.H.**

KATHERINE TEGEN BOOKS
*Imprints of* HarperCollins*Publishers*

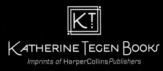

HarperAlley is an imprint of HarperCollins Publishers.

Katherine Tegen Books is an imprint of HarperCollins Publishers.

The First Cat in Space and the Soup of Doom

For information address HarperCollins Children's Books, a division of HarperCollins Publishers, 195 Broadway, New York, NY 10007.
www.harpercollinschildrens.com
Shawn drew the pictures in this book with pencils and charcoal,
and colored them digitally, with flatting assistance by Claire Sweeney and Kelly Fry.
Thanks to Michael White, Leslie Sage, and Karl Ziemelis
for talking to us about black holes.

---

ISBN 978-0-06-308411-7

---

Typography by Shawn Harris
23 24 25 26 27 EP 10 9 8 7 6 5 4 3 2 1
First Edition

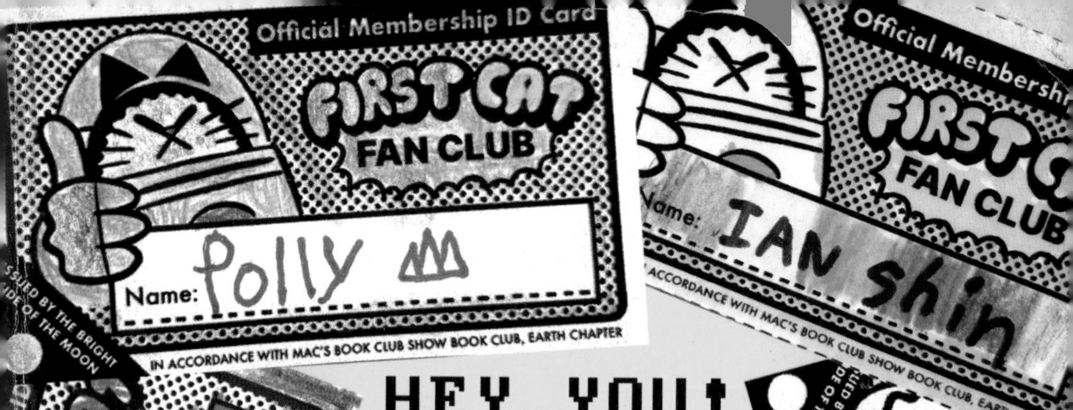
Official Membership ID Card
FIRST CAT
FAN CLUB
Name: Polly
ISSUED BY THE BRIGHT SIDE OF THE MOON
IN ACCORDANCE WITH MAC'S BOOK CLUB SHOW BOOK CLUB, EARTH CHAPTER
Official Membership
FIRST CAT
FAN CLUB
Name: IAN shin
IN ACCORDANCE WITH MAC'S BOOK CLUB SHOW BOOK CLUB, EARTH CHAPTER

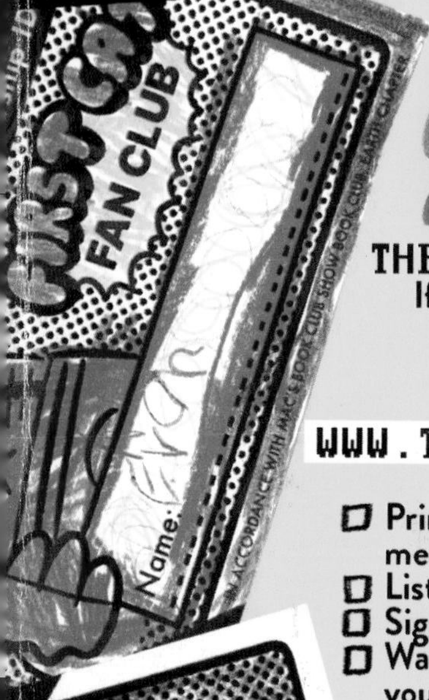
FIRST CAT
FAN CLUB
Name: Evan
IN ACCORDANCE WITH MAC'S BOOK CLUB SHOW BOOK CLUB, EARTH CHAPTER

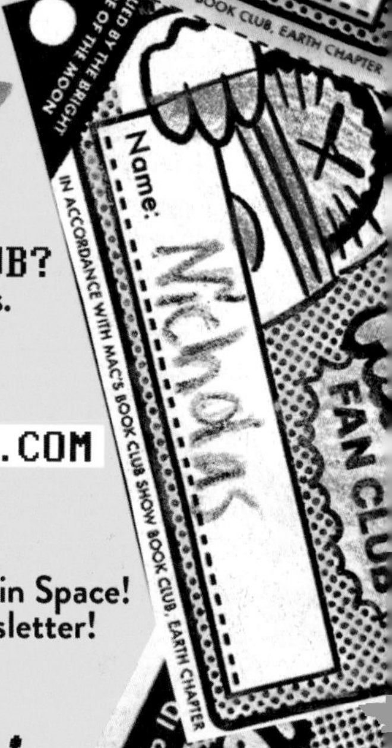
ISSUED BY THE BRIGHT SIDE OF THE MOON
Name: Nicholas
IN ACCORDANCE WITH MAC'S BOOK CLUB SHOW BOOK CLUB, EARTH CHAPTER
FAN CLUB

# HEY YOU!

## Yes, You!

Are you a member of
THE FIRST CAT FAN CLUB?
If yes, please skip the rest of this.
The book is done!

If not, what the snap?! Visit
**WWW.THEFIRSTCATINSPACE.COM**
right now so you can:

- ☐ Print out your very own membership card and certificate!
- ☐ Listen to songs from the First Cat in Space!
- ☐ Sign up for the First Cat Fan Newsletter!
- ☐ Watch "Live Cartoons" featuring your favorite TFCIS* characters!

*And much, much more!*

These are actual cards
from actual kids who are
actual members of the club.
We're not this good at coloring!

*A.K.A.[†] "The First Cat in Space"
†A.K.A. "Also Known As"

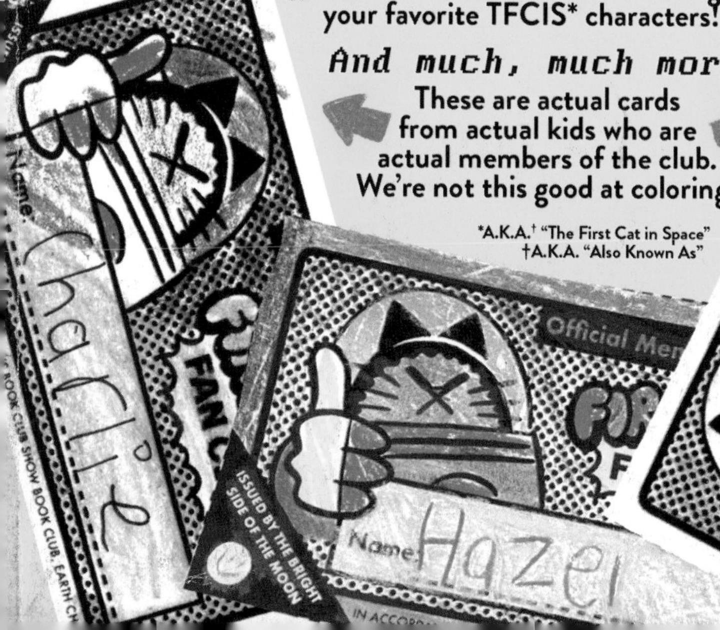
Name: Charlie
FAN C
Official Mem
Name: Hazel
ISSUED BY THE BRIGHT SIDE OF THE MOON

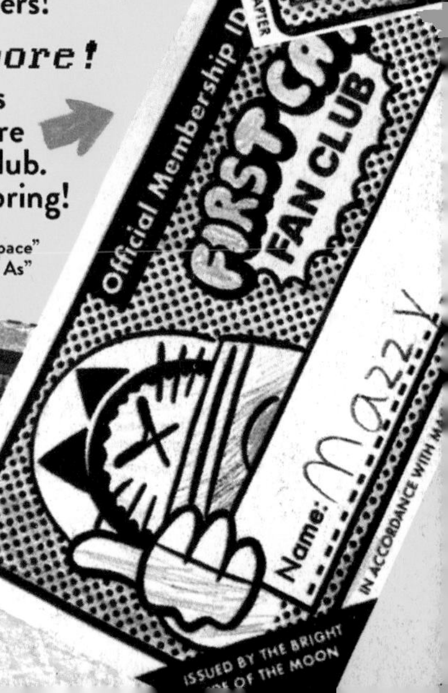
Official Membership ID
FIRST CAT
FAN CLUB
Name: Mazzy
ISSUED BY THE BRIGHT SIDE OF THE MOON

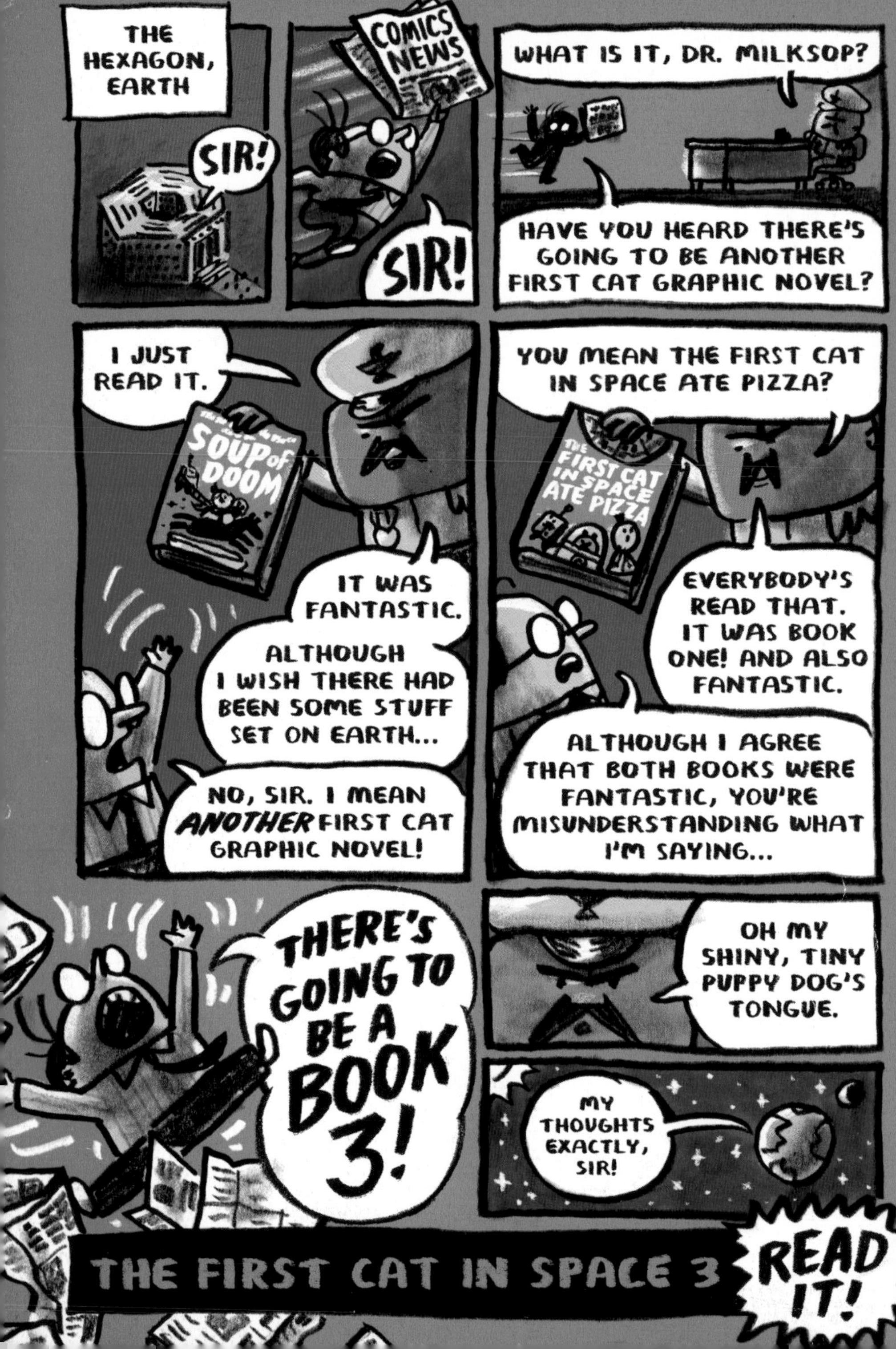
THE HEXAGON, EARTH
SIR!
COMICS NEWS
SIR!
WHAT IS IT, DR. MILKSOP?
HAVE YOU HEARD THERE'S GOING TO BE ANOTHER FIRST CAT GRAPHIC NOVEL?
I JUST READ IT.
SOUP of DOOM
IT WAS FANTASTIC.
ALTHOUGH I WISH THERE HAD BEEN SOME STUFF SET ON EARTH...
NO, SIR. I MEAN *ANOTHER* FIRST CAT GRAPHIC NOVEL!
YOU MEAN THE FIRST CAT IN SPACE ATE PIZZA?
THE FIRST CAT IN SPACE ATE PIZZA
EVERYBODY'S READ THAT. IT WAS BOOK ONE! AND ALSO FANTASTIC.
ALTHOUGH I AGREE THAT BOTH BOOKS WERE FANTASTIC, YOU'RE MISUNDERSTANDING WHAT I'M SAYING...
THERE'S GOING TO BE A BOOK 3!
OH MY SHINY, TINY PUPPY DOG'S TONGUE.
MY THOUGHTS EXACTLY, SIR!
THE FIRST CAT IN SPACE 3
READ IT!